Demon
Copperhead

ALSO BY BARBARA KINGSOLVER

Fiction

Unsheltered

Flight Behavior

The Lacuna

Prodigal Summer

The Poisonwood Bible

Pigs in Heaven

Animal Dreams

Homeland and Other Stories

The Bean Trees

Essays

Small Wonder

High Tide in Tucson: Essays from Now or Never

Poetry

How to Fly (In Ten Thousand Easy Lessons)

Another America

Nonfiction

Animal, Vegetable, Miracle: A Year of Food Life

Last Stand: America's Virgin Lands

Holding the Line:
Women in the Great Arizona Mine Strike of 1983

Demon Copperhead

A Novel

Barbara Kingsolver

HARPER LARGE PRINT

An Imprint of HarperCollinsPublishers

HarperCollins books may be purchased for educational, business, or sales promotional use. For information, please e-mail the Special Markets Department at SPsales@harpercollins.com.

FIRST HARPER LARGE PRINT EDITION

ISBN: 978-0-06-326746-6

Library of Congress Cataloging-in-Publication Data is available upon request.

22 23 24 25 26 LBC 6 5 4 3 2

For the survivors.

"It's in vain to recall the past, unless it works some influence upon the present."

CHARLES DICKENS, *DAVID COPPERFIELD*

Demon
Copperhead

1

First, I got myself born. A decent crowd was on hand to watch, and they've always given me that much: the worst of the job was up to me, my mother being let's just say out of it.

On any other day they'd have seen her outside on the deck of her trailer home, good neighbors taking notice, pestering the tit of trouble as they will. All through the dog-breath air of late summer and fall, cast an eye up the mountain and there she'd be, little bleach-blonde smoking her Pall Malls, hanging on that railing like she's captain of her ship up there and now might be the hour it's going down. This is an eighteen-year-old girl we're discussing, all on her own and as pregnant as it gets. The day she failed to show, it fell to Nance Peggot to go bang on the door, barge inside, and find her passed out on the bathroom floor with her junk all over the place and me already coming out. A slick fish-colored hostage picking up grit from the vinyl tile, worming and shoving around because I'm still inside the sack that babies float in, pre-real-life.

Mr. Peggot was outside idling his truck, headed for evening service, probably thinking about how much of his life he'd spent waiting on women. His wife would have told him the Jesusing could hold on a minute, first she needed to go see if the little pregnant gal had got herself liquored up again. Mrs. Peggot being a lady that doesn't beat around the bushes and if need be, will tell Christ Jesus to sit tight and keep his pretty hair on. She came back out yelling for him to call 911 because a poor child is in the bathroom trying to punch himself out of a bag.

Like a little blue prizefighter. Those are the words she'd use later on, being not at all shy to discuss the worst day of my mom's life. And if that's how I came across to the first people that laid eyes on me, I'll take it. To me that says I had a fighting chance. Long odds, yes I know. If a mother is lying in her own piss and pill bottles while they're slapping the kid she's shunted out, telling him to look alive: likely the bastard is doomed. Kid born to the junkie is a junkie. He'll grow up to be everything you don't want to know, the rotten teeth and dead-zone eyes, the nuisance of locking up your tools in the garage so they don't walk off, the rent-by-the-week motel squatting well back from the scenic highway. This kid, if he wanted a shot at the finer things, should have got himself delivered to some rich or smart or Christian, nonusing type of mother. Anybody will tell you the born of this world are marked from the get-out, win or lose.

Me though, I was a born sucker for the superhero rescue. Did that line of work even exist, in our trailer-home universe? Had they all quit Smallville and gone looking for bigger action? Save or be saved, these are questions. You want to think it's not over till the last page.

It was a Wednesday this all happened, which supposedly is the bad one. Full of woe etc. Add to that, coming out still inside the fetus ziplock. But. According to Mrs. Peggot there is one good piece of luck that comes with the baggie birth: it's this promise from God that you'll never drown. Specifically. You could still OD, or get pinned to the wheel and charbroiled in your driver's seat, or for that matter blow your own brains out, but the one place where you will not suck your last breath is underwater. Thank you, Jesus.

I don't know if this is at all related, but I always had a thing for the ocean. Usually kids will get fixated on naming every make and model of dinosaur or what have you. With me it was whales and sharks. Even now I probably think more than the normal about water, floating in it, just the color blue itself and how for the fish, that blue is the whole deal. Air and noise and people and our all-important hectic nonsense, a minor irritant if even that.

I've not seen the real thing, just pictures, and this hypnotizing screen saver of waves rearing up and spilling over on a library computer. So what do I know about ocean, still yet to stand on its sandy beard and look it in the eye? Still waiting to meet the one big thing I know is not going to swallow me alive.

Dead in the heart of Lee County, between the Ruelynn coal camp and a settlement people call Right Poor, the top of a road between two steep mountains is where our single-wide was set. I wasted more hours up in those woods than you'd want to count, alongside of a boy named Maggot, wading the creek and turning over big rocks and being mighty. I could go different ways but definitely a Marvel hero as preferable to DC, Wolverine being a favorite. Whereas Maggot tended to choose Storm, which is a girl. (Excellent powers, and a mutant, but still.) Maggot was short for Matt Peggot, related obviously to the screaming lady at my birthday party, his grandmother. She was the reason Maggot and I got to be next-door-neighbor wild boys for a time, but first he'd need to get born, a little out ahead of me, plus getting pawned off on her while his mom took the extended vacay in Goochland Women's Prison. We've got story enough here to eff up more than one young life, but it is a project.

Famously, this place where we lived was known to be crawling with copperheads. People think they know a lot of things. Here's what I know. In the years I spent climbing around rocks in all the places a snake likes to lie, not one copperhead did we see. Snakes, yes, all the time. But snakes come in kinds. For one, a common spotty kind called a Water Devil that's easily pissed off and will strike fast if you make that mistake, but it's less of a bite than a dog deals out, or a bee sting. Whenever a water snake gets you, you yell all the curse words you've got stored up in your little skull closet. Then wipe off the blood, pick up your stick, and go on being an Adaptoid, thrashing on the mossy stump of evil. Where, if a copperhead gets you, that's the end of whatever you planned on doing that day, and maybe with that part of your hand or foot, period. So it matters a lot, what you're looking at.

If you care, you'll learn one thing from another. Anybody knows a sheepdog from a beagle, or a Whopper from a Big Mac. Meaning dogs matter and burgers matter but a snake is a freaking snake. Our holler was full of copperheads, said the cashiers at the grocery whenever they saw our address on Mom's food stamps envelope. Said the school bus driver, day in, day out, snapping the door shut behind me like she's slamming it on their pointy snake faces. People love to believe in danger, as long as it's you in harm's way, and them saying bless your heart.

Years would come and go before I got to the bottom of all the heart-blessing, and it was not entirely about snakes. One of Mom's bad choices, which she learned to call them in rehab, and trust me there were many, was a guy called Copperhead. Supposedly he had the dark skin and light-green eyes of a Melungeon, and red hair that made you look twice. He wore it long and shiny as a penny, said my mother, who clearly had a bad case. A snake tattoo coiled around his right arm where he'd been bit twice: first in church, as a kid trying for manhood among his family's snake-handling men. Second time, later on, far from the sight of God. Mom said he didn't need the tattoo for a reminder, that arm aggravated him to the end. He died the summer before I was born. My messed-up birthday surprised enough people to get the ambulance called and then the monster-truck mud rally of child services. But I doubt anybody was surprised to see me grow up with these eyes, this hair. I might as well have been born with the ink.

Mom had her own version of the day I was born, which I never believed, considering she was passed out for the event. Not that I'm any witness, being a newborn infant plus inside a bag. But I knew Mrs. Peggot's story. And if you'd spent even a day in the company of her and my mom, you would know which of those two lotto tickets was going to pay out.

Mom's was this. The day I was born, her baby daddy's mother turned up out of the blue. She was nobody Mom had ever met nor wanted to, given what she'd heard about that family. Snake-handling Baptist was not the half of it. These were said to be individuals that beat the tar out of each other, husbands belting wives, mothers beating kids with whatever object fell to hand, the Holy Bible itself not out of the question. I took Mom's word on that because you hear of such things, folks so godly as to pass around snakes, also passing around black eyes. If this is a new one on you, maybe you also think a dry county is a place where there's no liquor to be found. Southwest Virginia, we're one damn thing after another.

Supposedly by the time this lady showed up, Mom was pretty far gone with the pains. The labor thing coming at her out of nowhere that day. Thinking to dull the worst of it, she hit the Seagram's before noon, with enough white crosses to stay awake for more drinking, and some Vicodin after it's all a bit too much. Looks up to see a stranger's face pressed so hard against the bathroom window her mouth looks like a butt crack. (Mom's words, take or leave the visual.) The lady marches around through the front door and tears into Mom with the hell and the brimstone. What is she doing to this innocent lamb that Almighty God has put in her womb? She's come to take her dead son's only child from this den of vice and raise her up decent.

Mom always swore that was the train I barely missed: getting whisked off to join some savage Holy Roller brood in Open Ass, Tennessee. Place name, my own touch. Mom refused to discuss my father's family at all, or even what killed him. Only that it was a bad accident at a place I was never to go called Devil's Bath-tub. Keeping secrets from young ears only plants seeds in between them, and these grew in my tiny head into grislier deaths than any I was supposed to be seeing on TV at that age. To the extent of me being terrified of bathtubs, which luckily we didn't have. The Peggots did, and I steered clear. But Mom stuck to her guns. All she would ever say about Mother Copperhead was that she was a gray-headed old hag, Betsy by name.

I was disappointed, wishing for a Black Widow head of kick-ass red hair, at the least. This being the only kin of my father's we were likely to see. When your parent clocks out before you clock in, you can spend way too much of your life staring into that black hole.

But Mom saw enough. She lived in fear of losing custody, and gave her all in rehab. I came out, Mom went in, and gave it a hundred percent. Gave and gave again over the years, getting to be an expert at rehab, like they say. Having done it so many times.

You can see how Mom's story just stirred up the mud. Some lady shows up (or doesn't), offers me a better home (or not), then leaves, after being called a string of juicy cusswords (knowing Mom) that would have left the lady's ears ringing. Did Mom make up her version to jerk me around? Was it true, in her scrambled brain? Either way, she was clear about the lady coming to rescue a *little girl*. Not me. If this was Mom's fairy tale: Why a girl? Was that what she really wanted, some pink package that would make her get her act together? Like *I* wasn't breakable?

The other part, a small thing, is that in this story Mom never spoke my father's name. The woman is "the Woodall witch," that being my dad's last name, with no mention of the man that got her into the baby fix. She found plenty to say about him at other times, whenever love and all that was her last stop on the second six-pack. The adventures of him and her. But in this tale as regards my existence, he is only the bad choice.

2

My thinking here is to put everything in the order of how it happened, give or take certain intervals of a young man skunked out of his skull box, some dots duly connected. But damn. A kid is a terrible thing to be, in charge of nothing. If you get past that and grown, it's easiest to forget about the misery and pretend you knew all along what you were doing. Assuming you've ended up someplace you're proud to be. And if not, easier to forget the whole thing, period. So this is going to be option three, not proud, not forgetting. Not easy.

I remember I always liked looking at things more than talking about them. I did have questions. My problem was people. Thinking kids are not enough full-fledge humans to give them straight answers. For instance. The Peggots next door in their yard had a birdhouse on a pole that was a big mess of dangling gourds, with holes drilled for the bird doors. It was the bird version of these trailer pileups you'll see, where some couple got a family going and nobody, not kids nor grandkids, *ever* moved out. They're just going to keep shacking up and hauling in another mobile home to set on blocks, keeping it one big family with their junkass porches and raggedy flag over the original unit. One Nation Under Employed. The Peggot birdhouse was that, a bird-trailer clusterfuck. But no birds lived in it, ever. There were bird nests galore in the trees behind the house, or they'd build one in some random place like under the hood of Mr. Peggot's truck. Why not move into a house already built, free of charge? Mr. Peggot said birds were like anybody, they like living their own way. He said he'd known government housing that didn't cost much more than a birdhouse to move into, just as unpopular.

Fine, but why keep the thing up there, growing mold? Maggot told me Humvee had made it in Shop. Humvee being one of Maggot's uncles, last seen near a schoolhouse around the time of the Bee Gees or Elvis. By now it's the nineties. The Peggots kept this reject birdhouse up its pole all those years for what, to remember their son Humvee by? I didn't buy it. The

Peggots had seven kids altogether, living as far away as Ocala Florida or as close as a mile away. Cousins without number roamed through that house like packs of half-broke animals with meal privileges. Every family member got talked to or talked about on a daily basis, except two: (1) Maggot's mom, (2) Humvee. One doing time in Goochland, one dead, for undiscussed reasons.

Besides the birdless birdhouse, they had a dog pen with no dog. Mr. Peggot used to run hounds before he got too tired for it like all the old men we knew, back whenever they still had the lungs for it, and dogs had foxes or bears to chase up a tree. In fall time he'd take us to the woods to hunt ginseng or dig sassafras because those can't outrun you. But mainly just to be out there. He knew bird tunes the way people know who's on the radio. After we got old enough to handle a rifle, nine or ten, he showed us how to take a buck, and how to heft up the carcass on the tree branch over the driveway to dress it out, letting loops of guts fall out steaming on the gravel. Mrs. Peggot cooked venison roast in the crockpot. You've not eaten till you've had that.

The empty dog pen stood between our trailer and the Peggot house. Maggot and I would put a tarp over it and sleep out there, usually if falling trees someplace took out the lines and we couldn't watch TV. One summer we did that for maybe a month, after a Nintendo Duck Hunt challenge where I accidentally let fly the controller gun and busted the screen. Maggot took credit for that deed so I wouldn't get sent home and skinned alive. Mrs. Peggot pretended to take his word for it, even though she heard the whole thing. Probably everybody has had some golden patch of life like that, where everything was going to be okay thanks to the people that had your back, and sadly you wasted it, by being ticked off over some ignorant thing like a busted TV.

The Peggot house sat up at the top of the road with woods all around. They had chickens at one time, including this rooster with the mind of a serial killer that gave me bad dreams. But not farmers proper. Likewise not the churchiest of people, but they were the ones that took me. Mom despised church, due to some of her fosters getting carried away with it, but I myself didn't mind. I liked looking at the singing women, and the rest you could sleep through. Plus that thing of being loved automatically, Jesus on your side. Not a faucet turned on or off, like with people. But some of the Bible stories I minded, definitely. The Lazarus deal got me mentally disturbed, thinking my dad could come back, and I needed to go find him. Mrs. Peggot told Mom I ought to go see Dad's grave in Tennessee, and they had a pretty huge fight. Maggot calmed me down by explaining Bible stories were a category of superhero comic. Not to be confused with real life.

As a kid you just accept different worlds with different rules, even between some houses and others. The Peggot home being a place where things got put where they went. Mr. Peggot would come home with the groceries and right away, in they'd go to the refrigerator. Maggot and I would get done having our World War III in the living room, and those Legos and crap got picked up before we went outside, or else hell would be paid. Not so at my house, where milk seemed like it had its own life to live and would sit out on the counter till it turned. Mom always said she'd lose her mind if it wasn't screwed in, and she wasn't wrong. Her work ID badge on the back of the toilet, makeup by the kitchen sink, purse outside under a chair. Shoes wherever. That was just Mom. In my room I tried to keep stuff put away, mainly my action figures and the notebooks I kept for my drawings. I asked Mom one time how to fix the bed so it was covered up like you see them on TV, which she thought was dead hilarious.

We kids roamed wide, sometimes as far as the old coal camps with the little row houses like Monopoly, except not all alike anymore due to idle mischief and the various ways a roof can cave in. We'd play king of the hill on the tipple cones and come home with white eyelids in coal-black faces like old miners we'd seen in photo albums. Or we'd mess around in creeks. Not the unmentionable one of Devil's Bathtub, which freaked Mom out, and anyway was over in Scott County. The best place by far was the little branch that ran right behind our houses, as a place for a boy to turn invisible. Water with its own ideas, moving around under all those rocks. And underneath the water, a kind of mud that made you feel rich—leaf smelling, thick, of a color that you wanted to eat. Peggot's Branch, it was called, the Peggots being who had lived there longest. Their house was built by some previous Peggot before any other houses were up there, whenever it was one big farm where they plowed their tobacco with mules. So said Mr. Peggot. Mules being the only way you could farm on land that steep. On a tractor you'd roll it and kill yourself.

The trailer where Mom and I lived was technically a Peggot trailer, former home of Maggot's aunt June before she moved to Knoxville. Mom rented it from the Peggots, which was probably why they kept an eye and helped her out, like Mom was the second-string sub that came in off the bench after their own A-team daughter left the game. Maggot said June was still their favorite, even after she got her nursing degree and moved away. Which is saying a lot. Most families would sooner forgive you for going to prison than for moving out of Lee County.

To be clear, me and Mom were no kin of theirs, so this was not one of those family trailer pileups. Those shabby type of places show up on reality TV a lot more than reality in general, I think for the same reason people like to see copperheads where there aren't any copperheads. The Peggots just had their house and the one extra single-wide. Nine or ten other families had their places up and down our road that were kept up very decent, and again, no relation.

But the Peggots were a thundering horde, no question. I was jealous of Maggot for the wealth of cousins he totally took for granted. Even the hot older girl cousins that were all "Oooh, Matty, I'd kill you for your eyelashes! No fair God wasted a face that pretty on a boy!" Then squealing because Maggot's trying to give them arm burns, these buff cheerleader babes that honestly could kick his puny ass any day. There's no way they were scared. It was just this routine they had, the girls saying their girl shit to Maggot, and him acting like he hates it.

And I'd be like, Really man? Yes, I get that *pretty* is one of those words a guy has to treat like it's the clap and he's got his balls to protect. The whole manhood situation with Maggot being complicated, to put it mildly. But this would happen with nobody around to judge him, just the cousins. And me, the cousinless jerk that would have paid money for some girl making that kind of fuss over me, and lying halfway on top of me in a dogpile once they've all settled down on the living room floor to watch *Walker, Texas Ranger*. Me, the jerk sitting by himself on the couch looking at my friend down there in that pile, thinking: Dude. Who hates being adored?

I've been saying Mrs. Peggot this and that, so I'll go on writing it that way because the truth is embarrassing. I called her Mammaw. Maggot called her that, so I did too. I knew his cousins were not my cousins, nor was Mr. Peggot my grandpa, I called him Peg like everybody did. But I thought all kids got a mammaw, along with a caseworker and free school lunch and the canned beanie-weenies they gave you in a bag to take home for weekends. Like, assigned. Where else was I going to get one? No prospects incoming from Mom, foster-care orphan dropout. And the mother of Ghost Dad, already discussed. So I got to share with Maggot. This seemed fine with Mrs. Peggot. Other than my official sleeping place being at Mom's, and Maggot having his own room upstairs in the Peggot house, she played no favorites: same Hostess cakes, same cowboy shirts she made for us both with the fringe on the sleeves. Same little smack on the shoulder with her knuckles if you cussed or wore your ball cap to her table. Not to say she ever hit hard. But Christ Jesus, the tongue-thrashings. To look at her, this small granny-type individual with her short gray hair and mom jeans and flat yellow sandals, you're going to think: Nothing at all here to stand in my way. The little do you know. If you're going to steal or trash-talk your betters or break her tomato plants or get caught huffing her hair spray out of a paper bag, the lady could scold the hair off your head.

She was the only one to use my real name after everybody else let it go, Mom included. I didn't realize until pretty late in life, like my twenties, that in other places people stick with the names they start out with. Who knew? I mean, Snoop Dogg, Nas, Scarface, these are not Mom-assigned names. I just assumed every place was like us, up home in Lee County, where most guys get something else on them that sticks. Shorty or Grub or Checkout. It's a good guess Humvee was not Humvee to begin with. Mr. Peggot was Peg after he got his foot crushed by one of those bolting machines they use in the coal mines. Some name finds you, and you come running to it like a dog until the day you die and it goes in the paper along with your official name that everybody's forgotten. I have looked at the obits page and thought about how most of these names are harsh. Who wants to die an old Stubby? But in life it's no big deal, you can buy a beer for your best friend Maggot without either one of you giving it a thought.

So it was not usual for Mrs. Peggot to keep my born name in the mix after others had moved on from it. It's Damon. Last name of Fields, same as Mom's. At the time of filling in the hospital forms after my action-packed birth, she evidently had her reasons for not tagging me to my dad. From what I know now, there's no question, but looking like him was something I had to grow into, along with getting hair. And in those days, with her looks still being the main item in Mom's plus column and the words "bad choice" yet to join her vocab, maybe there were other candidates. None on hand to gentleman up and sign over his name. Or drive her home from the hospital. That job, like most gentleman-up stuff in Mom's life, fell to Mr. Peg. Was he happy about it or not, another story.

As far as the Damon part, leave it to her to pop out a candy-ass boy-band singer name like that. Did she think she'd even get me off her tits before people turned that into Demon? Long before school age, I'd heard it all. Screamin' Demon, Demon Semen. But once I got my copper-wire hair and some version of attitude, I started hearing "Little Copperhead." Hearing it a lot. And look, no red-blooded boy wants to be Little Anything. Advice to anybody with the plan of naming your kid Junior: going through life as mini-you will be as thrilling as finding dried-up jizz on the carpet.

But having a famous Ghost Dad puts a different light on it, and I can't say I hated being noticed in that way. Around the same time Maggot started his shoplifting experiments, I was starting to get known as Demon Copperhead. You can't deny, it's got a power to it.

3

From the day Murrell Stone walked up our steps with his Davidson boot chains jingling, Mom was like, He's a good man. He likes you, and you like him. I had my instructions.

Stoner is the name he went by, and if he said nice things to Mom, she was all ears. By now she's been sober long enough to keep her Walmart job through all restocks of the seasonal aisles: Halloween costumes, Santa crap, Valentines, Easter candy, folding lawn chairs. She's up on the rent and has her drawer full of sobriety chips that she takes out late at night and looks over like a dragon sitting on its treasure. That much I remember. Mom getting home from work and into her cutoffs, cracking open a Mello Yello, sitting on our deck smoking with her feet up on the rail and her legs stretched out trying for the free version of a tan, yelling at Maggot and me down in the creek not to get our eyes put out from running with sticks. Life is great, in other words.

What I don't remember is what I didn't know: How does it feel to turn legal drinking age, and already be three years into AA? How much does it suck to have a school-age kid and a long-termed relationship with the Walmart party-supplies aisle while the friends you used to have are still running around looking to get high or drunk or married, ideally some perfect combo of all three? All Mom had to work with were middle-aged type people in their thirties at least: sobriety buddies and Walmart buddies that would tell her "You have a blessed day, hon," and go home to their husbands and buckets of chicken and *Jeopardy*. She'd tried and failed at more boyfriends by this time, post me getting born, which all dumped her because (a) they got her off the wagon and into hot legal water with motherhood, or (b) she was no fun.

Then along comes Stoner, claiming he respects a clean woman. Looking something like Mr. Clean himself, cue-ball head, big biceps, gauges instead of the earring. Mom said he could grow hair if he wanted to, but liked shaving his head. To her mind, a ripped, bald guy in a denim vest and no shirt was the be-all end-all of manhood. If you're surprised a mom would discuss boyfriend hotness with a kid still learning not to pick his nose, you've not seen the far end of lonely. Mom would light me a cigarette and we'd have our chats, menthols of course, this being in her mind the child-friendly option. I thought smoking with Mom and discussing various men's stud factors was a sign of deep respect. So I came to know such things: a whole head with a five o'clock shadow, dead sexy. But Stoner ran out of steam on his shaving at a certain point because he had a full beard, the biggest and blackest you'll see outside of a Vandal Savage comic.

One of the above powerful figures has plagued the earth with misery since before all time. And one makes Mr. Clean's Clean Freak spray that will take the mold off your crappy shower curtain and make it like new. According to Mom, Stoner was door number two.

She started coming home from work and getting into more makeup instead of less, in case he showed. And he did, passing out compliments. Mom is gorgeous, she's killing him with it, prettier than two peaches. Me, he called His Majesty. What is that supposed to mean, for a kid that owes most of his growth so far to signing his mom's name on the SNAP free-lunch forms? Stoner said my trouble was, I'd gotten used to being a mama's boy. If he caught me lying with my head on Mom's lap while we watched TV, he'd say, "Oh look. The little king is on his throne."

But he owned a late-model Ford pickup and a Harley FXSTSB Bad Boy, both completely paid off, and that part of the Stoner deal was hard to despise. He'd kick down the stand on the Harley and go inside to see Mom. Cue for me and Maggot to spend the next solid hour touching that hog, looking at our own stupid faces in its chrome, daring each other up onto its seat. Fully believing if Stoner came outside at that moment, we'd get the electric chair.

So the day he roared up and asked if I wanted a ride, just down to the highway and back, Christ on a crutch. Why wouldn't I? Maggot looked at me like, *Man*, you have all the luck. Mom yelled down from the deck, "You hang on to him, Stoner, I'll tar you if you get him hurt."

My problem was no shoes. It was a Saturday, and we'd been doing target practice with Hammerhead Kelly, that was some form of Peggot-cousin add-on by marriage, older than us. Quiet kid, Mr. Peggot's favorite to take deer hunting. He'd brought over an air rifle, with our creek being full of items to shoot at, anyway the point being I had to think where my shoes were. Maggot's house probably. Mom seemed to think I needed them and said go get them on, so I did.

But not without Mrs. Peggot first grilling me about what was up. She was watching out her window. Mom had walked down to the road and Stoner was bent over kissing her like he was trying to suck something out of her guts with a straw. And her a willing party to the crime.

Mrs. Peggot gave me the advice that I would probably fall off that boy's motorcycle and crack my head wide open. "And the worst of it is, he might drive off and leave you," she said.

Jesus. As much as I'd wanted to climb on that Harley and tear down the road for all to see, now I couldn't stop picturing my head lying open like the halves of a walnut shell, neighbors all crowded around, Stoner speeding off for the blue yonder. I mean, Mrs. Peggot was not one to blow smoke, the lady knew shit. What a boy's brains look like laid open, I had no idea of at the time, which now I do. It's high on a list of things I wish I could unsee. But my little mind had a brutal talent for pictures. I went outside and told Stoner my stomach hurt. Maggot would have sold his own nuts to go in my place, but being a true friend, he just told Hammerhead we should all go inside and play Game Boy till I felt better.

"Suit yourself," Stoner said. But it was how he said it, like "Shoot yourself." Standing with his arm draped over Mom's shoulders like he'd already made the down payment.

The day would come though, for me to ride on that hog, crammed between him and Mom like the cheese of a sandwich, getting a better look than needed at his neck tattoos. Mom behind me with her yellow hair flying and her arms reaching around to hold on to Stoner's ripped abs. The neck tattoos ran quite a ways up onto his scalp. I wondered if those came before or after the idea of shaving his head. The dumb things a kid thinks about instead of the bigger questions, like, Where is this joy ride taking the three of us in the long run?

The first time, it was to Pro's Pizza. Stoner ordered us an extra-large with everything, a pitcher for himself, Cokes for me and Mom. After we'd put a pretty good hurt on the pizza, Mom excused herself for a minute to the ladies'. These two friends of Stoner's came over and sat down in our booth like it was no big deal, they were just taking the next shift.

I didn't know these guys. In Lee County they say you have to look hard for a face you've not seen before, which surely was true for Mom, who'd directed any-body that could walk to where the Solo cups are kept on Aisle 19. But it's different for a kid, where you stick closer to your own. I'd noticed these men looking Mom up and down, but I didn't see how they were part of our group. The one that slid in next to Stoner was pale and white-haired, with a lot of ink, including an extra eye on the middle of his throat, don't ask me why that's a good idea. The one sitting by me reeked of Axe spray and had the small type mustache and goat you'd normally see on the devil and Iron Man. My brain with its kid obsession of superheroes and evil supervillains wandered off to how I would draw them. The inked one I would name Extra Eye, that could see your thoughts. The other was Hell Reeker, with the power of slaying you with his smell.

They got in a conversation with Stoner. What's this one called. A little Demon, huh? Demon Spawn, jokes I'd heard a million times. Then Reeker came up with "Spawn of the Centerfold," and Extra Eye said, "A fox is going to whelp her pups, Stoner. You're lucky it's just the one." And Stoner said he'd better watch it because some people are smarter than you think.

"Oh yeah, who's that?" Extra Eye asked. I was curious too.

"Bear," Stoner told him, which was a letdown. I thought maybe he'd meant me.

"Bear who?" they wanted to know.

Stoner did a fast little wink. "Mr. Grin's friend, you damn idjits. Mr. Bear It."

"Oh, I got ya," Reeker said. "Mr. Cross-to-Bear."

I already knew at my tender age a decent list of assholes, but none by the name of Bear. These guys laughed about him until Mom got back, which was taking forever. They got cups out of the dispenser and helped themselves to Stoner's beer, and asked about his drilling project. If Stoner drilled wells, that was news to me. Stoner asked what they would do if they found a cherry Camaro they wanted to buy, but it came with a trailer on the back.

"To *buy*, or just take for a hard run?" Extra Eye wanted to know, and Reeker asked, "How firm is the hitch, man?" All three of them laughing their asses off. I sat there sucking my Coke down to the ice till my throat froze to a hard round hole, confused by all that was said.

After school let out for summer, the Peggots offered to take me to Knoxville. They were going to see Maggot's aunt June, staying two weeks. She was a hospital nurse and doing well for herself, living in an apartment with a spare room. For a person not even married, that's a lot of space.

My first question: Is Knoxville near the ocean. Answer: Wrong direction. I've mentioned I was a weird kid regarding this seeing the ocean thing. So that was a letdown. Virginia Beach wasn't out of the question, just to be clear. Not like Hawaii or California, impossible. Seven hours and a tank of gas gets you there, according to Mom's coworker Linda that went for a week every summer with her husband and stayed in a condo. But the Peggots were going to see their daughter and letting me tag along, so I should be polite about it. And really the idea of going any place other than school, church, and Walmart was pretty exciting. Up to then, I hadn't.

What about Mom, was my next question. "She'll be late to work if I'm not here to remind her to set the alarm," I told Mrs. Peggot. I had a lot of concerns, like finding her work shoes for her and her ID badge, and remembering to go to the grocery. Mrs. Peggot was not really getting the situation of me and Mom. Who would get her Mello Yellos for her out of the fridge, and who would she talk to? Mrs. Peggot said I should go ask Mom myself, which I did. I was sure she would say no, but she lit up and started on how much fun that would be, me in Knoxville with the Peggots. Almost like, not surprised.

The night before we left, I stuffed my pillowcase full of underwear and T-shirts and my notebook of superhero drawings, and slept in my clothes. In the morning I was out on the deck an hour before they packed up their truck, which was a Dodge Ram club cab with the fold-down back seats that face each other. Maggot and I would play slapjack and kick each other's scabby knees all the way to Knoxville.

Mom sat out there with me waiting for the Peggots to shine, and the sun to come up over the mountains that threw their shade on us. Living in a holler, the sun gets around to you late in the day, and leaves you early. Like much else you might want. In my years since, I've been amazed to see how much more daylight gets flung around in the flatter places. This and more still yet to be learned by an excited kid watching his pretty mom chain-smoke and listen to the birds sing. She tried to pass the time by asking the bird names, which I'd told her before. I only knew some few, Mr. Peg knew them all. Jenny wren, field canary, joree bird. If we'd splash our armpits and faces in the sink instead of a real shower, he'd say we were taking a joree bath. Which is what I did that morning, in my big hurry to leave Mom. It's all burned in my brain. How she kept thinking of things to remind me about: act decent, remember please and thank you, especially whenever they pay for stuff, and don't go poking around June's apartment. Things you'd need to tell a kid before he goes out of state. I told her to set the damn alarm clock. Which made her laugh because I'd already stuck a note on the refrigerator: SET THE DAM ALARM CLOCK. She said she loved me a whole lot and not to forget about her, which was weird. Mom was not usually all that emotional.

Finally Mr. Peg down at the road hollered "All right then, we're fixing to go." I started down the steps, but Mom tackled me with all of them watching, kissing on my neck until I was pretty much dead of embarrassment.

And that was it, we left her. Mr. Peg waved, but Mrs. Peggot just stared at her, making a long kind of face. I could still see it any time she turned around to ask us if we were buckled up and did we want any cookies yet. She wore that face well over the state line.

4

Knoxville had a surprise in store: a girl named Emmy Peggot that lived with Aunt June in her apartment, the daughter of Maggot's dead uncle Humvee. Of the birdhouse. She was a skinny sixth grader with long brown hair and this look to her, cold-blooded. Carrying around at all times a Hello Kitty backpack that she looked ready to bludgeon you with, then tote around your head inside. Getting to the bottom of all that was going to take some time.

Right away we piled into Aunt June's Honda to take us all to lunch at Denny's, except Mr. Peg that needed to put up his bum leg after the drive. Aunt June made us belt up, which was the first I'd seen of three functioning belts in a back seat. Emmy sat in the middle not talking to us, fishing hair scrunchies and whatever out of her backpack, making a show of not letting us see what else was in there, like it might be something too shocking for our young minds.

Aunt June let us order anything we wanted, so it was like a birthday. We sat by the window and it was hard to concentrate, with everything going on out there. I might have been the only kid at school that hadn't been to a city before, other than a girl with no parents and epileptic by the name of Gola Ham. Other kids my age had mostly been to Knoxville because people have kin there. Now I was getting my eyes full. If something went by like a cop cruiser with a dog in back, or a tow truck pulling a crushed Mustang, I'd yell, Oh *man*, look at that! And Emmy would cut her eyes over at me like, *So? People don't total their fucking cars where you come from?* Aunt June was busy talking to Mrs. Peggot about her job. She had to go in to work after lunch until the next morning: day and night shifts back-to-back. She talked about the long hours and what she saw in the ER, like a pregnant lady that came in gut-stabbed with her baby still inside. Which if you think about it, would make a crushed Mustang not that big a deal.

More ER stories were still to come, told to Maggot and me by Emmy after she got over herself and started speaking to us. It turns out, the worst shit people can think of to do to each other up home is also thought of and done in Knoxville. Probably more so. The thing about a city is, it's huge. Obviously I'd seen city on TV because that's all they ever show (other than Animal Planet), so I was expecting something like Knoxville. Only I had the idea you'd go around a corner and you'd be out of it. Back to where you'd see mountains, cattle pastures, and things of that kind, alive. No dice. Whenever Aunt June took us out, we'd drive down twenty or thirty streets with buildings only. You couldn't see the end of it in any form. If you are one of the few that still hasn't been, let me tell you what a city is. A hot mess not easily escaped.

Did Maggot already know about Emmy, before we came? Yes. Everybody in his family knew, and so did my mom, which freaked me out. For some reason the subject of dead Humvee having a daughter living with Aunt June was not to be mentioned back home, ever. Maggot said I could talk to Mom since she already knew, but not Stoner. I said I was pretty sure he and Mom would break up by the time we got back, so. Not a problem. This conversation was on our first night, with Emmy asleep. We'd stayed up watching *Outer Limits* and finally she conked. Maggot crawled over and took her backpack out of her hands to make sure she was really asleep.

So Aunt June's spare room was actually home to the

Ice Maiden. She had to move out of it for her grand-parents to use for our two weeks visit. We kids slept in a giant nest we made in the living room out of pillows and sheets. We called it a fort, but Emmy corrected us that it was our "ship." The SS *Blow It Out Your Anus*, Maggot suggested, which got him demoted. She had all these tiny stupid dolls in tiny stupid suitcases, and in Emmy's world they had ranks: lieutenant, private, etc. Maggot usually ended up below the entire suitcase-doll militia as something like dishwasher, whereas I was in the middle. We tried involving her dolls in robberies and murders, which she surprised us by being totally into. She said there was a place outside Knoxville called Body Farm where they buried dead bodies and then dug them up after they'd rotted, to study the scientific aspect of crimes. Fine, we played by her rules and slept in a pillow ship. I asked if she'd ever seen the ocean. Never and no thanks, was her answer. She'd been to Undersea Wonders Aquarium in Gatlinburg, and the sharks terrified her.

If you asked me, her building was scarier than any sharks. Like being trapped in a Duke Nukem doom castle. A thousand other families living there, every front door opening into one hallway. Stairs going down past other hallways. Outside the main front door, a street full of cars and cars, people and people. There was no *outside* anywhere. I asked Emmy who all these other people were, and she said she had no idea but you couldn't talk to them due to stranger danger. Doom castle was normal to her. Supposedly she had school friends with Nike Air Maxes, Furbys, etc., meaning cooler than us grimy fourth graders, but where were they? Nowhere. She couldn't see them all summer. They lived in other doom castles. There was no running wild here like we did at home, adults around or not, ideally not. Emmy was not on her own for one second, due to all the unknown people and murder potential. After school she went to a lame place where they did crafts until the moms showed up, with kids that were not at her level. Her words. On Aunt June's night shifts, because they kept that ER going around the clock, there was an old lady downstairs with two stink-eye cats where Emmy went for sleep, breakfast, and TV watching, meaning one neighbor at least was not a criminal mind. Her cats, possibly. That was the life of Emmy: school, making crap out of Popsicle sticks, sleep.

Aunt June had days off coming, and said we'd do stuff then. In the meantime, Mr. and Mrs. Peggot sat at the table with the lights shut off, not wanting to use up their daughter's electricity. Mr. Peg didn't know the streets, and there wasn't any yard. I mean, none, because I asked. I didn't believe the world would even have a place like this. Not just from the kid viewpoint of no place to mess around. Where would these people grow their tomatoes?

The apartment itself was nice, if you overlooked where it was. Classy, like Aunt June, with her shiny fingernails and short brown hair like Posh of the Spice Girls. Little freckles. Definitely hot, or so I'd have thought if I wasn't calling her Aunt June. Her furniture was a cut above what people usually have, matching. A fridge where ice and cold water came out the front, and a kitchen counter with stools. Bookshelves with books. One bathroom for everybody and another one for Aunt June only, in her bedroom, with a tub. I was still scared of those somewhat but didn't let on. She also had a closet with a shoe rack on the door, twenty-one pairs of shoes, actual count. On our first day Emmy made a point of showing us all these special features of the place, which took maybe an hour. Then we were pretty much lost for stuff to do. Mrs. Peggot poked into June's closet and got to mending. She could mend anything at all to where you couldn't tell it was ever ripped, and made all Maggot's clothes, one of her powers. Mr. Peg read the *Knoxville News Sentinel*, including obituaries of a thousand people he didn't know, and griped about having no place to go smoke. Then figured out to go downstairs on the sidewalk in front of the building with more people he didn't know, all smoking hard in a friendly way. Maggot and I took turns on his Game Boy while we waited for Aunt June to finish up saving people from their code blues and their GSWs. Or I drew in my notebook. I made one drawing of Aunt June in the bra-type outfit like she was Wonder Woman, with the superpower of what Aunt June actually did in real life. It would get so quiet we could hear people in the other apartments, or their TVs. A city is the weirdest, loneliest thing.

Aunt June's bedroom closet was carpeted, the inside of a closet if you can believe, and big enough for the three of us. We'd sit in the dark with stripes of light coming sideways through slits in the door, me and Maggot and the twenty-one pairs of shoes, hearing Emmy's ER stories. Some guy's cut-off leg that got buried with the wrong body. Also Aunt June stories. Guys at Jonesville High that had wanted to screw her but got kicked to the curb, even after one or more of them begged her to marry him. Same thing, different guys, in nursing school. We kept waiting for the part about what happened to Emmy's parents and why she's living with Aunt June, if the lady was so hot to get away from the would-be husbands and babies. No mention. Emmy had other concerns, like her secret stash under some loose carpet. The first time she went digging around, I saw the light-striped face of Maggot looking at me like, What the hell? And up she comes with flattened packs of cigarettes and gum. Asking did we want gum. We said okay.

She said, "How does it feel to want?"

We watched her peel the foil off one stick of gum, very slowly. Watched her put it in her mouth, hypnotized by the weirdness of this chick. Drooling, even if we didn't want any in the first place. She pushed her hair back over her skinny shoulders. We smelled the fruity smell.

"Rude," Maggot said after a minute.

She said, "Talk to the hand."

Aunt June was the opposite of Emmy. She gave us our own special bowls for snacks we could eat any time we wanted. She finally got her days off, and took us all over: a trampoline park, putt-putt golf, the hospital. The zoo, where we spent a whole day. Tigers, giraffes, and all like that. Monkeys, which Maggot and I figured out how to get all riled up until Aunt June said knock it off or we were going straight home. She was extra nice, but the lady took no shit. It was a stinking hot day, which probably the animals were liking no more than us. The only happy campers were these small-size penguins that slid down rocks into their not-so-clean pool, over and over. I was like, Hey, the life! I'd take it, penguin shit and all. I asked Aunt June if there was an ocean part of the zoo, which there wasn't. I might have asked a few times.

Then she got this idea. She took hold of my ears and stood looking at me, like she had me by the handles. "I know what you'd love," she said. In Gatlinburg they had a giant aquarium place that was full-on ocean. Sharks and everything. I didn't mention Emmy already telling me about this place, that she was definitely not a fan of. Aunt June let go of my ear-handles and said just as soon as she had more days off, we'd drive over there. And Emmy gave me this look like, You were warned, so don't cry when you wake up with your nuts ripped off.

But we were going, sharks and all, even if Emmy was afraid. Every dog gets his day.

Aunt June was working all hours, plus taking us places, and being a kid I gave it no real thought until one night she came in late, or early morning maybe. I was awake but didn't want to spook her by saying anything. Then after a while it was too weird for her to know I was lying in the pillow pile watching her. She poured herself a glass of water and took off her white shoes and sat down at the table and just stared at the glass. Pulled both hands through her hair like she was combing it, exactly a thing Maggot did sometimes. She had his same eyes, the blue and the dark lashes that his girl cousins wanted to kill him over. I'd never seen Maggot's mom, but now I thought about her being Aunt June's little sister. Those two playing together. Now here was one of them trying with all her might to put people back together, and the other in Goochland serving ten to twelve for trying to cut a person to pieces, damn near with success.

Aunt June stretched her legs out under the table and leaned back in the chair and stayed that way for so long I thought she must have fallen asleep, but she hadn't. After a while I could hear her letting her breath out, long and quiet like an air mattress with a slow leak. It was unbelievable, how much she had to let out. It went on forever.

The aquarium turned out to be the best day of my life. If I ever get to see the real ocean and it turns out better than Undersea Wonders in Gatlinburg, I'll be amazed. You name it, they had it: seahorses, octopus, jellyfish that swam upside down. Shallow tanks you could reach in and touch stuff. The main attraction was the Shark Tunnel, where you walked under a giant tank with the bigger individuals: sharks, rays, turtles. But turtles the size of a Honda. A Saw Fish, which is like a shark except sticking out of its face is something like a chain saw. I kid you not.

Mrs. Peggot came with us that day. One or the other always had to stay behind so the rest of us could fit in the car. If Mr. Peg stayed, he'd fix something. Or Mrs. Peggot would stay and have supper ready for us, which made Aunt June homesick. On the Gatlinburg day Mrs. Peggot and Aunt June never stopped talking, even though there was amazing shit they should have been paying attention to, such as a Saw Fish. Also she'd paid some crazy amount of money like a hundred dollars to get us in. But we were leaving soon, and I guess mom and daughter still had ground to cover. Such as how hard June worked, which Mrs. Peggot was opposed to, and something about her rotation or moving to a different hospital. A guy named Kent she was thinking of going out with, that she called a drug rep, which I figured must not be the same as a dealer, Aunt June being all on the up and up. None of it of course any of my business.

We saved the Shark Tunnel for last because it was best, and because Aunt June and Emmy were in mortal combat all week over whether Emmy was going in there. She started out refusing to go to Gatlinburg, period. Her next failed plan was to stay in the car while we all went in. Aunt June had this way of being dead calm, but it's her way or the highway. You could see her in the ER saying, "I'm sorry about the bullet holes in you sir but I've got a job to do here." Long story short, Emmy was going in the damn Shark Tunnel. Aunt June said she'd been too young that first time, but she needed to get back on the horse and see there was nothing to fear.

So in we went, Aunt June ignoring Emmy, while Maggot and I got our minds blown by a million tons of water over us with huge things swimming in it. The floor itself moved. I was not expecting that. Pulled by our own shoes into the briny deep. I turned around to see what Emmy thought, and holy Moses. The girl was dead frozen. People with their strollers and drinks jostling around her to get into this thing they paid good money for, and Emmy, scared out of her mind.

I didn't really think, just headed back. But the floor was moving, so I was going nowhere, somewhat like a dream in how it felt like time was not time. Her scared eyes watching me. I shoved through the people all looking up at sea creatures, basically Aquaman in the Lagoon of Atlantis, until I was on solid ground with Emmy hanging on me like a true drowning person.

"It's okay," I told her. "We weren't going to go off and leave you."

"She did, though. She didn't even look back."

"She wouldn't have left the building. She was coming back for you after the tunnel."

Emmy was shivering. "She didn't act like it."

"She was," I said. "Aunt June is perfect like that. She keeps track."

I figured on having to wait with her till the others came back, then hearing about the Gatlinburg fucking Shark Tunnel from Maggot for the rest of my natural life. But for whatever reason Emmy said okay, let's do it. I had to hold her hand. She kept her eyes closed.

It was true about Aunt June keeping track. Which was not true of my mom in any way, shape, or form. So that was me promising Emmy that life is to be trusted. I knew better. I should have let her go with her gut: Never get back on the horse, because it's going to throw you every damn chance it gets. Then maybe she'd have been wise to the shit that came for her later on, and maybe it would have turned out better. Which is me saying too much, for now. Sorry.

Aunt June gave us all five dollars to spend in the gift shop. Maggot bought a plastic hammerhead shark, Emmy got rock candy, and everybody was waiting. On snap decision I bought this thing for Emmy, a little silver bracelet with a snake as part of it. The package said moray eel, whatever. I gave it to her while we were walking to the car. I said probably she hated snakes, but it was like her bravery badge. She just said thanks. Then on the drive home she mentioned she was in love with me and we would get married whenever we got old enough. Okay, I said. I was pretty much used to the chain of command by then. But to tell the truth, kind of shocked. I asked her, Why me? Why not Maggot? And she said, Duh. Matty's my cousin.

That gave me the usual sting of not having my own cousins. But I hadn't considered there being a plus side, like Emmy eligible to be in love with me. I told her I didn't know how. She said no worries, it was easy, she did it all the time with boys at school and the Popsicle stick place.

Maggot said that just proved she was a slut. I think he was feeling left out.

The day we packed up to go home, Emmy pounced with all these instructions. I was to talk Mom into letting me call her. This being the nineties, no Facebook, no texting. Emmy said if I didn't call, she'd drop me and be in love with somebody else. Might as well learn that one early, I'm going to say. But I hadn't thought much about Mom since we left. Even though she was all, Don't forget me, which I thought was stupid. Who forgets his mom? But yet I had.

I made up for it by thinking about her a lot on the way home. It's two hours, but we stopped for gas and Cokes at Cumberland Gap, and at the park where they have the bison. Mr. Peg was the slowest driver imaginable. Finally we chugged up the driveway at a mind-shattering five miles an hour, and I was ready to open the door and roll out before he got to a stop. But Mrs. Peggot turned around and laid a hand on my arm while the others got out. She said she had something she was supposed to tell me. She was nervous, which I didn't like one bit.

"Well, you're not going to tell me she's dead, because I can see her," I said. Mom must have heard the truck because she'd come outside. She was up there waiting on the deck.

"No, nobody's dead. It's good news," Mrs. Peggot said. "You've got a daddy."

"And he's *dead*," I said. Even though trying to be respectful.

"Well, no, he isn't. Not the one I'm telling you about."

I thought about the grave where he was buried, which had been much discussed as regards my seeing it, and I blurted out, "Lazarus isn't real!"

She gave me a funny look. "No, not him. A new one. Now I've told you, so go on."

I didn't understand, even after I was up on the deck getting attacked by Mom's hugs and kisses. Then Stoner came out of the house. For a split second I wondered what he would think of me having a new dad, and then I got it.

5

In the two weeks I was gone, Mom did these things:

1. Got married to Stoner.

2. Took off work for a weekend honeymoon to Luray Caverns.

3. Moved the furniture around.

My bedroom was the bigger one, and now according to Mom we had to swap, because it was her and Stoner versus one of me. She said we'd get a better house pretty soon because Stoner made a good living. I walked around my house that wasn't my house while

Stoner with his boots up on the coffee table paged through his *American Iron,* not even in a shirt, just his wifebeater. Like it's his kingdom now and he's got nobody to impress.

In my room that wasn't my room, the bed was under the window where I hated it, and my action heroes were put on their shelf in the stupidest way imaginable, the reds together, greens with greens, nothing to do with their actual alliances or powers. It looked like some brainless ghost kid had been locked in here while I was gone, lining up his stuff in meaningless ways.

Also, Maggot's and my fort had a dog in it now. Like Vandal Savage's beard, huge and black, with hate in its eyes. It barked and flung itself at the chain link any time you got close.

School was starting in a few weeks, and for the first time ever I wanted summer over with. Who knew that was possible? Meantime, I spent all hours over at Maggot's, telling him how lucky he was not to have parents he had to live with, Maggot being in total agreement. From his room upstairs we'd watch Stoner at the dog pen having his "sessions" with Satan. In case you thought I was being a crybaby, asshole names his dog Satan. Trains it to the path of murder using raw steak: shaking it, yanking it away, dog is going full apeshit. Stoner getting off on that.

"Mother H. Fuck, you better stay over here till that dog rips out the master's lungs," was Maggot's advice, not at all needed. That was my plan for the rest of the summer. After that, my time there would be limited to the after-school hours. I assumed the Peggots would be on board.

Who was *not* on board was Mom. She started asking questions. Were the Peggots trying to turn me against Stoner? No trying needed, job well done by the man himself, I told Mom. She smacked me for having a smart mouth. But that was by no means the end of it. She acted like the neighbors' opinions of her new husband mattered more than mine. Or hers either.

Finally I got mad and told her what Mrs. Peggot had said one time, about Stoner not caring if I fell off the back of his Harley and busted my brains. Mom got this wide-eyed look, and said I was not to go back over there the rest of the week. Mom was a small person, tiny really, which according to Mrs. Peggot was from Mom having me before she was done growing herself. The upshot of this being, by age ten I was catching up to her, heightwise, and had started on certain occasions to tell her, "Try and stop me." This was one of those occasions.

This time her answer was maybe she couldn't, but

Stoner sure as hell could. And maybe *that's* what she needed a husband for, if I was wondering.

We were in other words turning into a domestic shit show. I was too mad to care, but I think Mom was having her doubts. With Stoner always grilling her on why she dressed like a whore, who was she flirting with at work, where did she go afterwards, which was nowhere. He didn't even like her going to her AA and NA meetings because it was mostly men. He passed up no occasion to remind her she was married now, so there'd be no more playing the field.

So maybe Mom's pep talks were as much for her benefit as for mine. How lucky we were, because Stoner had a good job. Not a point to be argued in Lee County, I'll grant you. The business he worked for was picking up, he'd be making good money, we would be safe.

This job that made Stoner the second coming of Jesus? A CDL driver. Meaning he drove a semi, with a special license so he could drive not just ordinary everyday shit around in his truck but *beer.* Or as Stoner called it, Product. Distribution truck driver for Anheuser-Busch. He had to pass an annual test proving he could lift and move Product weighing up to 165 pounds. All this and much more I never wanted to know, he told me while lying on the floor pressing his XMark free weights that had moved in along with certain bad smells and Satan. The weights took up most of the living room, all the more so if he was lying among them in his sweaty undershirt and leather bracelet, neck veins ready to pop, grunting on each press like he's taking a shit. "Rotating and merchandising beverages at more than fifty customer accounts," he says, like he's a professor of whatever the hell. "Driving the routes to completion regardless of road conditions."

"Medical and dental" was the part that got Mom excited. I would have coverage now in case I needed my tonsils out or got hit by a car. Or the ADHD drugs that some teachers had been wanting Mom to put me on from day one. Stoner said oh, yes, the riddling or whatever would take me down a notch. Mom was on the fence. But she said definitely I was going to the dentist now, whether needed or not. Which I wasn't thrilled about. I'd heard kids say it was like a torture chamber, and I'd heard others say it wasn't that bad, the dentist. I'd never been.

Soon I found out that teeth drilling was the best of what I could expect now. A whole new life for young Demon was Stoner's plan, described to me one morning at breakfast after Mom left for work. I was going to learn self-discipline, like they teach you in the army.

Not that Stoner had done military service, mind you. I reckon he saw the movie.

My mom has been too lenient with me, says Stoner, leaning over to take another slurp of his Cheerios and milk, and I'm thinking how much he eats like a dog. Even the red plastic bowl he's eating from, how that could be a dog bowl. My mother has been letting me get away with 'tude. Now I'm going to learn how righteous people live, with discipline and respect for others.

I have nothing to say to this.

Stoner reaches forward lightning fast and decks me in the jaw. My spoon flies out of my hand onto the floor. One ear is ringing, my cheek burns. I stare at him. "What did I do?"

"Arrogant little piece of shit. It's not what you did, it's what you were thinking."

What was I thinking? That Stoner ate his breakfast like a dog. A dog with gauges in its ears. That I'd like to clip a leash in one of those holes and take him for a hell of a walk.

"Here's the thing," Stoner explains calmly, like nothing just happened. Wiping milk out of his beard with the back of his wrist, scratching his tattooed head. He says it's no surprise, me being so screwed up. How would Mom know how to raise a kid? She grew up in foster care. It's inevitable she's going to raise up another total loser. And I'm thinking, if he just called Mom a total loser, then he married her why, exactly? Losing track of where he's going with this chat about how lucky we are, Mom and me. That Stoner came along to get us both straightened out.

I sit with my fists on the table, cereal bowl between them, my red-haired head still on my neck. Stoner finishes dog-slurping his cereal, I don't blink, I don't move. I've seen the army movie too. The milk in my bowl can go sour, day can turn to night, it's nothing to me. I stay. Stoner shoves back his chair, throws his bowl in the sink, and goes out. The screen bangs shut.

Then I pick up my spoon off the floor and eat my cereal. That's the win I get, if there is one. Filling up like a bowl under a dripping faucet. Filling with hate while I wait the man out.

I told Mrs. Peggot about Stoner, and she said she'd have to talk to Mom, either that or call DSS. I picked Mom. So they had their talk. I could tell Mom was hurt at Stoner. Maybe she didn't realize how bad it was getting as regards the man-to-man shit. She tried pushing back on him some. One night she brought home a pizza, and while we were eating in the living room with the TV on, she used this bright, birdy little voice to say she still had opinions about things, and ought to be able to say them in her own house. It was during a commercial.

About what, was Stoner's question, and her answer was: Me. That I was still her son. Stoner said nothing. The show came back on, which was *Law and Order*, and I didn't want to eat any more. The pizza was a Hawaiian from Pro's with the ham and pineapple, my favorite, which Mom of course knew and Stoner didn't. This pizza was like a message in code from Mom to me, meaning: Don't give up the ship, I'm still on it with you. But now with Stoner going quiet and all brutal in his eyes, I felt like I'd be lucky to keep down what I'd eaten so far.

The show ended. Stoner got up and turned off the TV and sat back down facing Mom. "I see," he said. "Because drunks and pill heads are so good at taking care of their kids."

Mom's eyes went to mine. *The house is on fire*, is what they said, *and I'm so sorry about it that I could die.*

I knew she was sorry. We'd been over it a hundred times. That's Step 9, apologizing to all the people you've hurt. That and the higher power, the moral inventory, the practicing of the principles, we'd been through it all. She'd tried, and to be fair I guess she was trying still.

"Mom is sober," I said. "She got sober so she could keep me."

"And who the hell asked you?" He leaned over the coffee table and closed the pizza box and slid it away from where I was sitting on the floor. Like I was an animal he was training that had just lost my privileges. He turned back to Mom.

"You love your kid so much, you let the neighbors fucking raise him. Even though we've discussed this. I have talked. And you have not listened. He's still over at the damn Peggots' more than he's in his own house. Am I wrong?"

"No," Mom said.

"No I am not. You sit here turning a blind eye while he runs around with that little queer next door, with the jailbird mother. Am I wrong?"

Mom said nothing.

"The little queer's whore mother that is in the *pen* for shanking her goddamn *boyfriend*." Stoner leaned over close to Mom and yelled, "Am. I. Fucking. Wrong?"

She nodded, then shook her head. Confused, due to being terrified. He turned to me.

"Is that your plan, Demon? To grow up and be a fag?"

"I don't have a plan," I said. I couldn't even believe this conversation was happening.

"No? You're not thinking you'll find yourself a

boyfriend, and then shank him and wind up getting gangbanged in prison? Is that the kind of people we are in this family?"

I wondered how Stoner would feel about getting vomit for an answer, because that's where I was headed. But he didn't care, he turned back to yell at Mom. I was starting to run low on sorry for Mom by that point. Marrying the asshole was not my idea.

"Tell him," Stoner yelled at her. "Right now, so we can all hear it. He's not going back over there to play with the queer. Not tomorrow and not ever. Or there will be consequences."

She said it, and I didn't see forgiving her for it.

I hardly went outside again until school started. It rained the whole week, which made it feel that much more like detention. I watched a thousand reruns of *X-Men, Iron Man, Exosquad, Spawn,* and *Hulk.* Whenever Stoner wanted the TV, I went in my room and read them in the comics versions. I drew pictures in my notebook of Stoner as a supervillain getting crushed in various ways. At some point the shows, comic books, drawings, and my dreams all got mashed up so it was like there wasn't any me anymore. Just a quiet boy that looked like me with a beast inside, waiting to burst in a gamma warrior rage explosion.

What I said about people, that if they care, they can tell one kind of a thing from another? Big *if.* Possibly the biggest *if* on the planet of earth. Why notice zero on snakes, and a thousand percent on certain things about people?

You don't know me or Maggot. If you saw the two of us let's say in second grade, you'd see two of a kind. Two white boys more or less. My dead father being Melungeon, which passes generally for white, mixed with my little blondie mom. So I'm not as white as some, but enough to say so. Two little rascals then, in Walmart tennis shoes and dirty fingernails: if you're from the city, I guess you'd say a couple of little hillbillies. Matched pair.

Now I'm going to jump ahead, which is breaking my promise, but just for a minute. Ninth grade. I've got a lot of growth on me and a tiny red mustache. Maggot has grown his hair to his shoulders and started stealing eyeliner and nail polish from his cousins, worse case Walgreens. He's got spending cash, but a boy can't walk in and buy those things. Because he aims to use them. To switch out the tennis shoes also. Mrs. Peggot's homemade clothes we had turned against hard, no-thank-you on the fringe cowboy shirts. But now Maggot's tastes have started circling back around to the eye-catching.

Now take a look at us: a straight boy and a queer. No matter who you are, whatever else you might say— "Good for him," or "I want to kick his face in," or even "I don't give a damn"—you still saw what you saw. A boy and a queer. The eye sees what it cares enough to see. Even though I'm exactly the same kid I was, and so is Maggot. He was always the same Maggot.

It was me that started calling him that. We were little, and it was hilarious. And it was me that kept it up. Because Matty Peggot goes to school, and what is he going to be there but Matty Faggot? I tried to make an end run around that one. I can't say the other names never got called, they did. But apart from that night with Stoner, they weren't said where I could hear them.

I wasn't clueless to people's thinking. But a thing grows teeth once it's put into words. Now I felt that worm digging, spitting poison in my brain, trying to change how I saw Maggot. How I felt about people seeing the two of us together.

Up to then, I was a casual collector of reasons to hate Stoner. That night a fire got lit. For what he'd done to my head, I would burn the man down.

6

How Maggot's mother got to prison. How much of that story did I even know, at this point in time where Maggot and I are still running around with our little pink brains and buzz-cut pencil-eraser heads? Mrs. Peggot tried to keep the worst of it from both of us. But if a story has all the elements, it will be legend around here, where we love our neighbors so much we can't stop talking about them. It gets to be known to anybody with ears. Those we had.

It starts the usual way, a girl falling hard for the wrong guy. That was Mariah Peggot. According to everybody, she's got no business running around with the likes of Romeo Blevins. He's way too old for her and also, let's be honest, too good-looking. There's nothing wrong with Mariah, but she's not the beauty of the family. The Peggots had four girls, with the older three tying up the homecoming and everything-festival-queen side of things in Lee County for most or all of the eighties. Cheerleaders, sweethearts. June the straight-A student, and still popular enough to date any guy she wanted, which is unheard of. The Peggot girls slayed. Then comes little Mariah, flat-chested, raw-boned, stubborn as dirt. Not ugly, but she's not going to be crowned queen of anything, due to that look she had. Like: Don't even ask if I'm one of the fucking Peggot girls.

Whereas this Romeo is a stud menace. Magazine-model looks, like the dudes in the J. C. Penney's ads that would not in a million years be wearing those dad clothes if not getting paid the big bucks for it. He's dead fit, killer smile, lion-king mane, the whole pic-ture. Who knows what turned Romeo's eyes her way, but Mariah felt like she'd won the lottery, and Romeo acted that way too: like she'd won the lottery. If she wished to hang on to her luck, she could be on the for-tunate receiving end of his golden dick at his personal convenience, and at all other times run his errands without complaint. A date with Romeo might involve going over to his house to do his laundry. He has a two-bedroom A-frame home in the woods, up on the mountain outside of Duffield, and a successful business as an auto mechanic with his own gear in a panel truck. Not standard grease-monkey shit, we're talking electronics. Diagnostic capabilities. This is the era of cars beginning to get the fancy circuitry in everything from power windows to brakes, just so they can lose their complete minds at the drop of a hat. And Romeo brings this auto shop to you, is the thing. So handy in times of a breakdown, he can charge what he wants. Because you won the lottery, just by letting his pretty face show up.

Mrs. Peggot being no fool says "Glitter ain't gold, hon," and puts her foot down. Mariah being still in high school sees no choice but to sneak around. Maybe little sister needs to be queen for a day after all, or maybe she really loves him. Doesn't matter, she's not quitting him. If she even thinks about it, he lays that smile on her and she melts. Her junior year is one long argument in the Peggot house of "You don't know him, he's real sweet," and "Real sweet my hind foot, he's a fox in the henhouse," and "He's different whenever it's just him and me," always ending in the same place: "I've warned you, girl, so don't come crying to me." Until chapter 2, Mariah is pregnant and moves into his A-frame in the woods outside of Duffield.

This turns out to be not at all what Romeo had in mind. Before she's even had the baby, he's out running around in front of God and everybody with other girls. And suggesting Mariah is lucky to be carrying his seed. She's the one that went and got pregnant, was she not. Next comes baby, and Mariah is feeling not so much the lottery winner now, tired to death, nagging her man to stay home and help out or at the very least, quit chasing tail. For this kind of lip, she gets to be on the receiving end of quite a lot more than the golden dick and killer smile. One night after a blowout, she's threatening to call her sister June to come help her pack up the baby and get out of there. He rips the phone out of the wall, knocks her flat, and ties her hands behind her back with the phone cord. Drags her outside screaming, binds her good and well to the deck railing. Gets his Ruger and rolls it around in her mouth, asking how that smart piehole of hers likes sucking cold metal cock. Takes the barrel tip that's wet with her spit and draws a big smile across her face. Says she ought to try it sometime, it might make her less unsightly. Then rips her shirt open and with his cold spit pencil he draws a big heart on her chest, says she ought to try loving her man too. Wear something decently sexy instead of the ugly-ass nursing bras. Why is she still being a cow for that kid anyway, he's practically walking, it's disgusting. God-damn Mariah Peggot finally grows a pair of tits and they're the property of a goddamn infant.

Eventually Romeo gets bored, shoves the piece in his pocket, and drives off. Not in his panel truck either, Mariah's Chevy Monza being the better getaway car. This is not the end of Mariah's bad day. It's the beginning. The front door he's left standing open so she can see Matty in his playpen in the living room. She has to watch him getting hungry and scared out of his mind. He's far from walking yet, barely sitting-up age, always-empty age, crying out his heart and looking through the white mesh of the playpen, his little sad eyes asking *whymommywhy?*

The first time, it's two hours. Then Romeo comes back with his pretty smile and asks her if she's sorry. She says yes, she runs to calm down and feed poor Matty, and that's what passes for making up in this love nest.

Mariah can't go begging her parents to let her come home, because she was warned. Plus stubborn as the day is long. She begs her sister for help. June is still living at home but in community college now, and a genius. The whole Peggot family in fact is a shed of sharp tools, all these gifteds and talenteds. The exception being Humvee, of the birdhouse, that recently brought disaster on the family by getting himself killed. Dark clouds over the Peggot house.

Things get worse. Romeo leaves for days at a time, only to come home demanding his dinner and sex if he feels like it, but generally so toasted he passes out facedown on the bed where he'll sleep through hell, high water, and any number of pager beeps. Mariah looks forward to these times. Because he's threatened her with all manner of shit by now, knocked out a tooth, and the tying-up thing gets to be a habit. Again one evening he leaves her outside where she can see Matty in his playpen crying himself apart. It's winter now, cold, the door's standing open, and Mariah is sure this time her child is going to die. She can yell for help all she wants, with nobody up there but the owls in the trees to answer. She's yanked her wrists around till they're cut and bleeding, but Romeo is a careful man and knows how to tie a knot.

The first hour, the baby cries till he's lacquered his little red face with snot, eyelashes all stuck together, chin quavering. Second hour he goes quiet, lying still, looking at her with those eyes. Third hour, the eyes close and his little body's shaking. She's guessing on the time, it could have been three hours or thirty minutes, but once it starts to get dark, she knows, and this is the point where Mariah remembers how to pray. Something she'd forgotten how to do some while ago, around middle school where life gets mean and a girl starts to see how mad is better than sorry, and telling better than asking. Even where God is concerned.

Mariah is thrown back on her ass. Back to asking. Please God don't let my baby die. Her boobs are rock hard and burning, she's crying tears, crying milk, lowing like a cow. Matty starts to wail again in the dark, the special howl a baby keeps on reserve if the need should arise for exploding a mother's heart. Mariah feels it like a knife in her rib cage, lifting skin from bone, but she's thanking God her baby hasn't died yet of hunger or cold or the bad luck of getting born in this shit family in their shit two-bedroom A-frame outside of Duffield. Romeo will not be back before morning. This is the night that will break and make Mariah.

She's going to act real sorry, yes, to see him come back home with his big smile. She'll put on a show, let this man believe he's the answer to her prayers. But this night she remembers the other thing she was fool enough to forget: that mad is better than sorry.

Mariah will sneak a blade out of Romeo's truck, one of those X-Actos, and duct-tape it to her body where she can reach it the next time she finds herself back-handed, in need of a cutting edge. Taped to her butt, below the butterflies-are-free tramp stamp that her parents still don't know about. One more secret, this sweet blade she takes to wearing at all times. If she finds herself tied up again, this butterfly will get herself free.

It's the edge she will use on him too. The day Romeo finally deals out one too many shitfaced fuck-you-alls to herself and the baby prior to passing out cold, deep enough that she can flip him faceup and go to work. Slicing into his cheek from the corner of his mouth till she hits jawbone, both sides, for a shit-eating smile he can wear the rest of his life. And a big heart carved into the skin of his chest. She lets no gushing blood stop her, nor the sight of yellow cheek fat falling in little chunks out of cut-open flesh, nor the screaming as he comes around. She stops short of Lorena Bobbiting him (which was maybe not invented yet), but she does enough. She can grab little Matty and light out of there knowing Daddy will not be modeling any khakis for any J. C. Penney's.

It doesn't cross her mind that he would press charges. She's young, of course, raised around good people that aren't perfect but always own up. Mariah was taught that you lie in the bed you've made. She's sure this man knew what was coming to him, and will finally be sorry. After everything. But the wicked have a different head for numbers than most. Any bad they do will end up on the side of never-mind. What's done to them weighs double.

Romeo Blevins lawyered up and gaslighted the jury like he'd gaslighted Mariah and every other soul ever to know him. Making himself out the good Samaritan, Mariah the crazy jealous bitch. That baby is not even his, says the lawyer in the alligator boots and the gold watch. Mr. Blevins was minding his own business till she came around stalking him. This is not the first time he's had such trouble, young girls get notions and will try to pin down a man with means. These are other times, it's the eighties, where they haven't invented DNA all that much, and take a man on his word. And his means. Word was, Romeo took pity on a little single mother thrown out by her parents, with no place else to go. And then she got clingy. If he so much as went out at night to help some old lady with her Camry broken down on the interstate, Mariah would throw a fit. Too unstable herself to take decent care of a child, as the baby's doctor testified. For on two occasions she'd brought the little fellow in all weak and sick from dehydration.

The more Mariah wept and wailed on the stand about tortured and tied to a deck railing overnight with the baby in the house, these far-fetched things, the crazier

she was. He had ten witnesses to her none. The Peggots did their best for Mariah, but not to the extent
of alligator-boot lawyers, such men walking a different
cut of grass from the Peggots. They didn't know what
to think. All they'd ever heard was how Romeo hung
up the moon and every damn star, Mariah being too
proud to complain to anybody but her sister, and not
even June knew the worst of it. Nobody ever saw her
tied up. By the time Mariah got to the courtroom her
scars were healed. Not his. If you've noticed, it's the
prettiest people that everybody wants to believe, and
next after that, the most wrecked. Romeo was both.
The jury decided Mariah disfigured him and ruined
his life to keep other women away, so she'd have this
prize all to herself.

This is a story that came to me in pieces, over years.
People's doubts and regrets flavored the stew along
the way. They made much of how the assault with the
deadly weapon occurred so soon after Mariah's eighteenth birthday. No wishes were made on candles, you
can bet. Romeo was not one for romance, and the shape
Mariah was in, she probably forgot it herself. Still,
a girl comes of age. If her pride had cracked sooner,
the shacking-up-with-a-minor business would have
played louder, and Mariah might not have been tried
as an adult. She could have done some time in juvie and

grown up into a whole other life, as Maggot's mother. It's all she wanted to be.

For the start of her twelve-year sentence she got sent to Marion, an extra-special prison for the deeply disturbed. Which you have to reckon she was.

Nobody believed a word out of this girl's mouth at the time of her need. And today, her side of the story stands as gospel. The world turns. It would take no time at all for people to start fussing over little Matty, telling Mrs. Peggot what a pretty baby, he didn't suck those good looks out of his thumb, did he? The apple falls straight from the tree. Everybody's got their cross to bear. Mrs. Peggot would have to serve her own time with what she'd told Mariah, about making a bed and lying in it. And with what the whole town heard: a mother turning out her own daughter. Mrs. Peggot bore her cross, changed his diapers, and taught him to tie his shoes.

How all this fits with the story of me, hard to say. Romeo drove away in his panel truck to parts unknown, where he and his new face could tell whatever story suited. I never saw that scary smile except in my nightmares. And sometimes also wide awake, in my mind. Wondering how it would look pumpkin-carved on Stoner. You lie down with snakes, you get up with the urge to bite back. All I'm saying.

7

School started, and I was ready to bust out of home lockdown. The first day we had to catch the bus down at the highway due to our road getting washed out from all the rain. It didn't look that bad honestly, but bus drivers took no chances, being mostly older ladies and the school having no money to fix a busted axle. Anyway it was not a bad walk, maybe a mile from the top where we lived. There were nine of us for our bus stop, including these first-grade twins, and two sad high school guys of different families that we understood to be marked for life. Bus riders. Even at my young age I knew if you were sixteen and could get your ass to a fast-food job or bagging groceries after school, there were vehicles to be had. We all waited in a little gang watching adults drive out to wherever, work if they were the lucky few. Maggot and me grinning like pups, trying not to paw each other's shoulders because of all the pent-up shit we had to tell each other. Or not tell, in my case, with Stoner's words hulking around in my head.

School though was still school. Math class was like, *Hey kids, welcome back! Remember math? No, Mr. Goins, we do not.* And history as everybody knows is State of Virginia in fifth grade, so it's Jamestown of the Doomed and all on from there. It took no time for Maggot and me to get back in our groove: shooting rubber bands at a suicidal wasp that flung itself at the window all through English. Scouting the lunchroom for girls that would give up their fries. Little-known fact: Maggot was almost a year older than me, but due to the bad business he had to deal with infant-wise, it took him the extra time to grow up to kindergarten size. How we ended up in the same grade. Our good luck. Now, at school with Maggot, I was a thousand miles from Stoner. If his plan was to make my home life suck so bad I wouldn't want to lay out of school, it worked like a charm.

At the end of the day, first-grade-twin-mom was waiting at the bus stop with her ATV to take all the tiny tots up the hill, blue-ribbon mommy that one. The rest of us, left to our own device. It was unthinkable now to go back to the full ban on Maggot-association. We weren't even clear on where the ban zone started. In eyeshot of my house, you had to think. To play it safe we took a few hours screwing around before making it all the way up there. I poked my head in the door and hollered but nobody was home. I went in, got a Snickers out of the fridge, and went to my room. End of story. I wish.

Mom gets home from work, yells how she hopes I had a good first day, I yell back it was okay. Then Stoner gets home: "What in the goddamn motherfuck, *Demon*. Get in here *now*."

I had tracked in some mud on the kitchen floor, and Stoner was losing his shit. It was *mud*, okay? I am a *kid*, and we live in a place that is *made* out of *mud*. Fine, I took off my shoes and put them outside, then got the mop and bucket. I'd cleaned up worse. Mom in her times of lapse was a drinker of the toilet-hugging kind. Maybe where I got my weak stomach from. She's standing by the sink saying nothing, with her hand over her mouth in case it was to get any ideas. Stoner is in the doorway, hands on hips like he's the badass warden in *Escape from Alcatraz*.

I start mopping the floor, and Stoner asks what I think I'm doing. I tell him I am mopping the floor, spelled with a silent *As you can plainly see, dumbass*.

He says he doesn't think that's going to do the job. Honey, he says, do you think that mop is going to do it?

Mom looks at him. Shakes her head, no.

Stoner agrees that it is not. What he wants, I eventually figure out, is to see me down on my knees with a rag scrubbing the damn linoleum. With a bucket of water and *Clorox*, in case somebody wants to eat off that floor or maybe open a fucking tattoo parlor.

Fine, scrub the floor I did. Mind you, I'm still of an age where most moms don't want their kids messing with Clorox at all, my own included, as far as I knew. The fumes were getting me kind of high. I finished up and washed out the rags in the sink. Mom still right there with nothing to say about it. I looked at Stoner, needing to be done before I puked or passed out.

"Your boy says this is clean. Does that look clean to you?"

Mom looked over at him, surprised.

"Or does it look like his usual half-assed effort? Because I can still see his damn tracks on that floor. Can you not see the goddamn shit your son tracked in?"

Mom looked weird. I mean, she was in her regular work clothes, slacks and button blouse, Croc flats for standing in all day, hair in the ponytail she wore to look professional. But she had a glazed look, doped. Which she couldn't have been, I thought. Did I want her to whip out a blade and slice him up? No. But *something*. For her to wake up in there for godsakes and see how mad is better than sorry. But all the mad Mom ever could muster just leaked right back out of her in tears and puke. Finally she said, "Demon, you better go on and clean it again."

Bullshit. There was nothing to see. Mom's eyes were excellent. They were about the only part of her head that always worked right. Whatever, I scrubbed the floor again, and as much rage as I put into it, they'd be lucky if there was any linoleum left. I dumped the bucket again, rinsed the rags again, threw them into the bucket like a ball I was firing home from the out-field. Pushed past Stoner to get myself out the door. He caught me by the collar of my T-shirt and dragged me back inside.

Where the hell did I think I was going, was his question, because I wasn't done yet. Let's all take a look at the living room, he said. More muddy tracks on the living-room carpet. Mind you, that carpet was nasty and old to begin with, stained since the dawn of time. Me and Mom were far from the first to live in this trailer. Stoner asked me what I saw and I said, A shitty-looking carpet. He said, That's right. And he needed it clean. Because how was a man supposed to do his weight training on a floor that looked like that?

I had some suggestions that I kept to myself. Mom got out scrub brushes and the StainZaway, handed them over, and went off to hide in the kitchen. Stoner stood over me while I scrubbed at the stains with the Clorox rags and sprayed them with the carpet cleaner and by the way was getting krunked as a kite. Maggot and I had tried out StainZaway for this exact purpose one time, and got educated. There are better and worse things to huff, and StainZaway is a fast train to puke-ville. Especially if there's bleach in the mix.

So now all I can think of is puking, and Stoner making me clean up puke, then the stains of that, and I'm going to be on my knees here huffing StainZaway till somebody kills somebody. It shouldn't take long. I've got snot pouring out of my nose and this insane ringing in my ears, the theme of the *X-Men* show in my head. That one tune over and over, soundtrack to me scrubbing fury holes in the goddamn carpet: *Da-na-na-na NA na na! Da-na-na-na NA na na!!* It's so loud in my head, I honestly can't tell if it's coming out of my mouth or not, but it must be because Stoner starts yelling at me to shut the hell up. And I'm screaming back at him *Da-na-na-na NA na na!* because by this point I've pretty thoroughly lost my mind.

All I remember after that is me throwing shit around

and him grabbing both arms behind me in a hammer-lock. His hand covering my mouth so I can't breathe. With nothing else to fight with, I bite down on his hand. Sweet Jesus how that feels to sink my teeth in the meat of his hand and taste blood. Like I'm Satan, and all of life has trained me to this achievement.

I wound up in my room nursing a busted lip and hopefully nothing busted inside, though it felt possible. I sat on my bed listening to all this clanking and thumping which was Stoner shoving a thousand pounds of his stupid free weights against the outside of my bedroom door so there would be no escaping from Alcatraz. I tasted blood in my mouth, mine and his. It crossed my mind to hope I wouldn't get hep C or some such shit, but Mom always swore Stoner was clean and didn't do any drugs. Just a lot of beer, in his line of duty. After he got me penned in, I heard yelling, mostly him, a little her, more him, then quiet. Maybe they went out. Maybe they sat down and had a bite to eat before *Home Improvement* came on. It was nothing the hell to me.

I curled up on the bed and cried, which I hated myself doing, and then got up and puked. In my trash can, since I wasn't getting out to the bathroom. Upchucked the Snickers and all the french fries I'd scored off the sweet Weight Watcher girls at school, which was a shame since prospects for dinner looked dim.

I thought of running away. Getting out the window would be no small trick, since it only opened a few inches. It could break, though. It was quite a drop from there, our trailer being set on the hillside, but I could do that, with probably a minimum of broken bones. After that I was at a loss. The only place I could see going was next door, obviously not far enough. Where else was there? I thought of Aunt June. The woman was known to take in strays. I was sorry I'd never called Emmy, but Mom wouldn't pay for long distance. Emmy probably had moved on by now. I thought of her anyway, stuck in her doom castle, and felt even sorrier now in my situation of lockdown. Hitchhiking as far as Knoxville without getting picked up by cops was a stretch, and once I got there, I didn't know any address. Doom castle, second floor. What a useless dickhead. Knowing basically from birth that my mom was not to be counted on. And still no plan B.

I didn't get let out for school the next day, even though I heard Mom telling him they had attendance officers that would be calling if I stayed out of circulation too long. He said if she knew so much about raising kids, how'd she wind up with a rabid biting dog for a son. Before she went to work, she tried to explain I would need bathroom visits and some kind of food. Then left Stoner to rule over me. Never did any two guys have less to say to each other.

Eventually I was allowed back to school, but on lockdown the rest of the time. A freakish existence. I told Maggot I was thinking of running away, which he advised against. He said I had nerves of steel and Stoner would be crushed in the end. I don't remember how many days this went on, three or four, plus a heinously boring weekend. It all ran together. In the evenings I was hearing shit being said between Stoner and Mom that I didn't like the sounds of. At all. The Peggots also were probably not liking the sounds of it, with windows being open at that time of year. I tried to blot them out by drawing in my notebook, inventing various genius ways to crush the Stone Villain. Eyeballs and gauges flying out of him with action lines and little cloud bubbles—Pop! Pop! Or I would bang on the wall with my baseball bat for hours at a stretch: thud, thud. To shut the two of them up, or drive them crazy if that was still an option.

Then one evening late, the door flies open and there stands Stoner. Surprising me in my T-shirt and underpants eating a bag of Cheetos in bed because why the hell not, if that's all there is. Reading an *Avengers* that I'd read, oh, nine thousand times already.

"Your mom wants to see you," he said.

Interesting, I thought, what's the catch. I had no intention of getting out of bed, but there he stood. I'd not realized he was home. Stoner had been going out in the evenings a lot, working some weird-shit hours or more likely carousing, because who needs their beer delivered that close to closing time? He must have come back to the house without my hearing his truck or his bike. Obviously. I asked him what Mom wanted, and he said she was wanting to show how much she loved me. A weird enough statement to make me nervous. I yelled for her. No answer.

"Mom!" I said louder, bolting out to the living room. Nobody, nothing. "MOM!" And now I'm thinking, Goddammit, she's moved out. She marries the bastard, and I get stuck with him. In the kitchen there's crap everywhere, dishes in the sink. A gin bottle on the table, oh shit. Oh hell. Empty. Not a new sight to my eyes. Stoner has this look on his face I could kill him for.

She's in the bedroom. Lying there in her clothes, shoes and all, passed out. Faceup, not dead because that's the first thing I checked. Breathing, so she didn't drown herself yet. There's pill bottles on the thing by the bed, closed, so I screw open the childproof caps one at a time, three bottles. I don't know what they are, Xanax and shit she should definitely not have around, but the bottles aren't empty, thank God. She didn't down the whole batch, so she's just going for a Cadillac high, not the total checkout. But God knows she could get there anyway. Mom being not the most careful driver.

"Call nine-one-one," I tell Stoner, and the damned fool asks why.

"Call nine-one-one!" I scream at him. "*Christ*, you ignorant asshole! She might have OD'd."

At this point I'm not even thinking what "ignorant asshole" will get me in the Stoner rewards program. I already know. Life as we've lived it is over.

8

I was the one to grab the phone, with Stoner slinging punches to stop me, the two of us loud enough to get Mr. Peg banging on the kitchen door. Stoner said I'd regret making that call. I've wondered. Would Mom really have died? Or just followed her true colors and hurled up the works, living on for more Seagram's-and-nerve-pill fiestas? Could I have lasted Stoner out? At the time, I thought my life couldn't get any worse. Here's some advice: Don't ever think that.

I rode up front with the ambulance driver, trying to get my shoes tied. I'd managed to pull jeans on before the EMTs got there, but had to run out of the house carrying my shoes. That's how fast it all went down. The Peggots' truck followed on our tail. Stoner got to ride in back with Mom, because by this time he's all

"Yes, sir, I am the husband," so much bullshit coming out of his mouth I was choking on the fumes, starting the minute they showed up and asked who made the call. Stoner did, of course. (Wait, what?) Patient's name, date of birth, pill bottles pulled out of Stoner's pocket where he'd stashed them quick. Names on the bottles confirmed by him to be Mom's coworkers, and they would be getting a piece of his mind. All respectful and *oh my gosh* and *those so-and-sos*, like he's a damn Sunday school teacher. It was the most words I'd ever heard come out of him without an "asshole" or "motherfucker." Was this a whole new Stoner, shocked by dire events into manning up? Not a chance.

We tore down Long Knob Road, siren screaming, past all the little settlements of people in bed. In Pennington Gap we ran straight through the red lights and then were at the hospital with all parties running around six ways to Sunday. I wasn't allowed in the ER, or the room where they moved her after that, due to being a child. I sat in the waiting room with the Peggots forever. We were starving, so Mrs. Peggot went to get whatever they had in the vending machines, and hot coffee for Mr. Peg. We ate four packs of nabs each, then Maggot stretched out on the connected plastic chairs and conked out. Mrs. Peggot felt we should go home, since we had school tomorrow. Right then the lady from DSS showed up, saying she needed to speak with me.

I didn't know this lady at all. She said her name, which I instantly forgot. She had on a green jacket and skirt, two different colors of green, and looked like she needed to go to sleep for a hundred years to get over what was eating her. Baggy eyes for real, like you could stash spare change under each eye. We asked for Miss Trudy that was my caseworker from a few years ago, and she said Miss Trudy was no longer with the department of social services. I'd get a new caseworker in the morning that might or might not be herself. She just happened to be on call at this hour, which I reckon explains the eyes. She told the Peggots they could go home, she would get me where I needed to go. Which freaked me out. Who the hell was she, to think she knew where I needed to go? I said thanks but no thanks, I'd go with the Peggots like usual if Mom was in rehab. The lady gave me this look like, Sorry kiddo, your money's no good where I come from.

Mrs. Peggot gave me more nabs to shove in my pockets and some money plus change for a pay phone, which existed then, and said to call as soon as they could come get me. And off we went to a little room for our discussion, Baggy Eyes vs. the Demon. She started with the usual questions they ask, then got serious about the Peggots: anything that had happened in that household that made me uncomfortable. I was confused, thinking she meant stuff I had done to *them*, such as busting their TV the one time, or swiping the small shit we traded at school for other small shit. We beat around a lot of bushes before I finally got what she was asking: had I been molested by Maggot or Mr. or Mrs. Peggot. Stoner must have put in his two cents. I said nothing of the kind had happened, the molester I wanted to discuss was Stoner.

She said okay, let's go into that, and I did. Mind you, it's three a.m. or something by now, I've eaten nothing I can recall that day other than nabs and Cheetos, I'm too tired to be polite, and madder at Stoner than a riverbank has rocks to throw. How would our relationship best be described, she wanted to know. I said maybe like two guys standing at the barrel and butt ends of one rifle, what relationship would you call that? And if you knew him, trust me, you'd want the trigger end. I even said something to the effect that if it was up to me, I'd not shoot the man all at once, I'd go kneecaps and elbows first to see him beg for mercy. She wrote all this down on her clipboard.

She had more questions around my stepfather, as she called him, which shows she was not getting our picture. Questions pertaining to my busted lip that I'd forgotten about, what with the newer reminders of our fight over calling 911. I could feel a shiner coming up on my left eye, and my right side hurt so bad I wished I didn't have to breathe so much. Baggy Eyes asked if I minded taking off my shirt and letting her have a look, which made me feel like a baby. She got a camera out of her bag and took pictures. She even asked was there anything going on below the belt. No way José to that, I said, pretty much wanting to die already. Losing a fight was bad enough without people putting it in their damn scrapbooks.

She wanted to discuss my assaults on Stoner, the so-called biting incidents. I said there was no *incidents*, plural. If I'd gone for a repeat offense, I'd have no teeth left. She wrote that down. I could have gone on till her pen ran out of ink, but she blew out her air in this drawn-out way that reminded me of the night I spied on Aunt June. The slow leak of women that mop up after guys have torn each other's soft parts out of their sockets. To this lady I was just one of those guys. I wanted to yell at her, It's no fair fight. Stoner is a psycho, and I am a freaking ten-year-old.

Next step was some kind of checkup. I told her I wasn't all that injured, but she said it pertained to the mental aspects, was I okay to be released. Or else *what*? I'm eyeing the clipboard where she's got me confessing to wishful murder. If you hurt or kill somebody due to mental disturbance, other than just being mad at them, I knew where you went: Marion. A prison for the insane, with razor-wire fences and guard towers according to Maggot. Where his mom got sent at first. Then after a while they decided she was just the normal pissed-off type of lady, not the insane type, and sent her over to Goochland Women's. He'd visited her both places.

I must have zoned out, because next thing I knew, a man had his hand on my shoulder. Shirt and tie, not the white doctor coat. The dreaded clipboard. I sat up and said "Yes sir," and asked were they sending me to Marion. I could see he was trying not to smile. He asked me what I knew about Marion. He looked tired but not the same tired as Baggy Eyes, more like, Let's not make things any harder than need be. I told him I didn't know anything about Marion except for definitely not wanting to go there. He said not to worry, he'd get me sorted out. He sat down and asked the regular things, and then got on the subject of Stoner. Was I just real mad at him right now, or had I ever really thought I wanted him to die. He asked if we were the hunting type of family, if we had guns, were they kept locked up or could I get them out. He asked if I had ever been so sad I wished I could go to sleep and not wake up. I said not really, I just usually went to sleep wishing I'd wake up in a different house. He said that was understandable.

Baggy Eyes came back later and said all righty. I was not going to Marion, evidently. But Mom's situation was such that we'd be looking at several weeks of me on my own with Stoner, which was not happening. We were going with a new plan they'd all signed off on. The plan where Demon doesn't get to go home. Mom evidently being conscious enough now to sign away her only child.

What were my out-of-home options, she wanted to know: trusted adults, Mom's coworkers, anybody at all I could stay with? I said the Peggots, over and over, period. Which was not happening. She said Stoner made a complaint on the Peggots that would have to be investigated before they could consider placing me there. Stupid. I wondered though if the Peggots had a couple of strikes against, what with Maggot's jailbird mom and the unmentionable Humvee. Not their fault, but people like to think the worst. The nut doesn't fall far from the tree, etc. Then I thought of Aunt June. What if I had a trusted adult in Knoxville, I asked, but she said I couldn't go out of state due to the paperwork. Maybe Emmy living there was some type of violation.

It would explain the secret-keeping, but Aunt June being an outlaw made no sense. I just wanted to go to sleep. She took me to another little room that had a bed with paper on it, where I could lie down.

At some point later on, a guy woke me up in the dark with a tray of food like a TV dinner. He was rolling a cart of them. I was starved. This man had on whitish scrubs, white cap on his head, white bags over his shoes, so you saw the clothes and not him. Like he was a ghost. I told him I couldn't pay. He said it was paid for already, but that hospital food oftentimes made people sick. He offered to eat the food for me. I was scared, and said okay. He sat down with the tray on his lap and ate it. He looked like a hungry ghost eating a TV dinner, which meant I had to be dreaming.

My new life started off bright and early with my new caseworker Miss Barks. She raised up the blinds and said, "Good morning, Damon. Let's take you home." For a split second I thought I had one, and was going there. Sometimes a good day lasts all of about ten seconds.

Miss Barks had the wrong name. No dog. She stood there smiling while I woke up and remembered all kinds of shit, and noticed also that she was a total babe.

I'd run through caseworkers galore, you don't get attached nor would you want to. But this one, another story. Younger than Mom, in a dress, not the jacket-type outfit that makes them look like wardens. That blond type of hair that's all curly in little waves falling down, like you'd normally see on TV actresses, mermaids, or angels. Maybe Miss Barks was my guarding angel. About damn time.

She saw the empty plastic food tray the ghost left on the chair (so, probably not a ghost) and commented on my good appetite. She said they'd found a temporary placement for me that was on a farm, so hopefully they'd feed me pretty well out there too. I could feel my stomach eating itself, I was that hungry. But didn't want to say anything she'd take the wrong way.

Outside it wasn't even full morning yet, just the gray time where lights were still on. She walked fast in her little boots, click-click. Her car was a Toyota with a DSS sign thing on the door, an older model with a lot of mileage from the looks of it. I got in the back and was surprised to see somebody in the driver's seat: Baggy Eyes. Christ, I thought. This lady must never go home at all. Miss Barks got in on the passenger side and we drove out on the same roads I'd covered on my ambulance ride. Why they thought it would take two of them to handle me, no idea. We passed by houses of people that had gone to bed and gotten up again, situation normal. Eating cereal now. All the kids with moms that had their shit together and dads that were alive.

Finally Miss Barks turned around with her elbow on the back of the seat and said let's talk about where we were going. I'd be staying with a gentleman named Mr. Crickson that took kids for short-term only. He had boys there now. The Cricksons had been regular fosters until his wife passed away, and now he just took in the odd hardship case. She had a nice way of talking, like I was not a child but a person. She was sorry I'd had to wait in the hospital all night. They had to cover too many bases and not enough facilities, basically a whole lot of kids in my boat.

Which was not news, at school you heard talk about what kid was homeless or sleeping on the couch of some relative none too pleased of it. What pretty or ugly girls in seventh or eighth grade were kicked out for being knocked up. So on and so forth. Never did I dream I'd wake up one day as one of those kids. Miss Barks seemed shocked by my sad turn of events. Her partner up there behind the wheel, Miss Night of the Living Dead, not so much.

This was turning into some drive. I asked if I would still be going to school, and Miss Barks said yes, same everything, just a longer bus route. The boys at Mr.

Crickson's would show me the ropes on that. And I said oh shit, and then, oops sorry. But I didn't have my history book or homework or anything, which was all back at the house. I didn't have a damn thing, actually. Not even socks, due to leaving the house in an ambulance. Miss Barks said she was really sorry, I would have to get by as best I could. She'd be checking on me next week, and would try to go by where I lived and pick up what all I needed. She said to make a list of important things, and she'd do her best. My hopes were not high. I pictured Stoner making a fire out back and burning my clothes and schoolbooks. Throwing in my comics and action heroes one by one.

Miss Barks and Baggy Eyes had a disagreement over which road to take, and had to turn the car around at one point. Baggy reminded her to discuss with me about Mom, and Miss Barks said, Oh, right, had I been brought up to speed on Mom? Nope. Well, it was good news, Mom was going to be released from the hospital directly into treatment, later that day. I hadn't asked about Mom after the worst of it was over last night, which was probably bad of me, but to be honest I was kind of fed up. Bringing a psycho into our home, then checking herself out: Who *does* that?

Miss Barks said Mom was looking at several weeks in a residential situation, and after that some home supervision before I could go back with her. So this was not going to be the quickie five-day rehabs like she'd done a few times before, which are more or less a tune-up. At this time I guess it was decided Mom needed the full engine overhaul. Miss Barks asked if I understood Mom had made agreements with DSS for keeping me safe. That she needed some extra support now to help her hold up her end of the bargain.

I still didn't get why I couldn't stay with the Peggots. But given how I'd ratted out Stoner, being next door to him now would scare the nuts off me. I thought of him in our house, going in my room, finding the note-book where I'd spent many an hour drawing wicked-good The-Ends for "Stone Villain." Beard, gauges, big shaved head, even Stoner would figure that out. There was one where I had an alligator bite off his dick. The man would be coming after me.

We turned up the dirt lane to a farm, almost there. I got up my nerve to ask how much trouble I was in from stuff I'd said. About Stoner, for instance. Miss Barks said nobody was mad at me, and I thought: Sure, lady. If kids say the wrong kind of shit, people will be notified and hell will be paid. That's how it works. We pulled up in front of an old farmhouse with grass so high in the yard, you could cut it for hay. Baggy put the car in park. Miss Barks asked if I had any questions before I went to meet my new foster. What would I ask? Here's this big old gray-looking house, like Amityville. I don't think it had totally sunk in yet, I wasn't going home.

Now we're just sitting. Those two staring each other down in the front seat, both of them like, *Nuh*-uh, *you*. Baggy finally says, "You're the legal on this one. You need to take him in."

Miss Barks is scared. Whatever is in that house, she doesn't want to be the one to take me in there and say, So long kid, sucks to be you. Probably this is her first day on the shit job of removing kids out of their homes for the DSS, and she's just figured out she doesn't even want to be on *her* end of the stick, let alone mine. So much for my guarding angel. I was her test drive.

9

C rickson was a big, meaty guy with a red face and
a greasy comb-over like fingers palming a basketball. Little eyes set deep in his head, pointy nose, your
basic dog type of face. But a meaner breed than the two
old hounds lying on the floor under the cold wood stove
in his kitchen. They looked like whenever frost came
around, they'd be right there ready.

The old man's voice came out in a Freddy Krueger
whisper, like it hurt him to talk so you'd damn best
listen. Yes I had seen that movie, at the drive-in, from
the back seat with Mom and Stoner thinking I'm asleep.
Education of many a Lee County kid. Scary guy says
sit, we sit.

Miss Barks meanwhile was working down her
checklist, nervous as heck. Would I sleep in the same

bedroom as his other fosters, was it inspected, was he briefed on me by phone that morning. He was like, Get this over with, lady. The other boys had left for school and he needed to be out seeing to his cattle. Miss Barks wasn't disagreeing on any of that. I sat tight, getting my gander at the inside of Amityville: nasty curled-up linoleum, yellow grease on the wall over the stove, open jars of peanut butter and crap all over the counter. A crust of scum on everything. I recalled her saying this man's wife had passed away. I wondered if her body was still lying somewhere back in that house, because I'd say there'd been zero tidying up around here since she kicked off.

Miss Barks finished up and handed over a big yellow envelope. He asked was his check in there. She said he could look for it in the mail like always. I couldn't believe she was going to leave me with Freddy Krueger, but she gave me those same eyes I'd seen on Mom a million times: *Sorry.* And off she went in her little boots, click-click. I wondered if DSS had anything like Step 9, where you eventually have to apologize to all the kids you've screwed over.

Once she was out the door, I thought the old man would run off to his everloving cattle, but he was in no big hurry, pouring coffee out of a dirty-looking pot into a dirty-looking cup. Under his flannel shirt he had on a long-sleeved waffle undershirt with the cuffs all frayed and grimy, like he lived in that one shirt day and night. Regardless Mom and her sloppy ways, she did not raise me to be unclean. I couldn't stomach watching the old man slurp his coffee.

He looked over at me like, questioning, so I said no thanks, I didn't drink coffee all that much. He said something in his creepy strangled voice, so quiet I couldn't make it out.

I asked him, "Sir?"

"I said, the other boys ain't liking a biter. I done told them. Ain't nobody likes a biter."

I looked at the dogs under the stove, trying to work out what he meant. They looked dead actually. Or so old, they would have trouble gumming down cat food out of a can. But this seemed like something I would need to know. I asked him, "Which one bites?"

He looked at me like I was an idiot. "You."

He watched out the window while the DSS car drove away. I noticed his fly was undone, or maybe the pants were so old the zipper had given up the ghost. After a minute he whispered, "A wonder nobody's yet filed off your teeth."

I had the day to get sick to my stomach, waiting to find out how much the other boys hated a biter. Stoner must have gone on the record. So I might as well have a sign on my back saying: Druggie Mom, Queer Best Friend, Hand Biter. Whatever Crickson told his fosters that morning, everybody at school was hearing now. I never wanted to go back there. Or be here. I was running on dead empty, but Crickson didn't ask if I'd had breakfast. The kitchen had this rank cooking smell, a cross between feet and bacon, and even that was making me hungry. But he just downed his coffee and said, "Let's go." And outside we went, for a day's work.

We started with haying the cattle. The barn smelled like cow shit, no surprise, but I mean this smell is a freaking storm front. Enough to make your eyes water. The cattle were muddy and black and pushy and of a size to kill you if you weren't quick on your feet, and that's about all I can tell you about haying cattle. A pitchfork was used, hay was thrown around. He said he had around two hundred head, most of them out on pastures. You don't hay your cattle in August except the pregnant heifers, which these were. He asked what I knew about cattle, which was nothing, and could I drive a tractor, ditto. I could see he was pissed about how worthless I was. He asked if I'd ever put up hay, because that needed doing if the damn rain ever stopped. Had I topped or cut tobacco, that was also coming. He said he kept the boys home from school for tobacco cutting because it was God's own goddamn piece of work to get it all in, so he hoped I wasn't keen on school or anything. I said yes sir, no sir, trying to ride it out.

I followed him around, carrying whatever he handed me. It rained on us off and on. All I could think of was home: Mrs. Peggot that would be worried sick about where I was. Our creek and its excellent mud. On the bright side, this guy would not be making me scrub any floor with Clorox. But I might at some point decide on doing that anyway. We moved cattle through gates. We walked for hours checking a ratty old fence for barb wire that had come loose off the palings. He had a giant staple gun that looked and sounded like a weapon of war, and he used that to attach the barb wire. He said pay attention because tomorrow I'd do fence lines on my own. Seriously. Putting that weapon in the hands of me, a known menace.

I was too hungry to think straight. Finally it was time to go have lunch, which he called dinner but who cared. It was bacon-tomato sandwiches. He fried up the bacon and tomatoes both, in a pan looked like it had lived its life without a wash, no fresh grease needed. I could see bacon was the gas for the engine of this house of boys. Big packages in the fridge. Loaves of bread still in the wrappers, stacked up like bricks on the counter. So, some good news.

After lunch we walked more fences and changed the spark plugs in a tractor engine. It was long in the afternoon before I spotted two boys walking up the lane from where the bus must have dropped them out by the highway. They went in the house to dump their backpacks, then came running out to the barn where Mr. Crickson had left me with a hose and a scrub brush, spraying out a bunch of slimy grain buckets, ready at this point to puke from nervousness. Sure enough, the littler one bared his teeth at me, let out a wolfman howl, and laughed like a kook.

I said Hey, I'm Demon. Trying my best to look like just, whatever. Not a person that bites. The bigger one said he was Tommy and this here was Swap-Out, and he grabbed the buckets I'd cleaned and started stacking them. The smaller kid went in the tool room for a shovel and went to work shoveling shit in the far end of the barn. This kid Swap-Out, everybody knew. He'd been in second grade with me, not his first time at it, and probably was still stalled out in the lower grades due to something going on with him that affected his mind and his growth. He was small in a freakish way, weird face, the eyes and everything not quite where they should be. People said it was from his mom drinking too much while he was in the oven. I always thought, And mine didn't? But Mom claimed she'd stayed on the wagon for the most part with me, at least in the early months, due to every single thing she looked at making her want to puke. My good luck.

"We knew you'd be coming," Tommy said. Which I said was interesting because I sure didn't. He said he didn't mean me exactly. Some tax bill comes due on the farm in April and September that the old man needs the money for, so usually there'd be an extra boy coming then. I had no idea what to make of that. I asked Tommy how long he'd been living here and he said a couple of years, off and on. Sometimes he was the April and sometimes the September. He said Creaky's wife had always liked him before she died, but Creaky hated him, so now Tommy came and went as needed. I just said, *Huh*, and left it at that.

This Tommy individual I'd also seen at Elk Knob Elementary, but he was some older than me, at middle school now. Last name of Waddell, so people called him Tommy Waddles, which he did. He was a chubby teddy-bear type of kid with big round eyes and brown hair that looked like it was too much for his head. It stood straight up. Some guys in those days were trying for the Luke Perry hair thing from *90210*, but in the case of Tommy you could tell that wasn't gel or trying, that was just all Tommy. Also too much Tommy for his clothes: sausage arms in his jacket sleeves, jeans straining at the belt. Now I knew why. Foster care. I don't reckon they look at you all that often and say Hey kid, you're busting out a little bit, let's go shopping.

But after all my fears over getting judged as a biter, Tommy was so nice. He showed me where to stack the buckets, how to go in the corn crib and get the corn for graining the heifers and calves, and various things we had to do before going in. The corn crib was a small barn type of thing, so full of rats you had to look where you stepped. Seriously, they ran over your feet. If something was hard to lift, like a grain bag, Tommy tried to do it. He explained things without acting like I was an idiot. He said the cattle were Angus, boy or girl either one, all called Angus. The cows got bred to have calves, and the boy ones would get castrated into steers and raised up in the pastures to about half grown. Before winter came on hard, they'd be sold to the stockyards and go out west someplace to get fattened up the rest of the way. From there, hamburgers.

Tommy talked sweet to the cattle whenever we were graining them and putting them up for the night, even though they were just dumb giant monsters. He was the same with me. Like he was trying to make up for all the bad things in our lives. At least I wasn't looking to get castrated and turned into hamburger, that I knew of. Tommy said you got used to it here. He called it the Creaky Farm, a name made up by Fast Forward because he was a genius at thinking up names. Fast Forward was the other foster kid here, not home yet because in high school and at football practice, a major star on the Lee High team, which are the Generals as everybody knows. To hear Tommy tell it, Fast Forward was the best-liked person of everybody alive, even by Mr. and especially the dead Mrs. Crickson. I would like him too, just wait and see. He'd been at this farm forever and was kind of like their real son, even though he hated Mr. Crickson. Or Creaky rather, which we were all supposed to call the old man, except to his face.

Tommy showed me where to wash up before we went in. By the porch with the screens hanging off, they had a spigot for hosing off your hands, shoes, whatever you could without getting too wet. I was already wet from getting rained on all day. But excited about getting to eat something. I wanted it to be true what Tommy said, that I could get used to this or at least lie low and get through it. Maybe at school not too much trash-talk about me would be going around, if it was only up to Swap-Out, a kid that was respected by nobody. I'd last out Mom's three weeks in rehab and go back home with nobody the wiser. Stoner, I had no plan for. Maybe the DSS did. Maybe there was a God in his heaven after all, and we would all fart perfume.

Tommy Waddles let me hang on him while I stood on one foot trying to hose the shit off my shoes. My shoelaces were all knotted up. I realized I hadn't had my shoes off since I put them on last night in the ambulance. No socks, same reason. Everything I was wearing was wet and smelled like cow shit. All the clothes I had. Tomorrow at school, I'd smell like cow shit.

Fast Forward got home as we were sitting down to dinner, and everybody acted like it was Captain America out there in a Ford pickup. "He's here!" and all like that. This kid has done no chores whatsoever, plus he's driving a Lariat F-150, two-tone red and silver with the square headlights. Sweet. I wondered if the vehicle was his, or borrowed from the farm, or what. I wondered if fosters were allowed to have anything belonging to them. I had much to know.

He came in the kitchen and even the damn dogs looked up. First they'd moved all day. He's long and lean with a look to him like somebody famous, all clean teeth and dark eyebrows and a head of hair not to be believed, like an explosion. Mad curly, like Mariah Carey in her mop-hair days, only not that long obviously. They'd not let you on a football team with long hair back then. "Hey Fast," all the other boys said, and "This here's Demon."

Fast Forward stops dead in his tracks like he's a comedy act, looking from the other kids to me, me to them, working out what to make of me. I'm ready for the biter remarks, bared teeth and snarl. But he smiles his rock star smile and says, "New blood! About time we upgraded the stock around here." And Mr. Crickson smiles and nods like he thinks so too, and I'd been all his idea. Nutso. A grubby little bunch of boys looking up to an older kid, that's the normal. But he's even got the old bastard under his powers. Demon, I'm thinking, watch and learn.

Dinner was hamburger meat with cans of Manwich poured on it plus macaroni and melted cheese, awesome. I would tell Mom about this. She never could think of a thing to make for dinner. Mr. Crickson asked Fast Forward how was practice and who was on defense and did he still think the Generals would go undefeated this year. So many words out of the old man's janked throat. He'd been saving it up all day for Fast Forward. After supper Mr. Crickson went in the other room and watched TV, aka fell asleep in his recliner chair, and Fast Forward scooted out. Leaving the rest of us to clean up in the half-assed way you would expect from three boys, one of them being quite a few bricks shy of his full load. Why that kitchen looked like it did.

Tommy showed me the rest of the house, our room upstairs, the bathroom we'd use, with Fast Forward getting first dibs obviously. He had more to do, like shaving. Our bedroom had two bunk beds, not much else. A closet for your stuff, if you were lucky enough to have any. A table for doing your homework if you felt like it. Tommy and Swap-Out shared one of the bunk beds and had a discussion of whether I should take top or bottom on the other one. Swap-Out didn't vote, with him being let's just say not a talker. But he liked climbing. I remembered from second grade, Swap-Out always getting up on the radiators like a freaking monkey, our teacher always yelling at him to get down, because one of these days the heat would come on and he'd get burned. And one of those days, yes he did. Such howling, you never heard. Whereas Tommy liked the bottom bunk so he could stash his library books underneath. He had piles down there: Boxcar Children, *Goosebumps*, who even knew they'd let you check out that many? He said the library at Pennington Middle was bigger, which was the only good thing about middle school.

I assumed all four of us boys would bunk together,

but wrong, Fast Forward had his own room down the hall. He'd lived here a long time. Mrs. Crickson while alive had started the procedures for adopting him, but she never got it finished up. So Crickson was still drawing the five-hundred-dollar check every month for keeping him as a foster. I didn't learn all of this right away. It's a complicated business to figure out, especially with the way Crickson and Fast Forward did it, having some kind of secret agreement to split the check between them.

We were not allowed in Fast Forward's room without permission, so I looked from the doorway. He had free weights of a different kind from Stoner's. Football trophies, newspaper photos of famous Generals moments taped on the wall over the desk (he had furniture). Pinned along one wall, a slew of ribbons he'd won for his 4-H calf projects, Tommy said, but that was history. Now Fast Forward had quarterbacking and a pickup truck and hot girls, everybody and her sister wanting a piece of this guy. I'd known him two hours and could already see how it was.

His real name was Sterling Ford. Who could want better? Something to do with silver, the best engines ever built. But he said the name Fast Forward came to him early, and it did fit.

He had the run of the house and keys to the gun

cabinet where the old man kept his rifles and the medicines Swap-Out was supposed to take every night if anybody remembered. DSS made him lock up the medicines evidently after some past event where his other foster kids were selling them. Uppers or downers, God only knows what Swap-Out was on, possibly both, the usual, half the kids at school had to line up for their pills from the nurse every day before recess. Fast Forward anyway had full privileges, whereas we three lower-life boys kept to our room of an evening. Nobody cared what time we went to bed, if we got ourselves up in the morning. That first night I was dead tired but worried about going to bed in my cow-shit clothes, and out of the blue Tommy asked did they bring me here without anything. Knowing the foster drill. He let me borrow one of his T-shirts to sleep in. This Tommy was not your usual type of kid.

He said Fast Forward would come in before lights out for drill. Sure enough, he came in saying: "Atten-*tion!*" Tommy and Swap-Out saluted and stuck out their chests and Fast Forward did inspection. I guess we've all seen that movie. It seemed dumb but I couldn't see *not* doing it, so I did. He gave me a good looking-over, saying, "Me oh my. Check out this green-eyed boy." He asked was I a Melungeon or a red-haired beaner or what. I told him my dad was Melungeon.

Next, Fast Forward asked what we had. Tommy dug in his pockets and came out with a pack of Chiclets, which Fast Forward took. Then he stood waiting in front of Swap-Out. Bent down and got in the little guy's face. Swap-Out says he's got nothing. Fast Forward pulls a fist and Swap-Out shrinks back in his skin. No punching was done, but you could see this kid knows what punched is. I'm looking over at Tommy like, *Is this normal?* And he's like, *Yeah it is.*

"Creaky gave you lunch money this morning," Fast Forward says in a slow way because of Swap-Out lacking on his mental side. "You had lunch money, and you took the nutbutter."

"I never," Swap-Out says.

"You did. I've got eyes in your school, not just in my head. If you lie to Fast Forward, you're letting down your brothers. You've got the cash Creaky gave you. Hand it over."

Taking the peanut butter sandwich for a normal kid meant they'd let their lunch money run out, or for a free lunch kid their mom forgot to sign the forms. Either way, the lunch ladies would lay that nutbutter on you like, *Here's your fuck-up badge.* Swap-Out had taken the sandwich of shame to pocket the money. His close-set eyes jumped around like a trapped rabbit's. Fast Forward snapped his fingers in the scrambled little face, held out his hand. Swap-Out shelled out the bills.

I was next. Fast Forward stared. I said, "Dude, I don't even have any fucking socks!"

I wasn't sure if this was an f-bomb household, nor if Fast Forward to me was a Dude or a Sir, but I risked it and the guys laughed. I told him I'd gotten dumped off with nothing.

Fast Forward got this look. "Nothing. You're sure."

"Positive."

"Holding out on Fast Forward is not how we do things here, Demon. I'm giving you another chance. Come clean, and all will be forgiven. Check your pockets."

I did, and pulled out some squashed nabs, which shocked me. Last night at the hospital seemed like a movie about somebody's sad mess of a life. But that was me, in possession of nabs, ten bucks, and phone change. If I'd remembered, I'd have eaten the nabs for sure. I felt my ears burning. One, because I hadn't had that much money in quite a while if ever, and two, I'd just lost it. Three, it looked like I got caught lying. Plus, how did he even know?

Fast Forward said he was proud of me for contributing to our goals and objectives. So that was good, him liking me. He said he held on to the valuables here to keep them safe. We'd celebrate by having a party as soon as he could get supplies. A farm party, he said. The others said, Yay, farm party! He explained we were the Hillbilly Squadron, which was like the Boy Scouts except not ass-kissers. He was our Squad Master and made the rules for our own good. He said don't let Creaky get us down. Then he said, "At ease!" and we were at ease. He left, and Tommy and Swap-Out climbed into their bunks. I put on Tommy's big T-shirt and climbed into mine. I chose the top. I was still thinking of the rats all over the corn barn and Creaky lurking around in the dark, maybe wanting to file off my teeth. The top bunk seemed advisable.

Hillbilly is a word everybody knows. Except they don't. Mr. Peg at one time had a sticker on his truck bumper, "Hillbilly Cadillac," but I was a small kid with no comprehension of anything. I mainly knew it from this one rerun that came on Nick at Nite, *Beverly Hillbillies*, which was this family running around a city wearing ropes for a belt, packing antique rifles, and driving a junkass truck. Dead hilarious. More so than most of the old black-and-whites they ran, *Gunsmoke*, *Munsters*. Then one time Maggot's high school cousin Bonnie saw us watching it and said we were clueless little turds. Bonnie was in Drama, Gifted and Talented, your basic all-around ass pain. She said be careful who we laughed at, that family was supposedly us.

Meaning what? There's not a person here that carries on like that or drives such crap, I assure you. Not even the Antique Tractor Club guys that tuck their shirts in their underpants and drive their ancient machines in the Christmas parade. Those guys are just old. But shooting the lights out, yodeling, keeping pigs in the house? Maggot told Bonnie to go screw her stuck-up boyfriend she met in Governor's School and leave us be. Which she did. But I did wonder.

For, like, years. Until one time Mr. Peg was smoking by his truck and I was out there messing around, and thought to ask him why he had that on there, Hillbilly Cadillac. I asked did it mean something bad, and his answer shocked me: *hillbilly* is like the n-word. And of course I said what everybody knows, n- is not a word to be used unless by assholes. He said all right, but some do, that aren't white guys being assholes. Which is true, Ice Cube, Jay-Z, Tupac. Mr. Peg was not a fan of those guys, in fact the opposite, but they still got heard in the house thanks to Maggot and me, so he would know. The n-word is *preferred* by those guys. Mr. Peg said other people made up the n-word, not Ice Cube. And other people made up *hillbilly* to use on us, for the purpose of being assholes. But they gave us a superpower on accident. Not Mr. Peg's words, but that's how I understood it. Saying that word back at people proves they can't ever be us, or get us, and we are untouchable by their shit.

The world is not at all short on this type of thing, it turns out. All down the years, words have been flung like pieces of shit, only to get stuck on a truck bumper with up-yours pride. Rednecks, moonshiners, ridge runners, hicks. Deplorables.

10

Tommy Waddles was a talker, and who wouldn't be, with a story like his to tell. He was not a case of screw-up parents, just the hardest luck imaginable. His dad was some kind of land surveyor that got killed in a small plane that crashed, and his mom had something go wrong with her heart even though not an old person. Tommy didn't remember either one, he was that young whenever they passed. He had a grandmother that lost her mind somewhat, in a nursing home way the heck out in Norfolk. Other relatives dead or just not there to begin with, his dad being an only child. So Tommy had been in some kind of care in the state of Virginia basically for life.

He said foster care gets worse the older you get, with the better homes preferring babies and kids still on the smaller side. Tommy I'm guessing was never that small. But the type to make the best of things, mostly by reading library books and ignoring the fact of people hating him. He was doomed at Creaky Farm because he was soft. The old man had no use for soft. Tommy wound up there time and again though, due to Creaky needing the money, and Tommy still with no permanent situation. He should have been adopted by some nice lady that would make cookies and let him explain the entire story of every *Magic Treehouse* ever written. But adoption is even worse than foster homes as far as people only wanting the littles. Life is brutal like that. And it's their loss, I'm going to say, because he was a kid you'd want around. Solid.

A thing about Tommy that we had in common is liking to draw. His doodling he called it. For him, though, it was like blood, this thing that came out of him whenever he got hurt. It took me a while to work out what was the deal of Tommy and doodling, but I got a clue the first night after Creaky called him out for eating too much of the hamburger and Manwich supper, saying this farm was for fattening up steers, not boys. He said worse actually, to the effect of Tommy being where he was because nobody wanted fat boys, and Creaky not running a foster home to take in rejects. I couldn't believe the shit that got said, but the other guys just went on eating like, There you go. Tommy got up and put his plate in the sink and went in the living room. I could see him in there curled up on the couch with a newspaper against his knees, leaning over and writing on it with a pencil. Hair standing up on his head like he's giving his all. I figured a cross-word or scramble like Mrs. Peggot always did. Later on, though, I went to have a look and what I saw was: Skeletons. Tiny skeletons covering all the edges where there wasn't print. You never saw so many. To look at Tommy you'd not think a Goth kid. Skeletons are the last thing you'd expect.

He also did his doodling on the bus using what blank spots he could find in his schoolbooks, if he was having a day that sucked especially, and again: skeletons. But usually he told me the story of his life. We sat together on the bus, with plenty of time for the telling. Because here was our day: rise and shine at five a.m., make breakfast if you're going to, walk the dirt lane to the highway and stand out there in goddamn moonlight to catch the bus. I thought the ride from Peggot Holler was long. The little did I know. From Creaky Farm we'd take a *first* bus to Lee High, wait in the caf-eteria with the other farthest-out country kids having spitball wars and free breakfast if we had our forms signed, then *second* bus to Elk Knob Elementary for

Swap-Out and me, or Pennington Middle for Tommy. Hours and hours, stops and stops. Moms yelling at the drivers for one thing and another as regards leaving a kid off in the wrong place, drivers yelling back. Falling asleep, waking up because somebody's telling you to shove over.

Riding the bus with high-schoolers was where you learned everything: how girls get pregnant, how to watch your back. Given the time we put in, the way-out country kids got the most education. I saw more than one guy fingering his girlfriend on a school bus, or her going down on him. More than one face slapped by a girl that wanted none of it. A lip or two busted. Once this fierce tiny towheaded girl got so fed up of a big guy calling her Q-tip, she stood on the seat behind him and cracked her Etch A Sketch over his head. Screen side down, the silver shit running down to cover his whole face. Picture Tin Man out of the Oz movie. That girl was going places. Probably she's the president of something by now. At the least, not pregnant.

And while we're all wasting our young lives on a yellow stinking bus, Fast Forward gets the extra hours in his rack every morning before getting up and cruising over to Lee High in his Lariat. Why every red-blooded boy dreams of turning sixteen with his own wheels: for the sleep.

At school I got to see Maggot again. He was like, My man! We thought you were abducted by aliens! Which is one way of looking at it. Maggot was my reason for living at that point in time. He saved my ass by getting clothes and stuff I needed from home. Mr. Peg had the keys, so they snuck over there like robbers while Stoner was out and stuffed my valuables in pillowcases, drawing notebooks included. Maggot brought it to school, a pillowcase at a time. They said Stoner was hardly showing his face around there anymore. So school was what I had left in the way of normal now, with Creaky Farm waiting at both ends.

Time went by, and promises were kept. First, the hay. Creaky did the mowing on his tractor while we were at school. Then came baling, with his tractor pulling this ancient baler machine that kept breaking down every fifty feet. It would make a hellacious grinding noise, and every single time in his raspy voice he'd yell: "Goddamn piece of Tazewell shit!" He must have bought it from somebody over there, while the dinosaurs still roamed in Tazewell County. He'd have to stop and shut everything down, and then he and Fast Forward, but mostly Fast Forward, would climb up on the baler and reach in and yank stuff around and then it would work again. The rest of us hauled and stacked the bales in the field, to get ready for loading them on the truck. These were the square bales a person can carry, not the giant round bales most farms went over to at that time, where tractors and forklifts do the work. No sir, Creaky had his slave boys, and we were a shit show. First of all, Tommy had his good points, but being strong, not one. He'd grab a bale with both hands on the twine, then stand there going red in the face like he's constipated, until I could get over to help. And Swap-Out, Christ. One hay bale weighed as much or more than Swap-Out, and all this kid wants to do anyway is climb onto the piles we're stacking, to where he ends up knocking things over and just general nonsense. We have to get all two hundred and some bales onto the flatbed, a load at a time, then unloaded and stacked in the barn, with more climbing, constipation faces, and nonsense. By then Creaky is cursing the fosters agency even worse than Tazewell County as far as trading in damaged goods.

That was my first weekend. Sunday night I never got to take a shower, due to Fast Forward taking his time in there. There was another bathroom downstairs with an old nasty tub, but the sewage backed up there on a routine basis, so I was not the only one scared of that tub. Even Creaky used the upstairs. It took all I had left in me to haul ass up into my bunk and lie there on fire, my whole body itching from getting scrubbed by two hundred Brillo pads of hay. I had three weeks to serve in this prison, and not one of them fully behind me yet. I wondered how Mom was doing. She always said drying out was the worst hell imaginable, and I felt sorry for that. Not now. *Tell me about hell*, I told her in my mind. *All you had to do today is your moral goddamn inventory and a lot of lying around. On nice clean sheets.*

Another promise kept: our Hillbilly Squadron farm party. Fast Forward had mentioned about getting supplies, and I'd thought maybe items from Aisle 19 of Walmart: Solo cups, paper plates. That's the dumb kid I was.

First he brought out the snacks, which I was utterly thrilled about. At night in those days I'd get homesick and torn up just thinking of the Snickers Mom kept in the fridge. So now I'm all, Reese's and cookies, yess! Thinking that's what this party is about. Fast Forward though was patient with my education. Like a big brother, honestly. He said this was my initiation. We had the party in his room, which was amazing, getting to look around and even touch some of his stuff. Which is how I found out those gold sports trophies they give you in high school are actually plastic. But they looked amazing. We had the lights shut off and a candle burning that we got from the kitchen stash for the power outages. Creaky, gone to bed. After he's taken his hearing aids out, they said, he'd just as well be a corpse.

Fast Forward's room had a window where you could see trees outside. The moon was almost but not quite round. He had a rug that same shape that Mrs. Creaky had made for him by braiding up rags whenever she was dying of her cancer. As sick as she was and on drugs galore, all she'd wanted to do was make him a rug for his room. We sat in our little circle on that rug, thinking of the dead lady that wanted to be Fast Forward's mom. We ate the candy and cookies. He passed around cigarettes and we smoked those. Creaky allowed smoking in the house, which was new to me. Mom always went outside. Mr. Peg same. Mrs. Peggot had rules about smoking, knowing of too many people that fell asleep in their recliners and burned a place down.

We didn't burn anything down. Tommy smoked like a kid, taking little sips of smoke and coughing them out, whereas Swap-Out was a natural. I was somewhere in between, this being my first nonmenthols. Fast Forward said every member of our squadron had a secret name he alone could give them, including some kids that weren't even here anymore. Now I was to get mine. Tommy was Bones, because of the skeleton doodles and also because underneath it all, Tommy had good bones. I could see that. And Swap-Out was Wild Man. So. What about the Demon.

He looked at me for the longest time. Head cocked back, the wild dark curly mane, his eyes squinted like he's rummaging around in my skull closet. Finally he said, "Diamond. He's bright and shiny and worth a lot. Harder than anything else there is."

For a guy to talk like this or even look that hard at another guy was not at all the normal. A straight guy that liked girls, which Fast Forward definitely did. But Tommy and Swap-Out just nodded their heads, yes, excellent. Diamond. Not even awkward, it was just the magic of this guy. You took his word for the gospel, and felt like a bigger person for having him notice you.

I said okay, but I thought diamonds were for rich people, or girls getting engaged.

He said, "That too. What you've got, the girls are going to want."

I was embarrassed of course and told him no way, but he said he was never wrong about such things. I would see. Just give it a few years.

We talked some then about movies we'd seen. Tommy told Fast Forward I had a talent of drawing superheroes, and he said Yeah? Let's have a look. I went and got my notebook, and Fast Forward was impressed. I only showed him my better ones, like where I'd drawn Aunt

June in the sexy Wonder Woman outfit. He wanted to know where Aunt June lived. He also asked if I had any sisters. Which reminded me of Mom's story of old lady Copperhead coming to carry off the baby girl me. I wondered why people thought I would be better in the girl version.

Fast Forward meanwhile got on the subject of some of the hotter girls he'd screwed, which of course we were all ears to that. This one chick Melissa always gave him blow jobs in his truck after football practice. She stayed late for band practice, which was convenient, and she played the flute. Also convenient, he said. We didn't get his meaning till he made his mouth in an O. That made Swap-Out go crazy, just screeching like an animal. I guess for all the misfortunate scramble of the little guy's brains, somewhere deep in there dwelled the concept of the blow job. Whereas I was thinking more about her and Fast Forward being in that truck in the school parking lot, right out in broad daylight. Jesus, the guy was something. No fear.

From there we strayed onto weirder topics such as zombies. What if Mrs. Creaky was still lying in a back bedroom of that house somewhere. Which was nuts. I told them I'd had that exact same thought the first time I ever came in the house. And the other guys doubled over laughing and said, Dope, you just told us that a minute ago. Then I had to think extra hard about whether I was just thinking my thoughts or saying them. Because I was high. I'd been high before on many things such as hair spray, magic markers, and a typewriter duster borrowed from the main office at school, but this was another level. Each thing I looked at or thought about or ate was like a series of time bubbles popping, one by one. I asked Fast Forward what the heck, and he said the cookies were special. A girl named Rose that was auditioning to be his girlfriend had made the cookies, and what did we think, did Rose pass the test? We're like, Well *yeah*. I looked at Swap-Out and Tommy, wondering if they were wise to all this, and the answer was yes, they were. Falling against each other, laughing like idiots, but also to me they looked like better versions of their everyday selves. More like a Bones, more like a Wild Man. You could see how even that cracked tiny kid had it in him one day to be a wild tiny man.

Fast Forward told us to close our eyes. I heard him digging around, a secret hiding place maybe, because after a minute he said, Booyah! And he was standing over us holding a hat. Just a regular green ball cap, but he's holding it in both hands like the bowl of treasure. He sits back down—from standing, just drops into a cross-legged sit while holding that hat in both hands—

and even in my messed-up state I'm impressed by the physical act of that. Exceptional motor skills. We all lean forward to look, and by the glow of the candle I can see it isn't gold in the hat but little dots, which are pills. Not all the same. And I get what a pharm party is.

He passes around the hat, and we each take something. I have no idea what I've got, although now in later life I could make a good guess. I recall it wasn't round but had pointed ends, scored in the middle, probably pink. I recall feeling it on my tongue, how I felt it going down, and then felt the rug and the floor all sweet and solid under my back as I lay there with my brothers and looked at the buttery light washing around on the ceiling.

A ten-year-old getting high on pills. Foolish children. This is what we're meant to say: Look at their choices, leading to a life of ruin. But lives are getting lived right now, this hour, down in the dirty cracks between the toothbrushed nighty-nights and the full grocery carts, where those words don't pertain. Children, choices. *Ruin*, that was the labor and materials we were given to work with. An older boy that never knew safety himself, trying to make us feel safe. We had the moon in the window to smile on us for a minute and tell us the world was ours. Because all the adults had gone off somewhere and left everything in our hands.

11

It's fair to say I was halfway in love or some damn thing with Miss Barks. And the other half of me was like, Lady, you are the ass-burn of my life, and I wish me and you had been born on different planets. I know, guy life. Get used to it. I got called to the office, and there she was for our first appointment. Easier than driving around to check on us out in the sticks. We used the attendance officer's office, with that lady's kids' pictures all over the desk, which made Miss Barks seem like she was playing dress-up. But she's all, Hey! Looking good, Damon! So was she, in this white sweater that seriously put the lady parts on notice.

Her news was not great. Things were not so simple as me going back home after three weeks. I would get supervised visits with Mom, but after rehab she'd have to go back to her regular life and get drug tests. Once she was on solid ground, we could discuss me moving back home. What about Stoner? That was a challenge, said Miss Barks. We would have to learn to get along better. Wonderful, I thought. Teach Satan some cute puppy tricks while you're at it.

She asked me about Creaky Farm, and I told her. The old man was brutal to Tommy, and Swap-Out should be in some other kind of situation. (Some other universe, honestly.) Had Crickson ever hit me, she asked. Answer: no, I myself had not been struck. And that was that. Miss Barks was sorry, but Tommy and Swap-Out weren't on her. Usually all kids in a home are from one foster company, but Crickson was an emergency-type place, and Tommy and Swap-Out belonged to a different foster company that Miss Barks didn't work with. So fostering was done by companies, and we, as Stoner would say, were Product. Rotating and merchandising foster boys at more than fifty customer accounts. Live and learn.

She said nobody was allowed to come visit me out there, but she could pick me up after school and take me to meet Mom someplace like McDonald's where we could talk. Then she'd drive me back to the farm. Creaky would be pissed at me for visiting Mom instead of barn chores. He never let us use homework for an excuse either. These were not things I went into with Miss Barks. She had a big stack of papers and was getting ants in her cute pants to move on. I wondered if other kids I knew of might be fosters, boys with Hillbilly Squadron secret names among us in math and gym. Miss Barks couldn't comment on that, except to say she had other kids to meet with, the most of them younger than me. She said she was super proud of how well I was handling everything, and that I seemed like a boy that could take care of himself. No shit. As I was about to leave, she looked up and said, Oh, wait! She'd just remembered about trying to go by my house, to get clothes and things for me. She asked if I'd made a list, like she told me to.

And I thought, *Damn*. This trying-hard angel with her eyebrows pinched in deep concern. What if I was depending on the Miss Barkses of this world, instead of my own bad self? I'd be a sockless little piss, still in the same reeking underwear I was wearing the night of Mom's OD.

"Don't worry about it," I told her. "I don't need anything."

The house at Creaky Farm had its own life to live. Loose gutters banging, boards creaking, leaks dripping. At night I would lie in my bunk listening to the kind of shit that gives no comfort. Mice rustling around. Or else the WWE of cockroach wrestling, maybe both. We knew that critter fiestas were had in the kitchen after hours because we found mouse poop all over, like they'd dropped turd trails to find their way back home. Obviously, a kitchen that's kept like a pigsty is going to attract the wrong crowd. What did we know? We're juveniles. Every day a fresh surprise. Many were the mornings I opened a new loaf of Wonder Bread, only to find something had tunneled through it from one end to the other. A mouse-size hole in every slice. Do you think Creaky let us throw that bread away? This man that saved every rubber band off the newspapers and called you a pussy if you didn't eat your apple whole, the core and all? Mouse sloppy seconds, no exception. He said the toaster would kill the germs. Maybe so, because here I am telling the tale.

So, digging and scritching was heard in the walls at night. Water moving around for no good reason in the pipes. Snoring. Long, sorrowful farts. Swap-Out oftentimes sounded like he was itching bad over there in his bed. I mean. Scratching himself half to death. It dawned on me that if this kid had done more than one year in every grade, he could have considerable age on him by now. He smoked like a fiend, among other signs of being older than Tommy and me, the tiny size deceiving on all counts. I'd have to be older myself before I got the full picture on what a boy does in his bed at night, to sound like he's itching himself to death.

We were our own messed-up little tribe. A squadron. We looked forward to inspections, filling up our hungers on Fast Forward attention. If he played favorites with me, which he did, that was the bread and butter in my otherwise butterless day-to-day. He found out I had every superhero that ever existed on tap in my brain, and would get me to reel out their full life histories. He looked at my drawings like they were true comic books, studying them over, asking why I put in this or that. He wanted me to draw him as a superhero. I said I needed to think about it, because a person's superpower wasn't always that obvious.

His was. I was playing for time. I practiced and threw away quite a few before I nailed it: Force Fastward, aka Fast Man, all hard-muscled in his tights and cape and football helmet. His superpower was the force of his will, that could make anybody do anything and feel glad of it because they all wanted to be on Fast Man's team.

The first one I showed him, he picked up and looked over for a long time. Terrifying. My drawing was stupid. But no, finally he said I had the gift. "You all see this here?" he said to the others, flipping the page with the back of his hand. "This shit can *not* be taught. It's a talent." Which made my entire dogshit life up to that point worth living. After that I just went to town. I drew Creaky as the supervillain Creak Evil. He had a light-bulb head, with a comb-over, that lit up whenever he thought of how to torture a boy. I did cartoons with three panels. *Bing!* goes the light-bulb head, and he's pulling a file out of his pocket, saying "C'mere and I'll file down your teeth." Or, "I'm here to fatten up steers, not boys," handing a plate to Tommy with just bones on it. Then Fast Man swoops in to trounce the dastardly Creak Evil and save the boys. I put my all into Fast Man. His Fastmobile was a Lariat pickup with gun turrets that could fly.

He started wanting me to draw a cartoon every night. Some of my best ones, he would take to keep. Some got tacked up in his room. The other guys lived for my cartoons also, it was an event of our day. I drew WildMan that could climb the highest anything, and SuperBones with the power of fixing people instantly if their bones got broken. I just made that up. Tommy's actual power was niceness, but it's hard to make that pay off in the superhero universe.

We'd sit around the table in our room where no homework was ever done. I drew, they watched. Sometimes I was tired and wished I could get a pass. But I did it anyway. Drawing was something Fast Forward couldn't do and I could. I'd have done anything to be on his team.

A supervised visit is some weird shit. Usually in Mc-Donald's, me and Mom eating our burger and fries. Four or five tables away, Miss Barks, drinking her Diet Coke and acting like she's reading, but keeping an eye on us. What do they think is going to happen here, Mom will haul off and shank me with a plastic knife? Put meth in my Dr Pepper? How screwed-up is it that the DSS can't be bothered about Creaky being hateful as a snake, but they're all high-beams and every step you take, as regards the druggie mother?

Recovering druggie mother, excuse me. Mom was bright-eyed and bushy-tailed, telling me how great she was doing at rehab, how everything was going to be different this time. I know this was not nice of me, but I asked her, How is it going to be different? Just saying. Oh, she had answers. She'd only ever before done the freebie rehabs, a long weekend in the tank, courtesy of DSS. This was a whole different level, with therapy sessions and so on. It cost money, and Stoner was paying. She said she never even realized before that the moral inventory meant taking stock of your entire life.

Wishes for the future included. She said her future was me. That I was one hundred percent of her reason for getting sober.

I could see how this was supposed to make me feel great, but honestly it hit me as one more thing to worry about. What if she turns around in a month and gets shitfaced again or starts using? What does that tell you? That I wasn't a strong enough reason. Stoner would be pissed off about the wasted cash and take it out on me. Mom was assigning me the superpower of getting and keeping her clean, and our family on track. It's a lot of pressure.

On the good side, she looked nice, for somebody living in a home for junkies. She had her makeup on, not so tired, and something different with her hair. She was wearing a new dress that Stoner had bought her. She said he'd come to see her three times already, the most visits allowed. He'd brought her the dress, flowers, and a card that he forgot to sign but it's the thought that counts. He knew her size for the dress by looking in the tags of her other dresses. This is all supposedly proof of Stoner being Mr. Wonderful. She said he loved me too, and we were going to be a better family now. We would do fun stuff together like maybe Dollywood. I told her I wanted to go see the ocean, and she laughed. Don't get carried away, she said.

Eventually she got around to asking about where I was living. They'd told her it was a farm, so she wanted to know how fun was that, were there animals to pet and such. Mind you, she never had one good thing to say about being raised in foster care herself, and now she thinks it's all rainbows? I told her, Yeah, Mom, it's exactly like a petting zoo where the main animals are roaches and mice. I told her for fun times we shoveled cow shit, and my foster was a creepy old man that threatened to file down my teeth. I didn't mention I'd started doing drugs. As far as I was concerned, drugs were not the problem in that home. Just the opposite.

She ended up getting weepy on me. I said, Look, I just want to get this over with and come home. You do your part and I'll do mine. She said okay. Probably she thought I was growing up to be one more prick in her life, a junior-varsity Stoner. It's not that I wanted to be mean. But any time I started feeling sorry for her, something in my brain said Don't go there, it's a trap. I'd tried all the options with Mom and had only one place left to go on her. Cold.

The next Saturday I got visitors at Creaky's. It was a normal day of Tommy and me pulling out an old fence, yanking crusty barb wire off of crusty palings and rolling it up to save for a rainy day because that was Creaky. Nothing but rainy days ahead, boys! Save everything, because life sucks and then you die! Fence work meant walking all the steep hills he couldn't climb, so on the good side it was a vacation from his shit. We were at the edge of the woods, taking turns pissing on an anthill, which Tommy felt bad about. He found these blue flowers coming up through the hay. Then we sat in the shade listening to what all was going on up in the trees. Birds having their discussions, a woodpecker making his little *tack-tack-tacks*, this whole other life of little beings out here minding their business and not actually giving a damn about yours. It could set you back on your haunches, in a good way. Why I liked the woods.

We heard a rain crow, which is not your everyday crow. It sounds like a two-cycle engine revving up, finally getting to this spooky *gulp, gulp*. A rain crow calling means you'll have a storm within the day. Tommy was surprised a bird would know that, but this came out of the bible of Mr. Peg, so he believed it. I'd already amazed him of countless things, like how chewing on sassafras stems tastes exactly like root beer. Or how squashing touch-me-not weeds like a washrag and rubbing it on your poison ivy will take the itch away. Amazing the hell out of Tommy with Mr. Peg lore was one of my pastimes.

He was sprawled on his stomach, holding a piece of grass up close to his face. His other fist was squashed against his cheek, propping him up. He had grass seeds in his hair and stick-tights all over his sausage-case jeans and shirt. I leaned over to see what he had, which was the smallest, smallest green grasshopper you can imagine with your brain. Like it came from the planet of smaller things. He said, "The storm thing, I get that. Birds would need to know, right? So they won't get rained on."

I agreed with him on that, caught in the rain would suck for a bird, hard for flying. Tommy and I could go into mental-type things like that, where with other guys, you just don't go there. Mainly we were stalling because we'd finished winding the fence, and ended up with giant wire rolls that were way too big for us to drag to the barn. Then what? At Creaky's we basically lived in terror of doing the wrong thing, and in terror of asking him what was the right thing, so we spent a lot of time debating on which would be worse. Finally, I said I would go ask if he meant to haul the wire out with his tractor, or what.

So. Halfway down the hill I saw what looked like Mr. Peggot's truck parked in front of the house. No way. Then I spotted all three Peggots up on the porch talking to Creaky. I whooped and tore down the hill, thinking for sure they had come to take me home.

Long story short, no. Just to visit. I wondered how they'd convinced the DSS they were not molesters. And Miss Barks had said no visits allowed here, so it blew out all circuits, seeing my old life and new one chatting on the porch. Mr. Peg and Creaky were figuring out they had some of the same cousins, which is what you do in Lee County whenever you meet somebody. First, how are your people related. Then you move on, in this case to silage, Angus cattle, beef prices. Creaky sounded like a different person talking to Mr. Peg in his raspy voice. You'd look at Creaky and ask yourself, How was this old cuss ever married and young and a human being at all? And there it was. Once upon a time, a nice piece of land and good prospects and a boy that loved his farming. Mr. Peg knew about that because back whenever he was a boy, his family did well with the corn and tobacco before they had to sell off their land a piece at a time for people to build houses on. Same with Mrs. Peggot, she started out as a little girl on a farm before their daddy sold his land for a certain number of hogs, one for each child. After that, their farm was a coal mine where her brothers worked, and Mr. Peg also. Mining is how he got his crushed foot.

Anyway I brought Maggot and Mrs. Peggot into the kitchen, where she had a near heart attack. She'd brought ham biscuits but said the tin was not to be opened until she cleaned up, and where did the man keep his Lysol. Good question. This was just skimming the surface, mind you. She had yet to see a bathroom. I introduced them to the two dogs Pete and Mike that were still lying where last seen. Maggot wanted to see some of the rank shit I'd told him about at school, sewage bathtub of doom, the mummified raccoon we found in the basement, but I skipped those. We got out clean towels to put on the couch so we could sit and eat Mrs. Peggot's amazing ham biscuits. I felt like, saved. They asked if I was coming home soon. They'd not even talked to Miss Barks. They found out where I was from our bus driver that was some kin to Mr. Peg, and just came over. Mrs. Peggot seemed pretty torn up. She leaned over and patted my knees and said I should go on saying my prayers. I thought of them going to the prison to see Maggot's mom. He never talked about it, but now I could picture them at Goochland in the visiting room eating ham biscuits, Mrs. Peggot telling Mariah, You hang in there, honey. Say your prayers, and we'll spring you.

Then Fast Forward pulled up outside, and I got excited for the Peggots to meet my friend that was a

Lee High Generals MVP. Out we all went. I could see Mrs. Peggot sizing up this good-looking young man, and Maggot just, gaah. Maggot that didn't give two shits about football. That was Fast Forward's powers at work. Creaky and Mr. Peg came back from the barn where they'd gone to look at the heifers, and Mr. Peg shook hands with him. I hate to say it, but I looked at the Peggots from a Fast Forward viewpoint, wondering if he might think they were a couple of old bumpkins, and that boy of theirs just a little bit odd, or what.

By the time they took off, the other guys had started on supper. Swap-Out for all his derpness could chop onions like a ninja. You just had to not watch. I came in, and Creaky asked where the hell was Tommy, and I said, Oh shit, oh Jesus. I'd left him up in the field with the rolls of barbwire. It had been hours, and Tommy would still yet be up there in the tall grass. He'd wait there till the sun went down, because I'd said I would be right back, and he believed me.

12

Mom graduated from rehab and got to go home. Now instead of McDonald's I could go sit in our kitchen, or in my room that was the exact mess I'd left it the night it all happened, visiting Mom with my chest hurting for how much I missed being a normal kid. Any minute Miss Barks was going to tap on the door and say, "Sorry, time's up." Then *bam*, back to foster life. Some years down the road it would be like this with the girls saying, *Pull out now, quick!* Honestly, give me all or nothing at all. Give me the damn visits at McDonald's.

But Mom said she lived for these times. Regardless the unfairness of her being allowed home while I wasn't. Me being *not* the one of us that screwed up. She still had drug tests to pass and a hard row to hoe, so Miss Barks said it was a realistic goal for us to get me home for Christmas. She didn't babysit us at the house, even though if Mom had wanted to do me damage there were a lot more options there than at McDonald's. Miss Barks said Mom was earning trust. She'd drop me off and sit outside in her car for the hour, doing her homework or her case files. Homework, yes. Miss Barks was seriously young. She was taking night classes to get certified for a teacher, which she said was her dream, because she loved kids. And I thought, What am I?

My first visit back home, I went after school while Stoner was at work. Mom said Stoner was still anti me moving back in, due to the stress of the three of us as a family making Mom relapse. You're going to say, What kind of shit is that for a mother to be telling her kid? Even I thought that, at the time. But Mom had milk and cookies out on the table for me, so probably she was trying to learn the drill from TV. She was nervous. I cut her some slack. She showed me the presents Stoner got her for coming home, including a new microwave that told the time in lit-up numbers. She asked if my foster was still being an asshole, and I told her a person could get used to anything except hanging by the neck. Something I'd heard from Mr. Peg.

After our time was up, Miss Barks came in and said I should get together anything I wanted to take with me. My first thought was to load up on stuff I missed like Snickers bars and my best comics. But anything valuable I would have to turn over to Fast Forward, so I ended up not taking much. Just two of my small-size action heroes that I could sneak in. I would hide them in Swap-Out and Tommy's beds, and they'd never know who put them there. God, maybe. The surprise toy in the shitburger happy meal of their lives.

On the drive back we rolled down the windows. "Just smell that," she said. "Fall time." Plowed-under silage fields, smoke from people's leaf burning, and something a little bit sweet, maybe apples that had rotted on the ground. She was a country girl. She showed me where her parents' farm was because we went past that road. The happiest I remember being that fall was in the car with Miss Barks. She was chatty and would ask questions like who were my caseworkers before, which I couldn't remember, honestly. I'd see one a couple of times, she'd be all like, *Hey, I've got your back.* Next visit, here's a new one reading my name off the files.

Given her looks, I figured Miss Barks would have a boyfriend wanting to get her knocked up and married, but she made no mention of that. She'd moved out last year and got her apartment with the roommate in Norton, which her parents thought was a waste of money, but she wanted that bad to be on her own. I asked why did she want to be a teacher, and she said you have to follow your dreams, plus it pays better than DSS. She wanted an apartment by herself because her roommate left dirty dishes and her crap all over. She said her two best high school friends had gotten their scholarships and gone away to college, but she didn't get one and it about killed her. Everybody knows there aren't that many to go around, but she was still ashamed. She'd thought she was as smart as her two friends were. But here's the thing, she told me, you don't give up, sometimes you just have to take second choice. In her case the job at DSS, slob-roommate apartment, and night classes at Mountain Empire Community College.

She asked me what I wanted to be whenever I grew up. I had to think about that. We went past some barns and tobacco fields with their big yellow-green leaves waving in the sad evening light. She looked over at me and said, Hey, why so glum, chum?

I told her nobody ever asked me that question before, about growing up and what I wanted to be, so I didn't know. Mainly, still alive.

Eventually I got to spend a whole Saturday with Mom, which was the day she told me her surprise: Mom was pregnant. Holy Jesus. I was as ignorant as the next kid, but knew enough to ask, How did you get pregnant in rehab?

She laughed, and said it was going on longer than that but she didn't know until they ran blood tests on her for other reasons. Now she knew. Next April I was going to have a brother or sister. Which blew my mind actually, to put it that way. Me, Demon, that never had even a cousin to my name, soon to be a big brother. Maggot would be jealous. He'd never had any brothers or sisters so far, with future hopes slim to none. Goochland being women only.

We had an amazing day, me and Mom. We went outside and raked up leaves and Maggot came over and we jumped in them. I wanted to run over and see Mrs. Peggot but Mom needed me all to herself, so I stayed. At one point she looked at me and said, Oh my god, Demon, I think you went and got taller than me! Which was impossible, so we measured ourselves with marks on the wall, the official way with a cereal box on your head. Of our two pencil lines, mine came out on top, by a hair. Mom always said she was five-feet-sweet in her two bare feet, but it turns out all this time she was only fifty-nine inches. Which rhymes with nothing, but now that was me too, plus a hair. Unbelievable. I was used to being taller than most kids, except the ones that had been held back a lot of grades. But taller than your own parent is a trip. We put on music and danced crazy, which was a thing we did, and sat on the floor and played dumb board games, which we hadn't done forever. I kept thinking about the baby. I asked her what we should name it, because I had ideas. Tommy was a good one. Also Sterling, which Mom didn't know was even a name.

I asked where its room would be, and she was vague on that. Actually it kind of killed the mood. It turns out she and Stoner had been having arguments on moving to a bigger house. They hadn't been married that long yet and he still liked the good times, so he was not keen on her having this baby. Which was ridiculous. If he wanted to run around with the no-kids version of Mom, he already missed that boat by ten years. Plus, the baby was on the way. You can't take it to customer service and get your money back, I told her, but she didn't laugh. Without really going into it, she told me that was more or less what Stoner had in mind.

I changed the subject by turning over the whole checkerboard and getting in a tickle fight, just basically acting like an idiot. We about peed ourselves laughing.

Stoner was supposed to get home around four, and it was required for me to wait and at least say hello. Our so-called work to do on learning to be a family. Miss Barks said she'd come in and get me at four thirty. I'd not seen Stoner since the night of Mom's OD, so I kind of froze up. He looked the same: denim vest, leather bracelet, gauges. I'd spent a lot of time making him die in my drawing notebook. Even if he never saw those drawings, I'd made them, and looking at him now, I felt like he knew. Not sensible, just an in-my-mind thing.

He gave Mom a kiss and asked what we two had been up to. She said nothing much. She got a beer out of the fridge and cracked it open for him, and asked why didn't he sit down and talk to me a little, to start things off on a new foot. Fine, he said. He turned one of the kitchen chairs around and sat in it backward, straddling it with his arms folded on the back, looking at me. Mom pushed her hair out of her eyes, edgy. She'd been happy and fun all day and now without even looking at her straight on, I could feel her change.

Stoner asked what I was learning in foster care. I said so far mostly putting up hay, working cattle, stretching fences, and riding the bus two hours each way to school. I told him basically everything else was the same as home, in terms of always having to watch my back. His eyes changed. He said he meant, how was I doing with the *attitude*.

I told him fine, thanks.

"Guess what!" Mom said. "I told him about the baby, and he's as excited as he can be." She was looking at me, mouth-smiling but not the eyes. Those please-save-me eyes. "Just think if this one's a boy, and Demon gets a little brother. They'll be two peas in a pod."

Stoner stared at her. "It wouldn't be a fucking mulatto."

"My dad was Melungeon," I told him. "Not a, whatever you said."

Mom tried to change the subject, asking where all Stoner made deliveries today, and why didn't we go in the living room because the chairs were more comfortable and her back hurt.

Stoner was still staring her down. "You wanted us to talk. We are fucking talking."

He had much to say. How I would have to be more considerate now, due to Mom's fragile situation. Stoner had learned a lot, he said, from him and Mom going to their counseling. New words to help us all get along. Opposition disorder being one of them. Supposedly that was a disease, and I had it. If I wanted to move in here, I'd need to go on the medication to knock some of the wind out of my sails. Evidently I had too much of that in my sails. Wind.

Mom acted somewhat like she didn't hear any of this and brought up the different subject of Christmas. How I would be coming home then, and that we would do something special. I remembered to tell her the Peggots were going to Knoxville again over vacation. Probably they would invite me to go too.

Not so fast, buddy, was Stoner's advice. He said I was still not to hang out with Maggot, which I could tell was a surprise to me and Mom both. I told him Miss Barks had checked out the Peggots and given the thumbs-up. It turned out Miss Barks had dated one of Maggot's cousins in high school. And Mom was like, Ha-ha, Lee County, wouldn't you know it.

Stoner slowly turned his head and fixed on her, like a big guard dog. "Since when does this Barks bitch make the rules about what we do as a family?"

I'd been thinking it was ever since the night Mom almost offed herself and Stoner gave me a black eye, but maybe that's just me. According to Stoner, the Peggots and me were a no-go. He said he was getting an injunction, so if I went over there the cops would arrest me.

I looked over at Mom like, Is this true? And she made just the tiniest, tiniest shake of her head. He didn't see it.

The microwave he'd bought her with the blue lit-up clock said 4:21. Nine minutes to go. I didn't want to be in that kitchen, and didn't want to go back to the farm. I sat still, trying to be nothing and nowhere, watching my minutes tick out.

13

Like the saying goes: They passed out the brains, he thought they said trains and he missed his. That was Swap-Out. Tommy, though. Smart as hell, he could think himself out of any hole, but then would crawl back into it and sit there. It was like he *chose* the shit end of the stick, so nobody else would get it. A hard thing to watch.

The day we had no water, for an example. This was a Sunday. We got up, flushed, nothing. Empty pipes howling. Bathroom sink, nothing. Kitchen, ditto. The guys said bad news, the well got drained. It would re-cover in a day or two, in the meantime look out. Sure enough, Creaky called us in the kitchen for his lecture on how farming is a war. All your livelong days, it's you and your livestock and machinery against the bank that wants to foreclose on you. If you waste one thing, that's a win for the bank. So, you do not waste one thing. Not food, not an ounce of grain, not water. I'm trying to be Christian here, he says, taking in orphan boys, and what does one of the damn idjits do but go and waste a whole goddamn *well* full of water.

I wanted to tell him I was no orphan, plus, if he was so Christian we'd all be in church right then discussing certain rules like, don't be pimping onto others as you wouldn't want to get pimped on yourself. But I was not the damn idjit of Creaky's concern.

The natural suspect was Tommy, because of how we divided up barn chores: Swap-Out was shovel, I was feed, Tommy was water. I grained and got the calves in the paddocks with their right mothers, Tommy hosed out buckets and filled the barn troughs. There was this blue-handled spigot thing called a hydrant you had to open up to let the water in the barn, and that same line ran out to fill all the troughs on thirty-some acres. If you went back to the house without remembering to yank the hydrant handle back down, the water ran on and on, overfilling the troughs all night, as long as there's water in the well. Not a minute more. It's the easiest thing in the world to turn off the hose and go on your way, forgetting to shut down the hydrant.

Tommy didn't make that mistake. He'd done it once,

and got leathered for it. After that he kept a clothespin on the hydrant handle. The brain of Tommy, as mentioned. He'd pinch the clothespin on his shirt whenever he turned the hydrant on. Finished, back it went on the handle. If he got to the house and somebody noticed a clothespin dangling on his shirt like an extra nipple, shit! Run back to the barn, it's all good.

Here's who had sucked the well dry: Fast Forward. Long after we'd finished chores, he was out there hosing off his Lariat, leaving no speck of mud on the chassis or whitewall tires, because Saturday nights were for cruising. Meaning every person in Lee County between the ages of sixteen and married drives up and down main street to see and get seen. Fast Forward had washed his truck and gone cruising and left the well to run dry.

So Fast Forward would tell Creaky that's what happened. I was sure of it. He knew how the damn hydrant worked, he'd been there longer than any of us. And Creaky wouldn't punish him, because as far as Creaky was concerned, Fast Forward's shit smelled like hand lotion. The old man would figure some way this water was a necessary sacrifice working to the benefit of America and Lee County football. So confess and get on with it, I'm thinking. Creaky is asking Tommy what a stupid wasteful boy has to say for himself, and Fast Forward is over by the stove getting his coffee.

I'm staring. Catching Fast Forward's eye as he turns around. Thinking, Squad master, yo. What in the hell?

Not a word. Creaky goes outside and fetches a piece of dirty old broken hose, like this is justice for a water-related crime, and makes us watch while he thrashes Tommy twenty licks on his sad big bottom. Fast Forward leaves the house. Tommy takes it for the team. He's bent over hanging on the counter, trying not to cry, but most of all he is not ratting out Fast Forward. I was amazed, honestly. I'm just not that good of a person. Not that brave.

We went on with our day the best we could, water-less, and later I found Tommy in the barn. There were nooks and crannies between the stacked hay bales, and he was curled up in one of those with his head hanging, doodling on an old paper grain bag. He always carried a pencil just in case, the way another person would carry Band-Aids or their heart pills. I sat down with him, wanting to ask why. But not really. I got it. Where in some universes you get reward chips for going X many days without drinking, in ours you got chips for getting through a day unhated. Creaky hating you was just background noise. But Fast Forward hating you would actually mean something. Anyway, the deal was done, with Tommy now going for the Guinness record of most skeletons ever drawn on a grain bag.

I watched him draw for a long while. "So, are you like a Goth kid?"

He looked surprised. He always did, of course, given the standing-up hair. But I don't think he knew what I was talking about. "Skulls and death," I said. "Usually isn't that a Goth thing?" We had this one girl in our grade that wore black lipstick and showed people where she'd cut herself, even back then in the nineties. Way ahead of her time.

Tommy said he drew skeletons because they were easy. He wasn't a talented person like me that could do faces and expressions, arms with muscles and all like that, so he stuck to skeletons. Whenever he wanted to see them, there they were, he said. His little buddies.

Mom was doing her recovering but none too cheerful about it. We had visits once a week, on a weekend if she could swing it but she had to work crappy hours. She was lucky and got her job back but had to start at the bottom again on taking the shifts nobody else wanted. Stoner made himself scarce whenever I came around, fine by me and Mom. She wanted to gripe about him. Stoner was not being all that supportive, babywise, saying it was her nickel if she wanted to do this. He didn't want to hear about her long days on her feet restocking Halloween costumes and candy, just wishing she could sit in one of the marked-down lawn chairs and go to sleep. Or throw up. She was doing a lot of that. She said don't ever be pregnant during the lead-up to Halloween because it will put you off candy corn for life. I told her thanks for the advice.

Hanging up Halloween costumes did not sound that bad. At the farm we were working like dogs. Tommy agreed on what Miss Barks said about Creaky's being an emergency type of foster where nobody stayed too long. He said after the farm work slacks off in winter, the old man wouldn't want us around. Nothing to me of course, I would be back in my own bed before snow fell. But that farm was starting to feel like my life. Cold mornings, a kitchen filling up with smoke while we stuffed newspapers in the stove to get it lit. Manwich suppers or shoe-leather steaks, not tender ones from the grocery but field beef. All meat we ate was previously known to us as Angus aka get your ass in the paddock. We were fed, but never quite enough, nor was our work ever quite done, nor our feet quite warm. We'd get up cold, go to bed cold, throw our filthy clothes in the machine in the basement and forget them down there for days. Even now, the smell of clothes gone rank in the washer takes me right back. That smell was our whole life.

We stayed alive for Friday nights, to pile in Creaky's truck and drive to the Five Star Stadium, home of the Lee High Generals. To wait in the stands, along with everybody else in the county, for our team to roar out of the Red Rage field house. Girls screaming their heads off, grown men right there with them. Creaky would let us buy chili dogs from concessions and we'd sit high in the bleachers to watch Fast Forward being freaking amazing. Yelling our lungs out for our own brother and the other Generals to murder the bastards from Union or Patrick Henry, first and ten, do it again! Knowing that we and nobody else, after it was over, would sleep under the same roof as QB1.

Seeing him in his white uniform with the giant shoulders and thin, fast legs, I got new aspects on how to draw Fast Man. And other designs in my head. Fast Forward thought I had good coordination. Possibly just compared to Tommy and Swap-Out, which God knows is no fair fight. But if he wasn't busy he'd show me things. Firing and receiving passes. Keeping a center of gravity. Down behind the barn where Creaky wouldn't see us slacking off, Tommy and Swap-Out would sit on grain buckets and watch, with manure-sogged jeans and stars in their eyes. I wasn't much to start with, being raised around old people and a mom that thought getting her empty pop can into the trash was a sport. But the shine I got from Fast Forward decided my future. One day I would be that guy, in that uniform, with those shoulders. Those cheerleaders.

Farms or anything else in the big world, I'd not seen much of back then. Or now either, to be honest. On TV I'd seen fields like great green oceans with men sailing through them on tractors and combines the size of the AT walkers in *Star Wars*. I never knew those were real, I thought it was make-believe. Because Lee County isn't flat like those ocean farms, not anywhere, not even a little. Here every place is steep, and everything rolls downhill. If you plowed up all your land, the most of it would end up down in the creek by year's end, and then you're done growing anything.

What farmers can do with a mountainside is what Creaky did, let God grow grass on it, and run cattle on it to eat God's grass. Then send them out west to be finished, because feedlots for turning cattle into burgers and making money are all out there. Not here. We just raise them big enough to sell for what Creaky called one kick in the ass per head. A few hundred dollars.

His only land flat enough for plowing was three acres, low in the valley. That's about average size for a tobacco bottom, lying alongside of the lane we walked out on to get the bus. The first day I came to that farm, passing that field, maybe I thought, there's some nice tobacco. More likely I gave no notice at all. Never will that happen again, any more than I'd fail to notice an alligator by the side of the road, or a bear. What a pretty sight, you'd say, if you're an ignorant son of a bitch. Instead of: There lies a field that eats men and children alive.

August they call the dog days, due to animals losing their minds in the heat. But the real dog days if you are a kid on a farm are in September and October. Tobacco work: suckering, topping, cutting, hanging, stripping. All my life I'd heard farm kids talking about this, even in the lower grades, missing school at cutting time. Some got to work on farms other than their own, and get paid for it. I envied them. The boy version I guess of how little girls are jealous of their big sisters for getting pregnant, with all the attention. I'd only ever known childish things, screwing around in the woods or Game Boy. Now I would be one of the working kids.

I had a list going in my head that fall, of what all I would tell my little brother one day. But time passed and eventually my mind had only one thought in it as regards childhood. For any kid that gets that as an option: take that sweet thing and run with it. Hide. Love it so hard. Because it's going to fucking leave you and not come back.

Topping starts in August. You have to break off the tops of all the thousands of plants that are head high or higher to a fifth grader. Walk down the rows reaching up, snapping off the big stalk of pink flowers on top, freeing up the plant for its last growth spurt. Those plants will be over all our heads before the season ends, and still yet we will have to be their masters.

My first day of topping was stinking hot. Creaky told us to keep our shirts on and wear the big, nasty leather gloves he gave us, but we shed our shirts the minute he was out of sight. I didn't want to wear the gloves, but Tommy said do it or I'd be sorry. Creaky set us all to topping our own rows, and moved faster than you'd think the old guy had in him. He and Fast Forward got out ahead of us. I worked hard and stayed close behind them, with Tommy and Swap-Out bringing up the rear. The reaching up made your arms ache. The sap ran sticky all over everything, the sun was a fireball on your head, and pity to you if you tried to wipe the sweat off your face with that gummy glove. I tried to use my left hand for topping, being a lefty, and right for sweat-wiping. Then the one arm gave out so I had to use the other, and let the sweat go on and burn my eyes out. All the while thinking, Man, tobacco is hard work. I'd seen nothing yet.

At some point I went back to look for Tommy and

Swap-Out because they were nowhere. Way back yonder I found them, and was like, Y'all, what the hell? Tommy was gathering up all the pink flowers that you were supposed to throw on the ground and walk on. Going back down his row, gathering up these flowers and carrying them in his arms like a freaking bride. Jesus, Tommy, I said. Your ass will be grass. He told me not to worry, he was almost done.

I followed him to the edge of the field, and out there by the lane were these two small dirt mounds, the size of bushel baskets dumped over. Side by side. I'd never noticed them before. Tommy put down his armload of flowers on the two little mounds, divided up between them. Saying nothing about it. Then he went back to work. I didn't ask.

But that night after we were in bed, he told me what it was for. His parents were buried out in eastern Virginia someplace, so he'd never gotten to see the graves, just like I hadn't ever seen my dad's. I would never have thought to do what Tommy did, though. He just made them up. Eight different homes he'd been in so far, that he could remember. In every one of them he'd left behind a little set of graves.

14

Cutting tobacco starts around a month after topping. Cutting is the bastard of all bastards. If
you've not done it, here's how it goes. First, the lamest
worker on your crew (Tommy) walks ahead, throwing
down the tobacco laths between the rows. Laths are
wooden sticks, three feet long, like a kid would use for
a sword fight. Which every kid up home has done, because a million of them are piled in barns waiting to get
used in the fall. You come along after him and pick up
the first stick, stab it in the ground so it's standing
up. Jam a sharp metal cap called a spear on the end of
it. If you fall, that thing will run you through, so don't.
Next, with a hatchet you chop a tobacco plant off at the
base. It's like cutting down a six-foot-tall tobacco tree.
Pick it up and slam its trunk down on the stick so it gets

speared. Chop another plant, slam it on. You'll get six plants pierced on that stick so it looks like a pole holding up a leaf tent. Then pull off the little metal spear point and move on. Jam the next stick in the ground, do it all again.

After the speared plants have stood in the sun and got three days' dews on them to heal the sunburn, you load them on the flatbed and haul them to the barn. Then carry them up into the rafters and hang them on rails to cure. Every stick gets laid up sideways with its six plants hanging down, like pants on a clothesline. They'll stay up there till all the plants are dry and brown. Only then will they get taken down, leaves stripped from the stalks, baled, and sold.

Climbing forty feet up into the barn rails to hang tobacco is a job for a monkey basically. Or the superhero that looks out for farms, instead of cities. Which, in case you didn't notice, there isn't a single one. So it's the typical thing of jobs that can kill you, this gets to be a contest among guys, how fast and reckless can you be with tobacco hanging. Everybody knows somebody, the near misses, the shocking falls, the guy in a wheelchair to this day. I can name names. No machine exists for any of this, the work gets done by children and men. Your chance to become a cripple or a legend. Fast Forward was excellent. But Swap-Out, holy Christ. He was a spectacle. Like they say, no child born without his gifts.

It's a full season of work to get a tobacco crop planted and set, weeded, suckered, sprayed to keep off the frog-eye and blue mold. If it rains so much you can't get the highboy in there, you slog around trying to spray by hand. And it all counts for nothing unless you can get it harvested before frost. So in October you're in the field all day every day, cutting for the life of you. Picking up the next stick, stabbing the ground. Chopping a plant, lifting, slamming it on. Stab-chop-lift-slam times six, and move on, forever amen and God help you. One loaded stick of plants weighs thirty or forty pounds, and you'll lift hundreds of them before a day is done. You do the math, because I've already done the job. What it adds up to is, everything hurts.

But you keep on, sunup to sundown in any weather, because if a farmer fails to get his crop in, he's lost it all. Land, livestock, the roof over his head. For some, a lousy day's work will get you yelled at. For farmers, it's live or die. A tour of tobacco duty can feel like a season in hell, and you come back from it feeling like an army vet: proud, used up, messed up, wishing to be appreciated. And invisible. You'll go back to school and get treated as another dumbass in history that doesn't know the difference between a state and a common-wealth.

Creaky kept us out of school most of October. Even as a kid, I'd never spent such long hours in the sun. I'd look in the mirror, shocked to see my pond-water eyes looking out of a face the color of walnuts. But we had to get that tobacco in the barn before month's end, or we'd be stripping green leaves in February. He threatened us like that was the fate worse than death. I would be so long gone by then, green leaves in February were nothing to me. But for now I was still in hell. Every day I thought: This has to be the end of it. Or the end of me. I thought: School was a better deal than I ever knew. Tobacco is its own education. How to get yourself out there again with everything already hurting, your back and sun-cooked ears and your goddamn teeth.

About a week in, midday, I discovered things could get worse. I started feeling sick, like a bad carpet-cleaner high. This was after a couple hours already of the meanest headache I'd ever had. Everything buzzing, like cicadas had gone in my ears and set up shop. I made myself keep working because I didn't want to be a wuss or let the guys down or any of those things. But I was starting to have crazy thoughts. Like, if I just lie down here in between the tall tobacco plants, nobody will know. Then I doubled over and puked oatmeal on my shoes.

I still had to keep up, because getting thrashed in that condition was unthinkable. But I must have been off my ball because Tommy found me and started yelling shit, like where were my gloves, oh crap, didn't he tell me to use the gloves? Oh crap, now I had the sickness and he had to go get Fast Forward. I told him not to, but off he ran. Then I don't remember a lot. Fast Forward and Creaky getting me in the house, making me lie down, drinking a bunch of water that I threw up, more water until I kept it down. Creaky was pissed, obviously. But since this was my first time, he said to learn my lesson from now on and wear the goddamn gloves.

Those things were so big and stiff, it was like trying to use tools while wearing baseball mitts. I'd seen Fast Forward working without his. So it wasn't my first day of going bare-handed, but that was the day it caught up to me, because it builds up in your system. Green tobacco sickness is what it's called. Nicotine poisoning. Kids get it all the time, more than adults, which is why Fast Forward could get by without gloves. If you're older and you've smoked more, your body gets used to the poison and takes everything better in stride.

What fool would want to put himself through all that, you're going to ask. For a crop that addicts people and tars their lungs and busts the grower's ass. Mind you, the government used to *pay* a man to grow it, with laws about how much he could grow, and where, with price supports to make sure there was plenty and also just exactly enough. The world needed our burley tobacco and wanted it bad. Philip Morris and those guys got their product, got the kids hooked, made their fortunes, and we all lived happily ever after, for a hundred years or something. Until people caught on to the downside of smoking and sued the hell out of somebody. And the government said, Well, never mind on that, and phased out the price supports.

I had only a kid's idea of anything at Creaky Farm, but losing those market guarantees was all men talked about. Getting their farms foreclosed, moving in with their kids or maiden aunts, going on disability because their piece of American pie went rotten. Only some few with superhero strength stayed out there trying to put in more acreage, busting their backs to break even. They said the most of our tobacco now was getting sold to China. Meaning I guess we were helping to kill the communists, so. God bless America and all that.

Why does a man keep trying? On long, cold days

in the stripping house I've spent many an hour listening to guys chew over that question. So yes, stripping green leaves would be my problem, in years to come. Used to be, the stripping house was a place to hear the best stories in the world. Guys saved them up all year. Now it's mostly just the saddest story ever told: where the world has left us. A farmer has his land, and nothing else. He's more than married to it, he's on life support. If he puts his acreage in corn or soy, he might net seven hundred dollars an acre. Which is fine and good for the hundred-acre guys, Star Wars farmers.

But what if he's us, with only three that can be plowed? In the little piece of hell that God made special for growing burley tobacco, farmers always got seven *thousand* an acre. A three-acre field is no fortune, but it kept him alive. No other crop known to man that's legal will give him that kind of return on these croplands, precious and small that they are. The rules are made by soil and rain and slope. Leaving your family's land would be like moving out of your own body. That land is alive, a body itself, with its own talents and, I guess you could say, addictions. If you farm on the back of these mountains, your choice is to grow tobacco, or try something else—*anything* else, it turns out—and lose everything. While somebody, someplace, is laughing at your failure, thinking you got what you deserved.

Around the time I topped and cut my first tobacco, we noticed the cigarette ads stopped playing. No idea why. If we'd known it was people thinking tobacco was dangerous for kids even to see on TV, with their eyes, we'd have found that dead hilarious. Our schools had smoking barrels. Teachers smoked on their breaks, kids at recess. The buyers were telling us the cancer thing was a scare, not proven. Another case of city people trash-talking us and our hard work, like anything else we did to feed ourselves: raising calves for slaughter, mining our coal, shooting Bambi with our hunting rifles. Now these people that would not know a tobacco plant if they saw one were calling it the devil.

If Philip Morris and them knew the devil had real teeth, they sat harder on that secret than you'd believe. Grow it with pride and smoke it with pride, they said, giving out bumper stickers to that effect. I recall big stacks of them at school, free for the taking. Grow and smoke we did, while the price per pound went to hell, and a carton got such taxes on it, we were smoking away our grocery money. We drove around with "Proud Tobacco Farmer" stickers on our trucks till they peeled and faded along with our good health and dreams of greatness. If you're standing on a small pile of shit, fighting for your one place to stand, God almighty how you fight.

15

November 19. A birthday never to forget.

I expected it to be a big nothing, since nobody knew. Mom would, obviously, but she hadn't scheduled any visit as far as I knew. Maybe trying to get off work that Saturday. Meantime I didn't plan on telling anybody, especially not Creaky, because he would hold it against me. Like, just from getting born I was expecting too much.

But the night before, lined up for squad inspection in our room, I blurted it out: tomorrow I'm turning eleven. This can be a monster thing for a kid to keep inside. And Fast Forward was a true brother. He'd thought I was already older than that, due to being tall for my age. He said it was too bad I didn't give him more warning because he would have organized something. But he would still try. Another pharm party was my guess, or the special girlfriend cookies. Life wasn't giving me a lot to go on right then. Regular cookies would have totally made my day.

I hung on to that thought, something good coming my way. Woke up, got dressed, waited on the bus with Tommy and Swap-Out in total and complete darkness because it's way down in the fall by now, and I'm thinking the whole time: Hang on Demon, today's the day.

Mrs. Peggot had to know, being the only person that had ever baked me a cake, but I saw Maggot at school and he had no clue. I didn't tell him either, because why make your best friend feel bad. Mr. Goins took attendance, and the announcements came over the intercom. And then they called my name, Damon Fields to the office. Yes! Somebody knew. My first thought was that Mom got permission to come take me out of school. Or maybe Mrs. Peggot had brought me something. Food, I hoped.

I got to the office and saw it was Miss Barks. Okay, she could bring me a package, no law against that. She looked upset though, and told me to come into the attendance office. She closed the door and sat down. I looked all around. If she'd brought me anything, I wasn't seeing it. I was still happy though. Obviously something was up. I sat down and looked at her across the big desk.

"Damon," she said, and then nothing. It was utterly weird. She did not look so good.

"I know," I finally told her, starting to get it. "It's okay."

She stared at me. "*What's* okay?"

"That Mom forgot my birthday."

Her blue eyes went big and round. "Oh my God. Damon. When's your birthday?"

"Today. But that's fine, that you didn't know. I'm used to it."

Miss Barks looked horrified and started crying. I mean, boo-hoo, grabbing Kleenexes out of the box next to the pictures of the attendance officers' kids. Nose blowing, black makeup running off her eyes. This was batshit.

"It's really okay," I told her. "I don't even care. Okay?"

She kept shaking her head, blowing her nose. "No, Damon, I'm sorry. It's not okay. I'm so, so sorry. It's your mom."

"*What's* my mom?"

"It's bad news."

Of course this is the point where I just lose it, saying

God*damn* it, I *knew* it, you don't even have to tell me, she got drunk again or took pills and I won't get to go home for Christmas because she is such a goddamn fucking *fuckup*!

I'm dropping f-bombs on Miss Barks left and right and she's putting out her hand saying No, no. That I really don't know. Listen.

Mom is dead.

No way to that, just, no.

I've got no more to say here, I'm getting up out of the chair to leave, like maybe I could go to the office and call Mom at work or I don't know what, while Miss Barks keeps saying yes, she's sorry but it's true. She is so, so sorry. I told her I didn't believe her, but if it was true, then what did she die of, and Miss Barks said oxy.

Believe it or not, I had to ask. What's oxy?

16

Maybe life, or destiny, or Jesus if you really need to put somebody in charge of things, had finally flung down one too many rocks in Mom's road and she called it a day. That's option one. Or two, maybe she didn't aim to die but miscalculated, to cap off her twenty-nine-year pileup of miscalculations, one of those of course being me. I could spend the rest of my life asking which it was, suicide or accident. No answer on that line.

I'll grant it did not look random, her clocking in as my mom and then out again on the same date. To hit the mark like that would take some looking at the calendar and getting stuff together, you would think. And that's the thing, Mom was not a planner. Plus I can't be sure she even remembered it was my birthday. Anybody that knew her would agree on that.

But now they were all sure she'd mapped it out. The wake and funeral being throwdowns of shame for this girl that had gone and abandoned her child. Bring on the fake nose blows, the eye-rolling towards me and shutting up if I came close. The child mustn't hear. Like I didn't know whose fault this was. Mom had promised to stay clean as long as I was a good enough son to make it worth her while. Nobody was hiding *that* from me, I knew shit. I was eleven now.

Everything about the funeral was wrong. First of all being in a church, which I guess is required, but church and Mom were not friends. This went back to her earliest foster home with a preacher that mixed Bible verses with thrashings and worse, his special recipe for punishing bad little girls. Moral of the story, Mom always saying she wouldn't be caught dead in a church. And here she was, losing every battle right to the end, in a white casket from Walmart, the other place she most hated to be. Jesus looking down from his picture on the wall, probably thinking, I don't believe we've met, and *girl*, where'd you get that dress? It was this ugly flowered one somebody put her in. She was getting seen by half the town and buried in a stupid dress she only ever wore to work on Manager Appreciation Day, as her personal joke. Now she'd be wearing it for the boss-appreciating days in heaven, so the joke goes on. She probably would have wanted the dress Stoner bought her in rehab, but knowing him he saved the receipt and took it back.

Oh, but he was all tore up, was Mr. Stoner. I almost didn't recognize him in a tie, plus reflector sunglasses for the extra effect. People lined up to pay their respects, with Stoner standing at the casket so the ladies could hug him and tell him what a tragedy to see her taken so young, and him a widower. Then they'd walk away and say whatever shit they actually thought of Mom. I could see their faces change, heads leaning together, hustling back to the living.

The church was not one the Peggots or any of us had gone to, except for some of Stoner's family. Sinking River Baptist. Maybe that made it Stoner's home court, but I didn't see how it was his place to be up there beside the casket. He'd barely known Mom a year. It was me that had mopped her vomit and got her to bed and hunted up her car keys and got her to work on time, year in, year out. I could have put her together one last time, but nobody was asking.

The Peggots did what they could. Came and got me from school, fetched my church clothes from over at the house, kept me over the weekend. Mr. Peggot got out his electric trimmers and gave me a haircut, which I was needing in the worst way. Maggot even more so, like years overdue, but out of respect they called a truce this once and didn't have a hair war. Which just made me sadder. Like, what had the world come to if Maggot and his pappaw couldn't fight over a haircut. Some cousins came in from Norton for the funeral, and normally with a full house there would be yelling over TV channels and the last chicken wing, a certain amount of soft objects thrown around. But they were weirdly quiet. Eyeing me like I'd turned into a strange being that might break if you made any noise. Mrs. Peggot for her part kept feeding me and telling me how Mom loved me more than anything in this world, which was nice of her to say, even if I was thinking at the time: Not really. She loved her dope buzz more.

I had roads to travel before I would know it's not that simple, the dope versus the person you love. That a craving can ratchet itself up and up inside a body and mind, at the same time that body's strength for tolerating its favorite drug goes down and down. That the longer you've gone hurting between fixes, the higher the odds that you'll reach too hard for the stars next time. That first big rush of relief could be your last. In the long run, that's how I've come to picture Mom at the end: reaching as hard as her little body would stretch, trying to touch the blue sky, reaching for some peace. And getting it. If the grown-up version of me could have one chance at walking backwards into this story, part of me wishes I could sit down on the back pew with that pissed-off kid in his overly tight church clothes and Darkhawk attitude, and tell him: You think you're giant but you are such a small speck in the screwed-up world. This is not about you.

But I would be wasting my shot, because the kid was in no mood to hear it. I can still feel in my bones how being mad was the one thing holding me together. Mad at everybody but mostly her, for marrying Stoner and then ditching us both, running off to some heaven where she could throw her shit anywhere at all, and nobody would ever lay a hand on her again.

And I'd have to go on living with what an asshole I'd been to her, especially at the end that I didn't know was the end. Last time I'd seen her at the house, did I even say goodbye, or let her hug me? I can't tell you. I've tried and will go on trying to see those last minutes again, pounding on them sometimes like it's the door of a damn bank vault, but if there's anything in there at all to be remembered, it's not coming to me. Access denied.

Instead, I get to remember every single thing about

the funeral. That day sits big and hard in my brain like this monster rock in the ocean, waiting to wreck me. I wish to God it would leave my brain. It stays. All of it. The itchy black socks borrowed from Mr. Peg because I'd outgrown all but my gym socks. The smell of sweat and shoe polish. The toothpaste green of the walls, a color Mom hated. The sound of the quavery organ, old ladies stinking of perfume. The wasps, this whole slew of them, buzzing and buzzing at the colored windows way up high. It was a warm day for November and I guess they woke up. I watched them all through the service.

The people in the church looked like strangers. Some or most I'm sure I'd met before, but I wasn't seeing faces, just the rock-hard hearts. All of them thinking Mom brought this on herself, and was getting the last ride she deserved in that cheap white casket. A mean side to people comes out at such times, where their only concern is what did the misfortunate person do to put themselves in their sorry fix. They're building a wall to keep out the bad luck. I watched them do it. If that's all the better they could do for Mom, they were nothing at all to me.

What I had felt at the Peggot house with the too-quiet cousins wasn't wrong: I was a strange new being, turned overnight. Creaky liked to call us orphan boys, and I always felt *proud* inside for not actually being one. So that was me doing the same, building the wall with me still on the lucky side. Now I'd gone over to the side of pitiful, and you never saw a kid so wrecked. At the start of the service they did that song about Amazing God, and I felt exactly the opposite: I once could see but now I'm blind, was found but now I'm lost.

The preacher and his sermon, the sin and the flesh, all that I won't go into. I wasn't listening. I was thinking about my little brother being in that casket with her. That part hadn't dawned on me until I'd gone up to view her with Mrs. Peggot. She patted Mom on her dead hand and said, "Poor little Mama, you tried your best," and that's where it hit me: *my brother* was in that casket. I was robbed. What a goddamn waste.

I'd had no intention of going to look at her with Stoner up there holding court, and anyway what kid wants to get that close to a dead body, let alone his mom's? My plan was to hang back and let other people do the viewing. But Mrs. Peggot had her eye on me, and right before it was time to sit down, she told me I would always regret it if I didn't go say goodbye before they closed the casket. It hadn't really sunk in that they were about to shut her in there. Permanently. I let Mrs. Peggot take hold of my shoulders and walk me up the aisle.

And even still, I ended up not saying goodbye. Too shocked. Not just by her being dead, which was expected. And the part about my little brother, unexpected. The worst was how pissed off she looked. I've heard it said that the dead look peaceful after they're laid to rest, but they've not seen the likes of Mom that day. If I was burned about this, she was *righteous* burned. It messed with my head, as far as my theory of her running off and getting away with it.

So I sat in that church hating on the world. The service took forever, and the burial more so. To get to the cemetery, I ended up riding in a limo that was supposedly for the family. The funeral director put me in there even though the Peggots brought me, and Stoner being Stoner drove his precious truck. As far as Mom and family, I was it. In a car the size of a living room, with extra seats and push-button everything. Every kid dreams of riding in a limo at some point, prom or whatever, but count me out because I had my shot and it was the saddest ride of my life.

The driver was the funeral director's son and he had a girl riding with him up front. Her hair was all on top of her head in one of those clip things, and she kept playing with the curly blond baby hairs on the back of her neck while the two of them talked nonstop. I could hear something about a forfeited basketball game, something about somebody getting a restraining order, something about a guy caught cheating and getting slapped walleyed. High school type information. He was one of those overly tall kids you see with the too-big Adam's apple and giant hands, the backs of his ears red, even though it was late in the year for any work that would sunburn you. He mostly nodded and laughed while she talked. She took off her shoes and put her stocking feet up on the dash. My first thought was huh, she's not family, and my second was, she didn't go to this funeral at all, she's dressed pretty slutty actually, and they are *flirting* up there.

After a while his arm stretches out on the seat and it's *him* running his thumb over the back of her neck. He's putting moves on this chick, thinking of pussy while driving me to see my mom get put in the ground. It hit me pretty hard, how there's no kind of sad in this world that will stop it turning. People will keep on wanting what they want, and you're on your own.

Mom got buried over in Russell County in a plot with Stoner's dead relatives. Probably he already owned the plot, and with him paying for everything, the shots were his to call. But she should have been buried with my dad. It looked like I'd lost all chances now for seeing that grave, wherever it was, and I'd be damned if I was ever coming back to Russell County to hang around dead Stoner kin, so that was that. I was in the same boat with Tommy. If I wanted to visit my parents, I would have to make little fake graves to leave behind me on my road to nowhere.

What's an oxy, I'd asked. That November it was still a shiny new thing. OxyContin, God's gift for the laid-off deep-hole man with his back and neck bones grinding like bags of gravel. For the bent-over lady pulling double shifts at Dollar General with her shot knees and ADHD grandkids to raise by herself. For every football player with some of this or that torn up, and the whole world riding on his getting back in the game. This was our deliverance. The tree was shaken and yes, we did eat of the apple.

The doctor that prescribed it to Louise Lamie, customer service manager at Walmart, told her this pill was safer than safe. Louise had his word on that. It would keep her on her feet for her whole evening shift, varicose veins and all, and if that wasn't one of God's miracles then you tell me what is. And if a coworker on Aisle 19 needs some of the same, whether she borrows them legit or maybe on the sly from out of your purse in the break room, what is a miracle that gets spread around, if not more miracle?

The first to fall in any war are forgotten. No love gets

lost over one person's reckless mistake. Only after it's a mountain of bodies bagged do we think to raise a flag and call the mistake by a different name, because one downfall times a thousand has got to mean something. It needs its own brand, some point to all the sacrifice.

Mom was the unknown soldier. Walmart would have a new stock girl trained in time for the Christmas shoppers, to knock herself out with the inflatable Rudolphs, and be bored senseless before the Valentine's candy came in. One of those heart-shaped boxes would be purchased by Stoner for the underage waitress at Pro's Pizza he was squiring around on his Harley without her daddy's consent. Our trailer home would be thoroughly Cloroxed and every carpet torn out, so the Peggots could rent it to one of Aunt June's high school friends that got left flat by both her kids' daddies. Aunt June probably leaned on them hard to help out her friend, given how they got burned with the last hardship case. But wanting a fresh start for this girl and her little family, I'm sure they scrubbed the place clean of old stains, including the two pencil lines on the kitchen wall that proved I once stood taller by a hair than my mom. Her life left no marks on a thing.

17

Stoner and I ran out of steam on our supervised visit halfway through lunch. He'd take a bite, chew, stare at the foil wrapper, repeat, like he'd found religion in a combo meal. I kept picking up my extra-large beverage cup and looking down its throat like whatever I'd lost might be in there. Rattling ice. Your basic two guys that would like to be not looking at each other. I'd never at any time had much to say to the man, but we did have the Demon improvement program to keep us entertained. It used to get him worked up in a pretty good lather. Not today.

I kept looking over at Miss Barks, hoping she'd come bail us out, but she was reading a book. She'd made it clear Mom wanted this, Stoner and me patching it up. If you think a mother is a hard rock to run up against, try pushing back on a dead one. She and Stoner had gone to the counseling, and he'd agreed to starting over from the top, family of four and all that. But with two of the four now scratched from the lineup, heels were dragged. Miss Barks had badgered him into this visit. Now here we were, duty done. She was keeping her nose in her damn book.

"I guess you're moving," I said.

"I'll finish up getting my stuff out of there whenever I get time. They liked to killed me these last couple weeks with the long-haul deliveries. You'd think a man could get a break."

I wondered what else he meant to take from our trailer home, maybe doorknobs and copper wiring. According to Maggot he had already cleared out, lock, stock, barrel, and Satan.

"You thinking to leave Lee County?" I asked him.

Bite, chew. He looked up at me. "Who's asking?"

"Nobody. I just wondered. Where you meant to live and everything."

"I'm back over at Heeltown, same place."

"I thought somebody else was in that apartment now. Some guy you knew."

"Nah."

I pictured Stoner walking backward to where he'd met Mom, which was in Walmart, on his way to sporting goods. He could rewind his life to that spot, turn down a different aisle, and start new. Find some other girlfriend to jump on the back of his Harley with her hair flying. Off they go. I had to quit this line of thinking for fear of what might happen, crying in front of people or a punch thrown at Stoner. He was getting a complete do-over, and I was stuck with the leftovers of him and Mom, like paper torn off a package. Here, now, nothing.

Stoner took off his reflector sunglasses and rubbed his eyes. The funeral shirt and tie had gone back to whoever he borrowed them from, but the sunglasses indoors he seemed to be keeping as his new look. The grieving husband thing. Given the shaved head and leather jacket, though, the shades just leaned it all in more of the criminal direction.

"She could of been real happy," he said, out of nowhere. "Her and me. If things were different. Gal was a spitfire, all said and done."

Why I needed to hear my own mother called any name at all, by a guy that had mostly pissed on her flame, was a question. *If things were different.* The existence of me having screwed up his wonderful marriage: there it sat. Same pile of crap waiting to be stepped in. I looked over at Miss Barks again and was shocked to see her looking straight at me. I rolled my eyes towards the door like, Please? But she ratcheted her eyebrows together, that thing she did, meaning, You've got some fish to fry here, young man. Which I did, she wasn't wrong. The main one being, what the hell comes next for me, and will Stoner have anything to say about it.

The DSS had been on the fence at first, but now were coming in on the side of yes, Stoner could have a say, if he wanted to. He'd shown up to counseling with Mom, and acted agreeable to helping support me. What about my busted lip, what about my black eye, what about getting locked in my room for days at a time? Questions were asked. But Mom always took up for him, claiming I was a hard kid to handle. She said *she* was the one doing the child abuse, more so than Stoner. This fairy tale, reported to me by Miss Barks, made me so mad at Mom, I wanted her back just for the purpose of calling her a goddamn lying bitch. Which was not happening unless I meant to go dig her up out of Russell County clay. What I did instead was come close to busting out Miss Barks's passenger-side window, the day she told me. This chat of ours taking place in her car, parked out on Millers Chapel Road. All that got busted though was my knuckles. And my cred, I guess you could say. As far as being a kid that was hard to handle.

I wasn't forgiving Mom for it, but after Miss Barks talked me down, I could see the reasoning. No part of the Stoner deal was ever supposed to happen to me, and I'd told Mom that. Like, daily. A mother is supposed to protect a kid from being made to lick a man's boots and take his punches. Mom screwed up, and she knew it. I'd never in the past been a hundred percent on all her moral inventory blah-blah-blah, but I was getting it now.

The upshot of her taking full responsibility was that no charges were ever filed against Stoner. Leaving the two of us free to discuss our feelings in a burger place on 58. Normally with a stepdad I guess nothing is set in stone, as far as child support for the kid of the dead wife. But legal-guardian-wise, I was short on options. Not a great time for him to lose interest entirely.

I was waiting for him to ask about school, or anything else. Was I making progress in the discipline-and-respect-for-others department. Nope, nobody home, Stoner boot camp had closed up shop. This probably sounds nuts, but I started wishing he would make some insult of my character, to show interest. I was blurting out any random thing that might make me sound like a worthy person, which to be honest there wasn't much. Even my drawing, the one thing I was pretty good at, was over and out since Mom died. I couldn't even open my notebooks to look at my older stuff. Too sad, I guess. I was the opposite of Tommy, as far as sadness and drawing.

And now I was embarrassing myself, trying to dig up bones for Stoner. I said I was going out for JV football. And had started weight training. Which was not a complete lie, Fast Forward was psyched about me and football and was letting me use his free weights, teaching me the body parts lingo some guys had: quads, triceps, lats. Those words did get the tiniest spark of attention from Stoner. For about ten seconds, before he went back to opening up the layers of his Quarter Pounder and separating out all the pickles.

I decided to let Stoner make the next move. A boring game, since he didn't seem to notice I'd stopped talking. He ran out of anything fascinating to eat, and was looking around like maybe somebody better had showed up. It was mostly just parents with kids eating their value meals in what you had to assume were happier situations. Our table was by the door, so we got a fresh blast of December whenever anybody came in. Freezing rain type of thing. I didn't have any winter coat that fall. Mom kept meaning to get me one, but never did.

I said nothing, Stoner said nothing. I turned up my Coke and drank it down. I needed more ice in me right then like a hole in the head. Now my whole chest hurt. A couple came in with a kid, one of those good-looking families you just want to believe in, like a commercial. The little guy was in a puffy jacket and boots and looked like a tiny moon man, walking on his toes. The mom had on a purple coat and tall boots, cheeks red from the cold, young looking. Like Mom whenever she first had me. The husband or boyfriend went to order and she squatted down on her boot heels to unzip the kid out of his coat, flicking her shiny hair over her shoulders, talking to this kid, smiling in his face like there was no place else she wanted to be. I wondered if Mom was ever that thrilled with me. She'd fought tooth and nail with her fosters about not giving up the baby, and ended up having to move out on her own, pregnant, broke, and boyfriendless as she was. She always said I was the first good thing that ever happened to her. And seemed that thrilled about baby number two, even if Stoner wasn't.

He was running his fingers around the inside of the paper sleeve that his fries came in, and licking the salt off his fingers. I could see little grains in his black beard. I wondered if he ever thought about the baby he was going to be the dad of, or if he'd forgotten it completely, as part of his total reset. At the funeral no mention was made about this being a two-in-one, meaning probably nobody else knew. So now, in the entire world, there was only me left to lie in bed at night thinking about those two being dead forever. It seemed like a lot for one person to be responsible for. The whole life of my brother that never got to happen.

Miss Barks got my attention, pointing at her watch. Shit and hallelujah.

I folded the dead-meat mess of my lunch back into its foil, laying it to rest. Or on second thought, to save for later because I'd be starving in an hour. "So, report cards are coming next week and I'm looking good," I said. "Possibly honor roll." Even for a Hail Mary, this was dumb, Stoner giving no particular shit about school. Plus not true. But not totally false, either. I told him I'd busted my butt trying to make up a ton of work, due to missing a month of school.

He looked up at me from his little salt project, with no exact expression.

"October," I said. "I was cutting tobacco."

"Huh," he said. "So the foster parents don't care if you lay out of school?"

"Jesus *fuck,* Stoner."

He sat up like I'd kicked him, and looked all around for whatever Sunday school teachers might be present. "There's no call for language."

I glared at him. "There's no *parents.* It's one old guy running a slave farm for homeless boys. You know where I'm living. Miss Barks told you about it, and so did Mom. What were you, unconscious? I hate it there."

"Fine, sorry." He spread his hands.

"Anyway, I won't be there much longer because the

work is pretty much done for now. He doesn't keep boys on the farm through the winter months."

Stoner just nodded, like I was explaining how my sock drawer was full and I needed some place to stash my extras. Not at his place, was a good guess. I was wishing so hard for him to give a damn, and also for him to disappear from the planet of Earth. I wished both those things at the same time. And wish number three, not to be the eleven-year-old redheaded boy that everybody saw crying at the burger place on Route 58.

I had one weapon left. "So it looks like I'll be hanging out with Maggot. The Peggots invited me to go with them to Knoxville after school lets out. Next week. Over Christmas break."

Stoner looked blank. Did he not know schools let out for Christmas? Had his reset button truly erased everything, even the unrepeatable-word son of a jailbird next door?

"You all have a nice time," he said. And the bottom fell out of my stomach. That's how far he was willing to let things slide, as regards the kind of people we were in this family.

That was my last shot. The Peggots going to Knoxville, that was true. Me invited to come with them, that was not. But I would go. Because where else was there.

18

So I lied. On the last day of school, before the bus came for the Lee Lady Leaders Christmas party they give for the poor kids. Which is shaming in and of itself. Some of the kids at this thing are old enough to be boning each other, but still the Lady Leaders have one of their husbands coming out all fake-fat jolly in his cotton beard and we're supposed be like, Yay, Santa! One of these situations in life where you suck it up and eat your turkey and gravy. I did wonder how we got picked. Did the Leader Ladies ask our teachers to name the three topmost skanks and food-stamp kids of each grade? Okay yes, there are the Gola Hams of this world, and the Houserman kids that all six turn up with lice every year, rain or shine. But most of us do a fair job of passing. Then comes the day they call your name over the intercom to go get on the Christmas party loser bus, lucky you. That's what I was waiting on while we ran out the clock in homeroom. Me and Maggot were playing hangman. He asked where I would be on Christmas, did they do presents in fosters, and the story just rolled out. I said I'd be at the Salvation Army shelter or some church that takes in homeless. To be honest I had no idea, homeless church basement not likely. I just wanted that passed along to Maggot's higher-ups.

He was totally on board with me coming to Knoxville. Who was *not* was Mrs. Peggot. On the day we drove down there, I could tell something was changed. At Mom's funeral she'd been as much family to me as I'd ever had. But Maggot told me she'd had to debate on it overnight before she finally said all right, let him come on. Now the ride in the truck was too quiet. Mr. Peg ran the heat, and it got as stuffy as a closet. Maggot asked him to put on the radio, and he wouldn't, and that was that. Something was going on, to do with me. I realized I might not smell great due to barn cleaning the day before, and not getting my turn for the shower. I put my face to the window so nobody would see, if I tore up. Was this me now, for life? Taking up space where people wished I wasn't? Once on a time I was something, and then I turned, like sour milk. The dead junkie's kid. A rotten little piece of American pie that everybody wishes could just be, you know. Removed.

Emmy Peggot, Christ Jesus. In the months since summer she'd gone full Disney channel. Neon windbreaker jacket, bouncy ponytail, boy-band posters taped up all over her room with their pretty hair and pouty faces, to the point where Mrs. Peggot said she didn't feel right changing her clothes in there. Which confused Mr. Peg because of him thinking they were girls.

The evening we got there, Aunt June was still at work, so Emmy met us in front of the building. Shocking new development: Emmy stays home by herself now. I couldn't believe this girl, all hands-on-her-hips, telling Mr. Peg where to park his truck. Helping to carry up all our stuff in the elevator, saying "Make yourselves at home," and "Mom is thrilled to death you all could come." Aunt June now going by a new name, which was *Mom*.

So that was Knoxville again, more surprises. On the drive in, we'd passed this park with people skating on solid ice, even though they're having a warm snap. Sun blazing, people running around in track jackets and shorts. In any normal place, just try walking out on an iced-over pond on such a day: sorry friend, you're dead.

But in a city, the rules do not apply. It's like everybody is bored of all the normal things, out looking for the weirder option.

This extended to people doing things that ended them up in the ER, and Aunt June had had enough. She was moving back home. Big shock. We'd waited up for her to get home because Emmy said she had something to tell us. Did she ever. We sat at the kitchen bar eating barbecue wings she'd brought us for a midnight snack. Aunt June laughed and cried, blowing her nose with wads of Kleenex. She was done with being stuck out there in Knoxville, so far from everything. If she was going to work as hard as she did patching up nincompoops that had hurt themselves, she might as well patch up the nincompoops she grew up with, because everything a person could want was in Lee County. She was fed up with the head ER doctor mocking her in front of the other nurses, calling her Loretta Lynn. She'd finished some course at UT and got hired for a new job in the Pennington clinic that would be an assistant doctor type of thing. Mr. Peg slapped his leg and said he'd be damned, and Mrs. Peggot cried, both for the same reason which was happiness. Aunt June was the apple in their eyes. Her senior picture had the top spot in their living room. She was legend: June Peggot that broke all records by getting herself higher-educated instead of knocked up, and employed at the largest trauma hospital in the tristate area.

So that was the news. Aunt June had spent her life so far trying to kick the Lee County mud off her shoes, and come to find out all she really wanted was friendly faces and the smell of hay getting mowed and to have a dog she could take for long walks in the woods. Maggot wanted to know what she would name her dog. She laughed. She said maybe Rufus.

Emmy would be moving back too. They'd finished up the paperwork and she was adopted, Aunt June said, so the secret was out. She put her elbow around Emmy's neck and pulled her close, both of them just beaming, and damn if they didn't look it. Like blood.

I kept quiet, eating wings and getting my mind blown. To think life could turn around so. Being a dead person's child, then in seventh grade start calling somebody Mom. It gave me the strangest feeling. I just kept reaching in the box and taking more without a please or thank-you, forgetting for that short while to feel like the person nobody wanted.

A murder was all over the news that Christmas, and Emmy was possessed. She'd park herself on the floor in front of the TV and wait for the latest. It was a whole family dead. Their neighbors got interviewed and said what neighbors always say on TV after a shocking crime, about the victim or murderer either one: totally unexpected, you never saw a nicer person. In other words, they're paying zero attention to their neighbors. Not so where I come from, considering just for example how the Peggots had their eye out for me on numerous bad occasions of my life, starting day one.

What tore Emmy up was this baby that survived the ordeal. The killers left him for dead along with the rest of the family, on the shoulder of a highway where they got carjacked in the worst way. The police found him crying in the arms of dead Mommy, next to shot-to-hell dead Daddy and dead big sister. Every night on TV they showed the same photo of this family, all smiles, matching outfits, taken obviously prior to the shit road trip. You could tell they were something over the top, religionwise, like Jehovah Witness. But that little blond baby. You'd think he was Emmy's own. She'd asked Aunt June to find out what hospital had him so she could call about his condition. Answer: No ma'am, that was not happening, and Emmy needed to find something more appropriate to occupy her mind. She was not supposed to be watching the news, this being the permanent top story, but Aunt June on her evening shift was in no position to stop us. Then Mr. and Mrs. Peggot got interested, almost to the same degree as Emmy.

I'm going to say though, the news was bad all around, murders being only one aspect. From TV, I'd always thought people in cities have it made. Not true. The cold snap finally hit while we were there, and the news showed all these hard-luck cases trying to get in the library, bus station etc. To *sleep*. Like they didn't have relatives. I mean, it sucks to barge in on people that don't really want you. But you've not seen the like of these sad individuals with nobody to barge in on, and nothing to eat. Because where are you even going to steal an apple off a tree? In the city if you're out of money you are screwed, no two ways about it. Giving rise to mayhem, such as carjackings.

After Aunt June put her foot down on the murder-baby talk, Emmy needed somebody else to talk to. She picked me. It started a couple of nights after we got there. All the shit I had to think about had turned me into not the greatest sleeper, so I was awake, flopped on the sofa cushions with Maggot sawing logs. He slept like a dead person, only louder. Emmy, being too grown up now for sleeping with boy cousins, was bunking with Aunt June, while Mr. and Mrs. Peggot shacked up in her room with the Backstreet Boys.

Quiet as a cat, she slipped into the living room. Came and stood over me in the dark, little skinny thing in her white gown, like she'd crumple and leave dust on your fingers if you touched her. Where was Miss Salute-My-Shorts now? Was daytime Emmy a fake, I wondered, and this little moth-wing girl the real person? Was I supposed to say something? She sat down on the floor and started crying. Really quiet except for little gasps, like getting surprised over and over.

"Is it still about the murder thing?" I finally asked.

She didn't turn around but nodded her head.

"Sucks," I said. "People dying for no good reason. I hate that for them."

"He's so little, and all alone. I can't quit thinking about him. I know I should."

"It's not your fault. You can't really help what's in your brain."

She turned around and looked at me. I sat up. "I know everybody says that. Clean out your juvenile little head and put something nice in there. I get that all the time, and I'm like, Seriously? Just spray around brain-Lysol and get over it? How's that work?"

"Oh my God," she said. "Your mother. I'm sorry for your loss."

She sounded like an adult. I was surprised she knew

about Mom. I told her thanks, and I was sorry about hers too. "Before Aunt June, I mean. If there was a real one at some point."

"My birth mother. Yeah." She shrugged. "I can't really talk about her."

"But now you're adopted. So maybe it turned out for the best."

"Oh, totally. I'm lucky."

"Heck yes you are. I wouldn't wish foster care on anybody."

"It's really bad?"

"So far, yeah. I hate it pretty much every minute of the day. It's like a cross between prison and dodgeball. And there's not enough food."

"Dodgeball, like whenever you play with older kids that want to laugh at you?"

"Yeah. Hurt you, and then laugh at you."

She seemed to be thinking about this. I mean really turning it over. She whispered, "Do the kids get abused? I've heard that."

"My mom definitely had molester type shit done to her whenever she was little. In a supposedly Christian home. I just basically watch my back, night and day."

She blinked a couple of times. I was surprised how well I could see her in the dark. I knew I shouldn't shock Emmy, given she was already upset. But she'd asked. Nobody ever did. I told her I was sure there were good fosters out there that are God's angels, like everybody says. But I had yet to meet them because they didn't take kids like me.

"What do you mean, kids like you?"

I shrugged. "I don't know."

She took in a big breath and let it out. "I was so mean to you and Matty last summer. I'm sorry. This has been a year." Again, it was like she'd turned into somebody's mother or one of the nicer ladies at church. I couldn't figure out what I was dealing with. I wished I was older.

"You were okay," I said. "At times."

She smiled. "Yeah. After you saved me from the sharks." She pulled up her knees and showed me the silver bracelet I gave her that day. She was wearing it around her ankle. Leave it to somebody like her, to think of something like that. I couldn't believe she still had it.

"It's not like they were going to take you down. I never got why you were so scared."

"Because they're evil creatures with dagger-like teeth? Why were you *not*?"

"No reason. I'm just not. I like thinking about the ocean, and what all is living in there. It's like my brain-Lysol. It calms me down or something."

"Seriously. Sharks calm you down."

I could see pieces of the everyday Emmy sneaking back into the conversation, but I didn't mind. Maybe it meant this thing we were doing now, whatever it was, might not just go poof in the morning. "Not sharks specifically," I said. "The whole being-underwater thing. I put myself there and float. Just, you know. Inside my skull movie."

"You have a *skull movie*? You could see yourself *drowning*. That's relaxing."

"I don't, though. That's the one bad thing that for sure won't ever happen to me."

"Because what? You took Junior Red Cross swimming?"

I laughed. "No. To tell you the truth, I haven't ever been swimming that much. In water that was deeper than like, an inch."

"And still you're drown-proof, because?"

I'd never told anybody the weird way I got born. But being awake in the dark with a girl was outside my normal. The whole world quiet. I tried to put it in the best light: I took Mom by surprise, coming out so fast I was still in the water bubble that protects babies in the before-life.

"The caul," Emmy said.

"What?"

"You were born in the caul. That's the medical ter-
minology. Mom saw it happen one time and said it
even freaked out the doctors. You'd be amazed how
many babies get born in the ER."

Nothing at all would surprise me as far as Aunt
June and the ER. But I liked knowing what happened
to me was real, with a name. "Yeah, that. I had the
call. If that happens to you, it's a guarantee you won't
drown. So the ocean is this giant thing that won't ever
defeat me."

Emmy laughed. "That's just some old hillbilly su-
perstition."

I got a little hurt at her for that. Even if she was
right. "Your mammaw is the one that told me, so take
it up with her. Ask about Jesus coming back from the
dead, while you're at it."

We'd been talking so quietly, our faces were just a
few inches apart. Now I sat up. This whatever-it-was
was over. Probably in the morning it would be a never-
happened. But she didn't go away. She sat up too, looking at me a while, and then said the words I hate: "I'm
sorry."

"Yeah, well. No big deal."

"It is, though. I could understand why you'd want
to think about someplace totally safe. After everything
you've been through. Your mom and all."

"My mom dying is not even the worst part. If you really want to know."

She sat facing me, waiting. She smelled like fruit shampoo. I wanted to say something mean, or just the truth. I wanted to tell her about my baby brother that was technically younger than the murder-family baby, and dead. I said that word: *Sorry*. "But you know what? If that kid ends up dying, it's not the worst thing. Being dead is better than an orphan your whole fucking life."

"No!" she said, so loud she put her hand over her mouth. Then took it off and whispered, "He's got grandparents. They're in some other country, but they're going to come get him."

"Good for him. Somebody wants him."

She reached over and touched me on the head. No person had touched me since Mom. My hair was on its own devices at that point, and I knew the sorry sight I was. With every part of me growing out of my sleeves or growing fuzz or changing shape that year, even the bone part of my nose, some way. And I was still sleeping in Tommy's shirt.

"Poor Demon," she said quietly. "Can't they find anybody to adopt you?"

She'd only ever called me Damon before, like Mrs. Peggot and Aunt June, to show she was taking their side. I didn't want to be poor anybody. But I felt like kissing Emmy. Or throwing up, from how mixed up I was. Possibly both. You'd want to do it in the right order, though.

"Everybody thinks adoption is just automatic," I said. "But there's a lot more orphan kids in Lee County than people wanting them. My caseworker says it's nothing personal."

"Is she nice, at least? Your caseworker?"

Somehow, I knew not to mention that Miss Barks was a babe. Or that I saved up things to tell her week to week because she was the only person I talked to anymore. "She's got a ton of kids she's looking after. Mostly younger than me. So, you know. Nice, if she's got a minute."

"That must be so hard."

We both lay back down, and she looked at me in the eyes, and we were sad together for a while. I'll never forget how that felt. Like not being hungry.

19

I was the person not invited at June's house. That feeling hangs on you like a smell. I had put showers between myself and Creaky's barn, but this is not something that washes off. You get used to it, not in the good way, to the extent of the entire world oftentimes feeling like a place where you weren't invited. If you've been here, you know. If not, must be nice.

June didn't mind me though, or was good at being sweet whether she felt like it or not. Which they probably do teach you in nurse school. She read my mind, same as she had with going to the ocean place. Again she took us places I liked. The skateboard park, even though Maggot and Emmy weren't into it because all we did was watch. But Jesus God. For kids with zero sidewalks in our lives, watching skateboarders on TV is just cartoons or sci-fi, you don't buy in. But seeing them in real life? Shit. I about died of happiness. Like boys could fly.

So that was June, seeing my little moments. Putting extra food on my plate at every meal. Not in the Lady Leaders way of "watch me being nice," just on the quiet. I tried to use manners and not act like a person that's been wanting seconds ever since around August.

What I dreaded was Christmas morning. The Peggots had brought presents they piled under Aunt June's tree, but weirdly nobody discussed them, no shaking or checking tags to see who got the biggest. Because of me, the kid not supposed to be there. Awkward. I planned on making myself scarce Christmas morning. I'd fake a stomachache or take a really long shower until the presents all got opened. Mainly I just wished Christmas didn't exist.

The worst was at night, with me and Maggot lying practically under the tree with the presents. Which wasn't a tree, honestly, just fake, small, set up on a table. You'd expect better from somebody so classy. But where are you going to go cut a cedar in Knoxville? At home, any farmer will let you come get one out of his fencerow. At Creaky's we cut cedars out of the pastures to pile up and burn, because they're too many and a nuisance. Why Aunt June hated it in Knoxville, being so far away from everything: from free Christmas trees, just for example.

That's where I was, thinking about shit like our last cedar bonfire at Creaky's that got out of hand somewhat with Swap-Out and the gasoline. Maggot asleep. And all the sudden here's Emmy touching my back. I almost shit myself, rolling over to see her lying two inches away. I'd not expected her to come back. She wasn't just all about the murder baby this time, so that was a relief. We were quiet like before, and Maggot stayed asleep. Or else a good friend about it. He never said anything the next day, or any other day, because it happened every night after that. She didn't surprise me again, either. I was always on the lookout.

We talked about everything under the sun, lying on those pillows. What we liked, what we hated. I told her my bathtub thing, due to my dad dying at a place called Devil's Bathtub. Actually I said it was only whenever I was small, being scared of them. She didn't laugh though. She was scared about moving, leaving Knoxville. I couldn't believe it. I told her there's trees, mountains, rivers, birds singing in your ears, we've got the whole rest of the world over there, other than people, which are only one thing. Going wherever we wanted to without adults, even at night. The woods. I got caught up in telling her all this and almost forgot my messed-up life, because in some ways she was worse off than me. She'd never even seen a lightning bug. That is just tragic. I told her the different ones. One kind goes totally dark, then they all blink together, thousands, one big sparkly pop all up and down the creek. It can thrill a person senseless.

In time we got into the darker side of things. My dead baby brother, for one. How Emmy ended up with Aunt June, for another. Complicated as hell. Turns out she had a mother out there at large all along, girlfriend of her dad, Humvee, that was killed. I'd heard people say a hunting accident. Emmy said yes, he was supposed to go get Pampers one day but instead ended up turkey hunting with some friends. Three men, three twelve-gauges, and a handle of fireball whiskey being one handle too many for the close quarters of a turkey blind, as anybody knows, except them evidently. Oh my Lord. She said it was Humvee's shotgun but different stories, either he accidentally fired it or somebody sat on it. He was too messed up for the hospital in Pennington, they had to get him to Knoxville and too much blood loss on the way.

Poor Mrs. Peggot. Given the fireball whiskey aspects, no wonder her having her policies on what she called demon liquor. For Emmy's part, she said she herself felt somewhat to blame, as far as the stresses and strains of a baby on such a young dad. His girl-friend was home with her at the time, so not involved, just probably waiting a long time for those diapers. But being a teen mom and then total wreck from the incident, she turned into the all-around bad-news type of mother, so. The Peggots had to step in and take Emmy. Then the next year after Humvee was killed, their daughter Mariah went to prison on her own matters, and Maggot turned up needing to be looked after also. The family you could say hit a bad patch.

This was news to me, that Mrs. Peggot had taken in not just Maggot but Emmy before him. Two tiny tots to raise. That's the Peggots for you, doors wide open. I'd known them to take other cousins for whole summers before, including Hammerhead Kelly and his stepsisters after the parents split up, which was how Mr. Peg got him started on deer hunting. Emmy asked if Hammerhead still came around or had moved away with his dad in the split-up. I said he was still with the stepmom Ruby, June's sister, and Mr. Peg's favorite. I didn't bring up hunting, given Emmy's bad-luck dad, plus not knowing where she stood with the whole city-person outlook on shooting Bambi, but I knew Hammer and Mr. Peg still hunted together. Many a time in the fall I'd see Hammer dressing a buck in their driveway. It would kill you how big and gentle he looked, drawing his long knife up the middle of the carcass, easing the gut and lungs to slither out in a pile. Like he's being sweet to that deer, even though dead.

I told Emmy he went by just Hammer now, and came over to help with things Mr. Peg had got too old for, like gutters. He was basically a Peggot grandson, even though technically not all that related. I told her I was basically one too, raised by them as far as the more solid parts. I admitted that for the longest time I'd thought Mrs. Peggot was my real mammaw.

Emmy put her eyes square on mine. It scared me almost, getting looked at like that. "You're wishing she really was, aren't you?" she said. "Then they'd have to adopt you." She kissed her finger and touched my cheek.

"They probably wouldn't, though."

I wanted her to say I was wrong, but she rolled on her back, looking at the ceiling. I watched her thinking it over. I'd never had that close a look at another person's face before. She had brown-sugar freckles and a little silver line through one eyebrow where she said a cat scratched her. The tiniest furrow plowed through her eyebrow hairs, never to grow back.

She rolled back to face me. "I don't know. They didn't legally adopt either one of us. For Matty they're just guardians. His mom is still his mom."

"Not that she's doing much about it in Goochland," I said. "No offense to anybody."

But Emmy was off someplace else, thinking of her own messed-up past. I was pretty shocked of it. Given the Peggots being so decent. "Having both of us was too much," she said. "Think about it, he's a newborn and I'm a toddler. Poor Mammaw. She really needed Aunt June to take over with me. I never gave it much thought till lately, but I mean, who *does* that? Take over raising your dead brother's two-year-old, while you're still in nursing school."

June Peggot, was the answer. The Peggots had brought in the trailer next door so she could have her own place with Emmy and still be all one family while June finished up school. That was the same trailer that soon would be Mom's, then Mom's and mine, after June got her hospital job and moved with Emmy to Knoxville. Emmy's bad-news real mom still would turn up at the Peggots' every so often, threatening to go to court and get Emmy back. She was in no position now as an IV drug user, homeless etc., but that didn't stop her from showing up in the middle of the night, banging on the door, raising Cain to see her kid. The Peggots kept quiet about Emmy being in Tennessee so she wouldn't go after June and try to steal Emmy back. That's why the big secret. But Skank Mom had finally agreed to sign Emmy over for good. Amen and hallelujah on Aunt June finally winning the mom war.

I asked how that felt, given away by her real mother. Emmy said she had all the mom a person could want. She didn't care if she ever laid eyes on the other one again.

The upshot of all this talking was me getting pretty much in love with Emmy. She was beautiful and like a grown person. In the daytime we didn't let on. Hanging out with her and Maggot, I tried to be normal, but sometimes said things to impress her. Like how the other foster boys thought my cartoons were good. And the football hero Fast Forward that was my friend. She just said something polite, but Maggot chimed in on how awesome this guy was. I'd forgotten Maggot knew him from that time they came to the farm. This got Emmy interested to the extent of saying she'd like to meet this famous Fast Forward.

So we played it cool, and I wondered if the other was real or just some after-hours game she was playing. But then she would let me sit on the couch with her while she was reading, and under the blanket her feet would touch my feet. She'd look up from her book and smile at me and, oh man. Utterly wrecked. Back in the summer she'd announced the one time about us getting married, which was kid shit. Like somebody giving you

Monopoly money and saying "Here, go buy a house." But now all I had to do was think of Emmy, her face or her toothpaste smell, and it would give me these waking-up feelings as regards the guy downstairs. Not kid shit. At night we'd be talking and I'd get obsessed on kissing her, even though not having the nerve. It was her finally that did it. She asked if I wanted to go to second base, which of course I did, except for not knowing exactly where that base was located. I'd heard different things. I said okay, and she took my hand into the neck of her gown and put it on her chest. Nipple and everything, warm and soft. Christ. Now I had a whole new body function to be terrified of doing on accident, from being that mixed up and happy at the same time. But I held it together. I just told her I loved her and that kind of thing. I told her whenever she moved back to Lee County, we could take walks together with Aunt June's dog Rufus.

After that I had a new brain-Lysol to calm myself down: walking in the woods with Emmy. I'd picture us holding hands, maybe with our own dog. Being grown-ups. It would be so much safer than being a kid.

For Christmas breakfast they invited Mrs. Gummidge, which was the cat lady downstairs where Emmy slept over on Aunt June's night shifts. Emmy still wasn't old enough to be on her own in the stranger-danger building overnight, even though graduated from day-time babysitting and Popsicle-stick-type shenanigans. I figured this cat lady wouldn't get presents either, so we could sit together watching the others, and I wouldn't have to stay in the shower.

Emmy warned me about Mrs. Gummidge being a sad human being and not to laugh at her, or Aunt June would kill us. I said I was in no position, being star player on the sad-sack team. But listen, this lady was in her own league. We were all, Merry Christmas Mrs. Gummidge! And she's like, "Well, it might be, I don't know. I been feeling so poorly." Aunt June asked how are Cain and Abel, which were her cats, and she said, "Well, they've both been at death's door for a good while. But it's for the best. If I pass away first, I don't know who would take them."

Mrs. Gummidge was a sister of somebody the Peg-gots knew in Lee County, which was how they knew she was safe and not a stranger. She'd helped keep Emmy ever since they first moved here, so they were used to her, but man alive. She had a downer comment for every occasion. Wasn't the Christmas tree pretty? Well, she said, a lot of times they started fires. Yes, the weather had been warm, but that meant winter would last longer. She had on these thick brown stockings rolled up under her knees that she had to wear night and day for her varicose veins that hurt her something awful. She had some name for them like compressure hose. I didn't ask, trust me. It just came up. All through breakfast which was pancakes and bacon, Mrs. Gummidge discussed how she was forlorn in the world and too poorly to be fit company for anybody since Mr. Gummidge passed. Emmy stared at me with her shut mouth pulled wide like a fish, trying not to laugh. I don't think Aunt June was too far behind her.

But they were all sweet to her. The time came for presents, and surprise, they had some for Mrs. Gummidge and also me. She got a fuzzy pink bathrobe that she said was so pretty she might ought to get buried in it. For me they had things from "Santa" that obviously got new tags put on them last minute, like socks (I wore the same size as Mr. Peg), a Stretch Armstrong, a Bop It, and Pokemon cards I'm sure were for Maggot, and he'd okayed them getting reassigned.

But Aunt June got me something amazing: a set of colored markers for making comics, fine-tip on one end and thick on the other, in more colors than you'd think there would be. Eight entire flesh tones. Also a real book for making comic strips, with the panel dividers printed in. I couldn't believe my eyes. After Mom died I'd not wanted to draw any more at all, but now I couldn't wait to run off someplace and get started. I would make one of Aunt June as Wonder Nurse, putting a new heart back inside a boy that had his own torn out.

The last night before we left, Emmy went to pieces. I told her we would see each other all the time whenever they moved to Lee County. But Aunt June had to finish out her hospital contract first, so it wouldn't be till May. Forever, in other words. It had only been thirty-nine days since Mom and my brother died, and that felt like longer than the years I'd been alive.

I tried to dwell on the happier aspects, like being amazed of how the Peggots gave me presents. I asked her opinion of it being a sign they might want to adopt me. Emmy said I shouldn't get my hopes up, but it wouldn't hurt to ask. Too late, my hopes were up. Mrs. Peggot already had said I could stay at their house after we got back until school started up again, rather than go back to Creaky Farm. Which had to mean something.

Emmy though got all mournful, lying on her back with tears running down sideways, which pretty much killed me. She asked would I wait for her and not get another girlfriend in the meantime before May. I told her no worries on that. I used an old-lady voice and said "I'm too forlorn to be fit company, unless I can find me some almost dead cats." And she laughed, so that was good. We cheered ourselves up then by making fun of

Mrs. Gummidge, and got tickled. Which is terrible, but you know. We're kids. I asked how long ago Mr. Gummidge died.

"No idea," she said. "We've known her forever, and there's never been any Mr. Gummidge in the picture. I don't even know what he died of."

"He probably hung himself," I said. "With her compressure hose."

That cracked all of us up. Maggot included. He'd been awake all along.

We were back at the Peggots' a few days before I got up my nerve, but the time came. The house was quiet. Mr. Peg took Maggot and some cousins to go bowling with their church youth league. They invited me, but I said I didn't feel like it. After they left, I went downstairs to the kitchen where Mrs. Peggot was cooking her big pot of blackeye peas they always had for New Year's, for a year of good luck. A Peggot thing. Mom always said she'd never heard of that. But then, look at her luck.

I hung around the kitchen watching Mrs. Peggot put things in her soup. Onions, carrots, a lot more than blackeye peas, plus it had to cook all day and then some. She always put in the big bone from the country ham they ate at Christmas. This year they'd taken the ham to Knoxville for Christmas dinner, then wrapped the bone in foil and brought it back. So that bone had more miles on it than most people I knew. All that, for the luck. Steam rolled out of the pot, fogging up the window and making the kitchen smell amazing. I told her she was the best cook and this was the best house I was ever in. She looked over her shoulder at me, then went back to stirring. I thanked her for the presents she and Mr. Peg gave me for Christmas, that I wasn't expecting. I'd said thank you at the time, but I wanted to use all my manners before I got to the main question.

"We had us a good Christmas, didn't we?" she asked, and I told her yes, I'd had the biggest time in Knoxville and was glad she let me come. She went on stirring. I told her the soup smelled so good, I wished I wouldn't ever have to leave.

She set down her big spoon and stood still, looking out the foggy window. Then untied her apron and came and sat down at the table. Her glasses were so foggy I couldn't see her eyes, and for a second I got terrified. Thinking of Stoner in his reflectors and all other adults that seemed like they went blind if they really had to look at me. Then the steam cleared and I could see her blue eyes, still kind of cloudy. Maggot had told me she had the cataracts and needed an operation on her eyes. But she was looking at me straight.

"Damon, are you asking if we can keep you permanent?"

I was afraid to tell her yes. Because then I knew the answer would be no.

It turned out she and Mr. Peg had already discussed it. The week after the funeral Miss Barks came over to meet with them about a possible foster placement, since I was more comfortable with them than anyplace else. The DSS evidently had cleared up the Stoner lies, and they'd decided the Peggots were my best shot. So she and Mr. Peg had talked it over. Talked and talked, she said. But decided they couldn't. Not as guardians or fosters or anything official.

I hated Miss Barks for not telling me this. I wanted to die of embarrassment. Mrs. Peggot looked sad, and kept rubbing her head. Her gray hair stuck out this way and that, like she'd forgotten to comb it that morning, which maybe it didn't matter. Nobody really looked that much at a lady her age, including me usually. But I did now. She was my only chance.

She said I would always be welcome to visit. But she and Mr. Peg were getting old, with him having the arthritis so bad his leg hurt him day and night. Plus he had the sugar, that he took shots for in his stomach. She didn't mention her eye thing, but I got the picture.

She said it was only two more years until Maggot's mom was getting released, maybe sooner for good behavior. Not likely, considering it's Mariah. But at some point, she would come take Maggot and finish up raising him. I asked where, and Mrs. Peggot said they would have their own place.

I couldn't even imagine Maggot not living in that house. "Does he know about it? That he's going to have to move out?"

"Yes, honey. He does. We'll be a little sad, but a boy ought to be raised by his mother, and that's what she wants. Mr. Peg and I can't always do for him now that he's getting so big."

Maggot wasn't that big, to be honest. For his age. I was, though. I kept quiet.

"You and Matty will be teenagers here before you know it. Learning to drive, courting girls. Lord have mercy." She smiled and looked sad at the same time, waving one hand like shooing away mosquitoes. That hand looked a hundred years old. Knuckles and gristle.

I'd given no thought to what lay up the road for us. Maggot learning to drive, courting whatever he had in mind, disaster possibly. He was already in a war with Mr. Peg over his long hair, the music he liked, some of his weirder magazines. Attitude in general. Nothing like the attitude wars of Stoner and me. But you could see how low-level fighting went step by step, with more hazards at the higher levels like in Super Mario.

I wondered if Miss Barks had told the Peggots I was a hard kid to handle.

"I won't do any of those teenager things," I told her. "I would mind you. You and Mr. Peg both, I promise. I could probably get Maggot to do better."

Mrs. Peggot looked at the window instead of me. Snow was starting to fall, the whole world so damn quiet. I could hear their big clock ticking from the other room where it sat on the mantel with the picture of Holy Aunt June. She wasn't going to save me, either.

"But what if," I started, and backed up, started again. "I can be a lot of help, like carrying in groceries and heavy things. What if I just stayed until Maggot's mom gets out, and whenever he moves, I'd find another home too?"

Mrs. Peggot said they had discussed this too with Miss Barks. But she gave them the advice that it wasn't a great idea. She said teenage boys are the hardest of all to find homes for, and it was better to get them in some kind of permanent situation while younger if at all possible. She'd promised the Peggots she would keep working on it.

And that was it. Mr. and Mrs. Peggot wanted to try

out being regular grandparents for a change, and not be parents anymore. I needed to let Miss Barks find me some nice people that were younger and could take me in for good.

I shouldn't have been shocked. Emmy had warned me, and honestly I knew better, but something in me was holding out. Now it fell to pieces. I cried in front of Mrs. Peggot. That was horrible. She had to go hunt up a box of tissues and then rub me on the back like a baby.

"Honey, I'm sorry," she said, over and over. Words I hated so much I wanted to smash them with my fists.

Crying was the sickest part, in how shamefaced I felt. Even at Mom's funeral I never shed a tear, because of hating everybody. Hard as a rock. But with Aunt June being so nice and Emmy in love with me, I'd let myself get soft. Thinking the Peggots were not like everybody else, but special, as regards the Jesus thing of loving your neighbor as much as you love yourself. For fuck's sake, hadn't I learned that lesson? Sunday school stories are just another type of superhero comic. Counting on Jesus to save the day is no more real than sending up the Batman signal.

20

Starting from that day, in that kitchen, I was on my own. New year, new life, not yet in my own house making the payments, but that's how I felt: my own man. Not liking it a bit.

Miss Barks found me a new foster home, which was the McCobb family: Mr. and Mrs., first and second grade boy and girl named Brayley and Haillie, plus two babies with names I never did get straight due to everybody calling them the Twins. Screamer One and Two would cover it. One would fall asleep, the other would start up a fit, they'd get each other going and not a lot of sleeping happened in that house. Nor cheerfulness either.

This family's main problem was being flat broke. You never saw people so stressed out over money. Mr.

McCobb oftentimes did have work, but between one thing and another, Brayley needing the better kind of tennis shoes, Haillie wanting five dollars to try out for junior tumbling squad, the babies needing Pampers and so on, plus whatever was going on with the credit cards as far as robbing Peter to pay Paul, they ran out of cash every single month without one end meeting the other. Mrs. McCobb worried herself sick over Brayley and Haillie getting tormented at school for not having what the other kids had. Which is a legit concern, take that from me, a person that lined up every Friday of all times for the Backpacks of Love aka food sacks the church ladies sent home on weekends for free-lunch kids so we wouldn't starve. I never knew any different, I was always that kid, so I grew up being as tall and tough about it as I was able. But you don't want to go down that road if you can help it. Brayley being one of those small but chubby, grubworm type of kids, and Haillie in her own little world of troll dolls and rainbow ponies, they both had targets on their backs. If those two went over to the Backpacks of Love side of things, you'd fear for their lives.

Mrs. McCobb told me she'd never in a million years thought they would stoop to taking in a foster child. But hopefully having that little bit extra every month from the DSS would turn things around. Plus they were being good Christians, and if it came up at school I was to say that.

Mr. McCobb was big on ideas for making that little bit extra to turn things around, and had tried most of them: selling Amway, breeding AKC pups with fake papers, human advertisement, sperm donor, etc. Plus buying lotto tickets, obviously. His newest idea was taking in a foster. If I went okay, they might take in two, for twice the cash. It didn't hurt my feelings. Creaky made no bones about wanting that five hundred a month per head. I knew the score.

The trouble that Mr. McCobb didn't count on, though, was needing to spend money on me. For example, buying more groceries so I could eat. The first week I was there, he asked if I was going to chip in for my meals and so forth.

"Chip in, like what?" I asked. Not having the slightest idea what he was talking about.

"Just a little cash, buddy. For the extra food."

The two of us were sitting at the kitchen table doing an enterprise where I licked the stamps and sealed envelopes after Mr. McCobb put brochures in them. Every time he leaned over to reach himself more brochures, I saw pink scalp shining through his buzz cut on top.

"I am all about the fair and the square," he said.

"As far as your bunking quarters, that's going to be grateese." He explained grateese meant he wasn't going to charge me anything for my bedroom.

"Thanks," I said, even though it wasn't a bedroom, it was a dog room. The day Miss Barks brought me there, she inspected the DSS-approved cute bedroom that supposedly was for me, with cowboy wallpaper, bedspread of Woody from Toy Story, etc. But after she left, it turned out that was their son Brayley's room. Mrs. McCobb said not to tell Miss Barks or I would get sent back, so I didn't. Sleeping in the McCobbs' dog room was preferable to whatever DSS might cook up next. This room was attached on the back of the house with the washer and dryer and a seriously rotted-out floor where their old washer had leaked. You had to be careful where you stepped, or the linoleum would give way. It's where they'd had their AKC puppy enterprise some while back, and smelled like it. Plus noisy, due to the washer and dryer going all hours, what with all those kids and babies.

Mr. McCobb asked me how I was liking it in the so-called annex. His wife had bought me one of those air-mattress beds and a little cardboard dresser for my stuff, so I told him it was fine. But that I couldn't pay for my meals because I didn't have any money. Sorry.

Mr. McCobb stopped stuffing envelopes and squinted

his eyes, like he was working out the whole situation of me. He had those extra-dark brown eyes that were like looking down two holes. Intense. "That's a deficit, buddy. You've got a problem. But it can be addressed."

"Okay," I said.

I licked some more stamps for his enterprise. This one had to do with blue-green algae pills that supposedly could cure anything but a broken heart. (Which is what Mr. Peg always said about duct tape.) Brayley and Haillie were upstairs in their rooms having a loudness war between *Lion King* and Spice Girls on their CD player, and Mrs. McCobb was in her bedroom trying to feed the twins. All told, a good deal of commotion coming from up there.

I didn't feel that welcome upstairs, so I hadn't been, other than the once where Mrs. McCobb gave us a tour and showed Miss Barks my so-called bedroom. Downstairs, the kitchen was the only place to hang out, the rest being dark, with the living-room blinds closed at all times due to there being no furniture. The McCobbs lived on a busy road, and I reckon they didn't want everybody in the county knowing they didn't have any living-room furniture. Miss Barks was pretty surprised over it. Mrs. McCobb said they did have some, until a few months before. The nicest imaginable, from Goodman's Furniture, not Walmart, plus a bedroom suite in some certain style where all the pieces matched. At this point in time, though, Mr. and Mrs. McCobb's bedroom only had the mattress that luckily they got to keep, because the repo guys don't take mattresses back after they've been slept on.

The kitchen was an okay place, other than making me hungry. I was pretending the taste of stamps on Mr. McCobb's envelopes was something better, like strawberry Gushers, but my stomach was growling, to the point of embarrassing. Their bulldog Missy was flopped on the floor, not even bothering herself over the half-full bowl of dog food by the door. Red, chunky dog chow that looked like meat. Probably this sounds sick, but even *that* was making me hungry.

Mr. McCobb said I should think about getting a job after school. I told him my problem was, I was eleven. I'd always heard they don't hire you till sixteen. He said those rules only applied in certain cases, and that younger kids were allowed to work in family enterprises.

"Like I'm doing right now?" I perked up, thinking he might pay me. But no. He said this didn't count because of something called nefrotism. He couldn't pay me and be my foster father both, so I needed to look farther afield. He said he would put out his antennas.

Mr. McCobb was the straight shooter of the family,

according to himself, but half the time I couldn't make the wildest guess as to what he was saying. He'd always let you know he's been around the block and you haven't. He served in the military in Operation Bright Star and some other ones, which explained the haircut and how he dressed, not T-shirts but always button-ups like he's the boss of something. After he got home from the Middle East he used the benefits to get his business degree at Mountain Empire, which is how he knew about starting enterprises. He had a list of everything he was an expert on. Mrs. McCobb said anybody would be a fool not to hire him, which they did, about every other week: medical supply store, gas station, lawn and tree service, flooring company, and other places he worked while I was living there, the years before that, and still to this day, if I had to guess. The pay at those places was lousy and he was too overqualified, plus knowing a lot more than his supervisors. A man can't stay long in a situation like that.

What I remember most about that year is food. Not eating it, *thinking* about it. Meals at the McCobbs' were never enough to tide me over. Dinner usually was burgers that Mr. McCobb picked up at a drive-through on his way home, two each for the adults and one for us kids. Maybe some fries to share. Or Mrs.

McCobb would microwave some of the Lean Cuisines she had in the freezer, again one each for the kids and two for the grown-ups. She'd bought a slew of those little box-type meals on sale because of trying to lose her baby weight. After babies-times-four she was one of those ladies with the small, pretty face and everything else kind of pillowy.

She kept boxes of snacks on top of the fridge, and I mean the works: Pringles, Oreos, Dunkaroos, your basic snack festival going on up there. I kept waiting for somebody to give me my snack bowl like at Aunt June's, but nobody ever said "Make yourself at home" in the McCobb house. Even though I didn't have any other one. After school Mrs. McCobb would sometimes get down a box and dole out a snack to each of us, but not every day, and I knew not to ask.

Luckily Miss Barks kept up the forms for my free lunch at school, but I was off the list for Backpacks of Love, with the church ladies figuring out I was somebody else's problem now. At school I cruised the lunchroom with some other guys, picking off extra fries or whatever we could score. Maggot wasn't in on it anymore. He was getting fed at home on blackeye pea soup, ham biscuits, apple cobblers, and all the other best things ever known, and not all that thankful for it honestly. He and I were still best friends and blood brothers of course, but in January we got reassigned to new homerooms after too many homeroom make-out sessions between certain girl and boy parties, so I didn't see much of Maggot unless our lunch periods crossed. If we did talk, he'd bring up that Mrs. Peggot was asking about me. What was I supposed to say to that? I told him not to worry, I was in a new foster with my own room and it was awesome. I told him they had a dog, to make him jealous. I said, "We have a dog," even though their bitch Missy actually wanted nothing to do with me. Possibly due to getting kicked out of her room.

Our lunchroom visits never lasted long. I always downed my lunch fast and then hung out by the kitchen shelf thing where we put our trays. Some people and especially girls would bring back their lunch basically untouched, drop the tray, and waltz away like food grew on trees. Apples without one bite out of them, milk cartons not even opened. It killed me to think how this was happening at other lunch periods without me there to grab it. I mean, *first graders*, probably throwing away the best stuff. You want to cry for the waste.

In the day-to-day, I got by. Weekends were rough. I had dreams about food that went to the extreme. Like I'm eating a large pizza with pepperoni, smelling that peppery meat smell, the cheese with that great rubber feeling in my teeth, and then, bang! Awake. Back in the dog room, hungry. I'd go through the dirty clothes pile looking for edibles. Haillie sometimes would leave a box of Junior Mints or something in the pocket of her little shorts. I'd sniff it out like a dog.

I wanted to tell Mrs. McCobb how hungry I was, trust me. Maybe mention that being over five feet tall and wearing the biggest shoes of anybody in that house, I might be considered more of a two-burger person than a one-burger like their first and second graders. I had this conversation with her in my head, six ways to Sunday. It always ended like my last talk with Mrs. Peggot. I'd given up all hope of rescue by that point in time. I'd already complained to Miss Barks, and she discussed it, but the McCobbs acted all shocked, saying they fed me night and day, how could a boy still be hungry after eating as much as I did? Miss Barks bought their story. She said if I didn't get enough, for goodness' sake, ask for seconds. If it even crossed her pretty head that these people were lying, stealing cheats, she was short on options. She had to let it go.

She stuck with a different theory: I needed to be more pushy with them. Did she give up on *her* dreams? No, she worked hard for what she wanted. Did I expect anybody to look out for Damon if he wouldn't look out for himself? Life is what you make it! Here's where

Miss Barks didn't grow up: foster care. She had no clue how people can be living right on the edge of what's doable. If you push too hard, you can barrel yourself over a damn cliff.

Mrs. McCobb was not that bad a person, just going nuts with those kids on her every minute of the day. And I mean *on* her. The babies did all their sleeping or not sleeping, eating, screaming, diaper changing, etc. upstairs in her and her husband's bedroom, and most days she wouldn't make it downstairs till noon or after, in her pj's and robe. Or if dressed, it was the type outfit where you can't tell a hundred percent if it's clothes or pj's. Her hair she wore in a half-assed ponytail that got washed on rare occasions. She and I did our talking in the car, where she'd tell me her worries that I was to keep to myself, which I did. I did not follow the Miss Barks plan of Speaking Up for Demon at these moments. The idea of people wanting at all times to hear your problems, that's a child thing. I had eyes. I saw Mrs. McCobb was in no mood.

The reason of us being in the car was her taking me around to the pawnshops. You'd not think there would be a thing left in that house to pawn, but she'd come up with something. An entire string of pearls that had been her mom's. Nice stuff, jewelry she was aiming to keep, but then couldn't. Or one of the kids' two Walkmans that they each got from their grandparents. She decided they could share just the one. Conniptions were had. Little Haillie screaming bloody murder, her mother pulling it out of her hands, Mr. McCobb saying whatever price she gets for that piece of Chinese-made crap, he hopes it's worth the kid having her walleyed fit.

And baby equipment, my Lord. There wasn't even room for it upstairs, they piled it in the empty living room. All in like-new condition. You would not believe the tackle that's been invented for babies: swings, bouncy seats, so-called infant gym. Like an infant needs that. Somebody had spent a pile of money on those twins. Turns out it was Mrs. McCobb's parents, that were well off and lived in the city someplace far away. Ohio. She grew up over there and it seemed like she couldn't get settled in here, always wanting to buy the better kind of things, to impress who exactly, I couldn't guess. She didn't speak to her neighbors. She said her parents didn't approve of Mr. McCobb but loved to spend on the kids, and if they ever found out she was pawning it all, they would disown her. Considering the Walkman shitstorm though, it was probably a smart move to sell off the baby crap now, before those babies got attached.

Our pawn trips happened on the weekends whenever Mr. McCobb didn't need the car and could look after the two older kids. The plan eventually was to get a second car or ideally a minivan so she could take all the kids to fun places, but so far she was only getting as far as pawnshops. We'd go to different ones in Pennington Gap or drive all the way over to Jonesville or Rose Hill. Mrs. McCobb said she liked to spread the love around. The part I liked was on the way back stopping for a Sonic burger if the sales had gone okay. But those were some long drives, let me tell you. Rose Hill, with the twins in their two car seats caterwauling in stereo.

Even spreading the love that far, the shop owners mostly knew Mrs. McCobb, which is why she took me along. She would park up the street and send me into a shop with the jewelry or baby bouncer, and not go in herself. Seriously awkward, me trying to deal with these crusty old pawn guys. I offered to stay with the babies so she could go in, but no. She always told me what to say, genuine cubic zircomium, factory packaging, etc. I was supposed to say my mom was sick, aka some lady that was not Mrs. McCobb, but they still figured it out. I mean, it's Lee County, you can run but you can't hide. The guy at Here Today Loan and Pawn just shook his head and said he knew Eva McCobb was out sitting in her car, so I'd best go get her.

Which I did. A yelling match ensued, with him following her out to the sidewalk saying if she was too proud to come in his shop, she could send her husband instead of a boy to do a man's errand. And her yelling back that he was a damn low-baller, thinking she was so hard up she'd take whatever lousy price he offered. And him yelling she could do her whining closer to home. Etc. This being a Saturday in downtown Jonesville, they drew a pretty good crowd.

She didn't say a word the whole drive home, except to swear she would never divorce Mr. McCobb in a million years. This was something she would say, just out of the blue. With nobody asking her to divorce him, that I knew of.

I was hungry at all the hours, but nights were worst. I drew pictures of food, pages and pages. Roast chickens with their drumsticks. Pork chops, mashed potatoes. I spent hours getting the shading right. Putting highlights on the gravy. This one girl at school, Maisie Clinkenbeard, probably thought I liked her due to me sitting as close to her as I could. But it was to see what was in her lunch box. Actually, some few girls had their lunch contest going. Bettina Cook thought she owned it, with her personal pudding cups and sandwiches cut in triangles, Bettina that got dropped off at school by her daddy's secretary, and supposedly had a maid at home cutting those sandwiches. I was like, they throw away the crusts? It was Maisie Clinkenbeard for me. I guarantee you a mom packed those lunches, and we're talking something amazing every day, thick slices of ham, potato salad, homemade desserts. Peach cobbler cut in a little square. Right now, I could draw that cobbler.

Around the end of January I started sneaking into the kitchen at night to raid the snacks. I was careful never to take much out of any one box, and always rolled the package back exactly how it was. Then after a week or so, I came home from school to see the top of the fridge bare naked. Huh, I thought. I reckon Mrs. McCobb wants the whole family to lose their baby weight.

But no. The snacks weren't gone, just moved. Mrs. McCobb leaned over me at the sink washing her baby bottles, and she had Oreos on her breath. The kids would come bouncing downstairs with little pieces of Pringles stuck all over their damn pajamas. They had their own stashes. I beat myself up wondering how they knew I'd stolen. I was so careful, lying in bed till everybody was asleep. Thanking God for the food I was fixing to take. Then I'd slip in and take my holy communion: exactly two Pringles, one Oreo, one handful of each cereal. Never whole packs of Dunkaroos or anything they might keep track of. How the hell did they know?

The only way I found out anything in that house was from Haillie. For instance about the enterprise of registered English bulldogs that actually were a cross between their mutt and something that ended up not fooling anybody. He tried three or four litters with different dad dogs before giving it up. After that, Missy refused to go back in the dog room, so it wasn't me. Bad memories, more like. Haillie said the puppies were *so, so* adorable, and every time her dad took them away due to not getting sold, she'd cried to keep all of them. Every time. That was Haillie, thinking she could have anything and everything if she cried enough. That's what I had, this babyfied kid being the only actual straight shooter in the family. I was shooting in the dark.

Nevertheless I worked it, getting Haillie on my side. Oftentimes she would float into my room while I was sitting on my blow-up bed that was the only thing to sit on in there, other than piles of laundry. It was the size bed for a small kid, which maybe explained the not feeding me, so I wouldn't outgrow it. I'd be drawing my pictures, look up, and there she'd be watching me from the doorway, this tiny girl with a troll doll in one hand, dangling by its blue hair. I'd wonder how long she'd been standing there. Was this a girl thing, to sneak up on a guy while he's in his bed without his defenses? But this was different from Emmy obviously, Haillie being a child. She had the same brown eyes as her dad, like dark holes in her head. I would let her come sit and watch me draw. She made me draw puppies over and over, which was how the dog story came up, plus other stories that were just pitiful. The parents having bad fights, one time the mom throwing an entire blender at him with a diet shake in it. I let her use my colored markers to write her name in my notebook. Being new at it, she dotted all the letters in Haillie including the l's, which is how I know how to spell it. "Brayley," hell, that's anybody's guess.

Finally I asked her point-blank what was the deal with the snacks. She said her mom was letting her and Brayley keep food in their rooms now. She went on about this, that, and the other, how she liked picking the chocolate chips out of the Chips Ahoys, etc., till I thought I might pass out. Then a little light bulb went on in the tiny head. She leaned over and whispered, "Do you want me to bring you some?" I said yeah, if she didn't care. And she said what did I want?

I said maybe a sleeve of Oreos, and she was like, "SSHHH!" Putting her hand over my mouth. She got up on her knees and with her lips touching my ear, whispered in the tiniest voice, "I'll bring you a whole package, but don't tell. Don't eat them in here. Take them outside."

I asked why not. She pretended to zip her little mouth shut, and pointed up at the shelf over the washer. There was junk up there, all the usual stuff you'd not look at twice. Detergent bottles, a plastic bucket. Dryer sheets. And a baby monitor. The kind with the camera.

21

Mr. McCobb found me a job at Golly's Market, which is the little gas-and-go out on Route 58. The sign says "Mary's Mini Mart" left over from ages ago, before Mary McClary got her divorce and lit out to Nashville to try to make it as a singer. Another story.

My first day, Mr. McCobb drove me over and introduced me to the owner, Mr. Golly that was from overseas, with an accent. I was to ride the school bus out there every day after school, and Mrs. McCobb would pick me up. The place had snacks and food so I could eat my dinner there free as part of my pay, which turned out to be the one good thing about working at Golly's Market. Mr. Golly said it was a shame how much he always had to throw out in the way of hot dogs and such that he'd put under the heat lamp for the day. So I got to be his trash can, yes!

Other than food and gas, Golly's sold the usual things you'd want to pick up on your way home: Hostess cakes, beer, Tylenol, Nicorette gum, etc. The more expensive items like medicine and cigarettes he kept on a shelf behind the checkout. Mr. McCobb chatted with Mr. Golly, and I got nervous. Having no idea how to work a cash register, plus was I going to sell cigarettes and beer? Would I go to prison? Reaching the cigarette cartons was not the problem, I was some taller than Mr. Golly, that looked like a little brown tree somebody forgot to water. People were always mistaking me for older. Probably he didn't know I was eleven, and maybe Mr. McCobb was banking on that. But I was pretty sure they had laws about who could sell what in America.

It turned out I would not be selling anything. I would be working for a different business on the premises run by a person that was referenced to Mr. McCobb by Murrell Stone. I started backing out the door, saying, Nuh-*uh*, no way am I dealing with Stoner, and they said, No, not him. Some friend of his. I had no idea Mr. McCobb even knew Stoner, but again, it's Lee County.

He wished me luck and took off. I waited while Mr. Golly did something to lock the cash register, wiped off his hands, and took me outside, doing those things slower than you would believe. We finally got around to the back, and here was shock number one of my new career: the highest mountain of trash I'd ever seen, outside of the actual dump. My new situation of employment, and, I was soon to find out, hell on earth.

Not that there is anything wrong on principles with a trash pile. Like any boy, I liked them. Maggot and I always begged to go with Mr. Peg whenever he took the week's garbage to the county landfill. There was so much to see. People carting off more than they came with in the way of furniture, appliances that might have potential, etc. Actual fact: you could make an entire second world out of what people throw away. The landfill is where I figured out one of my main philosophies, that everybody alive is basically in the process of trading out their old stuff for different stuff, day in day out. The idea though is to be moving up the ladder, not down, like the McCobbs were. Landfill, pawnshops, Walmart. All places for moving things one way or the other along that road. I had this nonsense idea of a comic strip with no superhero, just some item of earthly goods like a chair that gets passed downhill from one family to another until it's a chair-shaped dirt pile. I would call it *Earthly Bads*.

I'd always thought every good American took his garbage to a landfill every week, but it turns out if you live in town, like the McCobbs did, there are people that come and take it for you. I was amazed. An entire truck existing for the sole purpose of garbage. Men working their way down the street, emptying people's cans. A town thing. Out in the county, obviously we're on our own. Mom and I toted ours next door for Mr. Peggot to haul away. At Creaky Farm we burned it, or if it wasn't burnable, tipped it into a steep gully on his back forty where he'd had a pile going for maybe a century. You'd see things like a wringer-washer machine poking out, fenders, bed springs, all rusting back into the ground, which is how I got my comic strip idea. That's the normal for a farm. But some won't have farms or any place for their trash other than the landfill, and that can be a hell of a drive, especially if you don't have a pickup.

That's where Golly's Market came in handy. People could pay a small price to dump their trash in the lot out back. That was the separate business, with boys hired to pick through it. Anything worth money like aluminum cans went in one pile, plastic bottles in another. Batteries another. My new boss wasn't around. Mr. Golly told me to wait there, he'd come back soon and get me started. Then he shuffled back to his register, and I had a look around. Behind the trash mountain I found shock number two, standing there washing out plastic pop bottles: Swap-Out.

"Wildman," I said. "What's going down?"

He stopped hosing out his bottle and stared at me. The spray nozzle was leaking all over the place, and the little guy was shivering, hoodie and jeans all soaked from where he'd sprayed himself. Then his face lit up and he screeched, *Diamond!*

I couldn't believe he remembered my Squad name. This kid that reliably did not remember to zip his fly. I wanted to hug him but of course didn't. We just stood there like lost boys on our own garbage island. I tightened up the hose nozzle for him and asked questions. He was working here now, every day. No more school, he was done. Meaning he might actually have been sixteen. Or else over at Elk Knob they figured they'd done their worst, and gave up. He wasn't at Creaky's now, living with some guys in an apartment, the who-what-where I couldn't really guess. Swap-Out's way of telling you anything was like his sentences got dropped and broken all to pieces. You had to take whatever you could pick up, and work backwards.

He wanted to know if I was working here now instead of Rotten Potatoes, whatever the hell. Is that a thing or a person, I asked him, and he said yes. Rotten Potatoes was a person. Was he our boss, I asked, and Swap-Out said no, a kid. He puked all the time and got fired. The boss guy wasn't there right now, and his name was Ghose.

Gose? I asked. No. *Goes?* No.

"Whoooo," Swap-Out said, flapping his hands, scary. "Ghose like a dead guy!"

Ghost. That was my new boss. We watched his truck pull in around front, but I couldn't see him go into the store, nor from there into the back room that Mr. Golly had told me was the headquarters of the recycling business, which I was not *ever* to go into because it was private. I didn't get a look at my boss till he came out the back door and gave me surprise number three.

Ghost was the pale, white-haired guy with the crazy ink, Stoner's friend that I'd met one time in Pro's Pizza. With the other one, Hell Reeker, that had come over and teased Stoner about foxes whelping their pups, Mr. Grin and Bear it, all that. Ghost was Extra Eye.

If I say I had to sort through people's filthy, crappy trash, I'm saying there were diapers. Human shit. If I say there were rats, I don't mean we saw one or two. Rats were part of how we got through our day. Target practice, company, whatever you want to call it. Some we named. Rinsing bottles and squashing cans was

Swap-Out's department, and Ghost put me on the jobs that took any brains whatsoever. He said finally the damn gook had hired him some help that was playing with a full deck. Evidently the kid he'd just fired, Rotten Potatoes, was missing the cards in his deck that tell you not to eat food that's been in the trash too long before you find it.

One of the first jobs Ghost showed me was how to drain the acid out of old car batteries. You hammer a nail through the bottom to puncture it. Most batteries have several compartments so you figure them out, punch a hole in each one, then turn it up and drain out the acid into something glass, like a jar. (Not plastic. Never plastic. Rotten Potatoes evidently was missing those cards too.) Ghost collected up all the acid into metal cans where he wrote "acid" on them, lined up alongside of his paint thinner cans outside the back door of his HQ, by the propane tanks. He said he didn't want all that shit inside stinking up the place.

Which is a joke because he'd come out of there stinking to high heaven, sometimes like rotten eggs, usually cat piss. He had window fans running all hours, even on cold days, and the cat piss smell coming out of there hung over the place worse than the stink of garbage. What Ghost was up to, anybody's guess. He'd have frying pans and bottles for us to hose out, and bottles he said to put straight directly in the landfill pile, do not mess around. We're talking things that are no friends to your skin or your clothes. I got some of the acid on my jeans, and after they ran through the wash, every stain was a hole. I got why Ghost had put me on the batteries instead of Swap-Out. Poor little guy, a few days of that and he'd be a window screen.

I got paid four dollars an hour, sixteen a day. Cash. I went straight from school, and Mrs. McCobb would pick me up around nine after she got the kids in bed, so it was more than four hours a day, but after dark Swap-Out and I would come in the store to eat Mr. Golly's leftovers. He had a bathroom where we could wash up. I helped him stock his shelves after deliveries came in, and saw what people around there were living on. Mainly beer, toilet paper, Campfire pork and beans. Cold medicine, holy mother. He'd get in a hundred boxes of Sudafed. Two days later it's gone. I didn't see people buying it, either. If Mr. Golly was having all those colds, you'd not have known it. Actually, if he was alive, you couldn't be sure of that. He had a grayish look to his skin, and would sit for hours not moving. Watching his little TV he had by the checkout.

Mr. Golly didn't at all mind us hanging around. He said he grew up working in a junkyard as a boy, just like us. But! Happy ending, now he lived in America and could send money back home to his family. He'd had a wife at some point, but lived by himself now in a small apartment in Duffield. He said he didn't need anything in his apartment because he lived at the store, cooked his food and everything, which was true. If he ever closed, I didn't see it.

There weren't any houses around that area. People stopped on their way to someplace better. Sometimes it would be a mom with kids, obviously unfamiliar with the layout and only there to get somebody into the bathroom ASAP. They'd buy a Coke or some little thing for a cover story, but you knew. Then there were the respectable types that would pay Mr. Golly their ten bucks, drive around back to drop off their month's worth of trash bags, maybe purchase a chili dog to celebrate. Other than that, it was a rough crowd. Some, and I'm saying more than one, did not use trash bags. The back of their pickup *was* the trash can, and after it got piled high, they'd drive over, pay their fee, open the tailgate, and rake it out. I'm discussing bathroom trash and all. You tried your best not to picture the homestead.

Worst were the regulars with no involvement in the trash enterprise. They'd get their beer and beans up front, then slip around back to do their business with Ghost. I was getting the picture. Golly's Market catered to lowlifes, and I was working there. So I was a lowlife too.

Some are going to say I was never anything better. Not even born in a hospital to a mom fixing to take me back to her mobile home, but born *in* the mobile home, so that's like the Eagle Scout of trailer trash. Kids like me with our teen moms putting whiskey on our gums to shut us up, Coke in the baby bottle, we're the pity of the world. But I started out as decent as any kid, saying please and thank you, doing my homework, figuring out how to get smiled at. I played to win, with all my little prides and dreams. So what if they were junior-varsity dreams, like marrying Carol Danvers and being an Avenger whenever I grew up. I got up every day thinking the sun was out there shining, and it could just as well shine on me as any other human person.

By fifth grade I was taller than everybody, including some teachers. Guys wanted me on their side for whatever we played in gym, and I'm saying *always*. Girls flirted. Emmy had said I was tenderhearted, good-looking, and everything. Plenty of poor kids got their faces punched in just for existing. Up to that point I'd not thought much about what I was, but I wasn't that. This was in the before-time, last days of. Still no internet with all the ways of saying, Let's us be better than those guys so we can hate on them. Our school had two computers in the library, one that worked. Some few kids did a project where they set up their mailbox address on there, to get mail from a robot we thought, ha ha. What existed at that time for calling people out was the cootie game, where little kids would touch some loser and then run around threatening to spread loser germs on you. In some cases, like the Houserman kids, genuine head lice could be involved, so. Heads up.

But in fifth, we weren't children. Loser boys got fists. Girls had their girl shit of no interest to me, like their slam books that got passed around. Skinny spiral notebooks like you'd have for a subject, but with SLAM BOOK and PROPERTY OF on the front to let you know it's not for a teacher's eyes. Some girl would poke me in the back with one, to pass on up the row. These were the enterprise of the popular girls with plucked-to-the-bone eyebrows and hair parted in the shape of a lightning bolt. Look, you're sitting behind some girl all day looking down on her head, you notice the hair. The notebooks though, I didn't, even after they were getting pushed at me. Even with girls writing in them and looking at me like something's dead hilarious.

Then came the day of Demon's education. Everybody was set for recess, unless on detention which I usually was, for fidgeting or drawing on my desk. We had the one-piece type with the tiny chair attached, pretty much hell for a kid my size, and the wooden desk tops all gray around the edges with the ground-in dirt of our forefathers. Our parents and grandparents used these desks, and had some of the same teachers, including the mummified individual Miss Huddles we had in fifth. Miss Huddles famously had leathered my mom in front of the entire school for faking a striptease in Christian Music Assembly. (Mom and God, it just never worked.) To look at the old bat now, though, a shrunken head in a dress, I had no fear. These desks had so many names, hairy penises, and doodles carved in them, it seemed senseless not to carry on the tradition. You're sitting there with a pencil. Hours to get through before you die. I prided myself on excellent cartoon characters for the enjoyment of prisoners to come.

So here's the bell and everybody files out. A yellow notebook is slapped down on my desk. Slap goes another one as they walk by, girls detouring past my desk on their way out, laughing because this is all so funny. A pile of slam books to cheer up Demon's detention.

The first page is numbered. You sign in next to a number, so that's your code. Turn the pages. Each page has one kid's name at the top. You write your opinion of them, signed with your number. This is all new to me and I'm thinking, pretty hilarious, using a number for your not-at-all-secret identity. On the page of every popular girl, everybody writes *Cute sweet nice fun to be with.* Always those words, in whatever order. The religious girls get *Too straight no fun.* Or else *L-7,* which is the known code for "square," which is the known code for *Too straight, no fun.* Guys have pages also. Popular ones being *Hella hunk the bomb all that home skillet.*

Maybe I didn't think these books would have a Demon page. Maybe I did. Either way I wasn't ready for that hot spreading feeling like I've pissed myself. *Shit eater loser trash jerkoff.* No exception. Somebody wrote *Asshole.* I mean. I'd gone quiet since Mom died, and probably hadn't said more than five or six words in that class since Christmas. It takes some doing to scrape together *asshole* out of that.

Nothing was different afterward except for my fresh loser eyes, noticing it all. People steering clear. Not touching me in gym, not even cheering if I sank a shot. Holding up their plate to my face in the lunchroom, like I'd eat off it like a dog. I wanted no sun shining on me now. I erased myself like a chalkboard. In my outgrown high-water jeans and the old-man shoes Mr.

Peg had loaned me at Christmas, I joined the tribe of way-back country kids with no indoor plumbing and the Pentecostals that think any style clothes invented since Bible times is a sin. My specialty, acid holes. Who was going to take me shopping for new clothes? Hair over my collar, and who's going to cut it? Miss Barks had noticed I was getting ratty, and kept reminding Mrs. McCobb how the monthly check from DSS should more than cover those things. And Mrs. McCobb kept saying she meant to get around to it, but just so busy with her kids.

I'd been thinking about Emmy moving here in a few months, the walks we were going to take. Hand-holding. Now I just hoped she and June would move to some far-distant part of the county where she'd be in a different school and never find out what I was.

It happened after one of these shit-most days of school, and more of the same on my shitpile job, that I kind of blacked out and threw some punches at the dash of Mrs. McCobb's car. Scaring the living piss out of her. All she'd done was ask if I had a nice day. I don't know why that set me off, but I landed my punches and she got quiet. Finally she said she was worried about me. I said maybe she should worry a hell of a lot more. It was dark, and I couldn't see her face, which helped. "You're so scared of Haillie and Brayley getting tormented at school," I said.

She said "Yeah." Sounding scared. Like she knew what was up.

"Well, take a look at me." I let her have it then, told her about the slam books, the getting shunned, all of it. Kids pretending to sniff around me, asking did somebody shit himself. "And guess what," I said. "They know who I'm living with. It's getting around."

I felt her going stiff over there behind the wheel, the McCobb family name going down.

On Sunday she took me to Walmart. I got new jeans, T-shirts, belt, shoes, and also a new toothbrush, which I hadn't had in a while, ever since Brayley launched mine into the toilet on accident. Those kids loved to goof around in the downstairs bathroom. I thanked her, and she told me not to tell Mr. McCobb we'd spent almost everything I earned at Golly's that month.

But at school the next day in my new clothes I still felt horrible. Not even proud. Embarrassed honestly, because nothing would change. Now they'd all think I was just that much more pitiful, because of trying. Loser is a cliff. Once you've gone over, you're over.

What few friends I had now were some high school guys on the bus I rode out to Golly's. "Friends," meaning they let me sit with them and didn't run me off.

Redneck guys that everybody knew to leave the two back rows of seats open for, no discussion. Mostly they talked about girls: which ones were skanks and whores, which to stay away from because of hep C or the clap. Also drugs, who had what and for how much. They didn't say a lot to me personally other than "Hey, how's it going" whenever we got on the bus. But I kept my mouth shut and got educated. They did ask some few things, like what grade was I. Thinking they wouldn't want a fifth grader in on those types of conversations, I said eighth. They asked was I doing JV football and again I lied, saying yes, and I was going out for varsity next year at Lee High. I told them I was friends with Fast Forward, and they were just amazed by that. These guys were on the team. Not first string, but still. They said they would be glad to have me on the Generals because I looked like I would make a good tackle or tight end. I remember which one of them said that, and the day. Due to that being the one nice thing anybody said to me that year.

Most days passed without a word coming out of my mouth. If I talked, it was to Swap-Out and Mr. Golly. Or Haillie, if she came in my room to play with my markers. I let her, even though they were all I had, so I was scared of them running out of ink. She wanted me to draw a cartoon of her, so I invented the Howliiie

Fairy that left Oreos under your pillow. If bad guys showed up, she screamed them off the planet. So that's what I had to work with: some gangbangers, a second grader, a foreign hundred-year-old man, and a guy with scrambled eggs for brains. Miss Barks mainly now just hounded me about school, why my grades had slipped. No big secret, I said. I hated school. I told her how ruthless the kids were. She said to hang in there, in middle school the kids would be nicer. I did not for one minute believe her.

It's hard to believe I could look back on Creaky Farm in any wishful way, but I missed having Fast Forward on my team. Fast Man that had made me feel hard and shiny as a diamond. I knew there was a dark side, he let others take his lickings, but that was him teaching us: a person can keep his head up and rise high, even if he wasn't lucky enough to get born up there. In all the years of no adult ever taking my side, he showed me it was possible to work them at their own game and win.

That summer I started getting the faintest red shine of hair on my upper lip, one more embarrassment. If I still lived with Fast Forward, he could have taught me how to shave. I'd have one person to talk to that actually knew what a kid like me was dealing with. He would have told me straight up whether it was true, what I'd started to think. That I was working for a meth lab.

22

Miss Barks had some big news. She was pumped. Picked me up from school to go for a long drive out in the country, which we both liked. Then dinner at a restaurant of Mexican food called Rancho something that didn't even have a drive-through.

Great all that, but you don't just run off with your caseworker and not show up for work. Ghost was not a guy you wanted mad at you. That tattoo eye staring at you from his throat, Jesus. I never forgot how I'd drawn him in my mind that first time at Pro's Pizza, as supervillain Extra Eye that could see your thoughts. Now I was like, What if that's real? What if he can even see this thought? I didn't discuss any of this with Miss Barks due to her not knowing about my job at Golly's Market. After I first started working there, I'd asked enough questions to figure out this was a what-DSS-doesn't-know-won't-hurt-me type situation.

But now it was just me and Miss Barks in the car having ourselves the biggest time, and I quit caring about Ghost. I was ready for a good day. We took the little winding roads through coal camps where the big blue coal chutes come down the mountainside over the treetops, like waterslides for giants. All the way out to those high white cliffs that run along the Kentucky line. It was one of your April days where you can smell the plowed fields and see the mountains greening up, like it's the world saying, Hey everybody, I'm not dead yet! We put on the radio and sang all the ones we knew. And I mean loud, windows rolled down, the two of us singing "You're Still the One" like we're wanting Shania to hear us over in Nashville.

Miss Barks said she never felt so free as she did behind the wheel of a car. I wondered how many years I'd have to work at Golly's before I could score some wheels. Probably a hundred, given how things were going. Two months had got me some T-shirts, the cheapest brand tennis shoes they carried at Walmart, and if anything more, I wouldn't know. The McCobbs were keeping my money for so-called safety reasons. Like Fast Forward did at Creaky's.

Miss Barks said I was looking handsome in my new

haircut, so technically that's two nice things said to me that year. But then she erased it by trying to take credit. Didn't she say I just needed to speak up? Ask the McCobbs for anything I needed, ask and ye shall receive, the usual nonsense. Smash your fist into somebody's dashboard and ye shall get noticed, is more like it. But I didn't want to kill the mood, so I let her think what she thought.

Out by the Cumberland bluffs we got out of the car to walk around that park they have, and stood looking up at the cliffs that go on and on, for the last hundred miles of Virginia. I wondered how it would feel to be way up there on top, looking down. My brain kept going back to that, over and over, wondering how it would feel to jump off. Not to die necessarily, just to see how it felt to be a boy flying through the air. Not that I would. Jump. Or fly either. You can't help what goes through your head.

That's where Miss Barks told me her news. Big shock. I had money I never knew about. After Mom died, the DSS filed the paperwork for me to get social security checks, which is the bright side of being an orphan: they pay you for it. Who knew? It wasn't a ton, some percentage of what Mom was making at Walmart, which is an insult according to Mr. McCobb. But it was still a check, and I would get it every month till I turned eighteen. Miss Barks said they'd set up for it to go into an account that I could use after I graduated from foster care. She said this tended to work out better than putting the foster parents in charge of the account. And I said something to the effect of, Lady, you got that one fucking right.

She wanted me to promise I would use the money to go to college. Like, *away* someplace, not auto mechanics at Mountain Empire. Which meant promising to do better with my grades. You don't get to college without passing elementary school, she said, like this was new information. I told her at Elk Knob you get promoted to middle school just for showing up, especially a kid of my size. They need us in the higher grades for the sports teams. She said that was not the attitude she was looking for. I tried changing the subject, but she was real stuck on that point: Just showing up doesn't get you anywhere in life. It was not too late to turn myself around, etc. I asked if it was required for me to use this money account for college, and she said technically no. But I would be a fool not to, because that would give me the same chances in life as other kids had.

She was just bitter about not getting to go herself. She'd been taking her night classes, but it wasn't the same as the away-type colleges where evidently you get to live on your own as a grown-up without even going to work, just reading and studying on whatever you feel like finding out about. I didn't know anybody that had done that. It didn't seem real, honestly. I was just trying to get my head around the orphan bonus. I wondered about Tommy Waddles. Was he getting paid double for having *both* parents dead? She said probably. Then I wondered about something else, which was my dad, that died before I was born. Had I been racking up the dough all these years, only to find out on my eighteenth birthday I'd won the freaking lottery?

Sadly, no. She said they'd looked into that, hoping to track down some line on child support, but there was no father on my birth certificate. I told her I did have one, though, and knew his name. I even knew where he was buried, due to Mrs. Peggot and Mom having their arguments over taking me to see his grave. The cemetery was in Murder Valley, Tennessee. I only heard them say it a few times, an age ago. But a name like that is not too forgettable.

Miss Barks said none of this was any use. It was my mom's mistake for not putting him on my birth certificate. And with him being dead especially, an expensive mistake. I said "Damn," even though I wasn't supposed to use language with Miss Barks, and for just that once she made a face and said, "Yeah, double damn." That was Mom and mistakes. She was a pro.

We got back to town before dark, to eat at the restaurant, but I started worrying about Mrs. McCobb driving out to pick me up at Golly's, me not being there, her being mad over the wasted gas, Mr. McCobb being mad I'd skipped out. And so on. I told Miss Barks I needed to be back before eight o'clock to have plenty of time for homework. There's always some lie that will make everybody happy, if you work at it. She was all smiles about the homework, and pretty like always. Pink sweater, tight slacks, that angel hair. I wasn't cheating on Emmy in thinking Miss Barks was hot, because (1) Emmy was popular, so if she ever saw me again would break up with me instantly, and (2) Miss Barks was a different category from girlfriend, i.e. legal guardian.

The restaurant was a trip. They had it decorated up like a different country and even had a couple of Mexican people in there bringing your food. Plus cooking it, you would have to think. I couldn't tell you the name of one single thing I ate, except rice and some lettuce, but it was all great and there was a ton of it and I stuffed my face like a pig.

Towards the end of dinner she told me she had more news. Not good, this time. Terrible in fact, but it took me a minute to work that out. She was so excited she was bouncing in her chair. She'd saved up enough to take summer classes full time and finish out her teacher degree. In the fall she would start her student teaching. After that, pretty much guaranteed of getting a job as an elementary or kindergarten teacher, and finally would start making some decent money.

Miss Barks was quitting her job at DSS so she could go have her wonderful new career. Quitting me. And all her other precious orphans, screw us. For the money.

She dropped me back at the McCobbs' before eight, like I'd asked, so they wouldn't drive out to get me from Golly's. I came in the kitchen and told Mr. McCobb some lie about how I'd had an appointment with my caseworker and she'd cleared it with Mr. Golly so I'd get paid anyway. Then I went to my stinking dog room and punched the washing machine. Wiped off the smear of blood with somebody's black T-shirt that was in the pile, shut off the lights, and planted myself face down on my motherfucking child-size air-mattress bed.

On second thought, I got back up and rummaged around the shelf over the washer, got the baby monitor, and put it in the mop bucket. I didn't need anybody watching me cry.

Maybe some kids are told from an early age what's what, as regards money. But most are ignorant I would think, and that was me too, till I was eleven and started pulling down a paycheck. Before that, my thinking was vague. If you had a job, you had money. If you didn't have a job, you had your food stamps or EBT card and basically, not money. I didn't really get that there were gray areas. Okay, I did know about rich people, that some few made the big bucks from being movie stars, pro football, the president, etc. These types of people living one hundred percent not in Lee County. Except for this one NASCAR driver that supposedly bought a farm near Ewing in the seventies. Also, the coal miners back in union times. Thirty or forty bucks an hour, old men still talked like those were the days Jesus walked among us throwing around hundred-dollar bills. But for the most part I thought a paycheck was a paycheck, whether from Walmart or Food Country or Lee Bank and Trust or Hair Affair or the Eastman plant over in Kingsport.

Obviously, you live and learn. Now I know, if you finish high school that's supposed to be a step up, moneywise. College is another step up, but with a major downside: for the type of job college gets you, most likely you'll end up having to live far away from home, and in a city. My point though is the totem pole of paychecks, with school as one thing that gets you up there, and another one being where you live, country or city. But the main thing is, whatever you're doing, who is it making happy? Are you selling the cheapest-ass shoes imaginable to Walmart shoppers, or high-class suits to business guys? Even the same exact work, like sanding floors, could be at the Dollar General or a movie star mansion. Show me your paycheck, I'll make a guess which floor. If you are making a rich person happy, or a regular person *feel* rich, aka better than other people, the money rolls. If it's lowlifes you're looking after, not so much. And if it's kids, good luck, because anything to do with improving the life of a child is on the bottom. Schoolteacher pay is for the most part in the toilet. I gather this is common knowledge, but I had no idea, the day Miss Barks said, So long sucker, I'm chasing the big bucks now. *Schoolteacher!*

I've had friends in places high and low since then, and some of the best were people that taught school. The ones that showed up for me. Outside of school hours they were delivery drivers or moonlighting at a gas station or, this is a true example, playing in a band and driving the ice cream truck in summer. They need the extra job. Honestly need it, just to get by.

So here is Miss Barks in her first real job, twenty-two years old, working her little heart out for the DSS. And hitting the books at all hours because she pretty desperately wants to live in her own tiny apartment instead of sharing with a slob, and for that she needs to climb up the paycheck pole to *first-grade teacher.* That's how they pay you at DSS. Old Baggy has been at it so long she's got no more reason to live, working two shifts a day, going home to her crap duplex in Duffield owned by her cousin that gives her a break on the rent. If you are the kid sitting across from her in your caseworker meeting, wearing your two black eyes and the hoodie reeking of cat piss, sorry dude but she's thinking about what TV show she'll watch that night. Any human person with gumption would have moved on to something else by now, the military or selling insurance or being a cop or even a teacher. Because DSS pay is basically the fuck-you peanut butter sandwich type of paycheck. That's what the big world thinks it's worth, to save the white-trash orphans.

And if these kids grow up to throw punches at washing machines or each other or even let's say smash a drugstore drive-through window. Crawl in and take what's there. Tell me how you're going to be surprised. There's your peanut butter sandwich back. Every dog gets his day.

23

Summer was coming, and I was counting the days down. Not that moving to full-time hours on the garbage mountain enterprise was any great shakes, vacationwise. But still, for a kid it's just ironed into you that summer is freedom. For three whole months, no more sitting in a too small desk trying to be not the biggest shit-eater in the room.

For the record, I didn't always hate school. I was once known to put in a decent effort. One of the better readers, as far as the boys at least. Maybe I thought Mom would be proud, or maybe I wanted to show her I wasn't going to be a dropout like her. Either way, it no longer pertained. Now I watched other kids raise their hands, get their answers right, and good for them. Topic sentences, Appomattox Courthouse, life cycle of a plant, what is all that? If all your brain wants to know is, where's the door out of here and wherever it goes, will you still be starving.

The teachers, principal, and Miss Barks all gave me the same lecture on how I was not working hard or living up to my potential. I had no fight with them. You get to a point of not giving a damn over people thinking you're worthless. Mainly by getting there first yourself. I wanted to tell them: This right here that you're looking at is my potential. What the fuck would *you* call it? Do you seriously think this is the person I wanted to end up living inside of?

But hard work? Let me tell you what that is: trying to get through every day without the gangling ugly menace of you being stared at, shamed by a teacher, laughed at by girls, or sucker punched. Again, if you've been there, you know. If you have to guess, you might not even be close. All these people had to keep on asking and asking: Why was I flunking out? What could I do but look at the wall and say nothing, just *sorry*. I was learning to love the brutal burnt screw-you taste of that word I'd been given to eat forever. *Sorry.*

But I still yet had a small fire in my belly for the first day of summer. Picture me with my big smile, turning up at Golly's at nine a.m. on a weekday, dropped off by Mr. McCobb on his way to wherever he hadn't quit from lately. I can see Mr. Golly inside the store putting his two-for-one Corn Dogs sign in the window. Over at the far side of the dump lot, I see Swap-Out lighting a cigarette one-handed while pissing against a tree in full view of the passing cars. And I think, *Jesus.* This is all there is. Walk around back to bang on Ghost's door and clock in.

The thing about school you don't realize is, everybody's moving towards something. Even if you're one of the screwups, you still participate. Okay kids, let's get through this lesson, this unit, this grade. In May we'll take our Standards of Learning tests, maybe our sorry-ass school will do better on the scores this year, the teachers will keep their jobs, and everybody moves on to the next grade. Every kid wants to be older anyway, so there you go, automatic improvement. It's like the escalator thing at the Knoxville mall. Step on, take your ride. There's always the chance you might run across something shiny and new on your way up.

Now I'd fallen off. At Golly's we didn't have any units or even weeks, we measured time in roll-offs. Which is a giant metal bin, like a railroad car, that you fill up with trash. Then a semi comes and hauls it off to the landfill. After we'd sorted people's dropped-off trash into what could be sold for scrap, recycled, pawned, smashed, drained, whatever, the leftovers were the trash of the trash. Also pretty toxic, but not the point. That's what we threw in the thirty-yard roll-off. It was nothing so easy as just tossing it in, either. The company charged four hundred dollars to haul it off and bring in an empty, so we had to be economical about it and get over a hundred ten-buck loads of people's trash leftovers crammed in that dumpster. This meant using all our superpowers of stomping, flattening, breaking, rebreaking, then piling it higher than the canopy over the gas pumps. Towards the end of a load, it took a serious pitching arm to get anything up there on top. Plenty would fall off too, as they hauled it away, leaving a trail of crap from Golly's to the landfill. Not our problem.

Here was our summer: filling that roll-off to the max, be it a month, six weeks, doesn't matter. Because it goes away, the empty comes back, and you're back where you started. Here was the real world where nobody and nothing gets better. Biding my time till I turned sixteen and could drop out of school, with a whole life ahead for applying myself to full-time shit work. Maybe I was Ghost's trainee, someday to graduate from battery-acid drainage assistant to the show he had going inside.

Meanwhile the McCobbs were in some serious shit. Their car got repossessed. It was a late-model Dodge Spirit, leased, sky blue, none of that I guess being the point. Mr. McCobb couldn't get to work anymore, so he lost his job, was the point. You tell me why it makes sense for guys wanting money from you to come and take your car, so you can't earn another dime. That's the grown-up version I guess of teachers yelling at you for hating school.

First the McCobbs didn't know what the hell they were going to do, other than possibly be homeless, because of already being behind on their rent. Next they fired up a full-time marital spat between (1) starting a couple of new in-home businesses with Mr. McCobb doing telephone surveys and Mrs. McCobb doing dog grooming, or (2) taking the kids and going to Ohio to live with Mrs. McCobb's parents, dog grooming my ass. I myself was banking on Mr. McCobb winning, because he definitely wore the pants. It mattered to me which way this went, obviously. Since I would not be moving my personal ass to any Ohio.

Or grooming any dogs, either. I was working full time at Golly's. It turned out Ghost lived over towards Fleenortown and drove right past, so he could pick me up on his way in. I wasn't crazy about the hours he kept, or being alone in a Chevy pickup with Ghost and the thoughts in my head. Christ. But I got to work most days, other than the weeks he'd disappear on some kind of bender. I had to stay longer in the evenings, due to Ghost doing a lot of his business in the after-dark hours. But I got used to it. Swap-Out had a reliable source of weed and a generous heart. Definitely it helped the time go faster. Or maybe slower actually, but you didn't care. Once in a great while he'd show up with a Glock 19 that belonged to one of the guys he lived with, and we'd set up a row of bottles on the edge of the roll-off for target practice. It was years since Mr. Peg had showed me how to shoot, so I wasn't that great, but my aim got better over time. Swap-Out's aim was scary as hell, permanently, improvement being not a Swap-Out thing. We kept an eye out for the aerosols, which over and above the huffing potentials made excellent targets. Big bang, for real. But we could get ourselves just as thoroughly entertained over some childish shit like stomping the bubbles of bubble wrap. Also you wouldn't believe the number of hot dogs two deeply baked boys could put away. Mr. Golly had to be making extras on purpose.

After Swap-Out went home of an evening, I'd be on my own to hang out in the store and help Mr. Golly. He liked talking about his childhood in India, where evidently a lot of people lived in the dump itself. In houses they built out of actual trash. If that sounds like some wack fairy tale, I'm just going to say he was not a guy to lie to you. He acted like this was no big deal really, getting born and raised in a dump. He had all these great stories about what boys did to mess with each other, like traps, stink bombs, etc. For their holidays (and we're talking some whole other Christianity) they built giant statues of their goddesses and elephants and such, out of—wait for it—stuff they found in the dump! God made out of garbage, you can't make that up. It seemed like the old man had been saving up these stories his whole life, waiting for somebody to listen. He'd had a wife in there somewhere, but at this point in time I'm pretty sure I was it for Mr. Golly. Technically it turned out that he was Mr. Ghali this whole time. I saw him write that on the thing you sign for deliveries. I was surprised, but he said I was not the lone ranger, everybody in the county thought it was Golly's Market. According to him, "Golly" meant "Gee, that is really great," so the name was okay by him. Part of his advertising scheme.

Hearing these tales of his dump boyhood, sometimes I'd think of telling Miss Barks, how she'd be interested in the whole situation of foreign orphans. Then I'd remember: nope. I was back to Baggy Eyes as my caseworker, a sadder sack of person than ever, plus seriously pissed off at Miss Barks for abandoning ship to go chase her dreams. That made two of us, and I guess we both decided out of bitterness to say as little as possible to each other. She would call the house once a month while I was at work, and Mrs. McCobb would tell some lie about me being outside playing. Baggy would be glad to hear it, no need to talk to me. Just to be clear: I'm eleven. She's my legal guardian. And her idea of a perfect ward of the state is one that's AWOL.

The McCobbs by this time were fighting like cats and dogs. I'd hear them going at it in the kitchen before I was even awake, and at night up in their room, voices raised to be heard above crying babies. And even still Mrs. McCobb sometimes would up and tell me for no reason, like while she's putting in a load of laundry, that she would never divorce Mr. McCobb.

If true, that's about all that could be ruled out in the department what the hell next. In July the landlord threatened to kick them out unless they paid their back rent. Which they did, by dipping into the cash I'd earned at Golly's. No confusion now about me chipping in. Did they plan to tell me? No. I found out from Haillie that heard her parents discuss it, taking *my* cash out of the drawer where they kept it. I went postal. The poor kid pissing herself, to see the level of catfuck she'd let out of the bag. I stormed upstairs, yelling how I was going to turn them in to DSS. How would I do that, without going into various not-legal things I'd done to make this money they'd taken? No idea, I just went with my gut. Some items in their bedroom got busted, including a lamp. The babies went off like a car alarm. Not a good scene. I took what was left of my cash, put it in a peanut butter jar, and said if they wanted my help they could fucking well ask.

What else were they going to use, though? Honestly, once I got over my Hulk moment I was more worried than mad. Without any car they were in pitiful shape. Sending their grocery list for me to bring home from Golly's, then freaking out over paying double for a can of beans, etc. But they couldn't very well walk the five miles to Food Lion. Mr. McCobb was getting whittled down to size. He still talked down to the wife and kids, but me he started treating like one of his buds. He was drinking a good deal of beer in the afternoons now, so I'd get home of an evening to find him in the kitchen wanting to share his tales of woe. Rarely was I in the mood. But if I went in my dog room he'd just follow me in there, which was worse. No place for two guys to sit, for one thing, underpants lying around for another. That weren't even mine.

He felt like a loser, not providing for his family. He

said it almost killed him to take my money and then get yelled at in front of his kids. He'd go all sorry, and the dog would look up at him with the whites of her eyes showing, and I'd feel like it was me that should apologize. Shame was a shithole I knew. He'd get in these sloppy moods of giving me life advice, like I was his real son. Which, even if beggars can't be choosers, would not have been my first choice. He always ended up saying the same thing: If you spend one penny less than you earn every month, you'll be happy. But spend a penny more than you earn, you're done for. He'd look at me with those dark, sad eyes and lay this on me. That the secret of happiness basically is two cents.

By late summer the dog-grooming side of the fight had gotten nowhere, signs pointing to Ohio. Mrs. Mc-Cobb's parents would call and she'd get the kids on the extensions, both crying. Daddy's so mean they can't have the littlest thing, no Barbies, no Lisa Frank, waah. My Lord, to think of Mr. McCobb moving in with those in-laws. A hot mess. They decided on leaving town before school started. Baggy would have to find me a new placement. And at least I'd finally be done worrying about that household, where the man of the house was the one sleeping in the dog room.

Now I could worry about my own next stop on the road to hell, with a caseworker that was not on the case.

I had to call her to ask, was I going back to Creaky Farm. She said Crickson, and no. The DSS had discovered he was committing infractions, so they removed his fostering privileges. They were looking for somebody else to take the hardship cases. "Our kids that resist permanent placement," was how she put it, and of course I thought of Tommy. He would not resist but throw his arms around a permanent placement. Never to draw a skeleton again.

Around this time I made my plan. Dangerous possibly, crazy for sure. All I can say is, you try living in crazytown for a while and see what you cook up.

All I had to my name was the jar of money I kept stashed in my backpack day and night. Every dollar I got paid, I stuffed in there on top of whatever the McCobbs had left me after paying off their landlord. I'd had no chance to make an exact count. No privacy at work, nor in my room at night, with the baby-cam. Those two watching me count my money, they'd pop a vein. But I got paid for eight hours most days, and had worked eight weeks that summer more or less. Less, due to Ghost going on some bad jags. It would have to be enough.

Because now it's August. Mrs. McCobb is packing anything as yet unpawned into cardboard boxes, Mr.

McCobb probably is weighing the pros and cons of a bullet in his brain, and still nobody can tell me where I'm going to live. Baggy's idea of working on it is asking the same questions again. Did I have friends that could take me in a pinch? She'd checked back with the Peggots, which was embarrassing. How many times did I have to hear it? No, they did not want me. They did say I could come visit for a few days before school started, to spend time with Matthew. Meaning probably Maggot was bored, wearing eye makeup around the house and driving everybody nuts, and it dawned on the grandparents that I might be a good influence. And I thought: Damn it, I *told* you this. What I said to Baggy was, "Tell them I'll consider it."

The other thing she kept asking about was relatives. Did I have any. Had we not been through this? Lady, look it up. Mom: orphan, foster care, no living relatives she knew of, plus dead. Dad: skip straight to the dead part. Also not existent, according to my birth certificate.

But he did exist. Mom was very clear on that. Her story about the day I was born and some old biddy coming for me, okay, questionable. But the older I got, the more people said I looked like him. That I came from somewhere, in other words. From somebody.

The first Thursday of August, the McCobbs had a

U-Haul truck sitting in their driveway pointed at Ohio. I'd told Baggy I was going to the Peggots. She wouldn't have to give me a ride, they were picking me up. I'd stay there until she sorted out my placement. My last morning in the dog room, I crammed what I could into my school backpack: clothes, drawing notebooks, money jar. The rest was trash. What toys I had, I'd given to Brayley. I let the plug out of my bed and sat on it to let the air out. I would miss those kids, especially Haillie. I'd bought them goodbye presents from Golly's: a plastic horse for Haillie and a pint of bubble-gum-flavor ice cream for Brayley. I rolled my bed up with the sheets and stuffed them in a laundry basket that I carried outside. I tried to say goodbye to the Mr. and Mrs. but they were yelling at each other over how to fit a queen-size mattress in the U-Haul. Whatever. Haillie gave me a hug. Brayley wiped off his pink ice cream beard and waved from the steps. Ghost rolled up and I got in his pickup and that was me, over and out on the McCobbs.

It was a weird day at work. My head was not in the normal place, but it wasn't just me. I mean, a lady leaning out her car window and yelling for a solid half hour about had we seen her motherfucking husband that had done hightailed it with her SSDI check. Also, finding a mother skunk with her four babies *inside* a twist-tied bag of trash. She'd made a little hole and got her family in there. This is *skunks*, right, so getting them all out is another story. Lethal Weapon III.

At the end of my shift the Peggots did not pick me up. I'd lied to Baggy, knowing she'd never in this life or the next one call up the Peggots to check. I told Mr. Golly I wouldn't be able to come in the next day, not a lie, so he gave me my week's pay early. I picked up some items I said were for the McCobbs, and to put it on their tab. Candy bars, Slim Jims, easy-to-carry type things. If Mr. Golly noticed this wasn't the usual McCobb grocery list, he didn't say anything. With a good hour of daylight still hanging, I turned my back on Golly's. Walked out to the junction, turned south on Highway 23, and stuck out my thumb.

It probably wasn't five minutes before a guy pulled over in a rusted-out El Camino, those half-car, half-pickup type of deals, with two muddy dogs in the back. I thought that was a good sign, as regards the guy not being a child molester. Why carry around dogs to crime scenes? Anyway, I got in. Wherever those dogs had been to get so muddy, this guy was right there with them. He had dried mud on the sleeves of his shirt and caked in his hair. But fine, not blood. I thanked him for picking me up. He asked where I was headed tonight, and I told him Tennessee.

He laughed. "Where at *in particular*, buddy? Tennessee's kindly big."

I said it was a place he'd probably never heard of before. Murder Valley.

He told me I was right, that was a new one on him. But that he'd not be able to forget a name like that, now that he'd heard it. I said no, sir. You never do.

24

The muddy guy was a preacher. He'd been camping out at some lake in Kentucky, and had to get
home and cleaned up before Sunday services. I'd say
he was wise to schedule in the extra time for that. He
said it was a small church in Carter's Valley where he
preached. I pictured those places you see on a Sunday
drive, out on the bendy back roads, people coming out
the door in their overalls and housedresses. Nothing
high or mighty about their God business. This guy was
like that. He said fishing was something he did to clear
his head. Sitting with his dogs at the water's edge listening to the birds and frogs all singing their praises, he
felt right close to God.

He asked me who all lived in Murder Valley that
I was going to see, and I said my grandmother. He

asked how long since I'd seen her. Not wanting to blow smoke on a guy that's just come from visiting God, I said I couldn't remember. Because look, if Mom was telling the truth about this lady showing up the day I was born, would I remember that?

I knew her name though: Betsy Woodall. It felt like a power to say that aloud, similar to how I'd gone all Hulk that time and claimed back my money jar. Snake handler or child beater the lady might be, but still mine to claim. People owe their kin. Her dead son should have been paying me his social security all these years, to name one example. Worst case, she'd turn out to be somebody that never existed, due to my mom making her up. Or if real, I might not find her. Knowing where my dad was buried was no guarantee of her living in the same town. Also, I might get picked up by the cops, if anybody was looking. So really there were quite a few worst cases, I wasn't stupid. None of them looked worse than the fix I was already in.

He asked how old I was, and I said going on fifteen. Again, not a lie technically, you're going on it till you get there. We shared his bag of sour cream and onion potato chips and he told me a lot of tips on fishing, which I didn't mind hearing even though I'd learned from the best. Mr. Peg knew the right lure for every hole, figuring in clouds or sun, what bugs are hatching out. His tackle box could keep a kid fascinated for life. Grown men, I'm saying all of them, wanted to know how he caught fish every damn time. His answer: You have to hold your mouth right. I never knew for sure if that was a joke. I'd sit holding my pole and watching him, working on my Mr. Peg face. Painful shit to remember now, due to being mad at the Peggots. But the preacher had a lot to offer as regards nightcrawlers versus hula-poppers. Carter Valley is far deep in the sticks, and it got dark on us, so he went out of his way to drop me off at a truck stop, thinking I'd have better luck at a place where things stayed busy all night.

He was not wrong about the all-night action. Being a godly type person, maybe he wasn't up on the particulars. I was trying to get my bearings under those weird pink lights, bugs flying all around, and this lady walks over wanting to know if I have any ice, and do I need a blow job.

She didn't mean the ice you get in the five-pound bag. That much I knew. But I was way outside my game. Gas fumes burning my brain like an aerosol-can high. This hag of a person, Jesus. Skeleton-skinny and older than you'd want her to be, given how she was dressed, like she'd got halfway through the job and quit. Black bra, little white undershirt thing, miniskirt, collarbones and stick-thin legs, putting it all out there. I told her no ma'am, but thanks anyway.

I should have run. I wish. But like any kid I'd just had it ground into me that you don't disrespect your elders, and she wasn't done with me. She said if I rubbed her the right way, she'd rub me back, and didn't I have a little something for her? Maybe an eighty, or even a forty?

Eighty or forty what, I asked her, and she said, "Honey, I'm wanting an oxy real bad."

No need to ask this time. I walked away. She followed me, which was awkward because I wasn't really going anywhere. I'd planned on taking a whiz by the road and then trying for my next ride, but after her special offer, no way was I whipping anything out. I headed for the truck-stop mini-mart and she stayed right on me, talking more or less to herself. She walked like she was having some trouble at it, with this giant bag of a purse banging her hip. My heart was jumping. It felt rude to blow her off but I did, hurrying through the glass doors, past all the shelves of snacks and souvenirs straight for the Rest Rooms sign at the back. The guy at the checkout was working his Willie Nelson angle, braids and bandanna, minus Willie's baked chill. He kept his eyes on me like I had "Runaway" on my T-shirt. My shadow disappeared in another aisle, but she was still over there. Never did I feel so saved to get in the door of a men's.

Two trucker guys were talking to each other at the urinals, so I went in a stall and peed. Then sat down on the throne, pants up, just to be someplace quiet and try to think.

"I *knew* the damn thing wasn't his, whenever I seen him with it," one of the truckers said. "I should of called the law on him right there."

"Son of a bitch is in Texas by now. You know he is."

They weren't discussing me, but I still felt jumpy as hell. The place smelled like Clorox and piss and was lit up like a nightmare. All that bright light on all those white tiles was making my ears ring. I had to stay put till my lady friend out there found other waters to fish in. Meanwhile it seemed like I should know how much money I had. I dug in my backpack and got out the peanut butter jar. Even before I stormed the fortress and got it back, I'd spent time that summer thinking about my hourly, times weeks I'd worked, which came out to a number that wasn't real. A lot of dollars. Obviously the McCobbs took a chunk for their rent, but I still hoped for something decent, in the hundreds. If I showed up at my grandmother's with cash on hand, she would see I was a person that could do a day's work and was worth something. Not trash.

I waited until the trucker guys left before I opened the jar and started pulling out the mess of cash. I was paid mostly in small bills and coins, so the jar was half full of quarters and probably weighed five pounds. My hands were shaking. I dropped some bills trying to flatten them out on my lap and sort them into kinds. The change I wasn't even messing with yet.

I heard the door open and somebody come in, but he didn't say anything so I kept going, trying to keep it all on my lap. The coins were noisy, so I set the jar on the floor. I got the ones into piles of ten and counted, a hundred and nine dollars total. Next I got through the fives, and was up over two hundred dollars before starting on the tenners. A *lot* of them. Damn. I was rich.

"Hey redhead. Come on out and play nice."

Christ Jesus, it was a lady in the men's room. Her. I held my breath as long as I could before letting it out. I heard her moving around.

"I see you got a jar of money in there. You fixing to buy me a diamond ring, honey?"

My eyes went fuzzy for a second. I held still. Then picked up the jar off the floor.

"I'm just kidding around with you, sweet thing. I'll suck your pretty cock for free. How's that sound? And then me and you can take that money and go have us a party."

I started stuffing the bills back in the jar but dropped a shitload of ones all over everywhere. Scooped it all up, jammed the jar in my backpack and zipped it, trying to be quiet. I leaned over and tried looking under the stall but couldn't see any feet.

"Whatsamatter, you mad at me honey? I didn't mean nothing. Just wanting to have fun with you is all. You look like you need to have you a little fun."

Not wrong. This was not it. I could hear her shoes clacking around. Nothing to do but sit tight. Enough of God's truckers in this world were needing to piss, surely one of them would get in here and run her off. But he was taking his damn time.

And then holy fucking shit she was looking down on me. Over the top of the stall.

I bolted. The shape she was in, it would take her a minute to get down from her perch or with any luck, fall in. I was out of the restroom and almost to the entrance before the screaming started: *Damn you little asshole give me back my money help police help me I been robbed!*

I got outside but my shirt was grabbed and I was pulled back in. The stink-eye cashier. A lot younger than Willie, stronger than he looked. He shoved me against a rack of magazines and asked where I thought I was going. I said outside. The lady was whooping and hollering about how I stole her money. He asked if we knew each other, and she said she'd never seen me before.

He eyed me up and down. She was doing the same, getting her first good look, probably surprised to learn she'd been chasing something in the line of grade-school cock.

"Do we need to call somebody, son? Or are you going to give this lady her money?"

"For Christ's sakes," I said. "It's my goddamn money."

"I don't think so," he said. "And your foul mouth isn't helping you any."

"Sorry. But it's my money."

The guy rolled his eyes. I was hugging my backpack in both arms like every friend I didn't have. He would have to kill me for it.

He looked around at the gang of late-night shoppers watching the show. "Did any of y'all see this boy mugging my customer?"

Nobody said a word. They got interested in the snacks or souvenir bottle openers at hand. His so-called customer was now in a righteous old-lady snit, giving a fair impression of sober. Somewhere between outside and now, she'd pulled on this pink housedress or shirt type thing that made her look like somebody's mammaw with a bad hand for makeup. She must have been living out of the giant purse. She buttoned her top button and sniveled. "It's my pin money I been saving up that I keep in a peanut butter jar. This here little boy grabbed the jar out of my purse."

This here little boy that one minute ago you wanted to party with, I thought. And not a person here was going to believe me. Because under the bright lights, this crap-jacked world is what it is and we were what we were: a grown-up and a kid.

"You were watching me like a damn hawk," I told the cash register guy. "You saw me go in the men's, and if you've got any eyes you saw *her* go in the men's. She followed me in there trying to talk me into a . . ."

"That's enough of that," he said, holding up his big knuckly hand. I was terrified he would put it over my mouth. Because I knew what I would do.

"Just look in his backpack thing," she said. "See if he's got my jar in there." Higher and mightier than you'd think possible for a truck-stop hooker. How could this guy not recognize her, if she was a regular? But what did I know. Maybe they shopped around.

"A Jiffy peanut butter jar," she said. "Full of dimes and quarters."

Holy shit. She didn't even know about the bills. She

must have seen it under the door while all the real cash was on my lap.

"Ask her how much money was in there," I said. "If she gets it right, she can have it."

That got her wailing. "I don't know, I don't know! It's all my spare change I been saving up forever, how am I supposed to know how much it is?"

Customers were now shuffling over to the register.

"Nobody thinks you're funny, kid. Give the lady her money and I'll let you go."

"It's my money. *Sir.* She came in the bathroom and saw me with it, and now she's scamming you, trying to get it away from me."

I tried staring him down. He crossed his arms, shook his head, all the signs of "We're done here and you are screwed." I considered bolting out the door, running away into the dark. I was faster than anybody here. And he'd get the cops out on me for sure.

"Do I need to call your parents?" he asked.

I laughed. "Good luck with that."

He didn't get the joke. "Can I see some form of iden-tification?"

"Form of identification like what?" I asked, and he named some things, driver's license, school ID, nothing I had or ever did have. It dawned on me that I could get run over flat on the highway out there, and nobody would know or care what to call the carcass. Roadkill.

By this time the whole place is on edge, crazy lady caterwauling, people shifting around in the checkout line, and Willie throws a sucker punch that doubles me over. Grabs my backpack. Professional-quality moves. I can't even catch my breath before he's pulled out the jar and is asking all high-handed, "What do you call this, you little fucker?" Shaking it in my face like now he's got me ha-ha, while the rage blows up in my gut, and the hooker bitch is all, I told you! Only she's wide-eyed, seeing we are talking money plural, major bucks. Her shrieking goes sky-high. Singing her happy song of getting shitfaced for the foreseeable month of Sundays.

It doesn't even seem real, seeing this guy put my money in her hands. With all those people watching, not one soul on my side. Nothing to do but punch the magazine rack so hard it crashes over, spilling free brochures all over the fucking welcome mat. Where the screaming is coming from, who knows, it doesn't feel like me telling this guy he's a Nazi and I worked all year at my job for that cash so he could give it to a lying fucked-up whore. Telling her off too, getting up in her little wrecked face, telling her to go buy herself a fucking overdose.

I did that. With all the hate in my heart, I told her

to go ahead and die like my mom did. Go have a party and get rid of her ugly self all alone behind a dumpster.

I walked out the door. It opened for me, and closed behind me.

My heart was pounding so hard I felt it in my eyes. I walked past the pumps where travelers in a haze of fumes were gassing up their cars. Past the big lot where the tractor trailers idled in their sleep, waiting out this godforsaken night. Shadows of people hung around the trucks, cutting their bargains. Part of me was waiting for somebody to come after me saying this hell is not real and you are not this person. It's a mistake.

That's how I left Virginia, walking down the shoulder of 26 with my thumb out, headed towards my grandmother with the exact same naked-ass nothing I'd had the first and last time she saw me.

25

My words came around to haunt me. Before another night passed, I'd be hunkered in the dark between a dumpster and the back of a gas station, wondering would I die there by morning.

I got shed of that hell-hole truck stop in a hurry, picked up by a long-hauler with a fist of skoal in his cheek and nothing to discuss. His radio was all Garth and Reba, fine, just no Willie please. I was wiped out from what had happened, so I told him I was Tennessee bound and then I guess fell asleep. Mistake. Tennessee turns out to be something ridiculous like four hundred miles long. We covered over half that before I woke up to see the sun rising over these skyscrapers like a freaking movie. One building had horns like Hellboy, I'm not even kidding.

Nashville, says the driver, and I'm like, Mother fuck, mister, *Nashville*? Simple as that. How I got farther away from Murder Valley than I'd ever been in my life so far.

This did not sink in right away. I asked if Nashville was anywhere close to Unicoi County, which was all I knew about where my dad was buried other than the valley with the downer name. The driver didn't know Tennessee counties but had a map that he unfolded all over the wheel. He gave it a good study at the same time he's roaring down the interstate, changing lanes, eating a sandwich. Scary. After a while he gave up and pushed the map at me. In due time I found Unicoi, and Nashville, and asked if he could let me out right there please because I'd spent the last five hours going the wrong way. Son of a bitch. Off to seek my fortune, and on day one I'd put myself in the hole by some-odd hundred dollars and half of Tennessee.

The trucker pulled over on an exit to dump me out. I stood breathing air that didn't smell like egg sandwich and farts. The signs said my options were three flavors of gas station, a Taco Bell, or a hospital. It was too much daylight for pissing in public, so I headed for a restroom. If I dared. I was starving. I dug in my pack for an apple and ate it as I walked along, thinking of Mr. Golly I'd stolen it from, charging it to the McCobbs. Thinking of Creaky calling us pissants if we didn't eat the apple seeds and all. Interrupting this report card of my happy life, somebody yelled "Hey brother!"

I jumped. I'd had my eye on the Phillips 66 and totally missed this couple camped by the road. The guy came staggering out of the tall weeds with his dirty Jesus hair and pale glassy eyes, asking am I his brother and am I saved. The girl tagging behind him was all hangdog, hair in her eyes, like he was the master. They both had the look that comes of hard living, clothes and skin all the same drab color of washed-out leather.

"I'm as far from saved as it gets," I told him and kept walking.

"Give me five bucks then," he yelled. "The Lord will bless you for it."

"I got no money." I didn't turn around. "Reckon the Lord's got nothing on me."

The guy came around and grabbed the apple out of my hand. He walked backwards in front of me, teasing me with it. "Repent!" he said. "Whosoever sows generously will reap!"

"Oh for fuck's sake. Really?" I stopped walking. "Somebody already stole everything I had, and you're going to take my last half an apple?"

That threw him. We stood in the empty gas station bay while he stared at my apple in his hand like he thought it might speak up and settle this. "Who is this coming from the wilderness?" he asked it. "Beneath the tree I awaked thee where thy mother was in labor and gave thee birth."

Hangdog girl came edging around behind him, looking at me and shaking her head, like: Seriously friend, be afraid.

She didn't have to tell me twice. I walked away fast while he and the apple were still working things out. Sidled into the men's, slammed the door. Luckily it was the one-person type around the back where you can lock it from the inside. It smelled like a cesspool, but I planned on staying there until homeless Jesus moved along. I stopped being hungry, due to the stink, but was dying of thirst. I drank out of the smelly tap, and sat on the trash can to face various facts. How I had no money now, zip. How hungry I would be, after I got out of that bathroom. How I was farther away from home than I'd ever been. And if I really had to go that many hundred miles on accident, *damn*: how I could have gone the other direction and been at the ocean by now.

Also, that being a long way from home isn't really your problem if you don't have one.

Twice somebody banged on the door and then went away. My brain wormed its way to the worst place and got stuck there: I'd cursed another person to die. She was probably better off than I was right now, if God or whoever was paying attention. Which probably they were.

Finally a guy came with jingling keys and hollered there'd be no loitering in his facilities, so I eased myself out and looked around. Coast clear. I told the attendant sorry, and headed out. Crossed the interstate to the other on-ramp to catch a ride headed east, but there wasn't a lot happening. An ambulance screamed by, and I thought of how one of those carried me off from home. The last day of my life I really had one. The little does anybody ever know.

The sun got high and I was still on the shoulder with my thumb out, wondering if I looked homeless yet. As long as I'd been in that bathroom, I could have changed out of the T-shirt and underwear I'd had on forever. Cars went by, business guys, moms with kids. Nobody looks you in the eye whenever they're leaving you flat. I kept thinking about the food in my pack that was all I had, so I needed to save it. Then ate the candy bars and beef jerky, one by one.

It did dawn on me, this was Nashville. Amazing, given who all lives there, Garth Brooks, Dolly Parton, etc. Carrie Underwood. Too bad, but without money the city is no place you want to be. I knew that much, even if this was only my second one. I remembered guys on the streets in Knoxville with their deer-carcass eyes and pitiful cardboard signs: "Help Please," "Hungry," "Disabled Vet." Or the name of someplace they wanted to get the hell out of there to. Bingo. I got out my drawing pad and made an amazing sign using all the colors: UNICOI.

Freaking unbelievable. The very next car to come along pulled over, a yellow VW, not a Beetle but one of those sporty sedans. Power windows. The girl driving it rolled down the passenger side and said, "Go you!" so I did. Headed the right direction at last.

Could this girl ever talk. The first subject she got onto was how she had a thing for unicorns, same as me, was that too bangin' crazy or what. I had no idea what to say, being actually not a fan, but I was not needed for this conversation. I watched the miles go by while her list of favorite unicorn items went in one ear and out the other. Bedspread, raincoat. I spent all that time trying to figure out how old this girl was. She had to be Miss Barks's age or so, because of driving a car for one thing, and for another her too-small T-shirt was showing off her bare middle part and plenty else. On the other hand, glitter nail polish, pouffy bangs, those little butterfly clip things like bugs in your hair, pretty much on par with Haillie McCobb, second grader.

She moved on eventually to TV shows, her favorite one being *Sabrina the Teenage Witch*. I told her I liked comics better than TV. It might have been the first thing I'd said since I got in the car a hundred miles before, and she was like, "Go you!" It turned out she said that a lot. If I told her I knocked off an old lady and hid her body in a thirty-foot roll-off, I'm pretty sure this girl would have said, "Go you!" She was slugging down a giant thermos of coffee and driving barefoot to keep herself awake, with her shoes up on the dash which were these red sandals with gigantic bottom parts made out of wood. All new shit to me, I was out in the world now. She'd been driving all night since Memphis, going to see her boyfriend in Knoxville that looked exactly like Paul from *Mad About You* except younger. Nerdy in the cute way.

Knoxville, damn. Probably Emmy had moved now. I would be in Knoxville soon, she'd be in Lee County, and whoever was sitting at control center of the universe, laughing his ass off.

My Unicoi sign was still on my lap, and it finally did hit me that she'd read it wrong, duh. Unicorns. The entire three hours of me in her car was a mistake. We started seeing signs of how many miles to Knoxville, countdown on me getting ditched by the roadside again like the stray cur I was: unwanted, not yet drowned. I'd gone past hungry into crazed, and was wondering if I had anything in my backpack I could sell this girl. If I'd learned one thing from Mrs. McCobb, it was that people will buy the weirdest shit. I had my marking pens, but was not parting with the best gift anybody ever gave me. I wondered if Aunt June even remembered.

Barefoot driver girl asked where I wanted left off, and I said anyplace but a truck stop. So that was that, an exit marked Love Creek. One last "Go you!" and off she flew.

The sky was dark, clouding up. I felt too beat up to stand on the shoulder getting ignored, and too hungry to think what else to do. I left the interstate and walked down Love Creek Road because, hell. You never know. It started pelting rain, and I ran for a little mini-mart similar to Golly's. I could see the lights on inside, an old guy at the counter settled in for a slow night. He would never know I'd been there. Around the back of the building, I curled up between the block wall and a dumpster where it was almost dry, and pawed through my backpack like an animal. I ate the last Slim Jim I had to my name, stolen from Mr. Golly.

The thing about him though. He loved nothing better than giving you food and watching you eat it. He made a big deal of handing customers their fried pie or corn dog, and had a sign saying people were welcome to eat in the store. It was for the reason of his childhood. This might be one of the weirder things ever.

He said his parents, sisters, and all their dump friends were so-called no-toucher people. Meaning if they touched food or anything at all, it was like, doomed. Regular people would have none of it. Same for bodies, no shaking hands. If he let his *shadow* touch a high-class person, they'd call the cops to come beat the hell out of him. He said a name for this kind of people that sounded like "dolly."

I was sure there had to be a catch. What about helping somebody get up out of the road, if they fell? No, he said, they would get run over before they'd touch you. What if you wanted to give them a present? Nope. What about money, buying something at a store? He said you'd leave the money on the counter and they'd do a prayer thing over it to clean it up, after you're gone. He and his little pals for their best prank would run up to some guy selling food on the street and put their hands all over it, so he'd have to throw it away. If they hid out long enough and didn't get killed first, they'd go back and eat it.

This was a million years ago obviously. But even after all this time, you could see how he had the biggest time handing people food. If the most important person imaginable was to come in his store, like the governor of Virginia or Dale Earnhardt, Mr. Golly could hand them a corn dog, and they would eat it. He said it felt like a magic trick. He said he never would get used to how nice Americans are to each other.

I told him yeah, I guess. But I had my doubts. A lot of people don't ever get touched. Not even high-fived after a rim shot. I should know. Little kids chase around yelling "Cooties," which are a made-up thing. But if we had a word for that type of person in America, it would get used.

I didn't die that night behind the dumpster. It took all the next day and three more rides to get to Unicoi County. First, another trucker on his radio the whole time. He left me off at the junction of 26 where I'd gone wrong the day before. Next, a peckerhead kid in a truck that was older than he was. Face like a country ham, chest like a cement block. He kept asking why didn't me and him go try and locate some women. I said no thanks, but he was kind of one-track. Finally I told him I'd sworn off hookers because the last one I tangled with took all my money. He slapped the steering wheel, laughing and laughing.

Ride three, a Caddy Deville. It was that dark brown color they call doeskin, and so was the man driving it. Another preacher. Suit and skinny tie, neat-cut hair, not young and not old. His car, definitely old. He had this way about him like whatever you've seen, he'd probably seen it too. He asked what was my burden and I told him: eleven years old without a dime, running away from nobody that gave a damn, probably headed for more of the same. He kept his eyes on the road, nodding his head, sometimes running a hand over his hair, while everything came out of me. Fighting with Stoner, Mom dying on me, getting sent to Creaky Farm, right up to two nights ago where I'd cursed a junkie hooker to die for stealing my money. He listened, now and again rubbing that hand back over his head like sweeping off the tears of heaven falling on us.

He'd heard of Murder Valley. He said he traveled pretty wide over those parts looking after his folks, and I could believe it. If he was in charge of my church, I would go. He never put on the hard sell about Jesus or anything. His only advice was to be careful in Unicoi because there were folks down there mean enough to hang an elephant. I said okay, thinking it was an expression his people had. But no. They gave the death penalty to an elephant there one time. He said if I was ever in a library to look it up, but try not to look at the photos because the sight of an elephant hanging was not an easy thing to forget. It was a circus elephant that got fed up and finally ran off after its drunk trainer whipped and tormented it to the point of going on a rampage, which, I could relate. But in the process of running off, it accidentally trampled somebody in town, and those folks were not going to be still until justice was done. Christ. Imagine the size of the noose. Plus what all they'd have to build, to hold it up.

The moral of his story was how you never know the size of hurt that's in people's hearts, or what they're liable to do about it, given the chance. I thought of Mariah Peggot carving her no-takebacks on Romeo Blevins. The preacher said this big type of hurting was the principal cause for prayer being needed in this world, as far as he'd seen, and he would sure pray for me. Then he gave me a dollar.

I got out at an empty crossroads and felt so sad watching that Caddy drive away, wishing for something I couldn't put a name to. Also a mini-mart where I could buy a dollar's worth of anything at all to put in my stomach. I'm sure he went out of his way some to drop me off there, at a little road he said ran straight on to Murder Valley. I didn't doubt that a graveyard lay at the end of it, because nobody alive was coming or going. I walked the whole afternoon into evening, with my shoes starting to come apart and blisters on both feet. I found an empty bread bag in the ditch that I tied around one of my Walmart tennis shoes so the sole wouldn't come off. I passed farms with pickups in their drives but nobody out and about except kids out tearing around on ATVs. I'd lost track of what day it was, maybe Saturday, if the kids weren't in school. I passed fields of tobacco in flower, and tried to feel happy that it wouldn't be me cutting it. A farmer came along and let me ride in the back of his pickup for a few miles before he turned off again. He reminded me of Mr. Peg by driving not a lot faster than I could walk, but my feet didn't mind the break.

I slept that night in a barn. The hay was put up, so I climbed on top of the stacked bales where I wouldn't be seen or shot at, if anybody was to come around. I was tireder than death, and fell asleep thinking of Tommy curled up in the hay, drawing skeletons. My stomach was too empty to let me float off entirely. Three or four times I woke myself up talking to Tommy, or hearing him talk to me. All mixed up in the pitch-dark, thinking I was back at Creaky Farm.

The next day was a Sunday for sure. I could tell by the people coming out of everywhere driving to church in their good clothes. Kids all washed and buttoned up in the back seats. A few families offered me rides, but I saw their faces as they got close and saw the hay-headed filthy mess I was. I said I was fine to walk, and asked how far to Murder Valley. Turns out I was there. It was a valley. Farms. And cemeteries, sure enough. The first I came across was small, in back of a little white church. I combed it from one end to the other but there was not a Woodall to be found. Everybody there had died in another age, 1950s or before.

I sat down in the middle of the graves and listened to the singing coming out of the church. The people inside sounded so glad of somebody looking out for them, never to be alone, so sure that promise was real. I'd have given an eye to be one of them.

I probably asked a dozen people if they knew any Betsy Woodall. I didn't see why I shouldn't. In Lee County if you were looking for some person by name, the odds are you'd hit a cousin or an ex by the third try. Not so in Murder Valley. Some gave me the brush-off, some jerked me around. A guy at the diner ran me off, thinking I was begging. There was a town with some stores still alive and lots more dead, boarded up. I don't think they got a lot of strangers through there. But I had no steam to go farther, so I kept asking. Even if treated like a pest.

"I got a wood-awl in my toolbox," one joker told me. Another one said sure, he knew the lady. Last seen riding a broom. This was at the feed store and hardware that wasn't open because of Sunday, but had quite a few guys hanging around the loading dock. The one that made the riding-a-broom crack was standing in the back of a pickup pitching hay bales into the back of another, with an audience of guys in overalls chewing their cuds. They all laughed. One of them piped up. "I'd say a boy that size, she'd put him on a spit and roast him for his brisket."

I was already walking away, but that made me turn around. It was like they were discussing a lady they knew, even if she was nobody you'd want to run into.

"Are you saying she's real? Like, a human person?"

They looked at each other, then me. Leery. A whole lot of pigeons were lined up on the wire overhead, all facing my way, and it felt like they were staring too. The guy up in the truck bed answered. "She's real, yessir. Reckon the jury's still out on the human part."

They all laughed. Other than the birds.

"Where would I find her?" I asked.

It was so still. I could smell hay and sweet feed. Everybody waiting.

"Bottom of Watauga Lake, if you're lucky," one of them finally said, laughing. But the others didn't. He was a younger guy, string bean. Acne that looked painful.

"You needn't to be disrespecting an old lady," I said. "What if I'm her kin?"

The jaws chewing tobacco all stopped at the same time. Damn. All these men with their hands tucked into their overall bibs, looking at me like some un-heard-of type of fish on their line. Finally an older guy said, "If that's so, I'd say you come honest by that red head of yourn."

But she didn't have red hair. According to Mom. "How do you mean?"

Now they all looked at him instead of me. Two guys headed to their trucks, wanting no part of this. One said, "Go on, Slim, give 'at boy what he's after." And Slim, which was a fat guy, said, "Look here, don't nobody say I done what I oughtn't to have," and the other ones said their opinions on feeding me to a man-eater, until my head was fixing to blow up.

"You all can go to hell!" I yelled.

That did it, they told me. All at the same time: take a left after the place that used to be the furniture store, or else used to be the schoolhouse, on a road that was called Janet Lane or the old donkey road. They didn't agree on a thing except that I would come to a yellow two-story. I left them fighting it out. Blisters be damned. I covered that last mile at a gallop.

There was no sign on the road, but a yellow house there was, lone and tall on a hill like it didn't want company. The place was kept up very decent, big windows, the yard crammed with flowers, a fence around it with a wire gate that I didn't dare open. I was filthy enough to scare the birds out of that yard. Looking at all the color and buzzing bees got me sort of dazed. That plus having not much to eat lately. For whatever reason I didn't right away see the lady pulling weeds, till she straightened up and put a hand to her back. Dang. Possibly the tallest old lady I ever saw, tanned dark, like a tobacco hand. Hard-looking in her features. No sign of the guys at the feed store being wrong. She had on a man's hat and shoes, a stout skirt. Lumpy legs in her stockings, like bagged walnuts. If she hadn't moved, I might have taken her for a scarecrow.

She saw me. Raised up her hand trowel like she was fixing to throw it. "Go away!"

I was frozen.

"I said *get.* No boys here!" She started chopping the air with her weapon.

If I opened the gate and took a step towards her, which I did, there was nothing brave about it. Just no choice. "I'm sorry," I said. "I'm your grandson."

She lowered the trowel. She had those wraparound sunglasses that old people wear, and she took them off. Underneath was another pair of thick glasses that made her eyes look like swimming fish. Green like mine, milky, surprised. She stood there looking me over from my busted shoe to the top of my wiry red head. Especially that.

"Oh, lord," she said. And sat down on the ground.

26

My grandmother had no use for anything in the line of boys or men. "Any of them that stands up to make his water," was how she put it. Bad news for me.

Her parlor smelled of stale cigarette smoke and old people and you never saw so much furniture in one room, from the olden times. The chairs had wooden legs with animal feet, and lace things on the arms so you wouldn't wreck them. She spread out a tablecloth on her sofa for me to sit on, same reason. Then pulled up a chair and looked me over, fanning herself with one of those funeral home fans with the stick handle. It was hot as hell in there, and crowded with knicknacks and whatnots all over the place. Big old clocks on the mantel, and I'm saying more than one. If you wasted this lady's time, she was going to know it.

"What are we going to do with you?" she kept asking. Like *I* knew.

She sounded like a man, with that deep type voice smokers get as their prize for the hundred millionth pack. But it was also what she said and how she said it. Like somebody that doesn't give a damn if you agree or not. In a while she got up and left me sweating like a pig, not daring to move. Came back with a plate of sandwiches and watched me stuff it all in. Not pretty.

She had questions. Starting with, had anybody ever told me I was the spitting image of my father. I told her yes, that people called me by his nickname, Copperhead. She shook her head over that like, No sir, not going there. Bad memories maybe, in the snake department. She said I'd about given her a heart attack out in the yard. "My own boy come back from the dead, is what I thought, come to me as a boy instead of a man to get back on my good side. But it won't work. Boys aren't a thing but just little men still learning what to aim at."

I wondered if this pertained to how we pissed, which seemed like a major sticking point. I told her I was sorry for all that, and asked what my father did that had put her out so bad.

"Lord, child, I don't have days enough left to tell you."

I said I hoped she wouldn't hold it against me. And that my mom had thought he was awesome, so maybe he'd cleaned up his act some in his later days. I wanted to ask if it was a true story about her coming to visit Mom, and seeing me getting born a boy.

But she was on her own track. "Church was his trouble," she said. "It started him off on the wrong foot." This was a new one on me, especially coming from an old person. I'd heard of course about the snake-handling, but she said it was worse than that. Men wanting to get back to the Old Testament, reaping virgin girls and using daughters for their slaves. "There's some I knew would have taken more wives than Jacob if they thought they'd get away with it."

"Did Jacob have more than one?" I asked. I was holding the empty plate that had a picture on it of Abraham Lincoln. I wondered how he got in here. It took some doing to keep myself from licking the sandwich crumbs off his face.

"Two wives and two concubines. You don't know the scriptures?"

It seemed like a trick question. I told her the truth, that Mom had gone sour on all that. And that as far as I knew, her son was probably not churchy either by the time he got to Lee County. Mom just wouldn't have tolerated anything like that in a boyfriend.

"You didn't know him," she said. "He died in July, and you weren't born till the fall."

I was a little freaked out by her knowing that.

"He was crazy over cars, too. He had the sickness. A car can kill a man faster than a snake. I've not driven one of those killing machines since 1961 nor had one in my possession."

This was a lot to take in. First, that my dad was into vehicles, the same fever I had in my blood. I was always that kid on the playground with my eyes turned out to the road, watching the metal roar by while the older boys yelled, Oh *man*, a Continental with suicide doors!

Second of all: since *1961*? How did a modern person not have a car?

She said she got her groceries delivered, and if she needed anything else in town, she walked. Or had one of her girls drive her, or run the errand for her. She'd raised and educated eleven girls total, some from wayward teens, a few from babies. So she was like a foster mom. She said she did it on her own steam, though, without paychecks or anything. She took a dim view on how they could mess things up at social services. I told her amen to that.

So, Mom's crazy story was true. Betsy Woodall must

have come to see her. The hell and brimstone she'd supposedly laid on was surely *not* true, just Mom's nightmares talking. But the plan of taking me was real. Did Mom agree to that? If I'd been born without the plumbing, would I have grown up here in this house as a whole different me, sitting around eating sandwiches in chairs with animal feet? My brain was pretty close to blowing a gasket.

I asked to use the bathroom, and she showed me what she called her washroom but luckily it did have a toilet. Even though a weird one that took a minute to figure out, due to a pull chain. She didn't stay to watch if I stood up.

It was a pretty terrifying afternoon on the whole. She asked if there were people I'd run away from that needed to be called. I said not really. But she pressed the point, not wanting the police on her, so I told her who needed to know I was alive and with a relative. After she made the call, she asked what on earth had possessed me to come find her.

I told her my sorry tale. I didn't want this lady being all "told you so" where Mom was concerned, it's not like she'd dropped the ball totally, so I said my life was great and everything until Mom took up with a guy that believed in educating with his fists, that bullied and brainwashed her till the day she died. Then came foster care with an old guy running a slave-boy farm. And all the while this lady's looking at me like, Told you so. I tried to work a different angle other than Men Are Satan, because honestly Mrs. McCobb was no great shakes, nor Old Baggy either. Not to mention Miss Barks that dumped me for better pay. And the truck-stop whore, definitely a bad character, but that was tricky to get into. I just wrapped it up saying I was a hardworking person and had started out with the money to prove it, but it got stolen.

All she said at the end of my story was, "That poor girl."

Wait, what? Not poor me? She didn't mean the money stealer, which I'd not mentioned being a hooker. She meant *Mom*. I was still pissed at Mom for dying on me, so I wasn't ready to take her side. But this lady seemed pissed off at her son for dying on *her*, which she said was a lowdown thing to do to Mom, leaving her in charge of a baby. I wondered if Mom had felt the same, and nixed his name off my birth certificate to get even. Definitely Mom stayed pretty torqued over whatever accident took him out, to the extent of refusing to talk about it. Maybe this lady had answers, but all the sudden she looked slumped and sad, all out of steam. We sat listening to the clocks tick. She also had a man's big round gold watch that she took out of her

pocket, looked at, wound up, rubbed against her sleeve
and put away again. A gray cat slunk out from under
a big cabinet thing and gave me the evil eye before it
oozed along the wall and ran out the door.

Then out of nowhere she stood up and said it was
time to bring out little brother dick.

Christ. *Mine?* To prove I was unfit for being adopted?

She didn't say another thing, just went out and left
me with Abraham Lincoln on my lap. In a few minutes
she came back pushing a wheelchair with a little man
in it.

Oh kay. Little brother Dick.

He was the size of a kid, but old and gray like her.
With the same Melungeon look as her, the light eyes
and dark, dark skin. These had to be my people. But
in all the ways that she was tall and sturdy, he was little
and crooked and pigeon-boned. It almost hurt to look
at him, his little feet both turned to one side, not even
reaching the footrests of his wheelchair. Shoulders
hunched one way, head cocked the other. They had the
exact same eyes though, the color of pond algae, hers
with the thick glasses and his bare-naked, staring at
me like a little child would. I sat still, letting those four
green eyes go all over me.

"This is your great-nephew," she told him. "Damon's
child."

His eyes got wider, and mine probably did too. I'd never known my name was from my father. The little man's mouth opened. It seemed like he was laughing, but nothing came out.

"A boy," she said. "Not much to be done about that, is there?"

Brother Dick's head shook sideways on its crooked track, agreeing with her, but he was looking at me with a kind of twinkle. Almost like, We're in this boat together, my man.

"What should we do with him?" she asked.

He did the silent laugh again, nodding his head. His eyes crinkled up and he worked his mouth until sounds finally came out. It sounded like "*Wortheemup.*"

She nodded. "All right. That's a good idea, I'll run him a bath. And then what?"

Brother Dick looked me right in the eyes, reading me like a book. I wanted to look away but he didn't let me. Then he looked the rest of me over like he could read that too. Every place I'd been, every damn thing I'd lost, the full shame and the pity of me. He seemed interested especially in my shoe that was wrapped in a bread bag. The nodding and working his mouth started again, like pumping a well handle until sounds came out: "*Henees noothoos.*"

"Oh, for the love of Pete. He does. I'll ask Jane Ellen

if she can hunt up some shoes to fit him. You have a sharp eye, little brother."

She marched me upstairs to a bathroom with a tub. Yes. Goddamn son of a bitch. No shower, and not just your average tub, this sucker was big enough for boiling a hog. She showed me how to turn the taps and said I'd better take a good long soak while this Jane Ellen person rounded up some things for me to wear. Supposedly she had brothers in all the sizes. I sat on the toilet thinking about the Devil's Bathtub that took out my dad, a hushed-up tale that had run rogue on my brain for all my days. I didn't know what that place looked like and never would, but probably nothing like this long white china bowl. I stared the thing down, thinking: Okay devil, it's you or me.

In the end I figured I'd probably live and be the better for a good soak, given the days of shit I needed to get off my skin. I ran the water, I held my breath, I stepped in. Eased my butt down into the deepest water I'd ever got into. Sat there, naked and not dead, letting a boatload of new info soak into my brain. My whole lifetime of having nobody, claiming a pretend mammaw, getting kicked to the back of every line while people with kin looked after their own: that was all a lie. I had *my* own. It's a lot to turn over all at once. I had no idea what came next. Maybe nothing more for my trouble than some hand-me-down shoes, but still. I had my father's name. These people looked like me. And had money, you had to think. I mean, that house. Parlors and washrooms, downstairs, upstairs, every room full of furniture. Chairs with goddamn feet. The *bathtub* I was sitting in had feet, that looked like scary bird claws. This is not a lie. If the devil had a bathtub, that would be the one.

Somebody had laid out so many clothes on the bed, it looked like an outlet store in there. I put on the most normal ones that fit and went downstairs to a big dinner cooked by my grandmother and this Jane Ellen individual, a heavyset girl with long, twisty black hair and a gap between her front teeth that she stuck her tongue in whenever she smiled, which was every time you looked at her. There was so much food. I was set to founder and die happy.

Jane Ellen was number eleven of the girls my grandmother had raised up and educated. She was in high school, worked part-time in the doctor's office, and had lived at this house since she was eight. No discussion of where she came from before that, a mystery given the brothers around someplace not far away, with clothes evidently to spare. Not a pure orphan like me. She acted like living with my grandmother was the happiest life imaginable. They both treated Brother Dick like their pet, asking his opinions on things, leaning over to wipe off his chin. Our dinner was chicken, sweet potatoes, and green beans. His was this green milkshake thing they brought him in a big glass with a straw because one of his problems was with swallowing.

Before we ate, my grandmother asked me, "Do you return the blessing?"

No idea how to pass that test. I froze. Fork stuck in a piece of chicken, heart in my gullet.

"We don't!" she said in her gruff voice. Jane Ellen and Brother Dick laughed, and we all dug in. She asked more questions, such as why Mom took up with such a bad apple after my father died. I could think of a few answers, starting with Mom having shit for brains, but due to politeness I just said lonesome I guess.

"*Lonesome!* Nothing lonesomer than getting shackled to a bully-man in his house of spite." My grandmother looked at Jane Ellen, and for once there was no smile there. I got the idea they'd both done time in the spite house. My grandmother with her snake-handling husband, and as far as Jane Ellen went, who knew. I wanted to tell them it's not just girls that end up inside four walls of hate and knuckles for breakfast, it can be anybody. Hate comes along and lays out the damn doormat and there you are. But I kept my mouth shut. It's safer knowing more about people than they know about you.

After dinner my grandmother and Brother Dick smoked cigarettes. His legs and the rest of him weren't much count, but his hands were amazing. Tiny and clean, the fingernails rounded off, holding the cigarette like a little white bird perched in his hand, singing its song of pretty blue smoke. I tried not to stare. The brother was more like a sister, and vice versa.

They put me up that night in the room with all the clothes, now folded and put away so I could sleep in the bed, which was the size of a ship, with tall wooden posts in all four corners, for what reason I have no idea. Like you might need to run up a flag in the night. The room smelled the same as the rest of the house, like dust and old people, and their doors had the old-fashioned keyholes like in the Peggot house. Maggot and I used to play around with those long iron keys because nobody at all cared if we buried them in the yard for treasure, tried melting them in a fire, or what. Not so here. My grandmother came and looked in on me after I was in bed. Then the door closed, and I heard the key turn and click. I was her prisoner.

But if I could run, where would I even go? Being locked in a room, or living my life in general, no difference. The only roads I knew were full of people that would sooner run me over than help me out. I could end up as dead as my mom and baby brother on any given day. I settled on being glad this was not the day. I had a full belly and wasn't getting rained on. Tomorrow, another story. Probably the story of getting kicked out due to being a boy.

But this Dick person she doted on, asking for his advice and even taking it. That one I turned over and over. Then remembered what she'd said about people making their water. How he did that exactly, I couldn't picture. But for sure, not standing up.

27

I t took some time for her to make up her mind about
me. She was one of these that is never going to be
wrong, period. As regards to me: (1) No flesh and
blood of hers was getting turned back over to the do-
nothings at DSS. (2) She'd sooner shoot herself in the
head than raise a boy, so. Getting her way was going to
be a problem.

Her opinion on her brother Dick: most people
thought he was brainless, but really he was the smartest person they knew. She wanted me to hang out with
him, which I was a little scared to do, honestly, due to
not knowing how. I asked what happened to him to get
in the wheelchair. She said he was born with a spinal
type of thing, but that life hadn't helped his case any
either. Whenever they were little, the boys at school

bullied him to the extent almost of death. Stuffing him in a feed bag, hiding him in a culvert, stunts like that, just for being so small he couldn't fight back. Also for liking to read and knowing the answers in school, which everybody knows is asking for it. She was the big sister and got handy at warding off the boys with whatever weapon fell to hand, but their father had other ideas and put him in a home in Knoxville. He didn't get a lick of schooling over there, so she took him books if they went to visit. The father wanted him out of sight, with people at church saying a cripple was punishment from God. Poor little Dick was there for years, until the rest of the family passed away and she could go get him out.

Damn. I was still nervous to go talk to him, but less so after she told me all that. One no-toucher kid knows another, you have to think.

His room was downstairs for the wheelchair, and usually the door stood open. The first time I went in, he didn't notice me because of reading a book. Not regular reading, I mean *gone*. He and that big book were not in this house, nor maybe this world. His room was basically a living room with a bed in it. Chairs, lamps, desk, plus some medical and bathroom stuff I tried not to look at. The desk had a lot going on there, including a kite. Every wall had shelves of more books than

I'd seen anywhere, school library included. Some few had the skinny spines and the colors I knew were kids' books. I'd not seen a lot of those. Somebody one time gave me the one where the boy is hateful and sent to bed with no supper, and in his head he's a monster and goes to this island where it's all wild monsters like him, seriously ticked off, making their wild rumpus. I loved that. But preferred comics, which I didn't see any of at all in Mr. Dick's room.

Finally I said, "Hey, Mr. Dick," and he looked up and smiled, not that surprised. He motioned me to come in. His throat or voice box was messed up, but you could get used to it and mostly tell what he was saying. It took me a minute though to get to that point. That first day I checked out his books, asking what this or that one was about, and pretended I understood the answer. I didn't find the wild boy one. His kids' books had the old-timey pictures that kids now would get bored of. He must have kept every book he ever read. I asked if those were the ones his sister brought him in the cripple home, and he said yes. Which kind of wrecked me, how tragic that was. Jesus. But here these two were now, living happier-ever-after than most.

Mr. Dick didn't take offense at much of anything, so in time I asked some nosy shit, like how did my grandmother get such a nice house (by outliving everybody else in the family), and what did the others die of (being meaner than snakes). Did he remember my dad? Yes! At the time of my grandmother fetching Mr. Dick back from the cripple home, after her husband died, my dad was a teenager. That tripped me out, to think of him walking around in this exact house, alive and a kid. I was used to thinking of my dad as another category of being, like Ant-Man or Jesus. But a real person. That looked like me. I wanted to know a million things, like what was his first car, what sports did he play. Mr. Dick was vague on that, saying just that he fought a lot with the religious father, and then without any dad in the house to lay down the law, fought with my grandmother. Then turned sixteen and moved out. What he did between leaving this house and taking up with Mom in Lee County, which was a lot of years, Mr. Dick had no idea. Possibly nobody did. I wished I could find the book of my whole dad in that house and read every page.

So, taking crap from a teenager that looked like me: Was this the start of my grandmother taking her dim view of boys? I had to ask. Mr. Dick smiled and shook his head no, motioning over his crooked shoulder like, way, way back. Of course. The big, stinking guys that shoved his little wishbone arms and legs in a feed sack, laughing their nuts off. She'd made up her mind long before she had her redheaded baby boy. He probably never had a chance.

It was after her son ran off that she'd started taking in girls for their so-called educations. I asked Mr. Dick what she taught them that they wouldn't learn in regular school. I'd already seen how Jane Ellen hit the books every single evening, homework spread out all over the kitchen table. My grandmother would quiz her or give pointers on history or even math, trig and such, which surprised me that an old person would know about. I'd thought it was a newer invention. Mr. Dick said she taught her girls to be the best in their class and not let anybody talk down to them. Same old song in other words: steer clear of the hateful boys. Mr. Dick said yes, that was it. I asked him how the girls graduated from their educations and moved out. He said generally by getting married.

It was a long couple of weeks I waited around. Some days she'd put me outside on garden chores. Jane Ellen also, if she wasn't at school or work. We spent a morning turning over dirt where she wanted to put in her fall collards. I could get Jane Ellen tickled over the smallest thing, talking worms etc. But that only takes you so far. There wasn't any TV. It was usually Mr. Dick or nothing. We guys had our laughs. Sometimes we made fun of my grandmother a tiny bit. He loved her of course, but to a certain extent, she was batshit. Our little secret.

One morning I found him wheeled up to his desk working on something, and he meant business. Not reading, he was writing. On the kite. I'd had dollar store kites as a kid, but his was not normal like that. It was homemade, out of tobacco lath and the plain paper in rolls. He said to pull up a chair, so I sat and watched him write on his kite. He had the neatest, littlest writing ever to come out of a human person. To be so crooked in his body, his lines of writing were straighter than straight. Also, slow as Christmas. It took forever for him to finish one sentence: *So wise so young, they say, do never live long.* Words that made no exact sense, but probably true. He'd written other sentences all over that kite. Like, a hundred of them. My eye picked out: *Dispute not with her: she is a lunatic.* Uh-oh, I thought, trouble with sister dear. But another one said: *I am determined to prove a villain, and hate the idle pleasures of these days.* I couldn't make heads or tails. *No beast so fierce but knows some touch of pity.* And in the center, in bigger print:

And if I die no soul will pity me.
And why should they since I myself
find in myself no pity to myself.

I asked what it was about, and he patted his book on the desk that he'd just finished. Did he aim to write out the entire book on the kite? No. Just certain parts he liked the best.

"And then what happens?"

He pointed out the window. His hand motioned up, up.

"You fly the kite?"

He nodded yes. He said after he read a book he oftentimes wanted to thank whoever wrote it, but usually they were dead. His book had a name on it I'd heard of, Shakespeare. Dead, evidently.

"So it's like returning the blessing?" I asked.

He nodded yes. Like that. Which my grandmother said they didn't do in this house. Not to God, anyway. Returning the blessings to Shakespeare and them, evidently okay. You had to reckon she was on board with it because there's no way he was going to go behind her back. Flying a kite from a wheelchair is bound to be a production.

What finally lit a flame under my grandmother's ass was school. That I wasn't going. Jane Ellen was already studying for tests, and I'd not even set a foot into— what grade was I supposed to be in? All the sudden she's acting like it's an emergency, and I'm wondering,

Where's the fire, lady? I'd laid out of school plenty, mostly due to grown-ups wanting to get some better use out of me. Not this one. She'd have no part in me growing up an ignorant bastard. She called me into her parlor and sat me down. Asked if I had any particulars on where I wanted to go. She was sitting at her big desk that I didn't know was a desk until she heaved open the top thing that rolled open. It took me a minute to work out what she meant by *particulars*.

What grade? No. School, county, state. I couldn't stay with her, but she wasn't sending me back to Lee County, if that's not where I wanted to be.

I wasn't used to choices. I only had a list of people I hoped not to see again this side of the grave, with Stoner on top. Next, Creaky and his farm. Old Baggy, but I already knew my grandmother's opinions on the DSS. What she had in mind was a different setup.

"I've been looking after children longer than you've been alive," she said, looking at me through the top of her glasses. The glass part was divided, like an F-150 two-tone.

"Yes ma'am," I said.

She turned a roller-wheel thing with cards in it that was her list of people. Names, phone numbers, but we're talking maybe a hundred cards in that thing. Imagine knowing that many people. She was an old person of course, fifties or sixties. Time enough to round up a posse.

"My girls don't usually end up staying in Unicoi," she said. "They have bigger fish to fry." I thought of what Mr. Dick said about them marrying, so maybe it was their husbands that had the bigger fish. But I was not about to pick any fights with the spider lady that had me in her web, deciding my fate. Because that's what this was about. One of her girls was going to take me in. We went over the different ones, what they did, if they had kids now. They lived all over. Two in Knoxville, one in Johnson City. Most had gone to college, she was proud of that. So naturally they'd end up in the city. I said I'd be real glad and amazed if anybody wanted to take me in, but please not the city. And my grandmother said okay, she understood.

Whatever we came up with, she said she would have to square it with Social Services on the legal stuff. I knew they wouldn't argue with her. They'd been beating the weeds for anybody to take me. Probably if she called and said, Hey, Demon is moving in with this nice ex-con child porn dealer I know, Old Baggy would say, Okay, tell me where to send the man his check.

She asked about social security, being wise to the business of me getting money for Mom being dead. I told her about the account they set up, which got me wondering about my dad as far as cash possibilities. She frowned at the wall, tapping her chin with the eraser of her pencil. She had a little bit of a mustache, if I didn't mention it. Maybe thinking the same. I liked the idea of her son owing me. It made me not so pathetic. We were all of us in this spiderweb.

But all she said finally was that I needed to stay in the state of Virginia. Legalwise.

I told her if I was going that far, I'd take Lee County or thereabouts. I didn't know I thought that, it just came out. Because of Maggot and a million other things I'd known all my life. The Corn Dog, where I swallowed a tooth. Five Star Stadium, the Generals. The mountain everybody says looks like a face, which it doesn't. Not seeing any of that again just made no sense. As far as Tazewell or other Virginia counties, all I knew about them was I wanted to see their asses kicked at the football games. Living there would make me a traitor.

My grandmother said Okay, she'd see what she could do. She had girls living over that direction, one in Big Stone Gap, one in Norton. Another one in Jonesville but sadly she was dead of the breast cancer. My grandmother got kind of woeful talking about her, tough old bat that she was. This girl Patsy was taken young, a little baby left behind. Patsy being one of the first girls my grandmother raised, so that was a while ago. She still kept in touch with the husband. She could call him up to see how he'd feel about a boy around the house. Mind you, she said, even if he says yes, this deal comes with rules. A trial run, for starters. She always paid the family something to help out, but I would be expected to be a decent young man and do my part.

Oh crap, I thought, here I go paying the rent. I did not like the sound of this house with the dead wife. Who's taking care of the baby? A husband ruling the roost on his own? There'd be nobody to remind him kids need shoes and haircuts and the shit they don't really want but you still have to have to qualify as a person, like toothpaste. New ring binders for school. Not to say I'd caught my grandmother's disease, but let's face it, guys can be dicks.

"He's a schoolteacher, so that's good," she said. "I think he's civics, or health. Land, it's been an age." She was flipping through her wheel of people, looking for his card. "And something with the sports. I don't know about that, but he'd not let it get in the way of your lessons. He's a pretty good one. Here he is, Winfield."

Dear Lord in Heaven. Sorry about the million times I took your name in vain because I didn't think you were actually there. Holy God. My grandmother was picking up the phone to call the coach of the Lee High Generals.

I was leaving them. Mr. Dick, my grandmother, and whatever was left of my dad in the graveyard she took me to see. There wasn't but a flat, shiny marker on the ground with his real name and how long he lived, start to finish. It spooked me to see my first name on a grave. It could have been all me, first and last, if Mom had forgiven him. The graveyard was behind a church that looked abandoned, down the road past her house. The weeds were a sight. She put on her gloves, got down on her knees, and put it all straight. She'd brought a jar of flowers from her yard to set down on him, and collected up jars that were left there before. I'd say she cared about my father more than she let on.

It was that fall type of day where the world feels like it's about to change its mind on everything. Cicadas going *why-why-why*, the air lying still, all the fight gone out of summer. My head kept telling me *Run! Go now!* But I didn't know from where, to what. She got up from her weeding, settled her hat on her head, and we walked back to the house on the gravel shoulder. She took big steps like a person crossing plowed ground, and I followed behind. It felt like she was mad at me. I still didn't know what to call her. After all my years wishing for a mammaw, I finally had one and the shoe didn't fit. I called her yes-ma'am. The sun was behind us. I shifted so my shadow touched her, falling across her skirt and fast, lumpy legs. No good reason.

Back at the house I put the clothes, toothbrush, and other things my grandmother gave me in the suitcase she gave me, wondering if this stuff was Demon now, and if so, was I erased. It's not that I didn't like the clothes or the suitcase. They were fine. The next day Jane Ellen was driving me to Kingsport, where Mr. Winfield would meet us at noon in the Walmart parking lot. After all those days and nights that about had killed me getting here, the trip home wouldn't take but an hour and a half. Crazy. That's Lee County for you. It pulls you back hard.

I went downstairs to Mr. Dick's room. He didn't like to start a new book till he finished his kite on the last one, but he wasn't doing that. Just looking out the window. I said I'd miss hanging out with him, and he said the same. I wondered if I would ever see him again. The Coach Winfield deal could fall through, of course, but one way or another it looked like I was Virginia bound. Would they come see me? Given her whole cars-equal-death thing, not likely. I told him I'd call on the phone or write, even though I had no idea how to buy a stamp or any of that. We sat quiet a minute. I wasn't one for hugging, or else I would have.

The clouds had bellied up since morning and a stout wind was kicking up outside, turning the leaves upside down and silvery. Mr. Peg always said that meant rain on the way. I asked Mr. Dick if his kite was ready to fly, and he said it was. Then let's do it, I said. I got a shiver in my spine. Maybe that's what my brain had been telling me all day: *Run. Go fly a kite.*

He looked pretty shocked, but he said okay, he just had one more thing to write on it. I tried to be patient, with him being the slowest writer. He said this one was from a different book, some words he wanted to put up there for me. He wrote them at the very top:

Never be mean in anything. Never be false.
  Never be cruel.
I can always be hopeful of you.

If that was from him to me, it was more man-to-man talk than I'd ever had in life so far. It beat the two-cents-equals-happiness thing, all to hell. I said, Okay, let's do this thing.

I didn't ask how he usually did it, who helped him or what, because I had my own plan. He wheeled outside, down the porch ramp and onto the flagstones of the front sidewalk, this being all the farther his wheelchair could go. But still in the yard. No running room. He motioned me to take the kite and go on with it, but I said, My man! We can do better. I wheeled him off the sidewalk onto the grass, which wasn't hard with him weighing probably not much more than a bale of hay. Out over the bumpy grass we went, Mr. Dick working his mouth until what came out was "*Heee, heeee!*" Which I took to mean *Hell yes!*

I unlatched the back gate and wheeled him plumb out into the stubble of the hayfield behind the house. Then the going got pretty rough, wheelchairwise, so we didn't go far, just to where I could get the runny-go I needed to send that sucker to the moon. The clouds were scooting by, throwing shadows like a herd of wild monsters rumpusing over the field, and I was right there with them. I hefted the kite and let out the string, more and more till it was not but a speck in the sky. I could feel rain starting to spit on us, and who cared. Let it thunder.

The string was pulling hard in the wind, but I towed it back to Mr. Dick and put it in his hand. "Hang on tight," I said, and flopped on the ground beside him, panting like a dog. He was quiet, holding that string and kite with everything he had. The way he looked. Eyes raised up, body tethered by one long thread to the big stormy sky, the whole of him up there with his words, talking to whoever was listening. I've not seen a sight to match it. No bones of his had ever been shoved in a feed bag. The man was a giant.

28

We sat in the parking lot waiting. Me with my gut full of rocks, Jane Ellen with her workbook opened out on the steering wheel, doing math problems. What is the deal with women, somebody tell me. A day can be going to hell in a hornet's nest, you're fixing to lose your breakfast, but she's still going to get her homework done.

"What if Coach Winfield doesn't show?" I asked.

"He will." Her pencil never stopped moving. I guess I didn't either. She'd already told me to stop fooling with the glove box before I busted it. An '89 Comet is what she drove.

"What if he doesn't?"

She erased something, then turned over her wrist to

look at her watch. "He's not that late yet. We got here early."

I wanted to go home. Which was nowhere, but it's a feeling you keep having, even after that's no place anymore. Probably if they dropped a bomb and there wasn't any food left on the planet, you'd still keep feeling hungry too.

"Je-*sus*," I said. A car had pulled in, and the guy getting out of it was *the* weirdest-looking human I ever saw, not counting comic books. Stick legs, long white arms, long busy fingers that twined all over him. Running through his hair, wrapping around his elbows while he stood looking around the parking lot. A redhead, but not my tribe. He was the deathly white type with the pinkish hair and no eyebrows. That skin that looks like it will burn if you stare at it.

"Great day in the morning." Jane Ellen shut her workbook.

"Snake Man to the rescue," I said.

She couldn't help herself smiling, with that tongue stuck in the gap of her teeth. We both stared, rude as you please. His car was a late-model Mustang with a big trailer hitch, normal. But this guy, my Lord. He stood there hugging himself with those arms, looking around. Then looking at us. He walked around to the side of us, checking out Jane Ellen's car.

"What's he looking for?" I whispered.

"I don't know," she whispered back. "What does a snake eat?"

She had her hand on the key, ready to start the engine. But then he came straight at us and we froze. Stuck his hand in the open window on my side. We both reared back.

"I reckon you all are Betsy Woodall's." Creepy voice. Too quiet.

"Who wants to know?" I asked.

"Coach Winfield got tied up this morning. Saturday practice can run real long."

"Then who are you?" Jane Ellen was getting back on her game. Not about to turn me over to some random freak outside Walmart.

He waved a long hand in front of him, like shooing flies. "I'm nobody. Assistant coach." He leaned farther in and reached his hand across to Jane Ellen, causing her to rear back again. "Ryan Pyles," he said. "They call me U-Haul."

She stared at the freckle-zombie hand. "Why is that?"

He pulled back his hand, ran it through his stringy pink hair. We waited.

"I move equipment for the team. Your pads, helmets, Igloo coolers. Coach wants it hauled, I'm the one gets it there." He moved his head backward on his neck like he had extra bones in there. The man was a reptile. "I didn't hitch up the trailer. You got a lot of gear, son?"

Being no son of his, I said nothing. He stuck his head in the window, checking out my one suitcase on the back seat. "Okay, let's get 'er done."

I looked over at Jane Ellen like, *Don't feed me to Snake Man!* And she was like, *What am I supposed to do?* She couldn't go back to Murder Valley with the boy-cargo still in tow, I knew that. Probably she'd get her education extended by twenty years.

I went, but not without a fight. Jane Ellen marched him over to a pay phone and made him call somebody to vouch. They didn't get Coach Winfield, but some secretary at the school evidently said, Yes, that sounded right. U-Haul Pyles will get the boy where he needs to go.

That turned out to be a mansion, sitting on a big hill overlooking downtown Jonesville. This place had a lot more going on than a normal house, extra parts jutting out with their own separate roofs and windows. Not a castle but headed that direction. Which stood to reason. If Lee County had a king, he'd be the Generals coach. U-Haul geared down to take the steep driveway, and all I could think was, No way am I going in. A *mansion*. I wouldn't know how to act.

"Home sweet home," he said, in this eat-me tone. He cut the engine and turned a glare on me that scorched. His brown eyes were almost red, like little round windows out of hell, no eyelashes for curtains. How did he look in the mirror with those eyes? He grabbed my suitcase, and with me thinking, *Shitshitshit no escape plan as usual*, I followed him in the front door.

Inside was a shock. It looked like a regular house, with junk all over the place. Boxes of cleats, resistance bands, rolls of athletic tape, dumbbells, a busted car mirror. An exercise bike in the middle of the room with clothes draped on it. There were certain castle aspects for sure, a gigantic fireplace chimney with the mantel made of a sawed log. And a gigantic dangling light over the gigantic dinner table, where nobody had eaten I'm going to guess since the invention of forks. Amongst the piled-up papers and magazines I counted three pairs of sunglasses, more dip cans than you want to know about, and one Nike Air Max. On the table. It made me miss Mom.

U-Haul said Coach would be down in a minute and to excuse him because he had things to do in Coach's office. He shook my hand in a sneak attack, then slithered off towards the back of the house. I felt slimed. I wished for a bathroom where I could wash my hands. There was a big staircase with the curved railing like in a movie. I wondered if it was the same pigsty all over, or just concentrated here in the end zone around the front door. The one tidy spot was the mantel with a photo of a girl, or lady actually. Young. Sad-looking, apart from having the hair explosion thing from the eighties going on, which no girl would be caught dead in now. So, she probably was. Dead. The tragic wife raised up by my grandmother and taken young. Just a guess.

I turned around and freaked out, due to a kid looking at me with the exact same face, the photo come to life. Scrawny though, almost my height but skinnier, wearing one of those dweeb flat caps that would instantly get a guy poundcaked at school, if not for the badass leather jacket and Doc Martins. Those things cost, meaning there's backup somewhere, so watch who you're punching. This kid looked sad, a little soft, a little scary. All of those, at the same time.

"Hey," he said. "I'm Angus."

"Angus like the cattle?"

His eyes shot sideways, and back. "Exactly like that."

"So, I guess I'm supposed to be staying here a while. With Coach Winfield."

"Yeah, I know. He's my dad."

Oh, the little orphan baby. Reset. I asked him what grade he was, and he said eighth.

"So you're on the JV squad?"

He looked me over with his big gray eyes like he's reading the instruction manual of me. With the plan of taking me apart or putting me back together, I had no idea. I started thinking over my options on who to call if they kicked me out of here before dark.

"No," he said finally. "Tragedy of tragedies. Not on the JV team."

Coach Winfield came down the stairway like something dumped out of a bucket, making a big man's racket, talking before he's even in the room. "Hey buddy, great to see you, sorry, practice ran long, we've got the Vikings Friday so you know what that means, Betsy said you're a Lee County boy, is that right? So you know the territory . . ."

He stopped at the bottom of the stairs, checking me out. He was big and broad, paunchy in that certain way of guys that start out all muscle before the beer takes over. Red cap, big black eyebrows. I couldn't honestly say if I recognized him from the games, or just recognized the red windbreaker. "How old are you, young man?"

I was so used to lying, I actually had to think. "Twelve next month."

He let out a long whistle.

"Sorry," I said.

"Not a problem. That's what she told me, starting middle school. I was expecting a different make and model. You look like a linebacker, son."

"Yes sir," I said, with my stomach doing a little *hell-yes* dance. God in his heaven kicking a field goal and the angels doing cartwheels in their twirly skirts. Home sweet home.

We didn't eat at the giant table piled with crap, thanks to the Winfields having another table in the kitchen where it was a lot tidier on the whole. A lady named Mattie Kate set out the meat loaf and coleslaw and finished wiping down everything in sight with the tail of her apron, then said good night and left the three of us to eat our supper.

They didn't say any blessing, just dug in. With Angus still wearing that hat at the table, and Coach in his, so this was not going to be one of those houses with rules. Maybe different ones, though. Too soon to relax. I fed my face, probably too much, too fast. The windows were open and I could hear a tractor and smell the hay that somebody was cutting outside. I was glad it wouldn't be me putting it up in the barn. I wondered if I'd get sent to a farm again, after here. Probably yes.

I'd started to see how being big for your age is a trap. They send you to wherever they need a grown-up body that can't fight back.

We did more eating than talking, with Angus keeping the big gray eyes on me at all times. Giant eyes like a manga comic. Coach for his part had giant teeth, like *too* big, some way. Too flat across, too white. He didn't smile much, and it looked like those teeth would hurt his lips if he tried. He asked the awkward things adults do if they're making the effort, like what was my favorite subject in school. I told him lunch, which wasn't a joke, but he laughed. I asked how the season was going so far, since I'd missed the first games. What I wondered was, How in hell is your son not doing JV football? It seemed like that would be a given. I mean, yes, I noticed the small hands and skinny shoulders, but still. It's only JV. They'll let anybody sit on a bench.

Afterward we piled up the dishes for Mattie Kate to do in the morning and Coach told Angus to get me settled in my room, which surprised me. My own room. I figured we'd be bunking together, but no. We went up the stairs and then more stairs and down a hall to a room that was one of the castle-type parts of the house, rounder than it was square. Six walls, painted dark green, white window trims. Three of the walls had huge windows.

"You can use that dresser," Angus said. "Mattie Kate was supposed to clear it out if she had time. If you find anything in there, just throw it in the hall and she'll get it tomorrow."

"Okay," I said, which I wouldn't. Throwing things on the floor for somebody else to deal with, seriously? Whatever else might be said about me, I was house-broke. There's no tooth fairy living here, so pick up your damn shit, being basically the motto of foster care. How Mom got through it, and still the way she was? One of God's mysteries.

Angus started dragging open the big windows, saying it was stuffy in there, but I didn't care. The smell reminded me of the Peggots' attic. In back of the house the view was hills and hayfields as far as I could see. The guy was still down there on his tractor, work-ing up and down his field in the yellow light of day's end. The middle window looked down the driveway, and the front one looked across the top of Jonesville to a big hill behind it. I could see why they built houses like this, back in the day. Whoever launched an attack, you'd see them coming.

It was the best room I'd ever been in, and also the best house. I said so, but Angus just shrugged. "It's too much house for us."

"I didn't think there was any such thing. Like too much money or too much food."

"A person can eat too much. Obviously. People die of it."

"Sign me up," I said.

Again the big sad eyes, puddles on a sidewalk.

"Kidding," I said. "Sorry. I won't eat you all out of house and home or anything."

"I don't think you'll get a choice. Dad likes the look of your frame, so he's going to bulk you up like his new prime steer."

"Snap," I said. "Next comes the slaughter."

He almost smiled. "That's one word for the game. Said you, not me, for the record."

"For the record, I never heard of anybody that died of being a linebacker. Maybe just fang-banged into a coma by horny cheerleaders."

His half smile yanked back in so fast, like a slug if you touch his little horns. All pulled back inside the pissed-off black leather and the blank eyes. Shit. I was piling stupid on stupid here, but didn't know how else to go. As far as I'd seen, the basis of friendship for guys past the age of bedwetting is trash talk. Throw "fuck" into any sentence and you're dead hilarious.

"Tell your dad thanks for the bed," I said. All else

fails, try kissing up. "The last place I was living, I got the floor of the laundry room."

"At Miss Woodall's? She made you sleep on the floor?"

"No, not there. You know her? My grandmother?"

My grandmother. It felt like casually pulling a hundred bucks out of my pocket. I saw something move behind the eyes of Angus, like, *Damn*, dude. One hundred bucks.

"My mother used to take me to see her," he said. "But I was too little to remember."

Right. Before all the cancer and the death.

Angus showed me a bathroom that was for me and nobody else. Shower-tub combo. I'd find a way. His room and his dad's were one floor down. I asked how many rooms were in the house total, which he didn't know. Unbelievable. Counting is the first thing I'd do. I asked did they ever switch around.

"Why? You don't like the room you're in?"

"No, I mean you or your dad. Like if you got bored and moved into another one."

He stared at me.

"Just every so often trying out different windows. I mean, it's all here, so why not?"

"I might not be able to find him, is why not."

"He's a pretty big person to lose track of," I said.

"You'd be surprised."

We were in the bathroom, both facing the mirror. I tried out his same medicine, staring him in the eyes. "I guess you could, in that holy hash of mess downstairs."

I saw him light up with a little bit of fight. Barely, but seeable. Underneath the screw-you was a kid that wanted to protect his dad. Maybe more than he got protected back.

He went downstairs to get towels and things for me, which took so long I forgot about it. I unpacked the clothes out of the suitcase and put them in the drawers. Empty. Go Mattie Kate. Shoved the suitcase under the bed, looked out all three windows: the guy *still* mowing hay, streetlights on in Jonesville. Put on a clean T-shirt and got in the bed. I was beat up. Almost asleep before Angus knocked on the door and came back in to say he'd left my stuff in the bathroom. I sat up spooked, like in the days of little Haillie popping up out of nowhere.

"Okay. Thanks."

Angus was altered. Ready for bed, out of the jacket and the hat, in some kind of white stretch outfit that showed the build, skinnier even than I'd thought and small through the waist. A lot of curly, sort of moppy blond hair. What I am saying is, girl hair. A girl build.

We stared at each other, then the door shut and

Angus was gone, leaving me to stuff my blown-out brain back in my head and remember what all I'd stupidly said to him, to her. I couldn't. There was too much. Other than, was she on the JV football squad, pretty memorable. Fang-banging cheerleaders. Had I said I thought we'd be sharing the same room?

I couldn't fall asleep for wondering how I was so stupid. I guess I'd not been around girls much lately, especially not in those boots. But still. The second I knew, it was plain as daylight. And my mind couldn't stop running back over every single asshole thing I'd said to Angus, the girl. Starting with, "Like the cattle."

29

The deal here was, I would get a do-over. Like
Stoner did, walking out of our mess to start his
clean slate. I'd planned on hating his guts permanently
for it. Now came my turn, and I kind of hated my own.
How was it fair to Mom, being still alive with all new
everything: clothes, room, killer amazing castle house.
New grade in a new school where I was the new boy.

The house alone, Mom would have killed for a peep
inside of. She used to tell me how she and her friends
would lay out of school and break into teachers' houses
in the daytime to see what booze they had, what was in
their bedroom drawers, like porn, vibrators, etc. I was
living with a teacher. God alone knows what was in his
bedroom, but you could open a store with the crap he
threw on his living-room floor. Plus beer in the fridge,

Jim Beam in the cabinet. Given how early he went to bed, the man was just asking me to teach him how to share.

But that didn't make life easy. At Jonesville Middle they had two little cement bulldogs on towers out front, like guarding the place, and on it went from there as far as being baby-town. An office lady in her clack-clack heels walked me to my new homeroom, and I'm thinking, Lady I hitchhiked to fucking Nashville, you think I can't walk down this hall by myself? All these puppy eyes looking at me like, *New boy! Please don't hurt me!* Was it a town versus country thing, I don't know, but these kids were oversize Haillies and Brayleys with their wet-combed hair and buttoned-up shirts, some with breakfast crumbs still around their mouths, I swear to God. Sixth graders. No comprehension.

Did they know more than me as regards pronouns and subjunctions, Roman civilization etc.? Yes. Being checked out of school mentalwise for the last year and then some, I was so far behind it looked like a race with my own ass. But the weirdness wasn't in what I didn't know. It's what I *did* know. How to watch your back at all times. What a hooker means by "fun" and an asshole means by "discipline" and a caseworker means by "We're working on it." And *money*. Christ. Watching these kids pull it out of their pockets in fistfuls of fives or ones or tens, holding out the whole wad for the lunch lady to pick through, like they don't know the difference. Or don't care. Outside at recess, betting and losing actual quarters over utterly ignorant shit, like who holds his breath longest or will that bee fly up Miss Wall's dress and sting her twat.

What stood between this pack of blind puppies and me was the education of how many batteries drained, bags of garbage hauled, hours clocked in and out, makes the difference between a oner and a ten. I was inked with the shit-prints of life: thrashings, lies told, days of getting peaced out on weed, months of going hungry. I didn't want to be like these other kids. But I didn't want to be the freak fish out of water anymore either, dead sick of that. Feeling every minute like somebody's going to call me out, tell me I've got no business walking around that place in expensive new shoes, and should go back to whatever shithole I crawled out of.

The Air Maxes, new jeans and all that, another story of weirdness. Angus took me shopping. Coach headed off to Saturday practice and said to go get me what I needed. Nobody asked me, we just took off in U-Haul's Mustang, Angus up front with Snake Man, me in the back seat fixing to shit myself. How far would this adventure go before they found out I had smoke-all in the way of cash, being the question. Pretty far, was the answer. I tried telling Angus I would stay and wait while they did their shopping, but she said not to be an idiot, get out of the car. U-Haul stayed. I followed Angus into Walmart, down one aisle after another with her throwing stuff in the cart. First groceries. What did I like to eat, she wanted to know. Anything that's not rotten, the more the better, I said. She rolled her eyes like I was purposefully being a dick.

"I'm serious," I said. "You don't want to know some of the crap I've eaten before."

"Like what?" She frog-eyed me. "Human livers? Used Tampax?"

Jesus. I meant things like the Mr. Goodbar I ate after it ran through the McCobbs' washer. But this Angus individual was like, frayed-electric-wire level of shocking. I think the boy version worked better, except for that not being a person. She leaned into the cart with her elbows sticking out and tore around the store playing her sick game. She'd hold up a box and yell, "Which do you like better, yo—this, or toe jam? This, or shark piss?"

We left some shoppers ready to lose their lunch and moved on to menswear. I told Angus I wasn't buying any clothes.

She stared. "What is your *deal,* dude?"

"No deal. Thanks all the same."

She shook her head like I was a mental case. Which pissed me off. I didn't yet know the rules here, fine, but I couldn't see Angus getting to treat me like a dipshit.

"I like what clothes I have, okay? I'm good. Can we just go?"

"You're *good*. This is the look you're going with, then. Color-blind scrub opens up a can of *Wayne's World*."

"Screw you!" I said. I laughed though, because the other choice was punching a girl, not allowed. Plus she wasn't wrong. That day I was passable, Bugle Boy T-shirt and army jacket, but I'd been sporting some too-wide collars and a lot of acid wash. Baby-shit-brown tennis shoes, shaped wrong, like shoes from some other century. "It's not really my stuff," I said. "I mean, it is. But I got it all free from this girl Jane at my grandmother's."

"You're going for drag queen then, in some Jane person's clothes."

"Not hers, her brothers'. Their hand-me-downs."

"Shut up. Miss Woodall has boys living in her house?"

"No. I never technically saw any brothers. Just their clothes."

Angus looked me up and down. "May I say the brothers of mystery have handed you down some weird-ass apparel?"

I told her to go to hell, for real. I didn't feel like explaining how you get used to people looking at you like trash, so it's hard to care what kind of trash you put on the trash every morning. Or that my other choice of shoes came with a bread bag. I told her I wasn't color-blind, not that it was any of her business. Just not picky.

"So be picky. Clothes make the man. What's the Demon angle?"

A coach's daughter in a castle house gets to have angles. It was not the flat cap today but an old-time man hat with a tiny orange feather in the hatband. And orange Chucks. So like, matching, she'd thought it out. But I had a boy brain, zero cash, and no possible Demon angles. Our cart was blocking traffic around a marked-down underwear rack, and Angus gave no shit.

"Shoes," she said. "Everything starts there. Essay question. What shoes would you want to wear to the ass-kicking of your worst enemy?"

It was tempting to picture that. Enemies I had. For kicking Stoner across a parking lot, right away my mind started drawing in extra features the shoes would need, like poison-dart spikes and jet packs for a quick getaway. Nothing real, in other words. I couldn't give any answer, and she acted again like I was being a purposeful irritant.

"Just say!" she yelled. "What the hell kind of shoes would make you happy?"

"Fine, Air Maxes!" I yelled back at her, because who wouldn't. "But I'm not getting any the hell kind of shoes today because I'm fucking broke, okay?"

Some shoppers hit their brakes, like they'd never heard an f-bomb before. To be fair, there were kiddies about. I notched it down. "I don't have any money," I said.

Her gray eyes got that water look they could have. She seemed worried, maybe running her mind backwards over her morning with this new broke-ass version of me, just like I'd had to do after the girl surprise. "Sorry," she said, and for once I didn't mind that word. It looked good on Angus. I'd been waiting for it.

"Forget it," I said. "Can we just get out of here?"

"No. I'm saying, sorry for not getting straight with you. My bad." She whipped a slice of silver out of her pocket and tilted it up and down in the light, like a mirror flashing code. "Meet the Master," she said. Kissed it, put it back in her pocket, and said yes, we were getting out of there. I would be kicking no ass in Walmart Nike knock-offs.

We flew that credit card all over the damn county. From Walmart Supercenter to Shoe Show to T.J.Maxx, ferried around by Snake Man. No cash needed, the Master did the talking, or in some cases just Coach's existence. Like at Hardee's for lunch. We walked in the door with a freaking force field of worship around us. Guy at the counter didn't even ring us up, just said on the house as usual, say hi to Coach. The manager came out to say the same, and asked if Coach was putting in some person to sub for QB1 with the elbow injury. U-Haul told him he was not really in a position to say, being only assistant coach, but don't be surprised if that substitution happened. Everybody in the place kept watching us while we ate. Like, if we dropped a fry on the floor, they might grab it up for a souvenir. Did I like all the attention? Maybe, if nobody knew the real me and I could pass for some person that just normally wore Air Maxes without a speck of dirt on them. U-Haul, definitely yes, on liking the attention. Angus was so chill, you couldn't guess.

Angus shocked me up one side and down the other. By being into cars, for one thing. It started with seeing a '57 Nomad, and after that we had a contest of naming anything cool we saw. U-Haul knew a lot, but damned if Angus didn't know her share. This chick was not your average. You'll say sure, being raised with a dead mom, but guess what, I grew up with a dead dad and you won't see me doing girl shit. Plus they had this Mattie Kate individual around the house at all times. Not just for chores, she'd sit with you in the kitchen after school and drink Cokes and talk if you had questions, which I had a few. Should I be doing my laundry, making my lunches? Answer: No. She did all that. I told her I was pretty used to doing everything for myself like laundry and worst case, paying the rent. She laughed and said not to be putting her out of her job. She said mine was just to be a little boy. Weird. I'd not had that job before.

She knew I was no tiny tot, though, because she asked if I needed her to get me an electric shaver. (Embarrassing, but yes.) And got me a thing of Old Spice deodorant without asking did I want it. (More embarrassing.) She was just this extra-nice lady with no husband and a little boy that played Pop Warner football. She had wrinkles around her mouth and wore the elastic-type pants like an older lady but not totally over the hill, you could tell. Her eye makeup she did like bird wings. The point being, if Angus had questions about girl-type things, vacuuming or eye makeup, she had somebody to ask. Pretty sure that didn't happen. Angus seeming more like the type to go get inked with some me-not-pretty thing like a barbwire necklace. But she picked no fights with

Mattie Kate or her dad. Nor even U-Haul, which was a concern. The man oozed slime. He was always touching and petting his face and grimy red hair and other things that were just wrong, like the seat of the booth where Angus had been sitting, after she got up to refill her drink. Creepster. But he'd been working for her dad forever, and people get used to things.

She did know he was a liar. That much she told me. The real assistant coach was Mr. Briggs, a paid teacher that taught history at Jonesville Middle and was JV coach, plus helping out with the high school team. In practices he coached defense, where Coach worked mainly with offense. U-Haul was just an errand boy, paid part-time out of the booster funds. Angus said he acted more important than he was, and got away with it by saying he was "nobody" while pretending he's assistant coach. Like bowing down and sweeping his lies behind him.

We got on okay, myself and Angus. After our tricky start. Fashion advice, no thanks, but she told me what to look out for at school, being two grades ahead, and I told her some of the history of me. How was I related to Betsy Woodall, where all had I lived. This would be after her dad went to bed at seven p.m., seriously. We'd do homework and watch TV in this upstairs bedroom with no bed in it that she called the den. Just beanbag chairs and the TV she rescued from the sports tornado downstairs. She had an absolute rule of no athletic equipment allowed in her den, penalty of death. As far as other entertainments, popcorn fights, throwing M&M's at each other's mouths, pretty much anything went in the Den of Angus. I felt bad for Mattie Kate having to clean up, but Angus said the same thing, she needed her job so don't take it away.

It was hard to get used to being tended to like that. And to rules. Homework gets done, period. No running around on school nights. Pharm parties, not on your life. I didn't even bring up the idea of getting into her dad's liquor. Angus had her whole tough act and called a lot of shots in the house, helping to make the grocery list, calling to get the heater fixed, that type of thing. Coach wouldn't notice till the fridge went empty and the pipes froze, the man was just all football. But Angus had no big worries that I could see. Everything in that house got taken care of, me included. If I stayed here, would I turn into one of these Jonesville Middle School babies? Not something to worry about, I knew. Nobody ever kept me that long.

30

I'd dreaded middle school for the reason of running up against bigger guys that might pound me. Up to that point in fourth and fifth being the tallest, I was the type of loser that people could hate on but were scared to mess with. The world turns though. School dumps you out from top drawer to the bottom again. It's true Jonesville Middle was a litter of pups, but not without its big dogs. In time I sniffed them out, hunkered around the smoking barrel, lazing in back of class with their big untied shoes propped up on empty desks. Guys that repeated enough grades to roll into eighth with respectable sideburns and pack-a-day habits. They could break my ass.

But sixth grade had tricked me out as a new Demon. I was still me but with sixty-dollar shoes, so. A loser in disguise. Living with Coach was like packing heat. I walked down the hall and the crowd parted. Not like pee-yew, I smell foster-boy ass, but like, Wow. There he goes.

Nobody at first knew what I was to Coach exactly. Me included. Not his kid, but he was the one to sign my permission forms, like was I allowed to watch the Family Life film. Not that he knew. We'd bring our forms to supper and he'd sign off with his eyes under those woolly eyebrows watching a replay in his mind, jaw grinding his dinner like a cow on grass. He'd have given the okay on me watching porn in study hall. Not saying I did. But if I was anybody's to claim, I was Coach's.

And then I was more so, because he let me help out at Saturday practice. Only as errand boy of the errand boy, but even still, freaking amazing. To be chalking hash marks and dragging sleds and body shields, me, Demon. On the grass of the Five Star Stadium where Creaky took us for Friday-night prayer meetings and we screamed for a Generals bloodbath. *Inside* the Red Rage field house, in the presence of greatness. Or the wet towels and jockstraps of greatness.

I only did Saturdays, not after school, with Coach having homework rules and Angus being the enforcer. She didn't like me being at practices, but Coach said a boy can't stay cooped up, so. I couldn't put my own clothes in the washer at the house, but I bagged up dirty team laundry like my life depended on it, and watched varsity guys running drills. Figuring out plays if I was able. Fast Forward was long gone, but these guys had good hands, hard hitters. Coach at practice was a different human. Knees bent in a crouch, eyes sharp, he'd watch guys run a drill or complete a pass, and I'm saying he *saw* them. Memorized them. Picking out a fumble or even the risk of one, yelling at them to run it again and not screw up this time. Run it again, they did. Twenty times if need be. Where was sleepwalker dad? That guy we had to step out of the way of so he wouldn't walk through us like doors? Not in the Five Star Stadium. There he fired on all cylinders, riding his Generals till they gave him the shine he wanted, then telling them they were the best of men. Clapping them on the back as he sent them off the field to go shower up.

And one of the men was me. I was three years from any shot at Generalhood, and miles from knowing my ass from any hole in the ground. But one day after he dismissed the team and we're loading up equipment, Coach yells, "Damon, heads up!" and here comes a ball at my face. I catch it, goddamn miracle, and go to put it with the other balls but no, Coach says let's throw some passes. Him throwing, running me down the field to see what kind of legs I have. What kind of wind. Now let's see your arm. I'm shitting myself trying to remember anything Fast Forward ever showed me about holding the ball, using my field of vision. Giving my all.

My all was no great shakes, but Coach made me want to die trying. The big teeth finally fit his mouth, and busted out shining like sun through clouds. Unforgettable. The way he looked past my arms and legs into the soul of the General I might be, totally tuned in on me and the ball between us, curve of a wrist, turn of a head. And I saw the General he'd been on this field once, pumping a crowd, flashing those teeth at some girl in the stands that would steam up his truck in the postgame ceremony. Angus's mom, I thought. Wondering, was she a cheerleader or what.

But no. Being one of Miss Betsy's girls, no window steamer. Angus said they'd met at UT Knoxville where he went on a football scholarship. Running back, one year, then tore up his shoulder and had to major in education. I wondered if Angus even knew this other person her dad woke up to being at practice. I hoped she did. Then I thought about it, and hoped she didn't.

School took a wild turn, thanks to this one teacher Mr. Armstrong. He was seventh- and eighth-grade

English, so not my teacher, but also guidance counselor, meaning he's looking out for the bigger picture on kids that are headed for trouble.

At Jonesville Middle they'd just dropped me into classes, and it took me one hot minute to go down like the *Titanic*. Math, pop quiz: "Simplify the expression using order of operations blah blah rational numbers." A page of numbers and stuff not even numbers, like freaking code. "Here's your simplified expression," I wrote on my blank answer sheet: "Fuck me."

I scratched that out before the teacher collected them up, so I didn't get sent to the principal. Just straight directly to the dummy class, where I got acquainted with the gentlemen in the sideburns and unlaced size thirteens. We all moved together, a big slow herd, from Howdy Doody math to remedial everything and a lot of study halls where our reading material was *Hot Rod Magazine, Muscle Machines, Car & Driver.* Or *Allure* and *Cosmo* if girls, because we had females among us. Instead of sideburns, some serious racks. Our destiny was the Vo-Ag track in high school where we'd shuffle to the vocational center for auto mechanic classes or if girls, beauty school. So who cared if we read magazines all day? Getting a jump on our career ladders.

Being new though, I was supposed to check in with Mr. Armstrong. It took him some weeks to work me in, due to other kids needing him to testify for them in juvie court. Busy man. I'd settled in with my new crowd of Jonesville dogs that were not pups but hot bitches and guys that could pass for beer-buying age. Friends with potential. And the freedom to draw in my notebooks all day, unpestered by education. Then comes Mr. Armstrong to rock my boat.

This much I'll give the man: he didn't lecture me about not living up to my potential. He'd got hold of my DSS records going back to the hospital interviews of Mom's OD, or before. I'd had one foot in the custody-removal shitpile since birth. I told Mr. Armstrong if he'd read all that, he knew more about me than I did. He said no, he didn't, that nobody ought to pretend to know how I felt. "Here's what I do know," he said. "You are resilient."

I'd heard quite a few fifty-dollar words for the problem of Demon. I asked Mr. Armstrong if he was wanting to put me on meds for that.

"It's not something to fix," he said. "It means strong. Outside of all expectation."

I looked at him. He looked at me. His hands were on his desk with the fingers touching, a tiny cage with air inside. Black hands. The knuckles almost blue-black. Silver wedding ring. He said, "You know, sometimes you hear about these miracles, where a car gets completely mangled in a wreck. But then the driver walks out of it alive? I'm saying you are that driver."

He was not from here, he had the northern accent. *Draee*-ver walks out a-*laeeve*. I could still understand him though. "You're saying I'm lucky."

"Are you lucky, if a drunk comes at you through a stop sign and totals your vehicle?"

"No."

"No, you are not. You got the wreck you didn't ask for. And you walked out of it."

I kind of shrugged him off.

"Well, that's how it looks to me. I see you here in my office. Showing up. Not out there someplace else trying to smash something or put a bullet in it or set it on fire."

I smiled, recalling Swap-Out and myself doing those exact three things to a deer head trophy in the garbage pile one time. Ten-point buck, in perfect condition before we had our way with it. Because Jesus, those glass eyes. But Mr. Armstrong was not smiling. He said he'd been advised of my classroom performance. But that people often know more than the teachers are able to measure with their tests. His job was to figure out what those things are, using other methods.

I said if he was aiming to torture me, I'd just confess right off the top: I hated school.

He nodded. "Understandably. Can you tell me what you like?"

Helping with football practice, but I wasn't giving that up to this guy. He'd probably take it away. I said I couldn't think of anything I liked doing that was legal for twelve-year-olds.

"So you're thinking life will get better in the years ahead."

"Well *yeah*."

He nodded. "I hear that."

Did he mean he heard *me*, or just that all kids say this, I couldn't guess. He was soft and hard at the same time, eyes like melted chocolate. No meanness to him. But he's not giving you a damn thing here if you won't go first. Heavy glasses, button shirt, more spiffed out than the usual for teachers. Or else a white collar looks that way on black skin. Not something you see much in Lee County. We were used to NBA or rappers on TV, rich guys with gold in their teeth.

Just by waiting me out, he got a few things off me. That I liked to draw. He asked if he could see some of my so-called work, and I said not at this time. Lately I'd been studying on the human form, aka this girl in all my classes they called Hot Sauce that sat in a chair the way ice cream melts. Soft porn basically. He gave me a pass, but said he would need to see some drawings by the end of the week, no excuses. Like it was an assignment.

That freaked me out. I went through all the notebooks I still had, going back as far as Creaky Farm and the every-night comics of Fast Man saving the kids. Nothing for a teacher to see. I got nervous, then pissed off, and then thought fine, the man wants to get in my skullbox, here you go. I brought him superhero shit. Kids getting saved. He studied over my drawings like he's reading the damn paper, then said he had some assessments for me to do. I thought, Good, we're almost done here: more tests, more Titanic of Demon going down in a shit ocean.

Wrong. The ones he gave me were all picture tests. Example: here's some connected squares that are an unfolded box, pick which box it would be after you put it back together. Pages and pages of this crap, so easy it's like a game. It was the only test I'd finished in forever. I thought it was a warmup for the real tests. Wrong again. Mr. Armstrong tricked me. These were the special ones they use for Gifted and Talented, which he said I was. Which is ridiculous. All the sudden he's talking about what catching up I'll have to do, and if I move into this track in middle school, I can take art class in high school instead of making birdhouses in shop.

I was pretty upset about it. Getting used to all new everything was screwing with my head. Clothes, people, house. The one thing I could still count on was being an idiot. Now I was supposed to trash what little there was left of Demon and be smart. Would I still be me? And the main question: Can a Gifted and Talented play football? Doubtful. But Mr. Armstrong moved me into the better English class and signed me up for math tutoring, which turned out to be just me and six righteously hot girls, so I decided what the hell. Next year I'd be on down the road in some other placement and school, where nobody would know how smart I ever was or wasn't.

My gifts and talents were discovered by others. The first was this guy Fish Head, that had perfected the exact combination of BO and Axe spray to fend off attackers. It was a normal day in math, with me covering notebook pages with drawings because we did smoke-all in that class. Mrs. Jackson would pass out her worksheets and then read a paperback or paint her nails for the rest of the period. To this day, adding up numbers puts that sharp polish smell in my head. This is still the dummy class obviously. I was doing the math tutoring, but it had yet to take.

"Hey Demon, drawl me some different kind of

pussies right quick!" Fish Head whispered, and by "whisper," I mean the entire back of the class laughed.

I was not that acquainted with pussies to know there were different kinds. I asked did he mean like shaved or not shaved, but no. He had names for different types. "Like tits," he said. "You know how they's as many kinds of tits as they is kinds of cars?"

I'd never really thought about it. Not that I was admitting to that.

"Like your long low ones." Fish Head, not being great with words, was trying to explain with his hands. Other guys jumped in to help. "Slab sides, pontoons," they said. "*Vans*."

Somebody had a *Playboy*, worth a thousand words like they say. I only got to keep it till the end of class, but I can study a thing and keep it in my mind's eye. I started charging guys for these drawings, fifty cents for parts, a dollar a whole body. Minus the face. For faces and hands I would have to charge extra because they take the most time, and there was no interest. Then I told these guys I needed to keep their magazines overnight, to get better familiar on the different makes and models. My chassis fixation took a new turn.

The one thing I could count on, surprisingly, turned out to be Angus. I'd not had any friend since Maggot, and that had been awhile. You don't just hang out with a girl normally, but in no way shape or form did Angus seem like one. It wasn't even the kick-ass boots or knowing cars. It was the zero bullshit. If you ever met a middle school girl, you know what they are: volcano eruptions of bullshit. Every minute a new emergency, the best friend turned enemy. Some guy that was flirting yesterday, now talking to some other girl. Every body part too big or too small and oh I hate this dress and Lord what if I'm pregnant. My own girl experience didn't run that deep, I mainly knew this from Angus. She had no tolerance, and needed to gripe. A lot.

"So I told Michaela, look, your ass is your ass. Simple fact. It's going to look that way whether you're wearing those particular jeans or not, so why keep asking me?"

" 'Or not,' " I said, "is something to picture."

"Don't go there, young friend."

Too late, I already had. Artist's rendition. Angus wouldn't know this, being no part of the Fish Head crowd, but the Ass of Michaela was a legend in its time.

Angus paused her gripe to hand me a leaf bag, Mattie Kate being on a tear that fall about raking up the yard. Maybe just wanting us out of her hair while she vacuumed, or not in Angus's room on PlayStation all hours. Raking leaves though. There's always more going to fall. I shoved leaves in those bags till they were dead packed, like bags of bricks. My disposal experience was vast. "Okay," I said. "You preached. Check Michaela off your ass-pain list."

"*Oh*, no. This is not Mario where you blast the Goomba and it's gone. Michaela is the undead of Monkey Island. She keeps coming back."

My choice for those leaves would have been arson, but the county had outdoor burning laws, and Angus as far as legal shit was a freaking cop. It made no sense, given the whole thugged-outedness of her, but her worry was Coach. He could lose his job in a heartbeat.

"So we're in PE, I'm minding my own beeswax, and here comes Donna." (Cue the Minnie Mouse voice.) " 'E*li*zabeth told me M*ic*ha*e*la said to tell you she's not *talking* to you.' And I'm like, I'm sorry, was Michaela under the impression I wanted conversation? I was *assigned* to her as partners on our Antarctica project because Mr. Norwood gives me the charity cases, and Michaela thinks penguins live at the North Pole with Santa's motherfucking elves."

You had to be amazed any girl would try, but some did. Maybe because of Coach, anything in his orbit being godlike. Or maybe it was Angus they wanted a piece of, the attitude, clothes, whatever. Doomed efforts. She did have guy friends, nerds and gamers, this

Sax individual that played drums. Most guys though were terrified of Angus. Me included. But with Coach permanently checked out, it left a gap. The deeper we went into fall, the less we saw of him at home. The Generals were undefeated, opponents falling one by one, and every soul in Lee County dead proud. At practice, the smallest screwup would mean an extra half hour of suicides up the bleachers and Coach shitting his mood all over the grass. One man's fail is every man's punishment, a team is a body, etc. At home he lived in his office watching replays. He never even knew about the Mr. Armstrong business, he just signed the forms without looking.

I admitted it to Angus, and it turned out *she* was a Gifted and Talented. No surprise, she was a reader like Tommy but more adult ones like sci-fi and female-type shit that could scare the hair off your balls, titles alone. Her scariness pertained to taking apart everything she looked at. Not just amateurs like Michaela, I mean people on TV. Like if we're watching some show and a girl is ugly, glasses, etc., Angus would say, Okay, watch. They'll make her the smart one. If a foreigner, possibly the villain. Angus could wreck a show like nobody's business. If a character ever turned up that talked like us, country-type person, he was there for one reason only, stupidness. Wait for it . . . joke! He's a dumbass!

If a girl, worse. She thinks condoms are party balloons and the guy trying to get in her pants is just the sweetest li'l ol' gentleman. Angus couldn't believe I'd never noticed this before. You get so used to not even being *anything* on TV, I guess I was just like, Yay, country kid gets invited to the party!

She gave me the advice of not freaking out over Gifted and Talented. No big deal, they pull you out of class to do stuff that's interesting. At Easter break you go on a trip. The ocean? She said possibly. One time it was to Stone Mountain, Georgia, which is practically as far. So the ocean was not out of the running. That would be something. *If* I was still around next spring, and got my math shit together, and pulled out of the bonehead zone. A lot of ifs.

In the meantime I had to figure out how to live in that big house with Angus, because Coach only came out like a bear from his cave to chew up dinner and crunch his PBR can in his fist and leave it on the table. The big square teeth looked to be hurting his mouth at all times. Angus told me they weren't his teeth, by the way. He'd worn dentures since high school after he lost his whole front row biting off more end-zone turf one time than he could chew.

Another by-the-way she told me was her real name. Agnes. Some kids in first grade turned it around to tease her, and to shut them up she said she liked Angus better. Then decided she really did. Likewise, her daddy used to take her to every practice and game, sitting her up on his shoulders. Coach's girl, in her tiny Generals jersey some lady made for her, riding high for all to see. Then in fifth grade he stopped letting her come to practices because it was no place for a young lady. She said fine, she hated football. Then decided she really did. And that's the story on a motherless girl named Angus. Unbeatable. Coach was a big guy with big hands holding the world by its neck, with every game a win or else the world ends. Storm in a shot glass type of thing. And Angus was the opposite. A whole ocean, dark and chill.

31

Through some cousin or another, the Peggots tracked me down in Jonesville and called the house. Mattie Kate passed the phone over without a word, and the voice of Mrs. Peggot knocked the wind out of me. Wanting to know was I all right. Oh, I had answers, starting with "*Now* you care," but instead I got choked up. Yes, I did want to see Maggot and her and Mr. Peg. I would see if I could get a ride over there. On Saturday, after football practice.

I knew Coach would make U-Haul drive me if I asked, and he did. U-Haul sat outside in the car waiting the whole time, so it was like the old days of supervised visits, only not really, because U-Haul had no power. I stayed for dinner.

The Peggots crowded around me like I'd come back

from the moon. Mrs. Peggot saying how big I'd got, Maggot shocking me with how different he looked, serious raccoon eyes with the makeup, two earrings in his bottom lip. They asked about Jonesville and Coach and my grandmother Betsy and how come she was to take an interest in me after all this time. I said probably because she didn't know I existed till I showed up in her yard looking like dog vomit.

"No," Mrs. Peggot said. "That isn't so. She knew about you."

They got quiet. Mr. Peg looked at her. She nodded. And then in the Peggot kitchen after twelve years of life, I finally got the true story on my grandmother coming to have words with Mom. Not the day I was born, but some weeks prior. A car came up the holler that nobody had seen before. "It was a Chevy wagon," Mr. Peg said. "With some sassy little gal a-driving it."

Mrs. Peggot swatted his arm because she wanted to tell it. "It was a little gal driving, and a great big tall lady that got out and went up there to see your mama."

"Then that little gal gets out and opens the back door, and what do you think is in there?"

Mrs. Peggot knuckled him again. "In the back seat, here sits the littlest old fellow you ever saw. A grown man, but he's real small, some way."

I knew that man. But didn't say so. Not wanting a swat.

"He didn't get out. Them two stayed down there the whole time smoking their cigarettes. Little sass of a gal, leaning on that big car like she just dared anybody to say a word about it."

"But did you . . ." I didn't even know what I wanted to know.

"Honey, we had never seen the like of these people. We just waited for that lady to come back out. And then they went on their way."

She said Mom got tetchy afterwards and told the neighbors it was none of their business. But Mrs. Peggot got out of her that it was her dead boyfriend's mother poking around, wanting to take away the baby. Back in summer he'd written her a letter saying he was partially sorry for everything, and going to be a daddy, come November. He asked, did she want to come see her grandbaby then. He and my grandmother were on the verge of making up their twenty-years fight. Then after he wrote her, he died, so. Bad timing. You could see how it would piss her off.

Maggot sat through all this with his mouth open like a hooked bass. Possibly I did too. It floored me that Mrs. Peggot knew this all along, and never told. It had to be Mom's fault. They'd fought like crazy over me going or not going to see my dad's grave in Murder Valley, Mom being dead set against. She didn't want me knowing about this lady that might take me away from her. No wonder she didn't put the Woodall name on me. That secret was the only power Mom had. She probably made Mrs. Peggot swear on a whole damn pallet of Walmart Bibles.

I didn't know what to say. Except yes, as far as staying for dinner.

Being back in that house was weird. Knowing every single thing, which stair creaked, what pictures of ancient Peggots hung in their frames crooked. The bathtub that scared the piss out of me whenever I was small. Little owl collection on the windowsill with dust on their tiny heads. It was like I was home, and also a stranger. Maggot and I hung out some in his room, and he was a little standoffy at first. He knew I'd been pretty mad over the Peggots not keeping me there in the family and everything. But I told him I was doing great, living in a castle house, and what the fuck was the deal with his hair. He said it was a "compromise."

"Between what and what?" The last I'd seen, it was down to his shoulders with Mr. Peg threatening to take the shears to him while he was asleep. Maggot said he'd agreed to cut it, but his own way. "His way" being dyed black, different lengths all over between short and medium long, all kind of feathery around his face. Not a normal girl or guy haircut, whatsoever.

"They did that at the barbershop?"

"No. This chick at school. Martha Coldiron. You remember her."

I did. Goth girl. "She's moved on from cutting herself? I hope she washed her scissors."

He made his mouth into a kind of fist and looked out the window towards what used to be my house. Martha was probably his best friend now. "Sorry man," I said. I didn't want to know about his new friends or what new shit he was into. It felt like the last bridge that could get me back to Demon had just blown up. I was watching it fall down in slo-mo.

I asked him how Mrs. Peggot hadn't killed him yet over the makeup and everything, but he just shrugged. "What are they going to do? Send me back to my mom?"

The news there was not good. He said she'd come up for parole but got denied for lipping off to a guard, which was totally unfair because this aggro bitch guard had singled her out. Writing her up as off the count even if she wasn't, calling her gay for the stay and all such shit, till one day there was no more shit she could take and she blew. The curse of Mariah Peggot.

At supper we got on the happier subject of star daughter June. She was a nurse practicer now at the Pennington Gap clinic, living in a house that was the craziest thing you ever saw. A geographic dome, Mr.

Peg said. Like a boat turned upside down, Maggot said. But with windows and an upstairs. Emmy supposedly thought it was the cutest thing ever. Mrs. Peggot said they'd have to take me over there to visit. June and Emmy asked about me all the time.

"She has a boyfriend now," Maggot announced.

"That Kent fellow," Mr. Peggot said. "He's been courting her a good long while."

"Not *June's* dork boyfriend. *Emmy* has one," Maggot said, looking at me. The makeup made it hard to tell exactly what expression he was making.

"Duh," I said. "Why wouldn't she? She's a babe."

"He's still based over in Knoxville but he travels a right smart," Mrs. Peggot said. "He's over here to see June all the time. He does the business with the pharmacy medicines."

"Kent sells drugs," Maggot said. Wide, black-ringed eyes. Clown of the dead.

For the first time all evening, I thought of U-Haul outside waiting. My creepster ticket home. I lost interest in eating for about ten seconds, but got over it. I mean. Pot roast.

"He does real well," Mr. Peg said. "I expect here any day he'll pop the question."

"I'm going out for JV football," I said. I wasn't old enough. But nobody was listening.

They kept their promise and I got to see it all: upside-down geographic boat house, Emmy the eighth-grade babe, drug-seller boyfriend of Aunt June. We went upstairs to Emmy's room and she told us her secrets, just like old times. But not in a closet. Geographic dome boat houses are short on closet space. The whole ceiling or wall or whatever is a bunch of triangles that make a curve. Not really explainable, you'd have to see it. We sat on Emmy's bed.

Long story short, she despised Kent. She said he barked like a seal whenever he and June were doing the nasty. He pretended to sleep on the fold-out couch downstairs on his stay-overs, waiting till they thought Emmy was asleep. I hated the idea of Aunt June stooping to monkeyshines. Maggot was putting on his whole act of Nothing-shocks-me-I've-got-lip-earrings-y'all. But I could tell he was. No surprise on Kent being a loud one, even upstairs with the door closed we could hear him talking to the Peggots in a TV voice, like they're watching Home Shopping Channel and he's the product. Maggot suggested Emmy could put something in his coffee like pee or Drano. He got off the bed and went to poke around in Emmy's makeup.

"You gank my Max Factor and you're busted, Mattress. That stuff costs a fortune."

"Okey dokey. Where's your lubricant for the stick up your ass?"

Emmy being dead gorgeous, I expected. But she seemed ten years older than us. She'd gone from Disney Chick towards the Madonna cowgirl end of things, ruffle skirt, jean jacket, dark blue tights. We were sitting on her bed. I wanted to touch her feet for being perfect, like little blue doves. She still had my silver snake bracelet on her ankle, over the tights. I wondered if she wore it all the time. She seemed cool as a creek, discussing June-and-Kent action with no embarrassment whatsoever. Like she didn't remember the two of us going thirty minutes past first base and a quarter till heart attacks ourselves, once upon a time. Never happened. She was perfectly nice to me but, meh. I was just some kid.

I tried not to remember it either, including the fruit smell she still had.

Maggot brought up the subject of Emmy's boyfriend, several times. I think it was overtime revenge, to show me he'd been wise to our Knoxville shenanigans. This hurtful side to him made no sense, the old Maggot wouldn't have hurt a fly. Except obviously to pull its wings off, which is just kid crap. Emmy refused to take the bait, saying she and Hammer were not dating, just friends. I kept thinking, *Hammer?* Flop-haired

Hammerhead *Kelly*, the super-polite cousin-not-cousin that seemed too tenderhearted for this world, even while he was gutting a deer carcass with a Bowie knife? But Emmy just kept steering us back to the boyfriend situation downstairs. I said I didn't get it. Aunt June was no fool, plus had already turned down half the guys in the county. This Kent person must have had something on offer.

Sex, was Maggot's theory. Giant pork sword.

Emmy said no, it was all the free stuff. This guy was Santa Claus Junior in a Ford Explorer, coming around to throw presents on all the receptions and nurses. Candy for the fat ones, coupons for Hair Affair if they were on diets. It was like Kent had spy elves telling him what they'd all want. The doctors got actual free vacations to Hawaii and such. Golf trips.

"Mother H. Fuck," said Maggot. "Get me Hawaii."

"You have to be a doctor or nurse practitioner. It's your prize for prescribing his pills."

"Okay, whenever Aunt June gets her Hawaii, make her take us. I don't care if we have to hear barking-man boning her all night, I'll still go." Maggot was putting Emmy's hair clips in his whiskery hair so it stuck out like tentacles. And navy-blue lipstick. He turned to show his work.

"Me too," I said. Not really expecting to get invited, but Jesus. The ocean.

Emmy said Aunt June couldn't earn rewards from him due to Kent being her boyfriend. She was just getting off on how popular he was. "Mom says if anybody on God's green earth needs a Hawaii vacation, it's a doctor in Lee County."

We reminded her about Knoxville. Gut-stabbed pregnant lady, baby inside. Emmy shook her head like the little did we know. "She doesn't regret moving back. But she says medicalwise, Lee County is the doorway to hell, with too many patients and Medicaid forms to ever get through it. The nurses and doctors she used to know have all moved to the city to make a buck."

The weather was brutal that day, otherwise we might have gone outside to do our dissing of our elders. Or not, because Maggot was having too much fun with Emmy's things. He had on her sparkly Madonna vest, no shirt, and these giant swishy pants he'd pulled on over his jeans because he was that freaking skinny. After a while we heard somebody calling for us.

"Shhh," Emmy said. Maggot stopped, dropped, and rolled while she went to the door.

It was Aunt June hollering up the stairs. The Peggots were wanting to get home. The rain pounding the roof now sounded like evil tree gnomes throwing rocks. This is a dome type house, so if I say "roof" we're discussing the whole banana. Maybe sleet out there, soon to get dark, with Mr. Peg's eyes so bad he meandered like the slowest drunk driver on the planet. Mrs. Peggot got her old eagle eyes back after the cataract surgery, but she didn't drive.

We stalled long enough for Maggot to undisgrace himself, and then went and sat on the stairs, because nobody was going anywhere till Kent finished his damn talk show on the medical establishment not taking pain seriously. "We *know* better than that now. Pain is the fifth vital *sign*. We invented the pain score so the patient can give an objective *assessment*."

"I know what you're worried about, Daddy," Aunt June said. "But there's absolutely no chance of you getting dependent on this medication. The company did all kinds of studies. I can show you the package insert."

She was in the kitchen which was part of the living room, the whole downstairs being one big room. I watched her down there, shiny Posh Spice hair, tight black shirt tucked into the waist of her jeans, and wondered how pervy was it that I still thought she was hot. That I thought she *and* her niece-slash-daughter were hot. She'd baked a chicken for our dinner, and a birthday cake. My birthday was the reason of us coming over that day. Fine, I was in love with the lady. Now she was packing up all the leftovers for them to take home. Mrs. Peggot would say no, now y'all keep some of it for yourselves, but June would win. This family was a story I knew.

Mr. and Mrs. Peggot had sunk together into the couch while Kent wore them down. A Burt Reynolds type, mustache, too dressed up for a Saturday, shoes like nobody from around here. Looking down on him, I could see a pink shine on top of his head with the dark hair pulled across it. Not a full Homer Simpson like Creaky's, just a little beginner's hamburger helper up there. But do you trust a guy that cheats on his own head? Aunt June was bottom-feeding.

Emmy was on the step beside me. My knee touched hers but she didn't notice. She was eyeing Kent like she wanted the right superpower to vaporize him.

"We ask the patients to look at the chart and put a number to their pain," June explained, scooping potato salad into an empty yellow butter tub. "Kent's company came up with that."

"We believe your pain is a fact," said Kent. "Not just an opinion. That's all I'm saying." Definitely not all he was saying. I looked at Emmy and made an oh-brother face.

"Our mission is to get every suffering patient to zero on that chart," said Kent.

Emmy made a finger-pistol and shot herself in the head.

Mr. Peg ended up accepting a free coupon for Kent's miracle pain pills, probably to shut him up. *Stronger than anything ever made. Not the usual stuff you have to take every four hours, this one lasts around the clock! For the first time in years, you'll get a good night's sleep!*

Outside in the truck, he barely got the engine turned over before Mrs. Peggot said, "Give that paper here, old man. If you try bringing them pills to the house, I'm flushing them down the commode."

32

Christmas was coming, and I was nervous of Coach getting done with me. This being the time of year people start noticing who's family and who's not. I asked Angus what they usually did for Christmas. She said nothing much. We were up on the roof cleaning the gutters.

"But what *do* you do?" I asked. "Like, where do you go cut your tree?"

She squinted her eyes at me. She'd worn her oldest, stickiest Chucks to climb out on the tin roof, while I stayed on the ladder. "You mean that stupid thing of a *tree* inside the *house*?"

Not even whenever she was little? Not even then. "We're not *religious*," she said, like I was the one being weird. And I was like, Who said religious, this is fucking

Christmas we're discussing. Who ever heard of a kid thinking it's no big deal?

Angus was that kid. If she wanted something, Coach always just said go buy it. No need to involve fat guys in fake beards. Another one of these Coach rules that was just normal to Angus, like no pets, always do your homework. She said Christmas was a downer for him due to her mom dying of her cancer right before or after, possibly the day of. She wasn't sure.

Normally this guy named Happy would have been cleaning their gutters, but Mattie Kate had called and called. Finally his wife answered and said Happy fell off a barn and broke his back, so call back in a few months. Coach didn't trust anybody else to work on that house, mainly due to nobody wanting to do it. It was over a hundred years old and had its dicey aspects. Imagine if some handyman screwed up Coach's house? He'd have to leave the county. But the gutters had gotten so clogged with leaves, the roof was leaking in our TV den. I told Angus I was going up. I asked her not to tell Coach if I screwed something up or, like, fell. She said she was coming too, if we screwed it up, he couldn't fire *us*. And I thought, Speak for yourself. Coach was out of town that weekend for the playoffs. I'd thought he might ask me to go with them to help out, but he didn't, only U-Haul. It was December. My days in that house were numbered. Which is what got me on the subject of Christmas and death.

"That makes two of us," I said. "As far as holidays wrecked by dead parents. Not that the Fourth of July is comparable, but that was Mom's downer. She'd always get moody over my dad being dead, to where she'd put the shuthole on fireworks."

Angus gave me a look. Maybe Coach had fireworks rules. That family was hard to figure.

"I'm saying not even *sparklers*. Let alone your better class of explosives."

"Are you telling me your dad died by exploding?"

"No, it was water. I never got the particulars, just the place. And the day."

"And then *she* died on your birthday. Fuck a duck, bro. You win."

I thought about my last birthday I'd had at Aunt June's. Mom didn't really enter into it. I told Angus my mom being dead wasn't something I pinned exactly on my birthday. "It's more like this bag of gravel I'm hauling around every day of the year. If somebody else brings it up, honestly, I'm glad of it. Like just for that minute they can help me drag the gravel."

"Huh," she said, raking brown glops of leaves out of the gutter with her bare hands, which was brave. I mean, things could dwell in that shit. Primordial life. My job was holding up the bucket until it got full. Then down the ladder I'd go to dump it on this swamp-stinking pile we'd started, far from the house. What implements Happy used for this job, we had no idea.

Angus said it was different for her, because she didn't remember her mom. Not a bag of gravel. "It's more like this shiny little thing I wear around my neck. Once in a while some lady will lean over and say, 'Honey, she was so pretty' or 'She was a jewel.' And I just say, 'Okay, great. Thanks.' " Angus slopped more glop in the bucket. "Ignorance is bliss."

I'd suggested that smoking pot could make this enterprise more enjoyable. I'd scored some respectable weed from a guy at school as payment for body-part drawings. Angus almost never took my suggestions, especially anything that could bring scandal to the house of Coach, but this time she was extreme. Was I crazy, did I want to fall off my ladder and end up like broke-back Happy? Etc. Turns out she'd never smoked pot in her life. That's how her innocent mind could fall prey to the whole weed-makes-you-go-insane theory the DARE cops promote at school, and I had to set her straight, explaining how it could make you pay *more* attention to your work, while not minding the shittier sides. No dice. She couldn't smoke anything whatsoever, due to asthma. I'd seen her use her inhaler, but never knew that's why her dad quit smoking and went over to using dip. She said it put her in the hospital a few times as a kid. Any time she got too emotional, good or bad, she'd break out in hives. I'd not seen that in Angus, the hives. Or the emotional.

So she'd missed out on all the best things in life: pot, having a mom, Christmas. Unbelievable. I told her I couldn't argue with bad luck as regards death and asthma, but that Christmas was still on the table. She said she didn't see the point.

"That's because you don't know what you're missing." I went to dump our bucket, and she sat up there shivering, knees to her chest, hands in her coat pockets, stocking cap pulled over her ears. Gray manga eyes looking out at the world like a small kid abandoned on a rooftop.

The point, I told her after I got back, is presents. Totally different from shopping. People give you stuff you didn't know you wanted. Or were scared to ask for because too expensive.

She said that sounded wasteful.

I told her *surprised* is the point. *Waiting* is the point. Watching wrapped-up secrets pile up under the tree, that you shake and poke till you feel like the cat that's going to die of being curious. So what if Mom never had two bucks to her name and got all my presents on employee discount, we fucking *did* Christmas. As far as being too excited to sleep, listening with all my ignorant little might for reindeer hooves on top of our chimneyless single-wide? Totally.

Angus didn't think Coach would go for it.

I was shocked. Generally speaking, Angus could be a giant ass-pain as far as looking on the bright side. "Demon," she was always saying, "life is a wild, impetuous ride. There could be good shit up ahead, don't rule it out." Which I mostly did, rule it out. But Christmas? I was not giving up that one. I told her we didn't have to get Coach involved that much, we'd just give presents to each other. She admitted there was maybe a point in time where she'd been jealous of kids that got to do Santa. But if she'd asked him, it would have been like betraying her dad. I listened while she talked herself through this. Maybe he was past that now. Maybe he didn't actually care one way or the other.

"Fine," I said. "I know where we're getting our tree."

We stole one.

Never mind realizing after we got it home that we had nothing to decorate it with. We hung whatever the hell we felt like on that tree: spoons, mint Life Savers, CDs, some earrings and shit that Mattie Kate had given

Angus over the years in a futile attempt to mold her fashion sense. Pretzels. It was our tree of utter ridiculousness. Epic.

We got so psyched over our presents, we couldn't wait. The round-the-clock Christmas movie reruns start playing well before, which makes you think it has to be already Christmas somewhere. Around midnight of maybe the twenty-third, halfway through our second or third Chevy Chase, we called it. Ran downstairs like kids, tore everything apart while Coach was asleep. Angus got me amazing comics including a manga series of a kid named Gon Freecss on a journey to find his dad that left whenever he was a baby, and was said to have superpowers. Obviously a hit. Also clothes, which sounds boring but this being Angus, was not. Not the badass stuff she liked, either. She thought out the angle of Demon, Popular Kid, from head to toe: a Members Only jacket, parachute silver, just for example. I would own the school in that jacket.

The thing about Angus. We both had our crap to live with, and her way was to give no shit whether you liked how she was doing it, or not. But if I wanted to be a different type person and try for popular, she wasn't going to stand in my way. She was going to *help*. Not very usual.

She also gave me a model ship, with tiny sails, tiny

ropes, an entire seafaring vessel made of painted wood and toothpicks and here's the killer part: inside a bottle. Not even big like a deuce, just the regular beer size. How in the holy heck somebody got it in there, she had no idea. She'd found it that way, at the antiques mall. She said it was me all over, my ocean thing, and also the thing of beating impossible odds, because someday I was going to go wherever the hell I wanted.

"If you say so," I told her. "But will I always still be in a bottle?"

She laughed. "The world's a bottle, Demon. Gravity and shit. Don't expect miracles."

I was more excited over my presents for her than getting mine. Also nervous, because let's face it, she was one rock-hard peanut to crack. Coach's credit card wasn't my money and felt like cheating, so I used my cash I earned from drawings, and went to pawnshops. I did wonder if the guy at Here Today Loan and Pawn in Jonesville would remember the street brawl, boy on a man's errand, etc. He never looked up from his magazine. I checked for McCobb booty, but it was long gone. They do a quick turnaround at those places, mostly guns and jewelry unless it's nonsense items or weird antiques, which is what I was looking for. I found an awesome hat, black velvet, with a veil that came down over the face part. More femmy than typical

Angus, but I had a hunch, and was right. She vamped around in that hat, saying she would be the funeral fox of Lee County. I also got her some old-time books including this advice one we read aloud, on what to do in every emergency: shipwreck, nightclub fire, plummeting elevator. What is a nightclub? She said it's like a bar, only in the city, so you're jam-packed in there with your face against the armpits of others. So in case of a fire, you're toast. I can't remember the advice.

My main thing, though, was her portrait. I put it in a serious pawnshop frame, glass and everything. I'd known for a long time what superhero she'd be: Black Leather Angel. A badass one, black leather angel wings. It took quite a few tries to make it not look like any form of Batgirl. But I got it. The main aspect of Angus being those gray eyes that look straight into what's eating you. The superpower of reading your mind and making you talk. She was floored. She carried it around with her all day, cuddling that big square frame like a freaking teddy bear.

Mattie Kate took off to be with her kid, but left the refrigerator full of things for us to pull off the tin foil and heat up, like unwrapping more presents. Green bean potato chip casserole, blackeye peas with pork rind. Apple dumplings. We ate whatever we felt like, whenever. I put on my new clothes and she put on her veil hat and we said "Darling" like we were the rich Howells on Gilligan or "Dope" like Fresh Prince, and ate and watched TV for three days straight. At some point I realized it was actual Christmas, the day of. And thought, maybe there is a God after all in his heaven. On the slow bus ride of my dogshit life, for some while I got to stop off here.

The best part of it all was getting our tree. No question. I'd convinced Angus it wasn't larceny to steal something that farmers spend half the year piling up and burning. We could have just asked. But taking from Creaky felt righteous. Sneaking out there with Angus, cutting a cedar by dark of night, one of the higher points of my young life. I was just sorry we had to get U-Haul involved for transportation, since he might rat us out, which would sully the perfect crime.

I made him cut the headlights before we got to the house. The place looked worse than ever, with no slave boys for the upkeep. Lights were on in one downstairs room, so he was in there, all by his deaf, butt-ugly self, I hoped. No sign of the Lariat.

Why did I want that so much, to go back to the place where my childhood got crushed? After we went, I knew. The reason was power. To face down Amityville and yell at whatever still crept or clawed inside, "Fuck you. Fuck your thrashings and starving us and making all of us but mostly Tommy wish we were dead. Fuck you for making me glad it was him and not me." To hocker and spit on the frozen grass. Turn my back on evil and walk away.

I had one surprise left, and it was from Coach, a few days after Christmas. He said to come on back to his office. He had to clear off a chair, his office being worse than the living room. He had a small TV in there to play VHS tapes. Teams we were fixing to play, to find their holes. Or games already played, but only the losses, to learn from. Coach was not one to dwell on the wins. I knew what tape would play today, because I'd been seeing it all my life. The clock had run out on us here, we gave it our best but it's a loss, good luck and all that. *Sorry.*

He said nothing, I said nothing. What you noticed on Coach, after the teeth bulging behind his shut lips, was the eyebrows and hard, blue-eyed squint. He wore his red Generals cap at all times, so it was a shock to see him that day without it. An old man's white hair sticking up uncombed, like I'd caught him in bed. I felt like I'd messed up already.

"How long you been here now?" The cap was on his

desk. He put it on. I half expected him to do the jacket and sunglasses too. Coach's angle was to not be seen. "Two, three months?"

"Yes sir," I said.

He picked up his silver whistle and spun it on its long lanyard, winding it around his pointer finger all the way to the end. Then spun it the other direction, winding it all the way up again. One of his habits. He did this on the field while pissed off or thinking, aka always. I felt like that lanyard was winding around my neck. I wanted to run out of there and not hear what was coming. U-Haul told him about the stolen tree, or Mattie Kate found my weed stash. There's a million roads a person like me can take to ruin, and none I'd found so far led anywhere else.

"You liked helping out at practice, did you?" he finally asked.

"Yes sir." I didn't look at him. I balled up my heart or whatever you want to call it and threw it out the window behind him. Hills, bare trees. The weak piss-yellow light of winter.

"You've got something," he said.

"Sir?" My pockets were empty. I didn't steal. All right, I had. Never from Coach, but my mind skittered helpless over the Oreos and Slim Jims I'd pilfered from my keepers.

"I saw that right away. Size, for sure. Speed, and a decent talent for finding a pass. I had you for a linebacker. But I believe what you are is a tight end."

I came back inside the window.

"What I didn't know was, will this kid show up." He wound the lanyard again. Unwound it. "I'll be honest, I see boys like you all the time, pissing away what God gave them. They've come from the trash of the trash. We all know it. The bad homes, the incarcerated parents. These boys just go looking for more trouble because it's what they know."

I stopped breathing again. No parent of mine was incarcerated. The trashier homes I'd lived in weren't really mine. But he'd said what he said. Not needing any answer.

"I don't care how much talent a kid has, if he's too proud to do as he's told, he's a waste of my time. Proud, stubborn, you tell me. They come in here wanting to be stars, wanting their glory. And think they'll get it by acting like the biggest thugs on the hill."

I looked at his freckled hands on the desk. His Generals hat. I looked at the big black hairs of his eyebrows that sprang out in all directions, some of them way too long. Terrible, wrongful eyebrows. I wasn't meeting his eyes, man to man, but it was my best effort.

He leaned forward on his hands. "I'm going to tell

you something, and I want you to hear it. A successful team is not made of leaders. It is made of followers."

"Yes sir."

"I don't care if it's picking up the damn garbage," he said. "If that's the job I give a member of my squad, I want to see it done."

He had no idea. As regards me and garbage. But he'd seen enough. My ears were ringing, but I got the gist. He said I would go on living there, and we'd see how it went. He would talk to Coach Briggs about putting me in JV practices next fall. Seventh graders could go up for practice, if they had the size. Football camp ran most of the summer. Technically they shouldn't play me before eighth, but that rule was not hard and fast.

The blood thrashing on my eardrums drowned out everything else. Summer and fall were forever away. Months. I would be here, for all of them. In this house. Going out for football.

33

What I said before about having some golden time of life where it's all good, your people have got your back, and you don't notice? That's how the cruel world bites you. I have bad days galore to look back on, the shamings and hard fists, and I'll tell you what. It's the golden times that kill me. I had two. And like a son of a bitch, I missed them both.

The first, childhood in general. Running wild on my bare feet, tramping the mud of the creek into Mrs. Peggot's kitchen, those places being two versions of boy heaven. A kid couldn't ask for better. Too bad though, because the kid was full-time fixated on asking for better, mostly in the way of unaffordable shoes and Game Boy.

The second time was seventh and eighth. Regardless

Jonesville Middle being baby-town, it grew on me. Not a soul there knew that one mere grade previous, I'd been a worthless piece of shit. Born again. Now I could speak to anybody and had friends in all the kinds: laid-back ones you score weed from, brainy ones to drag you from the death swamp of pre-algebra. Full friend gamut. Teammates you could grab in the locker room and lift off the ground in a reverse chinlock, all slippery with sweat, laughing your naked asses off. Girls ditto, minus the chinlock.

These kids did seem young. Outside of the dummy classes, you'd be hard pressed to find a kid in Jonesville Middle that had even held down a job. Being friends with such people entailed listening to made-up problems to some degree. I could tolerate that, much more so than Angus. Girls can surprise you by knowing more than they're letting on. Also for a guy it's different. If you sit still and let your ears take all that girl business, other body parts may get their turn.

So the impossible happened. In due time, a school would be owned by Demon Copperhead in his Members Only jacket. He should have been the happiest damn fool ever. But no, he's waiting for the shit to hit the fan, looking behind whoever is being nice to him that day to see what's coming. Still your jack-shit homeless orphan, just faking it in nice clothes. I'd done nothing to deserve good luck, and I knew what people are made of. Sooner or later they will turn on you. Or die.

Also, there was this thing that happened with U-Haul. This was in late January. Awkward as fuck. After Coach went to bed U-Haul would spend hours in his office. Putting receipts into the books, jerking off, who knew what he did. And he scooted around the house in his white socks, for reasons of stealth. U-Haul never came into a room, he *materialized*. In the doorway of our beanbag TV lounge that night. There he was, crooking a skeleton finger at me.

"Hey! What's up?" I said. Playing dumb as to the meaning of the "come here" finger.

"The playbook is messed up. Coach must have dropped it. The binder is busted." He rolled his head to the side, heaving stringy hair out of his eyes. "I thought you'd help me put it back in order. You and him are so tight, I'd say you've got it memorized."

I looked at Angus but she was like, Your funeral, pal. On the football front she'd made herself clear from day one. Not interested. I followed him downstairs wondering how a human could look that much like a reptile while walking down stairs. He slithered.

We got in the office and he closed the door. "Sit, sit," he said, slinking around to Coach's swivel chair behind the desk. I wanted to stay on my feet, but he burned the red-brown eyes into me and I gave in. Moved a box of kneepads and a mouth guard off a chair and put my butt in it.

He pulled the playbook out of a drawer. Nothing about it looked broken. He'd lied to get me in here. "So, is it Waggle, Bootleg, Shovel? On the Wing T plays? Or the other way around?"

He shoved the big binder across the desk and I opened it. Leafed through the pages and saw nothing out of the normal. Pages stained with fast-food grease, their worn-out holes mostly falling off the rings. Perfectly good playbook. U-Haul was staring at me.

"You think you're some hot shit. Don't you."

I'd never been clear whether I was supposed to "sir" this creep or not. I opted out. "I might be shit. That has been said. Temperaturewise, it's not really my call."

He smirked. "I reckon that's Gift-and-Talented for telling me to fuck off."

Damn. How did he find *that* out? Angus hadn't even told Coach, let alone U-Haul. She was honorable. "Whatever," I said.

"Right. What would I know? Just a nobody assistant coach, from a long line of nobodies. Mercy's sakes, don't let me be the one to stop you." He kept pushing his hand into the long red greasy hair, then running the hand down his face. Doing that one thing over and over.

"Stop me from what?"

"Oh, you know. Coming in here like one of the family. Using your tactics."

This time as the hand ran over his face I caught a stealth nose-pick, one finger scooting into the nostril. He took his eyes off me to see what he'd mined out of there. Rolled it on his fingertips into a little ball. U-Haul was a horror movie. Brain says *run*. Eyes can't look away.

"I don't know what you're talking about. Take it up with my grandmother, if you don't think I should be here. It was her idea."

"Well, sure it was. And Coach rolls over and takes it." He leaned forward, rolling his fingertips still, but eyes back on me. "*Eleven years* I'm here at his bark and call, running his errands. Driving you kids around like I'm your motherfucking babysitter. If I had tits you'd be sucking on them. And *I* get sent home at night to my mother's house. Why is that, I forget?"

I said nothing. It was hard to concentrate, Christ. I'd never seen his eyes blaze so red. And what was his plan for that booger?

"Oh, right. Because I'm a fucking nobody. Okay, that's it!" He leaned back in his chair.

I waited. He didn't move. "That's *what*? You're done, I can go now?"

"Consider this a friendly warning, if you think you're part of this family. They'll put out the welcome mat. Just watch out for the naked bootleg play that's coming to take you down."

I walked out of there wondering how long it would take to get the bad taste out of my mouth. Maybe forever. I needed no snake to tell me I didn't belong in that family or house or life. I was the tree of knowledge.

I didn't turn out to be full-gifted, only half. Still hanging on by the short hairs in math. But Language Arts held my interest. Mr. Armstrong the counselor was also a teacher. But he didn't do the usual teacher thing of making sure you know you're worthless. Or the Mrs. Jackson thing of, *We're all turds in this teapot kiddos so why don't I just paint my nails.* Mr. Armstrong would talk to us like humans. He was mainly Seventh and Eighth but subbed in for Sixth a lot that winter due to our regular English teacher getting shingles. His first day, he said let's get to know each other, you can ask me anything, maybe wanting kids to relax about what he was. Some smartass asks, does he get sunburned. I thought for sure not. I'm only Melungeon-dark, and I'd never burned. But he

said yes, he wore sunscreen to be outside, like mowing his lawn. He told us other surprising things. If a
person is black, you're supposed to write Black, because it's not an adjective but a category like Chinese
or American. All capitalized because proper nouns.
I asked what about Melungeons, thinking he'd not have
heard of them. Surprise again, he said good example.
Melungeon is a proper noun.

He was from Chicago, that's why the accent. He
came here after college as a Vista, which was this program where people from the city come help you out for
being poor. His wife was a Vista also, from some other
city. They met here and got married. No kids. They
played in a bluegrass band called Fire in the Hole,
him banjo, her fiddle. I thought of Mr. Peg. He'd be
glad his type music hadn't totally died of old age. Mr.
Armstrong never heard of bluegrass music before he
came here, but he fell in love with everything about
the mountains and stayed on.

I knew about the wife. If people don't approve of
something, it is discussed, and this was. She was white.
And an art teacher, my good luck. In middle school
they didn't have any art, she taught at Lee High. But
Mr. Armstrong took some of my drawings to show her,
and she came over one day to meet with me. Ms. Annie.
She talked in a voice that was almost like singing (which

she did, in their band) and dressed like a hippie. Long blue skirt, flowery scarf on her long hair, earrings with little rocks on them, four colors of blue. Blond eyelashes, which you don't see that much. We were in the empty teacher lounge that had a couch, but she put out some thick paper and pencils on the low table and sat on the floor, so I did the same.

She asked me different things. Could I show her how I went about drawing a face. Easy. Start with a circle, divide it with a cross with the sideways part below center. Eyes go on that, with a gap in the middle, same wideness as the eye. Different type eyebrows for surprise or love or mad. Then draw the jaw below the circle as a separate thing, like a skull and jawbone, because a face actually has a skull underneath it. (Something I learned from Tommy.) She asked me how I would decide what type of jaw to make. That's simple: small jaw for a kid or a lady, big for a man, bigger for a superhero. Which is why lady superheroes are dead tricky.

She wanted to know if I'd taken any class or seen drawing shows on TV, which I didn't know existed. She kept on being amazed until the bell rang and I couldn't believe an hour was up. She said I had a natural talent and did I want to work with her on improving it. Perspectives, composition, etc. Long story short, she would be my Gifted teacher. I could try out other media that she had a whole studio full of. Art supplies other than pencils. Jesus God.

If you've ever heard that song "She'll Be Coming 'Round the Mountain," that was Betsy Woodall coming to visit. No six white horses, but an occasion. Mr. Peg would say high dudgeon.

The first time was late that winter, to transfer over my paperwork. If she approved of how I was doing with Coach, they'd go to the DSS office and sign him on as my new guardian. Old Baggy would shed no tears. She hadn't called once since I'd moved in with Coach, taking her usual approach of, if the kid's not broke, don't fix him. And if he is, go whistle it out your ass.

My grandmother was not that easy. Getting moved up to the harder classes won me no prizes, she wanted report cards. Mattie Kate had busted her butt clearing up the living room, piling the crap in back rooms, so we all sat around the giant table, including Mr. Dick and Jane Ellen that drove them in the Comet. Miss Betsy wanted to know if the sports nonsense was going to interfere with my education. I looked at Coach: no lanyard twirling. Eyebrows on even keel.

"There's not any sports right now, football season is over with till the fall," I told her. My grandmother probably being the one person on God's earth that didn't know that. Obviously other ones did exist such as basketball, but not in Lee County. Any sport that's not football around here is like vanilla. Why even eat that, if they've invented flavors.

She asked Coach was this true, me being done with sports?

"Miss Woodall, you can leave this young man to me. I plan on doing my level best to enhance his full potential." Total poker face.

She eyed us one by one. Angus had on this gigantic green sweater that swallowed her entire body like that Scooby-Doo girl, and her hair in these pop-up knobs like devil horns. My grandmother was like, Hmmm, maybe this one needs my educating. But Coach wouldn't give her up. He might not say much, but he'd sometimes come up behind Angus and put his arms around her neck, chin on her head. Stand there leaning on her like a man saved.

All the sudden my grandmother hefted up her six-foot scarecrow self, and we all drew breath. She walked over and picked up the photo of Angus's mom. Wiped it with her sleeve, looked at it, set it back down. Then announced that I appeared to be on the uphill climb, and if I kept it up, all would be well. She discussed changing my last name to hers, which I wasn't wild about. Having the exact name of my dad seemed like asking for confusion. With a dead person, that could have consequences. Plus where was Mom in all this, erased? Otherwise, all good. I had legal kin and a guardian that didn't hate me. Mattie Kate brought out a roasted chicken, and we had the meal that table was made for, fit for a king.

I was on notice though, and she stayed on my case. Jane Ellen drove Miss Betsy and Mr. Dick up to visit every few months, and it never stopped feeling like *Survivor* where I was fixing to get voted off the island. I hung on. The bright side was, our living-room situation improved, with the mayhem transferred to Coach's office and other places Miss Betsy wouldn't see. Once in a great while they stayed the night. Mr. Dick used a fold-out couch in a downstairs room.

Angus said it wasn't too disgusting now for friends to come hang out, so we both did that, different friends. Hers being all guys, mine girls. Angus said just keep the drama out of her sight. She and Sax and them stayed upstairs gaming or watching old movies that Sax was into. He memorized entire scenes and had contests with Angus of trying to say all the words right. Crazy to watch. They were in the same classes, and he kind of egged her on into contests of everything, including best grade on every test. Meaning he ended up pissed at Angus basically at all times.

Downstairs meanwhile, the so-called homework club girls sat around our king table trying to fit variable expressions into the tiny mail slot of the Demon skullbox. They'd crack their gum and be amazed how hard it was for me to get higher math. If I flirted with any one of them on accident, the others would go brutal on her. They couldn't just relax and be regular human. Angus had a point, and I was seeing it. Then May Ann Larkins's older sister Linda came with them, being an alleged math whiz. Holy Moses. Long hair, long legs, long sideways looks out of those blue eyes like, *dude*, I'm in high school. I know shit. This is not algebra we're discussing. Try doing equations some time while trying not to get an under-table woodie.

Who these girls really loved though was Mr. Dick. If he was there, they made such a fuss I got jealous. Me with my excellent arms and legs, feeling sorry for myself because these girls are crowding Mattie Kate out of the kitchen, taking over the blender to make strawberry milk shakes for Mr. Dick. Or pushing his wheelchair outside, breaking branches off the crab apple tree for him to smell the first flowers of spring. Not that I wanted to be their little dolly. It's how sweet they were, in a way that didn't happen with regular guys. Not trying so hard. And not scared.

Coach saw my future, and it was tight end. Every kid of course dreams of being quarterback, and I did too, since my altar call in the church of Fast Forward. But I never forgot what Coach said: a team is made of followers. Your coach or QB calls the play, but it's not worth pissing on unless there is execution. That's what a tight end is about. He's fast, he's alert, good at catching a pass and holding the ball and putting it down. Big enough to be a force, to get around the end and open a gap for a running play. If he has what it takes to play both ways, D-line also, and if he says his prayers, then he might get to be one of God's diamonds. A General.

Football camp ran through a good chunk of summer, both JV and varsity. Coach had put in the word with Mr. Briggs, the JV coach. He agreed about me being tight end, and that's where he put me, as alternate to Collins that was in eighth grade, my height, thirty pounds heavier, headed up to Generals the next year. To be the next Collins, I would need to bulk up. Bring it on.

Mr. Briggs also ran defense drills for the high school team, and sometimes called me over to go in on the hamburger drill, which is man-on-man. If he needed to match somebody for size. U-Haul always noticed, trying to take me down with the Hellboy eyes. But too bad for U-Haul because I just kind of oozed my way into the kingdom, as young as I was. No more errand boy. Coach gave me full privileges in the weight room, and at camp we all used the field apparatus together. The chutes, which are a metal pipe contraption like cattle chutes but with a low ceiling, three feet high. You have to get your body down low and charge through there, duck-walk running without banging your helmet on the top. Four guys would run it side by side, trying to be first to get to the end and hit the blocking guard and push him up the hill.

The chutes were my superpower. On other drills I held my own, but on the chutes I amazed. Tall as I was, I could still make myself small. And then at the end, throw all my might against whatever stood in my way. Everybody saying, *Jesus look at him go, turbo-Demon.* To me it felt normal. Keep your head down, don't get seen, assail. My life was one long chute leading me there. By fall I was dressing out, wearing my jersey to school on Fridays, getting the full quotient of pep rally love. A damn seventh grader. In another year, I'd be playing for Coach.

34

A lot of firsts that school year. First scrimmage, first JV game, first tackle, first passing yards made. First school dance, with an eighth-grader girl that was dead serious about it so, my first real date evidently. Angus and Sax went together dressed as *Planet of the Apes*, loser of their grade contest (Sax) being the human on a leash. This is Homecoming mind you, not Halloween, so. Not a date. But Angus took mine over, ordered the corsage from Walmart, took me to Goodwill where we found this dope white suit from the sixties. In my size, unbelievable. I've grown into my hands and feet by this point and am pushing six feet, thank you Mattie Kate.

First time going to the dentist. I didn't see any need, but Angus said quit being a baby, it's just to get everything cleaned off and fillings if applicable, all normal people do this. Which was a hurtful thing to say. I knew plenty of other kids that hadn't been. It's not like Mom didn't try. Whenever I was little she'd drive me to the free RAM clinic they have every year, but those things are a madhouse. People camping out in their cars for days to try and get in. Mom was afraid of me getting trampled and going home with less teeth than I started with.

First time carrying a grown man up a flight of stairs. This was Coach, passed out in his office. It wasn't exactly a habit, but it happened. Fall wasn't bad, spring would get worse. In the off season without games to think about, he didn't have a lot to do back there, so he'd take a bottle for company. Angus just rolled with it, saying it was always something that came and went. You try walking in his shoes, she said. Your wife dying on you, leaving you with a baby to raise. And a girl baby at that. He never even got to try for having his boy.

It was also my first time thinking school could be halfway interesting. Coach Briggs for history was breather-pass, if you weren't a corpse he gave you the benefit of the doubt. If you were on the team, extra credit. Mr. Armstrong, not so much. He gave points for talking in class, this being Language Arts, but

Jesus. Ask where something is at, he'd say "Preposition crime." Say you're tired, he'd slump his shoulders and say, "And feathered." This was due to his accent, it can affect your hearing. "Tired" to him sounded like "tarred." He tried without success to convince us on things like subject-verb agreement, irony, etc., and spent the entire year explaining his opinion on "when" and "whenever" having two different meanings, which is just wrong, man. Give it up. The thing about Mr. Armstrong though. He would sit on his desk, take off the glasses and set them down, rub his eyes, and you'd never know what in the holy bejesus might come out.

In seventh he assigned us this Backgrounds project of finding out what type of people we came from. What kind of work. If they came from some other country, where was it. In fall we had to do interviews of old people in our families. In spring, writeups and presentations. The main old person I knew was Mr. Peg that had been a miner, but not my kin. Mr. Armstrong remembered my Melungeon question and said I should look into that. I thought, "Fat chance." The orphan habit dying hard. But! Now I had a scary grandmother. Better yet, Mr. Dick, that could probably write a book on any topic.

Mr. Armstrong pitched in some on his own backgrounds: first name Lewis, named after Kareem Abdul

Jabbar, figure that one out. His dad being a basketball fan and doctor, his mom in charge of libraries. Both with the opinion he'd lost his mind whenever he moved down here and didn't come back to Chicago. He said after ten years they were still asking if he was going to quit fooling around with that banjo and come home. We'd not known of a guy like him playing the banjo. To be honest, we'd not known of a guy like him doing much at all, given there were maybe twenty Black people total in Lee County. He said guess what, the banjo was invented by his people, it's similar to a thing their great-greats played in Africa. He said there used to be a ton of Black people living here, that came for the coal jobs. Not being allowed decent pay down south, plus oftentimes getting killed down there for the reason of Blackness. It had mostly all along been more free around here in the back-ass end of Virginia, not slavery, due to the farms being piss-poor tiny and not the big plantations. But then the mine jobs started petering out and they all went on to Chicago or someplace. For the jobs and also this thing of Great Migration, the far south being hell on earth with the Black-hater laws, and them wanting to put as much road as possible between themselves and hell. We asked why didn't the white people go too. He said it was a different story for them, some left but most didn't because of big families with relatives, already living here a long time and pretty dug in. Somebody said, "Ain't nobody gittin me off'n this mountain," which got a laugh.

He said that was a stereotype. Big subject with Mr. Armstrong. He read us these things in history that were written about the mountaineers: shiftless, degenerate. Weird-shaped heads. We thought that was dead hilarious, with Brad Butcher making a whole big thing of his pointy head, and Mr. Armstrong saying, "Not funny." He said they made us out to be animals so they wouldn't feel bad about taking everything we had and leaving us up the creek. But Mr. Armstrong wasn't from here, so we didn't believe him. We said if that's true, what all did they take? And he's like, Oh, let me think. All the timber and coal that fired up the industrial revolution and made America rich? Look at the railroads, he said. Built to move out the goods, one way only, leave the people behind. And we're all like, Okay, whatever. Brad Butcher has a pointy head, totally not deniable.

A lot of the time Mr. Armstrong would just cross his arms, sit back, and let us fire away. At each other, him, president of the fucking world, our choice. No such language allowed of course. He was okay on our sayings, though, like if we said somebody was crooked as a dog's hind leg, or born on the wrong side of the blanket. Ugly as homemade sin. These counted for Language Arts. But no f-bombs, no "them guys," and do not for the love of the Lord say you're laying down if you mean lying down. The man blew gaskets on that one.

It wasn't just the language factors, he was also big on history, for not being the history teacher. (Coach Briggs did worksheets only. Boring as death.) Like with the rebel flags, you see those around, nobody gives it a lot of thought. One of the times we saw them for instance was outside waiting for our buses, where this Chevy D/K pickup on lift-kit tractor tires comes roaring through the parking lot, tires screaming, bass thumping, shirt-less high school guys hanging out the windows ripping loose a rebel yell. The truck tore a big U through the lot and back out to the highway, flapping its glory from two poles zip-tied to the bed: American, Confederate. A lot of guys around me laughed, some few didn't. Some looked at Mr. Armstrong that was with us on bus duty, just standing over there in his button shirt, arms crossed, watching the whole yeehaw.

Then it got quiet. The ones getting on buses got on their buses. Everybody else found interesting shit to look at on the ground. Shoes, gravel, ABC gum. It was close to Halloween, I remember, because the pep squad had the front entrance all decorated up in pumpkins with bad faces drawn on in Magic Marker. So that was something else to look at. Most if not all of us being aware that this flag thing was kind of an *oh shit* situation. And wanting it to blow over.

"All right, let's start with the obvious here," Mr. Armstrong said. So, not blowing over. "The Confederacy and the United States were opposing sides in a war."

Still quiet. Among our kind there is stuff not talked about, and stuff not done, including insulting people straight to their faces. We knew of words that were not proper-noun capital Black getting used, we definitely heard those, from older guys or parents or whoever, people ticked off over something they'd never met first-hand and knew nothing about. No real person. Which to us in that parking lot, Mr. Armstrong was. We'd all had him in class or as guidance counselor steering us through the juvenile justice system, and nobody I knew disliked the man. I kept my eyes on the bad-faced pumpkins, wondering for the thousandth time how hard is it to understand, you put the eyes *halfway down* the face, not the top? Another bus pulled up and people ducked their heads and got on, probably including a few that didn't take that bus.

"*People*," Mr. Armstrong finally kind of yelled, like he did whenever we were ignorant in class. "Are you following me here? A *war.* Opposite sides. Flying both those flags at once makes no sense. It's like rooting for the Generals and the Abingdon Falcons in the same game."

Whoah. We were all like, *Crap.* Because that's unthinkable.

Some guys started mumbling *heritage* and *nothing personal,* and Mr. Armstrong took off his glasses and rubbed his eyes, looking as usual somewhere between interested and flat-out flummoxed. "Whose history are we talking about?" he asked. "Because Virginia voted to join the Confederacy, that's true. To support the plantation owners. But the people here in this county were not represented in that vote."

Nobody wanted to tangle with him. Of all of us still out there that hadn't yet got on buses or edged back into the building, I'm going to say not one person would have taken up a rifle for any plantation fat cats. We were actually glad of what he told us, that the mountain people of Virginia rounded up their own militias to try and fight on the other team, Union. He said we should feel free to pass on this info to certain guys, and we shook our heads like, *Those assholes,* regardless some of those assholes being brothers or friends or dads. Because that was Mr. Armstrong. Even if you didn't necessarily want to, you would end up on his side.

Melungeon **turns** out to be another one of those words. Invented for hating on certain people until they turned it around and said, Screw you, I'm taking this. These people were mixed, all the colors plus Cherokee and also Portuguese, which used to be its own thing, not white. The reason of them getting mixed was that in pioneer days Lee County was like now, with nobody having a pot to piss in. These folks being poor as dirt just had a good time and ended up with the all-colored babies. If they went anywhere else, these kids got the hate word, *melungeon,* which Mr. Dick said is some other language for mixed-up piece of shit.

Mr. Dick got into my Backgrounds project in a big way. It would have taken three or more kites to hold everything he wrote down. He explained how in those times a person would get called the n-word if they were even the smallest tad of not-white. Meaning they couldn't vote, have their own farm, etc. So these mixed-ups that everybody called melungeon went to the courthouse and said okay, *that's* what I am. Write it down. (Proper noun, capital M.) The courthouse people probably studied on it but couldn't find a thing in their books to say a Melungeon couldn't do this or that, so. Nice trick.

Those were my people. Mr. Dick and Miss Betsy's father moved away from here to find Jesus, but mainly to stop being one of these people. If his kids ever wondered about aunts or cousins, they'd get leathered for asking. They never heard the word *Melungeon*. But they still got wind of these dark-skinned, green-eyed people back in Virginia. My dad grew up asking if it was true. At the time he ran off, he and Miss Betsy were hurt at each other so not speaking. She never knew if he'd made it back here till he wrote the letter saying he was in Lee County with a girl, fixing to have a baby. The little green-eyed Copperhead he'd never see.

Mr. Dick wrote all this up and gave it to me in an envelope and said to read it later, by myself. And I've never been one to get choked up or weepy, even as a small kid. But after I read about my people and my dad, I shoved my face in the pillow and cried like a baby.

Angus said I'd better start a little notebook on my girlfriends, to keep them all straight. This was just Angus being Angus, not mad, more like she's proud of my success. I never had that many at one time, or for long. To be honest, the most interesting female type of person in my life right then was Ms. Annie, art teacher, obviously out of the girlfriend running. Also I might have been pretty far gone for Linda Larkins, the big-sister math genius and killer flirt from the homework club, but ditto, not a real thing. She was seventeen.

As far as these others that actually liked me, they kept me busy. We were too young yet to do anything in cars like normal kids, but where there's a will there's a couch and blankets or my bedroom, if everybody else in the house was asleep. Study sessions that ran long. It got to where if I wasn't doing something with a girl, I was thinking about doing something with a girl. My body went on wishing even if I managed to get the brain on something else. Exactly like it does if you're hungry. I'd been a no-toucher person for a lot of years. I vaguely recalled Mom being a big hugger, but then came Stoner, and family life turned into a whole other kind of contact sport. This skin-on-skin was all new. I did get nerves over not knowing what I was doing or what was allowed, these middle school girls being dead set against going all the way, like they'd made a girlwide agreement. But I knew where all the bases were now. I got tutored.

Once in the blue moon I'd go with the Peggots to see Emmy, but over and out on that onetime romance. Maggot swore she was dating Hammer Kelly now, which she denied. She made fun of Hammer's countrified haircut, and said the only person in love with him was Mr. Peg, that took him hunting. So Hammer was not the problem, Emmy was just not that hot on me anymore. I was hurt at first and then wasn't, because like they say, plenty of fish in the sea. Jump in there wearing your football jersey to school on a Friday and my Lord, it's like that Bible miracle. Fishes coming out of everywhere.

For the record, gifteds can and do play football. Some of the guys found me out, but they didn't give me that much grief over it. I never missed a practice. These guys were solid, future Generals all. Cush Polk for one, our JV quarterback, decent as milk, a preacher's kid from way the hell over by Ewing. Tall, blond, actual red cheeks, the type that still said "Yes ma'am" to teachers. He claimed he got his speed from being youngest in a family of nine, and his mom only ever cooked for eight. And Turp Trussell for another, that once drank a shot of turpentine for purposes that remain unclear. Big clown, built like a brick shithouse, boldness of a bull in rut. Brain of a deer tick, but that's not something to hold against a running back.

My main gifted thing was twice a week after lunch riding over to the high school with Fish Head and the Vo-Ag crowd. They did auto mechanics, I got an hour with Ms. Annie in her art room. I thought she would make me do fruit pictures, but no. If it's cartoons I cared about, she said, draw them. I just had to use the different media to see how they worked. One day she sat still and let me do her portrait. Which I'd been doing secretly anyway. She didn't always wear long skirts, sometimes it was these big balloon pants with all the pockets full of brushes, rulers, paint knife, pocket knife. Hippie food items like cereal bars. Always the scarf on her long blond hair, and the dangle earrings. She was a small lady in big, swishy clothes.

She had unheard-of things in her art room, watercolor, gouache. I got to try them all. She made me use perspectives, vanishing point, etc. She gave me human body charts to copy out for learning the muscles, because a cartoon isn't a realistic person but there's a real person *under* it. Like the skull and the face. That room, those hours. I can still smell them. I would be just getting into something before it was time to put away the paints and get on the bus back to middle school. Never in my life have I known time to fly away like that.

Angus got on a tear that year to start an academic team, which nobody knew what that was. She explained to me that it's like a sport, only between teams trying to know the most of all the different units like math, literature, etc. A victory of smartness type of thing. She was in high school now, with her big crazy dreams. I said it'll never fly, that bird has got no wings. She said it's already flying. They actually did this in other high schools. She heard of it from her friend Sax's cousin that lived in Northern Virginia. Kids up there evidently had brains coming out their ears, to the extent of needing to meet up with other kids for brain-to-brain combat.

I said what Mom always did if I wanted to do something extra like make my bed: Why make life harder than it is? Angus ignored me and wrote a proposal that Sax's cousin's teacher helped her with, over the phone. She had this whole presentation she practiced on me prior to giving it to a teacher's meeting. I said maybe tone down the outfit, which was a DC Brainiac shirt and giant glasses she found at Goodwill, but other than that, perfect. So she gave it for the teachers and then the PTA. Next, the freaking school board. I'm sure they thought, this weird girl is getting no dates, fine, let her fill her empty life. Then snoozed till the word *competition* came up, which meant going to other schools, on buses. Meaning money. They all said the same thing: This category is already covered in the budget. Gifted kids got to take a school trip in sixth or seventh. By high school, evidently if you're still gifted, you just need to get over that.

Defeat only made Angus more determined. I didn't get it. I asked if she was jealous over me getting all my art attention, and she said *art*, was I kidding? If I wanted to discuss unfairness, let's talk about football. Uniforms, equipment, buses to away games, state championships. The school board threw money at all that like water on a house fire. And I was like, Angus. It's *football*. Take that out of high school, it's church with no Jesus. Who would even go?

Sax had helped hatch this plan, but wimped out under pressure. Angus was on her own. You'd think at least teachers would back her up. This girl that aces everything she looks at, and reads books for actual fun. But they waffled. Granted, it's Angus, of the full metal clothes closet and opinions not kept to herself. Plus Coach was always pulling rank on teachers to keep his flunk-ass players eligible. Not Angus's fault, but complicated. Finally she went to her old Jonesville Middle pal Mr. Armstrong, that helped her get an assembly set up to present the idea at the high school. Which ended up being a small meeting in a classroom of any kids interested, aka wanting to get out of class for that period. Sax called in sick, aka gutless. It was my art time, so Ms. Annie and I went to the assembly of Angus. She gave her talk about improving skills, school pride, etc., all boss in her black T-shirt with green-skin Brainiac, plus combat boots, hair in fifty little ponytails representing nerve ends. (No hats allowed in school. The girl could push dress code to an inch of its life.) The only nervous part of her was her eyes. She gave examples of what some teams did, like making team shirts with math equations on them or the names of books they'd read, and wearing these to school. "Like football players wearing their uniforms on Fridays," she said. "But we could pick Monday or Tuesdays, so smart kids get their own day to be lords and masters of the high school social pyramid." That got a pretty huge laugh.

Only two teachers were there, plus the principal to make sure things didn't get out of hand. He looked like he was napping. One of the teachers frowned the entire time and took notes. Angus finished up, and Mr. Armstrong said he applauded Ms. Winfield's initiative and believed her project could notch up the culture of academics at their school. He had knowledge of how these teams functioned, and was there to answer any questions they might have.

Frowny teacher had questions, all right. Who pays for this. Are these kids taken out of class, and how is that made up. Are teachers expected to put in time after school. This lady looked like she'd gone to prom in the eighties and got frozen, big hair, big shoulders. Scary. But Mr. Armstrong stayed on his even keel, talking about cost-benefit ratio, teachers volunteering to prep students in their subject areas, making good use of resources we already have.

Miss Shoulder Pads wasn't sold. "I heard her say it involved having meets at other schools. You can't tell me you're not going to want a budget allocation for this activity."

Mr. Armstrong said yes, probably. Shoulder Pads asked what the school board said about it. The principal woke up and said they'd already made their decision, so we really had no say. He said it's not like we have any new information here, that those men don't know.

We kids had zoned out, waiting for something to happen, which finally it was. Mr. Armstrong was getting ticked off. We could always tell by his accent getting stronger. He said with all due respect to our school board, we all know who those gentlemen are. Which honestly, we kids did not. Miss Shoulder Pads probably did. She was in the back of the room, and Mr. Armstrong in front, with all the kids turning back to front, watching. You could actually hear the action. She asked him what he was implying. (Turn, shuffle.) Mr. Armstrong said, Only that most of the men on the school board were experienced in the corporate world and coal business. (Turn back.)

She said, And is there something wrong with business experience.

He said, All he meant was that these men weren't trained in education per se. They came up in another era when mining labor was the end game, and college was not on anybody's radar.

Angus meanwhile is looking at me like, *Help!* But what did any of us kids know? As far as school board, college, radar, our general thinking on that topic was: So what and who cares.

Mr. Armstrong made a point of asking who among us kids had participated in any school activity other than football that brought us into competition with other schools. Which was ridiculous. We had Science Fair once that some few kids had wanted to do, girls and nerds. But not in state competitions obviously. We said *duh*, no. We'd get creamed. Everybody knows this.

And he said that's right, we would. Because every school district to the east of us in this state has AP classes and science labs and other things our students have never had here.

That's where the bell rang, fight over. The principal had already slipped out with nobody noticing, Shoulder Pads packed up her business and left, but some few kids stuck around to disagree with Mr. Armstrong, remembering the fun times of seventh-grade Language Arts. No, they told him. Wrong. We'd get creamed because the kids in Northern Virginia and those places just have more brains. But outside of a schoolroom, we could whip their asses.

And Mr. Armstrong rubbed his eyes and shook his head and said, "Oh, my effing God." Which we felt was walking a fine line, languagewise.

I was sorry for the crushed dream of Angus, but art time with Ms. Annie was all the extra I needed. Other than it being another thing to want more of, Demon and his cravings: for food, for love and touch, and now her lit-up face seeing something I'd done right. I didn't really care about the main gifted thing, the spring trip over school break. All year we had to study on this certain place and write our papers so we'd be all wised up whenever we got there. Which makes no sense. I mean, why not just *go*? Whatever. Sixth-grade trip I couldn't, being not yet up to par on my grades. It was just science museum in Charlotte, no overnighter due to budget cuts, so. Rip-off. The teachers promised they'd make it up to us the next year, which I didn't believe for one minute. Angus said wait and see. Her failed victory of smartness thing was a setback, but in better days she was always one to tell me I should start trusting the wild ride, meaning life or whatever. Because it's not one hundred percent fucked up, once in a while it delivers.

And in seventh grade, holy God, it did. They said we were going to Colonial Williamsburg, plus an afternoon at Busch Gardens amusement park, and one entire day at Virginia everloving goddamn Beach. The ocean. For my paper I didn't even know where to start, but I narrowed it down eventually. Currents. They travel around the earth in gigantic circles, you seriously would not believe it. Then March rolled around and the school said there wasn't money after all for a bus. No trip. And I was the idiot for listening to Angus, trusting the damn ride.

But then came a last-minute save: some volunteer moms would drive us. Hot damn. The car I got assigned to was a Plymouth Eagle wagon of me, driver-mom, her daughter Lacey, and her two bffs Gleanna and Pristene. All being mad Christian from the same church, so they knew all these Jesus songs they sang back-to-back from the minute of pulling out of the school parking lot. Hand motions. *This little light of mine, I'm going to let it shine* (hold up a finger like a candle), *don't let Satan blow it out* (PHWOOF!). I thought of Mr. Peg saying a man can get used to anything except hanging by the neck. Fine. I was going to see the motherfucking ocean.

Then Gleanna said she didn't feel so hot, and without further ado puked all over herself and the two of us in the back seat. Sudden death on the songs of praise. We pulled off at a truck stop where Gleanna was issued a ginger ale and her victims took our overnight bags to the rest rooms to get cleaned up and changed. Then we headed out again, one carload of worse-for-wear Christians with Gleanna up front now, where she supposedly wouldn't get carsick. I had my hunches though on it being some other kind of sick, because this is I-81 we're on. The one straight highway between Jonesville and anywhere.

Sure enough, halfway through "I Have Joy Like a Fountain in My Soul," Gleanna hurls again, nailing Driver Mom. Who by now is disgusted with the whole business, and tells us at the next exit she's going to go find a pay phone and call the Super 8 Motel where we were supposed to stay. To let the others know our carload was turning around and going home.

My ocean quest ended in a rout, at Exit 114. Christiansburg. *Irony.*

35

Ms. Annie had a tattoo nobody knew about, on her shoulder. I could draw it for you right now. A goldfish, with its long fins and tail flowing and twisting like it was swimming on her skin. All the perfect scales, with each little curve edged in gold. In class she always wore big paint-stained shirts that were her smocks, probably Mr. Armstrong's that got too ratty for him. I tried not to think about him and her doing husband-wife type things. I saw her tattoo because after the weather warmed up, we'd go outside to eat our lunch. She'd do that in just her tank top.

We ate lunch together because of how nice she was, plain and simple. She saw that I never finished up in an hour, so one day she said instead of riding the Vo-Ag bus over from the middle school, I could come earlier during lunch period to spend extra time. Meaning, after Mr. Armstrong's class, straight over to Lee High and Ms. Annie's art room. That was trippy, sitting there watching him comment on somebody's Backgrounds presentation, thinking how the man would be unthrilled that I was crushing on his lady. He had no idea. She didn't either.

To get the earlier ride, she organized for me to come with the janitor Mr. Maldo that cleaned the Jonesville Middle bathrooms in the mornings, Lee High in the afternoons. He'd get me there before lunchtime, so. Two whole hours of art. Afterward, I'd walk over to Lee Career and Tech and wait with Fish Head and those kids for our bus back to the middle school. One thing about Tech, that place was crawling with recruiters. Army, navy, these guys with their accents and complicated uniforms that made them seem not quite real. They had tables set up, wanting us to come sit down and chat, probably not realizing we weren't yet of age, just bussed-over seventh graders. And I'm going to tell you something, these military guys could look you in the eye and shame your ass: Is your dad at home right now in his boxers watching Spike TV? Did your mom get you diagnosed ADHD so you could get your Medicaid and see a doctor for the first time? Did you know less than half the people in this county have

jobs? Evidently we take the prize of America, as regards unemployment. Answer to these problems: Let's
get you signed up. Probably Fish Head and them were
counting the days.

As far as my janitor ride, Mr. Maldo, he was quieter
than anybody you ever saw. He would talk some to Ms.
Annie and eat his lunch in her art room before getting
on with his bathrooms. But he never said one word to
me, all the mornings I rode in his truck. Otherwise a
regular guy, with something going on with his left hand
that was small and no muscle tone, but he still could do
everything as far as driving and janitor. Ms. Annie told
me he was always alone so she'd started taking coffee
breaks with him, and from there the lunch thing came
about. The other teachers wouldn't give him the time
of day, even though their pay was not much better. Ms.
Annie said all God's children have to take a shit, but
you'd never know it from the way they treat the ones
that clean it up. She actually said shit. You can see why
I was so gone on her.

In Mr. Armstrong's Backgrounds project we learned
one thing: if you throw a rock in Lee County, you will
hit somebody with a family that's worked coal. Almost
everybody in our class had great-grandparents that came
over from some country to work in the mines. Or they

were here already, and worked in the mines. They told stories of all the kids in a family ending up working in a mine underneath the same land that was bought from them. The coal guys came in here buying up land without mentioning the buried treasure under it. And then all that was left was to work. Even little kids, pushing tubs of ore from the coal face to the tracks. "Low coal" was working thirty-six-inch-tall seams, stooping under a mountain. The Pappaw stories were mostly along the lines of: How awesome was that, us busting our asses. Whereas the Mammaw stories leaned more towards, not awesome. Getting your paycheck in fake money that you had to use in the coal company's stores that charged you double. Breathing black dust all day, coughing up black hunks of lung all night. Husband and sons all dying in one day in a shaft that blew up.

One girl's presentation she called "The Other Side of the Coin." This is flippy-hair Bettina Cook with her posse of gal pals and her dad that owned the Foodland grocery chain, seven stores in the tristate area. Packed-lunch sandwiches with the cut-off crusts that flabbergasted me back in third grade, yep, same Bettina. Her family on her mom's side were major shareholds of the Bluebonnet Mine. She passed out brochures on all the good the company has done for Lee County in the way of town park benches, etc. Her great-grandfather won an award from the governor for buying one of the biggest coal veins under Kentucky and figuring out how to pull it out of the ground on the Virginia side so they didn't have to pay some certain tax. She had a slew of relatives that were senators and such in the State House, that she showed us pictures of on her computer. Yes, her own computer, brought from home. Also a Motorola phone. Queen Bettina, we all knew she operated at her own level. But Mr. Armstrong said okay, everybody gets a turn, just listen.

For the most part though we listened to the crushed-leg, dynamite-explosion type of stories. This was the oldsters' chance to complain to their grandkids that usually have no time for old-people shit. If a miner didn't get buried alive, the question was what part of him would give out first: lungs, back, or knees. I thought of Mr. Peg that was giving out all over, on disability ever since he got hurt. Another old-guy topic: how they didn't want handouts. They grew up hard-working men and that's what they believed in, working. Even if they were on disability now, goddammit to hell. They're not that person. They *hate* that person. They also talked about Union. But I mean, this word. Like it was a handshake deal between them and God. We had the general idea of workers wanting their pay, safety, and such. But where did that go, and what was the *or else*?

Or else they'd all walk off the job and let the coal bosses suck their own dicks, Mr. Armstrong said. Not his words, but he got it across. He showed us films. Obviously we loved teachers showing films: nap time, makeout time if applicable. But this one, Jesus, you needed to see how it came out. Men calling a strike, the company calling in the army to force them back to work, the miners saying guess what, we've got guns too. Serious shit. Battle of Blair Mountain, that turned into the biggest war in America ever, other than the civil one. Twenty thousand guys from all over these mountains, fighting in regiments. They wore red bandannas on their necks to show they were all on the same side, working men. Mr. Armstrong said people calling us rednecks, that goes back to the red bandannas. Redneck is badass.

Anyway, it was all in the past, nobody in class had parents working in the mines now. We'd heard all our lives about the layoffs. The companies swapped out humans for machines in every job: deep-hole mines went to strip mines, then to blowing the heads off whole mountains, with machines to pick up the pieces. Bettina was like, Get real, you all, companies are in business to make money, that's just a fact. The facts being, there's hardly any coal jobs left around here. Bettina also said there's no such thing as unemployed, just not trying. Her posse all stuck up for her side, and other kids said city people were the problem, for bad-mouthing coal.

I wasn't from mining people that I knew of, so it wasn't my fight. I drew a lot of pictures and kept quiet. I dreamed up the idea of a comic strip about an old time red-bandanna miner that's a superhero, busting the company guys' nuts. I could ask Ms. Annie for tips on how to make him look old-time, because she was amazing like that. She'd know exactly how to do it.

Mr. Armstrong as usual let the argument go rogue for a long while. *But,* he finally said. Didn't we wonder why there's nothing else doing around here, in the way of paying work?

Our general thinking was that God had made Lee County the butthole of the job universe.

"It wasn't God," he said. Just ticked off enough for his accent to give him away. I remember that day like a picture. Mr. Armstrong in his light-green shirt, breaking a sweat. We all were. It's May, there's no AC, and even the two cement bulldogs out front probably have their tongues hanging out. Every soul in the long brick box of Jonesville Middle wishing they could be someplace else. Except for Mr. Armstrong, determined to hold us there in our seats.

"Wouldn't you think," he asked us, "the miners wanted a different life for their kids? After all the stories you've heard? Don't you think the mine companies knew that?"

What the companies did, he told us, was put the shuthole on any choice other than going into the mines. Not just here, also in Buchanan, Tazewell, all of eastern Kentucky, these counties got bought up whole: land, hospitals, courthouses, schools, company owned. Nobody needed to get all that educated for being a miner, so they let the schools go to rot. And they made sure no mills or factories got in the door. Coal only. To this day, you have to cross a lot of ground to find other work. Not an accident, Mr. Armstrong said, and for once we believed him, because down in the dark mess of our little skull closets some puzzle pieces were clicking together and our world made some terrible kind of sense. The dads at home drinking beer in their underwear, the moms at the grocery with their SNAP coupons. The army recruiters in shiny gold buttons come to harvest their jackpot of hopeless futures. Goddamn.

The trouble with learning the backgrounds is that you end up wanting to deck somebody, possibly Bettina

Cook and the horse she rode in on. (Not happening. Her dad being head of the football boosters and major donor.) Once upon a time we had our honest living that was God and country. Then the world turns and there's no God anymore, no country, but it's still in your blood that coal is God's gift and you want to believe. Because otherwise it was one more scam in the fuck-train that's railroaded over these mountains since George Washington rode in and set his crew to cutting down our trees. Everything that could be taken is gone. Mountains left with their heads blown off, rivers running black. My people are dead of trying, or headed that way, addicted as we are to keeping ourselves alive. There's no more blood here to give, just war wounds. Madness. A world of pain, looking to be killed.

36

I was born to wish for more than I can have. No little fishing hole for Demon, he wants the whole ocean. And on from there, as regards the man-overboard. I came late to getting my brain around the problem of me, and still yet might not have. The telling of this tale is supposed to make it come clear. It's a disease, a lot of people tell you that now, be they the crushed souls under repair at NA meetings or the doctors in buttoned-up sweaters. Fair enough. But where did it come from, this wanting disease? From how I got born, or the ones that made me, or the crowd I ran with later? Everybody warns about bad influences, but it's these things already inside you that are going to take you down. The restlessness in your gut, like tomcats gone stupid with their blood feuds, prowling around in the moon-dead dark. The hopeless wishes that won't quit stalking you: some perfect words you think you could say to somebody to make them see you, and love you, and stay. Or could say to your mirror, same reason.

Some people never want like that, no reaching for the bottle, the needle, the dangerous pretty face, all the wrong stars. What words can I write here for those eyes to see and believe? For the lucky, it's simple. Like the song says, this little light of mine. Don't let Satan blow it out. Look farther down the pipe, see what's coming. Ignore the damn tomcats. Quit the dope.

Two thousand and one was the year I had everything and still went hungry. I was a General. A freshman, and already I had that. Fridays, being worshipped, wearing my number 88. Roaring out of the Red Rage field house with my herd of men. Big tackles, locker room wrestling, all that hard flesh on flesh was like feeding a whole other empty stomach I never knew I had. Even the bad felt good. Pushing myself in the weight room till every string in my arms was on fire, my chest clenched like a heart attack, the guy spotting me saying Jesus, man, your face looks like a damn hemorrhoid. Laughing because it's so fucking good to hurt that bad. Most people never get anywhere close to being that much alive.

Learning the plays by heart and then making them on the field, there are no words to describe. It's an act of magic to take an idea and turn it into bodies on bodies, a full-participation thing for all to see. Like what's said about the Bible, the word made flesh. Learning to read the QB's mind, knowing what he'll do almost before he does. The Generals were always a running team, but now the Demon was changing their game. Passes fired and completed, you'd hear the stands go dead for one heartbeat before they roared. Excuse me for saying, but damn, it's like an orgasm. To blow up a crowd by doing what nobody expected.

Coach Winfield was like a father. Just guessing on that obviously, but he was the first and only man that ever saw what I could do. Not just do *for him*, there were those, many in number. This kid can cut my tobacco, make me a buck, eat my shit. With Coach, everything we did, we did for God and country but specifically Lee County. More than once I got mentioned by name in the *Courier*, because who doesn't love the shooting star, "From Foster Homes to Football Fame." I got a tiny bit full of myself over that, but Coach was more so. If he had his eye on me at all times, driving me hardest, that was his patriotism. I knew he'd lost a lot in his life. The young wife, and before that, his career, getting hurt and messed up as a kid not much older than I was

now. I knew he went to bed too early, that he drank
to shut himself down. And I also knew that whatever
good a man like that could still feel for another person,
he felt for me.

So I had more than I deserved. Ms. Annie, for another example. In high school art was a real class, for
juniors and seniors, but she gave me special permission. I could take her class all four years if I wanted.
Assuming I stuck around that long. Lee High is where
kids like us come to our crossroads of life: walk up the
steps of the big brick box and turn right, through the
front door into the classrooms. Or left, down the long
chain-link tunnel, past a thousand army and navy re-
cruitment posters, into Lee Career and Tech. Nothing
arty down there, trust me.

Thanks to the September 11 thing that happened
that fall, the posters now were stapled on top of each
other, and the recruiters likewise. Let's go kick terror-
ist ass, they all said, and many answered the call. Why
not. Lured by the promise of one paying job at least,
between high school and death. Because the attack
itself didn't seem quite real. To us, skyscrapers are
just TV, so watching two of them fall down, over and
over, looked like the same movie effects of any other
we'd seen. We knew people died. We had our assembly,
flags down, sad and everything. I'd had nightmares of

falling like that from on high. I know it was real build-ings. And they still have lots more standing in those cities, so I guess that's a worry. Here, if any terrorists came flying over, they'd look down on trashed-out mine craters and blown-up mountains and say, "Keep going. This place already got taken out." It was hard to see how September 11 was my fight. As far as doing good for my fellow man, my better option was football.

Lee Career and Tech looked like a path to freedom, definitely. A shot at working in an auto shop, no more to be held prisoner at a desk? Yes please. But Mr. Arm-strong had nailed my destiny to the classrooms. Spanish, Geometry, Personal Finance, like I would have need for any of that. I stuck it out for one reason only, my daily hour of Ms. Annie. That was the plus side of being in her art class. Downside: having to share. She was sweet to everybody, it turned out, walking around the room saying "Nice composition," or "I like your use of color there," or at the least, "I can see you worked really hard on that, Aidan." I had to do the same assignments as everybody else, elements of design, linear and grid drawing, value shading. Life drawing. She had us take turns sitting as the model, but clothes stayed on, so. Not like my earlier art enterprise. This was about pro-portions and such, tension versus a body at rest. I won't say I didn't learn things. Oil paints, all these pigment colors with automotive names: titanium, cadmium, cobalt. For homework we did still lifes. Angus helped me think of excellent ones, like *False Teeth in Salad Bowl.* If I did cartoons now, they had to be on my own clock.

All the middle schools fed into Lee High, which meant I was back in school with my own people. A Maggot-Demon reunion. And Emmy, a junior like Angus. But all going our different ways, as you do. I was a jock. Maggot mainly hung with the Goth girl Martha that cut his hair. Emmy sang in the choir that Ms. Annie was director of, and ran with the popular end of the arty kids, Drama and them. What Angus had to say about the Drama girls, you can guess. But even still, I was sharing those halls with people that knew me. Some were my wingmen, some had put ice down my back. One of them still remembered my mom. It felt like I existed.

What I didn't have was the thing I thought about night and day. In high school now, a General, and I'd still not been laid. Not the full thing. For various reasons, it hadn't happened. My number-one crush being twenty-some years and a marriage outside of bounds. And a teacher. I knew they had laws, thanks to that home ec teacher scandal in Gate City that people won't stop talking about until the sun goes cold. No way. But girls my age seemed young, more heavily into show-casing the goods than backing up the inventory. Angus had tainted my judgment.

And then I fell face-first into Linda Larkins. Long-legged homework club flirt, older sister of May Ann. She was out of high school now, nobody I would run into, but out of the blue sky one day she calls me up. I'm waiting for "Sorry, wrong number," but she's dis-cussing Friday's game, how great I looked. And then without even a warmup stretch, she's talking about my tight end like *that's* a sight she'd like more of, she'd bet my ass is all muscle and hers is pretty tight as well, had I ever had my tongue up a pussy like hers. With Mattie Kate and Angus not six feet away pouring Cokes over their ice cream. This is the kitchen phone we're on, and me shitting bricks, saying I appreciate that, okay I'll think about that, thank you. I kept my front to the wall and made a break for privacy.

This was to become a regular thing. I would mumble something and run to take the call upstairs. We had a phone up there on a long cord we could drag into our rooms. I was a good liar. But Jesus. This girl. I'd have her breathing in my ear, I'm about to come, and Mattie Kate is outside the door hollering, "Do y'all kids have anything to put in a dark load?" Linda would not stop until we both got ourselves off. Full-color descriptions.

Sometimes I'd have to fake the big finish for safety reasons, like if I had people waiting on me and needed a hasty exit. But holy crap. For a young male, a blue-ball shutdown like that I'm pretty sure could be fatal.

I kept expecting her to give me the coordinates for a meetup, but no. Linda Larkins was phone-sex only. My entire freshman year. It never crossed my mind that I could just, you know, hang up on her. This older person had singled me out, and it felt like the NFL draft, you go where you're called. I spent a lot of time trying to think of things I could say to sound more adult. That year I also did the regular things with other girls, homecoming dance etc. But it put a weird spin on normal dates and conversations and the making out, if that happened, to know that this chick that could probably suck the enamel off a phone receiver was waiting to polish off my night.

Angus as usual felt free to weigh in on the immature type of girls I was going out with. But for once, Angus had no inkling. Of this older woman that had me by the cerulean balls.

The Peggots started taking me in their wing again. Asking me over for Sunday dinners, not worried anymore about me trying to worm in and get adopted. I'd forgiven them for all that. It worked out for the best, not just because Miss Betsy was rich and sending Coach checks every month for my upkeep. She was my true kin. Paying me back on what I never got from my dad.

Angus would drive me to the Peggot house, with U-Haul supervising. She was in driver's ed, needing her forty-five hours behind the wheel. She got curious about the trailer home where I was born and everything, so one time we walked up there but I got pretty sad. Big Wheels trike on the porch, toys left out in the rain. A naked doll half buried in dead leaves with all its hair cut off, just those hair dots all over the scalp. A whole new family in there. Mom and I were nowhere.

Mrs. Peggot always would ask if my friend wanted to stay for dinner, and a time or two Angus did, but it was awkward. That winter she was into this black leather motorcycle cap, like they wore in the old movies prior to helmets. Mrs. Peggot, poor little thing, just stared at that leather hat with no gumption to make her take it off. So over here is badass Angus, over there is Maggot with the eye makeup, black nail polish, and ever-expanding lip ring collection. Big shock, Demon is the nice-looking normal kid at the table.

They'd got so old, Mr. Peg worse than her. He always had the limp, but now it was the event of his day to get up out of his La-Z-Boy to come sit at the kitchen table. Maggot was taking his toll on them. He'd not say two words at dinner, just the black eyes bugged at me from time to time like, *Rescue me.* Which he was in no need of, Maggot did what he pleased. He laid out of school plenty, and I'd heard about the molly parties, the drugstore raids where he was ganking more than Max Factor. I wasn't sure anymore how I fit into the Peggot situation.

One evening Mr. Peg got me outside, shoving his walker out the kitchen door, huffing and puffing over to his truck, supposedly for my second opinion on his battery cable. Actually, to discuss Maggot. Same truck, the Ram. Pretty sure Mr. Peg would be buried in that vehicle. He said he and Mrs. Peggot couldn't handle Maggot anymore. They were getting almost scared of him. I didn't ask if Mariah was getting out of prison any time soon. I tried to stick to the positive, that Maggot was a tenderhearted person underneath the cosmetics and death metal business.

Mr. Peg asked, "What is he thinking of, to go around looking thataway?"

I said I didn't know. Not wanting to be a traitor to Maggot. But also, I really didn't.

Mr. Peg elbowed the truck to keep his balance while he lit a Camel with his shaky hands. He smoked and looked up at the sky. His bottom eyelids drooped so their red insides showed. "Whenever I's a boy," he finally said, "we just done like we's told. Is that so damn hard to do?"

I said we probably were more messed up nowadays due to TV and cable.

He asked why, though. What was so confusing? I don't think he was wanting me to throw Maggot under the bus, just really and truly wondering what was so hard for us. Now, versus the old days. I said maybe the difference was we could see now what all we were missing. With everybody else in the world being richer than us, doing all kinds of nonsense and getting away with it. It pisses you off. It makes you restless.

Mr. Peg finished his Camel and stamped it out on the ground, shifting the heel of his old leather shoe side to side, grinding in slo-mo. Even for that small thing, he was hard pressed. "Do you reckon we spoilt him?" he asked. "Me and his mammaw? Because I'll tell you something. She'll go to her grave a-wishing she done better for Mariah."

I told him Mrs. Peggot had always treated me with the exact same niceness as Maggot whenever we were small, and I was glad of it. That as far as home life went, I had run the full gamut, and theirs was the best by far. I didn't think Maggot was mad or spoiled or anything like that. Just trying out being a different type person.

"Well, what kind of gal is ever going to have him like that? If he keeps on?"

I said maybe he was just having his wild oaks and would come around in time. Or else he'd find somebody. I reminded Mr. Peg of that thing people always say: There's a shoe out there for every foot. Mr. Peg said he used to think that, but now he wasn't sure if Maggot even wanted to find any shoe to fit him. And I didn't say so, but I kind of agreed on that. Or if he did, because honestly don't we all, probably Maggot's kind of shoe hadn't been invented yet. Or if so, they didn't stock it in Lee County.

Weirdly, I kept thinking of Fast Forward, how he could look at us and name the true person inside us. Even if we were pathetic losers for the most part. Fast Forward was proof that a kid could keep his head up and survive, no matter how shitty the waters. He'd called me a diamond. I don't know what I thought he could do for Maggot. It just seemed like this was a situation for Fast Man.

37

What never changed was U-Haul Pyles despising me. Staring me down at practices, lurking around the house making sure I knew my place. I gave as good as I got. I hated him touching our mouth guards, and being the one to tape or ice us if we got hurt. I hated him going with us to Longwood for the playoffs, which is how far we got that year. State semifinals. I got more playing time than Collins, which I felt bad about because it was his last game. He was a junior, quitting school after the season ended due to his girlfriend having a baby. The other teams had the usual things of their cheerleaders making up special Trailer Trash cheers against us and the fans throwing cow manure on the field, which we were used to, any time we played outside our region. But we kicked ass pretty decently.

Semifinals would have been the highlight of my young life, if not for the Hellboy eyes burning me from the sidelines. And then later that night, U-Haul coming around to our motel rooms lecturing us about no partying, like we're infants, putting Scotch tape on the outside of our doors so he could check in the morning to see if we'd been out. The man could leave a layer of scum on any good thing.

Sometimes he'd make me go with him on nonsense errands, like running over to the machine shop to help him load up the tackle sled they repaired. Asking in front of Coach, so I wouldn't share my true feelings on where he could put his tackle sled. Sometimes he'd stop by his mom's over at Heeltown, which wasn't a single-wide but one of those built houses from the old days, small, front porch with the steps falling apart. So much crap on that porch, my Lord. Sofas and chairs stacked one on top of another, upside down and sideways. Cats crawling all over and through the piles like head lice. While U-Haul went in and did whatever he did, I would sit in the car and count the louse cats. As far as going inside, you couldn't pay me.

Mrs. Pyles would want us to drop her off at Foodland or Walmart. She was heavier set, not a skeleton like him, but had the same red eyes and weird bad manners, old-person version: *Honey, I'm just a little old nobody, now scooch 'at seat forwards and give me some room.* She had a creepy way of getting intel out of me. On the McCobbs for instance, that were back from Ohio, living in Pennington Gap. *Honey, is it true what I heert about her a-pawning off solit gold jewry, ain't nobody can figure how she come honest by them kind of things.* I was dumb enough to tell her about Mrs. McCobb's rich parents spoiling the grandkids, before it dawned on me what she was actually trying to find out: were the McCobbs trading in stolen goods.

Another couple she wanted to discuss was Ms. Annie and Mr. Armstrong. What made him think he deserved that beautiful woman for his wife. *They's a world a people a-wondering on that. Why she'd stoop to lowerin' herself thataway.* "Beautiful" in this instance meaning white, I wasn't stupid. Ms. Annie was a tattooed hippie. If she'd married any other guy in Lee County, they'd be asking why *he* had lowered himself. A kid of my raisings is not going to tell an older person flat-out, Lady, get the hell out of my face. But I came close.

Finally one day I told U-Haul that on errands involving his mom, he could count me out. He drilled those red eyes into me and said maybe he wasn't a Gifted, but he knew things. Who I talked to on the phone. Where

I hid my weed. How he knew, I can't guess. But if I mentioned to Coach about us going to his mom's house, he said, I'd be looking for a new place to live.

After the season ended, I had time on my hands. The Peggots sometimes would pick me up on a Saturday to go see June and Emmy. No more Kent. That show was over, and according to Emmy not just a breakup but World War III. Kent was a con man, June was a paranoid bitch, take it from there. I hated to think about it, but Maggot wanted details, what weapons were drawn, etc. Probably from living with grandparents he was action-deprived. This was a Saturday in February, cold as tits, and still the adults sent us outside to mess around in the woods. Probably so they could have this same conversation inside. We made a pitiful little band: Maggot freezing because he refused to wear the camo hunting coat the Peggots bought him. Emmy in her puffy coat that was black-and-white-printed like a cow, seriously. We dragged our feet through leaf slop, kicking up the smell of acorns. There was an old wrecked cabin on the property, logs and a fallen-down chimney but no roof. We would have called it a fort if we were kids, but now it was nothing. A stupid place we were forced to hang out because we couldn't yet drive.

Emmy said Kent and June didn't use weapons, just mouths, both parties packing serious heat in that department. Kent was a yeller, but mouthwise, June was an AR-15. Instant reload, engineered to kill. Maggot wouldn't let it alone, wanting to know what June was so mad over.

"I don't know. Him being a shiznet?"

Emmy's cheeks were bright pink and her eyelashes sticking together, so pretty and sad. We were sitting on the wrecked chimney, cold rocks freezing our asses. Emmy and Maggot both picking at their nail polish, me pitching rocks through the gaps. The logs were gigantic, stacked at the corners the way you'd twine your fingers together, with big spaces between. They'd had some mother trees to cut down up here, back in the day. I could see Emmy's weird house down below us through the trees, a giant wooden bowl upside-down with Peggots inside.

"Wait, correction," she said. "A weapon was drawn. Mom had her Ginsu knife and kind of waved it around. Not chasing or anything. She was trying to get supper before it all blew up."

What got the knife pulled on Kent was him telling June to leave it to the professionals because she wasn't a doctor, just a nurse. Snap. A nurse practitioner *is* a trained professional and *can* prescribe medications,

Emmy said, June was just choosing not to give out any more of Kent's poison. She'd organized a meeting on it over at town hall with the biggest crowd they ever had showing up, to sign a petition thing against Kent's company. Which he took to be a major backstab from his girlfriend. He said she was uncompassionate to people in pain. June said if he wasn't such a damn coward he'd come down to her clinic and see all these decent people with hepatitis from needles, and their family farms going bankrupt in six months. Which I didn't get honestly, about the needles. Kent's thing was pills.

We stayed up there a long time in the cold. If we were kids on TV we'd have been sitting in a booth of some shiny diner or at a swimming pool mansion, instead of dead-looking woods. I used to like being outside with all the little beings poking after their business, but at that moment I felt ripped off. All we had was this junk-bone cabin with its valuable parts, if any, long since stolen. Some squirrels to shoot at, if we'd been properly armed. The day would have been more tolerable if I'd brought a joint and we could get blazed, which Maggot would have been up for. Emmy, a question mark. June protected that girl like she was made of ice. Emmy was old enough to be driving, but June was all, No ma'am, these Lee County roads are teenage death traps, etc. You had to wonder why Emmy wouldn't push back.

I knew her and didn't know her, regardless our one-time marriage plans. I watched clouds of frozen breath coming out of her face while she worked her way through the drama of June and Kent like it was the end of the world.

Long story short, whatever supper June was working on with that Ginsu knife did not get made. Screaming happened, hightailing was done. Kent being top sales-man of his company had sold a gazillion of his pills in Lee County and actually won the giant bonus, Hawaii vacation for real, that he was going to take Emmy and June on over spring vacation, so. Bad timing on that one. The breakup rattled her so bad, June had asked Hammer Kelly to come over and spend a few nights at the house in case the bastard came slinking back around. Emmy said Hammer was so nice about it. He sat up on the couch all night, sleeping with his deer rifle in his arms.

I was and always will be an idiot. I just pray to get old enough one day to recall Linda Larkins without want-ing to curl up with my balls between my legs and die. It was her little sister that dropped the bomb, and the only saving grace was that May Ann herself had no clue. Just pokes me on the shoulder in class one day and says hey. Her sister got married.

"Your sister Linda?" I got an instantaneous half-mast. In fucking Algebra. Then the rest of it slowly dawned. "Married? Who to?"

"This guy from over to Hillsville, Loring Blake, that drives stock cars. I doubt you'd know him. My mom only met him the once, before Saturday. We all thought she was going to community college after she got that Rotary math-whiz thing. And then she *bam*. Married."

"Saturday," I said. It was the end of class, where we were doing our homework. Never mind a grenade had gone off in my brain, I was expected to keep my voice down.

"It was no big deal," May Ann said. "They just went to the courthouse and then we had the family over. They picked up ribs at Fatback's. And then Linda's all like, *That* was brilliant, barbecue *ribs*, because she's wearing a white dress, and . . . why am I telling you all this?"

"I give up. Why?" I was kind of seeing stars, the way a shock can make you somewhat go blind. As soon as that part was over, I knew I would feel like throwing up, laughing, crying, and jerking off in public. About equally.

"*Because*, Linda *said*," May Ann rolled her eyes, "Quote, do you still see that tall redhead kid Demon that's on the team, will you please tell him I done got married? Unquote."

"Why would she mention me?"

"How should I know? Send her a present for the damn baby shower."

I'd had no reason to think Linda had any feelings for me. None. She never even wanted to go get McDonald's or drive around or anything. But to find out she was playing me utterly? The mystery of her thinking, plus no more of those phone calls, cold turkey, and nobody ever even knowing about it, was a black hole of misery. A huge thing that basically didn't happen.

Angus came close in those days to knowing everything about me, but not this. I never told her about the Linda calls, too embarrassing. Even more so now. Dumb little horn dog boy that thought he was a man. The breakup, if you can call it that, weighed on me hard, and ended up wrecking the next weekend that happened to be our big road trip to Murder Valley. Angus and me only, no U-Haul, which should have been the happiest of events. Angus had gotten her license and wanted to celebrate by driving us someplace other than Walmart. She settled on wanting to see the house where she used to go with her mom, to visit Miss Betsy. On the drive down, she started up her usual teasing about my girlfriends, and I told her she could stuff a sock in it.

"I could," she said, grinning. "But how fun would that be?"

"It's not a joke. You are cordially invited to stay the fuck out of my personal business, for a term of one hundred years to life."

She said nothing. Eyes on the road, hands on the wheel at eight and four o'clock.

"If you think my love life is so interesting, Angus, why don't you get your own?"

"Why? Let me think. Because males are infantile, and females are exasperating? So, what does that leave me, animals? You know, I might get there. But so far I'm just not feeling it."

Silent treatment after that. For over an hour, which was hideous. We'd never really had a fight before, other than our nonsense ones that were purely for entertainment. I hated that I was harsh with Angus, but you can't help what you are. I spent some time idling on the memory of punching the dash of Mrs. McCobb's car. Eventually Angus tried to bring up another subject, of being worried about her dad. But Coach seemed the same as always to me, and I said so.

Things didn't lighten up till we got down there to the house. Angus jumped out of the car with a big smile, walking all around with her hand clamped on her hat like she's in shock, and it might fly off. Looking at things outside the house, inside the house, like this happy big-eyed fairy in a white T-shirt and leather vest, saying, Oh, I *remember* this! Which I'm sure she did, since nothing probably had changed in that house since God was a child. I hadn't really thought before about the place being special to her, like seeing my dad's grave was to me. The house where her mom grew up. The bed where she slept, the bathtub. A dead parent is a tricky kind of ghost. If you can make it into more like a doll, putting it in the real house and clothes and such that they had, it helps you to picture them as a person instead of just a person-shaped hole in the air. Which helps you feel less like a person-shaped invisible kid.

They were tickled at us for coming, and had cooked a feast. Mr. Dick had a kite to show me, not ready for takeoff. Miss Betsy wanted to have a discussion on our futures, and sat us down in her living room where old furniture goes to die. Angus went first, being older, junior year, which Miss Betsy said was time to think about college. Angus said she definitely wanted to do that, and study psychology or sociology, which I wasn't even sure what those were. But so what, because that was her plan, Angus had no intention of staying in Jonesville. Not that she'd made any promises, but I felt betrayed. She was leaving us. What about Coach?

So I was already upset whenever it came my turn to tell Miss Betsy my future. Plus I'd never given it a thought, other than hoping to be still alive. All I could come up with was maybe trying for college on a football scholarship. Miss Betsy said the same thing as always: "As long as you don't let the sports interfere with your studying." With no comprehension that on a football scholarship, sports are kind of the whole point. She wasn't opposed though. She said it was important to leave Lee County at some point and "take a look around."

At what, I wanted to ask. Cities? Harsh streets and doom castles where nobody lived that I cared about? I couldn't stand to live anyplace without Coach and Angus. And Mattie Kate, I included her. The Peggots close at hand, and my teammates, and all of Lee County chanting my name from the stands: *Dee-mon Copper-head!* To start over someplace from scratch, as nobody and nothing? I hated the thought. I was only just now starting to exist.

The drive home was no better. Well, Angus was better, chatty and cheerful. But I was still hurt at her, with more reason. Miss Betsy had got her off and running. She wanted to talk about the colleges she'd thought of applying to. There was one in eastern Virginia she had her eye on, so she might actually end up living near the ocean! That was just lording it over me, I felt. She was older, leaving first. Making sure I knew she wasn't scared of a thing. Worldly-wise.

I rolled down my window and tuned her out. I could smell the dirt of the fields waking up, see the mountains with every tree lighting up on top like a candle, first neon green of spring. It should have been enough for any human person. I did know that, I have to say. Give me a view, pretty as a picture, I'm still pissed that I'll never get to see the ocean. I wondered what would it take to stop me feeling like I had rotten fruit down in me instead of a heart.

All I could think about on that drive was my lonely runaway spree that got me down to Murder Valley the first time. I took notice of all the sorry attractions as we went past them: the barn where I hid out to sleep in somebody's haymow. The mini-mart where I curled up starving behind a dumpster, in the rain. The truck stop where I lost everything, and cursed a hooker to die. My entire life's savings, that probably amounted to less than Angus had spent on her latest change of clothes. I didn't point out any of those places to Angus. I'd been so young back then. And still was, I guess. She liked to tease me that if we lived to a hundred, she would still be the one to get there first. Which was true. No credit given for all the extra miles that take you nowhere.

38

Once I'd stopped being a kid, summers were nothing more than a crap job to clock into. That or school, same difference. But living with Coach, summers came back. I was a kid again, as far as somebody else taking care of the harder aspects, bill-paying, etc. I should have been thankful, and can't say why I wasn't, other than that growing up goes one direction only. You can't stuff a baby back where he came from, and on from there.

Oh, I said thank you. All the time. To Mattie Kate for feeding me, to Angus for driving me places, to Coach for every freaking thing. Saying thanks, but at the same time thinking, where can I hide my dope, how can I get out of doing all this homework, who is he to tell me I can't go riding around with my friends on a Saturday night, I'm not a damn child.

That summer, I wanted a job and my own money. Coach said there was no need to fool with that, just tell him what I wanted and he'd get it taken care of. Which was my whole problem, having to ask. He said to remember football camp started in July. That was two months away. I seldom pushed back on Coach, but this time I did. So he asked around, and found out Coach Briggs's brother that was managing the Farm Supply in Pennington needed somebody over there pronto. Briggs said the job was mine if I wanted it because his brother was in total charge, due to the owner having a heart attack. They needed an extra pair of hands and muscle enough for loading bags of feed into people's trucks. Muscle I had, plus I was fifteen, so having a job was legal now. Coach filled out some forms and I started the day after school let out. Seven bucks an hour to save up for a car.

Because that's the thing: until you have your wheels, you're still a child. Anyplace I went, I had to ask. Angus now had a '99 Jeep Wrangler that Coach gave her for the sole reason of turning sixteen. She drove me over to Pennington for my job. Or worst case, U-Haul would. If I wanted to go out someplace after work, I had to make that somebody else's business. Fifteen is the hardest age. Emmy had told me in Knoxville they had these city buses that could take you all over. Not just to school, but for people of every age to ride to the movies, skate park, wherever. Or if in a hurry, you could call up a taxi. I'd seen those things on TV, but didn't totally believe Emmy. That they would have all that for any regular person to use.

Farm Supply was the best job I'd had so far: decent customers, zero rats that I was aware of, nobody cooking meth. The whole store had this sweet-feed smell that's a cross between fresh-cut grass and Cheerios. They sold all the regular type things: calf and sheep wormer, horse tack, lawn chemicals, chain saws. In May they had tomato plants and the like, for people to get their gardens put in. I'd set all those on a table outside the store in the mornings, and move them back inside for closing. Next came the chicks, also my job: unloading them from the cardboard shipping boxes into big troughs in the store where people could see and buy them. Keeping up their feed and water, the heat lamps on at all times, changing out the newspapers under them because man could those little dudes poop. The life of a chick: eat, shit, peep such a ruckus inside those galvanized troughs, you could hear it from the parking lot. Hard to believe every old beady-eyed hen starts out that way, as a little fuzz ball, yellow or black or spotted. Mornings before we opened, it was my job to scoop out the ones that had died overnight, cold and flattened out from being walked on. Each one I took out back to the dumpster was its own tiny sadness.

This girl Donnamarie that ran the register was the one to train me, nice as could be other than acting like she's my mom, all honey-this and honey-that and "You think you can remember all that, sweetie?" Just three or four years out of high school herself. But she did have three kids, so probably she'd wiped so many asses she got stuck that way. I didn't hold it against her. Coach Briggs's brother stayed upstairs in the office. Heart attack guy was a mystery. First they said he might come back by the end of summer. Then they all stopped talking about him.

As far as customers, every kind of person came in. Older guys would want to chew the fat outside in the dock after I loaded their grain bags or headgates or what have you. I handled all the larger items. They complained about the weather or tobacco prices, but oftentimes somebody would recognize me and want to talk football. What was my opinion on our being a passing versus running team, etc. So that was amazing. Being known.

It was the voice that hit my ear like a bell, the day he came in. I knew it instantly. And that laugh. It always made you wish that whoever made him laugh like that, it had been you. I was stocking inventory in the home goods aisle, and moved around the end to where I could see across the store. Over by the medications and vaccines that were kept in a refrigerator case, he was standing with his back to me, but that wild head of hair was the giveaway. And the lit-up face of Donnamarie, flirting so hard her bangs were standing on end. She was opening a case for him. Some of the pricier items were kept under lock and key. I debated whether to go over, but heard him say he needed fifty pounds of Hi-Mag mineral and a hundred pounds of pelleted beef feed, so I knew I would see him outside. I signaled to Donnamarie that I'd heard, and threw it all on the dolly to wheel out to the loading dock.

He pulled his truck around but didn't really see me. Just leaned his elbow out the open window and handed me the register ticket. He'd kept the Lariat of course, because who wouldn't.

"You've still got the Fastmobile, I see," I said.

He froze in the middle of lighting a smoke, shifted his eyes at me, and shook his head fast, like a splash of cold water had hit him. "I'll be goddamned. Diamond?"

"The one," I said. "How you been hanging, Fast Man?"

"Cannot complain," he said. But it seemed like he wasn't a hundred percent on it really being me loading his pickup. He watched me in the side mirror. The truck bounced a little each time I hefted a mineral block or bag into the bed. Awesome leaf springs on that beauty. I came around to give him back his ticket, and he seemed more sure.

"I'd have taken you for a stranger," he said. "You're twice the man you used to be."

Weightwise, possibly true, and at least a foot taller since fifth grade. "Doing my best," I said. "You taking all this to Creaky's cattle?"

"Hell no. That shithole ran itself into the ground some while ago. Tempting as it was to stay and watch the old man cry, I did not."

"So is he dead now?" The last time Angus and I were out there to steal another Christmas tree, we'd seen bank auction signs stapled on the gate.

Fast Forward took a drag on his cigarette, eyes sliding sideways. "Maybe. For all the shit I give." I just stood there burning it all to my brain. Dragging like that, not giving a shit like that.

"So, where you living at now, man?"

"Got my own place. Close to fifty acres up by Cedar Hill."

"Sweet, your own farm. Is it over by where they have the bison?"

"A few miles shy of that. North side of 58."

"Sweet," I said. Again. Just struck dumb, because holy crap. A foster kid going that far in life, not even all that old yet. "You got a tobacco bottom?"

"Two-and-a-half-acre allotment, so it's just about right. Manageable."

"Well, if you ever need help cutting or anything. You know I'm there."

"I appreciate it. But what I need to know is, can the boy keep the damn gloves on."

He smiled, I laughed. The times we'd had. I mean, yes, this was getting poisoned that we were laughing about. Every minute of those days had sucked. But with another person knowing it was hell, you had something. I wanted to ask if he ever saw Tommy or Swap-Out, but really I wanted to be the only one that mattered to him. I saluted him, as in times of old. I needed to get back to work, but my feet were glued to the ramp. Fast Forward, human magnet. And his F-100.

He threw the butt of his cigarette onto the cement pad. "Like I said, I almost didn't know you up close. But I have seen you on the field."

"You've seen me play?"

"What do you think, Eighty-Eight? I'm a General. It's not something you get over."

The engine engaged, the Lariat pulled out, and I waited to see if my heart would settle down. He'd seen me play.

He made a point after that of speaking to me any time he came in. Often he was just picking up Ivermec or syringes, small things, not needing me to load his truck, but he'd find me and ask how was it hanging. I'd look up from tagging cultivator handles with the price gun, and here would be that movie-star smile coming my way. Almost like a friend thing. Even still, it surprised the heck out of me the day he asked if I wanted to hang out that evening. On a Saturday, which meant cruising. This being the Saturday-night enterprise of every human person in Lee County between age sixteen and married. Dragging Main. Right away I'm thinking, does he know I'm only fifteen, no vehicle, how will I meet up with him and all such as that. But he was chill, saying he'd pick me up here at five and we'd go see what kind of action we could scare up. He said some guys that were Generals from his day wanted to talk to me about the new direction we were taking on the field. I said sure. I was nervous to call Coach's house and tell them not to come pick me up because I was going out on my own. The hard part I mentioned of feeling like a child. But it was U-Haul that answered, so I just told him. I owed nothing to U-Haul. The rest of the day dragged, due to not having my head in the feed store game. Bored with filling chick waterers, ready for action.

Pennington Gap is where we went, naturally. Because let's face it, cruising Jonesville is small-time, the whole of Main being a mile and a half, tops. Federal Street in Norton has its pros and cons. But in Pennington you cruise all the way through town on Morgan, then swing around and come the whole way back on Joslyn, a giant circle with the vehicles moving so slow it might take a full hour for a circuit. You could walk it faster. Car windows are down, bodies are hanging out, conversations are had. People flirting between vehicles, or between the cars and bystanders. A lot of girls hung out in front of Lee Theater or at the turnaround by the dry cleaners, staked out in one locale to see the show go by. Some brought lawn chairs. Wanting to get the bigger picture, plus your outfit will not be seen all that much if you're inside a vehicle, if that's your main selling point. Not just the clothes but, you know. How they fit.

It was my first cruise from the vantage point of a

vehicle, and we were the star attraction. Like the convertible in the parade with the homecoming queen in her fluffy dress, waving. In our case there was no waving, and really no "we," it was all about Fast Forward. Hands resting loose on the wheel, head tilted back, eyes half closed, that smile. *Ladies, come and get it if you dare.* The girls came alive in a wave whenever that Lariat came into view. Up and down like fishing bobbers. Skintight jeans and halter tops and bare midrifts that hurt your crotch to look at.

We were four of us: Fast and me, a girl by name of Rose Dartell, and Big Bear Howe that played all four years with him as left tackle, so you know what that means. No tighter pair than a QB and the defender of his blind side. The girl, another story. Not to be mean, but this Rose person was not in Fast Forward's league. Sharp elbows and eyes, sharp snaggled teeth, dirt-color hair teased out to the breaking point. She had this whole look about her like: *Go ahead and try, pal. Can of whoop-ass at the ready.* She sat in the middle and Big Bear shotgun, so after they picked me up, it was me and the door handle trying not to get too acquainted and fall out. We talked football, Big Bear wanting to know my thinking on our defensive lineup this year. Then we got to Joslyn and pulled into the string of cars, and Big Bear stamped shoe prints on the knees of my jeans on his way to squeezing out the window and swinging his big self onto the hood of the Lariat. He's our damn hood ornament. With ants in his pants, whooping at girls, pounding the metal really fast on both sides of him. Monkey drummer. It's a credit to Ford engineering and the support struts in that hood, because Big Bear is 250, easy. It was a time-tested arrangement evidently, and Big Bear a spectacle in his own right, about like the Hulk would look in Carhartt overalls and no shirt and a buzz cut with an epic rattail. They say Big Bear used to coil up that rattail in his helmet during games, for safety reasons. In this fashion we made our way around the town, clockwise I guess you would say if looking down at us from the standpoint of God. And let's hope God wasn't, this being open season on shady transactions, PDA, and language. "Where the fuck you been at lately asshole" being the usual hello.

It was all eyes on Fast Forward, but second to that, who was with him. I saw girls elbowing each other and pointing. The second time we rounded the corner by Lee Theater, Fast Forward surprised me by getting out of the truck. Middle of the street, engine running, door standing open. He's saying, Get the hell out here, Demon, so I do. He's got people for me to meet. Guys he played with and their girlfriends or wives or whatever, some with babies, Fast Forward being a few years out of high school now and some of these guys even older. The names went around too fast and loud to remember, this one guy Duck or Buck had a praying hands tattoo on his shoulder, his girlfriend wearing a Miss Thing T-shirt, another guy missing his pointer finger, I noticed. All retired Generals, here a tight end, there a cornerback. Fast Forward told them I was his prodigy that he'd discovered as a diamond in the raw. It happened more than once, him throwing the door open with the truck still rolling in some cases, me trying to keep up. Sometimes the younger people knew of me already, more really than they knew Fast Forward. He said you have to keep the legacy connected, old with the new, and I could see that. People come and go through school, there's a danger of them forgetting the greatness of Generals of old. It was awesome plus terrifying. Would all these people expect me now to be that cool, or make touchdowns on every pass, or loan them money? Jesus. Fame is a lot to handle.

This girl Rose meanwhile was mystery cargo. I recognized the name, recalling the dope cookies some girl had made for our long-ago Squad parties. If this was the same one, we were looking at the longest girlfriend audition of history. What I'm saying is, she still didn't have the job. They were more like brother and sister, having this fight the entire evening where she says, "I'm stupid obviously, but Jaylene Glass says it's not how you said," and he's like "What isn't," and she's like "You know what, the mouse deal," and he's like "Cry me a river," and she's like "You talk to her then," and he's like "I don't think so."

At a certain point he finished his Marlboros, crumpled the pack in his fist, and dropped it in her hand. Rose told me to let her out, and off she marches up the sidewalk, stick-thin girl with big farm-girl strides in her tight jeans and high-heel sandals. One block and two minutes later, she's back in the Lariat with a fresh pack and he's lighting up without word one of thanks. And I'm wishing I'd been quick enough to jump out and get them myself. That's how it was with Fast Forward, you wanted to be his foot soldier. I was proud to be a General of the present day, but would have given anything to be as old as Big Bear, and the one to have been his left tackle.

It wasn't till Rose got back in the cab, giving me a full front view, that I saw the scar running up the left side of her mouth. It dragged through both lips, leaving them out of whack in a kind of snarl. She was one of those heavy-makeup girls, majorly covered up, with the color boundary where the face meets the neck. Due to the scar, you have to think, but really it was not hideable. I wondered what that was like. For guys, it's just war wounds. We had this defensive tackle Davy with a serious scar on his forehead from where he was playing in the driveway as a tiny tot, and his dad ran over him partway with the car. And Davy was A-okay girlwise, a babe magnet to be honest. But for a girl like Rose, did this scar put her out of the running? Or middle-tier girlfriend level, so she could try all her life with Fast Forward but still remain doomed? I didn't know the rules. Something was going on between these two, but love was not it.

Not my problem. I was living the life I'd been waiting for. From time to time Big Bear would step from the Lariat hood onto another vehicle and lie on the roof, leaning over the window to talk to the driver. From time to time somebody would give him a joint, he'd take a couple of drags, then walk back over onto our hood and pass it inside to Fast Forward. We'd pass it across, and I'd hand it back out the window to Big Bear. The sun hung low over the mountains like a big red tit, the lights blazed green and red off the glass store windows, the girls bent their beautiful faces together keeping their secrets, their bodies of sweetness, Fords and Chevies, the river flowed. This is how it's done, I thought, and I am doing it. Dragging Main.

39

I don't know why, and God help me. But whatever it was Maggot needed, I thought Fast Forward could put him together with it. If I was a friend to both, I was duty-bound. So I invited Fast Forward to come with us to Fourth of July at June and Emmy's.

Word was out on this being the party of parties. Regardless June Peggot being no friend to fireworks, happy to sit you down and tell you all she'd seen professionally in the way of blown out body parts. No matter. Emmy crossed all normal lines of popular, hanging out with certain of the geeks, plus drama kids. Put those together and stand back. They'd been going to Tennessee for the banned-in-Virginia items, your aerials and laterals. Collections were taken up. Angus was like, Idiots with gunpowder, no thanks. But I was jacked for the day to come.

Fast Forward picked me up with two passengers already, surly Rose and this chick called Mouse, due to her tiny size I'm guessing. Not shyness. She had on a silver bodysuit thing like MTV-wear, already in the middle of a story as I climbed in. Full Yankee accent: "So he's on air in two minutes, I am losing my shit and *ohmygod* I get it, this is a comb-over on *top* of a toupee! I am supposed to do *what* with this? So I pick it up and lob him with the powder so he won't shine through and then pop it back down, you *guys*, I could be a very rich woman if I decide to extort."

Fast Forward said he thought she already was a rich woman. She laughed and hugged her giant purse. Turned to me, blinked her huge eyelashes. "I don't believe we've had the pleasure."

Mouse told me she did hair and makeup for celebrities, in case I'd missed that. Fast Forward told her I was the rising star of our football team. To anybody else he'd say "of the Generals," so this Mouse individual had to be from a galaxy far far away. Filly she said, which is a girl horse and made no sense until she clarified it was a town, Philadelphia. I gave the directions to Maggot's house, and then we were five in the cab. Cozy. Mouse hops in my lap with her feet dangling. She's pretty, I guess, her head too big for her small body, snub-nosed, but makeup obviously at the pro level. Her hair was this exploded whale spout situation that got in my face. She was like a doll on my lap. Still running at the mouth, she's got a gig coming up for a Britney show or whatever, constantly interrupting herself to remark on some ramshack place like she's never seen poor. Her big purse was on the floor at this point, rolling and clanking. I saw the end of a Pringle can sticking out. In case you were wondering what does a mouse eat.

Maggot was twitchy as hell. I saw Fast Forward checking him out sidewise. I was used to Maggot, to the extent you can get used to the black-dyed hair curtains, the neon mesh sleeves and giant black pants that he and his Batcave pals got at their Goth outfitters place over to Christiansburg. Chains all up and down the legs, so if you needed to put the boy on a leash you'd find many convenient attachment points. Maggot would always be my blood brother, but at that moment I was embarrassed. Mouse was staring at his makeup and dye job like she might not live through the experience. It could have been worse, Maggot was known to turn up at school with his scalp dyed black on accident. I gave directions to June's. Fast Forward drove with one hand on top of the wheel, cigarette out the window, eyeshades at Slim Shady half-mast, while Chatty Cathy ran her travelogue, *ohmygod* that dog is chained up, how can people be so cruel, what is that green shit growing on the side of that house (it was normal moss) *ohmygod*. Half a mile out from June's the line of vehicles started, parked all sigoggling on both sides of the road. We pulled over and walked down the gravel road, already hearing music through the woods.

"Nice sidewalks you have here in East Jesus Nowhere," Mouse said, grabbing Fast Forward's arm, teetering in her giant platform sandals. She was barely waist-high to him, toting that gunny-sack purse. Rose fell back into walking alongside Maggot and me, but looked like she'd snatch us baldheaded if we tried striking up a chat. Maggot checked out her dog-snarl scar, which maybe he thought was wicked, who knows. At the bottom of June's driveway he stopped to light a joint. Rose said "Bogart much?" so Maggot passed it to her in a futile gesture of friendship. He probably needed to balance out whatever he'd taken for pregame. The lad was wound tight. NoDoz crushed and snorted was a Maggot go-to, a grade school discovery I'd needed to try no more than once. I mean. Is life not menacing enough without feeling like ants have moved into your skin? Not if you're Maggot. He moved on from there to Adderall, which is doctor-legal, anybody can get it from anybody. And lately, smurfing Sudafed from drugstores to sell to the cookers. Probably getting paid in merchandise.

Rose took her time with the joint, waving bugs away from her face and her big cloud of hair. I took a couple of hits and headed in. Two guys ran through the woods wearing shoes and nothing else, yelling about swimming. There was no pond around. Guys were shooting bottle rockets at each other. Leggy girls slumped among the trees like wilted daisies, probably running replays of failed attempts, like we did with football games we should not have lost, but did.

I wanted to find June so she could meet Fast Forward, but he and Mouse were already gone. Maggot spotted his friend Martha aka Hot Topic in a little fist of kids in their chain pants and fingerless gloves, and made a beeline. If this was a Maggot rescue mission, I was failing. I spied June on the upstairs deck of the dome house, looking as usual hotter than a truck stop shower. Little red shorts, tall drink, fluffing the hair off her neck. She had a gang of ladies with her, some in nurse scrubs, and Ms. Annie in her hippie attire acting like she's one of their crowd. She was Emmy's choir director, but invited to parties now? That seemed like showing off.

June's house had no real yard, just a clearing in the woods, now crowded with people yelling at each other over top of Eminem. Extension cords ran from the house to some big speakers borrowed from school, because drama kids got away with shit like that, so the cattle in the neighbors' farms were now trying to chew or moo over top of Eminem. The trees were shaking, and the dirt under our feet. I shouldered in to find the keg that Emmy's parties were starting to get famous for, regardless June keeping Emmy in the egg carton. June would not have us driving the winding roads to get our drinking on. Do it here and sleep it off, was her policy, and she meant it. Start slurring or tripping and she'd take your keys, ordering you to sleep on whatever floor you could find, and please not on your back. Live to see another day. She was convinced the population of Lee County was headed for zero, because in any given year she saw more people dead of DWI-wrecks and vomit-choke than babies born.

Near the keg were folding tables strewed with paper plates and leftovers of a feast I was sorry to have missed. And Emmy, bent over a giant sheet pan cake decorated like the flag, flipping her long hair back over her bare shoulders, trying with a too-big knife to cut out little blue squares with one star each. She was a shiny star herself in her little white top, white hip-hugger jeans, some prime real estate in between. I got a rush to recall touching that belly under the blankets. You don't forget your first, even if we're only talking the minor bases. She was in the big leagues now, laughing, padding around in Chinese-looking flip-flops, giving out cake squares on napkins. I wondered how it would feel to like who you are, changing it up as needed to stay on top with ease. While other girls went on trying too hard, wearing the hair big, the makeup bright, the baby-blue sweatsuits with the whale-tail of thong showing in back above the pants rise. I felt safer in those waters, honestly. Technically Emmy was like me: dead dad, messed-up mom. But damned if you'd ever guess. She seemed like a person born to have sidewalks under her feet.

I chugged my beer and said hey a lot because I knew every Dawnella and Preston in this place. Mash Jolly, one of the rough kids I rode the bus with long ago, pounded me on the back and said "Damn, man, tight end! I totally fucking called that one." I said yeah, he totally fucking did. He said some of them later were driving over to that waterfall place with the swimming hole in Scott County, Devil's Bathtub. The hair on my neck stood up. But I just said Sure, man, knowing full well they'd be shit-faced and doing no swimming in the dark.

I watched the smile and curly head of Fast Forward moving through the crowd like the slick fish he was. Guys were pushing in to speak to the famous QB. Girls, more so. I saw Emmy hand him a piece of cake, arching her back in that girl way, where you notice the ass. Him laughing, her laughing, the little bow he made, taking the cake. So much starshine between those two, sunglasses needed. I wondered if she knew I brought him here. Well, that he'd brought me.

"Demon! Where the hell you been hiding at?"

I racked my beer-lubed brain for the name of this girl that had popped me too hard on the arm. One of the Peggot cousins I'd not seen in dog's years. Jay Ann. Ruby's daughter, Hammer Kelly's stepsister. I was still working through this while she told me she heard I'd moved away, and then I turned up on the football field, what the hell and so forth. I filled her in.

"Coach *Winfield*? In that house that looks like the frickin Disney Castle?"

I told her the house wasn't that big on the inside, which was a lie.

Ruby was the oldest of June's sisters, and those kids were the crustier end of the lot. But good as gold, like all Peggots. I thought of Hammer sitting up with his rifle, protecting June and Emmy. Jay Ann asked me did I know about Hammer and Emmy, which everybody did: he'd been wanting to go out with her ever since they moved back here. Maggot always teased Emmy about it. She always threatened to rip out a nose ring, or geld him. "Hammer's a brave man," I said.

"He has done swallowed the rubber minner, hooks and all. Slow and sure wins a race."

"Points for trying," I said.

Jay Ann said the party had started at noon as a family picnic with some aunts and cousins. Then June's nurse friends showed up after their shifts, and then the rest of the county, so this wingding was officially out of control. Right on cue, June came walking down among us with a metal first aid kit the size of an overnight grip. Somebody cut the music.

"Y'all listen here. I am off work today, so if you're intending to blow a hole in yourself, there's some gauze and Betadine in here. Help yourself."

Somebody up in the woods lit a string of firecrackers, *tat-tat-tat*. Everybody laughed.

"If the damage runs to eyes or limbs, you can come in the house and call the ambulance. That's all. I love ya and I mean it, try to keep what you came here with. I'm talking to you, Everett." She aimed a finger pistol at her brother.

Everett raised his Solo cup. "No problem. I'll find me one of your pretty nurse friends."

"No sir you will not. They're here to wind down after twelve-hour shifts, so if you ask them to doctor you, I will personally ruin your life. Got it? Happy Fourth. Have a big time."

Everybody cheered like she'd given the speech of all ages. She walked back up to the house waving one arm, not in a bad mood, just being June. I had yet to say hello, so I swam through bodies to the house. It was almost as crowded as outside, mostly with Peggot kin. Aunts standing close in the kitchen like cigarettes in the pack, uncles splayed on furniture like butts in the ashtray. Ruby could always be found under her smoke cloud, hair sprayed to moderate fire-hazard level, sporting on this occasion a top made out of a bandanna that probably mortified her kids. Old homecoming queens never die. She and June were standing with Maggot and Emmy and, it took me a second to realize, Hammer, that was with Emmy. I'm saying *with* her. He had his arm draped around Emmy's shoulders. Looking sure enough like the fish that swallowed the rubber minnow. I made my way over, shooting Maggot a look, wondering what the hell I'd missed here.

"Demon, *hey*," Emmy said, leaning forward to give me a hug, then holding out her droopy hand like I was supposed to kiss it. "Isn't it precious? It's a garnet. My birthstone."

I stared at Emmy's hand. June laughed at me. "The *ring*, hon."

"Oh." A garnet must be a tiny chip you'd sweep up after breaking a glass that was red in color. "So you two are what," I said. "Engaged?"

Emmy laughed, the aunts laughed, Hammer's fish smile got wider if possible, and June clarified they were just going out. The ring was a birthday present. Was this a birthday party? Ruby in her gravel voice said, "Hammer's been stuck like a tick on this gal for *years*. I reckon he finally done wore her down." More laughing. Maggot shot me a look like, I have *told* you this.

June was tickled. Tall, polite, flop-haired Hammer Kelly that the Peggots all adored since the day he came on board with Ruby's husband. (Now ex.) Not one of your hard boys to handle. Seeing June dote on him put me in a mood to break something. I needed to get out of there.

I saw Ms. Annie across the room, not with Mr. Armstrong but, big shock, Mr. Maldo. If there's any less of a party guy than Mr. Maldo on the planet, pray for him. Maybe she meant to fix him up with some Peggot bachelorette. Out of his janitor coveralls, in a pink long-sleeved shirt that mostly hid his shrunken arm, it was him all right, even if I had to look twice to be sure. Then right at that minute something caught my eye through a back window, moving in the woods. People. Fast Forward and Mouse booking it up the hill with a crowd behind them, mostly older kids I didn't know.

I slipped outside. They were all headed up to the wrecked cabin. I got close enough to see Mouse holding court in her silver jumpsuit, dealing out something from a Pringles can that was not Pringles. Small black disks. People with money in hand, Fast Forward watching over everything like he's the Squad Master. I got a bad feeling and split.

The fireworks had started. Not Roman candle shit but the real deals that shriek up and burst. Fire flowers. I found a gap in the woods and sat on the ground to watch them crack open. Flowers making other flowers, taking turns with the colors. I wondered how you'd go about that, painting the sky. It's Chinese people that do it. Their writing is on the boxes, with only the names in English: Waterfall Mountain, Peony Diadem Comet, Aerial Dragon Egg Salute. Maybe in Chinese they're all called Orgasm with Lots of People Around. Because that's the sum of it.

I had myself a moment there, against a poplar trunk, in the woods where once on a time I was happy. Fat trees with fat green leaves, fat boomer squirrels full up with the fat of the land. July being God's month. And the end of the road for my dad. I'd spent so many Fourths mad at Mom for being a killjoy, without thinking of the man that gave me life, signing off from his. Never taking a minute to count up all I'd seen, that he never got to see. Yes, life sucks, hungry nights and hurtful people, but compared to buried in a box, floating in a universe of nothing and never? I wouldn't trade. I watched a pinwheel of green fire swirl up over the treetops throwing white sparks. My dad, mom, and little brother were missing out on a lot of amazing shit.

I guess I took a small snooze, because a crack of fireworks woke me. It was full dark now. I went back up to the cabin, too curious for my own good, and sorry for it too. There was no more action up there, just guys lying on their backs, and girls that should have fixed their dresses before passing out. Mash Jolly and some other guys sat against the log walls with their heads slumped on their chests. I felt sick. Needles have always rattled me like that. Kit on the ground, or still in people's hands. No Mouse, no Fast Forward.

I got back down the hill quick. Somebody had made a bonfire, and I was glad to see Fast Forward squatting on his bootheels, feeding sticks to the flames. It was the stage of a party where the keg has run dry, Solo cups roll sadly in the dirt, cans and bottles turn up from emergency supplies. The Peggot aunts must have seized the equipment because the music was oldies, Michael Jackson and Prince. People sat in lawn chairs watching the fire like a TV show. Maggot was standing by himself. I smacked him from behind, harder than I meant to.

"Damn, you spilled me brother. Beer." He was woefully drunk, looking down at his chain pants. You have to wonder how they'd wash. Pretty sure that was up to Mrs. Peggot.

"What happened to the lovebirds?"

He cogitated. "Give it up, man. Emmy's a Britney, and you sir. You are a SpongeBob."

"Fuck you. I'm a General, first string."

"'Scuse me. A SpongeBob with a number on his SquarePants whaddayacallit."

"Jersey. Eighty-eight."

A long pause. "Jer-sey. Ten-four."

"Explain to me how Hammer Kelly gets to fly in the Britney zone."

Another pause. "I have a theory. He found Aunt June's G-spot."

Coming from a position of solid shitfaced, that was a pretty good one I thought.

Fast Forward was watching us from across the bonfire. I didn't wave or anything stupid, just wished. Until he stood up, flicked his cigarette butt into the fire, and came over.

"Gentlemen." He stood between us, an arm around each. I grew a couple inches, Maggot pushed hair out of his eyes. I asked if he got the chance to meet June, that was giving this party.

"The gracious hostess that invited us to use her Band-Aids?"

I laughed. He dropped his arms from our shoulders, seeing people noticing us. He did talk to June, he said, and she seemed like a nice lady. But he hadn't met the daughter.

"She's the one that was passing out the cake." I knew they'd spoken. I'd seen it.

"With the giant snuggly boyfriend attached," Maggot added.

Fast ignored him. "I know which one she is. Just didn't get a proper introduction."

That was on me, I'd screwed up. "We can go find her now," I said, but he didn't seem keen. "Or some other time. We're over here a lot. She and Maggot are like brother and sister."

Fast Forward was watching people around the fire that were all watching him back. Like at any moment he was going to bust an astounding move. *Feels so empty without Fast Man.* Maggot piped up that if he wanted to meet the hotcake cousin, he'd have to clear it with the boyfriend and his deer rifle. Of all the times in my life I wanted to punch Maggot, that one was memorable. I could feel the energy of Fast Forward pulling away from us.

Then Rose intercepted out of nowhere, worming through the crowd to bring him a beer. I was buzzed enough to watch it as a football play: Rose finds her gap, assesses the depth of coverage. Turns her numbers to the receiver and makes a quick slant for a run/pass combination.

He took the bottle from her and drained it. Rose watched him without kindness. If she was a football player, she'd be the one that gets you on the bottom of the pile and spits in your helmet. He handed the bottle back and told her it was time we hit the road. She dropped the bottle and walked away. Yikes. Maggot had decided to stay the night at June's. I went to hunt up Mouse.

I found her sitting in lawn chairs with June and Ruby, explaining something that involved a lot of pointing to their chins and cheeks.

"Fast Forward says it's time to go."

She looked up, her head cocked like a bird's. June and Ruby too. They all three gave me that look women get, *Who died and left you boss, mister?*

"So, what should I tell him? Do you want a ride?"

"When I am finished talking with these ladies about foundation contouring, yes."

"I'm not sure I like the sound of this Fast person," June said. "Is he drinking?"

"No ma'am," I said, glancing at Mouse. "You'd like him. Everybody does."

Mouse pushed herself off the lawn chair, which was actually a drop for her short legs. We found Fast

Forward and made our way out to the road. Most of the parked cars were still there, even with the party dying out. June's house would be wall-to-wall carpeted with drunks tonight. We walked in the middle of the road, hearing people in the woods. The saggy skin of pup tents glowed in the moonlight. A waste of a starry night I thought, to sleep in one of those. Then I heard a couple going at it hard, so privacy was the reason. Sorry to say, their secret was out. Mouse and Fast were talking, too quiet for me to hear. He seemed to be asking for some kind of intel. She was louder, so I caught answers without the questions: "High school, I'm positive," and "It better be, because I am going to be seeing bad spray tans in my nightmares."

I caught up, and asked Fast Forward didn't he think the Peggots were a good bunch.

"Bunch." Mouse said. "What comes in bunches, let me think. Grapes. Bananas."

"Honey bunches," Fast Forward said.

"Of *oats*! That's it. Oat party! Watch out for the horses." She slapped his ass.

I told Fast Forward I was sorry he didn't get to talk to June or Emmy.

Mouse asked if we were discussing Mrs. Robinson and Elaine, and I told her I didn't know them. "Are they Lee County Robinsons?"

She snorted.

Fast said the lady had her shit together, and the daughter was attractive. But the boyfriend was a knuckle dragger. "Chucklehead," he said. "Serious bumpkin seed."

"*Ohhh* yes," Mouse agreed.

I wasn't thrilled with the new situation, but Hammer was good people and I said as much.

"He's screwing his own cousin," Mouse said. "I guess that's normal for you people."

I tried to explain how they were divorce cousins and not blood kin, but I was exactly the wrong degree of sober. Which is just enough to hear how stupid you're sounding.

"Still gross," she said. "Like Woody Allen and his adopted kid. Eggs in the same nest."

I said it wasn't that kind of eggs. Mouse clearly thought I was an idiot. Up ahead of us was some commotion, guys yelling "*Go, go, go!*" Tearing towards us, and then a blast. A rain of something fell around us in the dark.

"What in *the* holy *mother* fucking *hell*," Mouse inquired.

"A kyarn blow," I said.

"A cornblow. Of course," she said.

"Not corn, *kyarn*, like roadkill. It's this thing where

510 · BARBARA KINGSOLVER

you bury an M-80. They used to put a dead animal in the hole, but now mostly it's just gravel and sticks. So it throws shrapnel."

I couldn't see her face in the dark, and didn't need to. Burying M-80s was ignorant. Fast Forward yelled at the guys to ask if the coast was clear, and they said yes, they'd only lit the one. Mouse walked fast, grabbing his arm. "A do-over of the fucking Civil War. Charming."

"Or practice for the next one," he said. Which was true, a lot of these guys would sign on to go blow up Afghanistan the day they were old enough. Their shot at seeing the world.

"Oh, my, gawd. Don't they have anything better to do?"

"Not really, no," is what I told her. "Welcome to Dixie."

I hate that I said that. Looking back. As hacked off as I was at her, I still just took it. There will always be those that look down on your station in life and call it a sty, but if you get in there and wallow, that's on you. Plus, to hear Mr. Armstrong tell it, this is not even Dixie. Our ancestors here had to save their hides from Confederate gangs that rounded them up and drove them shackled to the lines, to shoot Yanks and save somebody else's fat-ass plantations. There's north and there's south, and then there is Lee County, world capital of the lose-lose situation.

Nobody rides you like you ride yourself, they say. But we get more than our share of help. These people and vegetarians and so forth that are all about being fair to the races and the gays, I am down with that. I agree. But would it cross any mind to be fair to *us*? No, it would not. How do I know? TV. The comedy channel is so funny it can make you want to go unlock the gun cabinet and kill yourself. Do they really think that along with being brainless and having sex with animals, we don't even have cable?

There's this thing that happens, let's say at school where a bunch of guys are in the bathroom, at the urinal, laughing about some dork that made an anus of himself in gym. You're all basically nice guys, right? You know right from wrong, and would not in a million years be brutal to the poor guy's face. And then it happens: the dork was in the shitter. He comes out of the stall with this look. He heard everything. And you realize you're not really that nice of a guy.

This is what I would say if I could, to all smart people of the world with their dumb hillbilly jokes: We are right here in the stall. We can actually hear you.

40

O ne look at her and I was gone. This is the truth, it was first sight. I fell down a well into some shiny dream, and if somebody had thrown me a rope, which some few eventually did, you couldn't have paid me to climb it. Some call that addiction. Some say love. Fine line.

I wasn't looking, either. After the Linda Larkins cockup I was ready to sign on to the Angus theory on love, i.e. save yourself the trouble. Just minding my business, making my bucks at the farm store. It was their summer's end blowout, everything lawn and garden half off, plus free snacks and soda. The cashier Donnamarie lived for this shindig and organized the hell out of it, like the wedding she never got to have. Employee-zilla. Door prizes, balloons, sunflowers from her dad's farm set all around in buckets. She bought pink Solo cups and drew pig nostrils on the bottoms with a marker, so that holding the cup up to your face to take a drink made you look like a pig. I know how that sounds. But you get twenty people in a big circle talking and chugging, and the effect is pretty good.

We were slammed, people stocking up on their pesticides while the kids tanked enough free Dew to keep them wide-eyed for the week. Tearing around knocking tools off the racks, trying to bite the dog chews. I was busy as heck. Restocking, keeping track of the discount stickers that people were known to switch around. Mainly kids, you have to think. A three-hundred-dollar hand tiller marked fifty cents, this is not a criminal mastermind. Anyway for whatever reason I never saw her come in. Donnamarie had mentioned that heart attack store-owner guy, Vester Spencer, would be coming in with his daughter, and I didn't give it a thought. Until I looked across an aisle of irrigation supplies and there she was. Small, slender, long in the waist like a mermaid. Silvery purple hair cut short on one side and long on the other. Face of an angel. I wanted to draw her. Sandals with crisscross laces running up her perfect legs. I watched her talking to Donnamarie, threading her hands around, touching her dad on the shoulder. He was in a wheelchair, and that's all I saw because his girl had me hypnotized. I doubt I could have stood up without passing out.

Then Donnamarie yelled, "Demon, come here and meet Vester and Dori!" Her glittery dark eyes latched on to me, and I staggered over. "Dori," I said. "Hey. Mr. Spencer." Hell, I don't know what I said. Donnamarie couldn't believe we didn't know each other, with just the one high school. Dori's voice was like a low-running creek, deeper than you'd expect. She said she'd had to lay out of school most of last year to take care of her dad, driving him to his doctor visits and everything. And with him being still so peaked, she probably wouldn't be able to go back. They had to drive to Tennessee for the heart specialist, there wasn't one closer.

What small part of my brain hadn't turned into Jell-O worked out: no mom in her picture, like me. And she was sixteen at minimum, driving, not like me. Not good. I'd done the older woman thing, God help me. I did have my permit. I'd learned to clutch and shift years ago on Creaky's ancient International with little to no guidance, but now I had to take the wheel of U-Haul's Mustang with him saying blinker this or check my mirrors that, and me ignoring him. No license, so still a kid for practical purposes. I had no chance here. But her eyes. They were not just dark but shiny black like deep water. I wanted to go skinny-dipping in there.

I felt the minutes sliding away towards the part where she wheels her dad out the automatic doors, and I die.

I went frantic trying to pop out some reason to get her to myself, far from these shoppers and pigface cups. An old lady wearing what looked like pajamas, I swear, came over asking did we carry Snake-B-Gon. I tried to play dumb but Donnamarie gave me the mom stare, so I went to show her. With my heart banging, for fear of never seeing the fairy girl again. A nymph, I knew those from anime. Heaven's lost angel. I never took my eyes off her, while PJ Mammaw ran on about the snake she seen in her tater hole and her boy that didn't believe her. Yes ma'am, I kept saying. Watching those pretty arms and legs that were begging to be touched.

I got back in time to say a few things, all stupid. If she needed anything, she should let me know. Too bad the chicks were sold out, those little guys were cute as buttons.

"August is late in the year to be counting your eggs," Dori said. Which seemed like something a nymph would say. I said true, but you never know what a customer will want.

She gave me this amazing smile, black eyes glittering, raised eyebrows that were the same silver lavender as her hair, and said, "Snake, begone!"

Then the dad had a coughing spell and they left. For

the rest of the day I wondered if she knew the name I went by, Demon Copperhead. Was she vanishing me? I might never know.

I was a fool to tell Angus, but so afraid Dori would disappear. Like the dreams you wake up from with your heart on fire because some dead person you cared about was alive, and then by noon it's just vague nonsense. I couldn't stand for that to happen. I told Angus I was in love.

"Hold the phone," she said, not even taking her eyes off the TV. We were splayed on our beanbags in not much more than our underwear. The AC had gone out, and we were pretty shameless with each other, litter pups. Or what Mouse said, eggs in a nest. At the commercial she picked up one of my notebooks and pretended to page through it. Licked her make-believe pencil. "Okay, number five hundred. What's her name? I'll enter it before you forget."

"Fuck you," I said.

"Oh no, sir, not me. Let's keep this focused on the object of your momentary affection."

"Go to hell. Forget it."

We bickered like this every day. It was not a real fight. We'd only had one of those, and it was over. Angus was thinking now she'd go to community college, not applying to her go-away universities. For all her boss talk, we didn't know one person that really did that, so probably she got cold feet about jumping off the end of the world. Coach was her excuse, that he would fall apart if she moved out. So we were good again, at that moment watching *Survivor*, with me thinking how on an island with Dori I could outshine the city guys as far as making her a house, spearing fish. Idiotic thoughts, in other words.

After a while Angus piped up. "So who is she?"

"Nobody you know, and I don't want to talk about it."

"No problem. I'll find out next week when she's crying in the bathroom. Another victim fallen to the fleeting crushes of Demon."

I had no more to say, because she was wrong about everything: school bathroom, fleeting crush. *Too bad for you, Angus, is what I thought. You're never going to hear how this is the real deal, a whole new feeling.* Not another full day would pass though before I spilled my guts. Angus being the only human on the planet that could calm down my wild stupid heart.

A few weeks later, I would see her again. Crazy. I live fifteen years in the same county with this magical girl, never to cross tracks, and now she's the air I'm breathing.

Maybe because I was finally ready for something that good to happen for me. To trust the wild woolly universe, as Angus was always saying I ought. Tenth grade had started righteously, two shut-out games in a row. I played every minute of both, ran four TD's. Cush Polk was as solid a QB as the Generals had seen in years, and a solid friend. Maggot, sadly, not so much. High school has its razor-wire walls between these and those. I don't make these rules, they just are. My teammates were my guys. Horsing around pantsless in the locker room, to the point of naked feeling normal. Or eating in the lunchroom with covetous eyes on our wide-receiving shoulders. We cruised the top waters. Girls swam in our wake, eyeing us as the direct route to female power. Again, just the rules, ask anybody. (Other than Angus.)

It wasn't that I believed myself to be hot shit particularly, the opposite in fact. I was the same worthless turd as ever, just a turd as it happened that could catch a thirty-yard pass. I did speak to Maggot if I saw him in the hall with his dark people, but he'd just roll an eye at me through the hair curtains like, Don't do me any favors. Until I quit trying. I faked my cred, expecting every day to be busted and sent back to orphan class, but they let me stay, until I started feeling like, Fine, this is me. I deserve this.

Did that make me an asshole? Probably yes.

After hours, I was flying the Fastmobile. Coach knew nothing about it, being dead strict once the season started. Training was not just weight room and practices. Training was clean living. Getting our sleep. Fast Forward would swing by and pick me up after Coach was in bed.

That night, we'd pulled in at the drive-in just ahead of the second feature, as you do. First is always a Disney thing, second is the slasher. The idea being let the kiddies have theirs, then put them to sleep in the back seat before the real movie starts. Fair enough, where else can a family go for fun, but trust me, those kids are not sleeping. Mom and Stoner used to put me down like that, and the nail-head guy from *Hellraiser* got burned on my tiny brain for life.

But you can see the screen from all over, so why not hop from this to that tailgate to be sociable. Fast always came well supplied, just like in the days of our pharm parties. Or on this night, that I will remember to my grave, it was tequila shots and PBR chasers. I took a stroll around on my own and found a couple of teammates, Clay Colwell and Turp Trussell. Clay had a kid brother in a wheelchair, and drugs of choice coming out Clay's deadlift-ripped ass. They were breaking curfew like me. I felt restless. We found another crew that were second string, not guys we hung out with a lot, but they offered their bong and I took a few hits, to be Christian about it, before moving on. The weed smoke throughout the establishment was sufficient for a modest buzz. It was cold for September. Some kids had built a fire at the back end of the gravel lot, where they let you do pretty much anything you can think of. Past that was the woods, where people brought blankets and did the rest of what you can think of. I stood shivering in the dark, letting the weed hit, watching the movie, which was *Demon Island*. Memorable name, but this movie was dead idiotic. These rich teenagers on some island vacation, handcuffed together in couples, running around for unknown reasons trying to find underpants hidden in the jungle. Told you.

And there she was, swanning her way between the cars. I swear she glowed in the dark.

"Dori?" Saying her name was like begging, please-godplease. She stopped and turned, the longer side of the silvery hair turning towards me, then away. Fairy nymph deer fox, if I moved closer she might run away. "It's me, Demon," I said, so quietly, like a baby might be asleep between us. "We met at your dad's store. That day you brought him in for the party."

She didn't move.

"Is he doing okay?"

She moved closer, and I could see the little heart shape of her face. The silver eyebrows and pointed chin, the mouth I wanted to suck on. I smelled menthol, or maybe imagined it.

"He's not ever going to be okay. I left him alone tonight. I shouldn't be here."

"Isn't there anybody else that can help you all out?"

No answer. Her whispery creek had stopped running. Maybe she had no idea who I was. "Sucks," I said. "I grew up just me and my mom. I had to take care of her a lot."

"How is she now?"

I wanted to lie. And I didn't. "Dead. They both are, her and my dad."

"Shi-it," she said. "And here I thought the football heroes came from the nicer homes."

"Even a lowly orphan can be a mighty General," I said, and God forgive me for what I thought: She knows I'm Eighty-Eight. Girls give it up for that. She shifted her weight, a bird fixing to fly away. I nearly blacked out from how bad I wanted to hold her.

Finally she spoke. "No lie, you're state property? DSS guardianship and everything."

I felt more stoned than I was, swimming around in my head for a place to land. I asked how she knew about that, and she said the DSS had their doubts on her dad raising a girl alone. He never lost custody, but it was touch-and-go. She actually knew Old Baggy. I'd forgotten the lady's name, but she said it. She knew things I kept locked up. My eyes had made friends with the dark and I could see all of her now: the little white dress and lace-up sandals, the bag of popcorn. I wanted her to throw it on the ground and run off with me. Not to the woods. Some better place.

"So. I better go find my people," she said. If *people* meant person, like a boyfriend, I needed to vaporize him. She stretched her head to one side. "They'll be wondering."

"Me though," I said. "I could be your people. If you want. Like, next time, or whatever." I was not normally this terrible at asking a girl out. Never, honestly. This was epic.

She laughed. "What in the world is scaring you so bad?"

"That I won't see you again."

"Oh, my goodness, Demon. You don't have any idea, do you?"

I asked her, idea of what. Even in the dark I could see her black eyes finding me out.

"You're the one all the girls will be writing to in prison. Oh, my Lord. They'll roll on the ground pulling each other's hair out to get on your visiting list."

Then she was gone. And I was a mess. She knows my name. That's what I was thinking. Not, *that* was weird, what a righteously fucked-up thing to say, that I'm going to end up in prison. What can I say. Love. It's an unexcusable train wreck.

For the next while I had weight and occupied space, too shocked to think. I watched the handcuffed movie couples having their bad day. This squatty monster thing beat one of the guys with a shovel till his head came off. Another guy tried to fight, and it ripped off his nuts. I'm not making any of this up. For about fifteen minutes I'd wanted this night never to end, now I was ready for it to be over. And then. Here comes Tommy Waddles. Walking along all fretful, balancing a flimsy box of tall cups. My first thought: Who buys drinks from the concessions, cheaper to bring your own, and my second thought: Damn. It's Tommy. How did I know it was him? The hair. Still too much for his head, standing straight up. I hollered and he said who's that, and I told him. I told him I still had his T-shirt he gave me to sleep in at Creaky's.

He almost dropped his concessions box. We hadn't seen each other in close to five years. The Lee County drive-in evidently is a portal to other dimensions.

Tommy was still the best of men. He wanted to know everything. I told him my living situation now was the type of fosters we never believed existed: good food, nice people, not in it for the money. He himself was eighteen so out of foster care. He never did get adopted, but that's okay, he was living in an apartment with friends. He had a job and a girlfriend. Tommy goddamn Waddles. I came with him to meet his roommates, eight in number, all in one Camaro. At the drive-in you paid per vehicle, which led to any number of pile-in shenanigans. The concession drinks were because they'd forgotten mixers. These guys were discussing their plan of buying old horses from farmers and selling them for dog food in Canada. After my first Jack and Coke I remembered to tell Tommy I was hanging out with Fast Forward now. I invited him to come say hello, but he said that's okay, he'd better stay and look after his ever-more-shitfaced roommates.

After my second Jack and Coke I spilled my guts about Dori, that I was in love and everything. Just talking about her made me want to run off and find her, to settle this *people* question. Tommy got it. He'd fallen for his girlfriend over the computer. His job was at the newspaper, emptying wastepaper baskets and cleaning their coffee room, but they let him have his own account on a computer and that's how he found this girl. She was awesome and in Pennsylvania. It sounded like the sex potential was pretty limited there, but probably

Tommy was more of a gentleman and not as fixated on that aspect of the girlfriend enterprise.

The movie was winding down, the squatty demon had done about all the damage one movie allows, and I didn't want to miss my ride home. The Lariat was easy to spot because of this battery camping lantern he always set up on the tailgate, kind of festive. Bugs bombing around the light. Fast Forward had his arm around a tall, skinny girl that guys called Car Wash, not to her face. She had on a silky type dress with her hipbones jutting out like furniture under a sheet. Fast Forward was ignoring her, arguing with Big Bear and some other ex-Generals over who had the better offensive game, Riverheads or Surry. Nobody making very good points. To be honest, the tequila shots had won the day, but neither was any man giving an inch. They were going to die on their hill of Riverheads or Surry. Fast Forward tried repeatedly to say "onside kick recoveries," and for the first time ever, I wondered if he was okay to drive. I could get us to my house, no problem, but getting the keys would be the trick. Unless he passed out first.

And then who should appear but Rose Dartell. Like I said, a portal. She stomped out of the nowhere darkness into our little circle of light. Fast Forward with deep feeling was saying words like *sourced overtime* and *legal lorward flateral* so he didn't notice Rose until she chucked down something heavy in a paper bag, on the tailgate. I felt the clank of the metal in my teeth.

Fast looked at her, wide-eyed, a notch more sober.

She glared back. "I had to drive halfway to fucking Kentucky. BJ's closed at eleven."

He shook his head fast, like he'd caught a shiver. "*What?*"

"You're *welcome.*"

"Oh, where are my manners." He ashed his cigarette too close to the silky hip of Car Wash. She edged away from him. "I am *so* thankful, I'll tolerate your mess of a face and let you ride around in my truck. But just so you know, less hideous girls have done more to get there."

We all went dead quiet. Rose turned towards the rest of us, her pointy teeth glittering. "Just so *you all* know? Sterling Ford is the worst mistake his dead whore mother ever made."

And off she went into the dark. I couldn't believe what just happened. We all have our secret stores of poison, but to strike outright, calling a girl hideous to her face? The other guys seemed to give no shit, they were pulling out round two of Jose Cuervo and poking into the empty bag, with somebody saying "Didn't you give her a fifty, man?" Fast Forward saying "That bitch." And me saying "I'll go get your change." It just came out of me. I went after her.

She was moving fast, headed for the back of the lot, but her frizzed-out hair was catching the light some way. And then the red glow of whatever it was that she lit up. She bypassed the campfire circle, a bunch of kids that looked too young to be out here, and disappeared into the trees. It was a joint she'd lit. I tracked her by the smell of it. I didn't want to scare her, so I called out hey.

"Fuck you," she said. "Who is that?"

"Me, Demon." I came closer. She held out the joint, but I passed, feeling the need for a clear head. Some bargaining was called for. "Nobody should talk to a girl that way. I'm sorry."

"Wasn't you that said it." She inhaled and blew out, mad, ragged puffs. "Has he been telling you he owns his own place now? Over by Cedar Hill?"

I didn't answer. I wanted to ask her a lot of things. Her face was a scribble of rage.

"Well, he doesn't own squat. He feeds the horses and cleans their barn over there. Some dude ranchers that moved here from New York. He lives in what they call their guest house, and you know what? It's a fucking barn. He is exactly equal to a horse's ass."

Then why keep coming around? Rushing the scrimmage, bringing him whatever he wants? I settled on one question I could ask. "Did you know his mom, for real?"

She shook her head, holding her smoke. Then blew out. "Before my time. My mother took her on as a rescue. She died whenever he was real little, and we adopted him."

I tried to square this with everything else I knew about him. "He's your adopted brother?"

"*Was*," she said. "Until he was nine. They feel guilty over it to this day, but my parents had to unadopt him. Can you believe that?"

"Jesus," I said. "How come?"

"The safety of their other kids. Sterling tried to kill us, any number of times."

"Jesus. Seriously?"

"Oh, yeah. We would do anything he said. We idolized him. My youngest brother Ronnie, he liked to of hung himself. Sterling had him up on a chair and the rope around his neck, wanting him to jump off. Tells little Ronnie this is going to be fun, like a swing."

"Jesus," I said. Not at my original best.

"He's the one that gave me *this*." She jutted her face at me. "Claw hammer. He threw it at me on purpose and caught me plumb across the mouth. Let me tell you something, cut-open faces bleed like a motherfucker."

So much madness crowded my brain. Maggot's mom slicing into Romeo Blevins. Good people, bad people, what does that even mean? Get down to the rock and the hard place, and we're all just soft flesh and the weapon at hand.

"Sorry," I said. "But that's between you and him. He's still my friend."

"His new toy, is what you are. And he does not take care of his toys." She licked her fingers and pinched out what was left of her joint. Pocketed the roach. I couldn't see much in the dark, but something told me she was pleased with herself for dropping all this on me. And that I would not be getting any change back here.

"Here's what should scare you," she said. "After he laid open my face? I told Mama I fell and cut myself on the corner of my Barbie house. Thirty stitches worth of Barbie fucking dream house. He flashes that high-beam smile, and nothing's going to be his fault. If you asked him right now, I bet you money that's what he'd say happened to me. Barbie house."

And you're still here, wanting first position. She had to be lying. Maybe jealous. Even if he did game her family some way, he would have his side of the story. Fast Forward always outsmarted the people that made it their job to throw kids like me in the trash. That was truth. He'd showed me how to make good on places with no good in them, like Creaky Farm. How to survive. For some of us, that's everything.

"Yo! Eighty-Eight," somebody was calling through the woods. Big Bear. I heard him fall down, curse, get up again. "Come out come out wherever you are."

"Over here," I said, practically running towards him. That keen to get away.

I did not drive anybody home. I got back to the Lariat, the guys passed me Rose's brown-bag delivery, and I did my best to drown what she'd told me in a deep well of tequila and PBR chasers. Nobody seemed to remember about Fast Forward's change, and in due time I forgot about it too. That and more. I don't recall leaving the drive-in or getting into the house. On my own steam I must have made it halfway up the stairs, because that's where Angus found me in the morning.

I wanted to die. She used an entire roll of paper towels to mop up piss and vomit. I was no help, due to how bad it hurt to open my eyes. She got me out of my nastier clothes and into bed and went downstairs to get me a Coke. Some remedy thing she swore by, you shake up the bottle to make it go flat. She came back and put the cold glass in my hand. I felt her sit on the bottom of the bed, and even that hurt. "I didn't see Coach, so he's not up yet," she said.

"Thank God."

"Yeah, God and all his elves. Your ass otherwise would be grass."

Breaking curfew and rowdy drinking, at all, let alone in public, were grounds for getting benched or even thrown off the team. It was not just about our ability to perform, Coach said. We were Generals. Kids looked up to us. "I can't drink this," I said. "I'll puke it right back up."

"No, it's flat. It'll stay down. I told Mattie Kate you've got the flu. But I think she's onto you. Her kid told her you and some other guys pissed in their fire at the drive-in last night."

Did we? Oh, Jesus.

"She's none too pleased, but she won't rat you out. And U-Haul knows nothing."

U-Haul was practically at the house 24/7 now. Coach had finally promoted him to a real assistant, salaried, for unknown reasons. Even Coach seemed unhappy about it. Something liquid rolled over in my gut. I groaned and took careful stock of my bowels. "What time is it?"

"I don't know. Morning. It's okay, you're covered. Find your flu vibe."

If it had been anybody but Angus seeing me like that, with my puke-stiff hair and dumpster breath, I would have had to die. "You rock," I told her. "My guarding angel."

She was quiet a minute. The grasshoppers whining outside sounded like chain saws.

"Listen, Demon? I know you're in no mood. But can I just say, you're fucking up here?"

"Called it. Not in the mood."

"Okay. But some of your angels out there are not guarding. All I'm saying."

The disaster of me was not on Fast Forward. I was in charge of myself. If I had too many worries right then, pressure of the game, of being first string, of dying if I couldn't get Dori—it was my own shit to handle. U-Haul being out to get me, that also. It was a lot. I tried opening my eyes a tiny slit, and the brightness hit me loud. Like light itself was making a sound. I saw the bleary angel of Angus at the bottom of my bed in her white pj's, and behind her on my desk, that ship she gave me. Just like me, she'd said. A long way to go, and stuck in the bottle.

I ended up promising her I wouldn't touch alcohol for the rest of the season. Given my condition, an easy vow to make. For tequila at least, the promise was kept. To this day.

41

Where does the road to ruin start? That's the point of getting all this down, I'm told. To get the handle on some choice you made. Or was made for you. By the bullies that curdled your heart's milk and honey, or the ones that went before and curdled theirs. Hell, let's blame the coal guys, or whoever wrote the book of Lee County commandments: Thou shalt forsake all things you might love or study on, books, numbers, a boy's life made livable in pictures he drew. Leave these ye redneck faithful, to chase the one star left shining on this place: manly bloodthirst. The smell of mauled sod and sweat and pent-up lust and popcorn. The Friday-night lights.

In my time I've learned surprising things about the powers stacked against us before we're born. But the way of my people is to go on using the words they've always given us: Ignorant bastard. Shit happens.

This is how. Late October, deep into the season, we're up six against Powell Valley at home, running a sweep, our third or fourth of the night. I've got eyes in the back of my helmet for the defensive end, Ninety-Six, one of those assfists you can spot in the lineup before you ever go head-to-head. It's in how he stands, his whole resentful body bent around what he's missing. Anything you might have in the way of luck or love was stolen from his share, and he aims to get it back by drilling into the best man he sees. He's had his eye on me all first quarter.

In this sweep I'm blocking for the tailback, to let him come around me between the outside hash marks, looking for daylight. Ninety-Six gets a full head of steam and hits me low, taking me down from the side, legs first. The first thing I feel is breathless, no wind, with him and others on top of me, nothing unusual. Legs pinned. A normal tackle with some extra hate for me to remember him by. He takes his time getting up, an elbow in my kidney, pissing me off.

Pain doesn't get to your brain as fast as other things. Like being mad, and a little shamed, that you're down with other men still on their feet. The third or fourth thing I know is my knee is bent the wrong direction.

I see it. Fuck the devil's red ass, does that son of a bitch hurt. Getting my legs under me is the plan, but the knee won't execute. The knee is roaring. My teammates are yelling, Coach is yelling at somebody offsides, and I'm not liking how they're looking at me. I'm hurt, okay, but in this game, pain is not the enemy. Failure is your enemy. Being too slow, missing an opening, miscalculating a pass, these things you control. Doing it right is your only friend, messing up is your foe, and the distance between them is all you are here to care about. The rest is landscape. Pain is the turf under your cleats. Pain is weather. You pull your legs under you and heave up thinking: Rainy day. Walk it off. Don't pull me out, Coach, I'm good to go.

That's not how it went.

Pain can scramble you. If it is weather, it can be a storm tearing off the roof of your mind. The hours and days after that tackle are like a deck of shuffled cards. Maybe they're all still here in my brain, but damned if I could tell you which way they came about. I know the game ended in a loss. I was toted off the field to let that happen. Me telling Coach it's not that bad, put me back in the game: that's probably half the cards in that deck. Pleading, while I sat under my five-pound icepack. U-Haul's red eyes on me. He's eating this up, that this happened to me. I recall his use of unnecessary force while icing and wrapping my leg. No doubt thinking salaried men don't tend the injuries of pissants.

I recall trying to watch the game, losing focus. The ringing in my ears. Pain is a sound, a pull. It's fire. Then I'm at the house, at the bottom of the stairs looking up. Coach bracing me up on one side, Angus the other. Those stairs. Me bottoming out in a helpless bawl. Coach almost falling apart too, saying not to worry, Dr. Watts would come in the morning and he'd get me right. Angus quietly making up Mr. Dick's downstairs sofa bed for me. The cripple bed.

I wasn't awake all night but didn't exactly sleep. I kept looking under the sheet, feeling a pool of blood that wasn't there. At some point I turned on the light to be sure. It had turned black and was deformed, like a leg with a basketball stuffed inside. I was in my underwear. Somebody must have cut off my uniform pants, that card was gone from my deck, good riddance. If I dozed off I had nightmares. Going at my leg with a hacksaw, trying to get rid of it. Biting different body parts till they bled. A weird sound would snap me out of it, and it would take a minute to understand the sound was coming out of me. Pain is water, of a drowning kind. You waterboard awhile, come up for air, go back down. You're afraid you'll die, and then you're afraid you won't. That's where I was, at the time of Doc Watts showing up in the morning.

Watts was team doctor. He didn't make it to many games, but was friends with Coach since they played together at UT. He and Coach said things I wasn't really hearing, ACL this, meniscus that. To rule out a fracture I needed to go to the hospital in Norton to get x-rayed. I thought: You and what goddamn army are moving me out of this bed. Possibly I said this out loud. Angus was hovering in the doorway big-eyed, listening. He said I also needed an MRI, for that we'd have to go to Tennessee, and they're slammed down there so a three-week wait. He'd get me in to see an ortho, which is a bone specialist, again a two-week wait. The prescription would hold me till then. I stopped caring around this point because the little white submarine-shaped pill he'd given me to swallow was starting to sing its pretty song in my head. Cool relief, baby, let's you and me go cruising Main. Just hold my hand. Lortab was her name. Blessed, blessed lady.

I laid out of school and practice for a week. I can miss one game, I thought. Nobody was pleased, except probably U-Haul, but all I had in me was a ten-yard gimp hop through the living room in my sad droopy drawers to the downstairs head. Mattie Kate in the stands. Otherwise sleeping my life away on the couch bed. Every four hours I'd wake up, empty the tanks if needed, goddamn the whole mess to hell, and cruise away again, thank you Lortab. Doc said to double them up, and set an alarm and keep that good stuff in my blood around the clock. Eating I don't recall, though I must have. Only the bottles of lime Gatorade standing by to wash down the pills.

Coach and Doc Watts launched an offense on the bone doctor (or rather, his poor receptionist) and got me an appointment for the next Monday, early, before the busy man went into his surgeries. I wasn't excited for it. What if he wanted to cut on me? I was in no mood. Coach said not to worry, the bone guy would get me fixed up. Maybe in time for next Friday.

At school the rumors flew. Absent Demon was way more interesting than the real me. Angus came home to report my leg was: (1) broken, (2) not broken, (3) sprained (*sprung*, if we're technical), (4) amputated (above the knee and below, pick one), (5) I was medivacked by helicopter to the brain hospital in Nashville and in a coma. Angus laughing. Me, just watching the clock. She had the rumors list written down her arm in marker, reading it all out. I was still an hour out from my next date with Lortab, and in no version of reality was I going to hold out that long.

Angus got quiet then, studying my sheet-covered leg. This was up in my room, after an assisted crawl up the stairs for privacy and better bathroom access. A guy needs his dignity. Angus was cross-legged on the bottom of my bed in her denim overalls and red socks. Hair up in the devil-horn knobs she'd taken on as her favored look.

"Hurts, huh."

I laughed, just a bark: ah*huh*. I told her I used to think I knew what hurt was. But this leg I would trade for the worst busted face and ribs my stepdad ever gave me. I'd even throw in cash. Her gray eyes edged up from my leg to my face. "That is one screwed up economy, bro."

"Meaning what."

She shrugged. Scooted over a little and recrossed her red sock feet, making herself at home on my bed. "You don't have to trade one cockup for another one. What about like, trading up? Just get this shit over with, looking to better times ahead."

"Gee, never thought of that. I bet next week the doc will wave his wand over this fucked-up knee and I'll run a seventy-yard touchdown and we'll all fart perfume. Why don't you go out for cheerleader, miss sunshine?"

She shook her head, a small, quick move, not looking at me but out the window. What to do with Demon, the hard kid to handle. Age-old question. I felt meanness bubbling up inside me, like a burp of sour vomit. I made myself swallow it back down. "Sorry," I said.

She looked back at me. Lord, those eyes. "What the hell are you so scared of?"

Dori had asked the same question. Clearly I needed to shore up some leaks. "You don't know what it's like to be me, is all I'm saying. To be sidelined, with no family or anything."

Her eyes changed color, I swear. Light gray to darker. Didn't say a word, but I knew what she thought. Coach was trying to give me things I refused to take. Maybe family was one of them. That and the silver money card she flew around on. I leaned over and grabbed the little orange pill bottle I'd hardly taken my eyes off of in the last half hour. Press-screwed the cap, gulped down my Lortabs and Gatorade. Closed my eyes, breathed. The pill itself tasted of rescue. I opened my eyes to the stare of Angus. She was weirdly patient, in a manner that could wreck you.

"Don't take this the wrong way," I said. "Coach is great and everything. Because I'm the best tight end he's had coming up in a lot of seasons. That's the reason I'm here."

"You *really* think that's all."

"Christ, Angus. He put me through tryouts, right after I came here. He checked me for speed and ball handling and I did pretty good, or I guess more than pretty good, and he told me I could stay. You didn't know that? It was right after Christmas, down in his office. Deal struck."

She didn't know that, it was plain to see.

"Don't act shocked. The man's got his job to do. And right now, my speed and ball handling are for shit. Not a great position to be in."

She started picking a loose thread in the sheet, really pulling at it. She would maim the sheet if she kept that up. The type of thing that kids get smacked for in certain homes, starved for in others. Punishments vary widely among households. "I've always expected to pull my weight here," I told her. "That's all I want. I'm not one to ask for handouts." Maybe I sounded like an old man. Mr. Peg, former miner, hillbilly pure. Why wouldn't I.

"For God's sake, Demon. You're a *kid*."

"Am I, though?"

She shook her head, small and fast again. I wasn't trying to be difficult, just straight. It's all I knew how to be, with Angus. "He's not going to kick you out because you got injured, playing *his* game," she said. "Give my father some credit."

I'd not known her to call him "my father" before, ever. He was Coach. I told her I didn't think he'd give up on me, because I was important to the team. I planned on finishing out the season, with two years left to make my name as a General. I didn't spell out to Angus what she couldn't understand: that without football I'd be nobody again. That the loser Demon was still right there under the surface, and if I lost the shine, I was nothing. I'd never get Dori.

Somehow Angus decided she'd cheered me up. She went back to her list of my rumored sorry fates. "On the good side, you're rocking the vote for homecoming court."

"Bullshit, I'm only a sophomore."

"I'm just the messenger here. You, sire, are headed for coronation."

"Not happening. Anyway, I don't want the pity vote. If I win, it's got to be for my ripped physique and shallow personality."

She nodded thoughtfully. "I see that. But you'd better take what you can get. It's not a pity vote if you're injured in the line of duty. Like that soldier thing. Purple cross."

"Purple *heart*," I said. "Shit for brains."

She smacked the flat bib of her overalls. "*Dope!*"

Her clowning was known to pull me out of a mood, but in this case it was the Lortabs. I was nodding off to happyland. Should take a piss first. Bedwetting was an ever-present danger on this regimen. You aim for that brief window where the pain is tamped down to bearable, but you're not yet too dopeshit to haul ass out of bed. She watched me tilt and lever myself off the mattress, knifing in loud breaths until I was upright.

"Aw jeez, Demon. You gotta update the under wardrobe."

She wasn't wrong. The old cottonbottoms had lost all hope of whitey or tighty.

June must have got it through the school pipeline via Emmy, so there's no telling what injury she thought I had. But I woke up and there she was, staring at my pill bottle. Straight from work, in her white coat with the plastic name tag. Under the coat, a black sweater and pants. The sexy way she bent forward straight-backed, like a hinge from her narrow waist, put Dori into my head. If not for the pain I could have pitched a tent right there.

"Hey!" I said, sounding hoarse and groggy. I might

have double-doubled up the Lortabs. Doing the same thing day in, day out, you can forget if something happened an hour ago or yesterday.

"How long have you been taking these?"

I thought about it. "What day is today?"

She blew out a puff of air and swiveled around. Coach was in the doorway, red hat, lanyard and whistle around his neck, looking like any minute here he might make June run suicides. "Who put him on these?"

"I think the boy's in good hands," Coach said. "Watts has been a doctor since you were cheerleadin' in your little skirt and bobby socks."

She turned back to me. "Demon. Would you like me to have a look at that leg?"

I said okay, and she sat down on the bed. I could smell her soap, the same fruity sweetness that followed Emmy around, and again I thought of Dori, wishing I knew what she smelled like. "How much you going charge me?" I asked, vaguely realizing I was slurring.

She gave me a wink. "Friend of the family discount. After you're all better, you can come clean out my gutters."

Upside-down boat houses have no gutters. I had to claw through some brain cotton to get the joke. She pulled the sheet down and whistled, long and low, like calling a dog. She was supposed to have a dog by now. What happened to Rufus? What does it mean if a doctor sees your injury and whistles? Not good. She touched and pressed on different parts of my leg, feeling the pulse at my ankle. If I'd ever imagined June feeling me up, not saying I did, this wasn't it. She was all business. I was glad Angus had talked me into some decent gym shorts.

She covered me up and rested both hands on her lap, looked at me. Biting her lip. I wished I was asleep. Waiting to wake up from this assfucked turn of events.

"I saw your radiology report," she said, "and I'm not very happy with it. I know you're still waiting for your MRI, but I don't think it's going to be good news. I'm sorry, I hate this for you. But the only thing that will help this injury is a diagnosis and the right course of treatment. Not wishful thinking. Trust me. I've seen too many patients try."

"There's no fracture." This was Coach.

She twisted around to face him. "I'm not happy with the X-ray because there could be trouble in the growth plate that got overlooked. It wasn't a perfect angle, and there was no lateral mediolateral. If Watts or whoever's supposed to be looking after Damon has neglected to order a follow-up, I can call that in for you right now."

Coach said nothing. Twirling the lanyard around and around his finger. June turned back to me. "What would *you* like?"

To stop hurting like hell. I shrugged. "To be good enough to play by next Friday?"

"Oh, hon." She put her hand on top of my hand, and something rushed my chest so hard I held my breath to stop from tearing up. She was shaking her head. I focused on the shiny mink pelt of her hair, and let the words turn to bubbles over her head. Out for the rest. Of the season.

Coach's orbiting lanyard dropped dead. He said something. She said something. He dropped the nice and told her whose house this was. She grabbed up my pill bottle and shook it at him. "Playing with fire," she said. And so on. I was the little kid wishing Mom and Dad would quit fighting. At one point she came back over and asked me, close to my face, did I know what I was taking. She said it was hydrocodone and something. Not oxy then, I said, and she said it was really no better than that. I was struggling for words and possibly catching the asshole bug from Coach because I asked her whatever happened to Kent's "pain is a vital sign" and all that.

She hissed at me: "Kent Holt is a fucking hired killer for his company."

Those words, from her mouth, stopped my clock. She and Coach left the room, but I heard them out in the hall. Coach using his fifty-yard-line voice, and she was also plenty loud enough, telling him she used to see two or three narcotic patients a year and now that many every day. Then she gave up on him and came back to work on me. Telling me how pain is a body's way of taking care of you, letting you know when to stop. Telling me to think of my future. She had no clue. My future was football. Playing through the pain is what you do.

She left, I slept. Woke up confused, then ticked off. I wasn't some child, having my little pharm party. I was going by the book, doctor's orders. Being a General was serious work. Coach knew. She didn't.

By the time I got in to see the bone doctor, the basketball-size knee was down to a softball. All week it had been parading its bruise rainbow: black-green-yellow-brown. Coach found me some crutches and I was getting around. It felt good to move. Except for hurting like hell.

The bone doctor turned out to be a long-jawed man with skeleton hands and no time to spare. He checked me over in the hospital waiting room, on his way to a day of cutting people up. All I could think of in those plastic chairs was the night Mom OD'd and I got thrown in the deep end of the foster shitpool. I'd been swimming ever since. I wished I was five and could hold Coach's hand while I dropped my sweatpants and let Dr. Bones poke my leg. He said the same as June about not trusting the first X-ray. Even without the MRI he could see surgery was indicated. Meniscus this, ACL that, the leg needed to be stabilized, my PCP should get me into a cast and PT. More letters than you want to hear. He reupped my Lortabs and said to come back after I got the MRI. I thought Coach would ask him how soon I could get back to playing, but he didn't.

After we got out to the car, I told Coach I didn't want those skeleton hands cutting me open. He looked over at me, the square teeth behind his lips, freckled hands gripping the wheel. Rarely had I told him, flat-out, what I did or didn't want. Any foster kid can tell you why.

"I hear you, son," he said. Then he called Watts on his car phone and we went straight to the pharmacy to pick up my new prescription. Coach was going to run in, but I said I'd go. Wanting to prove something. I got out and crutched across the lot, all stupid proud. *I got this*, I'm thinking, as the doors swoosh open. *I got this*, down the aisle to Pharmacy. They said fifteen minutes.

I browsed magazines and condoms and found a place to sit down on a crate of Ensures.

Finally they yelled my name. I paid with Coach's card. The white paper bag had a thing stapled to the outside, pretty obvious, that said OxyContin. That shook me. I was still trying hard, playing *I got this*, but on my way out I stumbled, running smack into a homeless guy.

"Whoah, you blind?" he said, in such a pitiful way that I sorried myself all over him: sorry, careless, my bad, sorry. Coach was watching from his car. I gave the guy another look and almost lost my breakfast. He must have said *I'm* blind. He had no eyes, just two caves in his wrinkled face. A big nursey dog on a harness. Not homeless, just a person going into Walgreens for whatever drug they give a guy so he can stand his life in the hopeless fucking darkness.

I got in the car feeling rattled. Those empty caves. *Blind, blind, blind.*

42

This was legitimate, not using. With all the blood pumping through my heart, I believed that, and vowed as much to Coach. I would follow doctor's orders to the T, and he'd let me play.

And he did. Four weeks on, the mess I still was, idiot that I was, I got in there. Not every minute of the game like before, obviously. Key moments only, was the idea. Coach would save me for a sweep or a long-pass play where we needed it most. My first Friday back, there was no need. Against Northwood he generally let the second string have the run of the playground, we couldn't lose to those jackasses if we ran backwards. I was dressed out on the sidelines till the last quarter, we're up by 28, four minutes to go. Coach jerks his thumb at me, sends me limping onto the field just to light up the stands. All the cheering and stomping is practically dry-heaving the bleachers, Dee-*Mon!* Copper-*head!* Foster-to-fame poster boy, better than ever. Angus wasn't wrong. While sleeping it off, I'd been crowned king of Lee County.

The next Friday was to be no such walkover. River-heads, away. I got serious in the weight room. I was okay on upper body, but weighted front squats, nope. Even still, I would not let down my men. Or the school, Christ. My first day back, walking into the lunchroom: heads turn, trays clatter, everybody stands up clapping. Lunch ladies in hairnets are clapping. Most of me is thinking: They don't know me. Free lunch kid. But one other small part of me is thinking: I have killed myself for this.

So I took my meds. And played like a guy on meds, slow on the uptake. Coach didn't say anything, but he saw, and directed the play towards faster legs and less buttered fingers. That hurt me more than my leg, honestly. I tried cutting back, less butter on the bread. Just a hair, stretching to five or six hours on the Lortabs or the Percocets, a day and a half on the oxys. I was supposed to alternate or sometimes double up, as per written in-structions. Doc had me well doped for practice, tapering off for game nights, giving me some of my marbles back to play with. Counting on me to play through the pain. Lord, I did. Hard enough to tear up whatever that knee had left to its name. Pain wasn't even the main event anymore, I was numb some way, enough to try easing back on the meds. But if I stretched it out too far, especially between oxys, I'd wind up feeling tackled before I even dressed out. Bone ache, gut ache, puking in the locker-room head. And worse things, hard to discuss. I was shitting myself. This would come on hard and fast, chills and shakes and everything inside turned full-blast to running water. Which is so weird, because for the most part oxy constipates you like a motherfucker. Till you're in withdrawals, and it doesn't. So far I'd only gotten the runs at the house, before I left for practice. Scary as hell though. I might get them just from worrying about it. Homecoming was coming up. Not just the game, which is a big scramble anyway of mud, grass stains, piss, guys peeing in cups or towels or behind the benches, sorry if you didn't already know that. I was thinking more of the halftime thing, homecoming court. Parading around the field with a girl on my arm in front of the entire Friday-night congregation. Home game, obviously. White uniforms.

I went back to taking the oxys on the clock.

Homecoming was a whole ridiculous thing. Yes, I would be crowned. So it was a lot of pressure as regards asking a date: the queen is mandatory. Girls laid it on thick. Food left in my locker, cookies, fine all that. But then came photos. Pouty lips and stiff nipples, thumb hooked in the unzipped jeans, and all I could think was: Who the hell *took* this picture? You're halfway there already, go to homecoming with *them*. Maybe I'm a fool. But I liked the idea of starting from the top of the chase scene, not jumping in last second before the vehicle explodes.

My locker was easy to access. Angus, Maggot, various teammates and weed connections all had the combination, for practical purposes. So if these valentines turned up anonymous, which most did not, I only had to ask around. Sorry to say, I didn't. Just not that into it. Who *was* into it was Turp Trussell. He had the locker beside mine and scored a lot of free snacks, since I didn't feel right eating the cookies of a girl I wasn't going to ask out. I don't like owing anybody. Turp felt by the same line of reason, he should take possession of the photos. But I drew the line.

Then comes the day where Turp is waiting by my locker like a big red balloon fixing to pop. Kid was blessed with the pimply, boiled-meat type skin that gives you nowhere to hide. He's dying here, busting a gut, saying "Open it, man! Open it!" Like it's my damn birthday. He saw something go in, obviously. I felt like telling him to take it, whatever it is, just eat it. But now I was curious. Scrolled the lock, opened, and saw no cookies. No envelope with girl writing. Just a black scrap of something thrown in haste, hooked on the wire of a spiral notebook. I took a second to untwine it, and then I about shit. Underwear. A thong. I'd not ever seen one of those without the person inside. Nothing to it, lacy front, absentee the rest. Meanwhile Turp is doing something halfway between end-zone dance and asthma attack, like he's not seen panties before, or no, evidently because he has. He keeps asking me if the safety seal is broken.

"Do what?"

We've got an audience now, watching Demon being a full fledge idiot. What Turp is asking me is: Clean, or did she wear them first? How the hell I'm supposed to know this, no idea. He snatches them from me, all scornful. "Dude," he says. "*Inhale!*"

He pushes the crotch onto my face, and I get it. Full pussy, right between the eyes. And after this I'm supposed to go learn civics. The back of my locker is lipstick-signed, this is Vicki Strout. From that day forward to be known as Scratch-n-Sniff.

I feel bad for Vicki. This was a gamble on her part. To this very day, her kids' nasty little friends might be calling her Scratch-n-Sniff behind her back, and that's on me. If these ladies had caught me sooner, I would have been the dog on the bone. But now I was wrecked for anything but the best. If I went to homecoming at all, I'd have one queen only. Not Vicki Strout.

And I didn't even have the guts to call her. Because I knew about life. As long as you haven't yet asked, you can still have another day with some answer in your head other than "Go fuck yourself." So it happened the way it probably had to. Dori came to me.

This was a Monday. I'd been laying low at home a lot, which maybe she knew from asking around. I was in bed, trying to go over plays in my head, winding up someplace between sleep, not sleep, Dori dream lap dance. Not that it was all sexual thoughts, you don't just bang a fairy nymph. Or if yes, I'd not seen that particular manga. Anyway I was dead spooked to roll over and see her looking at me from the doorway. Zoo wee mama, standing there on her lace-up sandal feet like she'd flown in on my brain waves.

"Hey," she said. That deep, running-water voice.

I sat up too fast, bunched the sheets around for adequate coverage. Shit. "Hey," I said. "Where do you know me, I mean. Where I live?" Shitshitshitshit.

"How many other Coach Winfield mansions do you think I tried, before this one?"

"Sorry," I said. "Weird time to be asleep. They've got me on stuff that kind of licks me."

She came around the end of the bed to where all my crap was on the night table. Picked up the pill bottles one by one and checked the labels. Then sat down on the bed facing me, with one knee and foot hitched up, the other leg dangling. Not really dressed for winter, it must have been warm out. She had little silver rings on two of her toes. "So. How bad are you broken?"

"Most of me still works. The rest I reckon will come around."

She grinned at me. Lord, that face, like scoops of vanilla, all rounded cheeks and creamy skin. Little pixie nose. Shiny eyes, like the black middle had swallowed the rest. Her pink dress was made of something soft, a second skin, with a low, round neck smiling at me above the double scoop of her tits. I was afraid of crying if I couldn't touch her.

"I brought you something." She slipped the strap of her purse off her shoulder.

"You needn't to have."

"Oh, I did. You have no idea. It was life and death."

I felt cottony in the mouth and brain as I sorted through my many regrets. I'd gotten lazy about showers: that was one among the many. Her dark eyes were shimmying with a question.

"What? Am I supposed to guess?"

"You'd never."

"But if I do," I said. "I get to ask you out."

Help me Jesus, her smile. A tiny dent in each cheek, and her bottom lip held out a little way out from her teeth, like the juiciest smile possible. Inviting you in.

I rifled the messy mental locker. Not underwear, surely. "Is it something I need?"

"Definitely not." She looked tickled. The dangling foot bounced.

"Okay. So not a forty of Mickey's or my geometry homework."

She shook her head, solemn as church.

"Am I getting close though?"

"Very."

"A jar of pickled eggs. No, wait. A Furby."

Her laugh bubbled up. Like a glove box popping open and candy spilling out. I said a bunch more ridiculous things, just to watch that happen. Finally she gave me a hint.

"It's the one thing I knew you'd love. Because you told me."

No clue. I'd barely talked to her before this, in actual life.

"That time we first met at the feed store," she teased. "'Cute as buttons' . . ."

"Oh shit. No way you remembered that. Baby chickens?"

She reached in her purse and pulled out a pink Tampax box. The second she opened it the little guy started peeping. I took it from her, surprised by the strong little claws digging in. This one had real feathers, not like the day-old fuzzballs I'd handled at the store, both living and dead. I tried to calm him down, petting his walnut head. Dori watched us with that juicy smile. The foot still bouncing. Some part of her was always moving.

"Where'd you get it?"

"Where do you think?"

"Your dad's store? In November? That makes no sense."

"Right? Somebody special-ordered them and never picked them up. Donnamarie was shitting bricks over these dozen chicks, calling us at the house every day, so I had to go get them."

I could feel the heartbeat through the feathers. "Won't he miss the rest of his friends?"

"Okay, so. I told you this was life and death? This is the alive one. Sad story."

"The rest are *dead*? How?"

"So. I have this dog, Jip? He's the sweetest little thing."

"So sweet, he offs chickens?"

"I don't even know how it happened. I was outside

letting them run around, and Dad lets Jip out the back and next thing I know he's just *hoovering* the little fellas out of the grass."

Her smile turned upside down, the saddest of sad. I wanted to kiss her more than I wanted to live. "Survivor," I said to my little friend, giving his chest a tiny fist bump. "You and me."

Was I giving a thought to no pets allowed, the whole ridiculousness of a chicken in the house, any of that? What do you think? The bird was in the hand.

I went nuts, and spent too much money. Got her flowers not from Walmart but the true flower place in Bristol where they had one the exact color of her hair. Orchid. A new suit jacket, not from Goodwill. The homecoming rigamarole at halftime would be in uniform, but after that was the dance plus all other postgame action. It killed me that I couldn't drive over and pick her up, but my option was U-Haul's Mustang, himself supervising. I'd sooner take the riding mower. I tried to talk Angus into letting me use her Jeep, flying solo on my learner's permit just this once, because what cop in Lee County is going to ticket a General on game night? No dice. Angus was still teasing me about flavor of the week. All I could say was you wait and see. Dori's the one.

Angus called the baby chicken Dori's and my "love child." Like many a bastard, he ended up in a back room in a cardboard box. Dori brought him a waterer and scratch feed from the store. She came over every day that week, being pretty lonely, all on her own with her dad that turned out to be a lot sicker than just his heart. She said it's a losing battle trying to get in to see doctors. Only after the heart attack did they find the cancer in him that by that point was eating him up, lungs and bones. One day she closed my door and asked if she could lie down and cry a little bit, while I held her. Everything in me, my whole insides, turned over for this girl.

She was the one that took me shopping for our homecoming date and talked me into the new jacket, never even worn before. I told her I was not a wealthy man, but she laughed and said I had three hundred at least in my bedroom. Lortabs sold for ten bucks a pill, oxys for eighty. I wasn't about to part with those pills, but we bought the jacket. She lined up a neighbor to sit with her dad overnight on Friday. I was counting down minutes.

The ride problem turned out not an issue. Coach made us come out two hours ahead of kickoff for last-minute drills. I was wound so tight over so many things, getting the thunderous trots in public for one, I took every pill I was supposed to. Stood on the sidelines watching the hole in our game that should have been me. I was there and not there, the crowd noise and stadium lights melting into a long grasshopper whine in my ears. Feeling my heart thumping in the backs of my knees and my teeth. One sorry son of a bitch. Only one thing could save me.

She'd turned up looking like a wet dream. The purple-hair waterfall down one side of her face, the shiny blue dress also like water running down her perfect body. I wanted to drink it off of her. Before kickoff we'd met up in the parking lot so I could give her the flower thing. But really just to see her. I didn't fully believe she'd come. I fetched the clear box out of U-Haul's car and slipped it on her wrist and she was like a kid on Christmas morning. Holding it up to her hair. Perfect match. She'd not seen an orchid before, let alone anybody giving her one. It killed me to leave her. I told her to find the pep squad and they'd tell her where to line up for the halftime court. I'd already caused no small amount of drama, signing up a date that was not enrolled as a student. Seriously ticking off the cheerleaders and locker-cookies chicks. But Dori would never know about that, I'd make sure. I felt fifty years older than these kids in high school.

"See you on the field," she said. That open-lip

smile. "My liege." She reached up and kissed me, surprise attack, and I got hard. What that feels like inside
a jock and cup, oh man. Like a V8 under a Yugo hood.
I couldn't help wondering what I had to look forward
to later.

I got some idea at halftime. We did the whole pony
show, homecoming court, marching band, walking
out, our names over the loudspeakers. The runner-up
guys with their cheerleader dates in red hair bows and
mickeymouse skirts. Me, the king, with my mermaid
queen, as proud as it's possible to feel in shoulder pads
and a plastic crown from Halloween Express. They
honored the graduating seniors while the rest of us
stood out there smiling like our shoes were too tight.
All but Dori, that was sexy hot and lemonade chill. In
the middle of all that, she whispers she's got a surprise
for me later. Something she's been saving up, because
you only get one first time. Jesus.

Second half, not a story worth telling. You hate to
lose homecoming, hate worse to be the reason. Not that
I was blamed, the locker room afterward was all just,
Fuck it, next time we'll own those bastards. But I knew
the main event of the dance would be a consolation
party behind the gym. Dori of course was all about the
dancing and dress-up party, dying to see people she'd

not talked to in forever, whereas I was more in need of the frontal assault of Mountain Dew and vodka. I wanted to be outside with the team, standing where I could hold her close in front of me, one arm across her shoulder and chest like a seat belt. All the guys looking at me like, *Man*, no yards, no possessions, and still you get one of God's angels? Yes, I did.

So we were in and out. The usual gym smell of armpit and Lysol had a frosting of girl perfume that seemed flimsy, like the trellis thing loaned by Tractor Supply with Kleenex flowers on it for taking your photo. Sourpuss teachers doing their time around the refreshments table. Speakers rattling an ear-killing mix of Thong Song, Destiny's Child, Mariah Carey. Every so often, the shock of the whole gym falling into step for the Electric Slide. Dori tried to introduce me to her besties, but there was no talking over the din. It was plain to see she'd been popular, one of those that would have loved staying in high school if she could have. I begged off from dancing due to my knee, but really from not knowing how, my main dance partner so far being Mom that only knew the ridiculous ones: Robot, Worm, Macarena. Dori though. The first notes of every tune and she was a little bouncy ball, Yay, *this* one! Hopping all around in her shiny dress and smile, dancing with no one person, just all the moving bodies. Just once, a fast song trick-faded into "Beautiful Mess," and this asshole Keg Barnes oozed her into a slow dance. Then before I could go put his lights out, it finished, and everybody's flailing to "It's Gonna Be Me."

We stayed as long as I could stand, then took off in her dad's Impala SS. Seats like couches in that thing, front and back both. She said she had a place in mind for us to go parking, but first we had to stop by her house to check on Daddy. She had a neighbor staying over, so I didn't see the point, but didn't argue. The house was way out towards Blackwell. Deep country. She was talking a mile a minute, saying if her daddy was awake she would introduce us again because the time we'd met at the store didn't count, he hadn't paid any attention, not knowing I'd be taking out his daughter at some future time. I wondered if she was nervous like me but it didn't seem so, just glittery, the way she was. Talkative. I listened.

I ended up getting nowhere near Daddy. I opened the car door and this thing comes barreling off the porch straight at me like a heat-seeking dirty mop full of teeth. Dori just laughed, saying, "Jip you scamp, you are *rotten*," scooping him up, kissing his nasty toothy face, telling me how Jip was a little old sweetie. Unbelievable. I waited in the car.

The rest gets foggy. I hate this. Due to pills, booze, me being an idiot, all the above, that amazing night is a locked-up house I have to look into from outside, through the windows. I recall my arms around her, steering while she did the gas and brakes, Siamese drivers. Us laughing about that. And where we parked, some random place, a ridgetop gravel road that ended at a chain-link gate. Down below, a wrecked valley and stairstep tailings of an old mine with the reclamation trees planted the way they do, in rows, like the hair dots of a doll that's been scalped. The moon was out bright and hard, hitting these bean-shaped acid ponds down there, making them pretty. I was keyed up, nerves being my home turf. But less so after Dori said it was first time for her too. That she'd saved up for me. I could live on that forever, even if she dumped me tomorrow. Or so I thought. Until her surprise. It's the shocks that end up sticking with you, while all the rest melts away. I can still see her saying it, with her face lit by the moon.

"Daddy gave us a present."

I said I'd thought he was asleep, and she said yes. That's how come he gave it to us. He didn't know. Twinkly eyes, holding up a flat foil package, teasing me with it before tearing it open. Me trying not to wonder about Dori's dad having condoms. But it wasn't a condom. It was something like a Band-Aid. Evidently made out of money, given how careful she was with it.

"Shine," she said.

The shine I knew of was clear, in mason jars. Drinkable.

No, not that. Painkiller patch, she said, the extra-special kind. Fentanyl.

The next surprise won't ever leave my brain. The kit she took out of her purse. The spoon she used first, to scrape the patch. The lighter she held underneath. The cotton ball, the syringe, pulling the cap off the needle and holding it in her mouth like a nurse giving booster shots. I don't know what I said but she could tell I was scared, and she was sweet with me, the same voice she used with Jip. She'd been saving this, because the first time you do it with somebody, they say it's the best you'll ever feel in your life. Like having Jesus all up in your blood.

Jesus or not, I admitted to despising needles. She took the syringe cap out of her mouth and kissed me a long time. Then pushed the tip of the needle into the patch with such tender care. The way her tongue pressed the middle of her top lip, she looked like somebody concentrating on the best present a person could ever give. She drew something out of the patch, squeezed the clear drop of gel onto her finger, then put her fingertip in my mouth, under my tongue.

I stopped watching after she pulled her little foot up onto the seat and took off her shoe, to shoot herself up. We probably slept awhile afterward. I know enough now to say for sure, we would have. Curled together like two babies in a womb equipped with a steering wheel. Maybe her teeth chattered and she begged me to hold her tight, as would happen later, time and again. But I don't remember.

The back seat of that Impala was as good as any couch you'd want to have sex on. And we did, I'm guessing. I mean yes we did, but damn. You want to remember the pilot drill, but I only have this or that small view of it, like a peeping tom to my own event. I was pantsless at some point, I recall her being shocked by my poor busted knee, fussing over it. And for my part, the shock of seeing that dress come over her head in one sweep, balled up in her hand and dropped, no bigger than a pair of gym socks. The surprise of seeing her body all at once, the pale bikini of untanned skin like invisible clothes over the peaches of breasts and her cooch.

The rest is picture postcards. Her riding me, God yes, that laugh bubbling up out of her. Skin on skin, the electric shock of that. Touching her. My face up between her legs, her hands in my hair pulling hard.

Finding her clit with my tongue, the surprise of something really being in there, a slick little peanut. The phone-sex voice of Linda Larkins in my head being the reason I knew how to do any of this. Linda was a capable coach.

Maybe that's too much said. Wanting to protect Dori, that fire in me for saving her, will never go out, however late the day. But even if I were the bragging type, there's little to tell. Just that it was my first time for the whole thing, start to finish, if we did finish. I felt pretty sorry the next day, that I couldn't say for sure. But Dori was my girl, so. Nothing could hurt me now.

43

I got one week. To be the happiest man alive, my only care being how to get myself with that beautiful body again. We had it planned. Not Friday. That was the last game of the season, and I didn't want to be doing Dori on game-level dosage this time. Plus we'd be three hours on the bus getting back from Richlands, and I wasn't starting at midnight. I respected this girl. I'd take her out Saturday, starting at the drive-in. Early, because she actually liked the kid movies. We'd get in and out before all the socializing and booze. I'd buy her popcorn, we'd cuddle up to watch some Disney princess or other, then go park. Dori had a sitter again for Daddy, the same neighbor lady that was none too willing, hinting about getting paid if this turned regular.

The shit fell on Saturday afternoon, delivered by Maggot. I knew something serious had to be up, for him to call. We barely talked anymore. He said Mr. Peg was poorly, no news I thought, but Maggot said June was going over there and would swing by to pick me up.

"Not tonight," I said. "I'll go tomorrow, after they're home from church."

"Listen, Demon. He's not getting out of bed." Maggot's voice cracked. A late bloomer, finally coming hard into manhood, he'd gotten a wrathful stubble and that long-neck look with the big Adam's apple. All the more freakish for the eye makeup. Anyway, Maggot let me know I wasn't getting a choice, June had the bull by the horns as usual. So I called Dori to say I'd meet her at the drive-in. I'd make June drop me there afterward. How long could this take?

I was not in the best of moods on the way over. June was still in her doctor gear, stethoscope, no-fun shoes, the better to buckle me into her front seat and grill me: was I scheduled for the knee surgery, was I off those painkillers yet. I said Coach would be looking into it, now that the season was over. I didn't tell her to check with the devil about his establishment freezing over, because that's the day I'd let that bone doctor cut into me. She asked how long since I'd seen the Peggots, another sore subject. I'd passed on dinner invitations until Mrs. Peggot quit asking. You know, busy. Tomorrow is always another day.

I was surprised Emmy was not in the car with us. And that Maggot was, in the back seat, shrunk into his black hoodie like a mad turtle. I asked if Emmy was meeting us over there, and it was June's turn to go moody, saying Miss Emmy was now under the impression certain rules did not apply to her. And that Maggot had been staying at her house for a few weeks. She glanced over her shoulder like he might have something to add, which he did not. Fun outing.

The Peggot place was crowded with parked cars and an occupying Peggot invasion. Some I'd not seen since back in the day, cousins I'd crushed on Warcraft, now turned into their dads, same face hair and Buckmark tattoos. Hammer Kelly caught me off guard with a bear hug halfway between tackle and drowning man. I'd not seen him since the day of Emmy's not-engagement ring and all that. He looked wrecked. I told him cheer up, the world's not ended yet.

Which it hadn't, as far as I knew. But this was no normal Peggot hootenanny. Men out in the yard with their volume turned down, shuffling their work boots, blowing smoke at the trees. Aunts with faces like old pocketbooks, rolling the foil off covered dishes that nobody was eating. Maggot wouldn't come inside. His aunt Ruby nabbed me and said if I'd not been upstairs to see Mr. Peg yet, I could take my turn whenever somebody else came down. Which made no sense. I said we'd already spoken, and she eyed me with her tongue bulging out the side of her cheek, the exact thing her mom Mrs. Peggot did if she caught you lying. There we stood, Ruby with her dyed-to-death black hair coming in white at the roots, me wondering if some law says we all turn into our parents. If so, here's me signed up for death at an early age. And Maggot, damn. With a fucked-up snake like Romeo Blevins for a dad, you actually hoped the mom's jailbird genes would win out. I promised Ruby I'd hunt up Maggot and we'd both go upstairs to see Mr. Peg.

I found him down by the creek, playground of our mighty boyhoods. Squatting in the dark, side-arming rocks towards the water. "Yo, Storm," I called out. "What's the forecast?"

He craned his long neck around. "Wolverine. Get a fucking manicure."

I sat down, gave him a fake punch in the shoulder, and even that small violence made him shrink deeper into his hoodie. He tossed another rock at the invisible creek. "We were some pitiful Avengers," he said. "You know that, right? Vengeance was never ours."

"Speak for yourself. You're the one that always picked the lame-ass superpower."

"Okay. So even back then, me being Stormlady insulted your manhood."

"I'm just saying. You can pick anything, and you go for the power to make bad shit happen in terms of *weather*? It's like you're purposefully limiting your range."

"*Or* to make good weather happen. Always look on the sunny side!" He made a smiley leer at me that was terrifying, even in the dark.

"Right. Convince me that 'Have a nice day, for real' is that useful as a power."

"Like you'd know, big chief jockstrap. I've been waiting to have one of those nice days for, what. Eight or nine years?" He picked up a rock and threw it with such shocking force, we heard it connect with a sycamore on the other bank. *Thwock*, a random dead strike.

And then, shit. Maggot was crying. Breath racking out hard, like screaming with the sound off. I was scared to touch him. I just sat there wishing I could get something back for him, from our childhood days of people cutting us so much slack. Mr. Peg, my God. He had the patience of Job. Taking us fishing, setting down his own pole over and *over* again to rescue Maggot and me from our lines cast into the trees overhead or snagged on the bottom. Mr. Peg baiting our hooks with the worms Maggot wouldn't touch. It's possible Maggot hated fishing. If I knew, I wouldn't have let him say, for fear Mr. Peg would stop taking us. Now I watched him wring himself out like a rag, with no idea what powers existed to save him.

Mr. Peg passed away that night. The old man went out on the tide, while underneath his body and bed and oxygen machine and the floor, the wake of covered dishes and yard smoking flowed for most of the night. In the morning Mrs. Peggot and her sister washed him and clipped his hair. Then they called the funeral home to come fetch him out.

Maggot never did go tell him goodbye. We stayed out there by the creek till after the damn moon went to bed. The reason he was living over at June's now was the blowout they'd had, himself and Mr. Peg. Their last words amounted to inviting one another to go to hell. He said half of him was sorry over it, and the other half wasn't, so now he would stay cut in two forever. I might have gotten him up those stairs, if I'd known it was the last chance. I could have tried harder. Mr. Peg was the best part of Maggot's piss-poor lot in life. Both our lives.

So my second date with Dori was a few days late, and a funeral. She picked me up in her dad's Impala, nervous. She said she hadn't been to many funerals, not even her mom's, being too young. All she'd ever told me was that it was a wreck that killed her, kids drag racing on a Sunday evening, doing over a hundred in a commercial zone. Dori's mom had popped into Kwikmart to get a pack of AAAs for the TV remote, and pulled out at the wrong time.

My own mom's funeral was stuck in my craw that day. It hit me hard, how different this one was. In the Peggots' church, with the butt-polished wood benches and the colored glass windows like jigsaw puzzles of Jesus and sheep. Not one of these in-town churches with the fake steeple and signboard out front with God jokes, just your regular country church, small. But my Lord what a crowd. At the viewing, the line ran out the door and around the little graveyard, with people of all walks of life shivering in their overcoats waiting to say goodbye to a dead man. Not just Peggots and the Peggot-related, but people I'd not have guessed knew him. Donnamarie from the farm store. Coach Briggs. Even Stoner showed his ugly face, playing the good ex-neighbor, with his underage waitress now pregnant-child-bride. Her dad was the owner of Pro's Pizza, so

Stoner probably knocked her up for the free refills. I didn't speak to him. I walked around the graves and checked out the square hole they'd opened up for Mr. Peg, with a pile of dirt beside it that seemed twice too much to go back in. That church cemetery was so small, I'd say you had to be a lifetime member to get a spot in there. I was surprised to find Hammer Kelly standing off to himself at the edge of the woods. I introduced Dori and he was polite as always, all bad haircut and freckles and pleased-to-meet you, but he looked wrecked, like he had the other night. I felt like shit for what I'd said to him, that it was not the end of the world. Mr. Peg was the closest he had to a father.

Dori was too cold to stand in the line so we went inside and found June and Maggot. June had used her Wonder Woman powers to get Maggot into a coat and tie, so he looked like a nice young man slash zombie. Emmy, still AWOL. June knew everybody there to speak to, including old guys Mr. Peg had worked with in his mining days. Men he'd hunted and fished with whenever he was younger, not yet overrun with us brats crowding out the better company. I'd say half the county was there. Mr. Peg was a person. I felt proud to have some claim on him, but it took me down a notch to see all these other people that had the same claim, if not better. Dori and I got to sit in the family section of seats though. June put us up there with the kids and grandkids, and this is stupid I know, but it swelled me up. Similar to how I'd felt running onto the field in my jersey with all eyes on me. Like somebody of worth.

The service was so different from Mom's. This minister *knew* Mr. Peg. He told all these stories on him, and everybody was right there. Not slamming their heart doors on the misfortunate dead, but laughing and crying over a life. Boyhood shenanigans, like sneaking a calf into the schoolhouse, shutting it up in the principal's office overnight. Being ringleader of boys that fired pokeberries with their slingshots at the back side of this very church, making red splats on the white clapboards that looked like bullet holes. Then, ringleader of boys that had to repaint the whole church. Adult shenanigans also, like Mr. Peg and this minister's dad turning over in a boat on Carr Fork Lake, each of them claiming ever after that he'd saved the other man from drowning. Another time though, Mr. Peg did save a man's life, no question, while the two of them were castrating bulls. I never knew any of this. The person he saved was Donnamarie's grandfather. The whole idea of the sermon was how people connect up in various ways, seen and unseen, and that Mr. Peg had tied a lot of knots in the big minnow seine that keeps us all together. Dead but still here, in other words. That's what killed me the worst. At Mom's funeral, the casket closed on her and she was just over and out. Whatever good was still known about her, if any, was all on me, and I was too pissed off to do anything with it. I had even made fun of her dancing. Which was probably Mom at her best.

Dori held my hand the whole time. Her hand felt like a baby bird inside my fist, something I could protect if I tried hard enough. Something turned over, telling me to start my proper manhood there and then. Here's a knot I can tie, I was thinking. I will never let it unravel.

Normally after the burial comes dinner on the ground, meaning a church picnic. But this was winter, and way too many people for inside the church, so they had it at the basement fellowship hall of the funeral home. They were having a funeral upstairs that same day for somebody else I knew. Collins, that I'd replaced as first-string tight end. Not yet eighteen, with a girlfriend and a baby, that big strapping body: dead. Jesus. I'd never known his first name till I saw it on the sign in the hallway to the funeral chapel. Aidan.

Downstairs, Mr. Peg's people straggled in like a trail of ants carrying their casserole dishes, their sheet cakes, their green Jell-O rings with wrinkled Saran

Wrap skin. Nothing brings on the food like a person that's already had his last meal. Ruby was bossing her younger sisters over the setup, getting in a tiff with June. Too many hens in that coop. I wasn't keen to stay, but couldn't leave without speaking to Mrs. Peggot. She'd been sweet to me back whenever Mom died. I owed her for a lot of things, but especially that.

It took me awhile to find her, sitting quiet in her rumpled white hair and a black dress with shoulders way bigger than hers. Waving away all the people fussing over her. She'd been looking after people every minute since she was fifteen and married Mr. Peg, with all those kids and then Maggot. Now they were all saying she could finally get some rest, but if nobody was letting her lift a finger, she was as good as gone. That's how she looked to me, like the orphan of the world. If you think a person that's lost everything knows what to say to another one, I didn't. But I pulled a chair over and sat, and she gripped my hand so hard it hurt. Not even looking at me, just holding on. I meant to introduce her to Dori but she got whisked away, fresh cousin bait, all the younger girls asking her questions and coveting her pretty hair. That was Dori. Magical. I spotted her across the room talking with her hands the way she did, always in motion, pointing at me to show everybody I was the one she belonged to. If you want to discuss having Jesus up in your veins. For me, that was it.

It was a temptation to stay and eat, given all that food, so we did. Then midway through everything, Emmy showed up. A buzz ran through the place, plastic forks and chicken legs frozen midair. I'd not seen her earlier at the church, but she must have been there. She had one of those flowers they let you take off the casket. June shot her the get-over-here look, but Emmy turned on her heel and walked off, with that long-legged rose on her shoulder like a rifle.

I ate fast, and Maggot and I went outside for a toke. Dori was having a big time, but I'd had enough of this party, and Maggot needed a furlough from the war in his brain, with Mr. Peg now dead on his battlefield. I'm not saying Maggot's and my problems stacked up equal, but the same remedy applied. Weed is versatile. We were out there having an ignorant dispute over why a funeral home would need an entire row of dumpsters lined up at the back of the building (his view: excess bodies), and out of nowhere we heard a catfight. Major bad-bitch business, you could just about hear the fingernails sinking up to their hilts. We walked around the corner in our friendly fog, and were shocked to see Rose Dartell with a fistful of hair, and Emmy on the other end of it. Emmy screaming so hard, some of that pretty brunette had to be coming out.

My reflexes weren't top notch, but I managed to get around behind Rose and pull her away. The hair thing though, I had no skills with that. I shifted to a choke hold while Emmy worked both hands up over her head trying to untangle herself from Rose's fists. Finally Emmy staggered back, bloody nose, little flouncy skirt skewed sideways, stockings shredded, little gravels stuck in her knees. Eyes like flamethrowers. Rose twisted out of my hold with such force, I got a flash of her growing up with murder-boy Fast Forward, holding her own. She stomped across the lot, threw herself into a pickup, and tore out with a squeal that froze the black-dressed huddle coming out the front door. Emmy was gone in the same instant, down the alley in all her wrecked glory. Maggot and I watched her cut between the dumpsters, stomping off towards the laundromat and points west.

"What in the everloving hell?" I asked Maggot.

More of the upstairs funeral people started coming out, barely missing the brawl. Family of Collins, that thought about destroyed me. I saw which one of them had to be the girlfriend, with the baby and the wrung-out face, gripping that child like her last ten cents. Her hair was done in an old-style way, teased in the fat bump behind the headband. I remembered her now from school, one of the countrier girls. I knew I should go say something to her, but God alone knows what.

"Did you talk to Hammer?" Maggot asked.

"Just to tell him I was sorry. About Mr. Peg and everything."

"He's a sorrier fuck than that. Emmy broke up with him."

"Already? Well, hell. That was a flashbang."

"Thanks to you, man."

"I never touched the girl." I felt myself going red in the ears. "Since fourth grade."

"Not you, asshole. Your high-flying friend. Looks like his sidekick is pissed."

I was confused enough, he had to spell it out. They'd been seen. Emmy and Fast Forward. I got a squelched feeling in my chest, like a rotten apple in there. "Demon's friend, that Fast person," June called him, and had been asking if this young man I'd introduced to Emmy was decent. I told Maggot I didn't know him well enough to say. I wished it was the truth.

44

All the way up, or all the way down. That was me now, getting beat with both ends of that stick before any day's end, never both at once, and not much in between. Nobody but Dori knew what I was going through. Coach had told me to cut back on the percs, get off the oxys altogether, and stay off that knee as much as possible. If pain wasn't an issue, he said, I could taper out on the meds, get healed up, and he'd get me back in playing form in time for next fall.

I did what he said, or tried. Every day. Until I was hiding puke in my balled-up jacket and swamp-sacking my bed sheets. Then I'd give in, take a couple of pills and start again. Usually some percs and half an oxy in the morning would get me through school as a functioning being, and then afternoon and evening were just so many hours to get through until, until. Until the next hour that's not completely horrible, bought and paid for with another pill. Pain was not the issue. Pain is just this thing, like a noise or a really bad smell. Here's you, there's the pain, you bump fists and make your deal. What I'm discussing is a feeling up inside your blood and lungs, like you've been snakebit from the inside. Shivering, loose-boweled, a body you want nobody to get anywhere close to until you can get it fixed. The issue is: how soon will this bottle run out.

Late December, was the answer. Dr. Watts had renewed me a few times over, and I'd taken exactly what he and Coach told me to, right up to our sad defeat at Richlands. I won't pretend I've always been the obedient boy, but now I had people counting on me, and not just my teammates, this was a countywide situation. For the first time in my life I had a man's job to do, and the guts to hold my bargain. We didn't make it to semifinals, thanks to one mean motherfucker of a defensive end and God taking his regular dump on Demon. But even after I got hurt, I did everything in my power to be the man Coach thought I was. Now Coach was looking to seasons ahead, me getting off the meds and on my feet, so I'd die before I asked for another prescription. But dying felt like an actual option here. Day by day the orange bottle rattled its sadness at me, going down for the count.

Salvation was Dori. Everything was Dori.

I wanted a second first time with her, even if it was really our fifth or sixth. We were clocking them up pretty fast. But I wanted Dori to know I felt about her the way adult or married people do, if not better. To be together like that. Not in a car. It was a goal I set my mind to.

We spent most of our time looking after her dad, Vester, in their farmhouse that smelled of gas-stove pilot and adult diapers. Not sexy. Jip went berserk every single time I walked in the door, flattening himself to the linoleum like a rat-skin rug, his black beady eyes shooting murder. Vester's hospital bed was in the front room so he could watch the comings and goings, which were sadly few. They had home-care nurses a few times a week to do stuff Dori couldn't handle, catheters and such, and Dori would chat them up like crazy, being lonely. She was on her own for the most of it, even cutting the man's hair. She said all her friends dropped her like a hot rock after Vester got sick. Staying in school wasn't an option, it took all-day drives to get him to his different specialist doctors. At this point, those drives were probably the best part of her life.

Beeping the horn whenever they crossed the state line, having their big adventure.

If she had to run out for groceries, she'd let me baby-sit him, which mainly involved making sure his oxygen tubes didn't fall out of his nose. He'd want me to come sit close and hear the story of his life. The heart attack being least of the man's woes. I'd wondered about his age, this grandpa type of guy being Dori's father, and it turns out he did marry a wife ten years younger. But neither was he as old as he looked. Fifty-one. He'd worked for the mines prior to the layoffs, not as a miner proper but maintenance in the prep plant, longwall, I didn't really know what that meant. It put him in the way of coal dust and asbestos. He said he would come home with little white hairs of that all over him, like after you've had a haircut. Throw off his coverall on the kitchen floor by the washer and think no more of it, because nobody told him to. After he got bad lungs, they got a settlement from the asbestos, which was how he and his brother started the farm store. But now his brother was dead and he was as good as, so don't look for money to buy your life back, was his advice to me. And not that I said so, but I didn't think I'd mind giving it a shot. I'd buy a new knee, because one of mine was shot to hell. I just did my best with Vester to change the subject onto car engines or football plays, and try not to stare at the skull behind his face and the arm bones under the spotty skin.

One noticeable feature of their house was a horse on the roof. Plastic, semi-life-size. It used to be on top of the store, but little-girl Dori begged to have it on their house, so there it stood. This was after her mom died and various aspects of family life took a header. The whole upstairs was a dead Mom museum, dusty closed window blinds, closets crammed with dresses they never threw out. Dori's room was a different type of weird, rival to Haillie McCobb's as far as stuffed animals go, but with Christina Aguilera Dirrty posters and a Sims Deluxe Edition box where she hid her condoms. She said she got those free from one of the home-care nurses. We would make out on her bed because we couldn't help ourselves, but only to a point. Her dad was pretty much always asleep, so, not a problem. Jip was the problem. Adorable Jipsy Wipsy. If he wasn't barking his brains out at me, he was making a low chainsaw rumble and eyeing me with a view to clean castration. No way was I taking my pants off in that house.

My first choice would have been outside in the woods, on a blanket, with lightning bugs dancing around. Total Disney fuck, she'd go wild for that. But this was the dead of winter. I had to be creative. The special place I thought of was on Creaky Farm, which was foreclosed and sold now to some out-of-towner that never showed up to farm it. We heard of city guys buying and selling Lee County land they had no need of, just because it was dirt cheap and one more place to hide their cash. Creaky's tobacco bottom had been fallow for two seasons, the cattle pastures all grown up in thistles, and none of these problems mine to fix. With the old man gone, the snake had no fangs. I'd enjoyed the place, on the few occasions I'd gone back to plunder it.

The spot I had in mind was the stripping house, that used to be my boy cave. It was built into the ground like a cold cellar, with stone walls cool at all times of year and damp to the touch. The cool would keep the cured stalks soft so you could work through the winter, stripping the leaves from the stalks by hand. But I used to go there just to be off by myself, safe. Nobody ever found me there. The soft dirt floor and sweet tobacco smell in the dark always put a spell on me, like starting life over in the belly of some mom that was getting it right this time.

I took Dori there. With a bottle of Thunderbird and some candles I'd pocketed at Mr. Peg's funeral, which is how long I'd been planning this. I told her I had a surprise in store and she was all like, birthday girl. With anybody else it might have been a downer, driving out there on lonely roads, walking through dead weeds, no sound except some crows in a bald tree griping about the weather. Dori though. She'd get so excited for any small thing, it made you happy to be alive. I shoved open the heavy door like a castle keep. We spread out our quilt, and didn't even get the bottle cap twisted off before we were out of our clothes and on each other. Her cold lips and little teeth biting my ears, the shock of her breasts with their brown eyes staring. The slipperiness of putting myself inside her, the pull of that. No force on earth could stop it, once we'd gotten that far. I'd spent so much of my life hungry, and these days were no different. Every minute I craved that feeling with another person, being that close. I couldn't get air until I had Dori up against me again. Only then would the begging go quiet and let other good, strange things pass through my head. The beautiful slickness of all life, babies sucking tit, a calf getting born, pouring out of its mother the way they do, like blood from a pitcher.

Afterwards I lay looking up at the tobacco hanging above us like somebody's laundry left on the line. Well cured now, for sure. I thought of taking some to roll in Zig-Zag papers and pass around to my friends for a change, instead of being the broke-ass that bums. Random, peaceful thoughts. I only ever felt like this after Dori and I banged our brains out. She liked to stay on me, balanced on my slippery chest and stomach and sloppy wet dick. Sometimes she'd take a nap. At first I'd worried every time about doing things right, but she said I did. How she knew, what other guys had or hadn't touched her the right way, I had no wish to know. We were perfect together. She said before we were us, we weren't anything. That's why she could fall asleep on me, the perfectness of our fit. Or if not to sleep, she'd go all drifty, asking random things.

That day in the stripping house she asked if I ever noticed how those thousand-legger bugs, if you squash them, smell like cherry soda. Moving nothing but her mouth, this was her question. It shrank me up some. I mean, we're naked. I asked why, did she see one? And she said no, just wondering. She also asked if animals knew they were going to die someday. She had to be thinking of Jip, she was senseless over that creature, so I said no. "Maybe sometimes, right beforehand, if it's a situation," I said. "But for the most part I'd say your normal animal day is a happy little bubble, like being always stoned."

I felt her smile against my chest. She took my word on anything. She asked what did I think our baby chicken would be whenever he grew up. I said a rooster, if I had to guess. He was making sounds in that direction.

Angus had started calling it Lovechild to aggravate me, and I took up the name to spite her. Even though he was living in the tool shed now and getting no love to speak of, unless Mattie Kate remembered to go out there and throw grain at him.

Finally Dori slid off me. Her teeth were chattering, so I gave her my flannel shirt. She scooted against the wall, drew her legs up to her chest, and buttoned my shirt around her whole body, knees and all. She looked like a plaid pillow with her head on top and the little pink peas of her toes poking out the bottom. I wanted to take her in my arms and hide her someplace. Her shiny black eyes watched while I lit Mr. Peg's funeral candles and opened the bottle and poured the Thunderbird into paper cups. It felt like church, the part where they say, Remember who died for your sins. For Dori and me, all our best people died on us early, before we had any good shot at sin. So we had catching up to do. Maybe that's why nothing we ever did felt wrong.

We needed no more than the wine to get ourselves rosy. She'd already given me the smallest hit of something before we went out, so I'd be happy and not fiending. My stomach was always my downfall, running ragged these days on the daily ride of oxy-not-oxy, and I'm just going to tell you, nothing kills the buzz like bringing up Chick Fil-A all over the girlfriend's bralette. That only happened once, and she was so sweet about mopping me up, using her shirt to wipe scum off my chin. But all I could think of was her feeding Vester his babyfied meals, his gnarly hands gripping the bedrails as he strained towards the spoon, and I got in a mood. Walking like an old man with a bum knee already, I refused to be another mess for Dori to clean up. So after that, she always had something to tide me over. This or that, Xanax, Klonopin, a dab from one of her Dad's morphine patches if nothing else was on hand. But usually something was.

I thought I knew it all in those days. I'd seen people at school, in the locker room, even at Mr. Peg's funeral, with stains on their shirttails. Greenish grass stains, or pinkish brown like dirt. How could those people be so prideless, I thought, showing up in dirty shirts. I didn't know that was the coating of a pill that keeps this safer-than-safe drug from dissolving in your stomach all at one time. Coppery pink on the 80 milligrams, green on the 40s. Melts in your mouth like an M&M. Hold it there a minute, then take it out and rub it on your shirt-tail, and you're looking at a shiny white pearl of pure oxy. More opioid than any pill ever before invented. One buck gets you a whole bottle of these on Medicaid, to be crushed and snorted one by one, or dissolved and injected with sheep-vax syringes from Farm Supply, in the crook of an arm or the webbing of your toes. People find more ways to shut up their monsters than a Bible has verses.

You have to understand the rhyme and reasons of Dori. Why she was radical and fun like a little girl, even after all her friends left her flat. How she stayed patient with a wheezing, crying man gone old before his time. Why her foot kept bouncing. Her sparkly eyes were not really black, but blue. Bending down to kiss her, I'd see the thinnest crescent of sky blue around the huge black center. Living a life like hers, most people would have lost it a thousand times over.

Coach probably thought I was off the pills by now, headed for the gym to dead-lift my ass back onto the gravy train. Angus was getting pesky over Christmas, let's go steal a tree. I tried to steer clear of them both. I would make a hit-and-run for one of Mattie Kate's meals or a night's sleep, both badly needed, but mostly made excuses. Angus rolled her eyes at me. Which pissed me off. A guy does not need a reason to go screw his girlfriend, it's just a given. Dori was sweet to them, bringing over presents to the house from her dad's farm store like socks, chicken mash for Lovechild of course, Carhartt overalls, which Angus really liked, XL-size thermal shirts for Coach. Once, this little stool with a tractor seat. Somewhat random, but more sensible anyway than a chicken in a Tampax box. And none of it earned me a pass on blowing off family life and Christmas, even though I'd invented the whole concept for all Angus knew.

Too bad. My sole concern over Christmas was what to give Dori. I kept thinking of that first amazing Christmas with Angus, how I'd scoured the pawns high and low for exactly her kind of thing, and felt like a million bucks for finding it. I wanted that feeling again of really seeing a person and being seen. And wouldn't get it with Dori, she was too easy. If I wrapped a box of Trojans in Christmas paper, she'd say it was the best present anybody ever gave her. Which is kind of a letdown. You don't get points for hitting the side of the barn. But thinking of old times and the fun I'd had with Angus wasn't fair. I loved Dori with all my heart.

The femmy direction seemed like a safe bet, nail polish or makeup, which I knew zero about except that you won't find them at the flea market. Angus would be no help. I did know what CDs Dori liked, Christina, Avril Lavigne. Pink, that was Dori's hair idol. These were the things rattling around my skullbox the week before Christmas while I ran errands in town for Dori. Christmas shopping on the sly. She was particular about being the one to get Vester's meds, but I needed the car for my mission, so talked her into letting me pick up their mail and checks at the PO, then Walgreens to get the prescriptions. Last stop, groceries. They only ever ate frozen things: Vester lived on Bob Evans mashed potatoes and Dori on Mrs. Smith meringue pies. I argued for chicken nuggets and such, to level out the food groups. But either way, you don't let this shit sit in your car on a sunny day, even if it's December.

So that's where I was, waiting in a long line at the pharmacy pickup while gum-chewing counter girl with troll-doll hair had a discussion with a customer about her husband's anus surgery aftercare. The old lady had on those clear rubber rain boots that button over your shoes. Mr. Peg called them galoshes, a word Maggot and I used as a stand-in cussword. You galosher, I will so galosh you. I owed Mrs. Peggot a visit. The pharmacy consult dragged on. The girl tore a coupon off a booklet on her counter and started drawing a rendition of an anus on the back with a ballpoint pen. Behind her was an entire wall of cubbies exactly like the PO I'd just come from. Those PO boxes were all stuffed with disability checks, and these with the white paper bags of drugs that the checks paid for. What if you combined the two and cut out the hassle, I thought. One-stop shopping. Across the top of the Walgreens wall of cubbies, they'd stashed the boxes of every cold medicine ever known to man that has Sudafed in it: Maxiflu CD, Drixoral, Sinutab, Flu Maximum Strength, etc. There must have been five hundred boxes up there. Not on the shelves anymore. Thanks to Maggot and his smurfer pals.

While I was staring at the Sudafed motherlode, somebody tapped me on the shoulder. Heavyset guy, small goat-type beard, glasses, too much hair for his head.

"Tommy," I said. "What are you in for, man?"

Not drugs, he said, just a Dew and Doritos for his lunch. He caught me up on the months since we met at the drive-in. Still in his newspaper job, promoted from trash cans to doing stuff on the actual newspaper. Layout is what he said, setting out ads on the page to catch the reader's eye. Making enough to move out from the disaster roommates into his own place. I had to hand it to Tommy, coming out of the foster factory as a decent human. I said the new beard suited him, even though actually it added to the whole effect of what was standing up on his head, but you know. Old friends. I brought him up to speed on Dori, and asked if he still had the girlfriend. Surprise answer: yes. Sophie was her name, sweet girl, still in Pennsylvania so they hadn't met yet. Maybe next year.

The line started moving and Tommy had his ads to get back to, but told me to come visit. He wrote down his address and apologized that it wasn't the house per se, it was the garage. No bath or kitchen yet, but they were planning to put those in. He rented from a really nice couple that let him use their bathroom. With four kids, that he kept an eye on sometimes. I could see this meant the world to Tommy, being part of a family. He said he read them *Magic Treehouse*. The little girl liked books, not so much the little boy that was into *Grand Theft Auto*, and the other two just small. Twins. The girl was named Haillie. Not believable. It was the McCobbs.

The first thing I asked him was: Is your room really a garage, or is it a dog room with a washer-dryer combo? I had quite a few more questions after that. Yes, a garage. Yes, they worried all the time about money but Mr. McCobb had started a business selling weight-loss products called Wate-O-Way, mainly signing up other people for a three-hundred-dollar fee so they could also be part of the Wate-O-Way sales team. Tommy believed with his whole heart that Mr. McCobb would soon be a rich man. He hadn't seen any products yet, but they were supposed to be a whole new game in weight loss. Oh, Tommy.

He couldn't get over me knowing these people. My long-lost fosters. I wanted to say, Tommy, go pack your shit, walk out of that garage and never look back. But he was all over this family. I couldn't burst his bubble.

I said I would come over sometime with Dori and we'd take him and the McCobbs out to Applebee's or something, my treat. Which is insane. No idea why I said that. I wouldn't have minded to see those kids, Haillie especially, to see how she was holding up in that FUBAR family. But the main reason probably was me wanting to eat as much as I could in front of them. I'd stuff my face, two burgers. Some form of weird revenge.

I had to warn him, though, before he went on his way. About Mr. McCobb's enterprises. All fine and good on the Wate-O-Way, I said, but don't even think about putting your own money into that. Oh, Tommy. It turned out he already had.

45

The rest of that winter is hazy, like there's a cloud lying over me and tenth grade. All I can say for sure is that my home was with Dori, more and more. I kept my clothes over there and my meds. Having my night sweats in sheets that would not be Mattie Kate's secret to keep. I was trying to dial down the oxy but not too regular about it, with Dori's little add-ons throwing me off schedule. She couldn't help herself, just a caring person. She sang to Vester while she fed him, little kid songs like Twinkle Star. The care nurses came three mornings a week on rotation, and Dori passed me off as a cousin instead of a live-in boyfriend. Still worried about DSS. But it wasn't the nurses' job to keep tabs on us. They warned her to keep his pills and patches locked up in a safe place, probably thinking she was older, not a seventeen-year-old in charge of the man's narcotics. Just another case of everybody trying to do the jobs they're given.

Christmas came and went, with Dori of course loving the presents I gave her, and Angus making a good show of not sulking over the ones I didn't. After all, Angus was the one that swore to Christmas being no big deal. So I kept telling myself. That house was returning to its natural state. I was nothing more over there than a brief disturbance of the peace.

I missed her though, Angus. The easiness of her. I mean, sex is great and everything, as anybody will tell you. But there's much to be said also for lying around with a person on beanbags, firing popcorn penalties at each other for offside fart violations.

I had my driver's license, but no place to go. If I went to school from Dori's, she'd go with me to bring back the car, and pick me up later. Marooned on our island. My guy friends of recent years were my team-mates, and after the knee injury I fell off their map. That's high school for you, a bevy of people unfit for adult life encounters in any form. And my old standbys the Peggots were in disarray. So my whole life was Dori now, idling while she microwaved stuff to feed Vester or patted him down with a washrag. Other than that, she napped. I slid into my old lonely ways, drawing again in my notebooks, not superhero kid nonsense but things I saw while out and about. I did a three-panel cartoon of Walgreens Spy Girl passing secrets encoded in anus diagrams to undercover agent Galoshes, so. Whole different category of nonsense.

I was in Ms. Annie's art class again, if I bothered to go to school, but my former success had been largely crush-motivated. The repeat of last year was a letdown. Seeing her explain these amazing things of contrast and proportion the first time around was like watching a magical genius. Second time, she was just a teacher. She still thought I had talent but probably was all the more disappointed in me for zoning out. Fine. Special for Dori was all I needed to be.

Other than the useful parts like driver's ed leading automatically to the license, school faded from importance as is natural for a boy becoming a man. Civics, I actually cannot tell you what those are. Math I got to take from Mr. Cleveland that had his deal with Coach, football players got a grade that kept us eligible. I had to do the harder English, which was a time suck, reading books. Some of them though, I finished without meaning to. That Holden guy held my interest. Hating school, going to the city to chase whores and watch rich people's nonsense, and then you come to find out, all he wants in his heart is to stand at the edge of a field catching little boys before they go over the cliff like he did. I could see that. I mean, *see* it, I drew it, with those white cliffs on the Kentucky border where Miss Barks took me that time. I've not ever seen rye growing, so I made him the catcher in the tobacco. Likewise the Charles Dickens one, seriously old guy, dead and a foreigner, but Christ Jesus did he get the picture on kids and orphans getting screwed over and nobody giving a rat's ass. You'd think he was from around here.

The main event of that winter was Demon's big stupid adventure. The plan itself, what little there was of it, came from Angus putting it to me as a dare. Of the put-up or shut-up kind. I was spending enough evenings at Coach's to convince all parties that I still lived there. He was watching my limp, making noises about surgery, and I was doing my best impressions of a drug-free once-and-future tight end. Angus and I one evening were up in our den watching some nature planet show on the amazing leopard seal. I was in one of my moods. This being really the only major thing I'd wanted out of life, and I was never going to get any closer to the damn ocean than a damn Japanese-made TV. I said words to that effect. And I still remember her big gray ocean eyes, looking at me like, *What is wrong with you?* If Angus wanted to do something, she fucking did it. So maybe it was spite or pride. I told her: Fine, you know what? I'm going.

I started talking it up to Dori, which was just cruel. Of course she'd want to go, the beach would amaze her because everything amazed her. It wasn't so long ago she'd been this whole fun, popular girl at school, before her dad and his five-hour doctor drives ate her life. Now she was hard pressed to talk her neighbor into watching Vester so the two of us could go out parking. But she saw how bad I wanted it, and begged me to go without her. Take pictures, she said. This was before camera phones were in everybody's pockets. I borrowed a Polaroid from Angus.

Without Dori I would need transportation. Fast Forward wouldn't have been first choice, but he had wheels, and was generally up for adventure if the booze was adequate. On the phone he said he was covered up at the farm, tied up with his horses, which I'd been told were not his horses, but kept that to myself. I asked him to think about it. He said maybe. Next I brought it up to Maggot, knowing he'd be game for anything that got him out of the house. June was two inches from kicking him out, setting certain conditions he was not able to live with. She was pretty tolerant of his grooming, so it had to be more than that, and I didn't ask. Even a minor weed incident could really blow up over there, she was on some drug warpath ever since World War Kent, to the extent of Maggot coming over to Dori's just to roll a reefer.

In less than a minute, Emmy found out from Maggot and announced she was coming too. Which then got Fast Forward on board. I was never sure about the chicken or the egg on that one, but understood we were getting into some kind of love-hate triangle with June Peggot involved, which is not a geometry problem you want to be in. But damn. All that mattered to me was the ocean. I was going to Virginia Beach, Virginia. A town we chose solely for its name, having no idea where we would rest our heads after planting our asses on its grass. Or hopefully, sand. We had no money, no game plan, not enough supplies to get us five miles down the road, let alone the five hundred it was. Fast Forward had connections in a city he said was on the way, somebody that could hook him up with easy cash, and that was enough for four people high on youth and extreme inexperience.

I have to admit, another thing factored in. Some kids at school were peacocking around with their plan to hit the beach over spring break. This is the Bettina Cook crowd with their Abercrombies and Daddy Express cards and sixteenth-birthday cars with the big yellow bows from CarMax. Kids that only need to say the words, "Hey! Let's all get shitfaced at Myrtle Beach," and presto it happens. Half of them probably didn't care about the ocean, and the other half wouldn't notice it if they passed out tits-up on the fucking dunes. Not bitter or anything, me.

But to lose my mind that way, thinking I was in the league of those kids, wanting and getting? Dori had never been over a state line except to take her dad to heart-lung specialists, and lately was lucky to see the back side of Walmart. I was an asshole to dangle this trip in front of her, and then go, knowing she couldn't. I have no good excuse. Maybe all kids are like this, wanting too much. Like Maggot, working every angle too far, to blow the gaskets of his poor grandparents that married at fifteen with no bigger hope in the world than to have kids and not watch them die. Us though, give us the fucking world. We pretended we were as good as the Bettina Cook kids, while Bettina pretended to be a Kardashian. We'd all cut our teeth on TV shows where parents had jobs, and kids lived out big-city dreams in their wardrobe choices and rivers of cash. Even doing drugs, these forgivable schoolboys, and it's a comedy because they're not poor. In their universe, nobody shuts you down for being different and wanting the moon.

In ours, you live on a tether: to family, parents if

you're lucky, older people raising you if less so, that you yourself will end up looking after by and by. Odds are about a hundred to one, you are not destined for greatness. Your people will appreciate you all the same. On the other hand, if you poundcake someone or push them too far in the shame or shock direction, you will run into their people at Hardee's or the Dollar General parking lot, in all probability within the day. There will be aftermaths. Same goes for raising your head too high on your neck, the tall weed gets cut. So. You wind up meeting in the middle on this follow-your-heart thing, at a place everybody can live with. Show me that universe on TV or the movies. Mountain people, country and farm people, we are nowhere the hell. It's a situation, being invisible. You can get to a point of needing to make the loudest possible noise just to see if you are still alive.

The first night we made it as far as a place called Hungry Mother. Not kidding. We'd got off to a woefully messy start with everybody excited, needing their calm-down of choice. Then needing to sleep that off. And leaving Dori called for I'm-sorry-baby sex, which takes more time than the regular. So now we were only a few counties down the road, it was getting dark, and here was this highway sign. Hungry Mother turned out to be not a restaurant or sad female human but a park, with picnic tables and such. A lake. It was February, we didn't wait for spring break, being way out ahead of those rich kids plus more willing to ditch school. The park was empty, its picnic area and lake all ours. At the water's edge, a big patch of sand.

"Gol dang, children. It's the motherfucking beach," Maggot said, getting out of the truck, unfolding himself like a jackknife. He stretched his long arms wide and bounced on his toes.

"Let's not rush to judgment," I said. The sand was dark brown, like a worn-out welcome mat to the drab pavement of lake. But Emmy was singing "Beach, Beach, Baby!" and skipping sideways across the parking lot, a leggy colt in her skinny jeans and tall leather boots. The three of us climbed over a small fence onto the sand. The entrance was a locked gate beside a little block of rest rooms and vending machines, all deserted. Fast Forward lit a cigarette and leaned on his truck, watching us in his usual way, head tilted back, eyes narrowed.

This sand patch was no more than fifty or sixty yards wide, with log pilings holding a rope fence on both sides. Beyond that, the normal dirt and woods resumed. Somebody had just scooped up truckloads of sand and dumped it here, thinking no one would be the wiser. This fake beach moreover was pretty gross due to what all people had left there: flattened drink cups with red straws poking out of the lids, the black remains of a campfire. A torn white bra, half buried in sand. Maggot lit a joint and started singing about Margaritaville. Emmy formed big balls of wet sand one after another that fell apart as she threw them at us. Both those two were laughing like kids. I got a bad feeling as regards their interest in reaching the real ocean.

"You all, this is not the beach. You know that, right?"

"Stepped on a cow flop! Blew out my tip-top," yodeled Maggot, swaying his hips and tiptoeing across the sand in his weird boots.

Just to prove the entire world was against me, a seagull curved in and landed near us. Big, white, we've all seen the pictures. It stepped along the brown scum at the water's edge, keeping a mean eye on me. "Hell-o-o, this isn't the sea!" I yelled. The seagull paid no heed.

Our curly-headed Marlboro Man was still over there in his cowboy boots and tight white T-shirt tucked in his jeans. I didn't really trust him, but maybe never did. A kid in my shoes takes what power he can find. As far as him and Emmy, no guess. She'd been flirty all day, wearing a soft blue sweater that buttoned all the way up the back, seemingly designed to make you think about taking it off of her. How would she even get that on by herself? Fast Forward had driven left-handed with his arm draped around her, but seemed his usual self, like he's just waiting for a better offer. From time to time asking her to crack open another tallboy from the case at our feet.

Now we watched him flick away his cigarette butt and stroll towards us, getting over the fence in one motion like clearing a hurdle. No bad knees. Quarter-backs let others take the fall. "Me oh my," he said, taking it in. "What have we here? Ask and you shall receive."

"*Not* the ocean. *Not* the beach," I said.

He walked towards the water. I stared at his pointy-toed footprints in the sand. He leaned over and scooped up a squashed yellow Styrofoam clamshell stained with ketchup and held it up to his ear. "Shhhh." Finger to his lips. Eyes wide. "I can hear the ocean."

I picked up a crushed beer can and fired it at the seagull. The bird flew away.

Emmy laughed her starry laugh. Fast Forward grabbed her hand, twirling her around, and just like that they were doing a two-step: his left hand holding hers and his right spread wide on her shoulder blade, pushing her backward with little steps. Like they're hearing LeAnn Rimes singing "Can't Fight the Moonlight," and too bad for the rest of us if we're not. Maggot crouched on his long legs, elbows on knees like a praying mantis, looking pouty. They'd obviously done this, gone out dancing. Emmy would place her demands. They looked like a movie couple, Emmy matching his steps, her back arched, smiling up at him. The outline of a thick wallet was worn into his back pocket. They twirled around the beach and then he lifted her by the waist and set her on one of the posts of the rope fence. Emmy raised her pressed-together hands above her head and stood balanced with the bright moon rising through black pines behind her. She looked perfect up there. A church steeple.

Then Fast Forward grabbed her around the waist, flinging her over his shoulder like a grain bag, Emmy laughing and kicking her legs, and the beauty was over.

Hungry Mother was a joke on us. We'd not eaten all day. It was decided Fast Forward and Emmy would go into the town and pick up Pizza Hut or something. We pulled money out of our pockets to give Fast Forward, and Maggot and I were left behind like additional trash on the fake beach. We dragged a log to the water's edge to sit on. The moon was more egg-shaped than round, but seemed proud of itself regardless, laying out a shiny silver road across the water to our feet. Come on up, said the moon. Our faces and bodies were painted with silver. Looking at Maggot from the side, his nose and chin outlined in light, it dawned on me he wasn't a kid. He'd grown into his square, shaved chin and Adam's apple. And seemed to be dialing back the makeup. Maybe that was all just him now, the long, black eyelashes his cousins used to want to kill him for. I wondered if he was in love with Fast Forward. Like all of us.

Maggot and I sat like bumps on our log, letting the moon make us pretty. The whole place was, honestly, apart from me hating it for not being the place I wanted. On the other side of the sparkly water, a cone-shaped mountain with a pelt of pine trees rose halfway up the sky. The moon had a fuzzy ring around it. It was cold, and getting colder.

Maggot yelled across the lake at the mountain: "Who goes there?"

Like in our olden days, playing king of the hill. I yelled, "Nobody here but us hungry motherfuckers." For a long while after that, we yelled across the lake at the dark mountain to hear our echoes. "I am *one* HUNGRY *MOTHER*," we shouted.

Hungry hungry hungry. Mother mother mother.

The echoes were just in our minds, with the aid of a reefer. The truth is, it didn't matter what or how hard we yelled. Nothing was coming back to us.

Emmy and Fast were gone for an age and came back with a large cold pizza and their faces rubbed raw, like they'd been making out. Some dishevelment. I noticed the buttons up the back of Emmy's sweater were askew. We ate our pizza on the beach, which I don't recommend as a tourist option because, sand. We'd brought a pile of blankets on this trip with the plan of camping out, and now got them all out to wrap around us while we sat on the beach. Maggot and Emmy both had their quilts that Mrs. Peggot made for all the grandkids out of cut-up squares of their outgrown clothes. I used to lie on Maggot's bed staring at his, picking out all our good times. The green corduroys for instance that he'd wrecked playing on the Ruelynn coal tips.

After we ate, we cased a picnic shelter as a possible sleeping location, considering it for all of about ten seconds. The temperature was dropping like a rock. There was nobody around this park. We found some cabins and broke into one, which in our defense was not locked. The bunks had bare mattresses that smelled like mouse pee. A person can do worse.

The others were out like lights. Maggot's snore I noticed had changed with his voice. Fast and Emmy had claimed the loft and it was quiet up there, so the hankypank evidently had been gotten out of the way. All I could think of was Dori. What kind of day did she have with Vester, what kind of jerk was I to leave her. I was getting bad sweats also, even as cold as it was, so I got up and took a smidge of oxy to stave off midnight shits. I only had a few with me. Fast Forward was serious about us not getting busted on the road, and had ordered us to bring minor items only, weed and beer. Once we got to Richmond we'd be taking on valuable cargo, meaning his business arrangement, and he said he'd take care of it. Hubcaps I assumed, or duct-taped to body parts, he was worldly-wise. I wondered if the other end of this deal was Mouse, his tiny, bossy friend that had sold her goods from the Pringles can at the Fourth of July party. She'd said she was from Philly, but a Mouse nest relocation was possible.

Right away I felt the oxy quieting down my aching guts, but not my brain. I couldn't sleep. Too far from home, too much smell of mouse pee. I wrapped up in my blankets and went out on the porch. It was exactly the same cold, inside or out. They had rocking chairs and I sat in one, letting my eyes get friendly with the dark. I was surprised to see the door open and another blanket-cocoon slip outside, quiet as a cat. Emmy. I thought of those nights in June's apartment, her sneaking out to lie down with me on my pillow fort bed. Water under a long bridge. She sat in the other rocker. I couldn't see any part of her, just the burrito of her childhood quilt.

"Hey," I said. "The moon went to bed already. So what's wrong with us?"

She was quiet a long time. Then said, "Some guy threatened Mom's life."

"Christ. Who?"

"Some pillhead. He's not the first. But this was just a few days ago. Then Maggot and I take off without even telling her, so right now she's up at the house worried about us while some maniac off his nut could be creeping around with his Mac-10 fixing to blow her face off."

Her surprising knowledge of firearms made that sentence way too disturbing. "Why would anybody want to hurt June? She's Miss Popularity of the county."

The tube of quilt shifted down a little and Emmy's head came out of it. "You have no idea what she's dealing with. People come in every day just wanting her to write them. They'll say anything to get their painkillers. Kidney stones. They take the cup in the bathroom and prick their finger to put blood in the urine sample. She knows they're shopping doctors, but if she says no, some of them get really ugly. Screaming, calling her a ruthless cunt."

I couldn't imagine that. Or could, but didn't want to. The desperation was not unknown.

"That's the *men*," she said. "The women play it smart, they'll go into their exam room and duck out with her prescription pad before Mom can get in there to see them."

Emmy had one hand up to her mouth. I remembered how she used to bite her fingernails till they bled. June painted them with iodine to get her to stop. I had nothing to offer her now.

"Mom says half these people don't know they're addicted. They took what some doctor told them to, and now they're fiending and don't really know what it is. All they know is, Mom cut off their drugs and now they feel like they're dying. So why won't she help them?"

All this was making me hanker to go take more pills. Sick as that is. I wondered if Emmy knew how deep I was in. But she was wrapped up in her own shit. She said in Knoxville, June could refer these patients someplace for help, but here their insurance only covered the pills.

"You all never should have moved back. If things are so much better in Knoxville."

"No, she was miserable in that hospital. Their head

physician was this city guy from Johns Hopkins that treated the local nursing staff like they were half-wits."

I'd forgotten about that. He called her Loretta Lynn. Emmy's chair stopped rocking.

"Anyway, Mom says home is home. If people are in trouble, it's where she needs to be." Emmy put her face to the blanket, wiping her nose. I hadn't known she was crying.

"Sucks, though," I said. "She doesn't deserve people going off at her like that."

"Probably she's called Hammer to come over again. To protect her from getting murdered. He's probably there right now." She started crying then with no bother to hide it.

"What happened? With Hammer. You two were almost engaged there for a minute."

Bad move, Emmy went full waterworks. I said I was sorry, but she kept saying she was a terrible person. Over and over. I told her to stop it, she was a queen bee. Same as June.

"No, I'm not." She was doing that gasping thing that happens after crying. Mrs. Peggot used to call it getting the snubs. After a minute she asked if I knew Martha Coldiron.

"You mean Hot Topic?" Even in the dark, I could

tell I'd said the wrong thing. "Sorry, I forgot her name. Yeah, I know her. Maggot's barber."

"Martha got pregnant."

"Jesus. Maggot wasn't any party to that, was he?"

Emmy blew air out her lips.

"Okay, not Maggot. So what's she going to do? Marry the guy?"

"She despises the guy. She wouldn't tell me who, just that he's a bastard and now she had evil inside her like Rosemary's baby. She said if she couldn't get rid of it, she'd kill herself."

"Man alive. How'd you get mixed up with this?"

"She's at the house a lot. Maggot might be her only friend. I told her Mom could refer her to a free clinic and not be judgmental because it's her job. But Martha thinks if one adult knows something, they all will. Her dad finding out would be the end of her life."

"Damn. She's up a creek."

"It's called getting an abortion. I drove her to Knoxville so nobody would find out." Her chair started rocking again, in an agitated way. "Demon, I'm a horrible person. The sooner you realize that, the better off you'll be."

"Why? Because of Martha's baby?"

"No. That was probably the nicest thing I've done for anybody in ages."

"So?" Weirdly, I thought of my snake bracelet. Wondered if she still had it on her ankle.

"So, I lied to Mom. She thought we went to Knox-ville for a Kathy Mattea concert. I lie to Mom all the time. Me being here right now is lying to Mom. She hates Fast Forward."

"That's just June being June. She's always treated you like a china doll."

"No. It's him. It's not like she hates all guys, Demon. She likes *you*. She *loves* Hammer Kelly. I broke up with him because he's too good for me. I didn't deserve him."

I knew Emmy's moods. She would just have to talk herself out of this one. She told me June was worried to death about Maggot, no news there. But Emmy knew more than I did about where he was getting his crank. He was more into meth than oxy. We still talked like that, at the time, about what we were "into." Like it was a hobby. She told me things I didn't want to know, like who he was having sex with, to procure. My brain slammed the door on that one. Jesus. Maggot. This overgrown kid that barely had outgrown Legos and Avengers.

Eventually she went back to bed. I stayed outside until the sky started going white around the edges. Winter nights are too quiet, with all the little lives frozen or hiding out. My heart hurt for them. I thought of Mrs. Peggot making those quilts for all her kids and grandkids. The best people you could ever know. Save for the unlucky two, Humvee and Mariah. And among all the cousins, the only bad seeds turned out to be theirs, Emmy and Maggot, even though they were taken in by others and raised up right. I'd had some of the same kindness, the Peggots, Miss Betsy, Coach. And Fast Forward's story, the same. Many had tried their best with us, but we came out of too-hungry mothers. Four demons spawned by four different starving hearts.

46

Four of us in the cab were a crowd. Dragging Main for entertainment purposes, fine, but this was the entire state of Virginia we had to get across with legs going to sleep, breathing the stale beer breath of others. Emmy complained the most, even though cozied up by choice. It was decided that after our next gas-up, one of us would ride in the truck bed.

I was dead set on no more stops till we passed Christiansburg. I explained how my previous shot at seeing the ocean went down there in flames of Jesus songs and puke. They all said I was superstitious, and empty is empty. We took an exit with signs for the usual things, gas, food. And colleges. *Two.* You'd not think they would put two of them so close together. I thought of Angus. She was dead set on moving out after her two years at Mountain Empire, to go to so-called real college. Maybe she'd end up someplace this close, not the far side of the moon. Still though, who would her people be? College would change her. In due time she wouldn't come back.

Fast Forward told me to fill it up while he went inside to pay. Maggot and I rearranged the mess in the truck bed to make room for a passenger. We'd just thrown all our shit back there, since none of us had any suitcase. Well, probably Emmy did, but it would have looked suspicious. The Marathon station was bustling. At the pump behind us a guy in a suit and tie, blue hanky sticking out of his pocket like he's the president of something, tanked up his BMW. On the other side of the pumps, a Mercedes SUV pulled up with a bright green plastic boat of some small kind strapped on top. A tall, skinny kid with a man-bun sprang out of it like gassing vehicles is a sport event, bouncing on his toes as he fed in his credit card. He had on athletic shorts over black long johns, and these rubber shoes with individual toes. Seriously. He looked like he'd been genetically born with black rubber feet.

I helped Maggot make a nest in our blankets and grocery bags of clothes and cases of beer. He was riding in back. I'd have flipped a coin, but he volunteered. Trying to impress Fast Forward was bringing out a previously unseen side to Maggot: unselfish and agreeable. Also, he must have given himself a little bump of something to get through the day, because he was raring to get on with it. While I filled the tank, Maggot bounced on his pile of crap like he was bronco busting up there, pounding the back of the cab, yelling "Giddyup, let's get these dogies on the road! Yeehaw children," etc. Emmy told him repeatedly to shut up, and after that failed, went inside to use the ladies. I ignored him. President Hanky behind us snapped his gas cap shut and rolled his eyes as he got in his car. Man Bun stuck his head between the pumps and peered at us.

"What's this, guys, some deeply committed episode of *Jackass*?"

The kid is standing there in rubber feet, gassing up his eighty-thousand-dollar SUV for the purpose of hauling around his fucking kiddie boat, and *we* are the freaks.

Fast Forward and Emmy got back and we continued east. Atlantic Ocean, dead ahead.

But first, Richmond. Fast Forward had some written directions that led to confusion. We passed through the skyscraper and doom castle portion of the city, across a big river, through areas of houses, then back over the bridge. Fast Forward was pissed. Another slow start, then five hours of driving, now it was getting dark. He pulled over and made a call on his cell phone. Fast Forward was first of us to have one of those, him and Emmy. It was Mouse we were trying to locate. After the call we circled around through a whole other type of doom castle, rows of exactly-alike brick apartment buildings and more Black people than I'd ever known to see. Street lights were popping on. Fast Forward pulled over again, this time next to a paved square with benches and kid equipment and a tall chain-link fence around it. No guess as to what the fence was meant to keep in or out. There were kids inside, the older ones playing basketball, Black each and all, as entirely as we up home were white, and from the looks of that street, just about as broke. All of us living where we got born. Maybe you have to pay extra to mingle.

Fast Forward must have thought we couldn't hear him outside the truck cursing Mouse. A little girl let her yellow hula hoop drop to the ground, and stared at him through the chain link. Braids stuck out all over her head like a cartoon surprised kid. We watched the basketball boys in the fading light, admiring their interesting hair and superior tennis shoes.

The upshot of all this was arriving not in the best of moods at the Mouse abode. If it was even her house.

Two other guys were there, one being some form of giant, as tall as she was small. The other one, who knows, he never got off the couch. The house had a front porch, driveway, regular type place if you overlooked the fact of other houses standing just inches on either side of it. These people could lean out their bedroom windows and shake hands. The Bible says love your neighbor and you have to think city people have their ways of it, but in the two days we were there I saw no evidence. Closed blinds, the sound of dogs barking.

Mouse was unthrilled that Fast Forward had turned up with his underage fan club in tow, quote-unquote. She stood in the middle of her living room squinting up at us through her cigarette smoke, waiting for further explanation. Nobody on the planet talked down to Fast Forward, except for this four-foot-tall woman in her long pink claws and rhinestoned jeans. She was barefoot whenever we got there but hustled into her tall shoes, so. Four foot four.

"How do I know they're not going to narc me out to their mommies?" she asked.

Fast Forward suggested he would put a bullet in our heads if that happened. Emmy blew out a sharp laugh like she'd been socked in the gut.

"Our mothers are dead," I clarified.

Maggot bugged his eyes at me.

"Oh wait. One of them is in Goochland Women's. Sorry, man. No offense."

"None taken."

Fast Forward located his manhood and told Mouse he had lucrative connections in an untapped part of the state, and could certainly take them elsewhere. Mouse said if he was thinking we could all crash here, good luck finding a place to do it in this turdbone house. Which it was. The couch was broken in the middle and there were white kitchen trash bags, filled and lumpy, piled against one wall. A floor lamp stood bald and forlorn with no lampshade.

The giant guy was named Leon and not completely right in his head. He came out of the kitchen carrying a yellow cat and put it down on the glass table in front of the couch. "Here you go," he said, and smiled at us. He was in a hoodie and boxers and had the physique you come to recognize: bad teeth, caved-in chest, skinniest legs imaginable. After Leon broke the ice, Mouse rolled her eyes and said "Whatever." She threw the cat off the table and spread some powder for us all to get down there to snort lines. All except Couch Guy that was leaning over at an angle with his eyes closed and one hand over his face. I'd not seen Fast Forward do drugs before, only beer and weed. Emmy was hesitant, but Maggot got on it like a pro. Then I felt the peer pressure of Fast Forward glaring at me, and understood it was a politeness issue. Like Mrs. Peggot cooking you one of her hams: you better stay and eat or you're not one of her people. So I went ahead and got coked out of my brain box. I was already kind of awake-dreaming due to no sleep since we left home, and now it took on a nightmare aspect, with prospects of future sleep slim to none. For the record, I do not and never will relish the feeling of the engine outrunning the chassis.

I don't think much sleeping was done by anybody that night. Maggot and I were assigned to a room with no furniture in it other than a bicycle. We fetched our blankets and plastic bags of clothes to use as pillows, but the room smelled like gasoline and I kept seeing explosions in my mind's eye. Explosion, explosion. Maggot told me to chill out, it was just the smell of ass combined with bike tire. He could fall asleep on any amount of uppers, one of his superpowers. That and snoring. I had no idea what Fast might be up to. Part of me thought I should go rescue Emmy, and the rest of me felt like, Who did I think I was? Emmy had the world by the balls.

There were comings and goings all hours, car lights in the driveway. Music pounding through the wall. Somebody had a Ja Rule fixation, to the extent of "Always on Time" becoming the permanent brain soundtrack of my bad nights, probably until I'm dead. Voices were raised. Maggot roused after a while and went out to investigate. Came back and said it was nothing, just some guys in a fight over somebody shorting somebody, and Couch Guy screaming. I asked why was he screaming, and Maggot said they were moving a lot of furniture out in the yard and his couch was in the running. I understood this to be the type of place you hear about, where people get knifed and so forth as a routine. The longer I went without sleeping, the more visions I had of gasoline explosions and people getting knifed. Minutes were like hours, and hours were like large bags of shit delivered to my skull box. I got kind of beside myself and ended up taking all the rest of what I'd brought with me to calm down, plus a 1-milligram Xanax that Dori slipped in as a treat. Getting ahead of schedule. I'd be fresh out by the time we got to the beach, so. Puking and cold sweats down the road, waiting to crap on my golden moment.

The worst part, I saw coming. Fast Forward was losing interest in the beach. If he ever had any. Most of the next morning he spent making his negotiations with Mouse, and the afternoon lying under his truck with a metal box and a screwdriver and two rolls of duct tape. Maggot and I sat on the front porch smoking weed and watching the man at his labors. Person after person walked by on the sidewalk, paying no mind to the Tony Lama boots sticking out from under the F-100, like that was regular everyday scenery. If this was back home, trust me, you'd have a crowd inside of ten minutes, interested kids plus the old guys with their free advice and power tools. But these city folk just turned a blind eye.

Later on we went out driving around to see the various things they had in Richmond, statues, state capitol building, etc. We ate at Popeyes. That's where Fast Forward informed us we'd screwed around too much on the way up here, and now he had to get back. We were heading home in the morning. With the damn ocean no more than an hour away, two at the most, my dreams once again went down in flames. Son of a bitch. I was bitter and had nothing more to say to anybody, plus sick of smelling gasoline, so after we got back to the house I said I was sleeping in the cab of the truck. Mouse said I was crazy, she didn't feel safe sleeping inside this dump, let alone on the street. Giving the impression of this being not her house, and her being some incredibly bossy visitor, which stood to reason. Her fingernails alone had seen more maintenance than any part of that property. But I did it, went out on the street. And slept.

The drive home was hideous. Fast Forward was all

cocky over his score, the rest of us crashing from our various highs and expectations. The happy couple must have had a tiff, because Emmy wanted to sit by the window with me in the middle. Thankfully they made up at the first gas stop. But she was wrecked some way, I could tell. We all were. Maggot was borderline lunatic, either singing, unconscious, or blowing kisses at truck drivers from his throne back there. I was as mad as I'd been in my life. Mainly at myself, for believing in stupid dreams. And into withdrawals so bad, I had to embarrass myself by demanding unscheduled bathroom stops. If not for Dori waiting to rescue me, I was fit to drown myself in a truck-stop toilet.

Poor Dori, I'd left her for no good reason. We took forever getting back, with Fast Forward going the speed limit, thinking of his cargo I'm sure, plus you do not want to get pulled over with a boy-lunatic on open carry in the bed of your truck. There are laws. So I got dropped off late, in the dark. And there she stood under the porch light with her ice cream face and shiny hair, a big sweater buttoned up over her perfect body. We got inside and I was kissing her and then Jip got his teeth tangled up in the leg of my jeans to the extent of me punting him across the room, rolling and twisting.

"Sorry baby," I said, and she said Jip meant well, and

I let her think that. Clearly the little rat's ass thought he'd gotten rid of me for good. Right away Dori asked to see pictures, shit. I'd never thought to take any, and was hard pressed to say where Angus's camera ended up. Probably already pawned by one of Mouse's dirtball boyfriends.

Dori gave me what I needed and let me cuddle on her till I quit being sick and fell asleep in her bed and nothing was ever better. I woke up finally with no idea how many hours I slept. She'd shut Jip outside, possibly a first. Seriously, words cannot describe her and that dog. But I'd moved into first place. Various parts of me returned to the living. Vester asleep downstairs, no Jip, we were home free and starting to mess around, and, hell. The phone rang.

It was Angus. I stood in the freezing hallway in my underwear and partial erection trying to understand what was so important about me getting over to Coach's house. Today. Nobody was dead, *yet* she said, but Coach had gotten the robo-calls about me being a no-show at school all week. On further investigation, some or all of my teachers were unaware I was still enrolled. I asked what possessed Coach to start giving a shit about my off-season performance, and Angus said I was being a purposeful idiot. He cared, all right. He was making noises about putting me back on season rules. Curfew and lockdown. Angus said she'd run out of excuses for me, so I was advised to show up for dinner with my ass-kissing lips all shined up. I hung up thinking: I'm circling the bowl, and Angus for some reason is pleased of it. Damn her.

I promised Dori I would make it up to her, but I might need to spend the night over there. I took a pile of our dirty clothes because the washer at Dori's had died. Not all that recently. We needed to take some action on this, but Dori said that old Maytag had been her mom's and she was attached. Dori was a big one for letting things pile up. Too sweet for this world.

I didn't even make it to dinnertime before the shit hit the pan at Coach's house. I was back in the laundry room sorting out the whites and darks, trying not to mess up Mattie Kate's piles because she had her whole system, and suddenly, U-Haul. The old sock-feet sneak attack, and he's got me up against the Clorox.

"U-Haul," I said. "Can I offer you a shot of bleach?"

"Ha ha!" His laugh was like a fox barking. He craned his neck, leaning in too close. "The thing is, I got to put myself on the line here. For Coach. He has give me an obligation."

"Okay, nice. That and two bucks might get you a cup of coffee." I must have been past tired into some form of dead. Opened my mouth, out came Mr. Peg.

"A *job*," he hissed. "I'll keep this to easy-reader words for you."

"A job. This is on top of your higher calling of hauling around people's shit?"

The red eyes shot fire. "*Your* druggie ass. That's the shit I'm in charge of, and I don't like the view. Coach wants me keeping a close eye. To see if I can get you back up to speed, or if you're turning out to be a piece of trash like he thought."

U-Haul's eyes were closer to mine than anybody in their right mind would want. Freckles all over the face like spattered blood, even on the eyelids. I turned my back on him and shoved a wad of darks in the machine. Slammed the lid, and then faced him off again. "Okay. Remind me again why I'm scared of a fucking errand boy?"

He drew back like I'd kneed him in the balls. "As-sistant. Coach."

"Yeah, we've all been wondering whose cock you sucked for the promotion. Not Coach's, I know that much. The man has got standards."

"You don't know jack shit about the man."

"I'd say I do."

U-Haul rolled his head and shoulders around, then twined his arms together, holding hands with himself. "I'm saying you don't. If you can't work out how I got kicked up. He might be your legal fucking daddy but I'm the one keeping his books and counting his Beam bottles. I *know* him. And you hear me, boy. There's things he does not want known."

"The man gets shitfaced and passes out from time to time. No law against."

"Misappropriating of funds, let's try that one for size. Embezzling."

"You are so full of it." I tried to get past him, but he kept stepping into my way, blocking the door with his beanpole frame. I was contemplating a takedown, but finally he stepped aside.

"The hell do you know," he said. "Coach is just lucky there's a grown man awake at the wheel in this house, to look out for the merchandise."

"So I'm merchandise."

"You're dogshit. I'm discussing something a *who-ole lot* tastier." He pressed out his tongue over his top lip, grabbed the air in front of him with both hands, and pumped his hips. If there's a picture no human wants in their head, it's U-Haul performing the sex act. I was grossed out beyond all measure. And then got it, about the merchandise. He meant Angus. My sister. I was going to have to break his filthy face.

47

Vester died in dogwood winter. April, the month of the whole sorry world praying for deliverance, with dogwoods and redbuds all pretty on the roadsides and new green leaves lighting up the mountains. Then comes a late freeze to turn it all black, every fruit of the year killed in the bud. It's a fitting time to die, I reckon. If you're past believing in deliverance.

Dead people I had known, and so had Dori. But she showed no sign of getting over this one. She couldn't stop crying or worrying she'd OD'd him on accident. The nurses had left her in charge of so much, the morphine and fentanyl patches and pills she had to crush and give him in a dropper. Nothing was her fault, least of all the ice storm that took the power out. She was bleary and frantic on the phone, saying she'd been asleep and woke up with the house freezing and his oxygen had quit and she couldn't get the lights to come on. I told her to hang up and call the ambulance, but he was already gone. I should have been there.

The funeral was like Mom's, in all the bad ways. This Aunt Fred person with her L.L.Beans and mini-me daughter drove in from Newport News to take charge. Newport News what state, we had no idea, it sounds like a brand of cigarettes. Dori barely knew these people. They took one look around the house with their matching pulled-up noses and checked into Best Western's. The church, hymns, clothes he wore to the casket, all decided by Aunt Fred. The daughter that gave up her entire life to drive him to his appointments and spoon-feed him got no say. She sobbed through the whole service. They closed the coffin and put him in the ground, and I had to hold tight to stop her from crawling in there with him. In weeks to come, she'd go every day to sit on his muddy grave. I hate to say this. I got jealous of a dead man.

Once Aunt Fred got him buried, she called a meeting of the store employees and a lawyer to discuss the finances, not good. The store would be sold to level out the debts. The house was paid off, from the asbestos settlement years ago, and Dori could stay there if she chose, but was on her own as far as utilities. She could draw his social security till she turned eighteen, which was five weeks away. Not even time enough to file the paperwork. And that's Aunt Fred back to Newport News, over and out.

Taking care of Vester was Dori's whole life. The home health people came to take out the hospital bed and his sickness equipment, and she just howled. His oxygen machine was like a heartbeat at all hours pounding through the walls, you don't even realize. Now it was a dead house. She didn't know what to do with herself, and couldn't sleep without a lot of help. I tried mentioning the cheerful aspects, that we could be like other people now and go out partying or to the drive-in. She got hurt at me and said I was dancing on Vester's grave. All the party she wanted was to take another round of 80s and Xanax and ride that Cadillac back to dreamland.

In other bad news, our medical situation fell apart pretty fast. All these legit things that had been in steady supply, the patches, morphine pills, 80- and 40-milli-gram oxys, his different nerve pills of Xanax, Klonopin, and so forth: gone overnight. I'm not saying Dori took the man's medicine out of his mouth, good Lord no. But the way these doctors prescribe for a dying person, there's plenty to go around. And Dori was a smart little housekeeper, in that one regard. The oxys alone, he got a bottle of 80s every month that cost him one dollar on Medicare. If you know where to go, those pills sell for a dollar a milligram. Eighty times thirty, a person could about live on that for a month, till the next scrip rolls around. Could and did, come to find out.

Not that I was completely ignorant. She'd always been particular about picking up his prescriptions herself, other than the one time mentioned where I ran into Tommy at Walgreens. I knew she had to be going somewhere to trade some meds for other ones, according to what was needed. How else is an old man going to come by Mollys, I mean. You put two and two together. But I still had surprises in store, the first time I went along with her. She rounded up everything we could find in the house and said she was making a run. But she was in no condition. I told her I was driving and didn't back down, so. Our first date after Vester died: the pain clinic.

The one she used was out west of Pennington Gap in a strip mall that looked bombed out, as far as any other stores operating. Even still, there were probably two hundred cars parked in the lot. Seven o'clock on a Sunday evening, people lined up waiting to get in the door. Ladies and kids asleep in cars, men lying on the pavement. It was a rainy night and most were huddled under the awning but some of them were just out in the rain, like they no longer found it in their hearts to give a damn. I told Dori I didn't like the looks of this.

She was resting against the door, eyes closed, the seat belt running across her neck in a way that scared me. My little nymph. These vehicles are made for taller people. I leaned over and pulled the belt away from her throat so she wouldn't choke, kissed her and nudged her a little till she came around. She looked through the blur of rain and said, Oh. She said this was busier than normal. It was May, the first of the month, the entire county had just gotten their benefit checks. I told her I couldn't see waiting in that line, we'd be here till midnight, and she said, Don't be silly, we're not going in. All those people are waiting to see the doctor and get their prescriptions. Our scrips come from Daddy's doctors, we're just here to sell.

I stared at her, trying to work this out. She still had the mark across her neck from the seat belt, and looked about twelve. She'd quit wearing makeup since Vester died, because the crying just wrecked it anyway. I told her I should have been coming down here with her all this time, because I didn't think it looked very savory. We had an argument about keeping secrets, which she said she wasn't. She just knew I wouldn't like it, and now I was telling her I didn't, so that was the reason.

Also, supposedly the person running this clinic was somebody I knew.

Then she dipped out again, and I watched the comings and goings, trying to figure it out. There were the ones waiting to go inside, and the ones that pulled up in their old Chevies and got out with their white paper sacks and went away with money. Peddling the wares. You think of dealing as a young man's game, but a lot of these were older. I'm saying *old*, bum legs, walkers. A wad of chew in the cheek, flaps down on their hunting hats. Mr. Peg would have fit right in here. I thought of that night Kent gave Mr. Peg the coupon for free samples, and Mrs. Peggot said she would flush them down the toilet. The little did she know, they could have come over here and scored a month of groceries. These old hillbillies were using their resources, the same way Mr. Peg, back in the day with all his mouths to feed, used to sell venison roasts after he'd shot a buck, or tomatoes out of their garden. He'd made moonshine. You use what you've got.

It took me awhile to get up my nerve and go out there in the rain. I was thinking how Dori was a pro at this and I'm chickenshit, and then a guy came over pecking on the car window and I sold him half a bottle of oxy, lickety-split. Dori told me what to charge him for it. So that was good and we called it a day, headed out to Food Lion because she'd run completely out of everything at the house, t.p. and food. Planningwise, Dori was on the par with Mom.

I asked her what happens if you actually get inside that clinic. She said you just pay the money and he writes you. Everybody gets the exact same thing, holy trinity. Oxy, Soma, Xanax. But a lot of them end up having to wait so long, they're having their DTs in the waiting room. She always would fill Vester's prescriptions at Walgreens, count out what was needed for the coming days, then come straight over here to sell the rest. She said she made almost two thousand bucks one time in that parking lot. You look for the ones that are seizing or puking.

Technically I wasn't shocked, these pill millers were known about. Real doctors running their enterprises, the new philosophy of pain management as seen on Kent TV. They all would have started out as regular doctors, pediatricians or what have you. Sports medicine. That was the surprise. She said the guy running that clinic was Dr. Watts.

The hardest part of my day was leaving Dori and going back to Coach's house. But rules were in place, with U-Haul looking for any excuse to take me down, so for most of March and April I'd been sleeping over there to keep the appearances. But after Vester died, I didn't have the heart anymore to leave Dori. She'd never been alone in her life. Here she was this saint type person taking care of a sick man, and you'd never guess underneath it all was a child. A bedroom full of plush toys and a daddy that never said no. This was from a young age, starting after her mom died. Roller skates, Princess Di dress, horse on the roof, the occasional calm-down pill, what Dori wanted, Dori would have. It turns out, Jip started off as some old lady's puppy that she was carrying around in her crocodile purse one time at the 4-H haunted corn maze. Dori was eight or nine at the time. She saw that fuzzy little head poking out and started crying to have them both, the dog and the purse. Would not let up her caterwauling until Daddy laid out two hundred bucks to this lady, and they went home with a pup in a crocodile purse. I was starting to get to the bottom of Dori. I'd tried explaining to her about my responsibilities as far as Coach and my grandmother and all that I stood to lose if I went AWOL from over there. My future, etc. Dori would just blink her sad, sad eyes and ask why didn't I love her anymore.

Then my grandmother showed up. These were dark times. We'd had that late freeze that killed everything, including Vester technically, since ice took down the power lines and shut off his air. Then it warmed up a little and the rain set in. Now it was going on June, and nobody could remember a day where it wasn't raining. The day Miss Betsy came up, we all sat around the king table with thunder rolling overhead while she went down the list of my various fails, and Coach's face sagged, and it felt like the same black cloud had followed me all my life.

The problem was me and me alone, as far as Miss Betsy was concerned. Promises unkept. I'd flunked out of school past the point of all reason. She was stopping the monthly payments to Coach for my upkeep. As regards my staying there, playing ball or whatever, that was between Coach and me. Her interest was my education. She said you can lead the horse to water but the horse is not drinking. No need to waste more money. I was welcome to find my own way now, uneducated, and would soon find out there is more to life than kicking a ball. My grandmother never did get the mechanics of it, bless her heart. Thinking football is just the feet.

Even though I was the target, I could see Coach was taking it in the gut. In previous times she'd get on her jag about school, and Coach would wink at me behind her back. Now he was not looking me in the eye. Mr. Dick hung his head. Angus had her gray manga eyes boring into me, sending some instructions in code that I was failing to pick up on. My stomach felt like I'd been eating rusty nails. I was short on focus.

My grandmother though was loud and clear: no more support checks. "My reversed fortune," she called it. She said I shouldn't let it scare me, I'd just have to live it down. Some good was known to come out of bad luck, if you met it head-on. I said thanks for the advice.

Dori's position for some while had been: Screw them. They didn't love me like she did, so I should move in with her and be done with them all. I won't deny I'd considered it, to live with Dori for real, as a couple. But that was with Vester still alive, just idle thoughts. I had even asked questions testing her out on the practical side. Like, what if we wanted to cook a real dinner, not just microwave or frozen. She said what do you mean cook, and I said, you know, on the stove. Like a roast or something. Grill cheese. She said if I was hungry we had Slim Jims, and some of those juice packets. I told her it was more of a theoretical. She made her little frown that ran a line between her eyebrows and said the burners on the range were hard to light and she'd never tried out the oven, so I should probably go take it up with Mattie Kate.

But Dori was eighteen, and that's an adult, whether

you know how to work the range or not. People come at it from any number of angles. Some have buried both parents, some have their own kids. Some few probably get to that age without ever having worked any job or gone a day hungry or seen anybody die. Nobody gives you a test, is the thing. The day comes, they hand you a new rule book. Dori was living in her own house with a plastic fucking horse on the roof and her name on the deed, and I could live there too if I wanted. Miss Betsy was all gloom and doom about me going over the adulthood cliff with nobody's support checks to save me now. Like that was so scary. Ain't no hill for a climber, I said. I've been doing this all my life.

I came back right away to tell Dori. We microwaved some Xtreme butter flavor to celebrate and put the radio on, and she shut Jip in the kitchen so we could sit on the floor of the empty living room of the big house that was all ours now. I had some stellar weed from Maggot, and she'd saved back one of Vester's fentanyl patches for a rainy day, which this was, still yet and always. We leaned together with our foreheads touching and arms around each other and dipped off like that, listening to Tammy Cochran sing "Life Happened."

I still had to go back to Coach's house and get all my stuff out of there. Angus helped. She was peeved as hell, not at me. At my grandmother. "That bitch, lecturing you of all people about bad luck." She was emptying out the bureau drawers, throwing my T-shirts and balled socks into Jim Beam boxes. They had suitcases in that house, but it seemed like a complication.

"That's just old people shit," I told her. "The cost of doing business with them. They've got their rock-hard stools and dried-up old poon, what else are they going to wave in your face? They press the know-it-all thing as their sole advantage."

Angus worked through the bureau from bottom to top and slammed the drawers, *bam bam bam*, in a practiced way. Like she moved people out of her house for a living, and got paid by the job. "She was asking you to stick up for yourself. And you didn't even try."

"Try what?"

"Self-defense! What's happened to you, Demon? Somebody cut your balls off?"

"She had my report card in hand. I could have bled honey out of my balls, it wasn't going to change the permanent record."

Angus sat down on my sheetless bed, now former bed. I can still picture her there, in her khakis and white sleeveless T-shirt and one of those old-fashioned paper-boy caps. Watching me. She tucked one foot up under her. She had really high arches, like a person born with leaf springs. "You've had a serious injury. You're still limping around like Quasimodo."

"I don't really know what that is. But thanks."

"You need *surgery.* She's giving you no grace. Cutting you off in your time of need."

"I don't need any surgery."

I had almost nothing left to pack. I went over to the tall triple windows, the views I knew so well. Two dead wasps lay on the sill with their heads close together like a tiny murder-suicide.

"Your girlfriend's *father* just died. People miss school for a death in the family. Goddamned stuck-up old fart-breath bitch, where is the motherfucking compassion?"

Angus cursing somebody out was not casual. She applied herself. She became a creature of fierce beauty, like a thoroughbred running the Kentucky Derby of cursing. You just had to get out of the way. I let her run my grandmother up the devil's flagpole while I sorted out the weirder CDs she'd loaned or given me from the ones I wanted to keep. She wanted me to promise I would go back to school in the fall, but I couldn't see the point. She said it was only two more years, and would make all the difference in my future, etc. I asked her to name one great job I could do around here with a high school diploma, that I couldn't do now.

I watched her press both thumbs into the sole of her

bare foot, thinking. Finally she admitted she couldn't come up with anything off the bat, but that didn't prove she was wrong.

Her eyes darted to the doorway. Coach was there, leaning on the doorframe with one outstretched arm, looking at the floor. He wanted me to know the money my grandmother had been sending was of no consequence, this was still my home if I wanted to stay. I said nobody was holding any gun to my head, it just seemed like it was time I moved out.

A gun would have been kinder than the truth, that I was too messed up for football. He knew it. I'd kept myself thoroughly trashed of late, but occasionally I caught sight of it myself, lying out there in the weeds: what small greatness I'd had, I was not getting back. No further success lay ahead for me, and if I stayed here pretending it did, I'd be lying to Coach. Taking advantage of his free ride. I wanted to be a better man than that.

He said he wished things could have turned out different, but he accepted that I wanted to move in with my girlfriend. He wished me well, and ducked out.

Angus was roaming around the room now, touching the few things of mine still left. She picked up the bottle-ship she'd given me. Then set it back on the desk. "How deep are you into the junk?" she asked.

Prissy but trying to sound cool, the way a child would say "dog-doo."

I told her I was still on the painkillers Dr. Watts had prescribed, and that I still felt a lot of pain if I stopped taking them, so. I took them.

She just stared. "You don't have to bullshit me, Demon. I've got no power here."

I'd never perfected lying to Angus, so I went ahead and told her I was in a little deeper than that. It wasn't about my knee anymore. She asked, were we talking about meth or heroin. This may have been just DARE officer info, rather than real life, but she wasn't completely ignorant. I told her I was kind of all over the place, but not meth. And that I wasn't shooting anything because needles made me want to puke. She didn't seem surprised. She suggested maybe I could start backing out of this mess the way I got in, step by step. Maybe if I talked to an adult, they could give me advice. Not Coach obviously. Maybe June. Or Ms. Annie.

"Adult," I said. Ticked off, all the sudden.

She shrugged. Picked up the bottle again, turning it slowly, looking at the little sails and everything inside there. Oh, I was going places, she'd said. She did warn me though, about gravity and shit. Not to ask for miracles. She looked up. "You taking this?"

"Yes. I'm taking all the presents you gave me. I'm moving six miles away. I'll probably be over here for dinner twice a week because Dori lives on air and Reddi-wip and our stove doesn't work." I said that with pride: *our stove*. Regardless the rest of the sentence. I told Angus the adult in my life was me. A man, living with my lady. And something to the effect of childhood being a four-star shit show as far as I'd ever seen, so I was glad to be done with it. Angus took one of my shirts out of a box, rolled up the bottle-ship in the shirt, and set it into the box, gently. Like a baby in a cradle.

I asked her straight. "You don't like Dori, do you?"

She pulled out the desk chair and sat in it backward. Stoner used to do that, his arms draped over the back of the chair and his vile brain set on Demon-control. No two humans could be more different. Angus was sticking out her chin, tapping it with the flat of her hand, like there were words she was trying to get into her mouth, but they'd have to be just right. Not hurtful.

"I do like her," she said finally. "Remember how you were laid up in bed and she came over with presents all the time? That was great. The happy little Christmas elf. I *loved* that."

"You were not a fan of the chicken." Sad history of Lovechild: he got out of the tool shed and tangled with the neighbor's German shepherd.

"Okay, fair enough. Hate the gift, love the giver."

"Why, though," I asked. "*Why* do you like her?"

I'm not sure what I was fishing for. Angus folded her hands together. "I've known you how long, four years, going on five? And I never saw you happy, in all that time. Here and there maybe, but not for a whole day. And now you are. With Dori. I can see that."

If anybody else had ever wanted me happy, they could have fooled me. Possibly Mom, as long as it didn't cross tracks with her own maneuvers. That's all people really want, for you to fit into their maneuvers. Angus though, Jesus. Angus was a freaking wonder.

48

Emmy ran off with Fast Forward. All graduated
and scholarshipped to UT Knoxville, then drops
the bomb that she's not going. June was floored: so
smart, so beautiful, Emmy could be anything. Except
the girlfriend of that grass snake. June laid down the
law, Emmy stopped coming home. Age-old story.

But in this version, new to me, the mom doesn't rest
until she's turned over every rock on the planet. We
heard it all from Maggot, after he took up residence
on our couch. Emmy got three days' head start on her
getaway, supposedly hanging out with Martha Coldiron. June finally called over there and learned Martha
had been kicked out of her parents' house some weeks
prior. Now June was fit to be tied. She called the cops.
She called our house at all hours, in case Emmy showed

up there. June distrusted Maggot and would only speak to me. If I lied, she'd have my balls on the barbecue. I said yes ma'am. I gave her Fast Forward's cell phone number, which he wasn't answering lately. He'd left the Cedar Hill place. Rose was right, he was just a shit shoveler there.

I said all the things you say: Emmy will turn up, she's no fool. But had a bad feeling. Whatever Fast Forward had been to me, I could see he was bad medicine for Emmy.

"Don't be so sure," was Maggot's opinion. "I bet she's got him eating out of her hand."

This was around three in the morning, which seemed a safe hour to go on about our lives. We were sitting on the floor of Dori's bedroom. "Eating what?" Dori wanted to know.

"It's just a saying," I told her. Sometimes she would trip up on the smallest things.

"Eating vajayjay," Maggot clarified.

"Out of her *hand*?" Dori often got a little giddy at these times. Maggot put the 80 on the aluminum foil and Dori flicked the lighter underneath. The brown blob bubbled and melted and gave off its happy little smell of metal and burnt tires, sliding around on the shiny foil. I went first, then handed the metal straw to Dori and took over handling the foil. I might have been crap from the knee down, but still had my reflexes. You have to tip it this way and that, to keep it swimming around. Chasing the dragon, breathing its fire. We sucked smoke until nothing was left but a snail trail of melted rubber. And all I could think was: Eighty dollars.

Not a productive mindset, I know. But that pill was two days' work at the farm store, a week at Mr. Golly's. And I was doing neither. I had some money saved back, but it was going fast. I relied on Turp and my other guys for tips on who I could buy from that wouldn't take the car and leave me in some ditch bleeding from the ears. Dori argued in favor of the heroin that was all over the place now, just *bam*, overnight, it's smackland. Pretty cheap. We were buying our own now, not filling Vester's prescriptions on Vester's Medicare, so Dori was like, Why not get the best, baby? And I'm trying to keep us on the straight and narrow, pointing out what a beautiful thing it is to have no fear of the cops. They'd not bother you over oxy. You could have a hundred pills on you, no problem. If you had a prescription, they couldn't touch you.

Also, there was the problem of me and needles. Dori was so sweet and tolerant with me. Chasing the dragon was our happy medium.

Mostly it fell to me to call around, make a plan and

execute. Dori tried to help, she'd stayed friends with one of the home-care nurses named Thelma that had morphine patches to tide us over. Those were common as litter. Dori would shoot the gel, but it's mixed in there, with the drug not totally dissolved in the jello part. Thelma warned her about that. It's easy to OD. She and Dori cut and dyed each other's hair. Thelma being this older lady, divorced, big talker, with nobody to go home to so she would outstay her welcome, but what can you do. We owed her. Procurement is wearying, you're running circles to get where you started. I did think of going back to school in the fall, getting my head and body back in the game. Some part of me believed that would happen. September would come around, my knee would feel better. I would quit the dope. But for now we needed our own prescriptions. We had to go deal with the pain clinic.

Due to it being Dr. Watts, we agreed on me not going in. I waited in the car. Dori went nowhere without Jip, so he was sitting on the spot she'd just left, giving me a nasty eye. Gray whiskers around his mouth all yellowed, like an old man that chews tobacco. This was going to be a day. Heat waves over the pavement. It was the end of the month, so not a long line, but some. With the windows down I was getting that whiff of three days, no showers, too many cigarettes. Mostly men. I hated Dori going in there alone, in her little shorts.

She flew back out the glass doors looking slapped. Got in the car and fell to pieces. "Baby, baby," I said, trying to hold her and not panic while Jip growled. She had her hands pressed up to her face hard, like she's trying to hide lost teeth. "I miss Daddy," she said, which killed me. I wanted to be man enough. I pulled her hands away and kissed her wet cheeks and wide, scared eyes. She looked like she'd seen the dead. Told me that man in there was a piece of shit.

"I know he is, baby. We're just here to get a job done. Did he write you?"

She shook her head, holding Jip, not looking at me. "That motherfucker is gaming this whole county." Said Dori, that until last year probably put out the cookies for Santa.

An office visit was two hundred and fifty. Plus another hundred and fifty for so-called staff fees, to reduce waiting time. Dori said he spent thirty seconds explaining this to her, then thumped his pen on his prescription pad and stared at her tits, waiting for her to pay up or get out.

I told her we just needed a plan. After we got our

first prescription, we'd game the man right back, like she'd done before. Count out what we needed, then come back at the first of the month with the long lines and sell to people out here in the parking lot. I got her to stop crying and see the reason of my ways. Four hundred dollars up front, though. That was our problem.

"He said he could overlook the fees. *If*," she said. Staring out the windshield, stone cold.

"If what?"

"If he gave me an exam."

"What are you talking about?"

She looked at me. "Fucking me, Demon. That's what I'm talking about."

Two traffic lights and numerous stop signs stood between that pain clinic and the house, and I ran them all, a reckless driver crazed with rage, thinking life couldn't treat him worse.

A week or so later we got really hard up, and Dori said maybe she ought to go back there, go through with it. She loved me that much. She couldn't bear seeing me so sick.

I tried not to hate her for saying that. But ended up hating myself, for want of better options. I promised Dori I would get work and take care of her. She was all I had.

———

If you've not known the dragon we were chasing, words may not help. People talk of getting high, this blast you get, not so much what you feel as what you don't: the sadness and dread in your gut, all the people that have judged you useless. The pain of an exploded leg. This tether that's meant to attach you to something all your life, be it home or parents or safety, has been flailing around unfastened all this time, tearing at your brain's roots, whipping around so hard it might take out an eye. All at once, that tether goes still on the floor, and you're at rest.

You start out trying to get back there, and pretty soon you're just trying to get out of bed.

It becomes your job, staving off the dopesickness for another day. Then it becomes your God. Nobody ever wanted to join that church. A bad day is waking up with nothing, no God, no means. Lying in your stinking sheets, smelling what you hope is yourself and not your girlfriend. Someone has beat the tar out of you, it seems, and crushed some bones. Possibly a person, this comes with the lifestyle, but more likely it was the junk putting its fists through all your personal drywall on its way out of the building. Empty, you are a monster. The person you love is monstrous. You watch her eyes roll back in her head and her pretty legs racking, like the epileptic girl we all knew in grade school, Gola Ham. We were terrified of Gola.

I tried to quit, more times than Dori did. Thinking I was the stronger of us. That was me being stupid, she just knew more. One of the times we tried, we both saw guys in camo with assault rifles coming in the windows, where there couldn't have been any guys or windows. We came to despise our bed, for how little we managed to sleep in it. Day and night run together. You finally start to doze out of the misery and then your legs jerk, kicking you back to your wakeful hell. You might go twenty-four hours, thirty, countdown to the end of the world. At some point you'll look at this person that's your whole world and offer to go get something, the little hit that so easily brings her back. You do it as an act of love. I've known no greater.

Our housekeeping, oh my Lord. We were kids playing house. The frozen food boxes piled up, bags overflowed, trash doesn't leave a house by itself. The mice though will give it a shot. Due to the washing machine situation, Dori would leave dirty clothes piles to molder, and ransack the Dead Mom closets. Gypsy skirts, big-shoulder blouses, movie of the week was our girl Dori. I did my washing in the sink, till the plumbing went to hell. She had no sense about what could or couldn't be flushed. Let's say if Jip were to squeeze out his little circle of turds on my underwear left on the floor, true example. Dori would try to flush the evidence.

If I scolded her, it wouldn't go well. I'd yell, she'd get all pitiful. If I brought up looking for work, she didn't want me leaving her alone. We were storybook orphans on drugs. A big old apple tree stood out in the yard, and that summer we ate wormy apples off the ground. I can still see her, so hungry, dirt on her knees, kneeling on the ground in a dead person's housedress.

After we failed to pay the light bill, things got dire. I tried KFC, no luck. I'd have taken any shit job at all, other than a cashier. I wasn't entirely out of my mind. The oxy will put your hands in that till. I kept looking. I loved Dori and I adored her and sometimes I needed to get away from her. After another eventful day of feeling useless and unemployable, I'd go smoke a bowl with Turp, to hear about football camp and other guys living my childhood dreams. Or I'd go see Maggot, that had moved back in with Mrs. Peggot. Big pot on the stove, kitchen all spick-and-span, just like old times except with the guts scooped out. Mrs. Peggot was thin as a twig and walking in her sleep. Sometimes wearing her dress inside out. She'd ask me how I'd been keeping, set down her stirring spoon, walk in the living room, and stand by his empty chair. Then come back and ask how I'd been keeping. Maggot was no better, seriously strung out. I had orders from June to interrogate him as to the whereabouts of Martha or news of Emmy, but he knew nothing. It's like he and Mrs. Peggot both missed the train. Their only news was that Maggot's mom was getting out of prison. No date set, but the hearing was coming up.

The one person to cheer me up reliably was Tommy. One evening I went and found him in Pennington Gap, sure enough renting a garage from the McCobbs. Rack of garden tools on the wall, stained cement floor. He had a hose running from outside rigged up to a bucket for his washing. Hot plate, microwave. He put Dori and me to shame as far as tidiness, his books in shelves and his clothes folded in milk crates. A bed that was made. Bathroomwise, he had to use the one in the house. Weren't they supposed to be putting one in out here? He said well, the McCobbs didn't own that house, they rented. And their landlord wasn't aware he was paying them to live in the garage. There you go, the McCobbs. But Tommy threw his hands wide to indicate his hose-bucket sink, his bed beside a hand tiller with sod dangling from the tines, and asked if I could believe how far we'd come in life. "My own place!" he said. A man among men.

I was lucky to find him home, most evenings he was at the newspaper office. They had him come in at day's end to janitor up everybody's unholy mess. Then the ad lady quit and they gave Tommy her duties of laying out the paper and making up the ads. His boss was Pinkie Mayhew that wore men's trousers and drank on the job. People said the Mayhews had run the *Courier* since God was writing his news on stone tablets. Pinkie and two other people did all the photos and stories. Then Tommy came in nights and put the whole thing together. He said I could hang out over there any time, he could stand the company. So I did.

Tommy was carrying a lot of weight down there. Most of that paper was ads. The front page obviously would be your crucial factors, Strawberry Festival, new sewage line, etc. Then sports and crimes. They had other articles coming in over a machine, from the national aspect, and Pinkie would pick some few of those to run. All the rest was ads. Classifieds were laid out in columns, but the ones for car lots, furniture outlet, and so forth would be large in size, and Tommy had the artistic license of designing them. He had border tapes to dress up the edges, and what he called clip-art books that were like giant coloring books, on different subjects. Automotive, Hunting and Fishing, Women's Wear. He'd find what picture he wanted, cut it out, and paste it up on the ad. A sofa for the furniture store, or he'd get creative, like a pirate ship for Popeye chicken. It depended on what pictures he could find in those books, which got picked over and cut to shreds. They didn't buy him new ones very often. So he'd end up looking for the needle in the haystack, turning these pages of basically paper spaghetti.

Tommy was like a new person, a man in charge. He had clothes now that fit him, not the outgrown sausage-arm jackets of old. Plaid flannel shirts mostly, with the sleeves rolled up. He still had the girlfriend Sophie that worked at her newspaper in Pennsylvania, a much bigger operation than the *Lee Courier*, Tommy said. But he was proud of this one, showing me around: machines, computers, Pinkie Mayhew's office with a stale ashtray smell that could knock a man flat. If you've ever opened a drawer where mice have ripped up toilet paper to make a nest in there, the entire space filled with white fluff? Pinkie's office.

Tommy showed me how to feed print columns through the hot wax rollers and help him stick them on the pages. It was all done on a big slanted table with light inside. They had blue pencil marks showing where to line things up. The whole place smelled like hot wax. Little cut ends of waxy paper ended up all over everywhere, sticking to your shoes or the backs of your hands, like a baby eating Cheerios. This was the unholy mess that Tommy had to clean up. Honestly, he was holding that outfit together. I'd started coming in due to boredom, but he needed the help. He offered to pay me out of his check, but I said Jesus, Tommy, you have to quit being so nice to people. I still had his T-shirt.

One night I found Tommy pulling on his hair, looking for clip art he wasn't going to find. He had a Chevy dealer ad, with nothing left in the automotive book but tow trucks, Fords, and fucking Herbie the Love Bug. I said, Look, let me just draw you a damn Silverado. And knocked it out. Gave it extra shine, one of those star-gleams on the bumper. That's how it all started: clip-art Demon. I could do about anything. The *Lee Courier* started having a whole new aspect to its ads that probably was getting noticed. Tommy said I was a miracle art machine. I told him if there was ever a sale on skeletons, he'd have to take the wheel.

49

June wanted to see me. Emmy was two months AWOL, and she was at her wits ends. The scene of the crime was Fast Forward, everybody knew. But Emmy was well past the age of consent, and had gotten the message back to June that she was in no need of rescue.

I wasn't sure what dog I had in this fight if any, but June was never anything but good to me, so I drove over there. At a distance she looked the homecoming queen as ever, bare legs propped on the porch railing. I had to get close to see how two months had made her old. Lines by her mouth, tiny wires of white hair. She threw her arms around me, rocking like some sad last dance, her head on my shoulder. The women that loomed large in my life were all getting small.

"Sorry," she said, after she let me go. Wiping the corner of one eye.

"Lord, June, don't be. I spent the better part of middle school wishing for that."

"I believe it was Emmy you were after."

"I was not one to shut any doors. You pick that up in foster care."

She sized me up. "Look at you, all grown. After everything they put you through. An upstanding young man, living on your own. Where's Dori? I told you I'd feed you both."

"I already ate. She was tired. She said thanks."

I felt less than upstanding, and Dori was out for the count. I'd finally gotten a shift at Sonic, and Dori was cutting hair at some bootleg beauty parlor in Thelma's basement. We had our prescriptions. I'd snaked the drains and replaced the fill hose in the washer. Life was back on its keel somewhat, but we had different schedules. I aimed at functional for much of each day, whereas Dori set her sights on a couple hours of not poking out any eyes with her scissors.

"I've got a whole baked chicken I'm sending home with you, then."

My stomach did a little dance of hope. "You don't have to."

"I do, or it'll go to waste. Most of everything I cook,

I end up taking in for the girls at the clinic. I can*not* get the hang of living alone."

"I'm sorry." I hadn't thought of that. She never had. She'd started looking after Emmy at nineteen, while she was in nursing school. Living in the Peggots' trailer.

She put her hands in her back pockets. "You know I'd lay down my life for that girl."

"I know. I think she wants you not to, though. Anymore."

She looked at me, surprised. "That's just how it works, Demon. You should be as mad at her as I am. We give these kids all the advantages, and they won't stoop to pick them up. Emmy's acting like a child, and Maggot, good night. I don't know where to start."

"He'll be all right. He just needs more time than most to find his way out of the weeds."

"What he needs," she said, "is a boyfriend."

I might have blinked. "You'd be okay with that?"

"Of course I would. Even Mama would, I think. In time. If he could just find some nice boy to talk him out of his night of the living dead."

"I'm not sure he'd choose that wisely."

She spit out a bitter laugh. "We don't any of us, do we? Here, let's walk. There's a spot up the road where you can see the sun hit the ridge on its way down."

We walked out on the gravel road I'd once walked

with Fast Forward and Mouse, letting her trash-talk all I knew. I'd let summer get by me without notice. Here it was. The sun coming down through tall trees in long waterfalls of light, the birds starting up their evening songs. There's one like water trilling over rocks, pretty enough to make you cry. Wood robin. I thought about the night in Knoxville June told us she was moving back. Screw those doctors looking down on her, calling her Loretta Lynn. She could have crushed it there. But she wanted this.

As far as Emmy and Fast Forward, June knew as much as I did about where they were living, someplace in Roanoke. She said she woke up every day wanting to drive over there and bring the girl home. But this was Emmy. You'd want a SWAT team. June was desperate for anything I could tell her. I picked my words, but I didn't lie. I told her Fast Forward was one of these that has pull over people, like a magnet. And Emmy being a magnet-type person also, they probably couldn't help getting attracted. June asked if he was dangerous. I said the world is dangerous. She asked what drugs he was involved with, and I said to the best of my knowledge he himself wasn't doing a whole lot. That he was more into the money side of things.

"That is not going to help me sleep tonight," she said.

I told her I was sorry, but she was putting me between the rock and the hard place. We walked to where we could see the sun hit the ridge, and the dark start to pour down the valley. On the way back she asked about my knee. I said I didn't think about it anymore, which was a lie. I thought about it every single time I took a step. My own business.

"Just tell me this," June said. "Is she taking pills?"

"You want to sleep tonight? Or the truth."

"I'm asking."

"Then I'll tell you. I don't know a single person my age that's not taking pills."

June was quiet. I tried to decide if this really was true. Angus was the exception. Even Tommy popped NoDoz, due to the hours he kept. Late nights at work, and then the McCobbs had him up early taking the kids to school. We were halfway back before she spoke again.

"They did this to us. You understand that, right?"

I did not. Neither the who, nor the what.

She told me more of what I'd heard from Emmy, what she was seeing at the clinic. I asked if anybody was wanting to kill her lately, but she waved that off. "I'm not the one you need to worry about. It's not just people your age. You know what I'm saying? If they're old, sick, on disability? They need their scrip. If they're employed, they get zero sick leave and can't see me more than once a year, so there's no follow-up. They need their scrip. That *bastard.*"

I shouldn't have asked what bastard. Kent. And his vampire associates, quote unquote. Coming here prospecting. She said Purdue looked at data and everything with their computers, and hand-picked targets like Lee County that were gold mines. They actually looked up which doctors had the most pain patients on disability, and sent out their drug reps for the full offensive. June kept looking at me like she knew the parts of my business I wasn't telling her. But Kent was nothing to me. If I had problems, they were my doing.

Back at the house, she wrapped up a lot of food for me to take, and walked me to the car. Instead of saying goodbye, she stood with her arms crossed, looking at me. Weirdly, I thought of that time at the Knoxville zoo, how she took hold of me by the ears and said she knew what I needed. And was exactly right. Of all the good people I knew, she was probably the best one.

Tommy let me draw a comic strip for the paper. How that came about, long story. Starting with Tommy in a newspaper office. This was basically his first-ever contact sport, Tommy vs. the great big world. Where had he been, up till then? Magic Treehouse. Having a job suited him, not a problem. But the big world it-self? It was whipping Tommy's ass.

These national type articles that came in over their machine were a grab bag, as mentioned. Election, Olympics, earthquake, Lance Armstrong, what have you. But it was a Pinkie requirement to run any of them with mention of Southwest Virginia or anything close, like Tennessee or Kentucky. Which they mostly never did. But if so, dead guaranteed to be about poverty, short life expectance, etc. The idea being, we are a blight on the nation. Tommy showed me one with the actual headline "Blight On the Nation." Another one said "smudge on the map," that he'd highlighted with yellow marker. He was saving these articles in a folder. Seriously. Where was the Tommy of old, that took other people's lickings and kept on ticking? Over there on his spin-around stool was where, tugging on his stand-up hair, getting worked into a lather. I was like, Tommy. You didn't know this? Evidently not. He couldn't stop reading me headlines. "Rural Dropout Rates On the Rise." "Big Tom Emerges as Survivor."

"Technically that's one for our side," I said. "Our guy wins *Survivor.*"

Tommy held up the photo they ran of Big Tom. Okay, not good.

I tried to explain the whole human-being aspect of everybody needing to dump on somebody. Stepdad smacks mom, mom yells at the kid, kid finds the dog and kicks it. (Not that we had one. I wrecked some havoc on my Transformers though.) We're the dog of America. Every make of person now has their proper nouns, except for some reason, us. Hicks, rednecks, not capitalized. I couldn't believe this was news to Tommy. But I guess I'd seen the world somewhat, with our division games where they called us trailer trash and threw garbage at us. And TV, obviously. The month I moved out of Coach's, Chiller TV was running this entire hillbilly-hater marathon: *Hunter's Blood, Lunch Meat, Redneck Zombies.* And the comedy shows, even worse, with these guys acting like we're all on the same side, but just wait. *I dated a Kentucky girl once, but she was always lying through her tooth. Ha ha ha ha.* Turns out, Tommy had squandered his youth on library books and had zero experience with cable TV.

He kept wanting to know why. Like *I* knew. "It's nothing personal," I said.

He was fidgeting with his shirtsleeves, unrolling and rolling them to his elbows. Finally he looked up. With tears in his eyes, honest to God. "It *is*, though. I'm afraid Sophie won't ever want to come here. She says her mom keeps asking why she couldn't date somebody closer to hand. What if her whole family thinks I'm just some big, toothless dumbass?"

Damn. I hoped Sophie's family wasn't watching *Redneck Zombies*. Or *Deliverance*. You try to tune this crap out till it sneaks up and socks you, like the sad day of Demon's slam-book education. It's everybody out there. Reading about us being shit-eater loser trash jerkoffs.

"Your teeth are A-okay," I said. "She probably thinks you're the exception to the rule."

He looked defeated, shaking his head. "People want somebody to kick around, I get that. But why is it *us*? Why couldn't it be, I don't know, a Dakota or something? Why not *Florida*?"

"Just bad luck, I reckon. God made us the butt of the joke universe." At that point I knew it probably wasn't God. But I had nothing better on offer.

Where Tommy used to draw skeletons, now he collected proof of getting scorned. I told him to quit torturing himself, but he was as hooked on his poison as I was on mine. Even the comic strips were against him. Those came in a packet every week, and he had to pick out four to lay out on the last page. All lame, unfunny four-panels of kids acting rated-G naughty, talking dogs, yuk-yuk. Tommy could choose any three, but the fourth always had to be *Stumpy Fiddles* that they'd been running forever: lazy corn pones with hairy ears, big noses, patched clothes worse than any I wore as a foster. Old Maw nags, old Paw skips out on any threat of work to hide behind the outhouse with his shine jug. It wrecked Tommy to run this strip. I offered to draw in palm trees to make it Florida, which we both knew would not fool anybody. It was the same deal. This was the one comic strip of existence with so-called local interest.

"Local my ass," I said. "Whoever draws this has never been here. He's blowing his wad on us every week, everybody out there laughs, and we swallow the jizz. Stumpy fucking Fiddles is garbage." To prove it, I wadded him up and threw him away.

"Oh Lord," Tommy said to the trash can. "Pinkie's going to tan my hide."

"It's not even good drawing." I got it out, unwadded it, and flattened it on the light table. "Look how he puts the same face on every character. Men, women, babies. That's just lazy."

Tommy got this wild look. "Okay, let's see you do better. Superhero needed here. I'll watch." And he did. Just like in our Creaky Farm days of old.

I'd been thinking of this guy my whole life. And his universe. Not Batman's Gotham City or Superman's Metropolis or Captain America's New York or Green

Lantern's Coast City or Antman's LA. I'm discussing
Smallville, where Superman's nice fosters looked after
him till the day he got his wings and tore out of there.
I recall some ripping up of pages, as a kid reading
that. Not even understanding really why it broke my
heart. But Jesus, even a kid knows the basics. Why
wouldn't any of them want to look after *us*?

I made him a miner, with a pick, overalls, the hard
hat with the light on the front. I gave him a red bandanna like the old badass strikers that had their war.
No cape, he doesn't fly, just super strong and fast, running over the mountaintops in leaps and bounds. This
guy is old-school. I drew it in the vintage direction
where the characters are somewhat roundheaded with
long noodle limbs, in constant motion. Fleischer style
is the name of that, part Mickey Mouse, part manga.
It was a style I could do, and it felt like getting back to
the roots.

First panel: my guy spots an old lady crying in her
little home up in the woods, because she can't pay her
bill and the electric's gone off. Dark, stormy night.
Second panel: the hero grabs a lightning bolt out of the
sky and shoves it into the wires. You see it running all
the way into her trailer home, the lights and stove all
coming back on. In the last panel I made music notes
coming out of her radio and lights shining out the

windows into the night. The lady and her little old man are dancing outside on their porch.

Just kid stuff, obviously. That's all comics were, as far as we knew. I'd started with a different version where he swaps out lines at the pole, so instead of lightning he's stealing the power of a mansion house up on a hill. You see it all fizzle out up there, satellite TV, outdoor security lights, while the little trailer goes bright. But Tommy said that might get him in trouble with Pinkie, so I went with the natural forces. I put a lot of emotion and contrast shading in the last panel, where you see the miner hero out in the dark woods, watching the happy old couple on their lit-up porch. I named my strip *Red Neck*. Signed, Anonymous.

50

I got our light bill paid. Now we had a leaky gas stove and a furnace going to the dark side. I turned on the blowers to test it, churning up some bad business in there with the smell of burnt cat. Dori said the gas had always leaked, and it wasn't cold yet. We had a fight over why you'd turn on the furnace if it's not cold. My position being: It's freaking September. The world turns. Hers being: Why did I have to make everything so hard. Another day in our happy home.

In my first days of knowing Dori, I'd put in so much effort thinking of her around the clock, being amazed, planning how to get with her. I was high on wanting. Now I had her, and all the air hissed out. I was living life as a flat tire.

Generally speaking, I kept it together, dosing myself

to the sweet spot that gets you out of bed without knocking you ass-flat stupid. Making my fortune down at Sonic, one Red Bull slush at a time. Then going over to help Tommy. Some people must have noticed my comic in the *Courier*, because one wrote in to say it was the first they'd ever run that wasn't toilet paper. Tommy said why not do some more. Which I did, now and then. It took a lot of time to get one perfect though, and Dori wanted me home of an evening. Mornings also. Ideally all times of day. I tried mentioning how handy it was to have money, and that the hours might fly by if she tried doing something around the house. Huge fight. Why did I move in with her if I was going to be gone all the time? She threw a pout, shot half a morphine patch, and that's Dori over and out.

I'd made this bed of thorns, and needed to talk to the type of friend that doesn't tell you to shut up and lie in it. Angus had started community college, headed for the big leagues, so our friend days were numbered. I decided to cash in my credits before they expired. She said sure, let's meet at Hoboland, which was our name for the little park in Jonesville. It had the usual things of vet memorial, picnic shelter, steps up a hill leading to nowhere. A pine grove. One time we surprised a guy sleeping up there with all his worldly shit tied up in a Walmart bag, so. Hoboland. Our small imaginations ran wild in those days. We'd roused him from a safe distance.

I found her up there under the pines, wearing a leather hat like Abe Lincoln only not as tall, sitting on a blanket with a pile of Saran-wrapped triangles. I sat down on the other side like it was our campfire, and we stuffed sandwiches into our faces. Mattie Kate's BLT's are the sober man's smack. We asked questions with our mouths full, how was my knee, how was college. She said it was nice to swim in a bigger pond, she was meeting people with a lot in common. I looked at this girl in bike shorts and a top hat, and wondered how that worked exactly.

She said Coach was worried about me. I brushed it off, but she pressed the point. He was still my legal guardian for another year. Things were not great at the house. U-Haul was pushing ugly rumors at school. I recalled our standoff where he'd hinted about dark things he was holding over Coach, not to mention the heinous air-fuck. But Angus said these rumors pertained to Ms. Annie screwing somebody behind her husband's back. Mr. Maldo.

Christ's sakes, poor shy Mr. Maldo. You could sooner see him making a hit country single. But certain parents were jumping all over this, wanting people fired for their ethics. I said it was just the usual round of farts and the stink would pass. Angus said sorry, but there's worse. U-Haul was saying I was a party to the scandal and had witnessed the lovers together at June Peggot's house on the Fourth of July. If people didn't believe U-Haul, they were to ask me.

U-Haul's front teeth needed to make a date with the back of his skull. I asked Angus if he had ever made any moves on her, and she got a little wide-eyed. But didn't say yes or no.

In time I got around to telling her about my life with Dori turning into a shit show, as far as her keeping house or putting in any effort. I made the suggestion of Angus talking to her woman-to-woman, to get Dori to shape up. Angus laughed so hard she spit tomato, and said right there I just wrote the dictionary definition of what "woman-to-woman" is not.

I tried to make my case. Dori had looked after her daddy hand and foot, but now had no interest in the bigger picture. What picture, Angus asked. I said cleaning up the house, making decent food. Which admittedly Dori never did before. Also, as far as never wanting to be left alone at the house, not new. So, I had pantsed myself here. Angus leaned back on her elbows and watched with that smirky grin she had, where her mouth pulled completely over to one side.

"You chose her, Demon. This was the real deal. Remember? What was that about?"

I remembered. Watching Dori's face and body, feeling her hit my veins like a drug. Such a killing beauty. She still was. And sex was still great. Not the string of firecrackers it once was, due to us running on a half cylinder apiece. But sometimes we hit it right, and those were the Aerial Dragon Egg Salutes in the vast wasteland of our otherwise fruitless and constipated days. I spared Angus the details. She sat up and started packing up our picnic mess.

"Whatever you love about her, you get to live with. And the other stuff, you live with that too." Angus was this Yoda individual. It was probably good you talked to her, even if it wasn't.

I passed the high school on my way home, and without overthinking it, pulled in the lot. It was almost three. I found Ms. Annie's car. Stalky, but how else would I talk to her? A dropout, going in the building? Probably some part of your brain gets repo'd, like the *Dead Zone* movies.

Terrible idea. Here came the bell, and the lost life of Demon playing out in front of me. All my former brothers running onto the field for practice, punching each other in the head in the carefree fashion of youth. I rifled the glove box for a Xanax to buy myself another hour on the wanting-to-stay-alive clock. Pulled the Impala to the far end where I could see her car but not the football field. She was practically the last one out, moving fast in her long skirt, carrying her big flat folder. I eased my car around and tapped the horn, causing her to jump. Then she recognized me, and I was her cake full of candles. She opened the passenger door and slid in, all smiles.

"Please tell me you're coming back to class. I've got a folder of life drawings in here to grade, and they all look like they came out of bathroom stalls."

"I can see you worked really hard on this, Aidan."

She laughed. I could tell she wanted to lean over and give me a hug. My boyhood fantasies rearing to life, now that I was spoken for. "Damon. Just two more years. Is that impossible?"

"I'm not a kid. I have stuff to take care of now."

She stared at me. Some motion behind her caught my eye, Clay Colwell in a red scrimmage vest running after a missed pass. My eyes started watering like they'd been poked. I told her she was a great teacher, and I was sorry I wasted her time. She said plenty of kids wasted her time, but I was a shooting star. Her words.

"You know I don't do this for the money, right?" She frowned a little. "*Do* you know that? That I'm not even paid full-time here?"

I'd thought a teacher was a teacher, period, but no. She said art and choir director were her only two classes, and you don't get full salary for that. Science teacher was the same, only the two classes. "I'm not complaining, I get by on my art commissions and our band gigs."

"And the ice cream truck in summer." She and Mr. Armstrong traded off with that.

"And ice cream, right. What I'm saying is . . . What am I saying?" She tilted her head, the loopy earrings danced. "Okay, I like helping kids learn to see what they're looking at. But really and truly? I always hoped one day a spark would come along, that I could fan into a flame. Some whole new vision that the world actually needs." Supposedly, I was that spark. She said teachers spend years of their lives hiding out in the coffee room, trying not to give up hope on the likes of me being out there somewhere. It seemed like she might cry. Or if not her, me.

I told her I was sorry I let her down. But I'd come looking for her because I heard the sick pack of lies about her and Mr. Maldo, and wanted her to know I was no part of it.

She looked down at her lap, nodding her head slowly. "Normally I wouldn't give it a thought. That kind of thing goes around like a stomach flu. You want to talk about superheroes, my husband is a man of steel. This stuff just bounces off of him."

We both looked out the windshield at the last stragglers finding their cars, thinking our thoughts. Mr. Armstrong, rebel flags, all kinds of little uglinesses probably, that most of us never knew about. I'd lived long enough to know, that shit doesn't really bounce off. She glanced back at me. "I'll tell you something, the one I'm worried about is Jack. Mr. Maldo."

"Oh," I said. I'd forgotten his first name, if I ever knew it.

"It's like walking through fire for him right now, just to do his job. Kids making gestures. I'm scared he'll quit and lose his medical insurance. He's not well. Maybe you didn't know."

"I noticed the hand," I said, not sure there was anything you could take for such.

"You're sweet to worry about Lewis and me, but we've been through this so many times. There will always be some people around here that think our marriage is their business."

She said there used to be laws against the Black and white type of marriage, up till the 1960s. So, before any of us were born including her and Mr. Armstrong, but attitudes hang on. "Certain pitiful souls around here see whiteness as their last asset that hasn't been totaled or repossessed."

I wondered if the laws pertained to my people making their Melungeon babies way back when, or if we were too far backwoods for the higher-ups to give a shit. Age-old story, who gets to look down on who, for what reason.

I told her if it was any help, Mr. Armstrong was the MVP of grade seven. I told her how kids were always trying to get his goat, but then they ended up on his team.

She knew that. "Kids aren't the problem. It's parents. There's this whole little Armstrong haters' club that's practically a task force of the PTA. They won't admit to being bigots, so they want him fired for being a communist. Like they even know what a communist *is*!"

I said probably they were just scared he was going to put ideas in our heads.

She smiled. "Imagine that. A teacher, putting ideas in kids' heads."

She said the only person I needed to worry about was me. She knew I had pressures on me, and if I ever needed backup, I should talk to her and Mr. Armstrong. Whether I was in school or not, their door was still open. She started to get out of the car, but then looked back at me with a kind of twinkle. "Say hi to Red Neck for me. Tell him I like his perspective."

I felt my ears burning. "What makes you think I know him?"

She laughed in my face. "Damon. I know your drawing the way other teachers know your handwriting. Why in the world are you not signing your name to those strips?"

I needed her to go on about her day, get out of my Impala. But she stayed, half in and half out, waiting. "It's in the *paper*," I finally said. "Out there all over the place. If it's terrible, I don't want them all saying it was me. And if it's not terrible, I'd be bragging."

"For crying out loud. It's your *work*. Is it bragging if the guy at the garage does a good job fixing your engine and then bills you for it?"

I told her I didn't see the connection. She pulled her butt fully back in the car.

"Nobody else is going to tell you this. But art is work. People get paid to do exactly what you're doing. Guys a lot older than you, with less skill and very tired narratives."

I told her thanks, but my little strip was small potatoes. Who outside of here would give a rat's ass about the superhero that stayed in Smallville? She said, Don't be so sure. There's us, there's West Virginia and Kentucky. And Tennessee. We aren't any potatoes at all, small or large. She said if I was so keen to be a grown man, I should quit thinking like a potato.

I did what Angus said: went home to Dori and lived with it. I lived with dishes growing mold beards in the sink, trash bags sliding down in the cans, garbage mounting high. Jip running his victory laps around the house after every McMuffin wrapper or Jimmy Dean's box he found to tear in a million pieces. As far as living in a garbage dump, Dori and I were on the par with Mr. Golly's childhood. I was too busy to do much about it, between my Sonic job and the other shit that swallows you whole. Going into the clinic for our scrips. That man was not laying eyes on Dori again, and the sad part is, Watts didn't even recognize me. The bastard that got me started down this drain. After scoring our scrips, I'd have the phone calls and drives at all stupid hours to meet this or that lowlife to get our shit bought or sold, bills paid, the beast fed.

Sometimes I thought of Miss Betsy and Mr. Dick, what they'd think to see me now. The words he'd sent up on a kite, wanting to be hopeful of me. Sad case that I was, false or cruel I wasn't, if I could help it. And if hard work counts for anything, I was crushing it. Addiction is not for the lazy. The life has no ends of hazards, deadly ambushes lying in wait, and that's just the drugs, not even discussing the people. If I was a fuckhead, I was one that knew how to apply himself. It's what Coach had seen in me. He said discipline, I would use other words. Surviving. Giving it all up, day in, day out, from the very beginning. Keeping Mom in one piece, then outhating Stoner, then being fastest at whatever crap job was thrown at me, draining battery acid or topping tobacco. Football. I'd only ever lived one way, by devoting myself completely.

Probably that's why I got so mad at Dori for stealing from Thelma. I had my own warped honor. She started with nonsense things, scissors and conditioning products. Then she came home with some gold jewelry and a Vitamix. I had to scold her like a child. Not just the morals of stiffing your friend, morphine supplier, and quasi-employer, but the whole getting-caught aspect of things. Part of being a mature person is knowing your skill set, and neither of us had talents for larceny. Maggot, another story. Ace shoplifter, mastermind of which pharmacies had hidden cameras and where, he'd leave you in awe. Whereas Dori and I were incapables. I started a cartoon strip in my mind, called *The Incapables*. Yelling at her would only lead to disaster. Dori crying, saying I hated her. It broke me to pieces.

All she wanted in the world was to be loved. I had to think of her as my baby doll. You don't blame a doll for slacking. You watch the pretty eyes open and shut. You tuck it under the covers at night.

She remembered my birthday was coming, and asked what I wanted. I could name a few things. The Impala's transmission was grinding like nails in a bucket. But I said I only wanted my girl. Pretty as a picture and forever mine. She wanted to know did that mean getting married. I said why not. We were never getting married, we could barely pull our act together to buy a phone plan. But Dori wouldn't remember this conversation. She'd shot a patch and was lying on the bed with her feet over the edge. I got down on my knees and kissed the little rings on her toes. A dot of blood stood like a jewel on the top of her pale foot. I touched it, thinking of Maggot and me in another age, pricking ourselves, sharing our blood to promise brotherhood. As if it's only by hurting yourself that you can be true.

She was dipping out fast, all dreamy over our make-believe wedding. I was going out later, so I'd done a 40 and was letting the jangly ups and downs even out while I sat on the floor listening to her. Tommy would be my best man. Sweet. She wasn't always kind about Tommy, due to all the time I spent over there. But with the juice in her veins, she was all love. Jip would be our ring burier. Thelma and Angus, bridemaids. Or Angus could be my best man, she said. Kind of confused about where Angus came into it. My best girl-man, she said. She described the dress she'd wear and how everybody would say what a beautiful bride. How young we were.

Once she was out completely, I took care to turn her on her side and prop her with pillows before I left the house.

51

Another week, another shit show. Monday night. Maggot wants me to pick him up from Mrs. Peggot's and drive around. Fine, we're two guys getting away from women, as far as I know. He gives directions to this sketchy house in Woodway to pick up a friend, and who should that turn out to be but Swap-Out. News to me, that they know each other. Next thing I know we're behind Walgreens, they've put a cement block through the drive-through window and we're watching Swap-Out crawl in that tiny hole. He climbs up and clears the top-shelf boxes and we're out of there in under three minutes. I have to pull over on Duff Patt Highway to put my head between my knees. Maggot is skunked out of his skull, yelling that he's the fucking

Robin Hood of Sudafed. I drop them both back at Woodway and fly out of there.

Tuesday. Fast Forward calls, wanting to know if I'd like to take a ride for old time's sake. Where to? He says Richmond. I tell him not on your life, give my regards to the Mousehole, and by the way, how is Emmy? He says he and Emmy have parted company. I hang up and call June to find out if she's back home, which she isn't. June wants to know why. Shit. This is bad.

Wednesday. Not technically terrible, but as far as throwing me off my keel, yes, bad. Tommy tells me people are writing to the paper about Red Neck. He calls it an upswell of public opinion. Nobody ever writes the paper unless over something major, like after they took the soft serve machine out of Dana's Quickmart. Pinkie orders Tommy to keep running that strip every week, by all means and no matter what, forcing Tommy to confess it's not out of the regular package. "Contributed by a local talent," he says. Pinkie takes this to mean Tommy himself, and offers him a tendollar-a-week bonus. Tommy says he'll have a discussion with Anonymous as to where ten bucks per strip might get them. Every week would be a lot of pressure. Half of me says I'm already living on the knife edge between functional and dead meat blackhole junked, and this is the thing that's going to shunt me in. And half of me says, Ask her for twenty.

People in need of a hero, there's no shortage in the local supply. Ideas came at me from everywhere. It was fall now, topping and cutting time, so I did a series on tobacco. I drew little kids working to top the tall plants, girls in hair bows and short socks, boys in ball caps. All of them start seeing stars, reeling around dizzy with the green tobacco sickness. Red Neck swoops in and tears through the field, holding out a blade in each hand to top all the flowers at once. Then he piles the kids in the back of his pickup and takes them out for corn dogs. In the last panel you can see they've made a stop on the way: with the truck bouncing off into the distance, it's a close-up on tobacco flowers they've left on two graves. One is Pappaw, one is Little Brother.

I gave him a DeSoto truck, 1950s model with the fins. Just so you know. Not a Lariat.

That strip started a whole thing of people leaving tobacco flowers at their cemetery plots. Pinkie sent her photographer Guy Greeley out there to take pictures, so that was crazy. The newspaper making the newspaper. Tobacco flowers also got left on the front stoop of the paper office. Pinkie got calls from the Russell

County weekly and the daily over in Bristol, asking how they could run this strip, so she marched in to talk to Tommy. Pinkie coming in after-hours was such a rare event, it scared the living piss out of him, hearing that locked front door open. Half the storefronts in Pennington had been broken into lately, including ones you'd not expect to be all that rewarding. Extension office, H&R Block. This happened on an evening I wasn't there, due to a small bender after getting fired from Sonic. I'd never met Pinkie. Tommy said picture a pit bull with Dutch boy hair, lighting one cigarette off the last, staring you down like she's CIA special ops. Good with words, Tommy. She said it was time to formalize the Red Neck arrangement. There was money involved, so they needed a contract signed, a real person with a name. Still thinking it was him.

So he outed me. He blamed it on Pinkie being on the verge of getting physical, but I knew better. I'd seen Tommy take many a hard leathering back at Creaky's without squealing. Finally he admitted it was his decision to name me, and I ought to be glad of it, not mad. He said if the shoe had been on my foot, I'd have done the same.

Ms. Annie had given me her home number. The door is always open, etc. I wouldn't expect people really to mean that, they just feel guilty walking away from your mess, back to their lucky lives. But I called, and she said come over now, why not. For dinner.

There was no missing the house. The front was painted like a quilt. A dog barked inside but hushed after Mr. Armstrong told it to, not like Jip. He let me in and said they were getting supper on, so feel free to have a look around, which I did because there was a lot. Quilts on the walls. And these cloth pictures of mountain scenery, fall-colored trees and such, that Ms. Annie made on her loom, this contraption that took up half the living room. Paint I understood, but realistic pictures made of nothing but colored string, this was another level. I wanted to touch them, feel the grass and the bumpy rocks. One had a waterfall. She said it was Devil's Bathtub, had I been there? I went ice-cold in my belly and said no ma'am and didn't look at that one again. Their dog was named Hazel Dickens. Black, small, long hair, short legs. She followed me all around quietly, like she meant to pick up after me. The place was clean but not overly tidy, with music items all over, amps and such. I'd never heard their band. Not a young people kind of thing.

All over everywhere on the bookshelves and window-sills they had painted statues carved out of wood, almost like done by kids, but much better: smiling bear, Adam and Eve, IRS guy getting swallowed by a whale. Mr. Armstrong said he was a collector of those. People called it folk art, hillbilly art, self-taught, he called it just art. One was a hillbilly-art Superman that was Black, with his regular cape and insignia and everything. Big work shoes, fist in the air. And I thought, Huh, I am not the first to think of this.

It was trippy, seeing these teachers in their sock feet, being married. She had on the exercise type pants and her hair in a ponytail, this whole sporty Jane Fonda side to Ms. Annie you'd never guess. I saw him give her a sneaky pat on the ass while he was reaching behind her for the stirring spoon. Dinner was soup beans, salad, cornbread. I ate seconds of everything.

She was excited to give me advice on Red Neck, which was why I'd called. She said she would look over any contract before I signed, and I should think hard about the money. I could lose opportunities later on if I didn't drive a hard bargain from the start. She said syndication and words like that. I told her Pinkie had offered ten dollars per strip, and Ms. Annie said, Oh, honey, that's not even in the ball park. I told her it would feel weird pushing on the lady for more, not very Christian or whatever, and she said I needed to adjust my mindset. On second thought, she said, she'd call Pinkie herself to discuss my compensation. She would say she was my agents.

Mr. Armstrong said, "Tell her you're calling from Amato and Armstrong."

She gave him this look of mischief. "I'm going to do that." I always forgot that was her last name, Amato, different from his. They were crazy about each other though. You could see it plain as day in how they helped each other out, like mind reading. Mr. Peg would say, Like a mule team in harness.

I asked Mr. Armstrong how things were going over at Jonesville Middle, and he said same as usual, pissing onto the burning wreck. Not the type of language arts he'd allowed us in class. I was mildly stoned but trying not to let it throw me, being with them as people instead of teachers. Them treating me not as a kid. We got on the subject of why the school board was wanting to fire him. I asked if it was the coal company guys mad at him for blowing their cover, as far as them running all the other businesses out of town, and keeping the schools terrible so we'd be too dumb to fight back. He turned his head to the side, making this comedy face like, Oh shit, and Ms. Annie raised her hands and shook them in the air. They were having a big time, these two. With a complete poker face, he said he didn't recall saying anything like that in class.

"He can make more money playing his banjo," she said. "They keep him on at that school just to spite him."

I thought to ask her about Mr. Maldo. She said he'd moved away and was at some plant over in Kingsport now, free to clean bathrooms without the menace of adolescent spite. So that was good. I said I was sorry he got run off, and asked how she and Mr. Armstrong could stand living around gossips like U-Haul and his skank mom. Mr. Armstrong said Lee County had no corner on the market, because haters were everywhere. Being a mixed couple, they'd heard it all. "One time we got yogurt thrown at us from a car in downtown Chicago."

"*Yoplait* yogurt!" Miss Annie said, excited, like she's telling a joke. "That comes in those cute little containers, you know? What kind of a racist eats name-brand strawberry yogurt?"

I said I give up. The Chicago kind? And Mr. Armstrong said technically we don't know that he was eating it. Maybe he'd only purchased it as a projectile.

Even if it seemed like they were horsing around, something serious was going on here, like also dropping hints. Miss Annie said they loved what was good about this place, and had each other's backs for the rest, and that was enough. "One other person can go a long way towards making your world right," she said, "but the support has to run both ways." They ganged up on me then, as regards quitting school and shacking up with Dori. Ms. Annie said getting this contract was a break that doesn't come along every day, and if it were her, she'd want to meet the challenge with a clear head. Aka, I should quit the dope. Easier to do without the dopehead friends. They were polite, but still. Saying love has to come from a strong place, not just grabbing whatever's in reach. You can't choose your family, but a partner is your shot at a decent do-over. I sat there fingering a Xanax in my pocket, thinking, What the fuck. Have you people been looking in my windows. Maybe I was paranoid, which did happen if my tanks got low. But then again, they were teachers. As far as kids and families around here, they could write the book.

I left their house feeling so mixed up, I had to pop that Xanax before I started the car. Getting a good deal from Pinkie Mayhew, great. But I was also mad as hell. Dori depended on me for everything. If I abandoned her, she would in all honesty probably cry herself to death and starve. With Jip lying on her body thinking with me gone, he'd won the war. This teacher couple with their sly jokes and butt slaps and house full of beautiful things made by steady hands, who wouldn't want that. But how do you even get there from the normal place of business? I'd not known that many happy married people, especially to each other. Mr. Armstrong and Ms. Annie just gave me more to worry about, putting it in my head that I should break up with Dori. Because I never could. Good people don't give up on the ones they love.

I told Tommy all right, let's do this as a team. Ms. Annie hardballed Pinkie and got us fifty dollars per strip, with a bonus for every paper that picks it up. We'd deliver weekly, on a one-year contract. Tommy and I would split the money down the middle. These thousand books he'd read had to pay off at some point, he could help with story ideas. And the art itself. Going over it all in pen is the last step, and takes a steady hand. I told him we'd be mules in harness.

The truth is, I was scared blind to make a promise like that on my own. I'd been playing head games on how heavy I was using. Look at me, getting my ass up and out. Nothing out of control here. Tiptoeing around the morphine. I'd still never injected anything, for the sole reason of needles making my skin crawl, but I told myself that was a line between pastime and hard-core that I was refusing to cross. Pretending I could still show up on time as a human, even if I'd been fired from Sonic and more places after that. Not for slacking, I mashed orders double time. But you'd not have wanted to share space with me and a deep fryer, let's leave it at that.

Now, though, with Tommy backing me up, I would quit screwing around. The day we signed those contract things in Pinkie Mayhew's rat's-nest office, that's what I believed. What I wanted more than anything was to grow up. Hard to explain, given how I got short-sheeted on the childhood. Carefree, what is that? If I'd ever known at all, I couldn't remember. But I was still stuck outside of full adulthood, blowing smoke under its door, eyeing the windows with a cement block. It's all we want, we ragged boys of the world. To live as men.

By the time that contract expired, I'd be close to turning eighteen. I would get the money that was put away for me from Mom's social security, and start my life of freedom. As a man of work and talents, getting paid for my labors. I would marry Dori. I would get clean.

I went to bed thinking, Okay, Angus. I'll trust the wild ride, it is looking up. A few hours later my phone woke me up and it was the last person I wanted to hear from, Rose Dartell. I had no feelings for this strange girl, and assumed that was mutual. Wrong, she had feelings. She despised me. Because of Emmy and Fast Forward. Everybody put this on me, those two hooking up. Rose said to meet her at the little park above Ewing because she had something to give me, from Emmy. I told her I could probably get over there tomorrow afternoon. She said nope. Now.

The things you do to be decent. I put on my pants at three fucking a.m. and drove out to a no-name highway pullout to get what was sure to be bad news. It wasn't far from the park where Miss Barks took me years ago, the day she dumped me. Looking up at those white rock cliffs, weird thoughts took over my mind. Jumping off, flying or falling. Now the moon was hitting the jagged ridge up there. I sat on a cold cement piling waiting for headlights to come up the road.

Rose got out and stayed by her car, talking low. I couldn't really see her. She said Fast Forward had been living in Georgia. He'd decided to cut out Mouse and deal directly with Mexican traffickers in Atlanta. She mentioned various technical things, making it sound like Fast Forward was a businessman to be admired, making his smart moves to get promoted. Part of his business sense involved using Emmy for his lure. I was tired and shaky, and not hearing every word. I asked what did she mean, lure. All I could think of was Mr. Peg's tackle box.

That is what she meant. Bait. Having sex with guys, to attract them into dealing with Fast Forward. I told Rose that was impossible. If you knew Emmy, you could never picture that.

"I'm sure you can't," she said. Rose had lit a cigarette, and I watched the orange glow rise and fall. "She could walk up to you tomorrow and you'd not know her."

"I would know her."

"Not the mess she is at the moment, no sir you wouldn't. I did, and I can tell you, she's what they call ruint. Fast Forward got disgusted and left her down there." I saw the cigarette drop to the ground. "So that's two lives you wrecked, hers and mine. I would have stuck with him. I've got a good head on me."

I told Rose she could go to hell. I didn't believe a word she was telling me.

I heard steps on the gravel and then she was close enough to smell. Pushing a fist at me. Something dropped into my hand that felt slight and wet, like spit.

I watched her truck until it was gone in the dark, then got in my car. I was blinded for one second by the dome light. Opened my hand and looked. Snake bracelet.

52

I dreaded calling June, but I'd promised. I held back certain details. What killed me was how glad she sounded just to hear that Emmy was alive. Atlanta, not so much. June swore a blue streak, saying Atlanta was too much goddamn metropolis to go start knocking on doors, she was hoping Emmy had gone back to Knoxville. Which if you asked me was about on par, in the goddamn metropolis department.

What we had to do now, she said, was find Martha. June knew about the abortion and a good deal more, it turned out, and had taken Martha in her wings, getting her signed into a methadone clinic. But the nearest one was Knoxville, and Martha didn't know anybody there, and it was a mess. Martha would start getting on her feet, come back here to be with people she knew, then she'd relapse and disappear again. Maybe she was going to Atlanta. June had the idea that connecting with Martha's orbit would lead to Emmy. She was just thinking out loud at that point, not wanting to get off the phone, even though she was at work, with people waiting. I said call if she needed me.

I drove around a while to get June's worries out of my head, and look for a strip to draw. The best ideas usually came that way. My plan then was to go home to a quiet house, and get something done while Dori was at work. But that day I found her in bed eating one of those ice cream drumstick things with the crumbles that she bought in family packs. She'd finally blown off one too many hair appointments or stolen something obvious, and Thelma asked her not to come back.

"She said she was asking me as a *friend*," Dori clarified.

"Wonderful," I said. "You're bringing no money in, you screwed over your best friend, but it's all fine because she's not yelling at you."

Dori said I was a mean bastard with no understanding. Then she made kissing sounds at Jip and held out her ice cream for him to lick. White cream smeared in his old man whiskers, and the way his furry head moved up and down made me think of porn. I was a fully comprehending bastard. Thelma didn't yell at

Dori because you'd get just exactly as far yelling at a box of rocks.

After that, Dori stopped having reason to get out of bed, so I took her TV away. There was a time she could have dragged it back up the stairs, in her scrappy days of moving Daddy's oxygen and his wheelchair around, but now on her strict dope and ice cream diet, her weight was down to nothing. She and Jip stomped downstairs, not speaking to me, and from then on whiled away their days on the couch watching *View* and *Price Is Right* and *That's So Raven*. I'd stopped paying for cable, so we weren't getting anything but the channels that come in naturally. It made no difference, I'd come home and it might be *Mutant Ninja Turtles*. Her eyes like sparkly glass.

Then one day I hit the breaking point. I'd gotten a ridiculous estimate for the transmission job, came home to the bare fridge reeking from the last power outage, and I put an empty vodka handle into the screen. From across the room, I still had a good arm. Nothing really shattered, the surface just rumpled and the colors bled down the screen in lines. Idiot. I could have gotten a bottle of Xanax at least for that TV set. Not thinking like a head of household.

She stayed there, wrapped in her blanket, staring at a dead TV. Waiting for me to bring home the junk.

I had crazy thoughts of just staying away for a while, cutting her off. Let her start fiending, she'd appreciate me then. But I would never. She was my doll. I wasn't heartless.

Lonely, is what I was. Tommy saved me in those days, being the most interesting guy you'd ever want to talk to. He still read like it's an all-you-can eat buffet. Not kid stuff, now it was the news stories coming in. The *Courier* would run their toxic local items, much to Tommy's misery, but all the rest were going to waste, he felt, unless somebody got them printed out and read. Name it, he was up on it: tornado in Alabama, war in Iraq, Toyota moving into the number-three spot for American car buyers. Space, he was all over that. He said they're building a four-hundred-million-dollar vehicle to go up and crawl around Mars. I didn't believe him, but yet I did. You see what people do with money if they have it, it's two different universes. Theirs and ours.

At that time I was hanging on to a job at the farm co-op in Norton. Workwise, much the same as at Vester's old store, shelving, pricing, hauling feed. But the people, Lord have mercy. The manager Rita was not all that old but had already put away two kinds of cancer, double-ectomy this or that, and she's talking about bladder leakage before I've got my coffee down. While the cashier Les, former miner, had something wrong with every body part, including some I'm sure he made the hell up. Their contest never ended. If I had to referee, I'd go with Les, he used one of those sit-on walkers and his hands shook so bad, the customers always rushed to bag their own purchases before he could break a bottle of Ivermec. You wanted to ask, why not stay home, old man? Get your disability, let somebody else have the paying job. Probably his wife told him to get the damn organ recital out of the house or she'd finish it off.

It was a great comfort at the end of a day to drive over to the paper office and hear Tommy's national disasters.

He had suggestions galore for Red Neck. We did a whole series of doctor-theme ones. Red Neck rigging broken-down coal chutes into a giant roller coaster for wheelchair people getting to their doctors in Tennessee. A bunch on the free RAM clinics, with the volunteer doctors that fly in every year. I'd seen those tent camps myself, the craziness of it. Mom used to try to get me in, but we never did. People wait weeks for their place in line. I had Red Neck saving kids from the stampede. Red Neck stripping windows and rods from an old coal plant, bending them into glasses for kids that needed them. Red Neck making an old man a new set of teeth out of hard, shiny coal.

Regardless Tommy's worst fears, Sophie still yet hadn't dumped him for hillbilly reasons. They had plans to meet up in person if they ever saved up enough vacation time, and meanwhile sent computer letters to each other like two houses on fire. I'm saying, he could spend hours on that terminal, reading or writing either one. I asked how they came up with so much to say. He said they told each other everything they cared about, everything that got them sad, and what all made them happiest. That was about it. He said between those three, they could probably keep going till the end of time. If not, they'd come up with another category.

He couldn't have known he was putting a fist in my chest, telling me that. Poor Tommy, I'd been thinking, with his imaginary girl, while Dori and I had our fuck-fests. Then Dori and I had moved on to the fuck-yous, with no more categories out there that I could foresee. Tommy had something I never would.

And I had Tommy. We talked about most things under the sun, but I avoided certain topics, Dori, for one. Our not-so-happy love nest. Our extracurriculars, for another. But he was no fool. One night, and this was after we'd been hanging out for months, he told me he wasn't really supposed to have visitors at the paper office. So we should work on our strips someplace else. I figured this came from Pinkie, thinking I was a dopehead casing her premises. I said I was hurt at him, not standing up for me. Did he think I would steal shit from their office?

He was hunched over his slanted light table and kept his eyes down, one hand pulling on the little beard that I was finally getting used to. My guts went queasy. Tommy was a stand-up guy, the last one I probably knew, good to his bones. If he'd given up on me, I was a lost person.

"Not a lot here worth stealing," he finally said, shrugging at the pegboard on the wall, the giant mess of border tape rolls and X-Acto knives.

"Meaning what? If you did have, I would?"

He looked me in the eye. "I signed on to partner with you. I have to trust you, Demon."

"Okay," I said. "And?"

Tommy looked as sad as I'd ever seen him. And we'd seen some sad shit, we two. He told me it was about my capacity to function. He had to think about me possibly getting hurt, with all the machines in there, razor knives and such. I knew it was killing him to say this, and even still I said mean things. I was damn well functioning enough to live in a real house with my real girlfriend and not a garage with pitchforks and gas cans. Then I apologized and fell apart and admitted I was a little strung out on the junk. But was fully intending to clean up my act.

"How are you going to do it?" he asked. Elbow on the light table, chin on his hand.

"I'll just do it. Quit the dope. It's just, my knee. It still hurts like hell."

The sad hound-dog eyes, the chin propped on the fist.

"But I can cowboy up," I said. "It's time. I've been thinking that lately. I've been through worse, I mean, Jesus, Tommy. We got through Creaky's S&M camp."

"I don't think it's all that simple. I think it's better to have help."

I laughed. "Help. Where's that at."

"There's an AA in the church basement two doors down from here. A lot of nights of the week. If you started going, we'd probably be okay with you coming here after."

"So you're fucking bribing me to go to AA."

"I didn't mean it like that. Sorry. I know, it's supposed to be anonymous."

"What the hell do you know about it?"

He got up from his light table and walked around, hands shoved in his pockets. "Sophie," he said. "Both her parents were drinkers. But her mother got sober."

"Good for Sophie's mother. All mine got from A fucking A was the hard sell on giving it all up to a higher power. Which was the sum total of her life, Tommy. Never thinking she had any power herself. Just taking the shit life threw at her, till the last round of bumps took her out."

Tommy sat back down at the light table with his head in his hands. I told him I wasn't going to live like my mom did, letting everybody tell her she was worthless. I'd stayed alive so far by standing on my own feet, and wasn't about to give that up now.

"Another thing," Tommy said very quietly. "Sophie's mother had to leave her dad, to get sober. She says as long as you're living with an addict, you're addicted."

I punched my fist into my hand a couple of times and walked out of there before I did worse. Why didn't he just say it? Didn't matter. I wasn't leaving her.

Tommy was as good a man as I was not. That's all I can say. We had a contract. I went back over there the next evening, and we made our peace. Tommy gave me a key to his garage house, to prove he trusted me. I started working over there, just me and the pitchforks and gas cans, until he finished up his layouts, then he'd come home and we'd work together.

Being alone there was much like being back in the

McCobb dog room. Complete with surprise appearances of Haillie, popping in to scare the bejesus out of me. Thirteen-year-old version, picture the sparkle-Barbie vibe and hit fast-forward. She showed me the Howliie Fairie drawing she'd kept all this time. I was trying to work, but what can you do. I asked her what the squaller twins were up to, and she said kindergarten. The next night, came back with those brats on each hip like she's the little mama. I tried to ask the normal questions, how was Ohio, did she have a boyfriend. She said she had four. Toting those kids half as big as herself, giving me this sultry eye like I just might be number five. Shew-ee missy, I thought, you'll get there soon, no help from me. Eventually Mrs. McCobb would come shoo Haillie back to the house. Then *she* would stand there in her triple-XL sweatpants and mom hair and talk my ears off. Her husband is a genius, his Wate-o-Way enterprise is about to take off, same old same old. I wasn't depending any more on this nutbar family for my calorie intake or anything else, so I tuned it all out.

Except for this one crazy thing. She said she was scared Mr. McCobb had got into something over his head. Some deal he had with a man she didn't know, but he had come over and she did not like his looks. Given my football connections, she wondered if I might know this individual. U-Haul Pyles. Fuck me. I told her to steer clear by all means. But couldn't stop wondering. Was it real, was she trying to yank my chain. Was U-Haul trying to find me here.

Martha turned up, living in what June called "that crack house in Woodway" like it's a famous attraction. The place we'd picked up Swap-Out that time. June wanted me to go over there and collect her. I said Maggot was friends with those fine folk, so he was her man. Failing that, she should call the law. June said no dice. She'd gotten the tip from Juicy Wills, the sheriff's deputy that she'd dated in high school. Juicy had been coming over for debriefings ever since Emmy ran off, as full of himself as ever. June only tolerated him on the chance of a decent lead. Now that she had one, she was not blowing it by going over there with a damn peacock in a squad car. Her one goal was to find Emmy, and for that she had to get Martha to trust her enough to talk. Maggot had agreed to help, but only if I did too.

June was persuasive. She knew Martha wouldn't be glad to see her, even after all she'd done to help her. That was the reason, really. So it was decided Maggot and I should go over. If we could somehow fetch Martha back to June's, she'd take it from there.

We drove to Woodway in broad daylight, with Maggot

too stoned even to remark on my crap transmission. Pulled up to the house and sat in the car, admiring the porch that was its own twisted universe. Old rotten mattress, drawerless dressers, propane canisters, sawhorse, refrigerator on its side with four connected plastic chairs on top. Crutches. Fake palm tree. Little Tikes Cozy Coupe. Huge stack of firewood split by some man in his prime that surely was not around anymore to burn it. This was the dregs of three or more disappeared generations. It took me a minute to see the wisp of cigarette smoke, and Martha at the bottom of it, sitting on a Shop-Vac. We asked if she wanted to come ride around with us. Where to, she didn't even ask.

You never saw a more wrecked person. Hair, teeth, everything on her unwashed or coming apart. Old striped jeans with a busted zipper. Skeleton arms bare, in that cold. Maggot got in back so she could ride shotgun, and I got the full smell of her, like kyarn. Rotten meat. I made myself ask if she needed to eat, and she said yeah, but then dipped out before we got to a drivethrough. I got her a burger, but Maggot ate it, saying there would be more food at June's. Then he went to sleep too. We drove through the creepy stretch where the kudzu vines are hanging off the trees and reaching over the guardrails like they're wanting to get at you.

About a mile out from June's, Martha woke up, saw

where we were, and tried to throw herself out of the car. Forgetting she was belted in. I pulled over and let her go, because there was no escaping out there, just the banks of the Powell River where Mr. Peg used to take us fishing. A beautiful place, hemlock trees standing around like bored giants. She stumbled down the bank. I only then noticed she had one bare foot. Probably she'd shot up, dipped out, and forgot. I'd seen Dori do it many times. Having Dori and Martha both inside my skull at the same time scared the hell out of me. I left Maggot asleep in the car and went after her. I squatted on the riverbank, watching her shiver. All hunched, her face pressed to her knees, both hands in her stringy hair.

"I can't have her seeing me," Martha finally said. "She hates my guts."

"June? She doesn't either."

"She's the one made you come after me, ain't she?"

I said all June wanted was to take care of her. Martha shook so hard, I was afraid something in her might break. She said she wasn't taking any more of June's money because it made her more of a bad person and she couldn't go any lower. She'd tried to kill herself already a couple of times. "June thinks I'm the one that corrupted Emmy."

I told her nobody thought that. What struck me though was how Emmy had said this too, *I'm a terrible person.* Fast Forward was out there so cocksure he could do no wrong, with these women run over in the road behind him. I made myself touch Martha's back, rubbing my hand in a circle on her thin summer shirt, feeling the hard knobs of her spine. Dori's were like that now.

I told her June was not one to give up on people, ever. And if Martha had any way of getting in touch with Emmy, she needed to tell her that June still loved the heck out of her and wanted her home. Martha sat wiping her nose with the back of her hand, taking this in. I was trying to give her some usefulness, to keep herself going. But it wore me out. By the time I got her and Maggot dropped off at June's, it was dark and I was one more casualty of the day.

The whole drive home I thought of Dori, where she was headed. God help me if I'd just seen it. Dori was never going to get clean, she had no reason. I couldn't picture living without her, but neither could I go on being this lonely forever, waiting for Dori to wake up wanting to share my burdens. The only words we had left between us now were the foreplay to fighting.

She was asleep on the couch, on her back, with one hand on the floor like a storybook girl trailing fingers in the water from her boat. Jip on her stomach, beady-eyed watchman. He growled as I shook her gently.

"Baby, I'm going to get you something. Did you eat today at all?"

She rolled over on her side without opening her eyes.

"I need you to wake up. Sit up, okay? We have to talk."

Where to go, if I left, I had no idea. No place seemed possible. Maybe it would only be for a little while. I pushed Jip off her belly and helped her sit up. She blinked, focusing her eyes.

"What do you feel like eating?"

She put her hand on her stomach, shook her head. I said she had to eat. Her eyes opened wider, like my being there was dawning on her a step at a time. Then she looked at me like I was going to hurt her, and I felt like a terrible person. "Baby, baby," I said, stroking her hair. It had grown out every which way, finally her true color of blond. I said I loved her and would never, ever want to hurt her. And she said, The thing is, Demon. I'm pregnant.

53

I thought of it every minute of every day. This would get us clean. Now Dori had reason. It's simple, I said, think of the baby. It was not simple. Dori had never troubled to hide any part of her using. To her mind, it was all about love: sucking an oxy to crush and split exactly in half with me. Saving every patch she shot, for me to lick the leftovers. Now she got wily on me, only ever shooting up after I'd left the house. Sweet thing, that was Dori trying to be good. I might have been doing some version of the same.

Stupid is all the word I've had to cover much of my time on God's grass. But it's not stupid that makes a bird fly, or a grasshopper rub its knees together and sing. It's nature. A junkie catches his flight. That sugar on your brain cells sucks away any other purpose. You can think you're in charge. Walk around thinking this for hours at a time, or a day, till the clock winds down and the human person you were gets yanked out through whatever hole the devil can find. Learn your lesson, get your feet up under you. You will be knocked down again.

For Dori's sake, I went to talk to June. I knew she needed to be seen to. They have things they do for the pregnant now, heartbeat and such. Vitamins, I remembered Mom getting those. And just by the way, maybe also some help getting her off the junk.

What I didn't expect was to find June so pumped up on her own news, she wasn't all that excited over mine. Martha had a bead on Emmy's whereabouts in Atlanta. June actually had a street address, and was going down there. Some hellhole, no doubt. She was peeling potatoes while she told me all this, long slips of skin flying fast into the sink. The people I know are seldom idle with their hands. Men smoke or fix things, usually both at once. I once watched a man take down a dead poplar from the top down, working high in its limbs with a chain saw in one hand and a Camel in the other. Women fix a kid's hair or wipe a nose or sew on a button or peel potatoes. And smoke, though not June of course. I sat on a stool at her kitchen counter, wishing I could draw her hands. I asked, "What makes you think she wants to come home?"

No answer for half a potato. Brown and white peels mounding in the sink. And then: "Emmy is in no position right now to know what she wants."

"People get tired of hearing that," I said. "She's eighteen."

June's eyes flared, but she kept peeling, talking without looking up. "These aren't adult choices we're talking about. She's stuck down there with no means, getting used by terrible people keeping her strung out, whatever, raped. There's parts I can't even think about."

"Embarrassed," I said. "There's that part. She'd sooner die than have you know."

June's hands went still. "You need to come with us."

I almost laughed, for how doable it all seemed to June Peggot. Like she's Lara Croft, and we're going to go raid the tomb. I said no, I couldn't leave Dori for that long.

She narrowed her eyes at me, still working away, the *slip-slip* of the peeler sounding mad now. "Listen to yourself. Dori's a grown woman, soon to be a mother. What do you think she'll do if you leave her unsupervised, wet the bed? Burn down the house?"

I didn't want to admit that both were possible. I had other excuses, my job at the store, a strip I had to finish by Saturday. June said she was going on Sunday. *Slip-slip-slip.* I told her these were scary people, and she should go with somebody that packs heat, like Juicy Wills.

Hell no on Juicy, she said, multiple reasons. But damn straight on scary. She'd been getting threats from some Rose person that claimed Emmy had stolen her man, and if the bitch ever turned up back here she was asking to get her pretty face scarred up. June had no intention of going to look for Emmy without a sidearm. Her brother Everett had an open carry permit that he swore was good in Georgia, and he'd agreed to go with her.

I tried to picture this brother as Terminator 2. Everett. All the good looks and kindness that came with the Peggot package, a linebacker in high school. He and his wife owned the fitness club and tanning salon in Big Stone, so. He was pretty ripped, but still. June was batshit.

"Fine then, you don't need me," I said.

"But a friend, somebody her age. Like you said, she's humiliated. She trusts you."

That aggravated me, getting invited as the boy, not the man. "Take Hammer, then," I said. "Last of the nice guys. Deer rifle, pre-engagement garmin ring or whatever the hell."

June flew off the handle at me then, saying that would be cruel, pulling Hammer into this. All he'd ever wanted was to love that girl and keep her safe. If only they'd stayed together. She dropped her naked potatoes in the water to boil, wiped her hands on her apron, and used them to push her hair back from her forehead, one of those little habits that ran right down the Peggot generations. Those hands, that split second of babyish wide forehead laid bare, exact same look in their eyes. For one second I was seven years old playing Standoff with Maggot, our bare feet planted, trying to push each other over into the mud. Me winning, Maggot refusing to lose.

It was all doable. Myself in June's car headed south at an ungodly hour of Sunday. Atlanta was almost six hours each way, and she meant to get down there and do our business by daylight, before the vampires came out. Everett was napping in the passenger seat, his big head nodding forward, his Kel-Tec PMR-30 on the console between them. Concealed carry didn't cross state lines, and June did things by the book. I rode in back with the supplies she seemed to think necessary: old soft quilts, cooler of sodas, boxes of crackers, and such. So we've got two different movies running here, front seat tricked out for *Blade II*, back seat is *Lassie Come Home.*

I felt bad that I'd lied to Dori, or really just told her nothing, but she'd have gone to pieces to hear I was leaving the state. My bigger worry was getting through this whole day without a bump. I'd fueled up on the front end obviously, but with nothing additional for the road. Laws were laid down. We were taking I-75, the oxy expressway from Florida. June was so clean and prepared on all fronts, she probably *wanted* us to get pulled over.

June and Everett spent a full five hours bickering. Which way was faster out of town, Veterans Highway or 58. Whether the car was too warm or just right. Whether Easy Cheese was God's gift or a disgusting waste of a good metal can. June would put the radio on an eighties station, and Everett would drive us nuts singing in a ridiculous high voice with Eddie Rabbitt or Rosanne Cash, until she'd let him change it. Then June would grunt out her own made-up words to Beastie Boys and Jay-Z. "Ooh ooh bitch, gotta big dick for ya here."

"You are so far out of it, Junie. 'Song Cry,' it's this beautiful love story."

"Just playing it how it lays, brother. That's what it sounds like to me."

"Heartbreak of old age. Hearing's the first thing to go."

Everett and June were five years apart, and took no time at all getting back to seven and twelve. They argued over whether Everett peed on his shoes at the Peggot reunion one time, and whose fault it was the dog got run over, and an entire year of the older kids supposedly stealing Everett's lunches and convincing him their mom wasn't packing one for him.

"Oh my God Everett, are you never giving that up? That did not happen."

"Uh-huh, sad. I reckon it's the memory that goes first."

The surprise to me was Mrs. Peggot packing lunches at all. Maggot always bought school lunch. You could see how those seven would have worn her down before he ever got there.

By noon, we were looking at Atlanta. Cloud-high buildings spiking up in the distance, pointy or square on top, the colors of steel and sky. So much like a movie, your eye couldn't accept it was real. June's car was pretty sweet, I should mention, Jeep Cherokee, white leather upholstery. All of this briefly being cool enough to forget the FUBAR aspects of this road trip and pass around the snacks. I was still in the good part of my day, before fine and dandy edges over to sad and irritable. Then come sweats, yawning, itching, goose bumps, shaking and puking. These phases I could read like a watch. I was optimistic on getting home before fucked o'clock.

June had her maps and her battle plan. City driving didn't faze her, due to the Knoxville years. She was all center lane this, right on red that, arm-over-elbow turns through these hectic parts of town where there were more people in the intersections than cars. Peachtree Street, she announced, steering us down this video-game canyon of sky-high towers with few trees in sight, peach or otherwise. "Stopping for coffee," she announced, and parallel parked like no driver I've seen before or since. Slick as a rabbit finding its hole. I added it to the list of June's superpowers. We went in a tiny restaurant where she knew the rules, pay first, order off the long list of items that in no way shape or form sound like coffee, but are coffee. Tall flat frappo nonsense. She said this was to fortify our nerves, and bought me a blueberry muffin.

We sat at a tiny table and finally those two went quiet. I thought of the day I met June, the Knoxville restaurant where I couldn't eat due to everything going on outside. I'd felt like I did now, jumpy. Anxious in the back of my mind for a doorway out of all this, back to the green true world. But I wasn't a kid now, I knew things. For one, that Xanax would put much of that feeling to rights. A couple near us drank their coffee and had a whisper fight. Hundreds of people passed by outside hugging their coats around them, looking at their feet, walking fast. I wondered what they were taking for the brain alarm bell that goes off in a place like this, where not one thing you see is alive, except more people. Everything else being dead: bricks, cement, engine-driven steel, no morning or evening songs but car horns and jackhammers. All the mountains of steel-beam construction. And this, June informed us, was the *good* part of town.

After we got back in the car, she realized Everett had hidden his pistol in the glove compartment and said technically that was a conceal. He said technically he was not getting his five-hundred-dollar Kel-Tec stolen while she drank her fucking latte. I was about an inch from *You kids quit fighting or that piece goes out the window.* Irritable phase possibly under way.

The directions she'd written down got us to a neighborhood that was less crowded, in fact the opposite. Not a soul walking around. It looked somewhat like various parts of Lee County thrown together at close range. Bluffs, she called it. This is February so it's still pretty bleak, but you could see how it might green up in the right circumstance. Sad-looking trees, embankments, tall dead weeds standing up between the small houses. Junked-out porches to rival the Woodway crack house, other houses abandoned, boarded up, or burned out. About one in ten, though, were tidy and painted up nice. Old people like the Peggots, you had to reckon, that stood their ground while the youth went to hell. But everything was jammed together, a lot of houses with no space between. Tires lying on the sidewalks, trash blown up against chain link.

"Where the mothafuck are we?"

"Everett," June said. "You need to shut up."

The first human we saw was an old guy lying in the street on his side, slowly moving his legs like riding a bike. A few blocks later, some young guys in big clothes, carrying black plastic bags that pulled down with heavy weight, like full udders on a cow. Then another old guy in a hat and mittens parked on the street corner in a wheelchair, watching nothing go by. Here and there, a little store would have people hanging around, but mostly the streets were deserted. Maybe because it was Sunday, with the Godly in church and the rest sleeping off their sins.

"Damn, mothafuckers," Everett said now and again, until June blew up.

"Ever*ett.* You're one of about twelve men I know that aren't in any kind of trouble. Definitely not a thug. Could we just agree on that being a good thing?"

The address turned out to be a rough-looking place. We pulled up in front, killed the engine, and sat looking at this house. Low and wide, flat roof, moldy white paint, a lot of the windowpanes covered with cardboard. It looked like a brutal smile with missing teeth. Everett picked up his Kel-Tec and checked the safety. "You two stay in the car, I'll bake the cake."

June made this explosion, like a crying laugh. "I really am going to kill you with that."

Everett put the piece on his lap.

"I'm just going to knock on the door," June said. "If it turns out she's here, I'll ask if we can all come in and talk to her. For God's sake, Everett, behave yourself."

To get to the door she had to step over a pile of what looked like Pampers and blue plastic. In her jeans and red winter coat, she looked like a kid waiting outside for somebody to let her in. Normally she'd have her doctor outfit, with the whole authority aspect. She waited a long time. We had the car windows down, listening, ready to leap into action. I could hear Everett breathing. If I had to guess, I'd say he was terrified. More knocking, more waiting.

Anybody else would have given up. After about ten

minutes she went around and started knocking on windows, calling Emmy's name. I never fully believed we were going to find her, but watching June duck under hanging gutters, banging her knuckles on broken casement windows, I saw it was the opposite for her. No other option would fit in her brain. I got a full-body memory of the Undersea Wonders Aquarium, Emmy and June's standoff over the shark tank, nobody backing down. I'd helped Emmy into the tunnel that day, but I also lied to her. *If something scares you, get your ass out of there*, I should have said. *Everything will not be okay.*

The house next door was one of the nicer ones. Painted shutters, one of those whirligig garden things in the dead flowers. A guy was standing on the porch watching June. We hadn't noticed him until he yelled something like "Hey, lady," and both Everett and I jumped, and then we saw him. Old guy in a coat and cloth slippers. White ring of hair around his mostly bald brown head. June walked over to his porch and shook his hand. We watched them talk, June nodding, looking back at the grimace house. Touching her eye, asking questions, nodding.

She came back to the car, belted up, didn't start the engine.

"He said there were some people living there, and

they were evicted. Including some young women. One was white. Evicted is not exactly what he said." She shook her head fast, like trying to clear it. "There was a shooting. And they left."

"June. We should just go home," Everett said.

"He thinks they went to a house not too far from here. He doesn't know the address, but he said it's a brand-new place. Like maybe just built, with nobody technically living there yet."

"He's making shit up to get rid of you," Everett suggested. "Who'd build a house here?"

"I told him I was looking for my daughter, and he said he understood. He said this new house is a place they're using right now, I don't know for what. But she could be there."

"This is crazy, June. It's too dangerous."

"*Damn* you, Everett. Where's the gangland tough shit now?"

No answer to that.

She banged her open hands on the steering wheel. "There's not a damn thing messing people up around here that I'm not seeing in my office ten times a day." She threw the car into drive, and we drove. Up and down the blocks. The same old man still in his wheelchair, the other one still lying in the road. The leg-pumping had ceased. We didn't know what we were looking for.

Nothing looked remotely new. I was hungry and itchy, moving towards the sweats. Everett kept picking up his piece and putting it down, until June smacked his hand.

Then we saw the house. Like it had dropped out of the freaking sky of newness.

We all three got out of the car. A front yard of fresh bulldozed dirt, factory stickers on the windows. The front door was the modern type with an oval-shaped fake church window in it. June knocked, no answer. A little metal box type thing hung on the doorknob, sprung open, with a key sitting there in plain view. June tried the key in the lock, and then we were in.

It was all new everything: nice wood floors, strong smell of paint, no real furniture. Just a card table with bags and a scale, a white dust of coke. In the corner a guy was slumped on the floor with his back against the wall, head flopped forward. We held our breath, watching. The bill of his oversize black ball cap covered his face, so it was pure guess as to sleeping, dead, or dipped out. I thought number three, based on the splayed legs and open hands.

June touched Everett's shoulder, then his pistol, and pointed to the guy. Held up her flat hand: *Keep him there.* She and I moved through the house. A hallway, bedrooms. We made almost no sound, but the place was so empty it echoed anyway. I pushed open a half-closed door and almost pissed myself. Little kids, two of them, on a pile of opened-out cardboard pizza boxes. One was asleep and the other one sitting up, playing with the plastic rings of a six-pack. The awake one looked up at us wide-eyed, like June and I might be just the ticket. June stood with her hand over her mouth. I had to pull her back out the door.

We didn't check all the rooms, because the next one was where we found Emmy. She and another girl were passed out on a mattress, both half naked. I mean exactly half. Emmy had on a short skirt and snagged black tights and nothing at all on top, while the other girl had a blouse and jewelry, a shiny yellow jacket, and from there down just legs and pussy. Like they'd had to split one outfit, underwear and all. June still had her hand on her mouth and was looking at me, like *I* knew what the hell to do. Run, I thought. The room smelled ripe, like sex, and the sight of Emmy's bruised face and pasty skin made me sick. I walked over and scooped her up, more heft to her than Dori but not by much, she was maybe ninety pounds. I'd once been a man to deadlift three times that, easy. The man I was now got us out of there before any eyes opened.

June waved the two of us up front, got in the back seat with Emmy, and rolled her up in all the blankets.

Everett drove too fast, yelling "Fuck, fuck, fuck, I don't know where I'm going."

"My God. Those babies," June said. "What if one of them is hers?" And then in another minute, "What am I thinking? She's only been gone six months."

"We can call Georgia DSS," I said. All of us pretty far out of our minds.

Everett found his way onto a city freeway and pulled over. June gave him her map to figure out how to get back to I-75, then got out, opened the back, and fetched her medical bag. We sat on the shoulder with cars whizzing past, rattling us, while June crouched over Emmy in the back seat, listening to her heart, feeling her bones and organs. Emmy's hair was cut weirdly short in a scary way, with parts of it missing. Her eyes were open now, jumping around at all of us, but she didn't talk. Maybe in her opinion we were a dream. I took off my zipper hoodie and gave it to June to put on her. Then she wrapped Emmy up again and said, "Let's go home."

Too much adrenaline will age you before your time. I've heard that said. What I know for sure is, it will push you too fast through your day. I was into the sweats and beyond before we got out of Georgia. I had to ask Everett to pull over to save June's white leather seats. She made me get in the back, gave me a 7 Up and a pill to chew to settle my stomach, that she said would make me sleepy. Nothing for the shakes and sweats. She put a blanket around me and laid me on the dogpile so Emmy and I were dominoed onto June, our little back-seat rehab ward. June sat up straight with this look on her face like she wants to kill us both, but she's not going to let us die.

Everett was free at last to control the radio, and for a long time nobody said a word. I drifted in and out. Then somewhere around the Tennessee line, June started talking. Low, quiet. I was going to have my own child to think about, soon. She said she'd had this same talk with my mom before I was born. They were friends. I never knew that. June was the reason the Peggots took her into their trailer. They actually lived there together for a short while, before June moved away with Emmy and I got born. June had known my dad, too. She said you couldn't know one without the other, those two were joined at the hip. I asked what he was like. She said exactly like me. In looks, word, and deed. A beautiful man with too much heart for the raw deal he got.

That didn't sound like me. So probably none of it was true. I asked her how he died.

She frowned at me. "Are you testing me? Or do you really not know?"

I was too far gone to fake anything. I told her I knew it was on the Fourth of July, at Devil's Bathtub, and that was all. June told me he drowned or broke his neck. Probably both at once, because he dived from up high on the bank. I asked her why did it happen. She said there was talk that he was drunk or showing off, but Mom swore it was her fault, he was in so much hurry to get to her. She'd gone in the water without knowing it was deep. Mom couldn't swim.

June was in a place I'd never seen her go. Relieved, wrecked, talkative. Telling me things nobody else ever had. She said every time she saw me, it made her wish she'd tried harder with Mom, back in the time they were friends. But after the accident and everything, seeing my dad killed, Mom never wanted fully to be in the world. June said it was different for me, I had so many good reasons. She looked at me hard, like trying to read something written inside my skull. "Think of that baby coming. I know how hard it is, but you'll get clean."

I had my doubts on what June knew. But I was polite enough not to say: Get back to me after you've done time with your racking bones in your sweat-swamped sheets, crying for the lights to go out on your whole damn being.

June kept talking. As far as what lay up the road for

me and Emmy, she knew some things I didn't, and that part killed her, she said. She felt cruel every time she set somebody up with the methadone clinic in Knoxville. Martha being not the only one, far from it. She had patients getting up at three a.m. to get down there and back before work, with their kids in the car. No closer options. But something new was coming out, that she hoped she could prescribe right out of her clinic. A lot of paperwork involved. Suboxone. A word none of us knew yet.

The first thing we had to do, she said, was quit thinking this mess was our fault. "They did this to you," she kept repeating, like that was our key to salvation. Like there was even a door.

We got back after dark. Emmy had come around some by then, drinking a Coke, saying not much. June got some promises out of me before turning me loose. But I was so far gone by that point. I'm not proud of it. I had some stuff in the glove box of the Impala, and for the last many hours had been thinking of nothing else. Sitting in June's driveway, I did an 80 before I drove home to Dori.

54

I was surprised to find her awake, sitting up on the couch in bloody pajamas, face in her hands, crying. Jip tearing around in circles like a wind-up toy, out of his mind on the scent of blood and his little mother in pieces. I don't think Dori understood what was going on.

I got some wet towels to clean her up, and changed her out of the old striped pajama bottoms of Vester's she always wore now. Got her in a clean T-shirt and panties. Held her, rocked her, asked what all she'd taken that day and if she'd eaten. She just kept asking where had I been. Why didn't I come home, why didn't I answer my phone? I wasn't used to having that phone yet, and given what it cost, I was so scared of losing it, I mostly left it locked in the glove. That's where it had spent the day, buzzing to the expired insurance papers and oxy stash.

I tried to calm her down, saying I loved her, I was sorry to get home so late, and heartbroken of course. The pregnancy had to be over, with that much blood. This clouded her up. She wasn't crying over that, it seemed. Just so confused and ashamed of her mess. Maybe she'd forgotten. After I brought it up, a whole fresh storm blew in. She'd lost her baby.

She was begging to shoot a morphine patch, and I wouldn't let her. That's what it came down to, our love story. Dori trying to wiggle away from me to reach for her junk, me restraining her on the couch, my grip like handcuffs on her tiny wrist bones. More tears, more blaming. Daddy had never treated her so mean. I didn't love her, I wouldn't let her have what she needed. I felt like the villain of the world, but this was the truth, another fix could have been the end of Dori. I had no way to know how much she'd already taken. Her kit was all over the table, cotton balls, lighter and spoon, today's or yesterday's I couldn't tell. I smelled the vinegar she used with the fentanyl. Her patches scared the hell out of me, with those layers where the pure drug has to pass through the jelly to get to your skin. Poke a needle in there, it's a game of chance. At least five times already, I'd come home from Tommy's to find Dori thrashing on that couch, her lungs sucking hard and her eyes rolled back in her head. One of those times, she was blue around the lips. My blue fairy. I never hated myself more than those nights I had to shake and slap her to get her back. Throw water on her, pack ice on her neck if we had it. Things I'd not known how to do for Mom. For days after every OD, Dori would lie around whimpering, saying everything in her whole body hurt. I told her that was from her muscles trying so hard to draw breath. But I never truly knew if it was that, or what I'd done.

Let's just get through tonight, I kept telling her now, needing to relax my grip so it wouldn't leave bruises. It took no more than a minute for the fight to drain out of her. I stroked her hair and kissed her, saying we were okay, mostly talking to myself, trying to blot out the days ahead. Now we had no baby coming. No reason. I tried to ask her how sure she'd been about the pregnant thing. If she'd taken one of those home tests, I didn't see it, or buy it for her. Did we really lose something here, or did we never have it? She wouldn't talk about it. Dori always was embarrassed of her lady business and kept it to herself, but living with a person, obviously you know the basics. Her monthlies were all over the place, sometimes gone a long while and then back with revenge, hurtful and bloody. I would have to accept this as one more thing I was never going to know. Did this baby join up with my little brother in the black hole of lost and nameless, or was he lucky enough to skip the draft pick altogether.

Dori was like Vester now, a person that wasn't safe left alone. She'd stayed by his side for years, giving herself up totally, because in Dori's book, that was love. And mine too. It hit me then, holding her while she fell asleep, how loving Dori had swallowed me alive, from day one. She just couldn't see it. How I was her provider, facing down the world for our drugs and groceries, begging for further mercy at the co-op, where my job was on thin ice. Likewise our car, as precarious as everything else in our life. I carried a case of transmission fluid in the trunk that the Impala was knocking down like a wino. If I couldn't get the ring job done and paid for, we'd have to wait for somebody to find us starved in our bed. Even Jip's chow had run out. None of this would sway Dori. She would cry all day and sleep at night with the back of my shirt balled up tight in her hands. That sure I was going to leave her. Because everybody does.

Even after she fell asleep, I stayed with her on the couch a long time. But got more and more restless, feeling a near violent need to set things to rights. The soiled blankets, the kit, the plates on the floor with crumbs of her nothing meals. I made myself keep still as long as I could stand it, listening to her slow breathing. I watched brown beetles come out of the corners and move across the floor with their feelers twitching, hunting out their rewards.

Somewhere around two in the morning I carried her upstairs to bed. She weighed even less than the day before. She was turning into air.

I couldn't get in bed with her. Even as tired and wrecked as I was, after such a day. She was curled up so small with her knees pulled against her chest and her fists on her face like an unborn baby herself. I tucked blankets around her, then came back downstairs and stripped the filthy mess of clothes and quilts off the couch and stuffed it all in the washer. I picked up the dishes and put them in the sink. Came back to the naked couch and lay down and wished some flood would come and wash out the dry, grainy sockets of my eyes. My only job and purpose now was to keep Dori alive, and I didn't know how to do it.

55

June was sending Emmy away to some residence
place that would get her clean. None of this quickie
rehab business that Mom wore out like a doormat, nor
even the upscale three weeks that Stoner paid for, prior
to shaming her over it to the point of death. We're talking possibly years of Emmy's life, starting it all over
from scratch. In Asheville. There is no such reboot
camp around here. Lee County being a place where you
keep on living the life you were assigned.

June called to let me know if I wanted to say goodbye, this would be the day. What kind of bucks is
this gold-star cure going to cost, you wonder. But it's
rude to discuss money. I just asked the polite things
like, Does this establishment have bars in the windows because you know Emmy's going to try and bolt.

June was pretty confident Emmy would stay put. The reason: Rose Dartell. She'd contacted Emmy, offering to relieve her of some body parts. Holy shit.

I said I'd come over after work. I was still unfired at the co-op, probably because any other kid they hired would be as strung out as I was. I'd drag my ass in late, Rita and Les would hit pause on their Medicare war to join forces in eye-rolling. You get used to a routine. I needed the job, and if I lost my line on cheap livestock syringes, I'd be in trouble at home.

It was late winter now, where sunset puts its claim on much of the day. I drove up towards June's place, looking at pink sky through the black trees. June opened the door, looking worn out. "She's upstairs packing, hon. Hang on, let me go see if she wants you to come up there."

Emmy came downstairs with her coat on, wanting to go for a walk. We headed up to the ruined cabin. She pulled her hat on fast, but I saw attempts had been made to salvage the wreck. Some kind of pixie cut, spikes and wisps. It had been a few weeks since the rescue but she still looked too thin, too jumpy, old in a young body. Rode hard and put up wet, guys like to say. But in some other way, she was restored to full Emmy. She wanted a cigarette.

"She'll know you smoked, if you go back in there smelling like a chimney."

"She's bigger on forgiveness than permission."

"Fine then, let her blame me for corrupting you." I produced what was required. Emmy leaned against a tree and inhaled so hard the flame from my lighter pulled into the paper and crackled. Breathed in, breathed out, eyes closed, God don't I know it. That moment where nicotine has to stand in for all other things you're dying for.

"Late in the day for that, don't you think?"

For contributing to the delinquency, she meant. I wondered so many things: Was Fast Forward some kind of drug lord now, did he really just throw her away like trash. How does a person you've worshipped turn into a monster. And by the way Rose Dartell, what the fuck. None of this would Emmy want to talk about. We went into the skeleton cabin and sat on the log benches we'd dragged together as kids. She smoked and held her cigarette away from her, the way girls do to try and keep the smell out of their hair. Old habit. She put her face down on her knees for a while, then sat back up. "Demon, I'm scared to death."

"Of what?" I thought she'd say Rose, but no. She was scared to go away. Afraid they would brainwash her in this place. Afraid nobody there would understand her, she said. What she really meant was, nobody would know what she'd always been: queen bee, Emmy Peggot.

"You'll rock the house," I said. "You will rule rehab."

But I didn't really know. Here, all we can ever be is everything we've been. I came from a junkie mom and foster care, briefly a star, to some degree famous *because* of all that. Quick to burn out, right on schedule. Emmy grew up in Knoxville and moved back here out of the blue, but she landed in Lee County High with the full pedigree. Daughter of Peggots, homecoming royalty. In Asheville she might just be a pale, conceited girl with an air of broken beauty.

I remembered to give her the snake bracelet. She cupped her hands and dropped it from one to the other, staring at it like lost treasure. "I *wondered* what happened to that."

I left Rose out of this. "I never got why you kept wearing it."

She looked at me, surprised. Then leaned over, unzipped her little leather boot, and fastened it around her ankle.

"It's junk jewelry," I said. "June gave us five dollars to spend in that gift shop, and I probably got change back. Which I probably pocketed."

"Pocketed to take home to your mom."

"Well yeah. To buy her cigarettes and Mello Yello."

"And you wonder why I'd keep this."

I did. Wonder.

She leaned over and put her two cold hands on my cheeks, looking in my eyes like she meant to kiss me. But then sat back on her log bench. "Try to take care of Dori," she said.

"God, Emmy. I'm trying. I don't." There were no words.

"She doesn't deserve you."

"That's a hateful thing to say."

"I know you love her. I'm not being hateful." She shook her head, looking up at the trees. "It's why I couldn't be with Hammer Kelly. He's that same kind of good like you are. Like there's some metal or something in you that won't melt down, no matter what."

"Oh, I melt down. I could show you some fine broken shit."

She still wasn't looking at me. "I'm saying you wake up and you're still yourself, every day. I'm not like that, I give in. I change my recipe, to suit people."

Changing to suit people sounded like a good deal. Dori wouldn't, for me. She stuck to her plan of getting emptier every day. I'd stopped carrying her downstairs now, I just let her stay in bed. I didn't try anymore to talk about things we'd do after we got better. Dori that morning said we should have just been childhood sweethearts instead of trying to get grown-up about it. That way I could have moved on. I got so mad at her over that.

Pulling out of June's driveway, I saw a pickup pulled over on the roadside. It wasn't a vehicle I knew, and there was nothing wrong I could see, tires looked okay. I got out to see what kind of help was needed. It was Hammer. Elbows on the steering wheel, hair flopped forward in his eyes. Knuckles digging in his eyes.

I tapped on the window. "You good in there, man?"

He rolled down the window and looked at me, blinking. "I'm not going in that house."

"It's fine. I'm sure they both understand. You two have moved on."

"No. No, I haven't. She was the one, man."

"Okay." Serious damage here, nothing I could repair.

"Will you tell Emmy for me? Just goodbye, and that I'm sorry for everything. I don't blame her at all. Tell her I still love her."

My phone started ringing on the way over to Tommy's, and I ignored it. It was always Dori, wanting me home. I had a strip due tomorrow that I'd barely sketched out. Dori argued that I could just as well draw pictures at home. She would hold my pencils and ink pens. She'd talk the whole time, and want me to get her something, and cry. And Jip.

It kept ringing after I got to Tommy's. After an hour I'd almost finished the strip and was about to melt down my fucking inner wonderful metal, so I picked up.

Not Dori. Angus. "Oh my God Demon, where are you? Please come, right now."

Was somebody bleeding? Because I did not want to see Coach. You get past shame, into let's just pretend I'm dead now. But Angus was outside herself. I asked if I should call 911, and she cursed a blue streak. No cops. It was U-Haul, and she needed me if possible to kill him.

It takes twenty minutes to get over there and I was there in ten. Found the two of them in the living room cat-and-mousing around the table, circling one way, then the other, screaming, but I got no real indication of who was the mouse. U-Haul was red-faced, rope-necked, saliva flying out of him like a cartoon maniac yelling craziness. *I'm not waiting anymore, you can fucking give it over tonight or watch this whole fucking ship go down.*

She saw me. Then he saw me, and crouched like a different animal. Eyeing the door.

"Don't let him leave," Angus yelled. I tackled him and she grabbed some papers off the table and got past us, out the door. I listened for the car but she didn't pull out. I would have to sit on the asshole till further notice. U-Haul was pinching and clawing me with his long writhy arms. I asked where was Coach, and he said where do you think, drunk on his ass. Then shocked me by sinking his teeth in my thigh. Mother *fuck*. I punched him in the jaw, but it wasn't a great angle. I managed to get him turned on his stomach with some distance between his teeth and any of my parts, but he was still writhing and spitting. I couldn't understand why Angus hadn't driven away. Then heard in my ears, like tape delay, what she'd said. *Don't let him leave.*

I couldn't hold him there long. The way he was squirming under me, it felt like sitting on a floor of rolling baseballs. Also I'd medicated between June's house and now, so was not in top fighting form. The wily bastard went for the weakness, giving a savage backward yank on my bad knee, mother *fuck*. And scrambled away like a crab, out the door.

Outside in the dark I was blind, no porch lights on. Her Wrangler was in the drive. My Impala, blocking Coach's Caddy, both still there. U-Haul's precious Mustang also, with the man himself circling it, pounding on the windows. Angus had to be inside. They always left keys in the cars at home, it's what we do, barring the methier necks of the woods or situations of outstanding debt. I saw a glint of light: Angus inside his car, shaking a bouquet of dangling metal at me. She'd collected up all the car keys and locked U-Haul out of his mothership.

I edged in close, decked him, and scooted around to the passenger side. She unlocked, I dived in and locked it behind me. The car was thick with the oily smell of him.

"Shit," I said, trying to breathe. His screaming was damped down some through the glass. "He'll get a tire iron and smash a window."

She stared at me. "Not his sweet baby Mustang, surely."

"No, you're right. The love of his life."

Her eyes got very wide. "Demon, he wants *me*."

"What do you mean?"

"You tried to tell me. I didn't want to hear it."

He'd come on to her. Told her he'd been keeping things of hers ever since she was a little girl, underclothes. Watching her in the tub. He wasn't waiting any longer. To have sex with her, he meant. Because now he could make her do it.

"What the hell kind of sick madness is that?" I felt like puking. My ears were ringing.

"Blackmail." She got weirdly quiet. I watched her walking herself back from frantic to that place where she could go. Like this was happening to some other Angus. U-Haul had told her he could go to the school board and get Coach fired for drunkenness and worse. Embezzlement of school and booster funds. That would happen, unless she had sex with him.

He'd stopped banging on the car. We didn't see him, and it was too quiet. My brain was having trouble turning over, like the fluids were cold. "Shit. He's gone to get another key."

"There's no other key. He's been pissed over that, he lost the other set."

"You're sure."

"Yeah. But the tire iron is still in the running."

"This is all bark and no bite," I said. "He's just making shit up. Jesus. Stealing from the boosters? That's like taking out of the church collection plate, Coach would never."

Wouldn't, she said, but did. Without knowing it. U-Haul kept all the books. He'd been moving football funds into his mother's bank account, for years evidently. I said if that was true, they'd have burned down their damn rat trap in Heeltown and gotten a life.

He was just waiting for the iron to strike, is what he'd told her. She'd been calling me for an hour, Jesus. How long was he chasing her around that table? She said not that long, it took a while to get to that point.

She'd gone in Coach's office that afternoon and found out he'd forged Coach's signature all over a ton of things, power of attorney and such. Stealing from Miss Betsy also, altering her checks. U-Haul came into the office then, she shoved this stuff in his face and one thing led to another, the blackmail and such, before it blew up into him trying to back her into the bedroom.

It was a lot to follow. Why would she go poking in Coach's office? Craziest thing. Some man had called the house saying U-Haul was putting a lot of Coach's money in his so-called enterprise, and he needed to check this out with Coach himself. Angus had taken the call. And that's how it came down. Damn. Mr. McCobb blows open another guy's con.

We sat in the car forever, waiting for the next moves of a crazed mind. Tire iron to the Impala being among my concerns. The coward must have walked home. Around midnight we called the coast clear. Checked on Coach, who'd slept through the show. I offered to take Angus someplace, but she was pulling it together. We went in the office and unlocked the drawer where Coach kept his Smith & Wesson 40 to take to bed with her. I made sure it was loaded and showed her the safety, which is a little tricky, a grip safety that has to be palmed. She knew.

I sat with her a while in her room, even though I'd

have hell to pay later on many fronts. I asked if Coach might have known this stealing was going on. She said no. He'd trusted U-Haul, then stayed too drunk for too long. "That part's killing me," she said. "U-Haul says I asked for this. I knew about Dad and didn't speak up. That's true, Demon. We knew."

"You asked for nothing," I said. "Jesus. You can't think that."

"I know."

"This was *done* to you. To you and Coach both." Words I'd been hearing.

"I *know.*"

She got a little wobbly, and I thought she might fall apart but she didn't. She sat on the bed talking through what she'd have to do, starting tomorrow. Money to repay, shit to sort out. Lawyers. She looked like a kid, curled against the headboard in her white stretch pj's, twirling a strand of her hair around one finger, talking like the head of the house. All I could think of was little Angus bearing those Hellboy eyes on her, all her life. Growing her skin of leather.

I told her to push the heavy chest of drawers against the door after I left. And waited to be sure she did.

56

It was April, not quite a year after Vester, and it happened the way I knew it would. I came home and found her. Early evening, not yet dark. Damn April to hell, I could be done with that one. November also. Birthdays, Christmas, dogwoods and redbuds, even football season. Live long enough, and all things you ever loved can turn around to scorch you blind. The wonder is that you could start life with nothing, end with nothing, and lose so much in between.

I almost didn't feel anything at first, cleaning her up like I'd done so many times, getting her decent. And then the house, cleaning up her mess and her kit. Hiding stuff, before I made any calls. There were few to make. Thelma had run out of reasons to know her. Like everybody else. I had no wish to see the aunt again, but the EMTs said they had to get hold of next of kin, so I turned over Dori's phone. Aunt Fred was in the contacts. I'd erased some other numbers first, but nobody cared to track down any mysteries. Another OD in Lee County. There'd been hundreds.

And just like that, I was "the boy that went in there and found her." People were saying I'd broken into the house, various things. Stories grow on the backs of others. Regardless my clothes and everything being all over the house. Aunt Fred didn't remember me at all. I watched her pick up a pair of my jeans off the floor like she's scrubbing a toilet, saying something to the mini-me daughter about Dori having a lot of men friends. I should have screamed the bitch to hell, but my throat had closed up. My baby girl. No words of mine were called for, because just like before, the aunt chose everything. Church, music, one funeral fits all. They buried her beside Vester and her mother. The only thing they got right.

I just felt like a rock through the service, or a hunk of ice. Not coldhearted against the handful that came out to show respects, it wasn't their fault. Mostly they were the care nurses that had helped with Vester. Also Donnamarie and them, from the store, and a few girls that might have been friends with Dori in school before they got bored of her. Guilty, curious, who knows what brings people out to view the dead. The funeral was so wrong, I couldn't see how it mattered. I'd already done everything in the world I could for Dori, and it added up to nothing.

Seeing Angus, that was a surprise. She came up behind me as I was going into the church, and pretty much steered me like a blind man through the day.

At the graveside, we all stood around waiting for over an hour, because Aunt Fred and Tonto got lost. Four or five miles, church to cemetery, and they're lost. They'd been up there the year before for Vester, but I drove. This time they were on their own, and couldn't be bothered with the directions I gave them, saying they had the navigator thing in their phones. But you get on these back roads, and that business goes off the rails.

The day itself was cruel, a blue sky to rip your damn heart from your lungs. Trees in bud, yellow jonquils exploding out of the ground, dogwoods standing around in their petticoats. Vester's people were in one of these little graveyards way back up the side of a mountain, where you look out across the valley to all the other ranges rising one behind the other in so many different shades of blue, it's like they're bragging. You have to reckon in the old days people had a more optimistic outlook on the death thing, and picked these places for the view.

People got chatty and impatient from waiting around, regardless the scenic overlook, but the minister was getting paid by Aunt Fred, so he wasn't having her miss any part of the show. Quite a few walked back to their cars and left. I had no wish myself to throw a handful of dirt on Dori's little white coffin. She'd had enough of that in life. Angus and I took a walk up the road past the cemetery into a little stand of pines. We sat on some boulders and watched birds hopping around on the ground looking for bugs, throwing the duff aside with their jerky heads. Angus asked if I was going to be okay, and I finally fell apart to some degree. She let me snivel.

I eventually found my manners to ask about Coach, the scandal and everything. She said she and Coach went together to the school board to explain things, and he might get suspended, but not till after the fall season. The Generals without Coach, there would be rioting in the streets. Angus said he was okay with whatever got decided, he was wanting to pay the piper. I asked what they would do for money if he lost his job. She was on top of it, aiming to sell or rent out that big house. She was looking at apartments in Norton where she could go to her community college classes and Coach could get dried out. They had AA meetings over there. She was putting him on the clock. She'd stay and help him for another year, and then it was sink or swim because she was going away to the other type of college. I asked her wasn't that a little harsh. She said no. She was not in the business of throwing her life away so other people can stay shitfaced.

She stopped herself. "I don't mean you, Demon. You understand that, right?"

I said I knew I was not their problem. She argued with me, saying Coach was still my guardian. How was it fair, me getting assigned to a shitfaced guardian? I said add it to the list. But I could see she was getting upset. She'd made all new life plans over the last couple weeks, while there was still a me and Dori. Now she'd have to rethink. Not necessary, I said. She asked where I was going to live. I said I'd figure it out. I wasn't mad at her. I wasn't anything. I heard what she was trying to say, that we were still family. I just wasn't feeling it.

She was wearing the little black hat with the veil that I'd given her our first Christmas. She'd joked at the time about how she was going to get known countywide as the funeral fox. Thanks, God. Nice one. We walked back to the burial in time to see it through. Thelma was one of the few that stayed. She was sweet and gave me a hug. But all told, other than Angus, not too many of the attendees gave me the time of day. Some few asked if I had known the deceased.

I had to move fast to get my things out of the house, because the Fred team came back after the funeral, pulled on yellow rubber gloves, and moved through like Haz-Mat with their Lysol and trash bags, clearing the place out. Furniture, pictures, precious Mom clothes Dori had kept for all time, all bagged and thrown outside. A guy was coming in two days' time to haul everything to the dump. Not even a yard sale. To their mind, our life was entirely trash.

Luckily they ignored the Impala, seeming to think it was mine. All my stuff fit inside it. The two days they were cleaning, I would drive a ways and then circle back, sleeping in the vehicle, watching the heap of black trash bags grow to a mountain. They were scrubbing this branch off their tree. It turns out, Newport News is in Virginia. Same state, different planet.

The other mystery nobody cared to solve was Jip. I'd found him, too, not lying on top of her as usual but under the sheet, curled up against her cold belly. Did he have the same junk in his veins she did, I'll never know. Accident or no accident, the question of my life. As part of my cleanup before calling 911, I'd picked up his hard little body that was curled like a cinnamon roll and wrapped it in the ratty striped towel he always dragged around the house. Pretending that rag was me, I assumed. Then later, with so much else going on, I forgot about him.

The little towel bundle turned up outside, on the black-bagged trash pile. This fierce tiny being that never stopped loving her, nor wanting me for dinner. I took him around to the back and buried him behind the tool shed. The one goodbye that was left up to me.

57

I'm not sure how many days I lived in my car before Maggot tracked me down. He was back living with Mrs. Peggot now. The kid had been bounced around in his time, but never homeless, because blood is thicker than water. I ought to know, born in the bag of water. No relatives, homeless, but at least I would never drown, yay! The gospel according to Mrs. Peggot.

She'd turned me out once, and I had my pride. I was not going back there begging. But now she actually wanted me to move in, and it took some convincing. Maybe she was hoping for the good influence on Maggot after all, or for somebody to fix busted hinges and everything else that was going undone with Mr. Peg sick for so long, then dead. Maggot's talents ran in other directions.

I didn't end up fixing much. There's not a lot to say about those days I was there, mainly because I don't remember them. Maggot and I went on a bender that obliterated the weekend and ran to the end of the month. Then we thought, who needs May?

All previous statements as regards junkies not really trying to get high, just trying not to get dopesick? Scratch that. After Dori was gone, I was chasing the big zero. With fair success. My job at the co-op finally joined the tits-up work history of Demon. And poor Mrs. Peggot, I did nothing around that house except to surface on rare occasions to drive her to the grocery. We'd have starved otherwise, since she didn't drive, and Maggot was useless on Mr. Peg's truck. One more strike on his blighted manhood: Maggot never learned to drive a manual.

I had the vague idea that if money became essential, tobacco season was around the corner and I'd make some then. People were hard up for labor. With most every kid in the county hammered, what few farmers were still on their land were having to scout high and low to get decent hands for the hard work. Mainly these were coming to us across the Mexican border. Along with all the heroin. No connection, as far as I know.

The one thing I was still holding together, by a thread, was Red Neck. I couldn't let Tommy crash and burn, he of all people deserved better. He was more than pulling his weight at this point. In the beginning we'd brainstormed a lot of ideas, and now he was sketching those into panel strips. Skeleton versions. At least once a week I'd get myself sober enough to go over and put flesh on the bones. My style was required by the fan base. But Tommy's rough drafts had their own weirdly terrifying vision, more truthful than any we ever put in the paper. Our people, our mountains, all our worries: a universe of ghosts. I called his drawings Neckbones, and asked if I could save them. Tommy said this was a dark inclination on my part, but he let me.

The day everything happened, the hitting bottom as it's known in our circles, came in June. One of those hot, rainy days where you feel like you're breathing your own breath out of a paper bag. But weather was not the worst of that day's evils. I'm pointing my finger now at Rose Dartell. Running into her that day would put the nail in the coffin. I'd give anything to have stayed home. If wishes were horses, like they say. We'd all have different shit to shovel.

Maggot and I were at the famous Woodway crack house where Swap-Out was still living with some other guys. People came and went through there like barn cats, you didn't always bother with names. Maggot needed to get hooked up. For my own part I was okay, I'd scored a pity bottle of oxy off of Thelma at the funeral and had multiplied the investment. Pain clinic, first Friday of the month: loaves and fishes. But I drove Maggot over to Woodway and made the effort to be social. Had a chat with Swap-Out, asked if he still had any doings with Mr. Golly, which he didn't, too bad. That man had a place in my heart. Then Maggot and the other crackheads got to the part of ring-around-the-rosy where they all fall down, and I went and sat outside, deeply cooked and making the best of it. Breathing the halitosis of summer, basking in the sick glory of that porch. The rotten mattress, the dresser with no drawers, the refrigerator on its side with its mouth hanging open, harboring a tiny waiting room on top of four black plastic chairs joined together. I remembered rescuing Martha from this very porch, a lifetime ago, and wondered what became of her. June would be getting her straightened out, for sure. Maggot and I weren't crossing our path with June if we could help it.

Half the porch was taken up by stacked firewood that had been there so long, it was covered with a shredded sheet of white dusty cobwebs. I watched a mother rat run in and out of the logs, carrying her babies by their napes from one part of the stack to another. She'd appear with them one by one, all business, like she's on the clock here, relocating her office space. How she decided one part of this wreck was less dangerous than any other, no guess.

A dirt-brown Chevy pickup came down the road, the first vehicle of any kind in over an hour, and surprised me by pulling up to the house. More surprise, Rose Dartell flung herself out of it, slamming the door and moving fast, carrying a pizza box.

"Damn, Rose. Did you bake me a pie?"

She pulled up hard to a stop. Her hair was different some way, less frizzed out, but the face was unchanged. That scarred-up sneer. "What the hell are *you* doing here?"

"I could ask you the same."

"I work for Pro's. That and the phone company, for a couple of years now."

"Pro's Pizza delivers all the way out here to fucking Woodway?"

"Regular customers. They pay cash. Any more questions, or can I do my job?"

"Knock yourself out."

I wondered if they'd be paying her more than cash in there. She stayed long enough. Mr. Pro probably had no idea where all she was driving on his dime. I couldn't help thinking of our last meetup, the dark highway pullout where Rose gave me the news of Emmy like a drink she'd spit in. I was just about to go in and advise Maggot that it was time to say grace and blow this dump, but she came back out. Sat down on the edge of the woodpile. Mother rat, look out.

"Did Fast Forward call you yet?" She mumbled it, lighting a cigarette.

"Why would he do that?"

She shrugged, wiped her runny nose with the back of her wrist. They'd tipped her in there, all right. "I don't know why he wouldn't. He's always needing something from somebody. He's back in Lee County, maybe you didn't know."

"Oh yeah? Whereabouts is he living?"

"This big old house belonging to some lady. They call it Spurlock around there, but it's not really a town, more or less by Duffield. It's a hard place to find."

Rose flicked at something on the knee of her jeans, adjusted the strap of her sandal. Thunder was rolling around between the mountains to the east of us. Then the sky got a lot darker, in that sudden way that feels like a power outage of God. I lit a smoke of my own, since Rose hadn't offered. We sat looking at the collection of vehicles that seemed to belong to the Woodway crack house. Some living, some dead, some fallen prey to target practice.

Rose blew out the last of her smoke and ground out the butt with her heel. "You know what, this is my last delivery and I'm going over there now."

"To where?" My mind had wandered.

"To Fast Forward's. If you want to follow me over there. Come by and say hello."

I told her not to do me any favors.

"I'm not," she said. "Actually, I'm thinking the next time he needs somebody to come scratch his balls, maybe he could whistle for you instead of me."

Maybe, if I still bowed to the pull of the Fast Forward magnet. But I'd decided some while ago, if I spoke to the bastard again, it would not be in kindness. A fallen hero shatters into more sharp pieces than you'd believe. Emmy was the one that finally stuck in my throat. I tasted bile in my gullet. Then surprised myself by going inside to collect Maggot. We tailed Rose's pickup out of Woodway.

Before we were back out to 58, rain started slapping the windshield in big fat drops. The Impala needed new wiper blades, but that was far down the list of what that Impala needed. The title transferred out of a dead man's name, for a start. I squinted through the blur, wishing I were a hair more sober, and tried to keep a bead on the red taillights ahead. She turned off the highway sooner than I expected, on Dry Creek Road, which went no place you'd want to be. Not a sensible way to Duffield, but maybe it was like she'd said, his place wasn't there exactly. About a mile in, we came on a stranded pickup halfway blocking the road. She edged around it, but I stopped, because I'd come across that vehicle stalled once before. This time I knew the owner and the damage was repairable. Hammer Kelly, left rear flat.

I rolled down the window and yelled hey. Not sure why rain makes you yell across six feet of distance, but it does. Poor Hammer, a drowned cat could not have looked more pitiful. Rain dripping off his nose, white T-shirt soaked like a second skin so his nipples and chest hair showed through. He pushed the wet flop of hair out of his eyes and stared at us, and I saw he was not a sober man. He had tools out but seemed stuck as far as next steps. I got out, assuming Rose would go on and leave us. She must have been watching her rear view, because she backed up.

I yelled at her that we'd have to make it some other time. But she said no, she'd wait, because how long could it take for three stooges to change one tire. It was quickly down to one stooge. I sent Hammer looking for something to wedge the tires on the opposite side, which he did, while I set the jack. But then Maggot yelled for him to come get in the Impala, and he did.

I could see Maggot getting out the goods in there. Of all casualties of the Emmy/Fast Forward disaster, the sorriest one was Hammer. He'd said he wasn't going to get over her, and was keeping his word. Getting ripped with him had become one of our pastimes, to the point of Hammer being one woeful, weepy shitfaced fucker. The guy did not hold his liquor. The downside to his keeping so much on the straight and narrow through his formative years: no conditioning. I'd warned Maggot against getting him into anything stronger, at least till he got his training wheels off. But at that moment while I was pulling the lug nuts off his flat, I saw him snorting crank from the dash of my Impala. Rose saw it too. She never missed a trick.

I was unthrilled to be out there by myself changing Hammer's tire in a frog-strangling rain, and coming to understand why this was called Dry Creek Road. It was a creek bed. Not dry at this time. Muddy water gushed all around me and under the car, getting me worried about whether the jack would hold. I got the tire off and the spare on, lickety-split, but then, goddamn it to hell, the lug nuts. I'd set them out in a neat line right next to the hubcap, as you do. Now they were nowhere, and the hubcap was bobbing away like a fucking duck. I got frantic, cursing the rain, feeling around with both hands under the rushing water, trying to find lug nuts in the wet rolling gravel. *Shit, shit, shit, shit.* I was aggravated to the point of murder. Threw open the door of the Impala and yelled for them both to get out there and help me find the fucking lug nuts. But even if any of us had been sober, it was a lost cause. Like noodling for crawdads. Our chance of finding crawdads actually in that mess would have been better.

We ended up having to abandon Hammer's truck. He could come back later with fresh nuts and a clear head. At the last second, he remembered to go back and get his rifle off the rack in his truck. Probably the firearm had more value than the vehicle. I told Rose we were taking Hammer home, but she said we were only a couple of miles from Fast Forward's so we could stop there on our way and dry out, smoke a joint to calm our nerves, etc. Then she took off, throwing a wake like a speedboat. Hammer lived in Duffield. I wasn't entirely sure where we were, only that I should get the hell out of that roaring creek, so I followed Rose. Hammer was in the back seat, in no way clued in to our plan. He and Fast Forward had only ever met one time, as far as I knew, at June's party. That brief shiny moment of Emmy belonging to Hammer, before she was stolen away. I remembered Fast Forward afterward laughing with Mouse, calling Hammer a chucklehead knuckle dragger. Nothing good could come from a reintroduction. The last sober shreds of my brain were saying this: Go home.

And for the thousandth time in a month I answered back: Go home where, to what person? Useless fuck that I am, who cares. The night I'd found Dori, I hate to say, some part of me was relieved, thinking now I wouldn't have to worry every minute about her dying. I thought I'd be better off without the fear. I was so wrong. Even with nothing else good left between us, that dread made me a person still attached to another person. Nobody needed me anywhere now.

The rain got worse. I'd never seen the like. We turned onto a side road that was not a running river, but the windshield was blinded out. I saw the faint red glow of Rose's lights pulling over and I did the same, thinking she meant to wait out the blitz. Then her lights went out and I saw the outline of Rose running from her truck towards the outline of a house, and next thing I knew, Maggot was out and running for it too. We all went. The car felt like a fishbowl we could drown in. We got to the porch and somebody let us in.

Rose had said the house of "some lady," and I'd thought, housedress, rent check. Nope. Her name was Temple, total and complete hotcake. Short shorts, long blond hair. No love lost between her and Rose, that was plain to see. But she made over us guys like rescue pups, went and got towels, made hot coffee, set us up in the living room with her bong that was a hippie pottery type of thing. It turned out she made these herself. Interesting lady, interesting house. Big old place, not a whole lot of furniture. Maybe they'd just moved in together. I thought of the Emmy wreckage, and wondered how long he'd take to chew this pretty girl up and spit her out. She and Rose discussed something in code which obviously was drug business, and Temple said he wasn't there, he'd gone out driving with Big Bear Howe and some other guys. She hadn't gone with them because it was boring as hell, those boys never talked about a thing other than football. And I thought, Huh, maybe there's hope for this one. She said Fast Forward was still catching up with his homeboys since moving back to Generals territory. They'd gone over to this place on the river they always liked to go, Devil's Bathtub.

My stomach did a somersault over those words. Over behind the bong, Hammer's eyebrows went high, late to the party but finally catching on to who we were discussing. Rose said it was a hell of a day to go swimming. Temple said for sure, but it had been pretty as a picture that morning, these summer storms could just blow up out of nowhere. True, all that.

Hammer stood up, knocking over an empty coffee

cup, and said we needed to go. Temple was a little shocked, reaching for the cup. She said we were welcome to wait out the storm. And he said, "We're going now." Just like that, the whole lifetime of Hammer, polite, bashful boy loved by all, for always doing just what they asked, was over.

58

It seemed like the storm might let up. But whatever of it was left, we were driving straight into, headed east into Scott County on a no-name gravel road. Hammer didn't believe this was my first time at Devil's Bathtub, and got in his head I was lying about it. He'd been here time and again with this or that batch of Peggots and was sure I was too. Maggot knew better and kept quiet. They both kept saying this is the road, keep going. Hammer meant to hunt down Fast Forward and have it out. Hammer on meth was a whole new man, cradling his rifle in the back seat with the air of a person in charge, and there's no way I was taking that man home right now. He lived with his stepmom Ruby and her daughter Jay Ann that had her new baby. The Peggots had a deep bench. They would blame me for this and skin me alive.

He and Maggot were passing a handle of gin between the front and back seat, another last-minute save from Hammer's truck. If he'd started it that morning, I was impressed to see Hammer conscious. Maggot was putting a good hurt on the remainder. I mostly passed, on principles. Being the driver. Best to keep the blood alcohol in the mid to upper teens.

I don't think they saw the dark clouds up ahead, in any full sense. I was steering us into combat. Hammer's case was clear-cut. Fast Forward stole his woman, and disrespected the goods. And he'd not even seen Emmy after Atlanta, he had no real idea of the damage. I'd go to my grave with the picture in my head of those half-naked girls on their filthy mattress, like somebody's thrown-away Barbie dolls. Not even human. Whatever happened down there had knocked the shine off Emmy, maybe forever. Her and June both. Emmy was never my girl, I was not the avenger here, but even still I was getting an itch in my fist, for a certain cocksure jaw.

That itch grew by the mile. The woods got deep and the road narrowed and I was gearing down and accelerating both at once, to take the steep uphill snake of curves in this rutted gravel track. Driving took more concentration than I had, but my brain was still bouncing around. Fast Forward at Creaky Farm. Squad inspections. That bully getting up in the faces of Tommy and Swap-Out till they nearly pissed themselves. And me acting like I didn't see. He was never anything but a total rectum to either one of them, and Tommy was so tenderhearted, feeling it all. Taking the stick for our so-called protector, every time. That self-centered prick. Making me his bitch. The goodness of Tommy, even after all that, the friend he was to me now. With any luck we wouldn't find Fast Forward. Because if we did, there would be blood.

We weren't dressed for any category of damn Sunday frolic in this pounding rain, and were cursing each other out from the time we got out of the car. I told Hammer to leave the rifle, on the argument of it getting rain damaged, in actual fact more concerned over the homicide aspects. But Hammer was not parting from his everloving Marlin 336C. I pressed the point, and he yelled at me that it was waxed and blued and what the hell did I think the pioneers did whenever it fucking rained? Maggot took a couple steps backward, to see our golden retriever boy go all fierce like that. Shit. Hammer on crank, tiger in the tank.

It turned out we hadn't parked in the best place. We

walked maybe a mile up a dirt road before we even got to the trail for Devil's Bathtub. I was debating between this being a flirtation with disaster or just an ignorant goose chase leading to three baked guys getting sopping wet. And then we saw the Lariat. Parked at a steep tilt up a bank, nobody's idea of a parking spot, as close to the start of a trail as a vehicle could get. None of us said a word.

Hammer led the way on the trail, and I went last, watching the rifle barrel nodding over Hammer's shoulder and the ponytail straggling down Maggot's back. (His haircutter Martha was long gone.) Suddenly it felt some high percentage of insane to be out here in the woods on this half-cooked Fast Forward bear hunt. I walked back in my brain to where the day turned: Rose Dartell. Pizza delivery to East Jesus freaking Woodway? It had to be a setup. She always knew where Fast Forward was, and it was easy enough to know where I was. It looked purposeful, Fast Forward using his lackey Rose to lure me to this place he knew I never wanted to be. To what purpose, was the question. Hammer and his Marlin 336C getting thrown into the mix, that was nobody's plan. We needed to turn around.

But Hammer was walking fast, less drunk than I thought, or a lot more cranked. My knee was hurting like the devil. Messed-up bones get aggravated by un-settled weather and walking on uneven ground. Jack-pot. We came to a creek with the trail running straight through it. No way was I wading through rushing water over slick rocks on my wobbly legs. I yelled at the guys that I couldn't do this. Hammer laughed and splashed right in and yelled back that this was crossing number one, there were ten more. Maybe thirteen. "Make like you've got the ball and run for the end zone, star man," he yelled, and I thought: He has been pissed at me for years, and holding it in. Pissed at the whole lot of us bad boys and adult-avoiders that let him do the hard part.

I pushed myself into the water.

The second crossing was faster and deeper than the first, and on from there it went. Maggot said he'd never seen it like this before. Normally it was a trickle, this was a flash flood. I had to go on hands and knees at times, feeling for footholds in the rushing water, everything slick and wobbly under there and me in my soaked, heavy jeans. The bones inside my knee were grinding like a bad transmission. Hammer and Maggot waded ahead of me with sturdy strides, or they balanced and hopped from rock to rock, and it choked me up to watch them use their bodies that way, without a thought. Something I'd probably lost for good.

I yelled and yelled at Maggot to wait up, but he'd taken his shirt off and wrapped that and his ponytail around his head like a turban, for reasons only a Maggot brain could know, and didn't hear me. Hammer I couldn't even see anymore.

I started looking for an escape hatch from all the water, but options were slim. Drown, or fly. Cliffs rose on both sides of the trail, walls of layered rock like giant sandwiches piled with their hard black ham and cheese. Down here it was all woods and creek, and up on top of the cliffs, more woods, deep and dark. Pines and laurel slicks, poison mushrooms, pillows of moss.

I would have turned around then, if not for two guys that came running down the path towards me. Not Hammer, not Maggot. They were shirtless and shoeless, carrying their bundled wet clothes and running in that dicey crisscrossed way people do over rocky ground, whooping. At each other or the rain or the windmills of their minds, whoop-whoop. I recognized them from the days of dragging Main and Fast Forward trotting me out to meet his former General brothers. One had the praying hands tattoo on his shoulder. They stopped whooping and yelled at me that my friends were up ahead. Thanks, guys. I thought they might have raptured.

"Yeah, okay," I said. "Is Fast Forward with you?"

"He's still back at the waterfall," the one said, and Praying Hands clarified that it was two of them still back there, Fast Forward and Big Bear. And I said, Where goest the QB, there goes his left tackle, and they laughed and said, Yeah, still married, those two. Praying Hands was squinting at me through his wet eyelashes.

"I've seen you on the field, right? You used to be like a backup receiver or something, years ago. Cornerback?"

I didn't have the heart to go into it. Plus, this bee was in my brain about it being a trap laid by Fast Forward, versus pure accidental nightmare pileup of bad choices. I asked what made them come swimming on a day like this. They said four guys with shit for brains are stupider than one, and laughed like that was the best joke ever, which it wasn't. It's a well-known fact. Signs pointing to accidental nightmare pileup.

I couldn't get a lot more out of them. Only that Fast Forward was still messing around at the waterfall, wanting to climb some ridiculous rock face. First he'd stripped naked and said he was going to dive in, which was madness, it was too much flood for swimming. Then he started climbing the cliff. They got fed up with him peacocking his ass around and were going back to the truck where they had dry dope. Fast Forward stayed, and Big Bear wouldn't leave him.

Ever-faithful Big Bear. They invited me to come with them to the land of dry dope, and believe me the call was strong. But Maggot and Hammer were out in this mess. I'd spent half my life trying to save Maggot from his nonsense, and now we'd gotten Hammer tangled up in it. I was the responsible party.

I finally caught up to them, even though it came down to scooting on my butt. The last stretch of trail was no more than a slick, butt-wide track in the damn cliff face above the roaring creek. Then it took me a second to understand this was it, I was there. Maggot was sitting on the bank ahead of me, rocking, holding his big wet shirt-wrapped head in his hands. Hammer was screaming. Standing on a rock with the water roaring around him like some type of Moses shit, the rifle still slung over his shoulder aimed at the sky, not a person, thank God. But Hammer himself was cocked, ready to go off. I saw nobody else around, no Big Bear, no Fast Forward, and couldn't get why he was screaming his lungs out at this roaring bathtub of hell. Of all the tubs I'd feared in my day, none came close. This was a giant round hole carved out of smooth rock, maybe forty feet across, with water pouring in. A long, high waterfall at the back end was spraying at us full blast down a long stone chute like a freaking waterslide. But water also flooded in from the sides and roiled around in the hole like a giant washing machine. A rope swing dangled above the roar, suggesting happier times where this was a place to swim. Right now you wouldn't wish it on your dirty clothes. And into that madness, Hammer was pouring all the hate he could get out of his lungs, *Fucking asshole you're not good enough to touch a hair on her head you don't deserve to breathe the same air you fucking animal.*

The animal was Fast Forward. It took me that long to work out there was a waterfall here *above* the waterfall. And high above that on the cliff stood the spectacle of him, naked, sure enough. The dark wet mop of hair and ripped abs and pubes and dick, that careless showoff attitude of body-flaunting that comes out of years in a locker room. He was a lean, pale slash balanced high over us in the dark woods. Behind him, black trees and sky and thunder having its war around us. I wondered if his friends had run off with his clothes, but no, I saw the jeans and shirt down below in a wet pile. He'd stripped, probably just peacocking like they said and not really planning to swim, and then got excited about something to mount.

Hammer was not letting up. I edged over to Maggot, scared out of my mind. I could lose my footing and slide in. I squatted next to him and leaned close. "What's going on?"

"Hammer said to get his naked ass down here because he had a crow to pick. And then *he* said the girl wasn't worth either of their trouble. He was trash-talking Emmy up there."

Shit.

Hammer carried on screaming, and Fast Forward ruled in silence, standing above us with his head cocked back in his everlasting question: *Is that all you've got?* I couldn't see Hammer's face but his body was shaking, hands and arms. From the cold, from the crank wearing off, from the pin pulled out of the Hammer grenade. Maggot leaned towards me till our shoulders touched.

"Remember that dog Stoner had? How he'd shake meat in its face to get it in a rage?"

"Hammer's not Satan," I said. I had to believe it. Frothing at the mouth at this moment, but not a killer. I spoke to him the way I would talk to a dog, saying his name as level as I could, over and over. *Hammer. Chill out man. Hammer. He's got nothing. This will be okay. Hammer. We're getting out of here. Hammer.* But there was so much sound, the roaring falls and thunder. My own blood rushing my ears. I have no idea what Hammer heard. If he heard me at all.

What happened in the next ten seconds is so clear in my head. Hammer looking back at us, then shifting his weight. Losing his balance I thought, but no, just slinging that heavy rifle off his shoulder and lifting it in both hands. Then, the red flag of a shirt appearing out of the woods way off to the right of Fast Forward. A person, big, scared, nowhere and then there, just in time to see the man and the rifle and scream, "Drop! Fucker's going to take you out!"

The terror in that voice is what did it. Coming from Big Bear, steadfast guard of his blind side. Nothing we could have done would have rattled Fast Forward, not words or even gunfire, but that voice warning him from offsides jolted the naked QB a quarter turn, enough to lose his footing and start to slide. The coordinated body going for its longest shot, center of gravity automatically dropping, arms close in, knees in a half crouch, Jesus, the terrible beauty of it, and then he lost control. As a rolling ball of limbs he could have saved himself, bones and flesh flailing down that slope of rock onto more rock, maybe a branch to break the fall, it would have been ugly and might have worked, but pride in the end made the call. He opened and pushed off in a dive, piked, head down, arms open, a reach for the water, fumbled. The contact sounded not very different from a watermelon on pavement.

After that, I don't know. I must have tried to get to Hammer and hold him back. Big Bear was still up in the cliffs. And Fast Forward, across the water from us, was a naked nothing facedown on rock. Legs in the water, one thigh-deep and the other slung out, submerged to the knee. An ugly arrangement of limbs he would not have allowed in life. That's how I knew. All the magic that made him had gone out of him. And Hammer now was yelling at *me*. His face was a flat wall of shock and he was talking about the rifle, saying he was just going to put it down. *Jesus, did he think I was going to shoot? I wasn't going to shoot, I was laying it down, I was going to climb up there. Jesus, Demon.* Saying it was his fault, saying the guy was hurt, sliding in over there, unconscious, we had to get him back from the water. I told Hammer to stay where he was. I could see more of the broken head I think than the others.

But Hammer was having no dead men here. He couldn't let that be. He said it three times, maybe four, I'm not letting a man die, and then he was in the water while Maggot and I screamed no and no and no. No to all of it. Hammer in that white roar like an explosion and the rest of us losing everything, time, hope, our frothing wrecked minds. He was close to these rocks he'd jumped off of, and then he wasn't. His head and shoulders bobbed up out of the water, went down, and came up again, once I saw Hammer's eyes open wide, straight at me, he came up and then he didn't. We heard thunder, far away. And then Big Bear was there with us, he'd gotten down the slope and across some way, he must have run back downstream to a place he could get over because now he was here, panting like a wild animal. All of us making those kinds of noises, howling at the water and death and Hammer, begging him to show up again.

He did, on the rocks downstream. I saw his white T-shirt down there, the broad back, legs pummeled by the current. The push of the water was slowly turning his long body like a compass needle, from sideways to straight downstream, aligned with its terrible force.

The other body didn't move. The naked one. I made myself look, and it must have scarred my eyes because I can still see every goddamn line of it, the unnatural angle of arm, the smooth, hard quads, glutes like a pair of onions. The well-oiled machine he'd worked so hard to keep, a long time after it really mattered. What a waste, a dead body, with most of its parts still ready and eager to work. The final humiliation of a man, that last layoff.

There was no arguing about who would go for help. Maggot and Big Bear could pound the trail and the crossings, double time. There was somebody's phone in the Lariat. They could drive out and find a signal.

The emergency rescue team that arrived, because in time it did, close to nightfall on the longest of all my days, would bring three stretchers. One for each of the bodies, one for me. I was reported among the casualties. I did the hard part, staying behind.

As soon as they were gone, I edged myself over to the Marlin and kicked it down the devil's damn throat. It sank like the carbon steel pipe it was. All the careful hours Hammer spent waxing and bluing that piece, what a waste. I actually thought that. A blown brain will reach for any sideshow to dodge the main event. The rifle had played no real part, but a weapon hanging around these situations never helps, so. I kicked that one down the road.

With the Marlin drowned, I scooted back down the cliff path to a spot where I could crab-walk over boulders to the other side. Then made my way to the gravel shoal where I could drag Hammer onto dryer land. All I could see were the years that body still had in it, *should* have had. For all the people that counted on his help. For finding some sweet girl to have his kids. He would have been the best imaginable dad. All the Hammer I could see, backs of his arms, hands, the back of his neck, was the color of carbon steel. I made myself feel his wrist. The flesh felt too hard, not human anymore. Like if a pulse had even been in there, it wouldn't get through. Dead bodies are nothing new to me, I kept telling myself. This is no hill for a climber. My mom in her white casket. Dori in our bed. I'd sat alone with Dori for over an hour before I let the rest of the world come. But however heartbroken I'd been that day, I knew Dori was where she needed to be. Hammer was not. This was a body robbed of all its righteous goods.

I hauled the waterlogged bulk out of the water, then stopped to take off my shirt and slip it under his head because I didn't want his face sanded off by the dragging. Mrs. Peggot would have to see him. June, Ruby, all of them. I had to save his face. Eventually I got him over to the same stone ledge where the other body was. Hammer's enemy. I hated them being on the same rock, once I had him there. By no means laid out side by side, still ten feet apart, but even that was too close. It felt like the one might contaminate the other. Different materials.

I didn't have the guts to turn them faceup. I knew their eyes would be open, and it felt possible they might watch me huddled up on that ledge, choking out pieces of lung, it felt like, such was my rage and grief and stupid regret. I think I knew, even then, such things are not survivable. For any of us. Nobody could have seen what was coming next for Maggot. But I'd spent enough seasons on the field to know what Big Bear was in for. The peace he might never make with himself. All because he had to take a piss. He'd gone up into the woods and got lost. Beat around the laurel hells, then emerged at a crazy wrong moment. Followed his best instincts to the worst of all possible ends.

I should have been the one to jump in the water. If it had to be done, then me, not Hammer. I'll never believe anything else. It's the one good promise I ever got. Not drowning.

59

The world had turned some by the time they got us all out. The sheriff drove over to tell Ruby in person. Hammer's dad would have to be called, wherever he lived. Texas. Maggot called June, and she drove over to tell Mrs. Peggot. Fast Forward had no next of kin, so I can't say who got the call, but Rose Dartell was waiting beside the Lariat to see him come down the trail. She went crazy and threw herself on the men she thought were carrying him, but they actually had Hammer. The bodies were well wrapped up.

Rose seemed not to realize one of the stretchers was me. My face wasn't covered but they had a thermal blanket over me, so I passed for a body. The first responder that carried my head end was named Nathan. Rock-solid guy, talked me down from the spookiness of being strapped in like that, levitating over rocky ground and roaring water. Embarrassing. I wasn't technically injured, just a lot worse for wear. They had two ambulances, and Nathan said I was going into one of them, period. They were duty bound to send me to the hospital and get me treated for exposure. I didn't know what all that entailed. I definitely had been exposed to some shit.

Both bodies went in the other ambulance. Different timetables, no rush on those guys. So Hammer had to take his last ride with the bastard that stole his woman and ruined his life. I was sick over that, and shaken up, and trying to get my keys to somebody that could drive my Impala out of there. That was the point where Rose figured out I was body number three and came at me, screaming while they were loading me into the ambulance. Banging her flat hands on the windows after I was inside. They had to pull her off the vehicle.

Maggot rode with me in the ambulance, both of us shaking hard, coming down from our different places. He slipped me a Xanax to tide me over. Then after I got to the hospital, what do you know, the nurse asked me for my pain number and brought me an oxy in a little frilly white paper cup. VIP service. God bless her. She said they were keeping me overnight for observing, but I did very little worth watching. Drank a gallon or so of Gatorade, put a very similar output in a plastic measuring cup. I did such an excellent job with my pain numbers, they doped me out for a cracking good night's sleep. Easiest test I ever aced.

In the morning a different nurse checked on me, and said I had a visitor. Was I up for seeing my sister, she wanted to know, and my heart jumped up, thinking that would be Angus. Shit. It was Rose. All set to go hunting, from the look of her. Camo pants, black windbreaker. She pushed back the hood and hissed at me: "Fucking murderer."

I hit the nurse button to report an impostor, but they must have had people around there to save. Rose strode back and forth, in dire need of a cigarette, I could tell. After about ten trips around the room she shucked off her rain jacket and dumped herself into the La-Z-Boy they had for visitors. "Tell me exactly what happened," she said.

"Sounds like you've already got your version worked out."

"Where's the rifle," she asked.

I said what rifle, and reminded her nobody got shot. Terrible accident, period.

She jumped up and started pacing again. I had cravings of my own, to go anyplace on earth other than back there in my head. It was easy enough here in the hospital, complete other world that it is. Clean as a whistle, all the drugs without the dark underbelly. I'd only ever been in the waiting room part of a hospital before, waiting for a stomach to get pumped. In here it was crowded and empty, clean and smelly, all at once. Pine-Sol, locker room, traces of pee. Rose had her own smell, flinty and sour with cigarette smoke, like she'd been pacing like this all night.

"I need to know exactly how it happened," she said. "How it was for him at the end."

I was too woozy for a fight. I told the truth, but just the point plays, like a football game recap. He climbed up a high cliff. Big Bear yelled and surprised him. He slipped and fell.

"Why would Big Bear do that?"

"Why don't you ask him?"

"Because he's gone over to Turp Trussell's and drank himself into a coma."

I suggested she should do the same. She stared at me. Then shook her head and looked out the window. There wasn't any view, just gray sky and clouds. I could hear the cackly gossip of some crows outside, making their deals on the roof somewhere close by.

"That wasn't the way it was supposed to happen," she finally said.

"What the hell does that mean? You've got it all written out, how everybody dies?"

She went on staring at me until I felt my feet and hands go cold.

"Son of a bitch. You're saying it was planned. You knew he was not at the house. What the *fuck*, Rose? I never wanted to go to the Devil's damn Bathtub. I mean *never*, in my life."

"It wasn't supposed to turn into Noah's goddamn ark."

"*Why?* He knew I hated that place."

She shrugged her skinny shoulders. But he did. Stoned boys tell their secrets, and Fast Forward had long known mine. I tried to get more out of her, what the hell he'd wanted from me, some proof-of-manhood thing, facing down my father's death, nothing there made any sense, and she wasn't giving it up. Maybe she didn't know. None of us ever would, now.

"You guys screwed it up by bringing Hammer," is all she would say. Then she jumped up to pace around some more. Interrogation over. She went to the other side of the room and nosed around without touching anything. They had somebody else in the room with me, hidden behind a brown curtain, but I'd heard zero out of them all night. Another dead body, for all I knew.

Rose came back and dropped into the chair. "You all are accessories to a death."

"He fell, Rose. Climbed too high for his own good, end of story."

"Not him. I mean Hammer."

"What are you talking about?"

"The deceased had taken illegal drugs. Supplied to him by you."

"You weren't even there. Get over yourself."

"Oh, I saw. Earlier in the day."

I made myself sort back through it. Okay, that. "You saw me helping a stranded motorist."

"I saw him hoovering meth in your Camaro."

I laughed out loud. "Star witness, doesn't know an Impala from a Camaro."

"Whatever." She chewed on her thumbnail, watching the door. "I know what I saw. If you're the supplier of drugs and somebody dies, it's a felony. I know that for a fact."

"What you saw was me out in the rain trying to change my friend's tire. If anybody goes looking, they'll find a drug in Hammer that I haven't touched but once in eighth grade. Anybody around here can back that up, so don't try lying. Just leave me out of it."

I rolled over and turned my back on her. I'd heard

of this, about supplying drugs to somebody that gets in trouble. The trouble being in this case death. She had nothing on me, but she could nail Maggot. I felt rage building up in my gut. She didn't leave. Nobody came to take my temperature. It came down to whether I could hold off exploding longer than Rose could go without nicotine. I lost. I sat up and yelled at her. "Why do you have to kick the fucking hornet's nest? You think the Peggots aren't punished enough? Hammer died trying to fucking save that snake-assed bastard. You want to cry over him, knock yourself out. But you're not good enough to clean Hammer's shoes." She sat through all this with no expression at all. Asked if I was done. Said this was not about Hammer, it was about the rest of us. She'd lost everything, and now she had to make sure we all knew how that felt. And *then* she got emotional, pulling out wads of Kleenex and blowing her nose. She said losing Fast Forward was like dying herself.

I tried to pull up the sheet. They had me wearing a stupid dress thing with snaps. "For fuck's sake, Rose. Look how he treated you. He was cruel to everybody that ever knew him."

She said I didn't understand him. But I did. Fast Forward had a beautiful poison inside him that infected people and got them hooked. I told her it was bound to end this way because Fast Forward was a dangerous animal, and they aren't known to have long lives.

Rose didn't deny that. But she could have been the one to save him. She looked straight at me with her wrecked face full of tears and madness and swore that's what she believed. That the scar he'd put on her was his way of making sure Rose would belong to him for life.

I'd watched Hammer Kelly die, and now I had to see it all over again with every Peggot that came through the door saying, Lord, it can't be true, having to hear that it was. I dreaded coming back from the hospital to face the family. But I understood. They needed somebody alive to tell the tale. They were grateful, and didn't blame me, and we all agreed there would be no getting over this. Hammer was the Peggots' MVP.

June came to stay with us at Mrs. Peggot's, padding around all week in her gray sweatpants, making coffee, making soup beans, running a hand over her mother's rumpled head. Mrs. Peggot sat dazed at the kitchen table. The rest of the family rolled back and forth in waves between the Peggot house, which was home base, and Ruby's, where he'd lived. They couldn't plan a funeral, still waiting for final say from Hammer's Texas relatives as to where the body was to end up. Hammer's dad hadn't visited in an age, and we'd pretty much forgotten about him having blood kin. But that's who holds the cards in the end. The Peggots were stuck, not able to move forward with the normal death matters of cooking and drinking. It was all just loose ends and talk. Like if they hashed through it enough times, they might get to a different ending.

Maggot went upstairs and got cooked for the duration, so it was entirely on me to get this story on the family's books. It's a lot of responsibility. I did my best, save for a few details held back. We were not avengers on the trail of Fast Forward. There was no handle of gin, no meth. The Marlin he must have left in his truck, possibly stolen. It was by pure chance we happened on Hammer with his flat tire. Lost lug nuts, those made it into the story. Plenty here is true. We stopped by the house of an acquaintance to dry off, and heard that some friends had gone over to Devil's Bathtub. Why not join them, ridiculous weather and all, boys will be boys, etc.

What matters in a story is the heart of its hero. With no thought for his own safety, Hammer dived in to save the young man that fell from the cliff. True. Always and forever true. I couldn't change that if I wanted to, and oh I did. We all did. My story left us wishing Hammer had been born with a selfish heart to keep him alive. Which made us remorseful and in awe of his goodness. That was the comfort I could give the Peggots.

Rose had no place in this story. I left her out. As far as her plan of ratting out Maggot for getting Hammer high before he died, I listened but heard nothing about police involvement or drug-testing any bodies. So I didn't even tell Maggot. Maybe her threats had no teeth.

For over a month now I'd been sleeping in Maggot's top bunk, and it had been pretty much like the sleepovers of our numbskull boyhood days, with better drugs. Mrs. Peggot had the habit of leaving the TV on all the time, ever since Mr. Peg died, for the company she said, and I got used to that. But after Devil's Bathtub, everything changed. The house was full of people, and the TV drone made my skin crawl, for the random weirdness of a perky voice in the living room plugging Tokyopop and cucumber-scented shaving cream. Ronald Reagan's funeral, Jesus. They showed bird's-eye views of the crowded streets, a million people boohooing over this famous old prune that lived a whole lot of years past firing on any or all of his pistons. More years than he needed, is what I'm saying. Salt in our wounds. Just a weird mix, TV and real life. Two or more women are sobbing their guts out at the kitchen table, while Everett sprawls on the couch watching the

US Open. Like golf is even a watchable sport, that anybody we know has ever played.

A major topic among the women was Emmy. With
half of them saying she needed to be told. Meaning: That
girl needs to feel good and sick over leaving Hammer
such a mess. The ringleaders here being the Jay Ann and
Ruby branch that spent years telling Hammer to give up
his hopeless quest, Emmy was never going to have him.
And then, after the shortest romance of all times, were
never forgiving her for walking away and busting the
guy's heart. They wanted payback. I thought about what
Rose said, wanting to see the rest of us hurt, because
she was hurting. You have to wonder how much of the
whole world's turning is fueled by that very fire.

The other side of this argument: No real rush on
telling Emmy that Hammer is dead, because he'll still
be dead next year. Emmy was on lockdown and would
not be let out for any funeral, if there even was to be a
real one, i.e. not in Texas. The whole business could
wait until Emmy was sturdier with her sobriety. This
was June's opinion. June being the only person on the
planet that Emmy was allowed to have contact with, so.
There was no argument.

It was hard for me to believe in a cure for what happened to Emmy. Never had I seen a person fall so far.

This place she'd been sent sounded like prison, and it's well known that prison cures nothing. Other than for the people that got hurt and are wanting to see others hurt, as mentioned. No getting out, even for a funeral? No phone calling anybody other than your mom? Even Mariah got more than that, in Goochland. But June seemed pretty cheerful about it. She showed me pictures, and it looked amazing, mountains and trees, castle type buildings, a lake. Horses. Great wide mowed yards with girls sitting around on the grass, being sweet to each other no doubt. Pictures didn't make me believe. There are no roads from here to there.

A snake with venom is going to bite. That's just one of the rules God wrote down for us. Rose didn't go away. Mrs. Peggot got a letter from the courts. I was there. I watched June read it, set it down on the table, and leave the house. The deaths were being investigated. The police had information about Matthew Peggot supplying illegal substances to one of the deceased, approximately three hours prior to the fatal accident. Nobody was saying murder, it was an accident. But Maggot was possibly looking at criminal charges, accessory to the death.

"Two boys dead already," June said, before walking

out the door, "and they think sending one more to prison is going to help a damn thing? God how I hate this world."

Hate it or not, June always came back. That particular day, after a three-hour drive to God knows where. She'd kept going into her clinic all this time, because sickness goes on, the need over there was dire. Soon she'd move back to her own house. But she was the head of the family now. She would lead the charge this time on getting lawyered up for Maggot.

The story of Romeo and Mariah was just legend to me: his terrible abuse, her X-Acto knife revenge, the alligator-boots lawyer that had tricked the jury and got Maggot's mom locked up. Now we watched it play out again, the Peggots back in that swamp, June determined to get them out alive. I knew Mrs. Peggot had her cross to bear over Mariah, but hadn't thought how it must have been for June all these years. After letting her sister down. Ruby at first was upset about Maggot giving Hammer drugs, but June was not going to let this tear the family apart. And Maggot's contribution was being barely too young or damaged or all the above to stand trial as an adult. Never did a household thank their God so joyfully for having a juvenile in their midst. His court date was set for the same month Mariah was due to get out.

I wouldn't be around for it. The day before June went back home, she called me upstairs and laid down the cards. She could get me into a Suboxone clinic. No probing questions as to what I was on, she wasn't beating around the bush. Not her clinic, this wouldn't happen here. Nor Asheville, there was no money for such. But she could reenroll me in Medicaid, a simple thing that none of my guardians had thought to do since Miss Barks dumped me. It would cover me in a rehab clinic for a couple of weeks. Nothing fancy, just to get me over the worst, and after that I could go into a halfway-house situation. All I could picture was half of a house with the front ripped off, exposing the chairs and bathroom fixtures inside.

June and I were in the little dormer room that had a twin bed and a low, peaked roof over the window. It had girl wallpaper from back in the day, and a window bench they called the catbird seat. Mrs. Peggot had made a cushion for it with all the kinds of birds. One of my oldest memories was sitting there watching Mom outside smoking on our deck. This week it was June's room again. Her things were all around, shoes, hair-brush, the fruit shampoo smell I'd loved since I fell for Emmy in fourth grade. I was in the catbird seat, and June was sitting on the bed, explaining my life to me. She brought up the social security money I could use after I turned eighteen. She could help me out until then, if need be, and the halfway house would involve a job. Nothing interesting, probably loading boxes in a warehouse, the idea being just to keep busy.

"It's all work and no play, for a while," she said, tucking her foot up under her on the bed. She was in her doctor clothes, ready to go in to work, but still barefoot. "The deal in these halfway houses is you can go to your job, and then you come straight back. No running around. Your friends are all other people in recovery. It's the best way to make it stick."

I sat letting her words happen, smelling her fruit, and it hit me between the eyes: It was always June. This thing I'd had for the Knoxville women, aka dome house women. All along June, never Emmy, not past the puppy love. This was the full-throttle type love that I never got figured out properly, due to being raised in shotgun fashion. What my twisted little raggedy heart had always, always wanted. A mother, simple as that.

I asked her why me, why not Maggot. She had her reasons. Meth addiction is tough, no medical remedy. She said with opioids you can swap out the bad one for a different one that won't get you high, but you won't be dopesick either. Just take a pill and get on with your life.

"Right," I said. Not mentioning the part about wanting sum-total obliteration of your life.

"I would do anything for Matthew, you know that. But rehab is something a person has to do on their own two feet, and he's not ready."

I sat on my two hands to keep from fidgeting. Wanting a little bump of something, so very very much. Maggot wasn't ready, and I was? She said she and Mrs. Peggot had their doubts on Maggot ever taking responsibility, he just wasn't cut out that way. So it would have to be somebody else making him stick to the program. Not voluntary. Meaning the law. They'd been waiting for that, assuming an arrest or a good scare was what it would take. "We thought a shoplifting charge," she said, shaking her head. "Not that somebody would have to die." She got kind of emotional then, but told me not to blame myself. She said there were a hundred people she could blame for what happened that day, and Maggot and I were not even on the list.

"I had my part in it," I said. "We all kind of lost our minds."

She looked at me like there was something written on my face that she was trying to read. "For God's sake, Damon. It's the same place your father died. You didn't start this fire."

I felt rage boiling up. My ears were ringing and I wanted to scream: *Yes*. It's the place I hate the most, and that's why I got lured out there. That's the mother-fucking deal I get. I turned away from her and looked outside at the deck where my blondie teenager mom used to light every cigarette off the last one. She saved all the Pall Mall coupons to get us free stuff. Once, a radio that looked like a jukebox. It was mostly plastic and quit working after a couple of months and I thought it was made by God's own hands.

Some minutes passed. June was not letting this go. "It's not *natural* for boys to lose their minds," she said. "It happens because they've had too many things taken away from them."

I asked her like what. She got up and walked around the room, upset. No decent schooling, she said. No chance to get good at anything that uses our talents. No future. They took all that away and supplied us with the tools for cooking our brains, hoping we'd kill each other before we figured out the real assholes are a thousand miles from here.

I told her I didn't hold with that line of reason. I knew plenty of assholes at close range.

She smiled in the sad way I knew well. The hard kid to handle. But instead of leaving, she sat down on the bed again. "The question you have to answer now is, What are you willing to do for yourself? And I won't lie, it's going to be harder than anything you've done before."

I doubted it. Getting smacked around daily for my betterment came to mind. Going hungry for the entirety of fifth grade. Did she think I was looking for a new personal best in the hardships department? I told her it was a lot to take in. I didn't say, *You think I'm strong, but I'm not. I will always want that next hit.*

She said she'd come back over tomorrow, and we'd talk some more.

I asked where all this would be happening and she said Knoxville, which freaked me out. Not my idea of happytown. She said it wasn't like I was thinking, not a big apartment building downtown. They have regular houses there, with yards and such. The kind of living situation I'd need would be more on the outskirts, she said. I could get used to it. "You'd have to. Because if you do this, I don't want you coming back here for at least a year."

"A year."

"I know. You can't see it. I couldn't either, I had to leave here, and then come back as kind of a different person." June looked so beautiful and kind. She was killing me.

"What if I like the person I am now?" Said with a straight face, no small trick.

"I'm not saying the problem is you. It's not the drugs either. It's a whole lot of other things that are wrong, and they won't get better as long as you stay here."

A year was not thinkable. Where I would go, who I would be. Damn her. If we were all such a mess, did she think the whole of Lee County should empty itself out? I pictured the long line of cars and pickups backed up on 58. Next in line behind us, our neighbors: Scott County, Russell, Tazewell. Half of Kentucky. Leaving behind empty houses, unharvested fields, half-full beer cans, the squeaky front porch rockers going quiet. Unmilked cows lowing in the pastures, dogs standing forlorn in yards under the maples, watching the masters flee from the spoiled paradise where the world's evils all got sent to roost.

I told her I would think about it. She had to know I was lying.

60

I packed up that same afternoon. The earthly goods were down to a couple of boxes now, I've known homeless guys that had less. Shirts, a spare pair of shoes. Football trophies won by a shiny kid with two excellent knees. I threw those out. I kept the notebooks and art supplies that filled up one whole box, and it weighed on my conscience. I'd been hiding from Tommy. My only real valuables were in bottles, stashed in an old leather shaving case that used to be Mr. Peg's. Maggot had taken it for his stash, then at some point it became mine. I rarely thought twice about using Mr. Peg's nice case for pharmaceutical purposes, but from time to time I felt his eyes on me, seeing the waste of flesh I'd become. Now being one of those times. Maggot was asleep or dipped off. I punched him in the shoulder to tell him I was checking out.

He rolled off the bed onto the floor, a surprisingly smooth move, and lay looking at the ceiling. "Checkout *time*, checkin' it out," he said. Sang actually, some tune I almost recognized.

"Serious, man. I'm going."

He raised his head off the floor and frowned at me in a fuddled way, like some zoo animal had subbed in as roommate while he was napping. Anteater, sawfish. His head dropped back to the floor. "Going where?"

"To be determined. Not really figured it out yet."

"Then don't figure. Saves wear and tear on the haggard brain cells."

"Nope. Can't stay here."

He sat up, drew his knees to his chest, and hugged them with his long arms. Lots of weird jewelry on the hands as well as the face, and still into black, but the Goth vibe was scaled way back. Probably more negligence than fashion choice. He oftentimes didn't smell that great.

"Nothing personal," I said. "You're the easiest person I probably ever cohabited with. Other than the snoring."

He rubbed his face with the back of his hand and watched me stuff underwear in a plastic bag. The black ring that hung down from his septum pierce gave the permanent impression of booger. "Not my fault. It's *adenoids*, brother. I was born this way."

I plopped the underwear bag into a cardboard box, and that was me, over and out on the Peggots. "I have to get out of here before I break something. It's this family. They're so goddamn nice, you end up feeling like you owe them. And then I get really pissed off, because there's no way I can ever get it right or pay it back. You know?"

He gave me a woeful look. He didn't. He wouldn't, ever.

What surprised me was the rage. That it kept coming, in waves. Why? Out on my ass was the normal for me. I'd never yet met the people that could keep me. June was not my mother, regardless the ten or so minutes I almost laid claim to her. She just wanted the better version, not the broken boy I was. Nothing new here under my sun, and yet here was this car and me at the wheel, taking all the curves too fast, hating everything I saw. The kudzu hanging off the trees, the ignorant caboose car in front of Pennington Middle, the bric-a-brac mammaw houses with flamingo birds in their yards. I'd have rammed my car into any one of them, but that would have stopped me, and I needed to keep moving. For the whole afternoon I leaned on my pissed-off heavy foot, because going nowhere fast is a kind of juice.

Then the energy started going out of me and I felt new kind of bad coming on. I stopped on a godforsaken road around Fleenortown to run inventory on Mr. Peg's leather bag and the emergency supplies I kept in the glove box, and took what I needed to stave off the pressure in my chest. That ache was an old, old story and it wasn't ending. In Jonesville I stopped to fill up the tank. If I kept driving I might stay ahead of the monsters. Back in the car, pointed west, I tried to think of one place on the planet of earth where I would feel happy to be. Came up bust. Then tried to settle on someplace I could *stand* to be. Nothing again. No house or vehicle or yard or pasture came to mind. No place. A guy could take this to mean he ought to be dead.

I was in and out, as far as paying any attention to the road. Which can run you into trouble as far as stop signs or speed traps, but we're not big on those here. I ended up way the hell out past Ewing, with no idea I'd gone that far till I noticed the white cliffs on my right side, lining the ridgetop, catching light. I kept on going and there they still were, laughing. *Up here asshole, we're up, you're down.* Those cliffs run on for a hundred miles. My car found the park where Miss Barks brought me, on that fateful day where my brain ran away with itself, thinking of being up there and jumping off to see if I'd fall or fly. And I mean really *seeing* it in my mind, because that's the troublesome brain I have, it's got excellent eyes. Look at him up there. The boy on the edge of the cliff, the widespread arms and piked legs, the crash-dive or the sail. Even before I watched the end of Fast Forward, I don't know how many times my brain had put me up there on those white cliffs, easily a thousand. To ask that question. Which, let's face it, is not a real-world question.

There was nobody around in the gravel lot where the trail started up. The sign said Sand Cave, White Rocks, so many miles. I didn't register details. I'd heard of people hiking up there to that cave, those white rocks. It was doable. I had nothing in mind that would pass for a plan, only the need to move. I left my keys in the car.

Not sure why I thought walking would be any better than driving. It comes down to velocity. This was a business of outrunning ghosts, and there was no end to my dead. Not even counting parents or Mr. Peg. Death of your olders is natural. I was losing people right out from under my living days. My doll baby, that I couldn't love well enough to make her stay. My childhood hero that was a dangerous animal. Hammer that finished last. Maggot that would surely die if they put him in prison, and Mariah on the outside, of heartbreak. I connected my worn-out rubber soles to the dirt of the trail, again, again, again. Knee bones grinding, heart pumping, unthinkable matters battering the skull door. My dad. For him I'd gone to that waterhole of hell, maybe finally to tell the man to go fuck himself, thanks for abandoning me and Mom. Or to prove something. Fast Forward dared me and I went, took the devil's bath and came out with blood on my hands. Where do you go after that? All I knew to do was keep putting my feet to the rocky ground, waiting to register something in the body instead of the brain.

Because I wasn't. Fifteen or so football fields up the trail I understood I wasn't feeling. Not just drug-numb to moods or heartaches, I mean heat, cold. Tasting. That deadness of tongue and skin and eyes that doesn't technically blind you, but you're not seeing. Like the man said, the day I ran out of the pharmacy with my first ticket to oxy-nowhere: *Blind blind blind.* It grows on you till you're darked out and don't care. Something in me was wanting to grind my bones against this mountain till the body picked a side. Give up the ghost, or get back in here.

Eyes on the trail, deer tracks, moss, nothing. I chewed on my age-old grudges. The body is the original asshole, it can put you on detention away from all pleasures, but still makes you write out the list of its needs, one hundred times. I will piss and shit. I will go hungry.

Thirsty was the one killing me at the moment. That parch like a bandanna pulled tight around your throat. It got so bad that the sight of water, a little creek, made me get down on my belly and drink like a dog. The water had taste, sweet. A little piney. People say you'll get a dread disease from doing that, due to all the animals that have pissed in it. I wondered: Do I give a fuck here about dread diseases? I polled the mostly dead players—skin, tongue, eyes—on the subject of checking out on all future days: What if anything would you miss? Came to no real conclusion.

I sat there on the fence about it. On a rock actually. One of those buzzy tiny hummer birds bombed in close. Not to be ignored, this guy. The air from his wings blew the weeds all around under him, like the choppers in the war movies, tiny version. He didn't land, just dipped around sticking his pointy nose into the flowers. The ones he liked were orange and dangly like ornaments, but shaped like little vaginas, lips and all. Go, tiny guy, I said. Eat your fill.

Touch-me-nots. That name popped into my head from another age. They grew all over the banks where we used to go fishing. Mr. Peg showed us how to touch the green pods and make them explode, throwing tiny shrapnel. Damn. Mr. Peg was there, sitting up the bank and a little behind me, out of my line of sight.

Sorry for everything, I told him. And he said, Is that so hard to do? His voice, his words. My ears. I'm not suggesting any of this makes sense.

I got up and moved on. Yes sir, it is. Hard to live, and hard to watch the opposite coming down the road at you. I left out the f-bombs, not being sure if he was still with me or not. I looked at the trail and the dirt and the moss. The woods were their own show, with mushrooms for jokes. Mushrooms like orange ears that looked like they'd glow in the dark. I was delirious, given the no fuel in my tank, other than painkillers. But I felt some things. The deer family that left their tracks in the muddy trail. As much venison as I'd eaten in my life, I felt I was some percentage of deer. I felt the kindliness of the moss, which is all over everywhere once you get out of the made world. God's flooring. All the kinds, pillowy, pin-cushiony, shag carpet. Gray sticks of moss with red heads like matchsticks. Some tiny dead part of me woke up to the moss and said, Man. Where you been. This is the fucking wonderful world of color.

After another hour I sat on a big old mossy log to catch my breath, and remembered the joint in my pocket, a going-away present from Maggot. I hadn't smoked much weed since Dori died, just not feeling it. Hard to explain the various levels of doping hell, but there's a dark territory past the pleasures that weed is made for. I fished it out and admired it before lighting it up. Maggot's perfectly rolled white twig, pointed as a pencil on both ends. I actually had a hankering to draw its portrait. Another itch I hadn't felt in an age.

I set no land speed records. The sun got low, running me up against the wire on to-be-decided. I wasn't getting to the top of the cliffs. Not this day. That original asshole, the body, took over then, harping on getting me through a night. Not even asking, did I want to do that. Just the gripes, no water or food or roof over my head. In dire need of a piss. The last was easily taken care of. The rest was yet to kill me. I'd known sketchy shelter, and had logged enough hours hungry to be licensed as a professional. Ain't no hill for a climber, I thought, trudging up an ass-kick of switchbacks that knocked the wind out of me. The trail wound above the trees to a gravel slope, and then the Sand Cave. Dark and cool under a wide arch, seriously big. You could set a single-wide in there. Evidence of previous escapades here and yonder littered the sandy floor.

If I were a Boy Scout, I'd have known how to make a campfire. I'd have thought to bring a can of beans for dinner. And a can opener. Water. Being an ignorant juvenile delinquent with little or no will to live, I had none of the above. The person I felt watching me now was Angus. Not like Mr. Peg, earlier, I knew she wasn't really there. But I told her to shut up, and she laughed some more. That was it, the one place I'd like to be: talking to Angus. Dopey, tougher than hide, generally if not always one to improve a situation. Always saying I had to start trusting the ride at some point, because life was not a total and complete dumpster fire, which she was wrong about. She said my messed-up childhood made me a better person, also wrong. She'd believed I would go far, regardless my drawbacks galore and un-savory habits.

I found a good rock and watched the sun melt into the Cumberlands. Layers of orange like a buttermilk pie cooling on the horizon. Clouds scooting past, throwing spots of light and dark over the mountainheads. The light looked drinkable. It poured on a mountain so I saw the curve of every treetop edged in gold, like the scales of a fish. Then poured off, easing them back into shadow. I got all caught up in the show, waking up from my long cold swim underwater. Breaking the surface is a shock, the white is so white, the blue so blue. The air that's your breath.

I shifted and felt the lighter in my hip pocket, and laughed at myself for forgetting it. Stand back Boy Scouts, I told Angus. Oh my Lord. I'd have paid money for a little bump of *her*. Angus that was solid while all the shiny objects I craved came and went. She was going away at the end of summer, to real college. She'd gotten an offer she couldn't refuse. I was pissed as hornets. Vander-something the hell, Nashville T-N. Who knew they could make country hits and brainiacs in the one convenient location.

Okay, my friend. I rifled around the mess inside me and found what I needed to wish her happiness. Fly away and don't fall back into the slime I'm trying to crawl out of here, and also drinking on the sly, calling it my life's blood. Too scared to leave the last place where people looked at me and saw their son or blood brother or their shot at a winning season. I knew what she'd say about that. Trust the road. Because nobody stays, in the long run you're on your own with your ghosts. You're the ship, they're the bottle.

I spent the night curled up on the sandy floor with my back pressed against cold rock, thirsty and hungry and in the end not sufficiently doped. Every cricket that inched along the cave face was a copperhead, every squirrel rustling dry leaves was a bear. If I lived till morning, I would walk down the mountain, find June, and tell her I was ready to fly.

61

A year was not a long enough time to stay away. Even three years might not be, I would find out. One of the many things June got right.

Is it the hardest thing I've ever done? No. Just the hardest one I had any choice about. Getting clean is like taking care of a sick person, versus *being* the sick person. They get all the points for bravery, but they're locked in. *You* have to get up every morning and decide again, in the cold lonely light of day, am I brave enough to stick this out?

Rehab is like being married to sickness in a lot of ways, really. Disgust comes into it. You try to deny that, swapping it out for a kindness you may not feel. You fake it till you make it. You watch other people being smug, because they made better matches than you did. You let them say all the stupid things, God never gives you more than you can handle, etc. You get comfortable with vomit.

So I had a head start, being well used to the no-toucher lifestyle before I started into the program. *Dalit*, is the word he was saying all that time. The untouchables of Mr. Golly's childhood are for real. I've read all about them now. It's amazing how much time you may find on your hands, once you're freed up from tracking down your next fix, chasing the means for your next fix, bootlegging scrips, dipping out, ganking, pheeming, chewing chains, raving with Jesus, trying to find a new dope boy, and steering clear of the old ones that would eat your liver with gravy if they could be bothered. The perks of sobriety.

The Halley Library branch on the north end of Knoxville was the other half of my halfway life, after I graduated from detox-and-therapy boot camp, learned respect for properly dosed Suboxone under the tongue, and settled into my residency situation. Sober living home is the preferred term of professionals, hard-knocksville among the natives. My roommates came and went to some distressing degree. Triggers are seeded into the dirt of your every day: a song on the radio, a taste in the mouth, the cherry-soda smell of methadone that can be injected straight from the bottle. Drug tests

are easier to fail at than any other subject. We weren't
even allowed to have mouthwash in that house. I thought
a lot about my mom's months- and years-sober chips
I used to screw around with like play money instead
of the damn gold doubloons they were. I thought of
Maggot, how dutifully he would apply himself to fucking this up. June and Mrs. Peggot were right, getting
him sober would take a higher power than Maggot had
in his list of personal contacts. Would and did. Juvenile
detention was his worst nightmare and best shot. After
two years he was out, living with Mariah now in Bristol,
Tennessee. Outcome to be determined.

The pillars of my sanity in hard-knocksville were
three guys named Viking, Gizmo, and Chartrain.
Gizmo and Viking were from two different Kentucky
counties, Bell and Harlan, both closer to Lee County
than the nearest outlet mall, similar broke-ass localities
up to their ears in oxy fiends with no place to go. The
Knoxville treatment enterprise draws from a wide
watershed of humanity. These two were not much older
than me, and an unmatched set. Viking being this big,
blond specimen, foulmouthed as they come, and Gizmo
a little guy with funny teeth and a mild stutter, polite
as a live-in aunt. They both shared my life's crushed
ambition of never living in a city. Our house, as June
predicted, was on the outskirts, in a neighborhood of

folks that didn't mind junkie has-beens in their midst. Not rich. Houses were small and close-set, fences were chain link, dogs had outside voices, and none of this was the problem. What set us on edge were all the human eyes that wouldn't look at us, out on the city streets. The continual sirens, the pinkish light shellacking the windows all night long. We were wonderstruck at the idea of anyone at all, let alone ourselves, staying sober in such a place.

Chartrain would be our savior. A Knoxville man born and bred, street genius, guiding light. We would not be aware of any of this for some while. *Don you go no mofuckin Beaumont, boi, my bruh got kilt dae, fa real dey gone show you what dey got*, Chartrain would tell us, and we would nod our heads as one. *If at'n up air don make ye wood burn, ain't naught will*, we would say to him. At some point around six months in, we made contact. All good after that.

Chartrain explained that city people don't look each other in the eye because they're saving their juice. A person has only so much juice, and it's ideally kept for your homeboys, not all pissed away on strangers before three in the day. Simple as that sounds, it was a game changer for me. I taught myself to save the juice. It's a skill, like weight training, you do reps. Tell yourself ten times each night, don't spend your juice on those sirens, worrying about the life screaming past on its way to getting tanked. Don't spend it on the customers around you at Walmart Supercenter, just do your job without feeling the madness or sadness, the moms on the brink of snatching their kids bald-headed. The carts loaded with cases of PBR and Pampers. The carts with nothing but off-brand beans and marked-down stale bread. Not even on the guy I watched once while I rounded up carts, outside in the parking lot, trying to stuff his huge armload of pink birthday balloons into his hatchback, damning them to goddamn hell as they kept bobbing back out in his face, finally pulling a coping blade out of his pocket and stabbing every balloon but one. He slammed the hatch and drove off with it, home to some sad, one-balloon birthday girl, and I confess to spending some juice on her. Rehab possibly in her future.

Chartrain didn't fully follow his own advice, he gave of himself freely, but it worked out because he had more juice than any normal human. He'd been a star athlete in his formative years, and it's not something I'd planned to talk about again, but we ended up bonding over high school sports. Chartrain was basketball, already the A-team shooting guard as a freshman, averaging twenty or more points per game. A meteor, to hear him tell it, Division 1 scouts with eyes on him. But no college offers were good enough to keep him from a quick tour of Afghanistan, and he came home without his legs. The shuttle van that took us to our jobs and our meetings also rolled Chartrain twice a week to the East City Y to play wheelchair basketball, and once again he slayed. I went pretty often to see him play. As a guy that played football only until I lost my natural advantage, I had great respect for a guy with no legs that still played basketball. In my new life of feeling all the feels, the cesspool of self-disgust felt like a deal breaker. The whole existence of Chartrain shouted: Watch and learn, my brother. In addition to juice, he had front teeth incomprehensibly edged in gold, and calloused hands like vulcanized tires from charging and pivoting his chair around the court. None of this did he owe to the Veterans Administration that was paying his way.

One thing about sober living facilities. You come in thinking you've lost all there is to lose, then find out there are things you never knew were on the table. Chartrain still had his mother alive out there thinking Chartrain hung the moon, but he was otherwise nearly my equal as far as dead dad, dead brother, dead baby mama, and had seen a whole lot of guys shot dead in front of his eyes, not just overseas. Plus the no-legs. Gizmo, for his part, had been in a car that wrapped itself around a family of five, turning them into a family of one. Gizmo's girlfriend, the only girl he'd ever dated and hoped to marry, left her good looks on the windshield and was doing time. She was driving because they had a fight and he'd deliberately crunked out, so. Lots to live with there. And Viking had lost something still more unexpected, his ears. He was tall and broad as a tree trunk and about that deaf. Thanks to oxy. He said it starts as a ringing, then one day you wake up to find the ringing is all you've got left. We all had the ringing. This fact was sobering in every regard. Viking wore hearing aids the color of dirty pink crayons and was impressive in that he still talked pretty well, just way too loud, and caught a lot of what you said if you spoke to him face-on. Doctors had told him it might come back if he stayed sober, and this was his higher power. He had a baby back in Bell County. He'd never heard her say "Daddy."

Viking and Gizmo both worked in a warehouse, where they shouldered the yoke of labor like good-natured mules. No questions to ask or answer, and at least one of them was unbothered by the all-day whine of the forklifts. They were allowed to smoke on the job. It's the one addiction they let us keep, don't ask me why. Maybe because it won't inspire you to rob a liquor store or wrap your vehicle around foreign objects.

I wouldn't have minded the warehouse, but lacked a

mule's good knees. I had been looked at now by more doctors than existed in Lee County, and advised that at such time as I ever found myself in a job with good health insurance, I'd be a candidate for knee replacement. Meantime, I followed my mother's footsteps and got hired as a stocker at Walmart Supercenter. Unlike Mom, I was probably the soberest cracker in the whole big box, and quickly worked my way up the career ladder to produce. I avoided the employee smoking room aka drug-exchange HQ, and found no real downside to the job. People buying apples and green beans usually have some degree of joy in their hearts. I counted down the fifteen-minute intervals and watched them flinch and shudder like wet dogs every time the machine came on with the fake thunder and spray to mist down the goods. I told myself I was laughing with them, not at them. But really, I was sad. It was the closest they probably got to real rain on a vegetable.

I'm going to tell you something, there's country poor, and there's city poor. As much of my life as I'd spent in front of a TV thinking Oh, man, city's where the money trees grow, I was seeing more to the picture now. I mean yes, that is where they all grow, but plenty of people are sitting in that shade with nothing falling on them. Chartrain was always discussing "hustle," and it took me awhile to understand he grew up hungry for money like it was food. Because for him, they're one and the same. Not to run the man down, but he wouldn't know a cow from a steer, or which of them gave milk. No desperate men Chartrain ever knew went out and shot venison if they were hungry. They shot liquor store cashiers. Living in the big woods made of steel and cement, without cash, is a hungrier life than I knew how to think about.

I made my peace with the place, but never went a day without feeling around for things that weren't there, the way your tongue pushes into the holes where you've lost teeth. I don't just mean cows, or apple trees, it runs deeper. Weather, for instance. Air, the way it smells from having live things breathing into it, grass and trees and I don't know what, creatures of the soil. Sounds, I missed most of all. There was noise, but nothing behind it. I couldn't get used to the blankness where there should have been bird gossip morning and evening, crickets at night, the buzz saw of cicadas in August. A rooster always sounding off somewhere, even dead in the middle of Jonesville. It's like the movie background music. Notice it or don't, but if the volume goes out, the movie has no heart. I'd oftentimes have to stop and ask myself what season it was. I never realized what was holding me to my place on the planet of earth: that soundtrack. That, and leaf colors and what's blooming in the roadside ditches this week, wild sweet peas or purple ironweed or goldenrod. And stars. A sky as dark as sleep, not this hazy pinkish business, I'm saying blind man's black. For a lot of us, that's medicine. Required for the daily reboot.

I understand this is meant to be a small price to pay for the many things you *do* get to have in a city. Employment. Better entertainments, probably, if you're not living in a recovery house with a curfew. City buses, library and grocery stores in walking distance, check, check, check. Here's another one: house keys. I'd never lived any place where people locked the front door at all times, whether inside of it or gone from it. Usually, we never even knew where the door key *was*. Chartrain did not believe this. We tried to explain, after the sixth or tenth time Viking or Gizmo or I left for work and forgot to lock up. He just thought we were idiots. He called us hillbillies and yokels and all the names, unfit to live in the real world. We knew Chartrain loved us. We'd all had turns at carrying him and helping with bathroom business, the legs being not the only part of him messed up down there. The names we could have called him back are not approved, so we didn't. But never did get what he thought would happen to an unlocked house like ours, so plainly short on things to steal. We weren't allowed drugs, couldn't afford electronics, and our only jewelry was hardwired onto Chartrain. Regardless, we learned that much about living in the so-called real world. How to lock up a house.

I've tried in this telling, time and again, to pinpoint the moment where everything starts to fall apart. Everything, meaning me. But there's also the opposite, where some little nut cracks open inside you and a tree starts to grow. Even harder to nail. Because that thing's going to be growing a long time before you notice. Years maybe. Then one day you say, *Huh*, that little crack between my ears has turned into this whole damn tree of wonderful.

It had mainly fallen to Angus over the years to crack some of the harder nuts of Demon, due to her always being around and putting up with me. Also Mr. Armstrong, notorious serial-nutcracker of Jonesville Middle brains. But the one you're never going to guess: Tommy. Going all the way back to woeful Tommy in the paper office pulling his hair, crushed by the news of us hill folk being the kicked dogs of America. Leading to the shocking demise of Stumpy Fiddles, the pencil thrust in challenge: *Let's see you do better.* We were just a couple of time-hardened foster boys shooting the shit. What good could ever come of that? You wait.

Tommy was lonely at the paper office now, that

much I knew, based on how much he was emailing. Still reading books, and emailing me about the books and ideas he got from the books, just like he used to tell me the entire plot of his latest Boxcar Children, down to the last detail I heard before conking off. Now he was all into the history of Appalachian everything. This Dog of America thing being a major sticking point, Tommy was not moving on. But we were good, like old times, discussing his girl Sophie, my new rehab pals, both of us in the same boat now as regards girlfriend action. Our *Red Neck* strip went on ice for a time. We got some grace from Pinkie, as long as we promised to come back eventually and finish the twelve-month agreement. This option was written into our contract by Annie. Evidently she saw my downfall coming.

As far as the books he wanted to discuss, I can't even tell you what they were about. I honestly wished for a good Boxcar with a beginning and end, because these went nowhere. Theories. I told him about the hard and surprising knocks of city life, and he explained it all back to me in book words. He said up home we are land economy people, and city is money economy. I told him not everybody here has money, there are guys with a piece of cardboard for their prize possession, so pitiful you want to give them the shirt off your back. (Which Tommy would.) And he was like, Exactly. In your cities, money is the whole basis. Have it, or don't have it, it's still the one and only way to get what all you need: food, clothes, house, music, fun times.

Maybe that sounds like the normal to you. Up home, it's different. I mean yes, you want money and a job, but there's a hundred other things you do for getting by, especially older people and farmers with the crops, tomato gardens and such. Hunting and fishing, plus all the woman things, making quilts and clothes. Whether big or small, you've always got the place you're living on. I've known people to raise a beef in the yard behind their rented trailer. I was getting the picture now on why June's doom castle had freaked me out. Having some ground to stand on, that's our whole basis. It's the bags of summer squash and shelly beans everybody gives you from their gardens, and on from there. The porch rockers where the mammaws get together and knit baby clothes for the pregnant high school girls. Sandwiches the church ladies pack for the hungrier kids to take home on weekends. Honestly, I would call us the juice economy. Or I guess used to be, up until everybody started getting wrecked on the newer product. We did not save our juice, we would give it to each and all we meet, because we're going to need some of that back before long, along with the free advice and power tools. Covered dishes for a funeral, porch music for a wedding, extra hands for getting the tobacco in. Just talking about it made me homesick for the life of unlocked doors that Chartrain called Not the Real World. You couldn't see him sticking around one day in Lee County. We all want what we're used to.

Tommy and I discussed this nonsense way too much, with all my emailing at the library involving some degree of shenanigans with a hot librarian named Lyra, more on her later. I expected nothing to come of it. Mostly, it was Tommy being aggravated. He pointed out how a lot of our land-people things we do for getting by, like farmer, fishing, hunting, making our own liquor, are the exact things that get turned into hateful jokes on us. He wasn't wrong, cartoonwise that shit refuses to die. Straw hat, fishing pole, XXX jug. Kill Stumpy Fiddles, along will come Jiggle Billy on adult swim. But all I could say was, Tommy, you know and I know, neither way is really better. In the long run it's all just hustle. So our hustle is different. So what?

And he said, I'm still figuring that part out.

62

Thanks to my orphan jackpot, I didn't work full-time like most of my housemates. June had offered to help if I needed it, and she was keeping tabs on me. But I was well used to paying my own way. The monthly house fees came out of my social security account, and part-time at Walmart covered the rest. The entertainments of sober living are all those best things in life that are said to be free. Breathing, sleeping, enjoying your newly regularized bowels. Eating your own bad cooking. Bumming Camels and playing penny poker, listening to two Kentucky boys tell Tennessee jokes that you grew up telling as Kentucky jokes. Listening to hair-raising tales of the hood, in a language you wish had subtitles. I spent a lot of time at the library.

The main librarian at our branch was Lyra. Not your

father's Oldsmobile. She had cherry-red hair with short, straight bangs, and a full sleeve tattoo representing the book of *Moby-Dick*. Sinking schooner, curling waves, wrathful whale. She wore shorts, spiderweb tights and motorcycle boots in all weather. Deadpan flirt. I hadn't been laid since Dori, not even once. It's a level of death, knowing another body that well, that's touched every part of yours, thinking about it now cold in the ground. Some days, that killed me. Others, I felt nothing. Sex was just a vague and troublesome part of the feverish life I'd put on the other side of a glass wall. The counselors warn you this may be the case, and advise against romantic involvements till you're on solid ground with your recovery. Triple underlined, if you're a young man with multiple mommy issues and a thing for hot-mess rescue cases that are doomed to suck you under. Lyra seemed pretty solid, but I knew me and involvements. I couldn't poke a stick at that beast without getting swallowed alive. This one came to work with weed on her breath and seemed in every sense a party girl. I opted not to find out.

We found other ways to share. She liked books obviously and pointed quite a few my way, some that made me smarter, some just weird. She helped me study for my GED, which turned out to be a hell of a lot easier than being physically present to two more years of disgrace and overpriced drugs cut with sheep wormer.

Which would have been my lot, as a fallen General. I think most of humankind would agree, the hard part of high school is the people.

Lyra's secret love was computers. She set me up with email, and showed me how to use the library's scanner to upload my drawings. Red Neck as mentioned had to sleep it off for six months, but as soon as I had two sticks to rub together in my brainbox, I got right back on the job. Tommy had what he needed at the paper office so we could trade sketches. He pitched story ideas, I drew them, he shaded and inked. With both operatives sober, our efficiency was first class. Pinkie wanted to renew us for another year.

With some sadness, we decided against. We were both moving on. Tommy finally met his girlfriend, and it was the real thing. Sophie was crazy about Tommy, and so was her mom's family, that threw a big dinner for all the relatives to check him out. Tommy came back home, gave Pinkie two weeks' notice, untangled himself from the McCobb utility space, and moved to Allentown, Pennsylvania. He and Sophie got married at the Polish-American Citizens Club, followed by a huge reception with a polka band. Get me a hankie, somebody, and I'm not kidding. Tommy had a family. Before I saw him next, he would be a father.

On my end, I'd outgrown superheroes, even the

much-needed hillbilly kind. The Fleischer style of *Red Neck* was hemming me in, those bulbous eyes and noodle limbs felt babyish. I wanted to try something harder-core. Lyra was educating me, and not in the ways my idle mind had toyed with. After turning me on to the adult comics and graphic novels section of the library, she showed me what was going on in the world of online comics, which rocked my marbles. She walked me through building my own website. Mainly this involved me getting out of her way so she could click furiously at the keys while I lost myself in the dramatic oceanscape of her left arm. I could upload my drawings to the site, and in this fashion I started my enterprise. Like most of Mr. McCobb's, it made no money whatsoever for the first year. Unlike him, I stuck to it. It was my own little universe, created under my alias, Demon Copperhead. I was far from the football field and Lee County lore now, and had gotten used to my mom's name again. Most people called me Fields. But I had this whole other part I didn't want to lose. My dad.

It started with my long-ago idea of Neckbones. With Tommy's permission, I did some of our famous local histories through the eyes of skeletons. Knox Mine disaster, Natural Tunnel train wreck. I also messed around with the idea I'd had in my saddest days with Dori: *The Incapables*, a strip about a junkie couple trying to keep house. The guy was Crash and the girl was Bernie, two teenagers trying to raise themselves. They grilled hot dogs on their car engine while driving around to find their connect, and did household repairs with bongs and roach clips. To the best of my abilities, I made it sad and true to the laughable mess of addicted youth. Also bitter. In one of my strips, Crash is filling his pill-mill scrip and the pharmacy lady leans over to warn him, "This one's strong, hon. The Purdue rep takes it so he can sleep nights."

I'm not saying there was a market for any of this. But the days of the big village were just starting. If there's a shoe out there for every foot, the lonely and oddball foot by means of the internet had a vastly improved chance of finding it. My weird cartoons got a little following that grew, and after a year I sold subscriptions. Not very many. Luckily, I wasn't in it for the money. One thing I learned from Mr. Armstrong while striving heartily to remain uneducated: a good story doesn't just copy life, it pushes back on it. It's why guys like Chartrain wear their clothes too big and their teeth edged with gold, why Mr. Dick puts words on kites and sends them to the sun. It's why I draw what I draw.

Angus stayed in touch. She followed my comics, which she liked, and sent updates from the Nashville front:

college was hard, college kids were a bunch of spoiled brats, and everybody including professors made fun of her mountain accent. She was there on scholarship, and hadn't understood she was going to be fraternizing with, as she put it, cake eaters and princes of capitalism. Good to see Angus holding on to her winning personality.

She told me what classes she liked, and what nonsense the rich sorority girls were up to, so needy of attention they would pretend it was too hot and take off their jewelry in class. And how certain skeezy teaching assistants were stealth-undressing those girls with their eyes. Nashville she liked, as a town. Dive bars, bookstores, amazing food from countries you've not even heard of. Both of us were in Tennessee theoretically, but a half-day's drive and a couple universes apart. She said in Nashville you could see anybody famous on a given day, Brooks or Dunn, Carrie Underwood etc., because even if not living there, they're hanging around town waiting to make their albums. She saw Dolly goddamn Parton one time in the grocery store buying head lettuce. I told her the celebrity I saw buying vegetables was Crazy Marv from the "At these prices you'll know I've lost my marbles" used-car commercials.

With Tommy finally living his life, his emails petered out. You had to reckon Sophie was the one getting her ears full now, theorywise. Apart from meetings and my counselors doing their jobs, Angus was the only person anymore to ask what I was going through. How much did I still think about using, how did I keep it together. How's that wild ride going, was I ready to trust it yet. I told her about the inspirations of black coffee and the deep black bottom I was terrified to hit again. And the pink pill I put under my tongue every morning to keep all the other ones out of there for the rest of my days, so far, so good. I confessed my secret itch to do a comics version of the AA Big Book. I told her about Viking, Gizmo, and Chartrain. On her end, she'd comment on somebody she studied with or partied with, this cat named Jacko she took a trip with over spring break. But no one name ever came to the fore. More often than not, she went home on her school vacations, sometimes going down to stay with Miss Betsy and Mr. Dick. That surprised me, her going back. I thought for sure in a place like Nashville with everybody working their angles hell for leather, Angus would find her people. But it didn't seem so.

Maggot meanwhile was back in touch, finally ready to forgive me for my brief fit of high school popularity. He thought *The Incapables* was dead hilarious, and was always sending me ideas that were too third-grade or too adult-raunchy to use. No in-betweens with that guy. He and his mom both had jobs at PetSmart, of all

places. He had a boyfriend he met at work. I said con-
gratulations, was he one of those smash-faced bulldogs
or what. He said no, skunk breath, he's the reptiles
manager. We were still Demon and Maggot.

My number-one fan though turned out to be Ms.
Annie, that now wanted me to call her just Annie. Mr.
Armstrong I was supposed to call Lewis. They both
put a lot of fan raves on my site, which I could always
tell were theirs even though under multiple fake names.
They used words like "innovative" and "visionary,"
dead giveaway this was teachers, not kids and junkies. Regardless Ms. Annie's prediction, I was nothing
but the lowest level of potato, but you'd think I was
the most dazzling success they'd ever had as a student.
Lewis was in big trouble with the school board as usual,
so the honor you could say was dubious.

What changed everything was Tommy calling me up,
out of the blue. The History of our People thing, he
hadn't let go. Maybe homesick. Or having trouble explaining us rednecks to his new family, as you do. Anyway, so excited on the phone he doesn't start with hello.
*Demon! I know why we're the dogshit of America,
it's a war, and it's been going on the whole time, and
nobody gets it, not even us. You have to do a graphic
novel about it.* This, at three motherfucking o'clock in

the goddamn morning. I said I couldn't wait to hear all about it tomorrow.

Oh, I did. He claimed he was on the right track as far as the two kinds of economy people, land versus money. But not city people against us personally. It's the ones in charge, like government or what have you. They were always on the side of the money-earning people, and down on the land people, due to various factors Tommy mentioned, monetize this, international banking that. The main one I could understand was that money-earning ones pay taxes. Whereas you can't collect shit on what people grow and eat on the spot, or the work they swap with their neighbors. That's like a percent of blood from a turnip. So, the ones in charge started cooking it into everybody's brains to look down on the land people, saying we are an earlier stage of human, like junior varsity or cavemen. Weird-shaped heads.

Tommy was watching TV these days, and seeing finally how this shit is everywhere you look. Dissing the country bumpkins, trying to bring us up to par, the long-termed war of trying to shame the land people into joining America. Meaning their version, city. TV being the slam book of all times, maybe everybody in the city was just going along with it, not really noticing the rudeness factors. Possibly to the extent of not getting why we are so fucking mad out here.

It took a lot of emails of Tommy telling me how far back it went, this offensive to wedge people off their own holy ground and turn them into wage labor. Before the redneck miner wars, the coal land grabs, the timber land grabs. Whiskey Rebellion: an actual war. George Washington marched the US Army on our people for refusing to pay tax on corn liquor. Which they weren't even selling for money, mainly just making for neighborly entertainment. How do you get tax money out of moonshine? Answer: You and what army. It goes a ways to explaining people's feelings about taxes and guns.

Tommy said the world was waiting for a graphic novel about the history of these wars. I told him the world could hold its horses then, because I didn't have the foggiest idea how to do that. Then went to bed, woke up, and started drawing it. He fed me story lines like kindling on a fire. I wanted to call it *Hillbilly Wars*, but he said no, people would think the usual cornball nonsense, hill folk shooting each other. Plus he pointed out there were other land-type people in the boat with us. The Cherokees that got kicked off their land. All the other tribes, same. Black people after they were freed up, wanting their own farms but getting no end of grief for it, till they gave up and went to the city.

Surprisingly, Angus was all over this. I'd been

trying to get her interested in comics for an age. Then in college she discovers graphic novels like she invented them. Always sending me the latest one she's crazy about. Not your run-of-the-mill sci-fi and crime, this girl was into dark. Jewish mice in the Nazi concentration camps. Kids growing up in a funeral home. *The Incapables*, she called fierce. I'd been telling her this forever, adult comics are all over the map. But not a single one out there has *us* in it, she said. Not wrong.

I ended up calling it *High Ground*. The two-hundred-years war to keep body and soul together on our mountains. I started putting up chapters on my site as I finished them, earning a weird and intense fan club, part history professors, part good ol' boys. Then a guy emailed to say his company published graphic novels and might be interested in mine, could I send him all the material I had. This guy was in New York. Did he seriously think I was handing over my goods?

I talked to Annie on the phone pretty regularly, but after this news she wanted to see me in person. A book deal, Christ on a bike, quote unquote. She would look at everything I had, and help me put together a proposal. She offered to come to Knoxville. At this point Annie is something like eight months pregnant, if I didn't mention that. You turn your back, shit happens. The sensible thing was for me to go to her.

Technically there was no reason I couldn't. In three and a half years as a sober living resident, month by month, I'd earned a life without curfew, driving my own wheels, weekends away. The house managers were actually dropping hints. Viking was back in Bell County now, and Gizmo was lining up his options. There was literally no end to the line of guys waiting to get in here. But I couldn't imagine going anywhere. Especially back there.

Driving wasn't the problem, I still had an active license, which the other guys in the house regarded as magical. They'd all DUI'ed out, many times over, and here's me without even a moving violation. I tried to explain Lee County, where all the cops are your relatives or dope boys or both. I did not have the Impala. My last act before leaving Lee County was to talk Turp Trussell into giving me two hundred dollars for the car and any pills he could find in there. In less than a month he ran it through a guardrail on that stretch of 421 people call "the hateful section." Turp was shockingly intact, the Impala, RIP. Getting this news was like hearing that a childhood dog had to be put down. But there would be other cars in my life. From a friend of Chartrain's mom, I scored an abused but affordable rescue Chevy Beretta, robin's-egg blue, to celebrate one year sober. A month or so after that, I got up the nerve to drive it downtown. A year is a long time away from the wheel. Straight into city driving, quite the plunge. I tried to keep my eyes open and channel June Peggot parallel parking outside the Atlanta Starbucks. I'm in awe of that maneuver to this day. Men have married women for less reason.

So I had a car. I had Annie's invitation, and my freedom. Means, motive, and opportunity, as they say on *CSI*. Nothing holding me back now but sheer terror. It's hard to explain how you can miss a place and want it with all your heart, and be utterly sure it will obliterate you the instant you touch down. I said this to the counselor I still saw every week, Dr. Andresen, that was part of the house arrangement along with water and utilities. As far from Miss Barks as they get. Older lady, gray sweaters buttoned to the top, black clog shoes, professional and educated and decently paid I assume. She was from Denmark, first name of Milka, and for all that, a very likable human. She'd talked me through a boatload of crap, and honestly it was less distracting to do this with a counselor that you couldn't remotely imagine doing anything else with. Dr. Andresen weighed in on the side of me going to Lee County. Or at least examining my fears. I asked her, what part of *obliterate* do you not understand?

She gave me the assignment of writing a story, in

which Demon goes to Lee County and sees friends who support his sobriety. What I turned in: "On a planet that exists only in Dr. Andresen's mind, a good time was had by all, and nobody got shitfaced." She gave me her tiny lopsided smile, being used to my attitude on assignments. Didn't stop her from giving them to me. Practically from our first meeting, she'd been after me to write a recovery journal. I told her I don't write, I draw. She said this would be for myself only. I could share it, but only if I chose to do so. The idea being to get clarity and process some of my traumas. On that particular ball of yarn I didn't know where to start. She suggested pinpointing where my struggles had started with substance abuse, abandonment, and so forth. She said many people find this is a helpful tool for reclaiming their narratives, and in fact wasn't this what I was doing with my comics?

Whatever. I've made any number of false starts with this mess. You think you know where your own troubles lie, only to stare down the page and realize, no. Not there. It started earlier. Like these wars going back to George Washington and whiskey. Or in my case, chapter 1. First, I got myself born. The worst of the job was up to me. Here we are.

63

In December Annie emailed to tell me the baby was skewed in some fashion and she might have to schedule the delivery soon. I needed to get my carcass over there pronto. I called her and said to forget about my nonsense, just worry about the baby.

"We're not *worried*," she said. "He's just defying the rules, trying to come into the world back-asswards. Whose child do you think this is?"

She sounded so much like herself, I couldn't picture the watermelon aspects. The baby of her and Mr. Armstrong would be a knockout, no way around it. Hardheaded, great beauty, high-octane fuel for the Lee County gossip engines. "*Please* come," she said. "I've started my leave already, but I'm too fat to sit at my loom, and I don't feel like cooking because eating one saltine gives me heartburn. I'm just wallowing around here like a landlocked walrus."

She needed distraction. She wanted to see drawings. Weirdly, I wanted to see the walrus version of Annie. I said I'd think about it overnight. Before we hung up, she mentioned the high school was having a big thing on Friday to honor Coach Winfield. Not just football players, this was the town. Coach had retired after the scandal to get his life together, and the guy they hired to replace him steered the Generals to something previously unimaginable: a 4–6 losing season.

"Winfield is a damn fallen hero," she said. "I think they're having this blowout for him because burning the new coach at the stake would be illegal."

She said she understood if I had hard feelings against Winfield. I'm sure June would second that. Undue pressures and pharmaceutical missteps, not deniable. But she never saw me sleeping behind dumpsters, looking for something steadier than the DSS greatest-hits box set. Coach took me in. I blamed Watts for the worst of what happened. For the best of it, I needed to lay eyes on Coach and tell him it mattered.

If I went, I might also run into Angus. She'd gone back after graduation to take care of some of Coach's loose ends, but was pretty clear on this being just a stopover. Bigger fish to fry, no doubt. I didn't email her. I told almost nobody, since my friends were all dead now or waiting on deck for their turn. Just Annie. And June, that would kill me if I was in town and didn't see her. I told Dr. Andresen I was going for it, and she did the rare thing of smiling with her whole mouth. "I think you are unlikely to obliterate," she said. And I said, You watch.

The drive alone threatened to defeat me. I should have taken some other random route, even if it took longer. To trick my body into believing we were headed someplace else. Every few miles a memory broke like an egg on my face. Cumberland Gap, our bathroom stop on the trip to Aunt June's where I was uninvited and smelled bad. Gibson Station, where Mrs. McCobb made me try to pawn dirty Barbies and a used toaster with black crumbs in it. Cedar Hill, where I believed my childhood hero had bought his own farm, prior to learning he was a liar. Prior to seeing his skull broken open. I was processing my traumas, like they say. Lately I'd cut my smoking back to negligible, just poker nights and blue rainy days. The occasional walk home from the library after Lyra was overly frisky. Okay but now I was chain-smoking in the car.

On the outskirts of Pennington I passed the dead

strip mall and former pill mill of Watts that I knew was shut down. June had told me the soulless pervert got his due, federal charges pending. This was the year of trials starting to go to the top, the oxy tides turning. Angus said even people in Nashville were talking about oxy now, but in comic-book terms only, evil corporate villains. No mention of all the little people scorched but staving off their living death thanks to places like that pill mill, buying and selling in the parking lot. I thought of my old reliable buyers. The guy with his walker and fur-flap hunting hat, the sad fat lady with her Chihuahua. How the hell were they getting by now? According to June, the recovery enterprise of Lee County was still limited mainly to church life groups, *Grapevine* magazine, and basement twelve-step meetings. It was best not to get her started on the subject. These megabuck settlements against Purdue, and not a dime of it ever getting back here.

Annie was set on me staying over with them, so she could lay out all my *High Ground* drawings on her kitchen table. I had a breakfast date with June the next morning. Otherwise, no strategy. I'd had vague thoughts of meeting up with friends, but turning that into a plan moved in the direction of what Dr. Andresen called suicidal ideation. Going to the Five Star Stadium on Friday for Coach's thing, seriously? Every person there would try to sell me dope, unless they loved me and gave it to me for free. Everything about that place was a trigger. Yard lines, goalposts, the chutes that were my superpower. The place where I'd made and lost my fortune.

I passed kudzu valley and the Powell River and the mountain that doesn't really look like a face. All of it a little homely in the dead of winter, but in that ugly-duckling way that you knew would turn around. The caboose in front of the middle school, the bric-a-brac mammaw yards. I saw people on porches, but my eyes shied away as they'd learned to do. Saving my juice. If it had been July, my heart already would have cracked for the beauty. As it was, I might die of loneliness. How could I be here with all these familiar things but not the people that looked me in the eye and called me brother, or God love ya, or You're *that* one, or Honey I remember you from the feed store. To be here was to be known. If Lee County isn't that, it's nothing.

Annie's house was no trouble to find. I was a little surprised every time the Beretta took a turn the right way, like it was the Impala and not me that had known these roads blindfolded. I knocked on the blue front door, and heard Hazel Dickens running around in there yapping. Nobody came. I opened the door and yelled hello. Hazel Dickens sat down and looked at me. I closed the door and knocked again. All this before I saw the note stuck to the doorbell: *Gone to the hospital, sorry. Might be a false alarm. Lewis will call you. Make yourself at home.*

And it sank in: they were having a freaking baby. I thought of the McCobb twins, the all-night wailing, the casual flopping out of tits. I seriously doubted Annie knew what she was in for. These people did not need me or my box of drawings in their hair at this time. I called June. She had patients and a staff meeting and after that some meeting at the health department, but said I was welcome. Take Emmy's old room. She'd see me, if not tonight then in the morning.

So I was cut loose without a safety net. I had no intention of sitting all day at June's. I gave the Beretta free rein and we wandered aimlessly. It was an in-your-face winter's day, so bright. I drove to the river bridge where I used to fish with Mr. Peg. Watched the glittery water till I had to drive on. Went to Hoboland and sat looking up the skirts of those hemlocks, thinking of Angus lying back on her elbows, seeing straight into me. I had to get up and leave. The sun shellacked a shine on the houses and mailboxes. Everything I looked at made my eyes water. It felt like being in love with somebody that's married. I could never have this. Staying here, alone and sober, was beyond my powers. And I still wanted it with all my hungry parts.

I stuck to the lonelier roads, and really couldn't tell you my thought processes, if any, but I ended up at the trail to Devil's Bathtub. Was it a Step 4 type thing, courage and moral inventory? I doubt it sincerely. More like picking a fight with a person you're ready to break up with. I needed to find the place that would make me hate it here and not come back.

The gravel lot had one other car, so. Still open to the public. Two more fatalities wouldn't shut the place down, given the long history of youthful male recklessness. And girls wrecked too. I'd never thought of that before, not once. *Mom was here.* Walking the same trail as me. Watching what I watched and worse, the end of the man she loved. His body. I felt a little shaky as I locked my car, with nothing valuable in it but my box of drawings in the trunk. City habits.

Devil's Bathtub turned out to be the first place I'd been all day that wasn't laid with mines. I recognized nothing. The trail was bone dry, the creek was easy to cross on stepping stones with white rugs of dried-up algae. I didn't get my shoes wet. The air smelled like sweet apples and something else, Pine-Sol or medicine. Little trees alongside of the trail were covered with brushy yellow flowers. Witch hazel, that blooms in winter. Mrs. Peggot used to make a salve of that and put it on our scrapes. All that just hit me, from the smell. Now the bees were all over it, rousted out from their winter nap, filling up the quietness with their buzz.

I kept waiting for the scary part that never came. The cliffs rose high along the creek, covered with bright-colored lichens that made them looked tagged, like the walls in my Knoxville neighborhood. Several times I sat down on a log because my knee hurt, because it always hurt. I was past sorry for myself. Like every boy in Lee County I was raised to be a proud mule in a world that has scant use for mules. I'd tried the popular solutions to that problem, which generally pointed to early death. The trick was to find others. I sat and watched little jenny wrens hopping along the water's edge pecking up bugs, ticking their heads side to side like wind-up toys. I heard a tom turkey up in the woods doing that bad-boy gobble thing the hens cannot resist. I saw a hoot owl. It was hiding, all the same colors as tree bark, but outed by a mob of loud crows that had their grudge against it. Probably something to do with eating their babies.

The trail got tricky eventually but never treacherous, and I came to the water hole before I expected it. The falls were a tame trickle and the pool itself a deep, easy blue. Taking art classes on repeat, you learn a lot about color, but I can't explain that blue. You see it in photos of icy lands. Peacock blue in the deep center, shading out to clear on the pebbly edges. The water was dimply and alive on top, perfectly still underneath. My eye kept going back to the turquoise middle. You so rarely see that, but children will color water that way every time, given the right choice of crayons. Like they were born knowing there's better out there than what we're getting.

I didn't have the place to myself, there was a family over on the other side. On the rock platform where I'd seen the scariest brain I've ever known, laid open. Also, maybe, the last spot where my two parents sat together stretching out their legs in the sun, kissing. He knew about me that day, my dad. That I was on the way. He'd written his mother. The family over there now was parents with two littles, the younger one at the squatting and poking age, big sister prancing back and forth at the water's edge like a border collie. Mom saying no, they did not bring her cozzie, Dad saying no, she did not want to go in, the water would freeze her dinger. These people were not from here.

I said hey. They said good day, and wasn't it beautiful. I asked what city they were from, and they said Australia, which amazed me. People from the other side of the planet coming here. I crossed the rocks over to their side and they offered me their water bottle. I distracted the border collie sister by showing her how to launch leaf boats, and then she was all over that, running around to hunt up the biggest ones. Sycamores were best, the size of football helmets. I liked having company there, this family of two alive parents and kids that looked like they didn't know the meaning of getting leathered. I ended up hiking back out with them, and they asked me what everything was, the witch hazel with the winter flowers, the jenny wrens. I gave them sassafras twigs to chew on, that taste like root beer. The little girl hugged me around the knees before they got in their car, and I wanted so much not to be alone.

Breakfast with June was shoehorned in between her late night and another long day. Energizer bunny, was our June. She was beautiful as ever, and tired, and she looked her age, whatever that was. We poured syrup on our pancakes and she told me things about oxy, the lawsuits she'd helped get started, starting with the town hall meetings and petitions that made Kent furious. It was still going. The worst offender drugs were going off the market, changed to be abuse-proof. She said this might help in the long run, but she'd still be here trying to mop up the mess for the rest of her days. A whole generation of kids were coming up without families.

I didn't say, *Right here, you're looking at it.* She knew.

Ruby had started a grief group in her church. Mrs. Peggot was hanging in, with kids or grandkids going over there every day so she could fix them dinner. Maggot and Mariah were both still working at PetSmart and staying clean. I promised to go see him soon. The whole family knew about Maggot's boyfriend now. Some of them prayed it was a stage he'd outgrow, most said hallelujah. June had met the young man himself. He actually *was* the store's reptile expert, and kept a lot of snakes in glass boxes at his trailer home. I said that sounded about right.

The apple in June's eye was still Emmy. She'd moved into an apartment in Asheville with some other girls in recovery, somewhat like my situation. Probably minus the poker nights and porn. June said it was in an older building where Grace Kelly had lived at one time. I didn't know who that was, but acted impressed. She got serious then, and asked if Emmy had hurt me.

"How do you mean?"

June did that thing of running both hands through her hair. "I don't know. She's such a charmer. You know what I mean. Guys are just moths to her flame. I've wondered if she was a little too dependent on all that."

I said I couldn't speak for others, but I was never Emmy's moth. "Well okay, maybe in the early days. She was my first love disaster. But I lived to fight another day."

June smiled. "You never were one to fall only half-way down the well, were you?"

"No ma'am," I said. "I fall all the way in." Then I asked how was *her* love life, and she reached across the table and pinched my nose, like I was twelve.

She told me Emmy loved Asheville to pieces. She had a job as a restaurant hostess and was in a sober and body-positive dance group, which believe it or not does exist. They put on shows. Emmy was thinking about going in the direction of theater, so. There's Emmy, wagon hitched back up to the stars. I asked if she ever got homesick down there.

June's coffee cup froze halfway up to her mouth. "All the time. That's what she says. But she can't come back here. Not to live." She said it with so much sadness. Age-old heartbreak of this place, your great successes fly away, your failures stick around.

June assumed I would be going to the program for Coach that night, and was relieved to hear I wasn't.

She still blamed him for my downfall. "The daughter, though, Angus. Are you two still friends? I ran into her yesterday at the health department."

In her emails, Angus had made her summer and short-term jobs here into dark comedies. The nursing home where people talked to the dead. The in-school aides that talked messed-up kids out of murdering their teachers. "An impressive young lady," June called her, which I'm pretty sure was the first time in history those words were used on Angus. Or maybe not, what did I know anymore. My stomach did a thing every time Angus came up, because I really wanted to see her and really didn't. Everything else had changed. So she would have changed. And I couldn't take it.

June hated to run off, as usual, but did. I got in the Beretta and sat with my hands on the wheel a good five minutes before it decided where to go. Murder Valley.

My grandmother and Mr. Dick couldn't get over it. Me! Showing up! Bygones definitely bygones, as far as failures to apply myself. Reaching the height of six foot four evidently gave me a pass on all previous sins. She kept saying she hadn't thought I could look any more like my father, but look at me now. Mr. Dick for his part had the hots for my car. He wheeled himself all the way around it, looking it up one side and down the other, saying "It's blue!" They invited me to dinner and asked if I was aiming to move in. I said just visiting, but thanks all the same.

I whiled away the day looking at Mr. Dick's newest kite and being handy. Got up on a ladder and cleaned their gutters. Unjammed a casement window that had been stuck open since August. Not the tight ship of its former days, that house. Miss Betsy told me Jane Ellen had graduated, and Mr. Dick winked at me, so I knew what that meant. By getting married. I wondered who did their driving. Dinner took forever because it was all on Miss Betsy and she was slowing down. The legs looking more than ever like bags of walnuts in stockings. A stool by the cookstove so she could stir sitting down. I know pain if I see it.

At dinner they wanted to hear about the book I was writing. I was floored. How did they know about that? Angus. She'd told them all about the stories I put out on the computer, and my history book that was going to get published. Never at any time did the word "cartoons" come up, or "the adventures of Crash and Bernie, teenage addicts," so Angus must have put a respectable spin on things, which I appreciated. I told them I would do a chapter in my book on the Melungeons, and was counting on Mr. Dick to help me with that. He looked tickled. At some later date I'd have to break it to them it was more pictures than words.

They told me some about Coach, more about Angus. Things she'd not told me herself, such as being one of the smartest in her college class and winning awards. Her major was psychology, which I knew, and she planned to go back for even more school, which I didn't. To be a counselor. I'd been around the block now, so was not like most guys I know, that would yell "headshrinker" and run for cover. Angus would be awesome at it. I told them I thought so.

After supper Mr. Dick went to bed, Miss Betsy put her apron back on, and I washed all the dishes while she sat on her wooden stool and watched. I told her just sit, I've got this. Miss Betsy acted like she'd never seen a man clean up a kitchen before, which maybe she hadn't.

I wanted to keep her talking about Angus, so I asked questions. How often did she come down here, did she still have her Jeep Wrangler. Was she still working her badass angle, not that I used those words. What I really wanted to know was, is she still the same Angus. What kind of question is that? Obviously, if she was married or pregnant or anything along those lines, she'd have told me. But Miss Betsy had been hearing parts of her story that I hadn't. I kept going at it sideways, like casting a line in the water and holding your mouth right. Getting no bites at all. Finally I asked Miss Betsy straight up: Does she have a boyfriend?

I was scrubbing the glass dish she'd baked the bean casserole in. I didn't look at her, just kept on digging with the steel wool. Finally she said, "I have my hunches about that."

I was careful not to drop the dish. I turned around. "What kind of hunches?"

She'd taken her glasses off, and her face was like a snail without its shell. Slowly, slowly she cleaned the two-tone lenses with the corner of her apron. "I oughtn't to say."

"Meaning what? She doesn't like guys?"

She seemed unshocked by the suggestion, which just slipped out. I'd wondered the same of Miss Betsy. But she said that was not her thinking.

"O-kay," I said, faking patience. I went back to the casserole dish and got that sucker clean as a whistle and nothing else was forthcoming from Miss Betsy. If she got up and left now, I'd probably shame myself by following her upstairs, wheedling.

"I really don't think she'd care if you told me," I said. "She's like my sister."

"But you've not asked her that question yourself."

"No," I said. Busted.

"Well, maybe you ought. I think she has set her cap for one fellow in particular."

With a statement like that, and Angus, you had to take it as cash on the barrelhead. She would set her damn hat. The guy would know. "Somebody she met in Nashville, then."

"I oughtn't to say. She never told me outright. But you know me, I'm seldom wrong."

I was a good sport. Good for Angus. I hope they'll be very happy.

That night I stayed in the same bed as before, the ship with a wooden flagpole on each corner. I laid awake half the night running up every flag I could think of. Help. Surrender. Angus was my sister. I couldn't want any more in the world than for her to be happy. So I would go to the wedding of her and Mr. Nashville. I would be her man-bridemaid, just like Dori in her sweet foggy brain had stood Angus up as my best girl-man in ours. Angus would have done that for me. My turn now, to throw popcorn at the happy couple. I let her go. It's what I had to do, so I could get up in the morning and go see Coach.

64

The road from Murder Valley back to Lee County made me uneasy. Again, too many IEDs. This drive was where Angus and I had our only real fight, because she'd confessed to wanting to skip out on us all, to go to college, and I was counting up the hardships nailing me to the cross I'd dragged down this road: Here I got robbed by a truck-stop whore. Here I slept in a haystack. Shaking my mean little piggy bank of wrath. It set my teeth on edge, that memory, along with the sound of the wiper blades scraping a rime of hard frost on the windshield. The temperature had dropped overnight.

I was so lucky, I realized then. That Angus put up with me as long as she did.

The **apartment** building in Norton where Coach lived was the nicest place around, to the extent it almost didn't belong here. Fancy paint job, gray with white trim on the outside stairs and porches. New planted trees and mowed grass all around the parking areas. *Sidewalks.* I saw kids out there tipping skateboards, like pavement was a normal thing. No clue.

I'd called ahead, so Coach wasn't surprised. The shock was on my side. Out with the red cap and whistle, in with the leather slippers and sad old man smell. The bushy eyebrows were white. He clapped me on the back and sat me in his living room on furniture I recognized from the old house. But the apartment looked as new inside as out. Carpet with vacuum marks, never-used fireplace. Coach was a whole new man in a tidy room. That's the deal of sober life: celebrate the fresh start, suck up your sadness for all that was left behind. In Coach's case, a shit ton of random sports equipment. Angus had told me about her hasty bulldoze of the big house, shoving the crap into back rooms before turning it over to some NASCAR group for office space. It rented for twice what they paid for this apartment. So they got by, after he stepped down from his job to focus on pulling it together. He'd been here the whole time Angus was away, and still looked like a bird perched in the wrong tree. He told me they'd decided to sell the house. The renters had cleared out, and Angus was trying to get it fit to show. She was over there now.

I told him I was sorry I didn't get to his party last night. Oh, man. He lit up, naming names of who all was there. Generations of Generals. Father-and-son linebackers on the field. It was something, he kept saying, I should have been there. I didn't tell him I would only have seen the missing teeth in that smile. QB1 Fast Forward. Cornerback Hammer Kelly. Big Bear, dead of a self-inflicted gunshot. My predecessor Collins. Cush Polk, a cruelty to make you tear your hair. He had OD'd on what must have been his very first step off the narrow path. That good family, that preacher father, facing a coffin in wonder at God's failed mercy. But Coach seemed content to dwell on another plane. He didn't bring up the new coach or the losing season.

Nor did we talk about U-Haul. He'd faced embezzlement charges, but it got complicated and he wiggled out with fines and probation. I got this news from Annie and Mr. Armstrong, that had tolerated U-Haul and his skank mother sliming them on rinse-and-repeat for years on end. Nobody was sorry to see those two slither away through the grass with no forwarding address.

I helped Coach drink a pot of coffee and make small talk around all the bigger things I wanted to say. That

I was thankful for what he'd seen in me, sorry for the parts I screwed up. His mistakes were no more than the common failing to see the worth of boys like me, beyond what work can be wrung out of us by a week's end. Farm field, battlefield, football field. I have no words for that mess. But Coach and I were twelve-step brothers, there's a code. I'd showed up.

I pulled up to the mansion with knots in my gut. Which made no sense, it was just Angus. Hello good-bye. The sight of her Wrangler settled me some. Old four-wheel friend, the worse for wear. She'd mentioned putting over two hundred thousand on it, back and forth from Nashville.

I stuck my head in the door just as she walked into the living room carrying a box, which she almost dropped, doing a surprised little two-step. "*Jee*-sus on a Popsicle stick."

"Back at you," I said. It was freezing in there, they must have already cut off the utilities. She had on a red turtleneck and fleece type boots that looked like they'd come from the sheep to her feet with minimal process-ing. One of those overly colorful knitted hats with the earflaps and yarn braids hanging down. "Your pipes could freeze," I said. "Want me to build you a fire?"

She set down the box and frowned at the castle-size

fireplace. We'd tried roasting marshmallows in there as kids, and it never ended well. "Nah. Let's not burn the place down till I've got the cash in hand."

She stood there sizing me up, as people did now. I looked taller than I would ever feel.

"On the other hand," she said, "I'd better get some free labor out of you. Before you sell your book and get too famous for me to talk to. How's Annie, by the way?"

"Oh crap." I'd learned from Mr. Armstrong that it was not a false alarm, and I should stay tuned. A call had come in while I was driving, that rolled over to messages. I read it now, aloud: Woodie Guthrie Amato Armstrong. Seven pounds, one ounce, twenty-two inches.

"*Seriously.*" Her mouth shifted completely to one side, my favorite of all her smirks. I'd borrowed it for my character Bernie. If Angus noticed, she never said. "Are they too old to know what that's going to be like, a little boy going to school with the name *Woodie*?"

"I wouldn't worry about it," I said. "By age five he'll be going by something else."

"Like Hard-On."

"Exactly."

Another pause. We were a cold engine, not perfectly hitting.

"Nice hat."

She pulled it off and looked at it. "Right? I bought it off a guy on the street in Nashville." Set free, her hair sprang into action, somehow girlier than it used to be. We were standing in the exact places where we'd first met. I felt reckless, like setting something on fire for real.

"Remember the first day I came here? And thought you were a boy?"

The smirk shifted. "Angus, 'like the cattle.' "

"Why?"

"Why what?"

"Why did you let me go on like that, the whole day? You could have just said."

She stopped smiling. "Late in the day to start asking now."

I sensed myself picking a fight. The kind that helps you break up with somebody, evidently. "Right. I forget these things. How you always have to be queen of all the bees."

The gray eyes went through several changes of weather before they settled. "Can you not think *at all* about how that was for me? I had no say in the matter. Some kid I've never met is moving in with us. Coach is finally getting his boy."

"So you're going to roll out the idiot carpet."

She shrugged. "It wasn't planned, it just happened. I remember thinking, maybe this is my chance. Like we'd get along better as brothers or something." She stared, waiting for me to catch up. "Being a girl in this house never got me anyplace great, you know?"

And I'd missed it all. The evil red eyes of U-Haul on her little girl body, her dad's neglect, one root cause. And then came me, regaling her with my conquests. "Damn," I said. "I'm sorry for all that. You were the brother of all brothers. Or sister, you pick. A-team."

She smiled, but it was empty. "We missed you at the hootenanny last night."

"You didn't even know I was in town."

"I did actually. June Peggot told me. And then you didn't show up. I figured you'd blow in and out of town without saying hello." She bent over to pick up her box. But I caught the thing in her eyes she was trying to hide.

"I wouldn't do that." I almost had.

I asked her if I could take a last look around the house. Really just to calm down. I went upstairs to the beanbag lounge, now a blank space with a stained ceiling. Came back downstairs and found her in Coach's old office, sitting on the floor with paper piles spread in a complete circle around her, trying to figure out once and for all what needed to be saved. I asked about her job and she told me some about it, in-school services for kids that were wound too tight.

"Miss Betsy said you're lighting out again for more school. For doctor or something."

"Social worker. I've already lit out, technically. It's a nonresidency thing, you do a lot of the coursework online. I'll only have to be there in person a few months at a time."

"In Nashville?"

"Kentucky."

I thought with a full heart of Viking and Gizmo. I took files she handed me and put them in a trash box. Getting up my nerve. "So. Miss Betsy tells me you've set your cap for some guy."

She gave me the longest, strangest look. So I changed the subject, trying to think of respectful questions to ask her about social work. Would it be in mental hospitals or what. She said her main interest was kids. Abusive situations, incarcerated parents. I said no shortage in the supply around here, and she said that's what she was thinking. Job security.

"You mean you're planning on staying. Here."

She nodded. "And it sounds like you're not. You could be a famous cartoonist from anyplace, you know. We got us some real broadband in these parts now."

"That's all I've been thinking about for the last day and a half. It's all I want, but I can't picture it. Staying here as, you know. Who I am now. How do you even do it?"

"I don't know. Day at a time? You just do what needs to be done."

"But you're *god* material, Angus. Not like the rest of us. You know that, right?"

Those manga eyes. Was it really possible she didn't?

Back in the day, we never touched each other. *Ever.* The rule was hard and fast. But something made me reach over and open her right hand. I drew a heart on it, closed it up, and handed the fist back to her. "I'm sorry, god-*dess* material. There was never any confusion in my mind, after that first snafu. Just so you know."

She called it quits on the papers and turned to a box of massively tangled resistance bands. Blew out her breath and lay back on the floor. "*Fuck* this shit. I don't guess you know anybody that could use a truckload of heavily used sports equipment."

"I might, actually." I was thinking of Chartrain's teammates. Legless Lightning.

She sat up. "Then I hope you're driving a huge motherfucking vehicle."

"Pretty small. But she's a cutie-pie. Want to come outside and see?"

"You and your cutie-pies." She shoved the box at me. "Take this out to the trash pile for me. First mountain on your left, can't miss it. I'll be out there in a sec."

Outside it had gotten colder, not even yet noon. I stood watching my steamy breath come out of my mouth, which I took to mean I was still alive on the inside. Snow started to fall, just a little spit here and there. I lit a cigarette. Thirty seconds later she came out, and I hid the smoking gun behind my back. She laughed and said she was telling Coach. And then we were okay. We studied the giant pile of crap she'd hauled out of there. I told her where she could get a railroad-car-size roll-off for three hundred dollars. She checked out the Beretta and said *of course* I would have a car that's the color of the ocean. I hadn't even thought of that.

"Did you ever get to see it? After the tragically aborted early attempt?"

Two attempts. The school-trip rout at Christiansburg she meant. I'd never told her much about the Richmond-Mouse debacle. I finished my Camel and ground out the butt. "I don't want to talk about it."

"Okay, that's a no. But it's still out there. Just so you know."

"Do tell?"

"Yessiree Bob. You can take that one to the bank."

"I'll have to take your word on that. Given the college degree."

For a minute the sun came out, while it was snowing. People say that means the devil is beating his wife. Then the snow stopped, which I took to mean she was leaving the bastard. I asked Angus what she and Coach were doing for Christmas.

She gave me a funny look, chin pulled back. "What *Christmas*. That was all your doing."

"But you seemed so into it. Am I wrong?"

"No. But we never knew how to do it before you came, and the magic went away again after you moved out. The magic was all you, Demon."

We were quiet for a minute. I warmed myself on a little bonfire of remembered ridiculousness, and hoped she was doing the same. "I still have that ship. In the bottle. Everything else I've ever owned, I've lost by now or thrown out. But I kept that. You thought I was going places. We just didn't see the bottle part coming."

She opened her mouth, then shut it. Opened her empty right hand and looked at it, like something was in there. Then put it behind her back. "I'm sorry you and Annie didn't get your book thing put together," she said.

"I'll get it figured out. And I'm sure she'll get back to me eventually. I mean, how long can one baby last?"

She laughed. But something was winding down here.

"We could give it another go," I said. "Christmas. What do you want?"

"A big fat check for this house."

"You know my price range. No real improvement there, sadly. I might have notched up a little on the naughty-nice scale, though."

She leveled me with a stare that stirred something up I couldn't name. Or was scared to admit to. "Okay. I have a present for you," she said. "It's not wrapped. I just thought of it."

"Okay. Where is it?"

"Um. Five hundred miles from here. Directly adjacent to a bunch of sand."

I laughed. "Thanks."

"I'm serious. I'm giving you the ocean."

"It's *winter.*"

"You know what? They don't roll it up and put it away. It's just sitting there. Take it or leave it, home skillet. One goddamn Atlantic Ocean on offer."

"Can I get that to go?"

She pulled down the earflaps of her hat with both hands, like she might otherwise levitate, and got up in my face. As nearly as she could, being a foot shorter, reaching up at me with the big gray eyes: *Not kidding.*

She said she had the week off work, due to testing schedule or something. She asked if I had a deadline on getting back to Knoxville. I didn't.

"So what do you say, Demon. Time to say grace and blow this dump?"

I followed her back to Coach's apartment so she could grab what she needed. We took the Beretta, as the slightly less risky option. She said that sea-blue car was asking for it, and she was a good sport about it smelling like an ashtray. We kept the windows down as far as Gate City, which was damn airish in that weather, but by the time we got on the interstate it was fine to roll them up. And I was still yet shivering for some reason, ready to jump out of my skin. Angus was a couple of steps out ahead of me, as she always and ever would be. So happy. Utterly chill.

She rifled through her bag of car snacks. Opened a bag of M&Ms and threw one that bounced off my face. I called a traveling penalty. She picked it up off the floor and popped it in my mouth. "So, to get this straight, as far as your motives. You're not in it for the suntan, right?"

I told her I was not. Just wanted to look at that big drink of water.

"Good," she said. "Because it's going to be cold. But there are lots of advantages to going in winter."

She named them: No crowds. No strutting peacocks in Speedos. We'd have the place to ourselves. Motels would be half price. This was Angus trusting the ride, we were staying in a motel. I was extremely unclear about where we were headed. Was she still my sister?

She smacked her forehead. "Oh my God. *Oysters.*"

"What about them."

"You can only eat them in winter! June, July, August, they're poison. You have to wait till the months that have the letter R."

This sounded highly doubtful. "Why is that?"

"Believe it or not, with my amazingly advanced degree, I don't know. It's one of these things you pick up. I went to New Orleans a few times with friends."

There he was, the friend. "And you're saying it's worth the wait? Because I'm saying Mrs. Peggot used to cook them in soup at Christmas, and I was not a fan."

"This is nothing like that. At the beach they're fresh. You crack them open and drink them right off the shell. Raw. Technically I guess still alive."

"And that's a good thing?"

"You won't believe how good. It's like kissing the ocean. *Demon.*" She leaned forward so I could see her face, and drilled those bad-girl eyes into me with a look that threatened my perfect driving record. "And it's kissing you back."

Oh my Lord. The girl has set her cap. Not my sister.

We talked the whole way through the Shenandoah Valley. The end of the day grew long on the hills, then the dark pulled in close around us. Snowflakes looped and glared in the headlights like off-season lightning bugs. Ridiculous nut that I'd been to crack. I drove left-handed with my right arm resting on her seat back, running my thumb over the little hairs on the back of her neck. The trip itself, just the getting there, possibly the best part of my life so far.

That's where we are. Well past the Christiansburg exit. Past Richmond, and still pointed east. Headed for the one big thing I know is not going to swallow me alive.

Acknowledgments

I'm grateful to Charles Dickens for writing *David Copperfield*, his impassioned critique of institutional poverty and its damaging effects on children in his society. Those problems are still with us. In adapting his novel to my own place and time, working for years with his outrage, inventiveness, and empathy at my elbow, I've come to think of him as my genius friend.

Many generous people helped me sketch out and color in the frames of this novel, offering their expertise on subjects ranging from foster care and child protective services to the logistics and desperations of addiction and recovery, Appalachian history, cartooning, and high school football. Mistakes are mine, authenticity is theirs: Camille Kingsolver, Reid Snow, Silas House,

Kayla Rae Whitaker, Linda Snow, Amanda Freeman, Christine Dotson, Sue Ella Kobak, and Art Van Zee. Beyond the scope of this novel, we can all thank Dr. Van Zee for his groundbreaking exposure of dangerous prescription opioids, ultimately bringing the crisis to public attention. I'm in awe of his dedication to his patients.

The Origin Project, cofounded by Adriana Trigiani and Nancy Bolmeier-Fisher, enriches our schools and inspired my fictional Backgrounds project. Parts of this story came from my own Mammaw and Pappaw, Louise and Roy Kingsolver, and great-aunt Lillian Wright Craft, who still speak to me with the confidence of the living, in a language that my years outside of Appalachia tried to shame from my tongue.

Every draft of this book was improved by advice from insightful readers, especially Sam Stoloff, Terry Karten, Silas House, and Louisa Joyner. Judy Carmichael calmed the stormy seas and kept my little boat from sinking. Steven Hopp, in addition to reading and talking me through every page, kept me fed at my desk, accompanied me on fact-finding adventures, and pulled me outside into the sun, time and again, to get me back from the dark places this story needed me to go.

For the kids who wake up hungry in those dark places every day, who've lost their families to poverty and pain pills, whose caseworkers keep losing their files, who feel invisible, or wish they were: this book is for you.

About the Author

BARBARA KINGSOLVER is the author of nine best-selling works of fiction, including the novels *Unsheltered, Flight Behavior, The Lacuna, Prodigal Summer,* and *The Poisonwood Bible,* as well as books of poetry, essays, and creative nonfiction. With her husband and daughters she authored the influential *Animal, Vegetable, Miracle: A Year of Food Life.* Kingsolver's work has been translated into more than twenty languages and has earned literary awards and a devoted readership at home and abroad. She is a member of the American Academy of Arts and Letters, and in 2000 was awarded the National Humanities Medal, our country's highest honor for service through the arts. She lives with her husband on a farm in southern Appalachia.

HARPER LARGE PRINT

We hope you enjoyed reading
our new, comfortable print size and found it
an experience you would like to repeat.

Well – you're in luck!

Harper Large Print offers the finest in
fiction and nonfiction books in this same larger
print size and paperback format. Light and easy to read,
Harper Large Print paperbacks are for the book lovers
who want to see what they are reading without strain.

For a full listing of titles and
new releases to come, please visit our website:
www.hc.com

HARPER LARGE PRINT

SEEING IS BELIEVING!